The Artists Edition is limited to twenty-six
special lettered and five hundred numbered
sets.   This is No.

MERRILL AND BAKER

Publishers

The Artists Edition of the Complete
Works of WILLIAM MAKEPEACE
THACKERAY in twenty volumes
with many new etchings and
reproductions of the original cuts
Vanity Fair
A Novel Without a Hero
In Two Volumes
Volume II
Lovel
The Widower

New York
MERRILL AND BAKER
Publishers

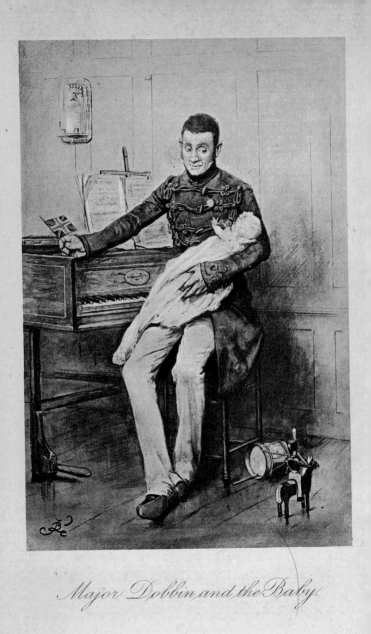

Major Dobbin and the Baby.

LIST OF ILLUSTRATIONS.

VOL II.

VOL III.

LOVEL THE WIDOWER.

CHAPTER XII.

THE heir of Crawley arrived at home in due time, after this catastrophe, and henceforth may be said to have reigned in Queen's Crawley. For though the old Baronet survived many months, he never recovered the use of his intellect or his speech completely, and the government of the estate devolved upon his elder son. In a strange condition Pitt found it. Sir Pitt was always buying and mortgaging; he had twenty men of business, and quarrels with each; quarrels with all his tenants, and lawsuits with them; lawsuits with the lawyers; lawsuits with the Mining and Dock Companies in which he was proprietor; and with every person with whom he had business. To unravel these difficulties, and to set the estate clear, was a task worthy of the orderly and persevering diplomatist of Pumpernickel: and he set himself to work with prodigious assiduity. His whole family, of course, was transported to Queen's Crawley, whither Lady Southdown, of course, came too; and she set about converting the parish under the Rector's nose, and brought down her irregular clergy to the dismay of the angry Mrs. Bute. Sir Pitt had concluded no bargain for the sale of the living of Queen's Crawley; when it should drop, her ladyship proposed to take the patronage into her own hands, and present a young *protégé* to the Rectory; on which subject the diplomatic Pitt said nothing.

Mrs. Bute's intentions with regard to Miss Betsy Horrocks were not carried into effect; and she paid no visit to Southampton gaol. She and her father left the Hall, when the latter took possession of the Crawley Arms in the village, of which he had got a lease from Sir Pitt. The ex-butler had obtained a small freehold there likewise, which gave him a vote for the borough. The Rector had another of these votes, and these and four others formed the representative body which returned the two members for Queen's Crawley.

There was a show of courtesy kept up between the Rectory and the Hall ladies, between the younger ones at least, for Mrs. Bute and Lady Southdown never could meet without battles, and gradually ceased seeing each other. Her ladyship kept her room when the ladies from the Rectory visited their cousins at the Hall. Perhaps Mr. Pitt was not very much displeased at these occasional absences of his mamma-in-law. He believed the Binkie family to be the greatest and wisest, and most interesting in the world, and her ladyship and his aunt had long held ascendency over him; but sometimes he felt that she commanded him too much. To be considered young was complimentary doubtless; but at six-and-forty to be treated as a boy was sometimes mortifying. Lady Jane yielded up everything, however, to her mother. She was only fond of her children in private; and it was lucky for her that Lady Southdown's multifarious business, her conferences with ministers, and her correspondence with all the missionaries of Africa, Asia, and Australasia, etc., occupied the venerable Countess a great deal, so that she had but little time to devote to her granddaughter, the little Matilda, and her grandson, Master Pitt Crawley. The latter was a feeble child: and it was only by prodigious quantities of calomel that Lady Southdown was able to keep him in life at all.

As for Sir Pitt he retired into those very apartments where Lady Crawley had been previously extinguished, and here was tended by Miss Hester, the girl upon her promotion, with constant care and assiduity. What love, what fidelity, what constancy is there equal to that of a nurse with good wages. They smooth pillows : and make arrowroot : they get up at nights : they bear complaints and querulousness : they see the sun shining out of doors and don't want to go abroad : they sleep on arm-chairs, and eat their meals in solitude : they pass long, long evenings doing nothing, watching the embers, and the patient's drink simmering in the jug : they read the weekly paper the whole week through ; and Law's "Serious Call" or the "Whole Duty of Man" suffices them for literature for the year — and we quarrel with them because, when their relations come to see them once a week, a little gin is smuggled in in their linen basket. Ladies, what man's love is there that would stand a year's nursing of the object of his affection ? Whereas a nurse will stand by you for ten pounds a quarter, and we think her too highly paid. At least Mr. Crawley grumbled a good deal about paying half as much to Miss Hester for her constant attendance upon the Baronet his father.

Of sunshiny days this old gentleman was taken out in a chair on the terrace — the very chair which Miss Crawley had had at Brighton, and which had been transported thence with a number of Lady Southdown's effects to Queen's Crawley. Lady Jane always walked by the old man ; and was an evident favorite with him. He used to nod many times to her and smile when she came in, and utter inarticulate deprecatory moans when she was going away. When the door shut

upon her he would cry and sob — whereupon Hester's
face and manner, which was always exceedingly bland
and gentle while her lady was present, would change
at once, and she would make faces at him and clench
her fist, and scream out, "Hold your tongue, you
stoopid old fool," and twirl away his chair from the
fire which he loved to look at — at which he would cry
more. For this was all that was left after more than
seventy years of cunning and struggling, and drinking,
and scheming, and sin and selfishness — a whimpering
old idiot put in and out of bed and cleaned and fed like
a baby.

At last a day came when the nurse's occupation
was over. Early one morning, as Pitt Crawley was
at his steward's and bailiff's books in the study, a
knock came to the door, and Hester presented herself
dropping a curtsy, and said, —

"If you please, Sir Pitt, Sir Pitt died this morning, Sir Pitt. I was a-making of his toast, Sir Pitt,
for his gruel, Sir Pitt, which he took every morning regular at six, Sir Pitt, and — I thought I heard
a moan-like, Sir Pitt — and — and — and — " She
dropped another curtsy.

What was it that made Pitt's pale face flush quite
red ? Was it because he was Sir Pitt at last, with a
seat in Parliament, and perhaps future honors in
prospect ? "I'll clear the estate now with the ready
money," he thought, and rapidly calculated its encumbrances and the improvements which he would make.
He would not use his aunt's money previously lest
Sir Pitt should recover, and his outlay be in vain.

All the blinds were pulled down at the Hall and
Rectory ; the church bell was tolled, and the chancel
hung in black ; and Bute Crawley did n't go to a

coursing meeting, but went and dined quietly at Fuddleston, where they talked about his deceased brother and young Sir Pitt over their port. Miss Betsy, who was by this time married to a saddler at Mudbury, cried a good deal. The family surgeon rode over and paid his respectful compliments, and inquiries for the health of their ladyships. The death was talked about at Mudbury and at the Crawley Arms; the landlord whereof had become reconciled with the Rector of late, who was occasionally known to step into the parlor and taste Mr. Horrocks's mild beer.

"Shall I write to your brother — or will you?" asked Lady Jane of her husband, Sir Pitt.

"I will write, of course," Sir Pitt said, "and invite him to the funeral: it will be but becoming."

"And — and — Mrs. Rawdon," said Lady Jane, timidly.

"Jane!" said Lady Southdown, "how can you think of such a thing?"

"Mrs. Rawdon must of course be asked," said Sir Pitt, resolutely.

"Not whilst *I* am in the house!" said Lady Southdown.

"Your ladyship will be pleased to recollect that I am the head of this family," Sir Pitt replied. "If you please, Lady Jane, you will write a letter to Mrs. Rawdon Crawley, requesting her presence upon this melancholy occasion."

"Jane, I forbid you to put pen to paper!" cried the Countess.

"I believe I am the head of this family," Sir Pitt repeated; "and however much I may regret any circumstance which may lead to your ladyship quitting this house, must, if you please, continue to govern it as I see fit."

Lady Southdown rose up as magnificent as Mrs. Siddons in Lady Macbeth, and ordered that horses might be put to her carriage. If her son and daughter turned her out of their house, she would hide her sorrows somewhere in loneliness, and pray for their conversion to better thoughts.

" We don't turn you out of our house, Mamma," said the timid Lady Jane, imploringly.

" You invite such company to it as no Christian lady should meet, and I will have my horses to-morrow morning."

"Have the goodness to write, Jane, under my dictation," said Sir Pitt, rising, and throwing himself into an attitude of command, like the Portrait of a Gentleman in the Exhibition, "and begin, 'Queen's Crawley, September 14, 1822. — My dear brother — '"

Hearing these decisive and terrible words, Lady Macbeth, who had been waiting for a sign of weakness or vacillation on the part of her son-in-law, rose, and with a scared look, left the library. Lady Jane looked up to her husband as if she would fain follow and soothe her mamma : but Pitt forbade his wife to move.

"She won't go away," he said. "She has let her house at Brighton, and has spent her last half-year's dividends. A Countess living at an inn is a ruined woman. I have been waiting long for an opportunity to take this — this decisive step, my love; for, as you must perceive, it is impossible that there should be two chiefs in a family : and now, if you please, we will resume the dictation. 'My dear brother, the melancholy intelligence which it is my duty to convey to my family must have been long anticipated by,'" etc.

In a word, Pitt having come to his kingdom, and

having by good luck, or desert rather, as he considered, assumed almost all the fortune which his other relatives had expected, was determined to treat his family kindly and respectably, and make a house of Queen's Crawley once more. It pleased him to think that he should be its chief. He proposed to use the vast influence that his commanding talents and position must speedily acquire for him in the county to get his brother placed and his cousins decently provided for, and perhaps had a little sting of repentance as he thought that he was the proprietor of all that they had hoped for. In the course of three or four days' reign his bearing was changed, and his plans quite fixed: he determined to rule justly and honestly, to depose Lady Southdown, and to be on the friendliest possible terms with all the relations of his blood.

So he dictated a letter to his brother Rawdon — a solemn and elaborate letter, containing the profoundest observations, couched in the longest words, and filling with wonder the simple little secretary, who wrote under her husband's order. "What an orator this will be," thought she, "when he enters the House of Commons" (on which point, and on the tyranny of Lady Southdown, Pitt had sometimes dropped hints to his wife in bed); "how wise and good, and what a genius my husband is! I fancied him a little cold; but how good, and what a genius!"

The fact is, Pitt Crawley had got every word of the letter by heart, and had studied it, with diplomatic secrecy, deeply and perfectly, long before he thought fit to communicate it to his astonished wife.

This letter, with a huge black border and seal, was accordingly despatched by Sir Pitt Crawley to his brother the Colonel, in London. Rawdon Crawley was but half pleased at the receipt of it. "What's the use of going down to that stupid place?" thought he. "I can't stand being alone with Pitt after dinner, and horses there and back will cost us twenty pound."

He carried the letter, as he did all difficulties, to Becky, up stairs in her bed-room — with her chocolate, which he always made and took to her of a morning.

He put the tray with the breakfast and the letter on the dressing-table, before which Becky sat combing her yellow hair. She took up the black-edged missive, and having read it, she jumped up from the chair, crying "Hurray!" and waving the note round her head.

"Hurray?" said Rawdon, wondering at the little figure capering about in a streaming flannel dressing-gown, with tawny locks dishevelled. "He's not left us anything, Becky. I had my share when I came of age."

"You'll never be of age, you silly old man," Becky replied. "Run out now to Madame Brunoy's, for I must have some mourning: and get a crape on your hat, and a black waistcoat — I don't think you've got one; order it to be brought home to-morrow, so that we may be able to start on Thursday."

"You don't mean to go?" Rawdon interposed.

"Of course I mean to go. I mean that Lady Jane shall present me at court next year. I mean that your brother shall give you a seat in Parliament, you stupid old creature. I mean that Lord Steyne shall have your vote and his, my dear, old, silly man; and that you shall be an Irish Secretary, or a West Indian Governor : or a Treasurer, or a Consul, or some such thing."

"Posting will cost a dooce of a lot of money," grumbled Rawdon.

"We might take Southdown's carriage, which ought to be present at the funeral, as he is a relation of the family: but, no — I intend that we shall go by the coach. They'll like it better. It seems more humble —"

"Rawdy goes of course?" the Colonel asked.

"No such thing; why pay an extra place? He's too big to travel bodkin between you and me. Let him stay here in the nursery, and Briggs can make him a black frock. Go you: and do as I bid you. And you had best tell Sparks, your man, that old Sir Pitt is dead, and that you will come in for something considerable when the affairs are arranged. He'll tell this to Raggles, who has been pressing for money, and it will console poor Raggles." And so Becky began sipping her chocolate.

When the faithful Lord Steyne arrived in the evening, he found Becky and her companion, who was no other than our friend Briggs, busy cutting, ripping, snipping, and tearing all sorts of black stuffs available for the melancholy occasion.

"Miss Briggs and I are plunged in grief and despondency for the death of our papa," Rebecca said. "Sir Pitt Crawley is dead, my lord. We have been tearing our hair all the morning, and now we are tearing up our old clothes."

"Oh, Rebecca, how can you —" was all that Briggs could say as she turned up her eyes.

"Oh, Rebecca, how can you —" echoed my lord. "So that old scoundrel's dead, is he? He might have been a Peer if he had played his cards better. Mr. Pitt had very nearly made him; but he ratted always at the wrong time. What an old Silenus it was."

"I might have been Silenus's widow," said Rebecca. "Don't you remember, Miss Briggs, how you peeped in at the door, and saw old Sir Pitt on his knees to me?" Miss Briggs, our old friend, blushed very much at this reminiscence; and was glad when Lord Steyne ordered her to go down stairs and make him a cup of tea.

Briggs was the house-dog whom Rebecca had provided as guardian of her innocence and reputation. Miss Crawley had left her a little annuity. She would have been content to remain in the Crawley family with Lady Jane, who was good to her and to everybody; but Lady Southdown dismissed poor Briggs as quickly as decency permitted; and Mr. Pitt (who thought himself much injured by the uncalled-for generosity of his deceased relative towards a lady who had only been Miss Crawley's faithful retainer a score of years) made no objection to that exercise of the dowager's authority. Bowls and Firkin likewise received their legacies, and their dismissals; and married and set up a lodging-house, according to the custom of their kind.

Briggs tried to live with her relations in the country, but found that attempt was vain after the better society to which she had been accustomed. Briggs's friends, small tradesmen in a country town, quarrelled over Miss Briggs's forty pounds a-year, as eagerly and more openly than Miss Crawley's kinsfolk had for that lady's inheritance. Briggs's brother, a radical hatter and grocer, called his sister a purse-proud aristocrat, because she would not advance a part of her capital to stock his shop: and she would have done so most likely, but that their sister, a dissenting shoemaker's lady, at variance with the hatter and grocer, who went to another chapel, showed how their brother was on the verge of bankruptcy, and took possession of Briggs for a while. The dissenting shoemaker wanted Miss Briggs to send his son to college, and make a gentleman of him. Between them the two families got a great portion of her private savings out of her: and finally she fled to London, followed by the anathemas of both, and determined to seek for servitude again as infinitely less onerous than liberty. And advertising in the papers that a "Gentlewoman of agreeable manners, and accustomed to the best society, was anxious to," etc., she took up her residence with Mr. Bowls in Half Moon Street, and waited the result of the advertisement.

So it was that she fell in with Rebecca. Mrs. Rawdon's dashing little carriage and ponies was whirling down the street one day, just as Miss Briggs, fatigued, had reached Mr. Bowls's door, after a weary walk to the "Times" office in the City, to insert her advertisement for the sixth time. Rebecca was driving, and at once recognized the gentlewoman with agreeable manners, and being a perfectly good-humored woman, as we have seen, and having a regard for Briggs, she pulled up the ponies at the door-steps, gave the reins to the groom, and jumping out, had hold of both Briggs's hands, before she of the agreeable manners had recovered from the shock of seeing an old friend.

Briggs cried, and Becky laughed a great deal, and kissed the gentlewoman as soon as they got into the passage; and thence into Mrs. Bowls's front parlor, with the red moreen curtains, and the round looking-glass, with the chained eagle above, gazing upon the back of the ticket in the window which announced "Apartments to Let."

Briggs told all her history amidst those perfectly
uncalled-for sobs and ejaculations of wonder with
which women of her soft nature salute an old acquaintance, or regard a rencontre in the street; for
though people meet other people every day, yet some
there are who insist upon discovering miracles; and
women, even though they have disliked each other,
begin to cry when they meet, deploring and remembering the time when they last quarrelled. So, in a
word, Briggs told all her history, and Becky gave a
narrative of her own life, with her usual artlessness
and candor.

Mrs. Bowls, late Firkin, came and listened grimly
in the passage to the hysterical sniffling and giggling
which went on in the front parlor. Becky had never
been a favorite of hers. Since the establishment of
the married couple in London they had frequented
their former friends of the house of Raggles, and did
not like the latter's account of the Colonel's *ménage.*

"*I* would n't trust him, Ragg, my boy," Bowls remarked: and his wife, when Mrs. Rawdon issued from
the parlor, only saluted the lady with a very sour
curtsy; and her fingers were like so many sausages,
cold and lifeless, when she held them out in deference
to Mrs. Rawdon, who persisted in shaking hands with
the retired lady's-maid. She whirled away into Piccadilly, nodding with the sweetest of smiles towards
Miss Briggs, who hung nodding at the window close
under the advertisement-card, and at the next moment
was in the Park with a half-dozen of dandies cantering
after her carriage.

When she found how her friend was situated, and
how having a snug legacy from Miss Crawley, salary
was no object to our gentlewoman, Becky instantly
formed some benevolent little domestic plans concern-

ing her. This was just such a companion as would
suit her establishment, and she invited Briggs to come
to dinner with her that very evening, when she should
see Becky's dear little darling Rawdon.

Mrs. Bowls cautioned her lodger against venturing
into the lion's den, "wherein you will rue it, Miss B.,
mark my words, and as sure as my name is Bowls."
And Briggs promised to be very cautious. The upshot of which caution was that she went to live with
Mrs. Rawdon the next week, and had lent Rawdon
Crawley six hundred pounds upon annuity before six
months were over.

CHAPTER XIII.

IN WHICH BECKY REVISITS THE HALLS OF HER ANCESTORS.

So the mourning being ready, and Sir Pitt Crawley warned of their arrival, Colonel Crawley and his wife took a couple of places in the same old Highflyer coach, by which Rebecca had travelled in the defunct Baronet's company, on her first journey into the world some nine years before. How well she remembered the inn-yard, and the ostler to whom she refused money, and the insinuating Cambridge lad who wrapped her in his coat on the journey! Rawdon took his place outside, and would have liked to drive, but his grief forbade him. He sat by the coachman, and talked about horses and the road the whole way; and who kept the inns, and who horsed the coach by which he had travelled so many a time, when he and Pitt were boys going to Eton. At Mudbury a carriage and a pair of horses received them, with a coachman in black. "It's the old drag, Rawdon," Rebecca said, as they got in. "The worms have eaten the cloth a good deal — there's the stain which Sir Pitt — ha! I see Dawson the ironmonger has his shutters up — which Sir Pitt made such a noise about. It was a bottle of cherry-brandy he broke which we went to fetch for your aunt from Southampton. How time flies, to be sure! that can't be Polly Talboys, that bouncing girl standing by her mother at the cottage there. I remember her a mangy little urchin picking weeds in the garden."

"Fine gal," said Rawdon, returning the salute which the cottage gave him, by two fingers applied to his crape hat-band. Becky bowed and saluted, and recognized people here and there graciously. These recognitions were inexpressibly pleasant to her. It seemed as if she was not an impostor any more, and was coming to the home of her ancestors. Rawdon was rather abashed, and cast down on the other hand. What recollections of boyhood and innocence might have been flitting across his brain? What pangs of dim remorse and doubt and shame?

"Your sisters must be young women now," Rebecca said, thinking of those girls for the first time perhaps since she had left them.

"Don't know, I'm shaw," replied the Colonel. "Hullo! here's old Mother Lock. How-dy-do, Mrs. Lock? Remember me, don't you? Master Rawdon, hey? Dammy how those old women last; she was a hundred when I was a boy."

They were going through the lodge-gates kept by old Mrs. Lock, whose hand Rebecca insisted upon shaking, as she flung open the creaking old iron gate, and the carriage passed between the two moss-grown pillars surmounted by the dove and serpent.

"The governor has cut into the timber," Rawdon said, looking about, and then was silent — so was Becky. Both of them were rather agitated, and thinking of old times. He about Eton, and his mother, whom he remembered, a frigid demure woman, and a sister who died, of whom he had been passionately fond; and how he used to thrash Pitt; and about little Rawdy at home. And Rebecca thought about her own youth, and the dark secrets of those early

tainted days; and of her entrance into life by yonder
gates; and of Miss Pinkerton, and Joe, and Amelia.

The gravel walk and terrace had been scraped quite
clean. A grand painted hatchment was already over
the great entrance, and two very solemn and tall personages in black flung open each a leaf of the door as
the carriage pulled up at the familiar steps. Rawdon
turned red, and Becky somewhat pale, as they passed
through the old hall, arm in arm. She pinched her
husband's arm as they entered the oak parlor, where
Sir Pitt and his wife were ready to receive them. Sir
Pitt in black, Lady Jane in black, and my Lady Southdown with a large black headpiece of bugles and
feathers, which waved on her ladyship's head like an
undertaker's tray.

Sir Pitt had judged correctly, that she would not
quit the premises. She contented herself by preserving a solemn and stony silence, when in company of
Pitt and his rebellious wife, and by frightening the
children in the nursery by the ghastly gloom of her
demeanor. Only a very faint bending of the head-
dress and plumes welcomed Rawdon and his wife, as
those prodigals returned to their family.

To say the truth, they were not affected very much
one way or other by this coolness. Her ladyship
was a person only of secondary consideration in their
minds just then — they were intent upon the reception which the reigning brother and sister would
afford them.

Pitt, with rather a heightened color, went up and
shook his brother by the hand; and saluted Rebecca
with a hand-shake and a very low bow. But Lady
Jane took both the hands of her sister-in-law and
kissed her affectionately. The embrace somehow
brought tears into the eyes of the little adventuress

— which ornaments, as we know, she wore very seldom. The artless mark of kindness and confidence touched and pleased her; and Rawdon, encouraged by this demonstration on his sister's part, twirled up his mustachios, and took leave to salute Lady Jane with a kiss, which caused her ladyship to blush exceedingly.

"Dev'lish nice little woman, Lady Jane," was his verdict, when he and his wife were together again. "Pitt's got fat, too, and is doing the thing handsomely." "He can afford it," said Rebecca, and agreed in her husband's farther opinion, "that the mother-in-law was a tremendous old Guy — and that the sisters were rather well-looking young women."

They, too, had been summoned from school to attend the funeral ceremonies. It seemed Sir Pitt Crawley, for the dignity of the house and family, had thought right to have about the place as many persons in black as could possibly be assembled. All the men and maids of the house, the old women of the Alms House, whom the elder Sir Pitt had cheated out of a great portion of their due, the Parish Clerk's family, and the special retainers of both Hall and Rectory were habited in sable; added to these, the undertaker's men, at least a score, with crapes and hat-bands, and who made a goodly show when the great burying show took place — but these are mute personages in our drama; and having nothing to do or say, need occupy a very little space here.

With regard to her sisters-in-law Rebecca did not attempt to forget her former position of governess towards them, but recalled it frankly and kindly, and asked them about their studies with great gravity, and told them that she had thought of them many and many a day, and longed to know of their welfare.

In fact you would have supposed that ever since she
had left them she had not ceased to keep them upper-
most in her thoughts, and to take the tenderest interest in their welfare. So supposed Lady Crawley
herself and her young sisters.

"She's hardly changed since eight years," said
Miss Rosalind to Miss Violet, as they were preparing for dinner.

"Those red-haired women look wonderfully well,"
replied the other.

"Hers is much darker than it was; I think she
must dye it," Miss Rosalind added. "She is stouter,
too, and altogether improved," continued Miss Rosalind, who was disposed to be very fat.

"At least she gives herself no airs, and remembers
that she was our governess once," Miss Violet said,
intimating that it befitted all governesses to keep
their proper place, and forgetting altogether that she
was granddaughter not only of Sir Walpole Crawley,
but of Mr. Dawson of Mudbury, and so had a coal-
scuttle in her scutcheon. There are other very well-
meaning people whom one meets every day in Vanity
Fair, who are surely equally oblivious.

"It can't be true what the girls at the Rectory said,
that her mother was an opera-dancer—"

"A person can't help their birth," Rosalind replied
with great liberality. "And I agree with our brother,
that as she is in the family, of course we are bound
to notice her. I am sure Aunt Bute need not talk:
she wants to marry Kate to young Hooper, the wine-
merchant, and absolutely asked him to come to the
Rectory for orders."

"I wonder whether Lady Southdown will go away;
she looked very glum upon Mrs. Rawdon," the other
said.

"I wish she would. *I* won't read the 'Washer-woman of Finchley Common,'" vowed Violet; and so saying, and avoiding a passage at the end of which a certain coffin was placed with a couple of watchers, and lights perpetually burning in the closed room, these young women came down to the family dinner, for which the bell rang as usual.

But before this, Lady Jane conducted Rebecca to the apartments prepared for her, which, with the rest of the house, had assumed a very much improved appearance of order and comfort during Pitt's regency, and here beholding that Mrs. Rawdon's modest little trunks had arrived, and were placed in the bed-room and dressing-room adjoining, helped her to take off her neat black bonnet and cloak, and asked her sister-in-law in what more she could be useful.

"What I should like best," said Rebecca, "would be to go to the nursery; and see your dear little children." On which the two ladies looked very kindly at each other, and went to that apartment hand in hand.

Becky admired little Matilda, who was not quite four years old, as the most charming little love in the world; and the boy, a little fellow of two years — pale, heavy-eyed, and large-headed, she pronounced to be a perfect prodigy in point of size, intelligence, and beauty.

"I wish Mamma would not insist on giving him so much medicine," Lady Jane said, with a sigh. "I often think we should all be better without it." And then Lady Jane and her new-found friend had one of those confidential medical conversations about the children, which all mothers, and most women, as I am given to understand, delight in. Fifty years ago, and when the present writer, being an interesting little boy, was ordered out of the room with the ladies after dinner, I remember quite well that their talk was chiefly about their ailments; and putting this question directly to two or three since, I have always got from them the acknowledgment that times are not changed. Let my fair readers remark for themselves this very evening when they quit the dessert-table, and assemble to celebrate the drawing-room mysteries. Well — in half an hour Becky and Lady Jane were close and intimate friends — and in the course of the evening her ladyship informed Sir Pitt that she thought her new sister-in-law was a kind, frank, unaffected, and affectionate young woman.

And so having easily won the daughter's good-will, the indefatigable little woman bent herself to conciliate the august Lady Southdown. As soon as she found her ladyship alone, Rebecca attacked her on the nursery question at once, and said that her own little boy was saved, actually saved, by calomel, freely administered, when all the physicians in Paris had given the dear child up. And then she mentioned how often she had heard of Lady Southdown from that excellent man the Reverend Lawrence Grills, Minister of the chapel in May Fair, which she frequented; and how her views were very much changed by circumstances and misfortunes; and how she hoped that a past life spent in worldliness and error might not incapacitate her from *more serious* thought for the future. She described how in former days she had been indebted to Mr. Crawley for religious instruction, touched upon the " Washerwoman of Finchley Common," which she had read with the greatest profit, and asked about Lady Emily, its gifted author, now Lady Emily Hornblower, at Cape Town, where her husband had strong hopes of becoming Bishop of Caffraria.

But she crowned all, and confirmed herself in Lady Southdown's favor, by feeling very much agitated and unwell after the funeral, and requesting her lady-ship's medical advice, which the Dowager not only gave, but, wrapped up in a bed-gown and looking more like Lady Macbeth than ever, came privately in the night to Becky's room, with a parcel of favorite tracts, and a medicine of her own composition, which she insisted that Mrs. Rawdon should take.

Becky first accepted the tracts and began to examine them with great interest, engaging the Dowager in a conversation concerning them and the welfare of her soul, by which means she hoped that her body might escape medication. But after the religious topics were exhausted, Lady Macbeth would not quit Becky's chamber until her cup of night-drink was emptied too; and poor Mrs. Rawdon was compelled actually to assume a look of gratitude, and to swallow the medicine under the unyielding old Dowager's nose, who left her victim finally with a benediction.

It did not much comfort Mrs. Rawdon; her counte-nance was very queer when Rawdon came in and heard what had happened; and his explosions of laughter were as loud as usual, when Becky, with a fun which she could not disguise, even though it was at her own expense, described the occurrence, and how she had been victimized by Lady Southdown. Lord Steyne and her son in London, had many a laugh over the story, when Rawdon and his wife returned to their quarters in May Fair. Becky acted the whole scene for them. She put on a night-cap and gown. She preached a great sermon in the true serious manner: she lectured on the virtue of the medicine which she pretended to administer, with a gravity of imitation so perfect, that you would have thought that it was the Countess's own Roman nose through which she snuffled. "Give us Lady Southdown and the black dose," was the constant cry amongst the folks in Becky's little drawing-room in May Fair. And for the first time in her life the Dowager Countess of Southdown was made amusing.

Sir Pitt remembered the testimonies of respect and veneration which Rebecca had paid personally to himself in early days, and was tolerably well disposed towards her. The marriage, ill-advised as it was, had improved Rawdon very much — that was clear from the Colonel's altered habits and demeanor — and had it not been a lucky union as regarded Pitt himself? The cunning diplomatist smiled inwardly as he owned that he owed his fortune to it, and acknowledged that he at least ought not to cry out against it. His satisfaction was not removed by Rebecca's own statements, behavior, and conversation.

She doubled the deference which before had charmed him, calling out his conversational powers in such a manner as quite to surprise Pitt himself, who, always inclined to respect his own talents, admired them the more when Rebecca pointed them out to him. With her sister-in-law, Rebecca was satisfactorily able to prove, that it was Mrs. Bute Crawley who brought about the marriage which she afterwards so calumniated: that it was Mrs. Bute's avarice — who hoped to gain all Miss Crawley's fortune, and deprive Rawdon of his aunt's favor — which caused and invented all the wicked reports against Rebecca. "She succeeded in making us poor," Rebecca said, with an air of angelical patience; "but how can I be angry with a woman who has given me one of the best husbands in the

world ?   And has not her own avarice been sufficiently punished by the ruin of her own hopes, and
the loss of the property by which she set so much
store ?   Poor ! " she cried.   " Dear Lady Jane, what
care we for poverty ?   I am used to it from childhood,
and I am often thankful that Miss Crawley's money
has gone to restore the splendor of the noble old family
of which I am so proud to be a member.   I am sure
Sir Pitt will make a much better use of it than Rawdon would."

All these speeches were reported to Sir Pitt by the
most faithful of wives, and increased the favorable impression which Rebecca made ; so much so, that when
on the third day after the funeral the family party
were at dinner, Sir Pitt Crawley, carving fowls at
the head of the table, actually said to Mrs. Rawdon, " Ahem ! *Rebecca*, may I give you a wing ? " — a
speech which made the little woman's eyes sparkle
with pleasure.

While Rebecca was prosecuting the above schemes
and hopes, and Pitt Crawley arranging the funeral
ceremonial and other matters connected with his future progress and dignity, and Lady Jane busy with
her nursery, as far as her mother would let her, and
the sun rising and setting, and the clock-tower bell of
the Hall ringing to dinner and to prayers as usual, the
body of the late owner of Queen's Crawley lay in the
apartment which he had occupied, watched unceasingly by the professional attendants who were engaged for that rite.   A woman or two, and three or
four undertaker's men, the best whom Southampton
could furnish, dressed in black, and of a proper stealthy
and tragical demeanor, had charge of the remains which
they watched turn about, having the housekeeper's

room for their place of rendezvous when off duty, where they played at cards in privacy and drank their beer.

The members of the family and servants of the house kept away from the gloomy spot, where the bones of the descendant of an ancient line of knights and gentlemen lay, awaiting their final consignment to the family crypt. No regrets attended them, save those of the poor woman who had hoped to be Sir Pitt's wife and widow, and who had fled in disgrace from the Hall over which she had so nearly been a ruler. Beyond her and a favorite old pointer he had, and between whom and himself an attachment subsisted during the period of his imbecility, the old man had not a single friend to mourn him, having indeed, during the whole course of his life, never taken the least pains to secure one. Could the best and kindest of us who depart from the earth, have an opportunity of revisiting it, I suppose he or she (assuming that any Vanity-Fair feelings subsist in the sphere whither we are bound) would have a pang of mortification at finding how soon our survivors were consoled. And so Sir Pitt was forgotten — like the kindest and best of us — only a few weeks sooner.

Those who will may follow his remains to the grave, whither they were borne on the appointed day, in the most becoming manner, the family in black coaches, with their handkerchiefs up to their noses, ready for the tears which did not come: the undertaker and his gentlemen in deep tribulation: the select tenantry mourning out of compliment to the new landlord: the neighboring gentry's carriages at three miles an hour, empty, and in profound affliction: the parson speaking out the formula about "our dear brother departed." As long as we have a man's body, we play our Vanities upon it, surrounding it with humbug and ceremonies, laying it in state, and packing it up in gilt nails and velvet: and we finish our duty by placing over it a stone, written all over with lies. Bute's curate, a smart young fellow from Oxford, and Sir Pitt Crawley, composed between them an appropriate Latin epitaph for the late lamented Baronet: and the former preached a classical sermon, exhorting the survivors not to give way to grief, and informing them in the most respectful terms that they also would be one day called upon to pass that gloomy and mysterious portal which had just closed upon the remains of their lamented brother. Then the tenantry mounted on horseback again, or stayed and refreshed themselves at the Crawley Arms. Then, after a lunch in the servants' hall at Queen's Crawley, the gentry's carriages wheeled off to their different destinations: then the undertaker's men, taking the ropes, palls, velvets, ostrich feathers, and other mortuary properties, clambered up on the roof of the hearse, and rode off to Southampton. Their faces relapsed into a natural expression as the horses, clearing the lodge-gates, got into a brisker trot on the open road; and squads of them might have been seen, speckling with black the public-house entrances, with pewter pots flashing in the sunshine. Sir Pitt's invalid chair was wheeled away into a tool-house in the garden: the old pointer used to howl sometimes at first, but these were the only accents of grief which were heard in the Hall of which Sir Pitt Crawley, Baronet, had been master for some three-score years.

As the birds were pretty plentiful, and partridge-shooting is as it were the duty of an English gentleman of statesman-like propensities, Sir Pitt Crawley, the

first shock of grief over, went out a little and partook
of that diversion in a white hat with crape round it.
The sight of those fields of stubble and turnips, now
his own, gave him many secret joys. Sometimes, and
with an exquisite humility, he took no gun, but went
out with a peaceful bamboo cane; Rawdon, his big
brother, and the keepers blazing away at his side.
Pitt's money and acres had a great effect upon his
brother. The penniless Colonel became quite obsequious and respectful to the head of his house, and
despised the milk-sop Pitt no longer. Rawdon listened with sympathy to his senior's prospects of
planting and draining: gave his advice about the
stables and cattle, rode over to Mudbury to look at a
mare which he thought would carry Lady Jane, and
offered to break her, etc.: the rebellious dragoon was
quite humbled and subdued, and became a most creditable younger brother. He had constant bulletins
from Miss Briggs in London respecting little Rawdon,
who was left behind there: who sent messages of his
own. "I am very well," he wrote. "I hope you are
very well. I hope Mamma is very well. The pony is
very well. Grey takes me to ride in the Park. I can
canter. I met the little boy who rode before. He
cried when he cantered. I do not cry." Rawdon
read these letters to his brother, and Lady Jane, who
was delighted with them. The Baronet promised to
take charge of the lad at school; and his kind-hearted
wife gave Rebecca a bank-note, begging her to buy a
present with it for her little nephew.

One day followed another, and the ladies of the
house passed their life in those calm pursuits and
amusements which satisfy country ladies. Bells rang
to meals, and to prayers. The young ladies took exercise on the piano-forte every morning after break-

fast, Rebecca giving them the benefit of her instruction. Then they put on thick shoes and walked in the park or shrubberies, or beyond the palings into the village, descending upon the cottages, with Lady Southdown's medicine and tracts for the sick people there.   Lady Southdown drove out in a pony-chaise, when Rebecca would take her place by the Dowager's side, and listen to her solemn talk with the utmost interest.   She sang Handel and Haydn to the family of evenings, and engaged in a large piece of worsted work, as if she had been born to the business, and as if this kind of life was to continue with her until she should sink to the grave in a polite old age, leaving regrets and a great quantity of Consols behind her — as if there were not cares and duns, schemes, shifts, and poverty, waiting outside the park gates, to pounce upon her when she issued into the world again.

" It is n't difficult to be a country gentleman's wife," Rebecca thought.   " I think I could be a good woman if I had five thousand a year.   I could dawdle about in the nursery, and count the apricots on the wall.   I could water plants in a green-house, and pick off dead leaves from the geraniums.   I could ask old women about their rheumatisms, and order half-a-crown's worth of soup for the poor.   I should n't miss it much, out of five thousand a year.   I could even drive out ten miles to dine at a neighbor's, and dress in the fashions of the year before last.   I could go to church and keep awake in the great family pew : or go to sleep behind the curtains, with my veil down, if I only had practice.   I could pay everybody, if I had but the money.   This is what the conjurors here pride themselves upon doing.   They look down with pity upon us miserable sinners who have none.   They think themselves generous if they give our children a five-pound note, and us contemptible if we are without one." And who knows but Rebecca was right in her speculations — and that it was only a question of money and fortune which made the difference between her and an honest woman? If you take temptations into account, who is to say that he is better than his neighbor? A comfortable career of prosperity, if it does not make people honest, at least keeps them so. An alderman coming from a turtle feast will not step out of his carriage to steal a leg of mutton; but put him to starve, and see if he will not purloin a loaf. Becky consoled herself by so balancing the chances and equalizing the distribution of good and evil in the world.

The old haunts, the old fields and woods, the copses, ponds, and gardens, the rooms of the old house where she had spent a couple of years seven years ago, were all carefully revisited by her. She had been young there, or comparatively so, for she forgot the time when she ever *was* young — but she remembered her thoughts and feelings seven years back, and contrasted them with those which she had at present, now that she had seen the world and lived with great people, and raised herself far beyond her original humble station.

"I have passed beyond it, because I have brains," Becky thought, "and almost all the rest of the world are fools. I could not go back, and consort with those people now, whom I used to meet in my father's studio. Lords come up to my door with stars and garters instead of poor artists with screws of tobacco in their pockets. I have a gentleman for my husband, and an Earl's daughter for my sister, in the very house where I was little better than a servant a few years ago. But am I much better to do now in the world than I was when I was the poor painter's daughter, and wheedled the grocer round the corner for sugar and tea? Suppose I had married Francis who was so fond of me — I could n't have been much poorer than I am now. Heigho! I wish I could exchange my position in society, and all my relations for a snug sum in the three-per-cent Consols;" for so it was that Becky felt the Vanity of human affairs, and it was in those securities that she would have liked to cast anchor.

It may, perhaps, have struck her that to have been honest and humble, to have done her duty, and to have marched straightforward on her way, would have brought her as near happiness as that path by which she was striving to attain it. But, — just as the children at Queen's Crawley went round the room, where the body of their father lay; — if ever Becky had these thoughts, she was accustomed to walk round them, and not look in. She eluded them, and despised them — or at least she was committed to the other path from which retreat was now impossible. And for my part I believe that remorse is the least active of all a man's moral senses — the very easiest to be deadened when wakened: and in some never wakened at all. We grieve at being found out, and at the idea of shame or punishment; but the mere sense of wrong makes very few people unhappy in Vanity Fair.

So Rebecca, during her stay at Queen's Crawley, made as many friends of the Mammon of Unrighteousness as she could possibly bring under control. Lady Jane and her husband bade her farewell with the warmest demonstrations of good will. They looked forward with pleasure to the time when the family-house in Gaunt Street being repaired and beautified,

they were to meet again in London. Lady Southdown made her up a packet of medicine, and sent a
letter by her to the Rev. Lawrence Grills, exhorting
that gentleman to save the brand who "honored"
the letter from the burning. Pitt accompanied them
with four horses in the carriage to Mudbury, having
sent on their baggage in a cart previously, accompanied with loads of game.

"How happy you will be to see your darling little
boy again," Lady Crawley said, taking leave of her
kinswoman.

"Oh, so happy!" said Rebecca, throwing up the
green eyes. She was immensely happy to be free of
the place, and yet loth to go. Queen's Crawley was
abominably stupid; and yet the air there was somehow purer than that which she had been accustomed
to breathe. Everybody had been dull, but had been
kind in their way. "It is all the influence of a long
course of three per cents," Becky said to herself,
and was right very likely.

However, the London lamps flashed joyfully as the
stage rolled into Piccadilly, and Briggs had made a
beautiful fire in Curzon Street, and little Rawdon was
up to welcome back his papa and mamma.

CHAPTER XIV.

WHICH TREATS OF THE OSBORNE FAMILY.

Considerable time has elapsed since we have seen our respectable friend, old Mr. Osborne of Russell Square. He has not been the happiest of mortals since last we met him. Events have occurred which have not improved his temper, and in more instances than one he has not been allowed to have his own way. To be thwarted in this reasonable desire was always very injurious to the old gentleman; and resistance became doubly exasperating when gout, age, loneliness, and the force of many disappointments combined to weigh him down. His stiff black hair began to grow quite white soon after his son's death; his face grew redder; his hands trembled more and more as he poured out his glass of port wine. He led his clerks a dire life in the City : his family at home were not much happier. I doubt if Rebecca, whom we have seen piously praying for Consols, would have exchanged her poverty and the dare-devil excitement and chances of her life, for Osborne's money and the humdrum gloom which enveloped him. He had proposed for Miss Swartz, but had been rejected scornfully by the partisans of that lady, who married her to a young sprig of Scotch nobility. He was a man to have married a woman out of low life, and bullied her dreadfully afterwards : but no person presented herself suitable to his taste; and, instead, he tyrannized over his unmarried daughter, at home. She had a fine carriage and fine horses, and sat at the head of a table loaded with the grandest plate. She had a cheque-book, a prize footman to follow her when she walked, unlimited credit, and bows and compliments from all the tradesmen, and all the appurtenances of an heiress; but she spent a woful time. The little charity-girls at the Foundling, the sweep-eress at the crossing, the poorest under-kitchen-maid in the servants' hall, was happy compared to that unfortunate and now middle-aged young lady.

Frederick Bullock, Esq., of the house of Bullock, Hulker, and Bullock, had married Maria Osborne, not without a great deal of difficulty and grumbling on Mr. Bullock's part. George being dead and cut out of his father's will, Frederick insisted that the half of the old gentleman's property should be settled upon his Maria, and indeed, for a long time, refused "to come to the scratch" (it was Mr. Frederick's own expression) on any other terms. Osborne said Fred had agreed to take his daughter with twenty thousand, and he should bind himself to no more. "Fred might take it, and welcome, or leave it, and go and be hanged." Fred, whose hopes had been raised when George had been disinherited, thought himself infamously swindled by the old merchant, and for some time made as if he would break off the match altogether. Osborne withdrew his account from Bullock and Hulker's, went on 'Change with a horsewhip which he swore he would lay across the back of a certain scoundrel that should be nameless, and demeaned himself in his usual violent manner. Jane Osborne condoled with her sister Maria during this family feud. "I always told you, Maria, that it was your money he loved, and not you," she said soothingly.

"He selected *me* and my money at any rate: he

did n't choose you and yours," replied Maria, tossing up her head.

The rupture was, however, only temporary. Fred's father and senior partners counselled him to take Maria, even with the twenty thousand settled, half down, and half at the death of Mr. Osborne, with the chances of the further division of the property. So he "knuckled down," again to use his own phrase; and sent old Hulker with peaceable overtures to Osborne. It was his father, he said, who would not hear of the match, and had made the difficulties; he was most anxious to keep the engagement. The excuse was sulkily accepted by Mr. Osborne. Hulker and Bullock were a high family of the City aristocracy, and connected with the "nobs" at the West End. It was something for the old man to be able to say, "My son, sir, of the house of Hulker, Bullock, and Co., sir; my daughter's cousin, Lady Mary Mango, sir, daughter of the Right Hon. the Earl of Castlemouldy." In his imagination he saw his house peopled by the "nobs." So he forgave young Bullock, and consented that the marriage should take place.

It was a grand affair — the bridegroom's relatives giving the breakfast, their habitations being near St. George's, Hanover Square, where the business took place. The "nobs of the West End" were invited, and many of them signed the book. Mr. Mango and Lady Mary Mango were there, with the dear young Gwendoline and Guinever Mango as bridesmaids; Colonel Bludyer of the Dragoon Guards (eldest son of the house of Bludyer Brothers, Mincing Lane), another cousin of the bridegroom, and the Honorable Mrs. Bludyer; the Honorable George Boulter, Lord Levant's son, and his lady, Miss Mango

that was; Lord Viscount Castletoddy; Honorable
James McMull and Mrs. McMull (formerly Miss
Swartz), and a host of fashionables, who have all
married into Lombard Street, and done a great deal
to ennoble Cornhill.

The young couple had a house near Berkeley
Square, and a small villa at Roehampton, among the
banking colony there. Fred was considered to have
made rather a *mésalliance* by the ladies of his family,
whose grandfather had been in a Charity School, and
who were allied through the husbands with some of
the best blood in England. And Maria was bound,
by superior pride and great care in the composition
of her visiting-book, to make up for the defects of
birth; and felt it her duty to see her father and sister
as little as possible.

That she should utterly break with the old man,
who had still so many scores of thousand pounds to
give away, is absurd to suppose. Fred Bullock would
never allow her to do that. But she was still young
and incapable of hiding her feelings: and by inviting
her papa and sister to her third-rate parties, and be-
having very coldly to them when they came, and by
avoiding Russell Square, and indiscreetly begging her
father to quit that odious vulgar place; she did more
harm than all Frederick's diplomacy could repair,
and perilled her chance of her inheritance like a
giddy heedless creature as she was.

"So Russell Square is not good enough for Mrs.
Maria, hay?" said the old gentleman, rattling up the
carriage-windows as he and his daughter drove away
one night from Mrs. Frederick Bullock's, after dinner.
"So she invites her father and sister to a second day's
dinner (if those sides, or *ontrys*, as she calls 'em,
were n't served yesterday, I'm d—d), and to meet

City folks and littery men, and keeps the Earls and the Ladies, and the Honorables to herself. Honorables? Damn Honorables. I am a plain British merchant I am: and could buy the beggarly hounds over and over. Lords, indeed! — why, at one of her *swarreys* I saw one of 'em speak to a dam fiddler — a fellar I despise. And they won't come to Russell Square, won't they? Why, I 'll lay my life I 've got a better glass of wine, and pay a better figure for it, and can show a handsomer service of silver, and can lay a better dinner on my mahogany, than ever they see on theirs — the cringing, sneaking, stuck-up fools. Drive on quick, James; I want to get back to Russell Square — ha, ha!" and he sank back into the corner with a furious laugh. With such reflections on his own superior merit, it was the custom of the old gentleman not unfrequently to console himself.

Jane Osborne could not but concur in these opinions respecting her sister's conduct; and when Mrs. Frederick's first-born, Frederick Augustus Howard Stanley Devereux Bullock, was born, old Osborne, who was invited to the christening and to be godfather, contented himself with sending the child a gold cup, with twenty guineas inside it for the nurse. "That's more than any of your Lords will give, *I 'll* warrant," he said, and refused to attend at the ceremony.

The splendor of the gift, however, caused great satisfaction to the house of Bullock. Maria thought that her father was very much pleased with her, and Frederick augured the best for his little son and heir.

One can fancy the pangs with which Miss Osborne in her solitude in Russell Square read the "Morning Post," where her sister's name occurred every now and then, in the articles headed "Fashionable Ré-

unions," and where she had an opportunity of reading
a description of Mrs. F. Bullock's costume, when presented at the drawing-room by Lady Frederica Bullock. Jane's own life, as we have said, admitted of
no such grandeur. It was an awful existence. She
had to get up of black winter's mornings to make
breakfast for her scowling old father, who would
have turned the whole house out of doors if his tea had
not been ready at half-past eight. She remained silent
opposite to him, listening to the urn hissing, and
sitting in tremor while the parent read his paper, and
consumed his accustomed portion of muffins and tea.
At half past nine he rose and went to the City, and
she was almost free till dinner-time, to make visita-
tions in the kitchen, and to scold the servants: to
drive abroad and descend upon the tradesmen, who
were prodigiously respectful: to leave her cards and
her papa's at the great glum respectable houses of
their City friends; or to sit alone in the large drawing-room, expecting visitors; and working at a huge
piece of worsted by the fire, on the sofa, hard by the
great Iphigenia clock, which ticked and tolled with
mournful loudness in the dreary room. The great
glass over the mantel-piece, faced by the other great
console glass at the opposite end of the room, increased and multiplied between them the brown
holland bag in which the chandelier hung; until you
saw these brown holland bags fading away in endless
perspectives, and this apartment of Miss Osborne's
seemed the centre of a system of drawing-rooms.
When she removed the cordovan leather from the
grand piano, and ventured to play a few notes on it,
it sounded with a mournful sadness, startling the
dismal echoes of the house. George's picture was
gone, and laid up stairs in a lumber-room in the

garret; and though there was a consciousness of him, and father and daughter often instinctively knew that they were thinking of him, no mention was ever made of the brave and once darling son.

At five o'clock Mr. Osborne came back to his dinner, which he and his daughter took in silence (seldom broken, except when he swore and was savage, if the cooking was not to his liking), or which they shared twice in a month with a party of dismal friends of Osborne's rank and age. Old Dr. Gulp and his lady from Bloomsbury Square : old Mr. Frowser, the attorney, from Bedford Row, a very great man, and, from his business, hand-in-glove with the "nobs at the West End ; " old Colonel Livermore, of the Bombay Army, and Mrs. Livermore, from Upper Bedford Place : old Sergeant Toffy and Mrs. Toffy ; and sometimes old Sir Thomas Coffin and Lady Coffin, from Bedford Square. Sir Thomas was celebrated as a hanging judge, and the particular tawny port was produced when he dined with Mr. Osborne.

These people and their like gave the pompous Russell Square merchant pompous dinners back again. They had solemn rubbers of whist, when they went up stairs after drinking, and their carriages were called at half past ten. Many rich people, whom we poor devils are in the habit of envying, lead contentedly an existence like that above described. Jane Osborne scarcely ever met a man under sixty, and almost the only bachelor who appeared in their society was Mr. Smirk, the celebrated ladies' doctor.

I can't say that nothing had occurred to disturb the monotony of this awful existence : the fact is, there had been a secret in poor Jane's life which had made her father more savage and morose than even nature, pride, and over-feeding had made him. This secret was connected with Miss Wirt, who had a cousin an artist, Mr. Smee, very celebrated since as a portrait-painter and R. A., but who once was glad enough to give drawing-lessons to ladies of fashion. Mr. Smee has forgotten where Russell Square is now, but he was glad enough to visit it in the year 1818, when Miss Osborne had instruction from him.

Smee (formerly a pupil of Sharpe of Frith Street, a dissolute, irregular, and unsuccessful man, but a man with great knowledge of his art) being the cousin of Miss Wirt, we say, and introduced by her to Miss Osborne, whose hand and heart were still free after various incomplete love affairs, felt a great attach-ment for this lady, and it is believed inspired one in her bosom. Miss Wirt was the confidante of this in-trigue. I know not whether she used to leave the room where the master and his pupil were painting, in order to give them an opportunity for exchanging those vows and sentiments which cannot be uttered advantageously in the presence of a third party : I know not whether she hoped that should her cousin succeed in carrying off the rich merchant's daughter, he would give Miss Wirt a portion of the wealth which she had enabled him to win — all that is cer-tain is, that Mr. Osborne got some hint of the trans-action, came back from the City abruptly, and entered the drawing-room with his bamboo cane; found the painter, the pupil, and the companion all looking ex-ceedingly pale there; turned the former out of doors with menaces that he would break every bone in his skin, and half an hour afterwards dismissed Miss Wirt likewise, kicking her trunks down the stairs, trampling on her band-boxes, and shaking his fist at her hackney coach, as it bore her away.

Jane Osborne kept her bed-room for many days.

She was not allowed to have a companion afterwards. Her father swore to her that she should not have a shilling of his money if she made any match without his concurrence; and as he wanted a woman to keep his house, he did not choose that she should marry: so that she was obliged to give up all projects with which Cupid had any share. During her papa's life, then, she resigned herself to the manner of existence here described, and was content to be an Old Maid. Her sister, meanwhile, was having children with finer names every year — and the intercourse between the two grew fainter continually. "Jane and I do not move in the same sphere of life," Mrs. Bullock said. "I regard her as a sister, of course" — which means — what does it mean when a lady says that she regards Jane as a sister?

It has been described how the Misses Dobbin lived with their father at a fine villa at Denmark Hill, where there were beautiful graperies and peach-trees which delighted little Georgy Osborne. The Misses Dobbin, who drove often to Brompton to see our dear Amelia, came sometimes to Russell Square too, to pay a visit to their old acquaintance Miss Osborne. I believe it was in consequence of the commands of their brother the Major in India (for whom their papa had a prodigious respect), that they paid attention to Mrs. George; for the Major, the godfather and guardian of Amelia's little boy, still hoped that the child's grandfather might be induced to relent towards him, and acknowledge him for the sake of his son. The Misses Dobbin kept Miss Osborne acquainted with the state of Amelia's affairs; how she was living with her father and mother; how poor they were; how they wondered what men, and such men as their brother

and dear Captain Osborne, could find in such an insignificant little chit; how she was still, as heretofore,
a nambypamby milk-and-water affected creature — but
how the boy was really the noblest little boy ever
seen — for the hearts of all women warm towards
young children, and the sourest spinster is kind to
them.

One day, after great entreaties on the part of the
Misses Dobbin, Amelia allowed little George to go
and pass a day with them at Denmark Hill — a part
of which day she spent herself in writing to the Major in India. She congratulated him on the happy
news which his sisters had just conveyed to her.
She prayed for his prosperity, and that of the bride
he had chosen. She thanked him for a thousand
thousand kind offices and proofs of steadfast friendship to her in her affliction. She told him the last
news about little Georgy, and how he was gone to
spend that very day with his sisters in the country.
She underlined the letter a great deal, and she signed
herself affectionately his friend, Amelia Osborne.
She forgot to send any message of kindness to Lady
O'Dowd, as her wont was — and did not mention
Glorvina by name, and only in italics, as the Major's
bride, for whom she begged *blessings*. But the news
of the marriage removed the reserve which she had
kept up towards him. She was glad to be able to
own and feel how warmly and gratefully she regarded him — and as for the idea of being jealous of
Glorvina, (Glorvina, indeed!) Amelia would have
scouted it, if an angel from heaven had hinted it to
her.

That night, when Georgy came back in the pony-
carriage in which he rejoiced, and in which he was
driven by Sir William Dobbin's old coachman, he had

round his neck a fine gold chain and watch. He said
an old lady, not pretty, had given it him, who cried
and kissed him a great deal. But he did n't like her.
He liked grapes very much. And he only liked his
mamma. Amelia shrunk and started: the timid soul
felt a presentiment of terror when she heard that the
relations of the child's father had seen him.

Miss Osborne came back to give her father his dinner. He had made a good speculation in the City,
and was rather in a good-humor that day, and
chanced to remark the agitation under which she
labored. "What's the matter, Miss Osborne?" he
deigned to say.

The woman burst into tears. "Oh, sir," she said,
"I've seen little George. He is as beautiful as an
angel — and so like him!" The old man opposite to
her did not say a word, but flushed up, and began to
tremble in every limb.

CHAPTER XV.

IN WHICH THE READER HAS TO DOUBLE THE CAPE.

THE astonished reader must be called upon to transport himself ten thousand miles to the military station of Bundlegunge, in the Madras division of our Indian empire, where our gallant old friends of the —th regiment are quartered under the command of the brave Colonel, Sir Michael O'Dowd. Time has dealt kindly with that stout officer, as it does ordinarily with men who have good stomachs and good tempers, and are not perplexed over much by fatigue of the brain. The Colonel plays a good knife and fork at tiffin, and resumes those weapons with great success at dinner. He smokes his hookah after both meals, and puffs as quietly while his wife scolds him, as he did under the fire of the French at Waterloo. Age and heat have not diminished the activity or the eloquence of the descendant of the Malonys and the Molloys. Her ladyship, our old acquaintance, is as much at home at Madras as at Brussels — in the cantonment as under the tents. On the march you saw her at the head of the regiment seated on a royal elephant, a noble sight. Mounted on that beast, she has been into action with tigers in the jungle: she has been received by native princes, who have welcomed her and Glorvina into the recesses of their zenanas and offered her shawls and jewels which it went to her heart to refuse. The sentries of all arms salute her wherever she makes her appearance: and she

touches her hat gravely to their salutation. Lady
O'Dowd is one of the greatest ladies in the Presidency of Madras — her quarrel with Lady Smith,
wife of Sir Minos Smith the puisne judge, is still remembered by some at Madras, when the Colonel's lady
snapped her fingers in the Judge's lady's face, and
said *she'd* never walk behind ever a beggarly civilian.
Even now, though it is five-and-twenty years ago, people remember Lady O'Dowd performing a jig at Government House, where she danced down two *Aides-de-
Camp*, a Major of Madras cavalry, and two gentlemen
of the Civil Service; and, persuaded by Major Dobbin,
C.B., second in command of the —th, to retire to the
supper room, *lassata nondum satiata recessit.*

Peggy O'Dowd is indeed the same as ever: kind in
act and thought: impetuous in temper; eager to command: a tyrant over her Michael: a dragon amongst
all the ladies of the regiment: a mother to all the
young men, whom she tends in their sickness, defends
in all their scrapes, and with whom Lady Peggy is
immensely popular. But the Subalterns' and Captains' ladies (the Major is unmarried) cabal against
her a good deal. They say that Glorvina gives herself airs, and that Peggy herself is intolerably domineering. She interfered with a little congregation
which Mrs. Kirk had got up, and laughed the young
men away from her sermons, stating that a soldier's
wife had no business to be a parson: that Mrs. Kirk
would be much better mending her husband's clothes:
and, if the regiment wanted sermons, that she had the
finest in the world, those of her uncle, the Dean.
She abruptly put a termination to a flirtation which
Lieutenant Stubble of the regiment had commenced
with the Surgeon's wife, threatening to come down
upon Stubble for the money which he had borrowed

from her (for the young fellow was still of an extravagant turn) unless he broke off at once and went to the Cape, on sick leave. On the other hand, she housed and sheltered Mrs. Posky, who fled from her bungalow one night, pursued by her infuriate husband, wielding his second brandy bottle, and actually carried Posky through the delirium tremens, and broke him of the habit of drinking, which had grown upon that officer as all evil habits will grow upon men. In a word, in adversity she was the best of comforters, in good fortune the most troublesome of friends; having a perfectly good opinion of herself always, and an indomitable resolution to have her own way.

Among other points, she had made up her mind that Glorvina should marry our old friend Dobbin. Mrs. O'Dowd knew the Major's expectations and appreciated his good qualities, and the high character which he enjoyed in his profession. Glorvina, a very handsome, fresh-colored, black-haired, blue-eyed young lady, who could ride a horse, or play a sonata with any girl out of the County Cork, seemed to be the very person destined to insure Dobbin's happiness — much more than that poor good little weak-spur'ted Amelia, about whom he used to take on so. — "Look at Glorvina enter a room," Mrs. O'Dowd would say, "and compare her with that poor Mrs. Osborne, who couldn't say bo to a goose. She'd be worthy of you, Major — you're a quiet man yourself, and want some one to talk for ye. And though she does not come of such good blood as the Malonys or Molloys, let me tell ye, she's of an ancient family that any nobleman might be proud to marry into."

But before she had come to such a resolution, and determined to subjugate Major Dobbin by her endearments, it must be owned that Glorvina had practised

GLORVINA TRIES HER FASCINATIONS ON THE MAJOR.

them a good deal elsewhere. She had had a season in Dublin, and who knows how many in Cork, Killarney, and Mallow? She had flirted with all the marriageable officers whom the depôts of her country afforded, and all the bachelor squires who seemed eligible. She had been engaged to be married a half-score times in Ireland, besides the clergyman at Bath who used her so ill. She had flirted all the way to Madras with the Captain and chief mate of the Ramchunder East Indiaman, and had a season at the Presidency with her brother and Mrs. O'Dowd who was staying there, while the Major of the regiment was in command at the station. Everybody admired her there: everybody danced with her: but no one proposed who was worth the marrying; one or two exceedingly young subalterns sighed after her, and a beardless civilian or two; but she rejected these as beneath her pretensions; and other and younger virgins than Glorvina were married before her. There are women, and handsome women too, who have this fortune in life. They fall in love with the utmost generosity; they ride and walk with half the Army-list, though they draw near to forty, and yet the Misses O'Grady are Misses O'Grady still: Glorvina persisted that but for Lady O'Dowd's unlucky quarrel with the Judge's lady, she would have made a good match at Madras, where old Mr. Chutney, who was at the head of the civil service (and who afterwards married Miss Dolby, a young lady only thirteen years of age, who had just arrived from school in Europe), was just at the point of proposing to her.

Well, although Lady O'Dowd and Glorvina quarrelled a great number of times every day, and upon almost every conceivable subject — indeed, if Mick O'Dowd had not possessed the temper of an angel,

two such women constantly about his ears would have
driven him out of his senses — yet they agreed between themselves on this point, that Glorvina should
marry Major Dobbin, and were determined that the
Major should have no rest until the arrangement was
brought about. Undismayed by forty or fifty previous defeats, Glorvina laid siege to him. She sang
Irish Melodies at him unceasingly. She asked him
so frequently and pathetically, will ye come to the
bower? that it is a wonder how any man of feeling
could have resisted the invitation. She was never
tired of inquiring, if Sorrow had his young days
faded; and was ready to listen and weep like Desdemona at the stories of his dangers and his campaigns.
It has been said that our honest and dear old friend
used to perform on the flute in private: Glorvina
insisted upon having duets with him, and Lady
O'Dowd would rise and artlessly quit the room, when
the young couple were so engaged. Glorvina forced
the Major to ride with her of mornings. The whole
cantonment saw them set out and return. She was
constantly writing notes over to him at his house,
borrowing his books, and scoring with her great
pencil-marks such passages of sentiment or humor as
awakened her sympathy. She borrowed his horses,
his servants, his spoons, and palankin; — no wonder
that public rumor assigned her to him, and that the
Major's sisters in England should fancy they were
about to have a sister-in-law.

Dobbin, who was thus vigorously besieged, was
in the meanwhile in a state of the most odious tranquillity. He used to laugh when the young fellows
in the regiment joked him about Glorvina's manifest
attentions to him. "Bah!" said he, "she is only
keeping her hand in — she practises upon me as she

does upon Mrs. Tozer's piano, because it's the most
handy instrument in the station. I am much too
battered and old for such a fine young lady as
Glorvina." And so he went on riding with her, and
copying music and verses into her albums, and playing at chess with her very submissively; for it is
with these simple amusements that some officers in
India are accustomed to while away their leisure
moments; while others of a less domestic turn hunt
hogs, and shoot snipes, or gamble and smoke cheroots,
and betake themselves to brandy-and-water. As for
Sir Michael O'Dowd, though his lady and her sister
both urged him to call upon the Major to explain
himself, and not keep on torturing a poor innocent
girl in that shameful way, the old soldier refused
point-blank to have anything to do with the conspiracy. "Faith, the Major's big enough to choose for
himself," Sir Michael said; "he'll ask ye when he
wants ye;" — or else he would turn the matter off
jocularly, declaring that "Dobbin was too young to
keep house, and had written home to ask lave of his
mamma." Nay, he went farther, and in private communications with his Major, would caution and rally
him — crying, "Mind your oi, Dob, my boy, them
girls is bent on mischief — me Lady has just got a
box of gowns from Europe, and there's a pink satin
for Glorvina, which will finish ye, Dob, if it's in the
power of woman or satin to move ye."

But the truth is, neither beauty nor fashion could
conquer him. Our honest friend had but one idea of
a woman in his head, and that one did not in the
least resemble Miss Glorvina O'Dowd in pink satin.
A gentle little woman in black, with large eyes and
brown hair, seldom speaking, save when spoken to,
and then in a voice not the least resembling Miss

Glorvina's — a soft young mother tending an infant and beckoning the Major up with a smile to look at him — a rosy-cheeked lass coming singing into the room in Russell Square or hanging on George Osborne's arm, happy and loving — there was but this image that filled our honest Major's mind by day and by night, and reigned over it always. Very likely Amelia was not like the portrait the Major had formed of her: there was a figure in a book of fashions which his sisters had in England, and with which William had made away privately, pasting it into the lid of his desk, and fancying he saw some resemblance to Mrs. Osborne in the print, whereas I have seen it, and can vouch that it is but the picture of a high waisted gown with an impossible doll's face simpering over it — and, perhaps, Mr. Dobbin's sentimental Amelia was no more like the real one than this absurd little print which he cherished. But what man in love, of us, is better informed? — or is he much happier when he sees and owns his delusion? Dobbin was under this spell. He did not bother his friends and the public much about his feelings, or indeed lose his natural rest or appetite on account of them. His head has grizzled since we saw him last; and a line or two of silver may be seen in the soft brown hair likewise. But his feelings are not in the least changed or oldened; and his love remains as fresh as a man's recollections of boyhood are.

We have said how the two Misses Dobbin and Amelia, the Major's correspondents in Europe, wrote him letters from England; Mrs. Osborne congratulating him with great candor and cordiality upon his approaching nuptial with Miss O'Dowd.

"Your sister has just kindly visited me," Amelia

wrote in her letter, "and informed me of an *interesting event*, upon which I beg to offer my *most sincere congratulations*. I hope the young lady to whom I hear you are to be *united* will in every respect prove worthy of one who is himself all kindness and goodness. The poor widow has only her prayers to offer, and her cordial, cordial wishes for *your prosperity!* Georgy sends his love to *his dear godpapa*, and hopes that you will not forget him. I tell him that you are about to form *other ties*, with one who I am sure merits *all your affection*, but that although such ties must of course be the strongest and most sacred, and supersede *all others*, yet that I am sure the widow and the child whom you have ever protected and loved will always *have a corner in your heart*." The letter, which has been before alluded to, went on in this strain, protesting throughout as to the extreme satisfaction of the writer.

This letter, which arrived by the very same ship which brought out Lady O'Dowd's box of millinery from London (and which you may be sure Dobbin opened before any one of the other packets which the mail brought him), put the receiver into such a state of mind that Glorvina, and her pink satin, and everything belonging to her, became perfectly odious to him. The Major cursed the talk of women; and the sex in general. Everything annoyed him that day — the parade was insufferably hot and wearisome. Good heavens! was a man of intellect to waste his life, day after day, inspecting cross-belts, and putting fools through their manœuvres? The senseless chatter of the young men at mess was more than ever jarring. What cared he, a man on the high road to forty, to know how many snipes Lieutenant Smith had shot, or what were the performances of Ensign Brown's mare? The jokes

about the table filled him with shame. He was too
old to listen to the banter of the assistant-surgeon and
the slang of the youngsters, at which old O'Dowd, with
his bald head and red face, laughed quite easily.   The
old man had listened to those jokes any time these
thirty years — Dobbin himself had been fifteen years
hearing them.   And after the boisterous dulness of
the mess-table, the quarrels and scandal of the ladies
of the regiment! It was unbearable, shameful.   "O
Amelia, Amelia," he thought, "you to whom I have
been so faithful — you reproach me! It is because
you cannot feel for me, that I drag on this wearisome
life.   And you reward me after years of devotion by
giving me your blessing upon my marriage, forsooth,
with this flaunting Irish girl!" Sick and sorry felt
poor William : more than ever wretched and lonely.
He would like to have done with life and its vanity
altogether — so bootless and unsatisfactory the struggle, so cheerless and dreary the prospect seemed to
him.   He lay all that night sleepless, and yearning to
go home. Amelia's letter had fallen as a blank upon
him. No fidelity, no constant truth and passion, could
move her into warmth. She would not see that he
loved her. Tossing in his bed, he spoke out to her.
"Good God, Amelia !" he said, "don't you know that
I only love you in the world — you, who are a stone to
me — you, whom I tended through months and months
of illness and grief, and who bade me farewell with a
smile on your face, and forgot me before the door shut
between us !" The native servants lying outside his
verandas beheld with wonder the Major, so cold and
quiet ordinarily, at present so passionately moved and
cast down.   Would she have pitied him had she seen
him ?   He read over and over all the letters which he
ever had from her — letters of business relative to the

little property which he had made her believe her husband had left to her — brief notes of invitation —
every scrap of writing that she had ever sent to him
— how cold, how kind, how hopeless, how selfish they
were!

Had there been some kind gentle soul near at hand
who could read and appreciate this silent, generous
heart, who knows but that the reign of Amelia might
have been over, and that friend William's love might
have flowed into a kinder channel? But there was
only Glorvina of the jetty ringlets with whom his intercourse was familiar, and this dashing young woman
was not bent upon loving the Major, but rather on
making the Major admire *her* — a most vain and hopeless task, too, at least considering the means that the
poor girl possessed to carry it out. She curled her
hair and showed her shoulders at him, as much as to
say, did ye ever see such jet ringlets and such a complexion? She grinned at him so that he might see
that every tooth in her head was sound — and he never
heeded all these charms. Very soon after the arrival
of the box of millinery, and perhaps indeed in honor
of it, Lady O'Dowd and the ladies of the King's Regiment gave a ball to the Company's Regiments and
the civilians at the station. Glorvina sported the killing pink frock, and the Major, who attended the party
and walked very ruefully up and down the rooms,
never so much as perceived the pink garment. Glorvina danced past him in a fury with all the young subalterns of the station, and the Major was not in the
least jealous of her performance, or angry because
Captain Bangles of the Cavalry handed her to supper.
It was not jealousy, or frocks, or shoulders, that could
move him, and Glorvina had nothing more.

So these two were each exemplifying the Vanity of

this life, and each longing for what he or she could not
get. Glorvina cried with rage at the failure. She had
set her mind on the Major "more than on any of the
others," she owned, sobbing. "He'll break my heart,
he will, Peggy," she would whimper to her sister-in-
law when they were good friends; "sure every one of
me frocks must be taken in — it's such a skeleton I'm
growing." Fat or thin, laughing or melancholy, on
horse-back or the music-stool, it was all the same to
the Major. And the Colonel, puffing his pipe and listening to these complaints, would suggest that Glory
should have some black frocks out in the next box
from London, and told a mysterious story of a lady in
Ireland who died of grief for the loss of her husband
before she got ere a one.

While the Major was going on in this tantalizing
way, not proposing, and declining to fall in love,
there came another ship from Europe bringing letters
on board, and amongst them some more for the heartless man. These were home letters bearing an earlier
post mark than that of the former packets, and as
Major Dobbin recognized among his, the handwriting
of his sister, who always crossed and recrossed her
letters to her brother, — gathered together all the
possible bad news which she could collect, abused
him and read him lectures with sisterly frankness,
and always left him miserable for the day after
"dearest William" had achieved the perusal of one
of her epistles — the truth must be told that dearest
William did not hurry himself to break the seal of
Miss Dobbin's letter, but waited for a particularly favorable day and mood for doing so. A fortnight
before, moreover, he had written to scold her for
telling those absurd stories to Mrs. Osborne, and had
despatched a letter in reply to that lady, undeceiving

her with respect to the reports concerning him, and assuring her that "he had no sort of present intention of altering his condition."

Two or three nights after the arrival of the second package of letters, the Major had passed the evening pretty cheerfully at Lady O'Dowd's house, where Glorvina thought that he listened with rather more attention than usual to the "Meeting of the Wathers," the "Minsthrel Boy," and one or two other specimens of song with which she favored him (the truth is, he was no more listening to Glorvina than to the howling of the jackals in the moonlight outside, and the delusion was hers as usual), and having played his game at chess with her (cribbage with the surgeon was Lady O'Dowd's favorite evening pastime), Major Dobbin took leave of the Colonel's family at his usual hour, and retired to his own house.

There on his table, his sister's letter lay reproaching him. He took it up, ashamed rather of his negligence regarding it, and prepared himself for a disagreeable hour's communing with that crabbed-handed absent relative. — It may have been an hour after the Major's departure from the Colonel's house — Sir Michael was sleeping the sleep of the just; Glorvina had arranged her black ringlets in the innumerable little bits of paper, in which it was her habit to confine them; Lady O'Dowd, too, had gone to her bed in the nuptial chamber, on the ground-floor, and had tucked her musquito curtains round her fair form, when the guard at the gates of the Commanding-officer's compound, beheld Major Dobbin, in the moonlight, rushing towards the house with a swift step and a very agitated countenance, and he passed the sentinel and went up to the windows of the Colonel's bed-chamber.

"O'Dowd — Colonel!" said Dobbin, and kept up a great shouting.

"Heavens, Meejor!" said Glorvina of the curl-papers, putting out her head too, from her window.

"What is it, Dob, me boy?" said the Colonel, expecting there was a fire in the station, or that the route had come from headquarters.

"I — I must have leave of absence. I must go to England — on the most urgent private affairs," Dobbin said.

"Good heavens, what has happened!" thought Glorvina, trembling with all the papillotes.

"I want to be off — now — to-night," Dobbin continued; and the Colonel getting up, came out to parley with him.

In the postscript of Miss Dobbin's cross-letter, the Major had just come upon a paragraph, to the following effect: —

"I drove yesterday to see your old *acquaintance*, Mrs. Osborne. The wretched place they live at, since they were bankrupts, you know — Mr. S., to judge from a *brass plate* on the door of his hut (it is little better) is a coal-merchant. The little boy, your godson, is certainly a fine child, though forward, and inclined to be saucy and self-willed. But we have taken notice of him as you wish it, and have introduced him to his aunt, Miss O., who was rather pleased with him. Perhaps his grandpapa, not the bankrupt one, who is almost doting, but Mr. Osborne, of Russell Square, may be induced to relent towards the child of your friend, *his erring and self-willed son*. And Amelia will not be ill-disposed to give him up. The widow is *consoled*, and is about to marry a reverend gentleman, the Rev. Mr. Binny, one of the curates of Brompton. A poor match. But

Mrs. O. is getting old, and I saw a great deal of gray in her hair — she was in very good spirits: and your little godson overate himself at our house. Mamma sends her love with that of your affectionate, Ann Dobbin."

CHAPTER XVI.

A ROUND-ABOUT CHAPTER BETWEEN LONDON AND HAMPSHIRE.

OUR old friends the Crawleys' family house, in Great Gaunt Street, still bore over its front the hatchment which had been placed there as a token of mourning for Sir Pitt Crawley's demise, yet this heraldic emblem was in itself a very splendid and gaudy piece of furniture, and all the rest of the mansion became more brilliant than it had ever been during the late Baronet's reign. The black outer-coating of the bricks was removed, and they appeared with a cheerful, blushing face streaked with white : the old bronze lions of the knocker were gilt handsomely, the railings painted, and the dismallest house in Great Gaunt Street, became the smartest in the whole quarter, before the green leaves in Hampshire had replaced those yellowing ones which were on the trees in Queen's Crawley avenue when old Sir Pitt Crawley passed under them for the last time.

A little woman, with a carriage to correspond, was perpetually seen about this mansion ; an elderly spinster, accompanied by a little boy, also might be remarked coming thither daily. It was Miss Briggs and little Rawdon, whose business it was to see to the inward renovation of Sir Pitt's house, to superintend the female band engaged in stitching the blinds and hangings, to poke and rummage in the drawers and cupboards crammed with the dirty relics and congre-

gated trumperies of a couple of generations of Lady
Crawleys, and to take inventories of the china, the
glass. and other properties in the closets and store-
rooms.

Mrs. Rawdon Crawley was general-in-chief over
these arrangements, with full orders from Sir Pitt to
sell, barter, confiscate, or purchase furniture: and
she enjoyed herself not a little in an occupation which
gave full scope to her taste and ingenuity. The renovation of the house was determined upon when Sir
Pitt came to town in November to see his lawyers,
and when he passed nearly a week in Curzon Street,
under the roof of his affectionate brother and sister.

He had put up at an hotel at first; but Becky, as
soon as she heard of the Baronet's arrival, went off
alone to greet him, and returned in an hour to Curzon
Street with Sir Pitt in the carriage by her side. It
was impossible sometimes to resist this artless little
creature's hospitalities, so kindly were they pressed,
so frankly and amiably offered. Becky seized Pitt's
hand in a transport of gratitude when he agreed to
come. "Thank you," she said, squeezing it, and looking into the Baronet's eyes, who blushed a good deal;
"how happy this will make Rawdon." She bustled
up to Pitt's. bed-room, leading on the servants, who
were carrying his trunks thither. She came in herself
laughing, with a coal-scuttle out of her own room.

A fire was blazing already in Sir Pitt's apartment
(it was Miss Briggs's room, by the way, who was sent
up stairs to sleep with the maid). "I knew I should
bring you," she said, with pleasure beaming in her
glance. Indeed, she was really sincerely happy at
having him for a guest.

Becky made Rawdon dine out once or twice on
business, while Pitt stayed with them, and the Baronet

passed the happy evening alone with her and Briggs.
She went down stairs to the kitchen and actually
cooked little dishes for him. "Is n't it a good *salmis?*"
she said; "I made it for you. I can make you better
dishes than that: and will when you come to see me."

"Everything you do, you do well," said the Baronet,
gallantly. "The *salmis* is excellent indeed."

"A poor man's wife," Rebecca replied, gayly, "must
make herself useful, you know:" on which her brother-
in-law vowed that "she was fit to be the wife of an
Emperor, and that to be skilful in domestic duties was
surely one of the most charming of woman's qualities." And Sir Pitt thought, with something like
mortification, of Lady Jane at home, and of a certain
pie which she had insisted on making, and serving to
him at dinner — a most abominable pie.

Besides the *salmis*, which was made of Lord Steyne's
pheasants from his lordship's cottage of Stillbrook,
Becky gave her brother-in-law a bottle of white wine,
some that Rawdon had brought with him from France,
and had picked up for nothing, the little story-teller
said; whereas the liquor was, in truth, some White
Hermitage from the Marquis of Steyne's famous
cellars, which brought fire into the Baronet's pallid
cheeks and a glow into his feeble frame.

Then when he had drunk up the bottle of *petit vin
blanc* she gave him her hand and took him up to the
drawing-room, and made him snug on the sofa by the
fire, and let him talk as she listened with the tenderest kindly interest, sitting by him, and hemming a
shirt for her dear little boy. Whenever Mrs. Rawdon
wished to be particularly humble and virtuous, this
little shirt used to come out of her work-box. It had
got to be too small for Rawdon long before it was
finished.

Well, Rebecca listened to Pitt, she talked to him, she sang to him, she coaxed him, and cuddled him, so that he found himself more and more glad every day to get back from the lawyer's at Gray's Inn, to the blazing fire in Curzon Street — a gladness in which the men of law likewise participated, for Pitt's harangues were of the longest — and so that when he went away he felt quite a pang at departing. How pretty she looked kissing her hand to him from the carriage, and waving her handkerchief when he had taken his place in the mail! She put the handkerchief to her eyes once. He pulled his sealskin cap over his, as the coach drove away, and, sinking back, he thought to himself how she respected him and how he deserved it, and how Rawdon was a foolish dull fellow who did n't half appreciate his wife: and how mum and stupid his own wife was compared to that brilliant little Becky. Becky had hinted every one of these things herself, perhaps, but so delicately and gently, that you hardly knew when or where. And, before they parted, it was agreed that the house in London should be re-decorated for the next season, and that the brothers' families should meet again in the country at Christmas.

"I wish you could have got a little money out of him," Rawdon said to his wife moodily when the Baronet was gone. "I should like to give something to old Raggles, hanged if I should n't. It ain't right, you know, that the old fellow should be kept out of all his money. It may be inconvenient, and he might let to somebody else besides us, you know."

"Tell him," said Becky, "that as soon as Sir Pitt's affairs are settled, everybody will be paid, and give him a little something on account. Here's a cheque that Pitt left for the boy," and she took from her bag and gave her husband a paper which his brother had handed over to her, on behalf of the little son and heir of the younger branch of the Crawleys.

The truth is, she had tried personally the ground on which her husband expressed a wish that she should venture — tried it ever so delicately and found it unsafe. Even at a hint about embarrassments, Sir Pitt Crawley was off and alarmed. And he began a long speech, explaining how straitened he himself was in money matters; how the tenants would not pay how his father's affairs, and the expenses attendant upon the demise of the old gentleman, had involved him; how he wanted to pay off encumbrances; and how the bankers and agents were overdrawn; and Pitt Crawley ended by making a compromise with his sister-in-law, and giving her a very small sum for the benefit of her little boy.

Pitt knew how poor his brother and his brother's family must be. It could not have escaped the notice of such a cool and experienced old diplomatist, that Rawdon's family had nothing to live upon, and that houses and carriages are not to be kept for nothing. He knew very well that he was the proprietor or appropriator of the money, which, according to all proper calculation, ought to have fallen to his younger brother, and he had, we may be sure, some secret pangs of remorse within him, which warned him that he ought to perform some act of justice, or, let us say, compensation, towards these disappointed relations. A just, decent man, not without brains, who said his prayers, and knew his catechism, and did his duty outwardly through life, he could not be otherwise than aware that something was due to his brother at his hands, and that morally he was Rawdon's debtor.

But, as one reads in the columns of the "Times" newspaper every now and then, queer announcements from the Chancellor of the Exchequer, acknowledging the receipt of £50 from A. B., or £10 from W. T., as conscience-money, on account of taxes due by the said A. B. or W. T., which payments the penitents beg the Right Honorable gentleman to acknowledge through the medium of the public press ; — so is the Chancellor no doubt, and the reader likewise, always perfectly sure that the above-named A. B. and W. T. are only paying a very small instalment of what they really owe, and that the man who sends up a twenty-pound note has very likely hundreds or thousands more for which he ought to account. Such, at least, are my feelings, when I see A. B. or W. T.'s insufficient acts of repentance. And I have no doubt that Pitt Crawley's contrition, or kindness if you will, towards his younger brother, by whom he had so much profited, was only a very small dividend upon the capital sum in which he was indebted to Rawdon. Not everybody is willing to pay even so much. To part with money is a sacrifice beyond almost all men endowed with a sense of order. There is scarcely any man alive who does not think himself meritorious for giving his neighbor five pounds. Thriftless gives, not from a beneficent pleasure in giving, but from a lazy delight in spending. He would not deny himself one enjoyment ; not his opera-stall, not his horse, not his dinner, not even the pleasure of giving Lazarus the five pounds. Thrifty, who is good, wise, just, and owes no man a penny, turns from a beggar, haggles with a hackney-coachman, or denies a poor relation, and I doubt which is the most selfish of the two. Money has only a different value in the eyes of each.

So, in a word, Pitt Crawley thought he would do

something for his brother, and then thought he would think about it some other time.

And with regard to Becky, she was not a woman who expected too much from the generosity of her neighbors, and so was quite content with all that Pitt Crawley had done for her. She was acknowledged by the head of the family. If Pitt would not give her anything, he would get something for her some day. If she got no money from her brother-in-law, she got what was as good as money, — credit. Raggles was made rather easy in his mind by the spectacle of the union between the brothers, by a small payment on the spot, and by the promise of a much larger sum speedily to be assigned to him. And Rebecca told Miss Briggs, whose Christmas dividend upon the little sum lent by her, Becky paid with an air of candid joy, and as if her exchequer was brimming over with gold — Rebecca, we say, told Miss Briggs, in strict confidence, that she had conferred with Sir Pitt, who was famous as a financier, on Briggs's special behalf, as to the most profitable investment of Miss B.'s remaining capital ; that Sir Pitt, after much consideration, had thought of a most safe and advantageous way in which Briggs could lay out her money ; that, being especially interested in her as an attached friend of the late Miss Crawley, and of the whole family, and that long before he left town, he had recommended that she should be ready with the money at a moment's notice, so as to purchase at the most favorable opportunity the shares which Sir Pitt had in his eye. Poor Miss Briggs was very grateful for this mark of Sir Pitt's attention — it came so unsolicited, she said, for she never should have thought of removing the money from the funds — and the delicacy enhanced the kindness of the office ; and she promised to see her man of business immediately, and be ready with her little cash at the proper hour.

And this worthy woman was so grateful for the kindness of Rebecca in the matter, and for that of her generous benefactor, the Colonel, that she went out and spent a great part of her half-year's dividend in the purchase of a black velvet coat for little Rawdon, who, by the way, was grown almost too big for black velvet now, and was of a size and age befitting him for the assumption of the virile jacket and pantaloons.

He was a fine open-faced boy, with blue eyes and waving flaxen hair, sturdy in limb, but generous and soft in heart: fondly attaching himself to all who were good to him — to the pony — to Lord Southdown, who gave him the horse — (he used to blush and glow all over when he saw that kind young nobleman) — to the groom who had charge of the pony — to Molly, the cook, who crammed him with ghost-stories at night, and with good things from the dinner — to Briggs, whom he plagued and laughed at — and to his father especially, whose attachment towards the lad was curious too to witness. Here, as he grew to be about eight years old, his attachments may be said to have ended. The beautiful mother-vision had faded away after a while. During near two years she had scarcely spoken to the child. She disliked him. He had the measles and the hooping-cough. He bored her. One day when he was standing at the landing-place, having crept down from the upper regions, attracted by the sound of his mother's voice, who was singing to Lord Steyne, the drawing-room door opening suddenly, discovered the little spy, who but a moment before had been rapt in delight, and listening to the music.

His mother came out and struck him violently a couple of boxes on the ear. He heard a laugh from the Marquis in the inner room (who was amused by this free and artless exhibition of Becky's temper), and fled down below to his friends of the kitchen, bursting in an agony of grief.

"It is not because it hurts me," little Rawdon gasped out — "only — only" — sobs and tears wound up the sentence in a storm. It was the little boy's heart that was bleeding. "Why may n't I hear her singing? Why don't she ever sing to me — as she does to that baldheaded man with the large teeth?" He gasped out at various intervals these exclamations of rage and grief. The cook looked at the housemaid: the housemaid looked knowingly at the footman — the awful kitchen inquisition which sits in judgment in every house, and knows everything, — sat on Rebecca at that moment.

After this incident, the mother's dislike increased to hatred: the consciousness that the child was in the house was a reproach and a pain to her. His very sight annoyed her. Fear, doubt, and resistance sprang up, too, in the boy's own bosom. They were separated from that day of the boxes on the ear.

Lord Steyne also heartily disliked the boy. When they met by mischance, he made sarcastic bows or remarks to the child, or glared at him with savage-looking eyes. Rawdon used to stare him in the face, and double his little fists in return. He knew his enemy; and this gentleman, of all who came to the house, was the one who angered him most. One day the footman found him squaring his fists at Lord Steyne's hat in the hall. The footman told the circumstance as a good joke to Lord Steyne's coachman; that officer imparted it to Lord Steyne's gentleman, and to the servants' hall in general. And very soon afterwards, when Mrs. Rawdon Crawley made her appearance at Gaunt House, the porter who unbarred the gates, the servants of all uniforms in the hall, the functionaries in white waistcoats, who bawled out from landing to landing the names of Colonel and Mrs. Rawdon Crawley, knew about her, or fancied they did. The man who brought her refreshment and stood behind her chair, had talked her character over with the large gentleman in motley-colored clothes at his side. *Bon Dieu!* it is awful, that servants' inquisition! You see a woman in a great party in a splendid saloon, surrounded by faithful admirers, distributing sparkling glances, dressed to perfection, curled, rouged, smiling and happy : — Discovery walks respectfully up to her, in the shape of a huge powdered man with large calves and a tray of ices — with Calumny (which is as fatal as truth) — behind him, in the shape of the hulking fellow carrying the wafer-biscuits. Madam, your secret will be talked over by those men at their club at the public-house to-night. Jeames will tell Chawls his notions about you over their pipes and pewter beer-pots. Some people ought to have mutes for servants in Vanity Fair — mutes who could not write. If you are guilty, tremble. That fellow behind your chair may be a Janissary with a bow-string in his plush breeches pocket. If you are not guilty, have a care of appearances : which are as ruinous as guilt.

"Was Rebecca guilty or not?" the *Vehmgericht* of the servants' hall had pronounced against her.

And, I shame to say, she would not have got credit had they not believed her to be guilty. It was the sight of the Marquis of Steyne's carriage-lamps at her door, contemplated by Raggles, burning in the

blackness of midnight, "that kep him up," as he afterwards said; that even more than Rebecca's arts and
coaxings.

And so — guiltless very likely — she was writhing
and pushing onward towards what they call "a position in society," and the servants were pointing at her
as lost and ruined. So you see Molly, the housemaid,
of a morning, watching a spider in the door-post lay
his thread and laboriously crawl up it, until, tired of
the sport, she raises her broom and sweeps away the
thread and the artificer.

A day or two before Christmas, Becky, her husband
and her son, made ready and went to pass the holidays at the seat of their ancestors at Queen's Crawley.
Becky would have liked to leave the little brat behind,
and would have done so but for Lady Jane's urgent
invitations to the youngster; and the symptoms of
revolt and discontent which Rawdon manifested at
her neglect of her son. "He's the finest boy in England," the father said, in a tone of reproach to her,
"and you don't seem to care for him, Becky, as much
as you do for your spaniel. He sha'n't bother you
much: at home he will be away from you in the nursery, and he shall go outside on the coach with me."

"Where you go yourself because you want to smoke
those filthy cigars," replied Mrs. Rawdon.

"I remember when you liked 'em though," answered the husband.

Becky laughed: she was almost always good-humored. "That was when I was on my promotion,
Goosey," she said. "Take Rawdon outside with you,
and give him a cigar too if you like."

Rawdon did not warm his little son for the winter's
journey in this way, but he and Briggs wrapped up

the child in shawls and comforters, and he was hoisted respectfully on to the roof of the coach in the dark morning, under the lamps of the White Horse Cellar: and with no small delight he watched the dawn rise, and made his first journey to the place which his father still called home. It was a journey of infinite pleasure to the boy, to whom the incidents of the road afforded endless interest: his father answering to him all questions connected with it, and telling him who lived in the great white house to the right, and whom the park belonged to. His mother, inside the vehicle, with her maid and her furs, her wrappers, and her scent bottles, made such a to-do that you would have thought she never had been in a stage-coach before — much less, that she had been turned out of this very one to make room for a paying passenger on a certain journey performed some half-score years ago.

It was dark again when little Rawdon was wakened up to enter his uncle's carriage at Mudbury, and he sat and looked out of it wondering as the great iron gates flew open, and at the white trunks of the limes as they swept by, until they stopped, at length, before the light windows of the Hall, which were blazing and comfortable with Christmas welcome. The hall-door was flung open — a big fire was burning in the great old fireplace — a carpet was down over the checkered black flags — "It's the old Turkey one that used to be in the Ladies' Gallery," thought Rebecca, and the next instant was kissing Lady Jane.

She and Sir Pitt performed the same salute with great gravity: but Rawdon having been smoking, hung back rather from his sister-in-law, whose two children came up to their cousin: and, while Matilda held out her hand and kissed him, Pitt Binkie Southdown, the son and heir, stood aloof rather, and examined him as a little dog does a big dog.

Then the kind hostess conducted her guests to the snug apartments blazing with cheerful fires. Then the young ladies came and knocked at Mrs. Rawdon's door, under the pretence that they were desirous to be useful, but in reality to have the pleasure of inspecting the contents of her band and bonnet-boxes, and her dresses which, though black, were of the newest London fashion. And they told her how much the Hall was changed for the better, and how old Lady Southdown was gone, and how Pitt was taking his station in the county, as became a Crawley in fact. Then the great dinner-bell having rung, the family assembled at dinner, at which meal Rawdon Junior was placed by his aunt, the good-natured lady of the house; Sir Pitt being uncommonly attentive to his sister-in-law at his own right hand.

Little Rawdon exhibited a fine appetite, and showed a gentleman-like behavior.

"I like to dine here," he said to his aunt when he had completed his meal, at the conclusion of which, and after a decent grace by Sir Pitt, the younger son and heir was introduced, and was perched on a high chair by the Baronet's side, while the daughter took possession of the place and the little wine-glass prepared for her near her mother. "I like to dine here," said Rawdon Minor, looking up at his relation's kind face.

"Why?" said the good Lady Jane.

"I dine in the kitchen when I am at home," replied Rawdon Minor, "or else with Briggs." But Becky was so engaged with the Baronet, her host, pouring out a flood of compliments and delights and raptures, and admiring young Pitt Binkie, whom she declared to be the most beautiful, intelligent, noble-looking little creature, and so like his father, that she did not hear the remarks of her own flesh and blood at the other end of the broad shining table.

As a guest, and it being the first night of his arrival, Rawdon the Second was allowed to sit up until the hour when tea being over, and a great gilt book being laid on the table before Sir Pitt, all the domestics of the family streamed in, and Sir Pitt read prayers. It was the first time the poor little boy had ever witnessed or heard of such a ceremonial.

The house had been much improved even since the Baronet's brief reign, and was pronounced by Becky to be perfect, charming, delightful, when she surveyed it in his company. As for little Rawdon, who examined it with the children for his guides, it seemed to him a perfect palace of enchantment and wonder. There were long galleries, and ancient state bed-rooms, there were pictures and old china, and armor. There were the rooms in which grandpapa died, and by which the children walked with terrified looks. " Who was grandpapa ? " he asked ; and they told him how he used to be very old, and used to be wheeled about in a garden-chair, and they showed him the garden-chair one day rotting in the out-house in which it had lain since the old gentleman had been wheeled away yonder to the church, of which the spire was glittering over the park elms.

The brothers had good occupation for several mornings in examining the improvements which had been effected by Sir Pitt's genius and economy. And as they walked or rode, and looked at them, they could talk without too much boring each other. And Pitt took care to tell Rawdon what a heavy outlay of money these improvements had occasioned: and that a man of landed and funded property was often very hard pressed for twenty pounds. "There is that new lodge gate," said Pitt, pointing to it humbly with the bamboo cane, "I can no more pay for it before the dividends in January than I can fly."

"I can lend you, Pitt, till then," Rawdon answered rather ruefully; and they went in and looked at the restored lodge, where the family arms were just new scraped in stone; and where old Mrs. Lock, for the first time these many long years, had tight doors, sound roofs, and whole windows.

CHAPTER XVII.

SIR PITT CRAWLEY had done more than repair fences and restore dilapidated lodges on the Queen's Crawley estate. Like a wise man he had set to work to rebuild the injured popularity of his house, and stop up the gaps and ruins in which his name had been left by his disreputable and thriftless old predecessor. He was elected for the borough speedily after his father's demise; a magistrate, a member of Parliament, a county magnate and representative of an ancient family, he made it his duty to show himself before the Hampshire public, subscribed handsomely to the county charities, called assiduously upon all the county folks, and laid himself out in a word to take that position in Hampshire, and in the Empire afterwards, to which he thought his prodigious talents justly entitled him. Lady Jane was instructed to be friendly with the Fuddlestons, and the Wapshots, and the other famous baronets, their neighbors. Their carriages might frequently be seen in the Queen's Crawley avenue now; they dined pretty frequently at the Hall (where the cookery was so good, that it was clear Lady Jane very seldom had a hand in it), and in return Pitt and his wife most energetically dined out in all sorts of weather, and at all sorts of distances. For though Pitt did not care for joviality, being a frigid man of poor health and appetite, yet he considered that to be hospitable and

condescending was quite incumbent on his station, and
every time that he got a headache from too long an
after-dinner sitting, he felt that he was a martyr to
duty. He talked about crops, corn-laws, politics, with
the best country gentlemen. He (who had been formerly inclined to be a sad freethinker on these points)
entered into poaching and game preserving with ardor. He did n't hunt: he was n't a hunting man: he
was a man of books and peaceful habits: but he
thought that the breed of horses must be kept up in
the country, and that the breed of foxes must therefore be looked to, and for his part, if his friend, Sir
Huddleston Fuddleston, liked to draw his country,
and meet as of old the F. hounds used to do at Queen's
Crawley, he should be happy to see him there, and
the gentlemen of the Fuddleston hunt. And to Lady
Southdown's dismay too, he became more orthodox in
his tendencies every day: gave up preaching in public and attending meeting-houses; went stoutly to
Church: called on the Bishop, and all the Clergy at
Winchester: and made no objection when the Venerable Archdeacon Trumper asked for a game of whist.
What pangs must have been those of Lady Southdown, and what an utter castaway she must have
thought her son-in-law for permitting such a godless
diversion! and when, on the return of the family
from an oratorio at Winchester, the Baronet announced to the young ladies that he should next
year very probably take them to the "county balls,"
they worshipped him for his kindness. Lady Jane
was only too obedient, and perhaps glad herself to
go. The Dowager wrote off the direst descriptions
of her daughter's worldly behavior to the authoress
of the "Washerwoman of Finchley Common" at the
Cape; and her house in Brighton being about this

time unoccupied, returned to that watering-place, her absence being not very much deplored by her children. We may suppose, too, that Rebecca, on paying a second visit to Queen's Crawley, did not feel particularly grieved at the absence of the lady of the medicine-chest; though she wrote a Christmas letter to her ladyship, in which she respectfully recalled herself to Lady Southdown's recollection, spoke with gratitude of the delight which her ladyship's conversation had given her on the former visit, dilated on the kindness with which her ladyship had treated her in sickness, and declared that everything at Queen's Crawley reminded her of her absent friend.

A great part of the altered demeanor and popularity of Sir Pitt Crawley might have been traced to the counsels of that astute little lady of Curzon Street. "*You* remain a baronet — you consent to be a mere country gentleman," she said to him, while he had been her guest in London. "No, Sir Pitt Crawley, I know you better. I know your talents and your ambition. You fancy you hide them both: but you can conceal neither from me. I showed Lord Steyne your pamphlet on Malt. He was familiar with it: and said it was in the opinion of the whole Cabinet the most masterly thing that had appeared on the subject. The Ministry has its eye upon you, and I know what you want. You want to distinguish yourself in Parliament; every one says you are the finest speaker in England (for your speeches at Oxford are still remembered). You want to be Member for the County, where with your own vote and your borough at your back, you can command anything. And you want to be Baron Crawley of Queen's Crawley, and will be before you die. I saw it all. I could read your heart, Sir Pitt. If I had a husband who possessed your intellect as he does your name, I sometimes think I should not be unworthy of him — but — but I am your kinswoman now," she added with a laugh. "Poor little penniless I have got a little interest — and who knows, perhaps the mouse may be able to aid the lion."

Pitt Crawley was amazed and enraptured with her speech. "How that woman comprehends me!" he said. "I never could get Jane to read three pages of the malt-pamphlet. *She* has no idea that I have commanding talents or secret ambition. So they remember my speaking at Oxford, do they? The rascals! now that I represent my borough and may sit for the county, they begin to recollect me! Why, Lord Steyne cut me at the levee last year : they are beginning to find out that Pitt Crawley is some one at last. Yes, the man was always the same whom these people neglected : it was only the opportunity that was wanting, and I will show them now that I can speak and act as well as write. Achilles did not declare himself until they gave him the sword. I hold it now, and the world shall yet hear of Pitt Crawley."

Therefore it was that this roguish diplomatist had grown so hospitable ; that he was so civil to oratorios and hospitals ; so kind to Deans and Chapters ; so generous in giving and accepting dinners ; so uncommonly gracious to farmers on market-days ; and so much interested about county business ; and that the Christmas at the Hall was the gayest which had been known there for many a long day.

On Christmas Day a great family gathering took place. All the Crawleys from the Rectory came to dine. Rebecca was as frank and fond of Mrs. Bute, as if the other had never been her enemy : she was

affectionately interested in the dear girls, and surprised at the progress which they had made in music
since her time : and insisted upon encoring one of the
duets out of the great song-books which Jim, grumbling, had been forced to bring under his arm from
the Rectory. Mrs. Bute, perforce, was obliged to
adopt a decent demeanor towards the little adventuress — of course being free to discourse with her
daughters afterwards about the absurd respect with
which Sir Pitt treated his sister-in-law. But Jim,
who had sat next to her at dinner, declared she was
a trump : and one and all of the Rector's family
agreed that the little Rawdon was a fine boy. They
respected a possible baronet in the boy, between
whom and the title there was only the little sickly
pale Pitt Binkie.

The children were very good friends. Pitt Binkie
was too little a dog for such a big dog as Rawdon to
play with : and Matilda being only a girl, of course
not fit companion for a young gentleman who was
near eight years old, and going into jackets very soon.
He took the command of this small party at once —
the little girl and the little boy following him about
with great reverence at such times as he condescended to sport with them. His happiness and
pleasure in the country were extreme. The kitchen
garden pleased him hugely, the flowers moderately,
but the pigeons and the poultry, and the stables when
he was allowed to visit them, were delightful objects
to him. He resisted being kissed by the Misses
Crawley : but he allowed Lady Jane sometimes to
embrace him : and it was by her side that he liked to
sit when the signal to retire to the drawing-room
being given, the ladies left the gentlemen to their
claret — by her side rather than by his mother. For

Rebecca seeing that tenderness was the fashion, called Rawdon to her one evening, and stooped down and kissed him in the presence of all the ladies.

He looked her full in the face after the operation, trembling and turning very red, as his wont was when moved. "You never kiss me at home, Mamma," he said; at which there was a general silence and consternation, and a by no means pleasant look in Becky's eyes.

Rawdon was fond of his sister-in-law, for her regard for his son. Lady Jane and Becky did not get on *quite* so well at this visit as on occasion of the former one, when the Colonel's wife was bent upon pleasing. Those two speeches of the child struck rather a chill. Perhaps Sir Pitt was rather too attentive to her.

But Rawdon, as became his age and size, was fonder of the society of the men than of the women; and never wearied of accompanying his sire to the stables, whither the Colonel retired to smoke his cigar — Jim, the Rector's son, sometimes joining his cousin in that and other amusements. He and the Baronet's keeper were very close friends, their mutual taste for "dawgs" bringing them much together. On one day, Mr. James, the Colonel, and Horn, the keeper, went and shot pheasants, taking little Rawdon with them. On another most blissful morning, these four gentlemen partook of the amusement of rat-hunting in a barn, than which sport Rawdon as yet had never seen anything more noble. They stopped up the ends of certain drains in the barn, into the other openings of which ferrets were inserted; and then stood silently aloof with uplifted stakes in their hands, and an anxious little terrier (Mr. James's celebrated "dawg" Forceps, indeed), scarcely breathing from excitement, listening motionless on three legs, to the faint squeaking of the rats below. Desperately bold at last, the persecuted animals bolted above ground: the terrier accounted for one, the keeper for another, Rawdon, from flurry and excitement, missed his rat, but on the other hand he half-murdered a ferret.

But the greatest day of all was that on which Sir Huddleston Fuddleston's hounds met upon the lawn at Queen's Crawley.

That was a famous sight for little Rawdon. At half-past ten, Tom Moody, Sir Huddleston Fuddleston's huntsman, was seen trotting up the avenue, followed by the noble pack of hounds in a compact body — the rear being brought up by the two whips clad in stained scarlet frocks — light hard-featured lads on well-bred lean horses, possessing marvellous dexterity in casting the points of their long heavy whips at the thinnest part of any dog's skin who dares to straggle from the main body, or to take the slightest notice, or even so much as wink at the hares and rabbits starting under their noses.

Next comes boy Jack, Tom Moody's son, who weighs five stone, measures eight-and-forty inches, and will never be any bigger. He is perched on a large raw-boned hunter, half covered by a capacious saddle. This animal is Sir Huddleston Fuddleston's favorite horse — the Nob. Other horses, ridden by other small boys, arrive from time to time, awaiting their masters, who will come cantering on anon.

Tom Moody rides up to the door of the Hall, where he is welcomed by the butler, who offers him drink, which he declines. He and his pack then draw off into a sheltered corner of the lawn, where the dogs roll on the grass, and play or growl angrily at one another, ever and anon breaking out into furious fight speedily to be quelled by Tom's voice, unmatched at rating, or the snaky thongs of the whips.

Many young gentlemen canter up on thorough-bred hacks, spatter-dashed to the knee, and enter the house to drink cherry-brandy and pay their respects to the ladies, or, more modest and sportsman-like, divest themselves of their mud-boots, exchange their hacks for their hunters, and warm their blood by a preliminary gallop round the lawn. Then they collect round the pack in the corner, and talk with Tom Moody of past sport, and the merits of Sniveller and Diamond, and of the state of the country and of the wretched breed of foxes.

Sir Huddleston presently appears mounted on a clever cob, and rides up to the Hall, where he enters and does the civil thing by the ladies, after which, being a man of few words, he proceeds to business. The hounds are drawn up to the hall-door and little Rawdon descends amongst them, excited yet half alarmed by the caresses which they bestow upon him, at the thumps he receives from their waving tails, and at their canine bickerings, scarcely restrained by Tom Moody's tongue and lash.

Meanwhile, Sir Huddleston has hoisted himself unwieldily on the Nob: "Let's try Sowster's Spinney, Tom," says the Baronet, "Farmer Mangle tells me there are two foxes in it." Tom blows his horn and trots off, followed by the pack, by the whips, by the young gents from Winchester, by the farmers of the neighborhood, by the laborers of the parish on foot, with whom the day is a great holiday; Sir Huddleston bringing up the rear with Colonel Crawley, and the whole *cortège* disappears down the avenue.

The Reverend Bute Crawley (who has been too modest to appear at the public meet before his nephew's windows), and whom Tom Moody remembers forty years back a slender divine riding the wildest horses, jumping the widest brooks, and larking over the newest gates in the country, — his Reverence, we say, happens to trot out from the Rectory Lane on his powerful black horse, just as Sir Huddleston passes ; he joins the worthy Baronet. Hounds and horsemen disappear, and little Rawdon remains on the door-steps, wondering and happy.

During the progress of this memorable holiday, little Rawdon, if he had got no special liking for his uncle, always awful and cold, and locked up in his study, plunged in justice-business and surrounded by bailiffs and farmers — has gained the good graces of his married and maiden aunts, of the two little folks of the Hall, and of Jim of the Rectory, whom Sir Pitt is encouraging to pay his addresses to one of the young ladies, with an understanding doubtless that he shall be presented to the living when it shall be vacated by his fox-hunting old sire. Jim has given up that sport himself, and confines himself to a little harmless duck or snipe-shooting, or a little quiet trifling with the rats during the Christmas holidays, after which he will return to the University, and try and not be plucked, once more. He has already eschewed green coats, red neckcloths, and other worldly ornaments, and is preparing himself for a change in his condition. In this cheap and thrifty way Sir Pitt tries to pay off his debt to his family.

Also before this merry Christmas was over, the Baronet had screwed up courage enough to give his brother another draft on his bankers, and for no less a sum than a hundred pounds, an act which caused Sir Pitt cruel pangs at first, but which made him glow afterwards to think himself one of the most generous

of men.   Rawdon and his son went away with the utmost heaviness of heart.   Becky and the ladies parted
with some alacrity, however : and our friend returned
to London to commence those avocations with which
we find her occupied when this chapter begins.   Under
her care the Crawley House in Great Gaunt Street was
quite rejuvenescent, and ready for the reception of Sir
Pitt and his family, when the Baronet came to London
to attend his duties in Parliament, and to assume that
position in the country for which his vast genius fitted
him.

For the first session, this profound dissembler hid
his projects and never opened his lips but to present a
petition from Mudbury.   But he attended assiduously
in his place, and learned thoroughly the routine and
business of the house.   At home he gave himself up to
the perusal of Blue Books, to the alarm and wonder of
Lady Jane, who thought he was killing himself by
late hours and intense application.   And he made acquaintance with the ministers, and the chiefs of his
party, determining to rank as one of them before many
years were over.

Lady Jane's sweetness and kindness had inspired
Rebecca with such a contempt for her ladyship as the
little woman found no small difficulty in concealing.
That sort of goodness and simplicity which Lady Jane
possessed, annoyed our friend Becky, and it was impossible for her at times not to show, or to let the
other divine her scorn.   Her presence, too, rendered
Lady Jane uneasy.   Her husband talked constantly
with Becky.   Signs of intelligence seemed to pass between them : and Pitt spoke with her on subjects on
which he never thought of discoursing with Lady Jane.
The latter did not understand them to be sure, but it
was mortifying to remain silent ; still more mortifying

to know that you had nothing to say, and hear that little audacious Mrs. Rawdon dashing on from subject to subject, with a word for every man, and a joke always pat; and to sit in one's own house alone, by the fireside, and watching all the men round your rival.

In the country, when Lady Jane was telling stories to the children, who clustered about her knees (little Rawdon into the bargain, who was very fond of her) — and Becky came into the room, sneering with green scornful eyes, poor Lady Jane grew silent under those baleful glances. Her simple little fancies shrank away tremulously, as fairies in the story-books, before a superior bad angel. She could not go on, although Rebecca, with the smallest inflection of sarcasm in her voice, besought her to continue that charming story. And on her side gentle thoughts and simple pleasures were odious to Mrs. Becky, — they discorded with her; she hated people for liking them; she spurned children and children-lovers. "I have no taste for bread and butter," she would say, when caricaturing Lady Jane and her ways to my Lord Steyne.

"No more has a certain person for holy water," his lordship replied with a bow and a grin, and a great jarring laugh afterwards.

So these two ladies did not see much of each other except upon those occasions, when the younger brother's wife, having an object to gain from the other, frequented her. They my-loved and my-deared each other assiduously, but kept apart generally; whereas Sir Pitt, in the midst of his multiplied avocations, found daily time to see his sister-in-law.

On the occasion of his first Speaker's dinner, Sir Pitt took the opportunity of appearing before his sister-in-law in his uniform — that old diplomatic suit which he had worn when *attaché* to the Pumpernickel legation.

Becky complimented him upon that dress, and admired him almost as much as his own wife and children, to whom he displayed himself before he set out. She said that it was only the thorough-bred gentleman who could wear the court suit with advantage; it was only your men of ancient race whom the *culotte courte* became. Pitt looked down with complacency at his legs, which had not, in truth, much more symmetry or swell than the lean court sword which dangled by his side: looked down at his legs, and thought in his heart that he was killing.

When he was gone, Mrs. Becky made a caricature of his figure, which she showed to Lord Steyne when he arrived. His lordship carried off the sketch, delighted with the accuracy of the resemblance. He had done Sir Pitt Crawley the honor to meet him at Mrs. Becky's house, and had been most gracious to the new baronet and member. Pitt was struck too by the deference with which the great Peer treated his sister-in-law, by her ease and sprightliness in the conversation, and by the delight with which the other men of the party listened to her talk. Lord Steyne made no doubt but that the Baronet had only commenced his career in public life, and expected rather anxiously to hear him as an orator; as they were neighbors (for Great Gaunt Street leads into Gaunt Square, whereof Gaunt House, as everybody knows, forms one side), my lord hoped that as soon as Lady Steyne arrived in London she would have the honor of making the acquaintance of Lady Crawley. He left a card upon his neighbor in the course of a day or two; having never thought fit to notice his predecessor, though they had lived near each other for near a century past.

In the midst of these intrigues and fine parties and wise and brilliant personages Rawdon felt himself more and more isolated every day. He was allowed to go to the club more: to dine abroad with bachelor friends: to come and go when he liked, without any questions being asked. And he and Rawdon the younger many a time would walk to Gaunt Street, and sit with the lady and the children there while Sir Pitt was closeted with Rebecca, on his way to the House, or on his return from it.

The ex-Colonel would sit for hours in his brother's house very silent, and thinking and doing as little as possible. He was glad to be employed of an errand: to go and make inquiries about a horse or a servant; or to carve the roast mutton for the dinner of the children. He was beat and cowed into laziness and submission. Delilah had imprisoned him and cut his hair off, too. The bold and reckless young blood of ten years back was subjugated, and was turned into a torpid, submissive, middle-aged, stout gentleman.

And poor Lady Jane was aware that Rebecca had captivated her husband: although she and Mrs. Rawdon my-deared and my-loved each other every day they met.

CHAPTER XVIII.

STRUGGLES AND TRIALS.

OUR friends at Brompton were meanwhile passing their Christmas after their fashion, and in a manner by no means too cheerful.

Out of the hundred pounds a-year, which was about the amount of her income, the widow Osborne had been in the habit of giving up nearly three fourths to her father and mother for the expenses of herself and her little boy. With £120 more, supplied by Jos, this family of four people, attended by a single Irish servant who also did for Clapp and his wife, might manage to live in decent comfort through the year, and hold up their heads yet, and be able to give a friend a dish of tea still, after the storms and disappointments of their early life. Sedley still maintained his ascendency over the family of Mr. Clapp, his ex-clerk. Clapp remembered the time when, sitting on the edge of the chair, he tossed off a bumper to the health of "Mrs. S——, Miss Emmy, and Mr. Joseph in India," at the merchant's rich table in Russell Square. Time magnified the splendor of those recollections in the honest clerk's bosom. Whenever he came up from the kitchen-parlor to the drawing-room, and partook of tea or gin-and-water with Mr. Sedley, he would say, "This was not what you was accustomed to once, sir," and as gravely and reverentially drink the health of the ladies as he had done in the days of their utmost prosperity. He thought Miss 'Melia's playing the divinest music ever performed, and her the finest lady. He never would sit down before Sedley at the club even, nor would he have that gentleman's character abused by any member of the society. He had seen the first men in London shaking hands with Mr. S——; he said, "He'd known him in times when Rothschild might be seen on 'Change with him any day, and he owed him personally everythink."

Clapp, with the best of characters and handwritings, had been able very soon after his master's disaster to find other employment for himself. "Such a little fish as me can swim in any bucket," he used to remark, and a member of the house from which old Sedley had seceded was very glad to make use of Mr. Clapp's services, and to reward them with a comfortable salary. In fine, all Sedley's wealthy friends had dropped off one by one, and this poor ex-dependant still remained faithfully attached to him.

Out of the small residue of her income, which Amelia kept back for herself, the widow had need of all the thrift and care possible in order to enable her to keep her darling boy dressed in such a manner as became George Osborne's son, and to defray the expenses of the little school to which, after much misgiving and reluctance, and many secret pangs and fears on her own part, she had been induced to send the lad. She had sat up of nights conning lessons and spelling over crabbed grammars and geography books in order to teach them to Georgy. She had worked even at the Latin accidence, fondly hoping that she might be capable of instructing him in that language. To part with him all day: to send him out to the mercy of a schoolmaster's cane and his

schoolfellows' roughness, was almost like weaning
him over again, to that weak mother, so tremulous and
full of sensibility.   He, for his part, rushed off to the
school with the utmost happiness.   He was longing
for the change.   That childish gladness wounded his
mother, who was herself so grieved to part with him.
She would rather have had him more sorry, she
thought : and then was deeply repentant within herself, for daring to be so selfish as to wish her own son
to be unhappy.

Georgy made great progress in the school, which was
kept by a friend of his mother's constant admirer, the
Rev. Mr. Binny.   He brought home numberless prizes
and testimonials of ability.   He told his mother countless stories every night about his school-companions :
and what a fine fellow Lyons was, and what a sneak
Sniffin was ; and how Steel's father actually supplied
the meat for the establishment, whereas Golding's
mother came in a carriage to fetch him every Saturday ; and how Neat had straps to his trousers — might
he have straps ? — and how Bull Major was so strong
(though only in Eutropius) that it was believed he
could lick the Usher, Mr. Ward, himself.   So Amelia
learned to know every one of the boys in that school
as well as Georgy himself : and of nights she used to
help him in his exercises and puzzle her little head
over his lessons as eagerly as if she was herself going
in the morning into the presence of the master.   Once,
after a certain combat with Master Smith, George came
home to his mother with a black eye, and bragged prodigiously to his parent and his delighted old grandfather about his valor in the fight, in which, if the
truth was known, he did not behave with particular
heroism, and in which he decidedly had the worst.
But Amelia has never forgiven that Smith to this day,

though he is now a peaceful apothecary near Leicester Square.

In these quiet labors and harmless cares the gentle widow's life was passing away, a silver hair or two marking the progress of time on her head, and a line deepening ever so little on her fair forehead. She used to smile at these marks of time. " What matters it," she asked, " for an old woman like me ?" All she hoped for was to live to see her son great, famous, and glorious, as he deserved to be. She kept his copy-books, his drawings, and compositions, and showed them about in her little circle, as if they were miracles of genius. She confided some of these specimens to Miss Dobbin ; to show them to Miss Osborne, George's aunt, to show them to Mr. Osborne himself — to make that old man repent of his cruelty and ill-feeling towards him who was gone. All her husband's faults and foibles she had buried in the grave with him : she only remembered the lover, who had married her at all sacrifices ; the noble husband so brave and beautiful, in whose arms she had hung on the morning when he had gone away to fight, and die gloriously for his king. From heaven the hero must be smiling down upon that paragon of a boy whom he had left to comfort and console her.

We have seen how one of George's grandfathers (Mr. Osborne), in his easy chair in Russell Square, daily grew more violent and moody, and how his daughter, with her fine carriage, and her fine horses, and her name on half the public charity-lists of the town, was a lonely, miserable, persecuted old maid. She thought again and again of the beautiful little boy, her brother's son, whom she had seen. She longed to be allowed to drive in the fine carriage to the house in which he lived ; and she used to look out day after day as she took her

solitary drive in the Park, in hopes that she might see
him. Her sister, the banker's lady, occasionally condescended to pay her old home and companion a visit
in Russell Square. She brought a couple of sickly
children attended by a prim nurse, and in a faint
genteel giggling tone cackled to her sister about her
fine acquaintance, and how her little Frederick was the
image of Lord Claud Lollypop, and her sweet Maria
had been noticed by the Baroness as they were driving in their donkey-chaise at Roehampton. She urged
her to make her papa do something for the darlings.
Frederick she had determined should go into the
Guards; and if they made an elder son of him (and
Mr. Bullock was positively ruining and pinching himself to death to buy land), how was the darling girl to
be provided for? "I expect *you*, dear," Mrs. Bullock
would say, "for of course my share of our papa's property must go to the head of the house, you know. Dear
Rhoda McMull will disengage the whole of the Castletoddy property as soon as poor dear Lord Castletoddy
dies, who is quite epileptic; and little Macduff McMull
will be Viscount Castletoddy. Both the Mr. Bludyers
of Mincing Lane have settled their fortunes on Fanny
Bludyer's little boy. My darling Frederick must positively be an eldest son; and — and do ask Papa to bring
us back his account in Lombard Street, will you, dear?
It doesn't look well, his going to Stumpy and Rowdy's."
After which kind of speeches, in which fashion and the
main chance were blended together, and after a kiss,
which was like the contact of an oyster — Mrs. Frederick Bullock would gather her starched nurslings, and
simper back into her carriage.

Every visit which this leader of *ton* paid to her
family was more unlucky for her. Her father paid
more money into Stumpy and Rowdy's. Her patron-

age became more and more insufferable. The poor
widow in the little cottage at Brompton, guarding her
treasure there, little knew how eagerly some people
coveted it.

On that night when Jane Osborne had told her
father that she had seen his grandson, the old man
had made her no reply : but he had shown no anger
— and had bade her good-night on going himself to
his room in rather a kindly voice. And he must
have meditated on what she said, and have made some
inquiries of the Dobbin family regarding her visit ;
for a fortnight after it took place, he asked her where
was her little French watch and chain she used to
wear ?

"I bought it with my money, sir," she said in a
great fright.

"Go and order another like it, or a better if you can
get it," said the old gentleman, and lapsed again into
silence.

Of late the Misses Dobbin more than once repeated
their entreaties to Amelia, to allow George to visit
them. His aunt had shown her inclination ; perhaps
his grandfather himself, they hinted, might be disposed
to be reconciled to him. Surely, Amelia could not refuse such advantageous chances for the boy. Nor could
she : but she acceded to their overtures with a very
heavy and suspicious heart, was always uneasy during
the child's absence from her, and welcomed him back
as if he was rescued out of some danger. He brought
back money and toys, at which the widow looked with
alarm and jealousy : she asked him always if he had
seen any gentleman — "Only old Sir William, who
drove him about in the four-wheeled chaise, and Mr.
Dobbin, who arrived on the beautiful bay horse in the
afternoon — in the green coat and pink neckcloth,

with the gold-headed whip, who promised to show him the Tower of London, and take him out with the Surrey hounds." At last, he said, "There *was* an old gentleman, with thick eye-brows and a broad hat, and large chain and seals. He came one day as the coachman was lunging Georgy round the lawn on the gray pony. He looked at me very much. He shook very much. I said 'My name is Norval' after dinner. My aunt began to cry. She is always crying." Such was George's report on that night.

Then Amelia knew that the boy had seen his grandfather; and looked out feverishly for a proposal which she was sure would follow, and which came, in fact, in a few days afterwards. Mr. Osborne formally offered to take the boy, and make him heir to the fortune which he had intended that his father should inherit. He would make Mrs. George Osborne an allowance, such as to assure her a decent competency. If Mrs. George Osborne proposed to marry again, as Mr. O. heard was her intention, he would not withdraw that allowance. But it must be understood, that the child would live entirely with his grandfather in Russell Square, or at whatever other place Mr. O. should select; and that he would be occasionally permitted to see Mrs. George Osborne at her own residence. This message was brought or read to her in a letter one day, when her mother was from home, and her father absent as usual, in the City.

She was never seen angry but twice or thrice in her life, and it was in one of these moods that Mr. Osborne's attorney had the fortune to behold her. She rose up trembling and flushing very much as soon as, after reading the letter, Mr. Poe handed it to her, and she tore the paper into a hundred fragments, which she trod on. "I marry again!—I take money to part from my child! Who dares insult me by proposing such a thing? Tell Mr. Osborne it is a cowardly letter, sir,—a cowardly letter—I will not answer it. I wish you good-morning, sir—and she bowed me out of the room like a tragedy queen," said the lawyer who told the story.

Her parents never remarked her agitation on that day, and she never told them of the interview. They had their own affairs to interest them, affairs which deeply interested this innocent and unconscious lady. The old gentleman, her father, was always dabbling in speculation. We have seen how the Wine Company and the Coal Company had failed him. But, prowling about the City always eagerly and restlessly still, he lighted upon some other scheme, of which he thought so well that he embarked in it in spite of the remonstrances of Mr. Clapp, to whom indeed he never dared to tell how far he had engaged himself in it. And as it was always Mr. Sedley's maxim not to talk about money matters before women, they had no inkling of the misfortunes that were in store for them until the unhappy old gentleman was forced to make gradual confessions.

The bills of the little household, which had been settled weekly, first fell into arrear. The remittances had not arrived from India, Mr. Sedley told his wife with a disturbed face. As she had paid her bills very regularly hitherto, one or two of the tradesmen to whom the poor lady was obliged to go round asking for time were very angry at a delay to which they were perfectly used from more irregular customers. Emmy's contribution, paid over cheerfully without any questions, kept the little company in half rations however. And the first six months passed away pretty easily: old Sedley still keeping up with the notion that his shares must rise and that all would be well.

No sixty pounds, however, came to help the household at the end of the half year; and it fell deeper and deeper into trouble — Mrs. Sedley, who was growing infirm and was much shaken, remained silent or wept a great deal with Mrs. Clapp in the kitchen. The butcher was particularly surly: the grocer insolent: once or twice little Georgy had grumbled about the dinners: and Amelia, who still would have been satisfied with a slice of bread for her own dinner, could not but perceive that her son was neglected, and purchased little things out of her private purse to keep the boy in health.

At last they told her, or told her such a garbled story as people in difficulties tell. One day, her own money having been received, and Amelia about to pay it over: she who had kept an account of the moneys expended by her, proposed to keep a certain portion back out of her dividend, having contracted engagements for a new suit for Georgy.

Then it came out that Jos's remittances were not paid; that the house was in difficulties, which Amelia ought to have seen before, her mother said, but she cared for nothing or nobody except Georgy. At this she passed all her money across the table, without a word, to her mother, and returned to her room to cry her eyes out. She had a great access of sensibility too that day, when obliged to go and countermand the clothes, the darling clothes on which she had set her heart for Christmas Day, and the cut and fashion of which she had arranged in many conversations with a small milliner, her friend.

Hardest of all, she had to break the matter to

Georgy, who made a loud outcry. Everybody had new clothes at Christmas. The others would laugh at him. He *would* have new clothes. She had promised them to him. The poor widow had only kisses to give him. She darned the old suit in tears. She cast about among her little ornaments to see if she could sell anything to procure the desired novelties. There was her India shawl that Dobbin had sent her. She remembered in former days going with her mother to a fine India shop on Ludgate Hill, where the ladies had all sorts of dealings and bargains in these articles. Her cheeks flushed and her eyes shone with pleasure as she thought of this resource, and she kissed away George to school in the morning, smiling brightly after him. The boy felt that there was good news in her look.

Packing up her shawl in a handkerchief (another of the gifts of the good Major), she hid them under her cloak, and walked flushed and eager all the way to Ludgate Hill, tripping along by the Park wall, and running over the crossings, so that many a man turned as she hurried by him, and looked after her rosy pretty face. She calculated how she should spend the proceeds of her shawl: how, besides the clothes, she would buy the books that he longed for, and pay his half-year's schooling; and how she would buy a cloak for her father instead of that old greatcoat which he wore. She was not mistaken as to the value of the Major's gift. It was a very fine and beautiful web: and the merchant made a very good bargain when he gave her twenty guineas for her shawl.

She ran on amazed and flurried with her riches to Darton's shop in St. Paul's Churchyard, and there purchased the "Parents' Assistant," and the "Sand-

ford and Merton" Georgy longed for, and got into
the coach there with her parcel, and went home exult-
ing. And she pleased herself by writing in the fly-
leaf in her neatest little hand, "George Osborne, A
Christmas gift from his affectionate mother." The
books are extant to this day, with the fair delicate
superscription.

She was going from her own room with the books
in her hand to place them on George's table, where he
might find them on his return from school; when in
the passage she and her mother met. The gilt bind-
ings of the seven handsome little volumes caught
the old lady's eye.

"What are those?" she said.

"Some books for Georgy," Amelia replied — "I —
I promised them to him at Christmas."

"Books!" cried the elder lady, indignantly, "Books,
when the whole house wants bread! Books, when to
keep you and your son in luxury, and your dear
father out of gaol, I've sold every trinket I had, the
India shawl from my back — even down to the very
spoons, that our tradesmen mightn't insult us, and
that Mr. Clapp, which indeed he is justly entitled,
being not a hard landlord, and a civil man, and a
father, might have his rent. O Amelia! you break
my heart with your books and that boy of yours,
whom you are ruining, though part with him you
will not. O Amelia, may God send you a more dutiful child than I have had! There's Jos deserts his
father in his old age: and there's George, who might
be provided for, and who might be rich, going to
school like a lord, with a gold watch and chain round
his neck — while my dear, dear old man is without a
sh— shilling." Hysteric sobs and cries ended Mrs.
Sedley's speech — it echoed through every room in

the small house, whereof the other female inmates heard every word of the colloquy.

"Oh, mother, mother!" cried poor Amelia in reply. "You told me nothing — I — I promised him the books. I — I only sold my shawl this morning. Take the money — take everything" — and with quivering hands she took out her silver, and her sovereigns — her precious golden sovereigns, which she thrust into the hands of her mother, whence they overflowed and tumbled, rolling down the stairs.

And then she went into her room, and sank down in despair and utter misery. She saw it all now. Her selfishness was sacrificing the boy. But for her he might have wealth, station, education, and his father's place, which the elder George had forfeited for her sake. She had but to speak the words, and her father was restored to competency: and the boy raised to fortune. Oh, what a conviction it was to that tender and stricken heart!

CHAPTER XIX.

GAUNT HOUSE.

ALL the world knows that Lord Steyne's town palace stands in Gaunt Square, out of which Great Gaunt Street leads, whither we first conducted Rebecca, in the time of the departed Sir Pitt Crawley. Peering over the railings and through the black trees into the garden of the Square, you see a few miserable governesses with wan-faced pupils wandering round and round it, and round the dreary grass-plot in the centre of which rises the statue of Lord Gaunt, who fought at Minden, in a three-tailed wig, and otherwise habited like a Roman Emperor. Gaunt House occupies nearly a side of the Square. The remaining three sides are composed of mansions that have passed away into dowagerism; — tall, dark houses, with window-frames of stone, or picked out of a lighter red. Little light seems to be behind those lean, comfortless casements now : and hospitality to have passed away from those doors as much as the laced lackeys and link-boys of old times, who used to put out their torches in the blank iron extinguishers that still flank the lamps over the steps. Brass plates have penetrated into the Square — doctors, the Diddlesex Bank Western Branch — the English and European Reunion, etc. — it has a dreary look — nor is my Lord Steyne's palace less dreary. All I have ever seen of it is the vast wall in front, with the rustic columns at the great gate, through which an old porter peers sometimes with a fat and gloomy red face — and over the wall the garret and bed-room windows, and the chimneys, out of which there seldom comes any smoke now. For the present Lord Steyne lives at Naples preferring the view of the Bay and Capri and Vesuvius, to the dreary aspect of the wall in Gaunt Square.

A few score yards down New Gaunt Street, and leading into Gaunt Mews indeed, is a little modest back door, which you would not remark from that of any of the other stables. But many a little close carriage has stopped at that door, as my informant (little Tom Eaves, who knows everything, and who showed me the place) told me. "The Prince and Perdita have been in and out of that door, sir," he has often told me; "Marianne Clarke has entered it with the Duke of ——. It conducts to the famous *petits appartements* of Lord Steyne — one, sir, fitted up all in ivory and white satin, another in ebony and black velvet; there is a little banqueting-room taken from Sallust's house at Pompeii, and painted by Cosway — a little private kitchen, in which every saucepan was silver, and all the spits were gold. It was there that Egalité Orléans roasted partridges on the night when he and the Marquis of Steyne won a hundred thousand from a great personage at ombre. Half of the money went to the French Revolution, half to purchase Lord Gaunt's Marquisate and Garter — and the remainder — " but it forms no part of our scheme to tell what became of the remainder, for every shilling of which, and a great deal more, little Tom Eaves, who knows everybody's affairs, is ready to account.

Besides his town palace, the Marquis had castles and palaces in various quarters of the three kingdoms, whereof the descriptions may be found in the road-

books — Castle Strongbow, with its woods, on the
Shannon shore; Gaunt Castle in Carmarthenshire,
where Richard II. was taken prisoner — Gauntly
Hall in Yorkshire where I have been informed there
were two hundred silver teapots for the breakfasts of
the guests of the house, with everything to correspond in splendor; and Stillbrook in Hampshire,
which was my lord's farm, an humble place of residence, of which we all remember the wonderful furniture which was sold at my lord's demise by a late
celebrated auctioneer.

The Marchioness of Steyne was of the renowned
and ancient family of the Caerlyons, Marquises of
Camelot, who have preserved the old faith ever since
the conversion of the venerable Druid, their first ancestor, and whose pedigree goes far beyond the date
of the arrival of King Brute in these islands.   Pen-
dragon is the title of the eldest son of the house.
The sons have been called Arthurs, Uthers, and Car-
adocs, from immemorial time.   Their heads have
fallen in many a loyal conspiracy.   Elizabeth chopped
off the head of the Arthur of her day, who had been
Chamberlain to Philip and Mary, and carried letters
between the Queen of Scots and her uncles the Guises.
A cadet of the house was an officer of the great Duke,
and distinguished in the famous Saint Bartholomew
conspiracy.   During the whole of Mary's confinement,
the house of Camelot conspired in her behalf.   It was
as much injured by its charges in fitting out an ar-
mament against the Spaniards, during the time of the
Armada, as by the fines and confiscations levied on it
by Elizabeth for harboring of priests, obstinate recu-
sancy, and Popish misdoings.   A recreant of James's
time was momentarily perverted from his religion by
the arguments of that great theologian, and the for-

tunes of the family somewhat restored by his timely weakness. But the Earl of Camelot, of the reign of Charles, returned to the old creed of his family, and they continued to fight for it, and ruin themselves for it, as long as there was a Stuart left to head or to instigate a rebellion.

Lady Mary Caerlyon was brought up at a Parisian convent; the Dauphiness Marie Antoinette was her godmother. In the pride of her beauty she had been married — sold, it was said — to Lord Gaunt, then at Paris, who won vast sums from the lady's brother at some of Philip of Orleans's banquets. The Earl of Gaunt's famous duel with the Count de la Marche, of the Gray Musketeers, was attributed by common report to the pretensions of that officer (who had been a page, and remained a favorite of the Queen) to the hand of the beautiful Lady Mary Caerlyon. She was married to Lord Gaunt while the Count lay ill of his wound, and came to dwell at Gaunt House, and to figure for a short time in the splendid court of the Prince of Wales. Fox had toasted her. Morris and Sheridan had written songs about her. Malmesbury had made her his best bow; Walpole had pronounced her charming; Devonshire had been almost jealous of her; but she was scared by the wild pleasures and gayeties of the society into which she was flung, and after she had borne a couple of sons, shrank away into a life of devout seclusion. No wonder that my Lord Steyne, who liked pleasure and cheerfulness, was not often seen after their marriage, by the side of this trembling, silent, superstitious, unhappy lady.

The before-mentioned Tom Eaves (who has no part in this history, except that he knew all the great folks in London, and the stories and mysteries of each family) had further information regarding my Lady

Steyne, which may or may not be true. "The hu-
miliations," Tom used to say, "which that woman
has been made to undergo, in her own house, have
been frightful; Lord Steyne has made her sit down
to table with women with whom I would rather die
than allow Mrs. Eaves to associate — with Lady
Crackenbury, with Mrs. Chippenham, with Madame
de la Cruchecassée, the French secretary's wife,"
(from every one of which ladies Tom Eaves — who
would have sacrificed his wife for knowing them —
was too glad to get a bow or a dinner), "with the
reigning favorite, in a word. And do you suppose
that that woman, of that family, who are as proud
as the Bourbons, and to whom the Steynes are but
lackeys, mushrooms of yesterday (for after all, they
are *not* of the Old Gaunts, but of a minor and doubtful branch of the house); do you suppose, I say " (the
reader must bear in mind that it is always Tom
Eaves who speaks), "that the Marchioness of Steyne,
the haughtiest woman in England, would bend down
to her husband so submissively, if there were not
some cause? Pooh! I tell you there are *secret reasons*. I tell you, that in the emigration, the Abbé de
la Marche who was here and was employed in the
Quiberoon business with Puisaye and Tinteniac, was
the same Colonel of *Mousquetaires Gris* with whom
Steyne fought in the year '86 — that he and the Marchioness met again: that it was after the Reverend
Colonel was shot in Brittany, that Lady Steyne took
to those extreme practices of devotion which she carries on now; for she is closeted with her director
every day — she is at service at Spanish Place, every
morning, I've watched her there — that is, I've happened to be passing there — and depend on it there's
a mystery in her case. People are not so unhappy

unless they have something to repent of," added Tom Eaves with a knowing wag of his head; "and depend on it, that woman would not be so submissive as she is, if the Marquis had not some sword to hold over her."

So, if Mr. Eaves's information be correct, it is very likely that this lady, in her high station, had to submit to many a private indignity, and to hide many secret griefs under a calm face. And let us, my brethren who have not our names in the Red Book, console ourselves by thinking comfortably how miserable our betters may be, and that Damocles, who sits on satin cushions, and is served on gold plate, has an awful sword hanging over his head in the shape of a bailiff, or an hereditary disease, or a family secret, which peeps out every now and then from the embroidered arras in a ghastly manner, and will be sure to drop one day or the other in the right place.

In comparing, too, the poor man's situation with that of the great, there is (always according to Mr. Eaves) another source of comfort for the former. You who have little or no patrimony to bequeath or to inherit, may be on good terms with your father or your son, whereas the heir of a great prince, such as my Lord Steyne, must naturally be angry at being kept out of his kingdom, and eye the occupant of it with no very agreeable glances. "Take it as a rule," this sardonic old Eaves would say, "the fathers and elder sons of all great families hate each other. The Crown Prince is always in opposition to the crown or hankering after it. Shakspeare knew the world, my good sir, and when he describes Prince Hal (from whose family the Gaunts pretend to be descended, though they are no more related to John of Gaunt than you are), trying on his father's coronet, he gives you a natural description of all heirs-apparent. If you were heir to a dukedom and a thousand pounds a day, do you mean to say you would not wish for possession ? Pooh! And it stands to reason that every great man, having experienced this feeling towards his father, must be aware that his son entertains it towards himself ; and so they can't but be suspicious and hostile.

"Then again, as to the feeling of elder towards younger sons. My dear sir, you ought to know that every elder brother looks upon the cadets of the house as his natural enemies, who deprive him of so much ready money which ought to be his by right. I have often heard George Mac Turk, Lord Bajazet's eldest son, say that if he had his will when he came to the title, he would do what the sultans do, and clear the estate by chopping off all his younger brothers' heads at once ; and so the case is, more or less, with them all. I tell you they are all Turks in their hearts. Pooh! sir, they know the world." And here, haply a great man coming up, Tom Eaves's hat would drop off his head, and he would rush forward with a bow and a grin, which showed that he knew the world too — in the Tomeavesian way, that is. And having laid out every shilling of his fortune on an annuity, Tom could afford to bear no malice to his nephews and nieces, and to have no other feeling with regard to his betters, but a constant and generous desire to dine with them.

Between the Marchioness and the natural and tender regard of mother for children, there was that cruel barrier placed of difference of faith. The very love which she might feel for her sons, only served to render the timid and pious lady more fearful and unhappy. The gulf which separated them was fatal and impassable. She could not stretch her weak arms across it, or draw her children over to that side away from which her belief told her there was no safety. During the youth of his sons, Lord Steyne, who was a good scholar and amateur casuist, had no better sport in the evening after dinner in the country than in setting the boys' tutor, the Reverend Mr. Trail (now my Lord Bishop of Ealing) on her ladyship's director, Father Mole, over their wine, and in pitting Oxford against St. Acheul. He cried "Bravo, Latimer! Well said, Loyola!" alternately; he promised Mole a bishopric if he would come over; and vowed he would use all his influence to get Trail a cardinal's hat if he would secede. Neither divine allowed himself to be conquered; and though the fond mother hoped that her youngest and favorite son would be reconciled to her church — his mother church — a sad and awful disappointment awaited the devout lady — a disappointment which seemed to be a judgment upon her for the sin of her marriage.

My Lord Gaunt married, as every person who frequents the Peerage knows, the Lady Blanche Thistlewood, a daughter of the noble house of Bareacres, before mentioned in this veracious history. A wing of Gaunt House was assigned to this couple; for the head of the family chose to govern it, and while he reigned to reign supreme; his son and heir, however, living little at home, disagreeing with his wife, and borrowing upon post-obits such moneys as he required beyond the very moderate sums which his father was disposed to allow him. The Marquis knew every shilling of his son's debts. At his lamented demise, he was found himself to be possessor of many of his heir's bonds, purchased for their benefit, and devised by his lordship to the children of his younger son.

As, to my Lord Gaunt's dismay, and the chuckling delight of his natural enemy and father, the Lady Gaunt had no children — the Lord George Gaunt was desired to return from Vienna, where he was engaged in waltzing and diplomacy, and to contract a matrimonial alliance with the Honorable Joan, only daughter of John Johnes, First Baron Helvellyn, and head of the firm of Jones, Brown, and Robinson, of Threadneedle Street, Bankers; from which union sprang several sons and daughters, whose doings do not appertain to this story.

The marriage at first was a happy and prosperous one. My Lord George Gaunt could not only read, but write pretty correctly. He spoke French with considerable fluency; and was one of the finest waltzers in Europe. With these talents, and his interest at home, there was little doubt that his lordship would rise to the highest dignities in his profession. The lady, his wife, felt that courts were her sphere; and her wealth enabled her to receive splendidly in those continental towns whither her husband's diplomatic duties led him. There was talk of appointing him minister, and bets were laid at the Travellers' that he would be ambassador ere long, when of a sudden, rumors arrived of the secretary's extraordinary behavior. At a grand diplomatic dinner given by his chief, he had started up, and declared that a *pâté de foie gras* was poisoned. He went to a ball at the hotel of the Bavarian envoy, the Count de Springbock-Hohenlaufen, with his head shaved, and dressed as a Capuchin friar. It was not a masked ball, as some folks wanted to persuade you. It was something queer, people whispered. His grandfather was so. It was in the family.

His wife and family returned to this country, and

took up their abode at Gaunt House. Lord George gave up his post on the European continent, and was gazetted to Brazil. But people knew better; he never returned from that Brazil expedition — never died there — never lived there — never was there at all. He was nowhere: he was gone out altogether. "Brazil," said one gossip to another with a grin — "Brazil is St. John's Wood. Rio Janeiro is a cottage surrounded by four walls; and George Gaunt is accredited to a keeper, who has invested him with the order of the Strait-waistcoat." These are the kinds of epitaphs which men pass over one another in Vanity Fair.

Twice or thrice in a week, in the earliest morning, the poor mother went for her sins and saw the poor invalid. Sometimes he laughed at her (and his laughter was more pitiful than to hear him cry); sometimes she found the brilliant dandy diplomatist of the Congress of Vienna dragging about a child's toy, or nursing the keeper's baby's doll. Sometimes he knew her and Father Mole, her director and companion: oftener he forgot her, as he had done wife, children, love, ambition, vanity. But he remembered his dinner-hour, and used to cry if his wine-and-water was not strong enough.

It was the mysterious taint of the blood: the poor mother had brought it from her own ancient race. The evil had broken out once or twice in the father's family, long before Lady Steyne's sins had begun, or her fasts and tears and penances had been offered in their expiation. The pride of the race was struck down as the first-born of Pharaoh. The dark mark of fate and doom was on the threshold, — the tall old threshold surmounted by coronets and carved heraldry.

The absent lord's children meanwhile prattled and grew on quite unconscious that the doom was over them too. First they talked of their father, and devised plans against his return. Then the name of the living dead man was less frequently in their mouth — then not mentioned at all. But the stricken old grandmother trembled to think that these too were the inheritors of their father's shame as well as of his honors: and watched sickening for the day when the awful ancestral curse should come down on them.

This dark presentiment also haunted Lord Steyne. He tried to lay the horrid bedside ghost in Red Seas of wine and jollity, and lost sight of it sometimes in the crowd and rout of his pleasures. But it always came back to him when alone, and seemed to grow more threatening with years. "I have taken your son," it said, "why not you? I may shut you up in a prison some day like your son George. I may tap you on the head to-morrow, and away go pleasure and honors, feasts and beauty, friends, flatterers, French cooks, fine horses and houses — in exchange for a prison, a keeper, and a straw mattress like George Gaunt's." And then my lord would defy the ghost which threatened him; for he knew of a remedy by which he could balk his enemy.

So there was splendor and wealth, but no great happiness perchance, behind the tall carved portals of Gaunt House with its smoky coronets and ciphers. The feasts there were of the grandest in London, but there was not over-much content therewith, except among the guests who sat at my lord's table. Had he not been so great a prince very few possibly would have visited him: but in Vanity Fair the sins of very great personages are looked at indulgently.

" *Nous regardons à deux fois* " (as the French lady said) before we condemn a person of my lord's undoubted quality. Some notorious carpers and squeamish moralists might be sulky with Lord Steyne, but they were glad enough to come when he asked them.

"Lord Steyne is really too bad," Lady Slingstone said, " but everybody goes, and of course I shall see that my girls come to no harm." " His lordship is a man to whom I owe much, everything in life," said the Right Reverend Doctor Trail, thinking that the Archbishop was rather shaky; and Mrs. Trail and the young ladies would as soon have missed going to church as to one of his lordship's parties. " His morals are bad," said little Lord Southdown to his sister, who meekly expostulated, having heard terrific legends from her mamma with respect to the doings at Gaunt House; " but hang it, he's got the best dry Sillery in Europe! " And as for Sir Pitt Crawley, Bart. — Sir Pitt that pattern of decorum, Sir Pitt who had led off at missionary meetings, — he never for one moment thought of not going too. " Where you see such persons as the Bishop of Ealing and the Countess of Slingstone, you may be pretty sure, Jane," the Baronet would say, " that *we* cannot be wrong. The great rank and station of Lord Steyne put him in a position to command people in our station in life. The Lord Lieutenant of a County, my dear, is a respectable man. Besides George Gaunt and I were intimate in early life: he was my junior when we were *attachés* at Pumpernickel together."

In a word everybody went to wait upon this great man — everybody who was asked: as you the reader (do not say nay) or I the writer hereof would go if we had an invitation.

CHAPTER XX.

At last Becky's kindness and attention to the chief of her husband's family, were destined to meet with an exceeding great reward; a reward which, though certainly somewhat unsubstantial, the little woman coveted with greater eagerness than more positive benefits. If she did not wish to lead a virtuous life, at least she desired to enjoy a character for virtue, and we know that no lady in the genteel world can possess this desideratum, until she has put on a train and feathers, and has been presented to her Sovereign at court. From that august interview they come out stamped as honest women. The Lord Chamberlain gives them a certificate of virtue. And as dubious goods or letters are passed through an oven at quarantine, sprinkled with aromatic vinegar, and then pronounced clean — many a lady whose reputation would be doubtful otherwise and liable to give infection, passes through the wholesome ordeal of the Royal Presence, and issues from it free from all taint.

It might be very well for my Lady Bareacres, my Lady Tufto, Mrs. Bute Crawley in the country, and other ladies who had come into contact with Mrs. Rawdon Crawley, to cry fie at the idea of the odious little adventuress making her curtsy before the Sovereign, and to declare, that if dear good Queen Charlotte had been alive, *she* never would have admitted such an extremely ill-regulated personage into Her chaste drawing-room. But when we consider, that it was the First Gentleman in Europe in whose high presence Mrs. Rawdon passed her examination, and as it were, took her degree in reputation, it surely must be flat disloyalty to doubt any more about her virtue. I, for my part, look back with love and awe to that Great Character in history. Ah, what a high and noble appreciation of Gentlewomanhood there must have been in Vanity Fair, when that revered and august being was invested, by the universal acclaim of the refined and educated portion of this empire, with the title of *Premier Gentilhomme* of his Kingdom. Do you remember, dear M——, oh friend of my youth, how one blissful night five-and-twenty years since, the "Hypocrite" being acted, Elliston being manager, Dowton and Liston performers, two boys had leave from their loyal masters to go out from Slaughter House School where they were educated, and to appear on Drury Lane stage, amongst a crowd which assembled there to greet the king. THE KING? There he was. Beef-eaters were before the august box: the Marquis of Steyne (Lord of the Powder Closet) and other great officers of state were behind the chair on which he sat — *He* sat, florid of face, portly of person, covered with orders, and in a rich curling head of hair. How we sang God save him! How the house rocked and shouted with that magnificent music. How they cheered, and cried, and waved handkerchiefs. Ladies wept: mothers clasped their children: some fainted with emotion. People were suffocated in the pit, shrieks and groans rising up amidst the writhing and shouting mass there of his people who were, and indeed showed themselves almost to be, ready to die for him. Yes, we saw him. Fate cannot deprive us of

that. Others have seen Napoleon. Some few still
exist who have beheld Frederick the Great, Doctor
Johnson, Marie Antoinette, etc. — be it our reasonable
boast to our children, that we saw George the Good,
the Magnificent, the Great.

Well, there came a happy day in Mrs. Rawdon
Crawley's existence when this angel was admitted
into the paradise of a court which she coveted; her
sister-in-law acting as her godmother. On the appointed day, Sir Pitt and his lady, in their great
family carriage (just newly built, and ready for the
Baronet's assumption of the office of High Sheriff
of his county), drove up to the little house in Curzon
Street, to the edification of Raggles, who was watching from his green-grocer's shop, and saw fine plumes
within, and enormous bunches of flowers in the
breasts of the new livery-coats of the footmen.

Sir Pitt, in a glittering uniform, descended and
went into Curzon Street, his sword between his legs.
Little Rawdon stood with his face against the parlor
window-panes, smiling and nodding with all his
might to his aunt in the carriage within; and presently Sir Pitt issued forth from the house again,
leading forth a lady with grand feathers, covered in
a white shawl, and holding up daintily a train of
magnificent brocade. She stepped into the vehicle
as if she were a princess and accustomed all her life
to go to court, smiling graciously on the footman
at the door, and on Sir Pitt, who followed her into
the carriage.

Then Rawdon followed in his old Guards' uniform,
which had grown wofully shabby, and was much too
tight. He was to have followed the procession, and
waited upon his Sovereign in a cab; but that his
good-natured sister-in-law insisted that they should

be a family party. The coach was large, the ladies not very big, they would hold their trains in their laps — finally, the four went fraternally together; and their carriage presently joined the line of loyal equipages which was making its way down Piccadilly and St. James's Street, towards the old brick palace where the Star of Brunswick was in waiting to receive his nobles and gentlefolks.

Becky felt as if she could bless the people out of the carriage windows, so elated was she in spirit, and so strong a sense had she of the dignified position which she had at last attained in life. Even our Becky had her weaknesses, and as one often sees how men pride themselves upon excellences which others are slow to perceive: how, for instance, Comus firmly believes that he is the greatest tragic actor in England; how Brown, the famous novelist, longs to be considered, not a man of genius, but a man of fashion; while Robinson, the great lawyer, does not in the least care about his reputation in Westminster Hall, but believes himself incomparable across country, and at a five-barred gate — so to be, and to be thought, a respectable woman was Becky's aim in life, and she got up the genteel with amazing assiduity, readiness, and success. We have said, there were times when she believed herself to be a fine lady, and forgot that there was no money in the chest at home — duns round the gate, tradesmen to coax and wheedle — no ground to walk upon, in a word. And as she went to court in the carriage, the family carriage, she adopted a demeanor so grand, self-satisfied, deliberate, and imposing, that it made even Lady Jane laugh. She walked into the royal apartments with a toss of the head which would have befitted an empress, and I have no doubt had she

been one, she would have become the character
perfectly.

We are authorized to state that Mrs. Rawdon
Crawley's *costume de cour* on the occasion of her
presentation to the Sovereign was of the most elegant
and brilliant description. Some ladies we may have
seen — we who wear stars and cordons, and attend
the St. James's assemblies, or we, who, in muddy
boots, dawdle up and down Pall Mall, and peep into
the coaches as they drive up with the great folks in
their feathers — some ladies of fashion, I say, we
may have seen, about two o'clock of the forenoon of
a levee day, as the laced-jacketed band of the Life
Guards are blowing triumphal marches seated on
those prancing music-stools, their cream-colored char-
gers, — who are by no means lovely and enticing
objects at that early period of noon. A stout countess
of sixty, *décolletée*, painted, wrinkled with rouge up
to her drooping eyelids, and diamonds twinkling in
her wig, is a wholesome and edifying, but not a pleasant sight. She has the faded look of a St. James's
Street illumination, as it may be seen of an early
morning, when half the lamps are out, and the others
are blinking wanly, as if they were about to vanish
like ghosts before the dawn. Such charms as those
of which we catch glimpses while her ladyship's
carriage passes, should appear abroad at night alone.
If even Cynthia looks haggard of an afternoon, as
we may see her sometimes in the present winter
season, with Phœbus staring her out of countenance
from the opposite side of the heavens, how much
more can old Lady Castlemouldy keep her head up
when the sun is shining full upon it through the
chariot windows, and showing all the chinks and
crannies with which time has marked her face ?

No. Drawing-rooms should be announced for November, or the first foggy day: or the elderly sultanas of our Vanity Fair should drive up in closed litters, descend in a covered way, and make their curtsy to the Sovereign under the protection of lamplight.

Our beloved Rebecca had no need, however, of any such a friendly halo to set off her beauty. Her complexion could bear any sunshine as yet; and her dress, though if you were to see it now, any present lady of Vanity Fair would pronounce it to be the most foolish and preposterous attire ever worn, was as handsome in her eyes and those of the public, some five-and-twenty years since, as the most brilliant costume of the most famous beauty of the present season. A score of years hence that too, that milliner's wonder, will have passed into the domain of the absurd, along with all previous vanities. But we are wandering too much. Mrs. Rawdon's dress was pronounced to be *charmante* on the eventful day of her presentation. Even good little Lady Jane was forced to acknowledge this effect, as she looked at her kinswoman; and owned sorrowfully to herself that she was quite inferior in taste to Mrs. Becky.

She did not know how much care, thought, and genius Mrs. Rawdon had bestowed upon that garment. Rebecca had as good taste as any milliner in Europe, and such a clever way of doing things as Lady Jane little understood. The latter quickly spied out the magnificence of the brocade of Becky's train, and the splendor of the lace on her dress.

The brocade was an old remnant, Becky said; and as for the lace, it was a great bargain. She had had it these hundred years.

"My dear Mrs. Crawley, it must have cost a little fortune," Lady Jane said, looking down at her own lace, which was not nearly so good; and then examining the quality of the ancient brocade which formed the material of Mrs. Rawdon's court dress, she felt inclined to say that she could not afford such fine clothing, but checked that speech, with an effort, as one uncharitable to her kinswoman.

And yet, if Lady Jane had known all, I think even her kindly temper would have failed her. The fact is, when she was putting Sir Pitt's house in order, Mrs. Rawdon had found the lace and the brocade in old wardrobes, the property of the former ladies of the house, and had quietly carried the goods home, and had suited them to her own little person. Briggs saw her take them, asked no questions, told no stories; but I believe quite sympathized with her on this matter, and so would many another honest woman.

And the diamonds — "Where the doose did you get the diamonds, Becky?" said her husband, admiring some jewels which he had never seen before, and which sparkled in her ears and on her neck with brilliance and profusion.

Becky blushed a little, and looked at him hard for a moment. Pitt Crawley blushed a little too, and looked out of window. The fact is, he had given her a very small portion of the brilliants; a pretty diamond clasp, which confined a pearl necklace which she wore; and the Baronet had omitted to mention the circumstance to his lady.

Becky looked at her husband, and then at Sir Pitt, with an air of saucy triumph — as much as to say, "Shall I betray you?"

"Guess!" she said to her husband. "Why, you silly man," she continued, "where do you suppose I got them? — all except the little clasp, which a dear friend of mine gave me long ago. I hired them, to be sure. I hired them at Mr. Polonius's, in Coventry Street. You don't suppose that all the diamonds which go to court belong to the owners; like those beautiful stones which Lady Jane has, and which are much handsomer than any which I have, I am certain."

"They are family jewels," said Sir Pitt, again looking uneasy. And in this family conversation the carriage rolled down the street, until its cargo was finally discharged at the gates of the palace where the Sovereign was sitting in state.

The diamonds, which had created Rawdon's admiration, never went back to Mr. Polonius, of Coventry Street, and that gentleman never applied for their restoration; but they retired into a little private repository, in an old desk, which Amelia Sedley had given her years and years ago, and in which Becky kept a number of useful and, perhaps, valuable things, about which her husband knew nothing. To know nothing, or little, is in the nature of some husbands. To hide, in the nature of how many women? O ladies! how many of you have surreptitious milliners' bills? How many of you have gowns and bracelets, which you dare n't show, or which you wear trembling? — trembling, and coaxing with smiles the husband by your side, who does not know the new velvet gown from the old one, or the new bracelet from last year's, or has any notion that the ragged-looking yellow lace scarf cost forty guineas, and that Madame Bobinot is writing dunning letters every week for the money!

Thus Rawdon knew nothing about the brilliant diamond ear-rings, or the superb brilliant ornament which decorated the fair bosom of his lady; but Lord Steyne, who was in his place at court, as Lord of the

Powder Closet, and one of the great dignitaries and illustrious defences of the throne of England, and came up with all his stars, garters, collars, and cordons, and paid particular attention to the little woman, knew whence the jewels came, and who paid for them.

As he bowed over her he smiled, and quoted the hackneyed and beautiful lines, from the " Rape of the Lock," about Belinda's diamonds, " which Jews might kiss and infidels adore."

" But I hope your lordship is orthodox," said the little lady, with a toss of her head. And many ladies round about whispered and talked, and many gentlemen nodded and whispered, as they saw what marked attention the great nobleman was paying to the little adventuress.

What were the circumstances of the interview between Rebecca Crawley, *née* Sharp, and her Imperial Master, it does not become such a feeble and inexperienced pen as mine to attempt to relate. The dazzled eyes close before that Magnificent Idea. Loyal respect and decency tell even the imagination not to look too keenly and audaciously about the sacred audience-chamber, but to back away rapidly, silently, and respectfully, making profound bows out of the August Presence.

This may be said, that in all London there was no more loyal heart than Becky's after this interview. The name of her king was always on her lips, and he was proclaimed by her to be the most charming of men. She went to Colnaghi's and ordered the finest portrait of him that art had produced, and credit could supply. She chose that famous one in which the best of monarchs is represented in a frock-coat with a fur collar, and breeches and silk stockings, simpering on a sofa from under his curly brown wig.

She had him painted in a brooch and wore it — indeed she amused and somewhat pestered her acquaintance with her perpetual talk about his urbanity and beauty. Who knows? Perhaps the little woman thought she might play the part of a Maintenon or a Pompadour.

But the finest sport of all after her presentation was to hear her talk virtuously. She had a few female acquaintances, not, it must be owned, of the very highest reputation in Vanity Fair. But being made an honest woman of, so to speak, Becky would not consort any longer with these dubious ones, and cut Lady Crackenbury when the latter nodded to her from her opera-box; and gave Mrs. Washington White the go-by in the Ring. "One must, my dear, show one is somebody," she said. "One must n't be seen with doubtful people. I pity Lady Crackenbury from my heart; and Mrs. Washington White may be a very good-natured person. *You* may go and dine with them, as you like your rubber. But *I* must n't, and won't; and you will have the goodness to tell Smith to say I am not at home when either of them calls."

The particulars of Becky's costume were in the newspapers — feathers, lappets, superb diamonds, and all the rest. Lady Crackenbury read the paragraph in bitterness of spirit, and discoursed to her followers about the airs which that woman was giving herself. Mrs. Bute Crawley and her young ladies in the country had a copy of the "Morning Post" from town; and gave a vent to their honest indignation. "If you had been sandy-haired, green-eyed, and a French rope-dancer's daughter," Mrs. Bute said to her eldest girl (who, on the contrary, was a very swarthy, short, and snub-nosed young lady), "you might have had

superb diamonds forsooth, and have been presented
at court, by your cousin, the Lady Jane. But you're
only a gentlewoman, my poor dear child. You have
only some of the best blood in England in your veins,
and good principles and piety for your portion. I,
myself, the wife of a Baronet's younger brother, too,
never thought of such a thing as going to court —
nor would other people, if good Queen Charlotte had
been alive." In this way the worthy Rectoress consoled herself: and her daughters sighed, and sat over
the Peerage all night.

A few days after the famous presentation, another
great and exceeding honor was vouchsafed to the virtuous Becky. Lady Steyne's carriage drove up to Mr.
Rawdon Crawley's door, and the footman, instead of
driving down the front of the house, as by his tremendous knocking he appeared to be inclined to do, re-
lented, and only delivered in a couple of cards, on
which were engraven the names of the Marchioness
of Steyne and the Countess of Gaunt. If these bits
of pasteboard had been beautiful pictures, or had had
a hundred yards of Malines lace rolled round them,
worth twice the number of guineas, Becky could not
have regarded them with more pleasure. You may
be sure they occupied a conspicuous place in the china
bowl on the drawing-room table, where Becky kept
the cards of her visitors. Lord! Lord! how poor
Mrs. Washington White's card and Lady Crackenbury's card, which our little friend had been glad
enough to get a few months back, and of which the
silly little creature was rather proud once — Lord!
Lord! I say, how soon, at the appearance of these
grand court cards, did those poor little neglected
deuces sink down to the bottom of the pack. Steyne!

Bareacres, Johnes of Helvellyn! and Caerlyon of Camelot! we may be sure that Becky and Briggs looked out those august names in the Peerage, and followed the noble races up through all the ramifications of the family tree.

My Lord Steyne coming to call a couple of hours afterwards, and looking about him, and observing everything as was his wont, found his ladies' cards already ranged as the trumps of Becky's hand, and grinned, as this old cynic always did at any naïve display of human weakness. Becky came down to him presently : whenever the dear girl expected his lordship, her toilette was prepared, her hair in perfect order, her *mouchoirs*, aprons, scarfs, little morocco slippers, and other female gimcracks arranged, and she seated in some artless and agreeable posture ready to receive him — whenever she was surprised, of course she had to fly to her apartment to take a rapid survey of matters in the glass, and to trip down again to wait upon the great peer.

She found him grinning over the bowl. She was discovered, and she blushed a little. "Thank you, Monseigneur," she said. "You see your ladies have been here. How good of you! I couldn't come before — I was in the kitchen making a pudding."

"I know you were, I saw you through the area-railings as I drove up," replied the old gentleman.

"You see everything," she replied.

"A few things, but not that, my pretty lady," he said, good-naturedly. "You silly little fibster! I heard you in the room over head, where I have no doubt you were putting a little rouge on ; you must give some of yours to my Lady Gaunt, whose complexion is quite preposterous ; and I heard the bedroom door open, and then you came down stairs."

"Is it a crime to try and look my best when *you* come here?" answered Mrs. Rawdon plaintively, and she rubbed her cheek with her handkerchief as if to show there was no rouge at all, only genuine blushes and modesty in her case. About this who can tell? I know there is some rouge that won't come off on a pocket-handkerchief; and some so good that even tears will not disturb it.

"Well," said the old gentleman, twiddling round his wife's card, "you are bent on becoming a fine lady. You pester my poor old life out to get you into the world. You won't be able to hold your own there, you silly little fool. You've got no money."

"You will get us a place," interposed Becky, as quick as possible.

"You've got no money, and you want to compete with those who have. You poor little earthenware pipkin, you want to swim down the stream along with the great copper kettles. All women are alike. Everybody is striving for what is not worth the having! Gad! I dined with the King yesterday, and we had neck of mutton and turnips. A dinner of herbs is better than a stalled ox very often. You will go to Gaunt House. You give an old fellow no rest until you get there. It's not half so nice as here. You'll be bored there. I am. My wife is as gay as Lady Macbeth, and my daughter is as cheerful as Regan and Goneril. I daren't sleep in what they call my bed-room. The bed is like the baldaquin of St. Peter's, and the pictures frighten me. I have a little brass bed in a dressing-room: and a little hair mattress like an anchorite. I am an anchorite. Ho! ho! You'll be asked to dinner next week. And *gare aux femmes*, look out and hold your own! How the women will bully you!" This was a very long speech for a man of few words like my Lord Steyne ; nor was it the first which he uttered for Becky's benefit on that day.

Briggs looked up from the work-table at which she was seated in the farther room, and gave a deep sigh as she heard the great Marquis speak so lightly of her sex.

"If you don't turn off that abominable sheepdog," said Lord Steyne, with a savage look over his shoulder at her, "I will have her poisoned."

"I always give my dog dinner from my own plate," said Rebecca, laughing mischievously ; and having enjoyed for some time the discomfiture of my lord, who hated poor Briggs for interrupting his *tête-à-tête* with the fair Colonel's wife, Mrs. Rawdon at length had pity upon her admirer, and calling to Briggs, praised the fineness of the weather to her, and bade her to take out the child for a walk.

"I can't send her away," Becky said presently, after a pause, and in a very sad voice. Her eyes filled with tears as she spoke, and she turned away her head.

"You owe her her wages, I suppose ? " said the Peer.

"Worse than that," said Becky, still casting down her eyes, "I have ruined her."

"Ruined her ? — then why don't you turn her out ? " the gentleman asked.

"Men do that," Becky answered bitterly. "Women are not so bad as you. Last year when we were reduced to our last guinea, she gave us everything. She shall never leave me, until we are ruined utterly ourselves, which does not seem far off, or until I can pay her the utmost farthing."

"—— it, how much is it ? " said the Peer, with an

oath. And Becky, reflecting on the largeness of his means, mentioned not only the sum which she had borrowed from Miss Briggs, but one of nearly double the amount.

This caused Lord Steyne to break out in another brief and energetic expression of anger, at which Rebecca held down her head the more, and cried bitterly. " I could not help it. It was my only chance. I dare not tell my husband. He would kill me if I told him what I have done. I have kept it a secret from everybody but you — and you forced it from me. Ah, what shall I do, Lord Steyne? for I am very, very unhappy!"

Lord Steyne made no reply except by beating the devil's tattoo, and biting his nails. At last he clapped his hat on his head, and flung out of the room. Rebecca did not rise from her attitude of misery until the door slammed upon him, and his carriage whirled away. Then she rose up with the queerest expression of victorious mischief glittering in her green eyes. She burst out laughing once or twice to herself, as she sat at work : and sitting down to the piano, she rattled away a triumphant voluntary on the keys, which made the people pause under her window to listen to her brilliant music.

That night, there came two notes from Gaunt House for the little woman, the one containing a card of invitation from Lord and Lady Steyne to a dinner at Gaunt House next Friday : while the other enclosed a slip of gray paper bearing Lord Steyne's signature and the address of Messrs. Jones, Brown, and Robinson, Lombard Street.

Rawdon heard Becky laughing in the night once or twice. It was only her delight at going to Gaunt House and facing the ladies there, she said, which

BECKY IN LOMBARD STREET.

amused her so. But the truth was, that she was occupied with a great number of other thoughts. Should she pay off old Briggs and give her her *congé?* Should she astonish Raggles by settling his account? She turned over all these thoughts on her pillow, and on the next day, when Rawdon went out to pay his morning visit to the club, Mrs. Crawley (in a modest dress with a veil on) whipped off in a hackney-coach to the City: and being landed at Messrs. Jones and Robinson's bank, presented a document there to the authority at the desk, who, in reply, asked her "How she would take it?"

She gently said "she would take a hundred and fifty pounds in small notes and the remainder in one note:" and passing through St. Paul's Churchyard stopped there and bought the handsomest black silk gown for Briggs which money could buy; and which, with a kiss and the kindest speeches, she presented to the simple old spinster.

Then she walked to Mr. Raggles, inquired about his children affectionately, and gave him fifty pounds on account. Then she went to the livery-man from whom she jobbed her carriages and gratified him with a similar sum. "And I hope this will be a lesson to you, Spavin," she said, "and that on the next Drawing-room day my brother, Sir Pitt, will not be inconvenienced by being obliged to take four of us in his carriage to wait upon His Majesty, because my *own* carriage is not forthcoming." It appears there had been a difference on the last Drawing-room day. Hence the degradation which the Colonel had almost suffered, of being obliged to enter the presence of his Sovereign in a hack cab.

These arrangements concluded, Becky paid a visit up stairs to the before-mentioned desk, which Amelia

Sedley had given her years and years ago, and which contained a number of useful and valuable little things: in which private museum she placed the one note which Messrs. Jones and Robinson's cashier had given her.

CHAPTER XXI.

IN WHICH WE ENJOY THREE COURSES AND A DESSERT.

WHEN the ladies of Gaunt House were at breakfast that morning, Lord Steyne (who took his chocolate in private, and seldom disturbed the females of his household, or saw them except upon public days, or when they crossed each other in the hall, or when from his pit-box at the Opera he surveyed them in their box on the grand tier) — his lordship, we say, appeared among the ladies and the children who were assembled over the tea and toast, and a battle royal ensued apropos of Rebecca.

"My Lady Steyne," he said, "I want to see the list for your dinner on Friday; and I want you, if you please, to write a card for Colonel and Mrs. Crawley."

"Blanche writes them," Lady Steyne said in a flutter. "Lady Gaunt writes them."

"I will not write to that person," Lady Gaunt said, a tall and stately lady, who looked up for an instant and then down again after she had spoken. It was not good to meet Lord Steyne's eyes for those who had offended him.

"Send the children out of the room. Go!" said he, pulling at the bell-rope. The urchins, always frightened before him, retired: their mother would have followed too. "Not you," he said. "You stop."

"My Lady Steyne," he said, "once more will you have the goodness to go to the desk, and write that card for your dinner on Friday?"

"My lord, I will not be present at it," Lady Gaunt said : "I will go home."

"I wish you would, and stay there. You will find the bailiffs at Bareacres very pleasant company, and I shall be freed from lending money to your relations, and from your own damned tragedy airs. Who are you to give orders here ? You have no money. You've got no brains. You were here to have children, and you have not had any. Gaunt's tired of you ; and George's wife is the only person in the family who does n't wish you were dead. Gaunt would marry again if you were."

"I wish I were," her ladyship answered, with tears and rage in her eyes.

"You, forsooth, must give yourself airs of virtue ; while my wife, who is an immaculate saint, as everybody knows, and never did wrong in her life, has no objection to meet my young friend Mrs. Crawley. My Lady Steyne knows that appearances are sometimes against the best of women ; that lies are often told about the most innocent of them. Pray, Madam, shall I tell you some little anecdotes about my Lady Bareacres, your mamma ?"

"You may strike me if you like, sir, or hit any cruel blow," Lady Gaunt said. To see his wife and daughter suffering always puts his lordship into a good humor.

"My sweet Blanche," he said, "I am a gentleman, and never lay my hand upon a woman, save in the way of kindness. I only wish to correct little faults in your character. You women are too proud, and sadly lack humility, as Father Mole, I'm sure, would tell my Lady Steyne if he were here. You must n't give yourselves airs : you must be meek and humble, my blessings. For all Lady Steyne knows, this cal-

umniated, simple, good-humored Mrs. Crawley is quite
innocent — even more innocent than herself. Her
husband's character is not good, but it is as good as
Bareacres's, who has played a little and not paid a
great deal, who cheated you out of the only legacy
you ever had, and left you a pauper on my hands.
And Mrs. Crawley is not very well born; but she is
not worse than Fanny's illustrious ancestor, the first
De la Jones."

"The money which I brought into the family, sir,"
Lady George cried out —

"You purchased a contingent reversion with it,"
the Marquis said, darkly. "If Gaunt dies, your husband may come to his honors; your little boys may
inherit them, and who knows what besides? In the
meanwhile, ladies, be as proud and virtuous as you
like abroad, but don't give *me* any airs. As for Mrs.
Crawley's character, I sha'n't demean myself or that
most spotless and perfectly irreproachable lady, by
even hinting that it requires a defence. You will be
pleased to receive her with the utmost cordiality, as
you will receive all persons whom I present in this
house. This house?" He broke out with a laugh.
"Who is the master of it? and what is it? This
Temple of Virtue belongs to me. And if I invite all
Newgate or all Bedlam here, by —— they shall be
welcome."

After this vigorous allocution, to one of which sort
Lord Steyne treated his "Hareem," whenever symptoms of insubordination appeared in his household,
the crest-fallen women had nothing for it but to
obey. Lady Gaunt wrote the invitation which his
lordship required, and she and her mother-in-law
drove in person, and with bitter and humiliated
hearts, to leave the cards on Mrs. Rawdon, the

reception of which caused that innocent woman so
much pleasure.

There were families in London who would have
sacrificed a year's income to receive such an honor at
the hands of those great ladies.   Mrs. Frederick Bullock, for instance, would have gone on her knees from
May Fair to Lombard Street, if Lady Steyne and
Lady Gaunt had been waiting in the City to raise
her up, and say, "Come to us next Friday," — not to
one of the great crushes and grand balls of Gaunt
House, whither everybody went, but to the sacred,
unapproachable, mysterious, delicious entertainments,
to be admitted to one of which was a privilege, and an
honor, and a blessing indeed.

Severe, spotless, and beautiful, Lady Gaunt held
the very highest rank in Vanity Fair.   The distinguished courtesy with which Lord Steyne treated her,
charmed everybody who witnessed his behavior, caused
the severest critics to admit how perfect a gentleman
he was, and to own that his lordship's heart at least
was in the right place.

The ladies of Gaunt House called Lady Bareacres
in to their aid, in order to repulse the common enemy.
One of Lady Gaunt's carriages went to Hill Street
for her ladyship's mother, all whose equipages were
in the hands of the bailiffs, whose very jewels and
wardrobe, it was said, had been seized by those inexorable Israelites.   Bareacres Castle was theirs, too,
with all its costly pictures, furniture, and articles of
vertu — the magnificent Vandykes ; the noble Rey-
nolds pictures ; the Lawrence portraits, tawdry and
beautiful, and, thirty years ago, deemed as precious as
works of real genius ; the matchless " Dancing Nymph
of Canova," for which Lady Bareacres had sat in her

youth — Lady Bareacres splendid then, and radiant in wealth, rank, and beauty — a toothless, bald, old woman now — a mere rag of a former robe of state. Her lord, painted at the same time by Lawrence, as waving his sabre in front of Bareacres Castle, and clothed in his uniform as Colonel of the Thistlewood Yeomanry, was a withered, old, lean man in a great-coat and a Brutus wig: slinking about Gray's Inn of mornings chiefly, and dining alone at clubs. He did not like to dine with Steyne now. They had run races of pleasure together in youth when Bareacres was the winner. But Steyne had more bottom than he, and had lasted him out. The Marquis was ten times a greater man now than the young Lord Gaunt of '85; and Bareacres nowhere in the race — old, beaten, bankrupt, and broken down. He had borrowed too much money of Steyne to find it pleasant to meet his old comrade often. The latter, whenever he wished to be merry, used jeeringly to ask Lady Gaunt, why her father had not come to see her? "He has not been here for four months," Lord Steyne would say. "I can always tell by my cheque-book afterwards, when I get a visit from Bareacres. What a comfort it is, my ladies, I bank with one of my sons' fathers-in-law, and the other banks with me!"

Of the other illustrious persons whom Becky had the honor to encounter on this her first presentation to the grand world, it does not become the present historian to say much. There was his Excellency the Prince of Peterwaradin, with his Princess; a noble-man tightly girthed, with a large military chest, on which the *plaque* of his order shone magnificently, and wearing the red collar of the Golden Fleece round his neck. He was the owner of countless flocks. "Look at his face. I think he must be descended from a sheep," Becky whispered to Lord Steyne. Indeed, his Excellency's countenance, long, solemn, and white, with the ornament round his neck, bore some resemblance to that of a venerable bell-wether.

There was Mr. John Paul Jefferson Jones, titularly attached to the American Embassy, and correspondent of the "New York Demagogue;" who, by way of making himself agreeable to the company, asked Lady Steyne, during a pause in the conversation at dinner, how his dear friend, George Gaunt, liked the Brazils? — He and George had been most intimate at Naples, and had gone up Vesuvius together. Mr. Jones wrote a full and particular account of the dinner, which appeared duly in the "Demagogue." He mentioned the names and titles of all the guests, giving biographical sketches of the principal people. He described the persons of the ladies with great eloquence; the service of the table; the size and costume of the servants; enumerated the dishes and wines served; the ornaments of the sideboard, and the probable value of the plate. Such a dinner he calculated could not be dished up under fifteen or eighteen dollars per head. And he was in the habit, until very lately, of sending over *protégés*, with letters of recommendation to the present Marquis of Steyne, encouraged to do so by the intimate terms on which he had lived with his dear friend, the late lord. He was most indignant that a young and insignificant aristocrat, the Earl of Southdown, should have taken the *pas* of him in their procession to the dining-room. "Just as I was stepping up to offer my hand to a very pleasing and witty fashionable, the brilliant and exclusive Mrs. Rawdon Crawley," — he wrote — "the young patrician interposed between me and the lady, and whisked my Helen off without a word of apology.

I was fain to bring up the rear with the Colonel, the lady's husband, a stout red-faced warrior who distinguished himself at Waterloo, where he had better luck than befell some of his brother red-coats at New Orleans."

The Colonel's countenance on coming into this polite society wore as many blushes as the face of a boy of sixteen assumes when he is confronted with his sister's schoolfellows. It has been told before that honest Rawdon had not been much used at any period of his life to ladies' company. With the men at the club or the mess-room, he was well enough; and could ride, bet, smoke, or play at billiards with the boldest of them. He had had his time for female friendships too: but that was twenty years ago, and the ladies were of the rank of those with whom Young Marlow in the comedy is represented as having been familiar before he became abashed in the presence of Miss Hardcastle. The times are such that one scarcely dares to allude to that kind of company which thousands of our young men in Vanity Fair are frequenting every day, which nightly fills casinos and dancing-rooms, which is known to exist as well as the Ring in Hyde Park or the Congregation at St. James's — but which the most squeamish if not the most moral of societies is determined to ignore. In a word, although Colonel Crawley was now five-and-forty years of age, it had not been his lot in life to meet with a half-dozen good women, besides his paragon of a wife. All except her and his kind sister Lady Jane, whose gentle nature had tamed and won him, scared the worthy Colonel; and on occasion of his first dinner at Gaunt House he was not heard to make a single remark except to state that the weather was very hot.

Indeed Becky would have left him at home, but that virtue ordained that her husband should be by her side to protect the timid and fluttering little creature on her first appearance in polite society.

On her first appearance Lord Steyne stepped forward, taking her hand, and greeting her with great courtesy, and presenting her to Lady Steyne, and their ladyships, her daughters. Their ladyships made three stately curtsies, and the elder lady to be sure gave her hand to the new-comer, but it was as cold and lifeless as marble.

Becky took it, however, with grateful humility; and performing a reverence which would have done credit to the best dancing-master, put herself at Lady Steyne's feet, as it were, by saying that his lordship had been her father's earliest friend and patron, and that she, Becky, had learned to honor and respect the Steyne family from the days of her childhood. The fact is, that Lord Steyne had once purchased a couple of pictures of the late Sharp, and the affectionate orphan could never forget her gratitude for that favor.

The Lady Bareacres then came under Becky's cognizance — to whom the Colonel's lady made also a most respectful obeisance : it was returned with severe dignity by the exalted person in question.

"I had the pleasure of making your ladyship's acquaintance at Brussels, ten years ago," Becky said, in the most winning manner. "I had the good fortune to meet Lady Bareacres, at the Duchess of Richmond's ball, the night before the battle of Waterloo. And I recollect your ladyship, and my Lady Blanche, your daughter, sitting in the carriage in the *porte-cochère* at the inn, waiting for horses. I hope your ladyship's diamonds are safe."

Everybody's eyes looked into their neighbor's. The famous diamonds had undergone a famous seizure, it appears, about which Becky, of course, knew nothing. Rawdon Crawley retreated with Lord Southdown into a window, where the latter was heard to laugh immoderately, as Rawdon told him the story of Lady Bareacres wanting horses, and "knuckling down by Jove," to Mrs. Crawley. "I think I needn't be afraid of *that* woman," Becky thought. Indeed, Lady Bareacres exchanged terrified and angry looks with her daughter, and retreated to a table, where she began to look at pictures with great energy.

When the Potentate from the Danube made his appearance, the conversation was carried on in the French language, and the Lady Bareacres and the younger ladies found, to their farther mortification, that Mrs. Crawley was much better acquainted with that tongue, and spoke it with a much better accent than they. Becky had met other Hungarian magnates with the army in France, in 1816–17. She asked after her friends with great interest. The foreign personages thought that she was a lady of great distinction; and the Prince and the Princess asked severally of Lord Steyne and the Marchioness, whom they conducted to dinner, who was that *petite dame* who spoke so well?

Finally, the procession being formed in the order described by the American diplomatist, they marched into the apartment where the banquet was served; and which, as I have promised the reader he shall enjoy it, he shall have the liberty of ordering himself so as to suit his fancy.

But it was when the ladies were alone that Becky knew the tug-of-war would come. And then indeed the little woman found herself in such a situation, as

made her acknowledge the correctness of Lord Steyne's
caution to her to beware of the society of ladies above
her own sphere. As they say the persons who hate
Irishmen most are Irishmen; so, assuredly, the
greatest tyrants over women are women. When poor
little Becky, alone with the ladies, went up to the fireplace whither the great ladies had repaired, the great
ladies marched away and took possession of a table of
drawings. When Becky followed them to the table
of drawings, they dropped off one by one to the fire
again. She tried to speak to one of the children (of
whom she was commonly fond in public places), but
Master George Gaunt was called away by his mamma;
and the stranger was treated with such cruelty finally,
that even Lady Steyne herself pitied her, and went up
to speak to the friendless little woman.

"Lord Steyne," said her ladyship, as her wan
cheeks glowed with a blush, "says you sing and
play very beautifully, Mrs. Crawley — I wish you
would do me the kindness to sing to me."

"I will do anything that may give pleasure to my
Lord Steyne or to you," said Rebecca, sincerely grateful, and seating herself at the piano, began to sing.

She sang religious songs of Mozart, which had been
early favorites of Lady Steyne, and with such sweetness and tenderness that the lady, lingering round the
piano, sat down by its side, and listened until the
tears rolled down her cheeks. It is true that the opposition ladies at the other end of the room kept up a
loud and ceaseless buzzing and talking : but the Lady
Steyne did not hear those rumors. She was a child
again — and had wandered back through a forty years'
wilderness to her Convent Garden. The chapel organ
had peeled the same tones, the organist, the sister
whom she loved best of the community, had taught

them to her in those early happy days. She was a girl once more, and the brief period of her happiness bloomed out again for an hour — she started when the jarring doors were flung open, and with a loud laugh from Lord Steyne, the men of the party entered full of gayety.

He saw at a glance what had happened in his absence : and was grateful to his wife for once. He went and spoke to her, and called her by her Christian name, so as again to bring blushes to her pale face — "My wife says you have been singing like an angel," he said to Becky. Now there are angels of two kinds, and both sorts, it is said, are charming in their way.

Whatever the previous portion of the evening had been, the rest of that night was a great triumph for Becky. She sang her very best, and it was so good that every one of the men came and crowded round the piano. The women, her enemies, were left quite alone. And Mr. Paul Jefferson Jones thought he had made a conquest of Lady Gaunt by going up to her ladyship, and praising her delightful friend's first-rate singing.

CHAPTER XXII.

CONTAINS A VULGAR INCIDENT.

THE Muse, whoever she be, who presides over this Comic History, must now descend from the genteel heights in which she has been soaring, and have the goodness to drop down upon the lowly roof of John Sedley at Brompton, and describe what events are taking place there. Here, too, in this humble tenement, live care, and distrust, and dismay. Mrs. Clapp in the kitchen is grumbling in secret to her husband about the rent, and urging the good fellow to rebel against his old friend and patron and his present lodger. Mrs. Sedley has ceased to visit her landlady in the lower regions now, and indeed is in a position to patronize Mrs. Clapp no longer. How can one be condescending to a lady to whom one owes a matter of forty pounds, and who is perpetually throwing out hints for the money? The Irish maid-servant has not altered in the least in her kind and respectful behavior; but Mrs. Sedley fancies that she is growing insolent and ungrateful, and, as the guilty thief who fears each bush an officer, sees threatening innuendoes and hints of capture in all the girl's speeches and answers. Miss Clapp, grown quite a young woman now, is declared by the soured old lady to be an unbearable and impudent little minx. Why Amelia can be so fond of her, or have her in her room so much, or walk out with her so constantly, Mrs. Sedley cannot con-

ceive. The bitterness of poverty has poisoned the
life of the once cheerful and kindly woman. She is
thankless for Amelia's constant and gentle bearing
towards her; carps at her for her efforts at kindness
or service: rails at her for her silly pride in her child,
and her neglect of her parents. Georgy's house is not
a very lively one since uncle Jos's annuity has been
withdrawn, and the little family are almost upon
famine diet.

Amelia thinks, and thinks, and racks her brain, to
find some means of increasing the small pittance upon
which the household is starving. Can she give lessons in anything? paint card-racks? do fine work?
She finds that women are working hard, and better
than she can, for twopence a-day. She buys a couple
of begilt Bristol boards at the Fancy Stationer's, and
paints her very best upon them — a shepherd with a
red waistcoat on one, and a pink face smiling in the
midst of a pencil landscape — a shepherdess on the
other, crossing a little bridge, with a little dog, nicely
shaded. The man of the Fancy Repository and Brompton Emporium of Fine Arts (of whom she bought the
screens, vainly hoping that he would re-purchase them
when ornamented by her hand) can hardly hide the
sneer with which he examines these feeble works of
art. He looks askance at the lady who waits in the
shop, and ties up the cards again in their envelope of
whitey-brown paper, and hands them to the poor widow
and Miss Clapp, who had never seen such beautiful
things in her life, and had been quite confident that
the man must give at least two guineas for the screens.
They try at other shops in the interior of London,
with faint sickening hopes. "Don't want 'em," says
one. "Be off," says another fiercely. Three-and-six-
pence have been spent in vain — the screens retired

to Miss Clapp's bed-room, who persists in thinking them lovely.

She writes out a little card in her neatest hand, and after long thought and labor of composition; in which the public is informed that "A Lady who has some time at her disposal, wishes to undertake the education of some little girls, whom she would instruct in English, in French, in Geography, in History, and in Music — address A. O., at Mr. Brown's;" and she confides the card to the gentleman of the Fine Art Repository, who consents to allow it to lie upon the counter, where it grows dingy and flyblown. Amelia passes the door wistfully many a time, in hopes that Mr. Brown will have some news to give her; but he never beckons her in. When she goes to make little purchases, there is no news for her. Poor simple lady, tender and weak — how are you to battle with the struggling violent world?

She grows daily more care-worn and sad: fixing upon her child alarmed eyes, whereof the little boy cannot interpret the expression. She starts up of a night and peeps into his room stealthily, to see that he is sleeping and not stolen away. She sleeps but little now. A constant thought and terror is haunting her. How she weeps and prays in the long silent nights — how she tries to hide from herself the thought which will return to her, that she ought to part with the boy, that she is the only barrier between him and prosperity. She can't, she can't. Not now, at least. Some other day. Oh! it is too hard to think of and to bear.

A thought comes over her which makes her blush and turn from herself, — her parents might keep the annuity, — the curate would marry her and give a home to her and the boy. But George's picture and dearest memory are there to rebuke her. Shame and love say no to the sacrifice. She shrinks from it as from something unholy; and such thoughts never found a resting-place in that pure and gentle bosom.

The combat, which we describe in a sentence or two, lasted for many weeks in poor Amelia's heart: during which she had no confidante: indeed, she could never have one: as she would not allow to herself the possibility of yielding: though she was giving way daily before the enemy with whom she had to battle. One truth after another was marshalling itself silently against her, and keeping its ground. Poverty and misery for all, want and degradation for her parents, injustice to the boy — one by one the outworks of the little citadel were taken, in which the poor soul passionately guarded her only love and treasure.

At the beginning of the struggle, she had written off a letter of tender supplication to her brother at Calcutta, imploring him not to withdraw the support which he had granted to their parents, and painting in terms of artless pathos their lonely and hapless condition. She did not know the truth of the matter. The payment of Jos's annuity was still regular: but it was a money-lender in the City who was receiving it: old Sedley had sold it for a sum of money wherewith to prosecute his bootless schemes. Emmy was calculating eagerly the time that would elapse before the letter would arrive and be answered. She had written down the date in her pocket-book of the day when she despatched it. To her son's guardian, the good Major at Madras, she had not communicated any of her griefs and perplexities. She had not written to him since she wrote to congratulate him on his approaching marriage. She thought with sickening despondency, that that friend, — the only one, the one who had felt such a regard for her,—was fallen away.

One day, when things had come to a very bad pass — when the creditors were pressing, the mother in hysteric grief, the father in more than usual gloom, the inmates of the family avoiding each other, each secretly oppressed with his private unhappiness and notion of wrong — the father and daughter happened to be left alone together; and Amelia thought to comfort her father, by telling him what she had done. She had written to Joseph — an answer must come in three or four months. He was always generous, though careless. He could not refuse, when he knew how straitened were the circumstances of his parents.

Then the poor old gentleman revealed the whole truth to her — that his son was still paying the annuity, which his own imprudence had flung away. He had not dared to tell it sooner. He thought Amelia's ghastly and terrified look, when, with a trembling, miserable voice he made the confession, conveyed reproaches to him for his concealment. "Ah!" said he, with quivering lips and turning away, "you despise your old father now!"

"O Papa! it is not that," Amelia cried out, falling on his neck, and kissing him many times. "You are always good and kind. You did it for the best. It is not for the money — it is — O my God! my God! have mercy upon me, and give me strength to bear this trial;" and she kissed him again wildly, and went away.

Still the father did not know what that exclamation meant, and the burst of anguish with which the poor girl left him. It was that she was conquered. The sentence was passed. The child must go from her — to others — to forget her. Her heart and her treasure

— her joy, hope, love, worship — her God, almost!
She must give him up; and then — and then she
would go to George; and they would watch over the
child and wait for him until he came to them in
heaven.

She put on her bonnet, scarcely knowing what she
did, and went out to walk in the lanes by which George
used to come back from school, and where she was in
the habit of going on his return to meet the boy. It
was May, a half-holiday. The leaves were all coming
out, the weather was brilliant: the boy came running
to her flushed with health, singing, his bundle of
school-books hanging by a thong. There he was.
Both her arms were round him. No, it was impossible. They could not be going to part. "What is the
matter, mother?" said he; "you look very pale."

"Nothing, my child," she said, and stooped down
and kissed him.

That night Amelia made the boy read the story of
Samuel to her, and how Hannah, his mother, having
weaned him, brought him to Eli the High Priest to
minister before the Lord. And he read the song of
gratitude which Hannah sang: and which says, who
it is who maketh poor and maketh rich, and bringeth
low and exalteth — how the poor shall be raised up out
of the dust, and how, in his own might, no man shall
be strong. Then he read how Samuel's mother made
him a little coat, and brought it to him from year to
year when she came up to offer the yearly sacrifice.
And then, in her sweet simple way, George's mother
made commentaries to the boy upon this affecting
story. How Hannah, though she loved her son so
much, yet gave him up because of her vow. And how
she must always have thought of him as she sat at
home, far away, making the little coat; and Samuel,

she was sure, never forgot his mother : and how happy
she must have been as the time came (and the years
pass away very quick) when she should see her boy,
and how good and wise he had grown. This little
sermon she spoke with a gentle solemn voice, and dry
eyes, until she came to the account of their meeting —
then the discourse broke off suddenly, the tender heart
overflowed, and taking the boy to her breast, she
rocked him in her arms, and wept silently over him
in a sainted agony of tears.

Her mind being made up, the widow began to take
such measures as seemed right to her for advancing
the end which she proposed. One day, Miss Osborne,
in Russell Square (Amelia had not written the name
or number of the house for ten years — her youth, her
early story came back to her as she wrote the superscription) — one day Miss Osborne got a letter from
Amelia, which made her blush very much and look
towards her father, sitting glooming in his place at the
other end of the table.

In simple terms, Amelia told her the reasons which
had induced her to change her mind respecting her
boy. Her father had met with fresh misfortunes which
had entirely ruined him. Her own pittance was so
small that it would barely enable her to support her
parents, and would not suffice to give George the
advantages which were his due. Great as her sufferings would be at parting with him she would, by God's
help, endure them for the boy's sake. She knew that
those to whom he was going, would do all in their
power to make him happy. She described his disposition, such as she fancied it ; quick and impatient of
control or harshness ; easily to be moved by love and
kindness. In a postscript, she stipulated that she

should have a written agreement, that she should see the child as often as she wished, — she could not part with him under any other terms.

"What? Mrs. Pride has come down, has she?" old Osborne said, when with a tremulous eager voice Miss Osborne read him the letter — "Reg'lar starved out, hey? ha, ha! I knew she would." He tried to keep his dignity and to read his paper as usual, — but he could not follow it. He chuckled and swore to himself behind the sheet.

At last he flung it down : and scowling at his daughter, as his wont was, went out of the room into his study adjoining, from whence he presently returned with a key. He flung it to Miss Osborne.

"Get the room over mine — his room that was — ready," he said. "Yes, sir," his daughter replied in a tremble. It was George's room. It had not been opened for more than ten years. Some of his clothes, papers, handkerchiefs, whips and caps, fishing-rods, and sporting gear, were still there. An army list of 1814, with his name written on the cover; a little dictionary he was wont to use in writing; and the Bible his mother had given him, were on the mantel-piece; with a pair of spurs, and a dried inkstand covered with the dust of ten years. Ah! since that ink was wet, what days and people had passed away! The writing-book still on the table, was blotted with his hand.

Miss Osborne was much affected when she first entered this room with the servants under her. She sank quite pale on the little bed. "This is blessed news, Mam — indeed, Mam," the housekeeper said; "and the good old times is returning, Mam. The dear little feller, to be sure, Mam; how happy he will be! But some folks in May Fair, Mam, will owe him a grudge, Mam;" and she clicked back the bolt which held the window-sash, and let the air into the chamber.

"You had better send that woman some money," Mr. Osborne said, before he went out. "She sha'n't want for nothing. Send her a hundred pound."

"And I'll go and see her to-morrow?" Miss Osborne asked.

"That's your look-out. She don't come in here, mind. No, by ——, not for all the money in London. But she mustn't want now. So look out, and get things right." With which brief speeches Mr. Osborne took leave of his daughter, and went on his accustomed way into the City.

"Here, Papa, is some money," Amelia said that night, kissing the old man, her father, and putting a bill for a hundred pounds into his hands. "And — and, Mamma, don't be harsh with Georgy. He — he is not going to stop with us long." She could say nothing more, and walked away silently to her room. Let us close it upon her prayers and her sorrow. I think we had best speak little about so much love and grief.

Miss Osborne came the next day, according to the promise contained in her note, and saw Amelia. The meeting between them was friendly. A look and a few words from Miss Osborne showed the poor widow that, with regard to this woman at least, there need be no fear lest she should take the first place in her son's affection. She was cold, sensible, not unkind. The mother had not been so well pleased, perhaps, had the rival been better looking, younger, more affectionate, warmer-hearted. Miss Osborne, on the other hand, thought of old times and memories, and could not but be touched with the poor mother's pitiful situation. She was conquered, and laying down her arms, as it were, she humbly submitted. That day they arranged together the preliminaries of the treaty of capitulation.

George was kept from school the next day, and saw his aunt. Amelia left them alone together, and went to her room. She was trying the separation, — as that poor gentle Lady Jane Grey felt the edge of the axe that was to come down and sever her slender life. Days were passed in parleys, visits, preparations. The widow broke the matter to Georgy with great caution; she looked to see him very much affected by the intelligence. He was rather elated than otherwise, and the poor woman turned sadly away. He bragged about the news that day to the boys at school; told them how he was going to live with his grandpapa, his father's father, not the one who comes here sometimes; and that he would be very rich, and have a carriage, and a pony, and go to a much finer school, and when he was rich he would buy Leader's pencil-case, and pay· the tart woman. The boy was the image of his father, as his fond mother thought.

Indeed I have no heart, on account of our dear Amelia's sake, to go through the story of George's last days at home.

At last the day came, the carriage drove up, the little humble packets containing tokens of love and remembrance were ready and disposed in the hall long since — George was in his new suit, for which the tailor had come previously to measure him. He had sprung up with the sun and put on the new clothes; his mother hearing him from the room close by, in which she had been lying, in speechless grief and watching. Days before she had been making preparations for the end; purchasing little stores for

the boy's use; marking his books and linen; talking
with him and preparing him for the change — fondly
fancying that he needed preparation.

So that he had change, what cared he? He was
longing for it. By a thousand eager declarations as
to what he would do, when he went to live with his
grandfather, he had shown the poor widow how little
the idea of parting had cast him down. "He would
come and see his mamma often on the pony," he said;
"he would come and fetch her in the carriage; they
would drive in the Park, and she should have everything she wanted." The poor mother was fain to
content herself with these selfish demonstrations of
attachment, and tried to convince herself how sincerely her son loved her. He must love her. All
children were so: a little anxious for novelty, and
— no, not selfish, but self-willed. Her child must
have his enjoyments and ambition in the world. She
herself, by her own selfishness and imprudent love
for him, had denied him his just rights and pleasures
hitherto.

I know few things more affecting than that timorous
debasement and self-humiliation of a woman. How
she owns that it is she and not the man who is guilty;
how she takes all the faults on her side: how she
courts in a manner punishment for the wrongs which
she has not committed, and persists in shielding the
real culprit! It is those who injure women who get
the most kindness from them — they are born timid
and tyrants, and maltreat those who are humblest
before them.

So poor Amelia had been getting ready in silent
misery for her son's departure, and had passed many
and many a long solitary hour in making preparations
for the end. George stood by his mother, watching

GEORGY GOES TO CHURCH GENTEELLY.

her arrangements without the least concern. Tears
had fallen into his boxes; passages had been scored
in his favorite books; old toys, relics, treasures had
been hoarded away for him, and packed with strange
neatness and care, — and of all these things the boy
took no note. The child goes away smiling as the
mother breaks her heart. By heavens, it is pitiful,
the bootless love of women for children in Vanity
Fair.

A few days are past: and the great event of Amelia's life is consummated. No angel has intervened.
The child is sacrificed and offered up to fate; and
the widow is quite alone.

The boy comes to see her often, to be sure. He
rides on a pony with the coachman behind him, to the
delight of his old grandfather, Sedley, who walks
proudly down the lane by his side. She sees him,
but he is not her boy any more. Why, he rides to
see the boys at the little school, too, and to show off
before them his new wealth and splendor. In two
days he has adopted a slightly imperious air and
patronizing manner. He was born to command, his
mother thinks, as his father was before him.

It is fine weather now. Of evenings on the days
when he does not come, she takes a long walk into
London — yes, as far as Russell Square, and rests on
the stone by the railing of the garden opposite Mr.
Osborne's house. It is so pleasant and cool. She
can look up and see the drawing-room windows illuminated, and, at about nine o'clock, the chamber in
the upper story where Georgy sleeps. She knows —
He has told her. She prays there as the light goes
out, prays with an humble, humble heart, and walks
home shrinking and silent. She is very tired when
she comes home. Perhaps she will sleep the better

for that long weary walk; and she may dream about Georgy.

One Sunday she happened to be walking in Russell Square, at some distance from Mr. Osborne's house (she could see it from a distance though) when all the bells of Sabbath were ringing, and George and his aunt came out to go to church; a little sweep asked for charity, and the footman, who carried the books, tried to drive him away; but Georgy stopped and gave him money. May God's blessing be on the boy! Emmy ran round the Square, and coming up to the sweep, gave him her mite too. All the bells of Sabbath were ringing, and she followed them until she came to the Foundling Church, into which she went. There she sat in a place whence she could see the head of the boy under his father's tombstone. Many hundred fresh children's voices rose up there and sang hymns to the Father Beneficent; and little George's soul thrilled with delight at the burst of glorious psalmody. His mother could not see him for a while, through the mist that dimmed her eyes.

CHAPTER XXIII.

IN WHICH A CHARADE IS ACTED WHICH MAY OR MAY NOT PUZZLE THE READER.

AFTER Becky's appearance at my Lord Steyne's private and select parties, the claims of that estimable woman as regards fashion were settled; and some of the very greatest and tallest doors in the metropolis were speedily opened to her — doors so great and tall that the beloved reader and writer hereof may hope in vain to enter at them. Dear brethren, let us tremble before those august portals. I fancy them guarded by grooms of the chamber with flaming silver forks with which they prong all those who have not the right of the *entrée*. They say the honest newspaper-fellow who sits in the hall and takes down the names of the great ones who are admitted to the feasts, dies after a little time. He can't survive the glare of fashion long. It scorches him up, as the presence of Jupiter in full dress wasted that poor imprudent Semele — a giddy moth of a creature who ruined herself by venturing out of her natural atmosphere. Her myth ought to be taken to heart amongst the Tyburnians, the Belgravians, — her story, and perhaps Becky's too. Ah, ladies ! — ask the Reverend Mr. Thurifer if Belgravia is not a sounding brass, and Tyburnia a tinkling cymbal. These are vanities. Even these will pass away. And some day or other (but it will be after our time, thank goodness), Hyde Park Gardens will be no better known than the celebrated horticultural outskirts of Babylon; and Belgrave Square will be as desolate as Baker Street, or Tadmor in the wilderness.

Ladies, are you aware that the great Pitt lived in Baker Street? What would not your grandmothers have given to be asked to Lady Hester's parties in that now decayed mansion? I have dined in it — *moi qui vous parle.* I peopled the chamber with ghosts of the mighty dead. As we sat soberly drinking claret there with men of to-day, the spirits of the departed came in and took their places round the darksome board. The pilot who weathered the storm tossed off great bumpers of spiritual port: the shade of Dundas did not leave the ghost of a heeltap. — Addington sat bowing and smirking in a ghastly manner, and would not be behindhand when the noiseless bottle went round; Scott, from under bushy eyebrows, winked at the apparition of a beeswing; Wilberforce's eyes went up to the ceiling, so that he did not seem to know how his glass went up full to his mouth and came down empty; — up to the ceiling which was above us only yesterday, and which the great of the past days have all looked at. They let the house as a furnished lodging now. Yes, Lady Hester once lived in Baker Street, and lies asleep in the wilderness. Eothen saw her there — not in Baker Street: but in the other solitude.

It is all vanity to be sure: but who will not own to liking a little of it? I should like to know what well-constituted mind, merely because it is transitory, dislikes roast-beef? That is a vanity; but may every man who reads this, have a wholesome portion of it through life, I beg: aye, though my readers were five hundred thousand. Sit down, gentlemen, and fall to, with a good hearty appetite; the fat, the lean, the gravy, the horse-radish as you like it — don't spare it. Another glass of wine, Jones, my boy — a little bit of the Sunday side. Yes, let us eat our fill of the vain thing, and be thankful therefor. And let us make the best of Becky's aristocratic pleasures likewise — for these too, like all other mortal delights, were but transitory.

The upshot of her visit to Lord Steyne was, that His Highness the Prince of Peterwaradin took occasion to renew his acquaintance with Colonel Crawley, when they met on the next day at the club, and to compliment Mrs. Crawley in the Ring of Hyde Park with a profound salute of the hat. She and her husband were invited immediately to one of the Prince's small parties at Levant House, then occupied by His Highness during the temporary absence from England of its noble proprietor. She sang after dinner to a very little *comité*. The Marquis of Steyne was present, paternally superintending the progress of his pupil.

At Levant House Becky met one of the finest gentlemen and greatest ministers that Europe has produced — the Duc de la Jabotière, then Ambassador from the Most Christian King, and subsequently Minister to that monarch. I declare I swell with pride as these august names are transcribed by my pen; and I think in what brilliant company my dear Becky is moving. She became a constant guest at the French Embassy, where no party was considered to be complete without the presence of the charming Madame Ravdonn Cravley.

Messieurs de Truffigny (of the Périgord family) and Champignac, both *attachés* of the Embassy, were straightway smitten by the charms of the fair

Colonel's wife: and both declared, according to the
wont of their nation (for who ever yet met a French-
man, come out of England, that has not left half a
dozen families miserable, and brought away as many
hearts in his pocket-book?), both I say, declared that
they were *aux mieux* with the charming Madame
Rawdonn.

But I doubt the correctness of the assertion.
Champignac was very fond of *écarté*, and made many
parties with the Colonel of evenings, while Becky
was singing to Lord Steyne in the other room; and
as for Truffigny, it is a well-known fact that he dared
not go to the Travellers', where he owed money to
the waiters, and if he had not had the Embassy as a
dining-place, the worthy young gentleman must have
starved.   I doubt, I say, that Becky would have
selected either of these young men as a person on
whom she would bestow her special regard.   They
ran of her messages, purchased her gloves and flowers, went in debt for opera-boxes for her, and made
themselves amiable in a thousand ways.   And they
talked English with adorable simplicity, and to the
constant amusement of Becky and my Lord Steyne,
she would mimic one or other to his face, and compliment him on his advance in the English language
with a gravity which never failed to tickle the Marquis, her sardonic old patron.   Truffigny gave Briggs
a shawl by way of winning over Becky's confidante,
and asked her to take charge of a letter which the
simple spinster handed over in public to the person
to whom it was addressed; and the composition of
which amused everybody who read it greatly.   Lord
Steyne read it: everybody but honest Rawdon; to
whom it was not necessary to tell everything that
passed in the little house in May Fair.

Here, before long, Becky received not only "the best" foreigners (as the phrase is in our noble and admirable society slang), but some of the best English people too. I don't mean the most virtuous, or indeed the least virtuous, or the cleverest, or the stupidest, or the richest, or the best born, but "the best," — in a word, people about whom there is no question — such as the great Lady Fitz-Willis, that Patron Saint of Almack's the great Lady Slowbore, the great Lady Grizzel Macbeth (she was Lady G. Glowry, daughter of Lord Grey of Glowry), and the like. When the Countess of Fitz-Willis (her ladyship is of the King-street family, see Debrett and Burke) takes up a person, he or she is safe. There is no question about them any more. Not that my Lady Fitz-Willis is any better than anybody else, being, on the contrary, a faded person, fifty-seven years of age, and neither handsome, nor wealthy, nor entertaining; but it is agreed on all sides that she is of the "best people." Those who go to her are of the best: and from an old grudge probably to Lady Steyne (for whose coronet her ladyship, then the youthful Georgina Frederica, daughter of the Prince of Wales's favorite, the Earl of Portansherry, had once tried), this great and famous leader of the fashion chose to acknowledge Mrs. Rawdon Crawley: made her a most marked curtsy at the assembly over which she presided: and not only encouraged her son, St. Kitts (his lordship got his place through Lord Steyne's interest), to frequent Mrs. Crawley's house, but asked her to her own mansion, and spoke to her twice in the most public and condescending manner during dinner. The important fact was known all over London that night. People who had been crying fie about Mrs. Crawley were silent. Wenham, the wit and lawyer, Lord

Steyne's right-hand man, went about everywhere praising her: some who had hesitated, came forward at once and welcomed her: little Tom Toady, who had warned Southdown about visiting such an abandoned woman, now besought to be introduced to her. In a word, she was admitted to be among the "best" people. Ah, my beloved readers and brethren, do not envy poor Becky prematurely — glory like this is said to be fugitive. It is currently reported that even in the very inmost circles, they are no happier than the poor wanderers outside the zone; and Becky, who penetrated into the very centre of fashion, and saw the great George IV. face to face, has owned since that there too was Vanity.

We must be brief in descanting upon this part of her career. As I cannot describe the mysteries of freemasonry, although I have a shrewd idea that it is a humbug: so an uninitiated man cannot take upon himself to portray the great world accurately, and had best keep his opinions to himself whatever they are.

Becky has often spoken in subsequent years of this season of her life, when she moved among the very greatest circles of the London fashion. Her success excited, elated, and then bored her. At first no occupation was more pleasant than to invent and procure (the latter a work of no small trouble and ingenuity, by the way, in a person of Mrs. Rawdon Crawley's very narrow means) — to procure, we say, the prettiest new dresses and ornaments; to drive to fine dinner parties, where she was welcomed by great people; and from the fine dinner parties to fine assemblies, whither the same people came with whom she had been dining, whom she had met the night before, and would see on the morrow — the young men faultlessly appointed, handsomely cravatted, with the neatest glossy boots and white gloves — the elders portly, brass-buttoned, noble-looking, polite, and prosy — the young ladies blonde, timid, and in pink — the mothers grand, beautiful, sumptuous, solemn, and in diamonds. They talked in English, not in bad French, as they do in the novels. They talked about each others' houses, and characters, and families : just as the Joneses do about the Smiths. Becky's former acquaintances hated and envied her : the poor woman herself was yawning in spirit. "I wish I were out of it," she said to herself. "I would rather be a parson's wife, and teach a Sunday-school than this ; or a sergeant's lady and ride in the regimental wagon ; or, oh, how much gayer it would be to wear spangles and trousers, and dance before a booth at a fair."

"You would do it very well," said Lord Steyne, laughing. She used to tell the great man her *ennuis* and perplexities in her artless way — they amused him.

"Rawdon would make a very good Ecuyer — Master of the Ceremonies — what do you call him — the man in the large boots and the uniform, who goes round the ring cracking the whip ? He is large, heavy, and of a military figure. I recollect," Becky continued, pensively, "my father took me to see a show at Brookgreen Fair when I was a child ; and when we came home I made myself a pair of stilts, and danced in the studio to the wonder of all the pupils."

"I should have liked to see it," said Lord Steyne.

"I should like to do it now," Becky continued. "How Lady Blinkey would open her eyes, and Lady Grizzel Macbeth would stare ! Hush ! silence ! there is Pasta beginning to sing." Becky always made a point of being conspicuously polite to the professional

ladies and gentlemen who attended at these aristocratic
parties — of following them into the corners where
they sat in silence, and shaking hands with them, and
smiling in the view of all persons.   She was an artist
herself, as she said very truly : there was a frankness
and humility in the manner in which she acknowledged
her origin, which provoked, or disarmed, or amused
lookers-on, as the case might be.   "How cool that
woman is," said one; "what airs of independence she
assumes, where she ought to sit still and be thankful
if anybody speaks to her."   "What an honest and
good-natured soul she is," said another.   "What an
artful little minx," said a third.   They were all right,
very likely; but Becky went her own way, and so
fascinated the professional personages, that they would
leave off their sore throats in order to sing at her parties, and give her lessons for nothing.

   Yes, she gave parties in the little house in Curzon
Street.   Many scores of carriages, with blazing lamps,
blocked up the street, to the disgust of No. 200, who
could not rest for the thunder of the knocking, and of
202, who could not sleep for envy.   The gigantic footmen who accompanied the vehicles, were too big to be
contained in Becky's little hall, and were billeted off
in the neighboring public-houses, whence, when they
were wanted, call-boys summoned them from their
beer.   Scores of the great dandies of London squeezed
and trod on each other on the little stairs, laughing to
find themselves there; and many spotless and severe
ladies of *ton* were seated in the little drawing-room,
listening to the professional singers, who were singing
according to their wont, and as if they wished to blow
the windows down.   And the day after, there appeared
among the fashionable *réunions* in the "Morning Post,"
a paragraph to the following effect : —

"Yesterday, Colonel and Mrs. Crawley entertained a select party at dinner at their house in May Fair. Their Excellencies the Prince and Princess of Peterwaradin, H. E. Papoosh Pasha, the Turkish Ambassador (attended by Kibob Bey, dragoman of the mission), the Marquess of Steyne, Earl of Southdown, Sir Pitt and Lady Jane Crawley, Mr. Wagg, etc. After dinner Mrs. Crawley had an assembly which was attended by the Duchess (Dowager) of Stilton, Duc de la Gruyère, Marchioness of Cheshire, Marchese Alessandro Strachino, Comte de Brie, Baron Schapzuger, Chevalier Tosti, Countess of Slingstone, and Lady F. Macadam, Major-General and Lady G. Macbeth, and (2) Miss Macbeths; Viscount Paddington, Sir Horace Fogey, Hon. Sands Bedwin, Bobbachy Bahawder," and an etc. which the reader may fill at his pleasure through a dozen close lines of small type.

And in her commerce with the great, our dear friend showed the same frankness which distinguished her transactions with the lowly in station. On one occasion, when out at a very fine house, Rebecca was (perhaps rather ostentatiously) holding a conversation in the French language with a celebrated tenor singer of that nation, while the Lady Grizzel Macbeth looked over her shoulder scowling at the pair.

"How very well you speak French," Lady Grizzel said, who herself spoke the tongue in an Edinburgh accent most remarkable to hear.

"I ought to know it," Becky modestly said, casting down her eyes. "I taught it in a school, and my mother was a Frenchwoman."

Lady Grizzel was won by her humility, and was mollified towards the little woman. She deplored the fatal levelling tendencies of the age, which admitted persons of all classes into the society of their

superiors; but her ladyship owned, that this one at
least was well behaved and never forgot her place in
life. She was a very good woman: good to the poor:
stupid, blameless, unsuspicious. — It is not her ladyship's fault that she fancies herself better than you
and me. The skirts of her ancestors' garments have
been kissed for centuries: it is a thousand years, they
say, since the tartans of the head of the family were
embraced by the defunct Duncan's lords and council-
lors, when the great ancestor of the House became
King of Scotland.

Lady Steyne, after the music scene, succumbed before Becky, and perhaps was not disinclined to her.
The younger ladies of the house of Gaunt were also
compelled into submission. Once or twice they set
people at her, but they failed. The brilliant Lady
Stunnington tried a passage of arms with her, but
was routed with great slaughter by the intrepid little
Becky. When attacked sometimes, Becky had a
knack of adopting a demure *ingénue* air, under which
she was most dangerous. She said the wickedest
things with the most simple unaffected air when in
this mood, and would take care artlessly to apologize
for her blunders, so that all the world should know
that she had made them.

Mr. Wagg, the celebrated wit, and a led captain and
trencher-man of my Lord Steyne, was caused by the
ladies to charge her; and the worthy fellow, leering
at his patronesses, and giving them a wink, as much
as to say, "Now look out for sport," — one evening
began an assault upon Becky, who was unsuspiciously
eating her dinner. The little woman, attacked on a
sudden, but never without arms, lighted up in an instant, parried and riposted with a home-thrust, which
made Wagg's face tingle with shame; then she re-

turned to her soup with the most perfect calm and a quiet smile on her face. Wagg's great patron, who gave him dinners and lent him a little money sometimes, and whose election, newspaper, and other jobs Wagg did, gave the luckless fellow such a savage glance with the eyes as almost made him sink under the table and burst into tears. He looked piteously at my lord, who never spoke to him during dinner, and at the ladies, who disowned him. At last Becky herself took compassion upon him, and tried to engage him in talk. He was not asked to dinner again for six weeks; and Fiche, my lord's confidential man, to whom Wagg naturally paid a good deal of court, was instructed to tell him that if he ever dared to say a rude thing to Mrs. Crawley again, or make her the butt of his stupid jokes, Milor would put every one of his notes of hand into his lawyer's hands, and sell him up without mercy. Wagg wept before Fiche, and implored his dear friend to intercede for him. He wrote a poem in favor of Mrs. R. C., which appeared in the very next number of the "Harumscarum Magazine," which he conducted. He implored her good will at parties where he met her. He cringed and coaxed Rawdon at the club. He was allowed to come back to Gaunt House after a while. Becky was always good to him, always amused, never angry.

His lordship's vizier and chief confidential servant (with a seat in Parliament and at the dinner table), Mr. Wenham, was much more prudent in his behavior and opinions than Mr. Wagg. However much he might be disposed to hate all *parvenus* (Mr. Wenham himself was a stanch old True Blue Tory, and his father a small coal-merchant in the north of England), this *aide-de-camp* of the Marquis never showed any sort of hostility to the new favorite; but pursued her with stealthy kindnesses, and a sly and deferential politeness, which somehow made Becky more uneasy than other people's overt hostilities.

How the Crawleys got the money which was spent upon the entertainments with which they treated the polite world, was a mystery which gave rise to some conversation at the time, and probably added zest to these little festivities. Some persons averred that Sir Pitt Crawley gave his brother a handsome allowance: if he did, Becky's power over the Baronet must have been extraordinary indeed, and his character greatly changed in his advanced age. Other parties hinted that it was Becky's habit to levy contributions on all her husband's friends: going to this one in tears with an account that there was an execution in the house; falling on her knees to that one, and declaring that the whole family must go to gaol or commit suicide unless such and such a bill could be paid. Lord Southdown, it was said, had been induced to give many hundreds through these pathetic representations. Young Feltham, of the —th Dragoons (and son of the firm of Tiler and Feltham, hatters and army accoutrement makers), and whom the Crawleys introduced into fashionable life, was also cited as one of Becky's victims in the pecuniary way. People declared that she got money from various simply disposed persons, under pretence of getting them confidential appointments under government. Who knows what stories were or were not told of our dear and innocent friend? Certain it is, that if she had had all the money which she was said to have begged or borrowed or stolen, she might have capitalized and been honest for life, whereas, — but this is advancing matters.

The truth is, that by economy and good management — by a sparing use of ready money and by paying scarcely anybody, — people can manage, for a time at least, to make a great show with very little means: and it is our belief that Becky's much-talked-of parties, which were not, after all was said, very numerous, cost this lady very little more than the wax candles which lighted the walls. Stillbrook and Queen's Crawley supplied her with game and fruit in abundance. Lord Steyne's cellars were at her disposal, and that excellent nobleman's famous cooks presided over her little kitchen, or sent by my lord's order the rarest delicacies from their own. I protest it is quite shameful in the world to abuse a simple creature, as people of her time abuse Becky, and I warn the public against believing one tenth of the stories against her. If every person is to be banished from society who runs into debt and cannot pay — if we are to be peering into everybody's private life, speculating upon their income, and cutting them if we don't approve of their expenditure — why, what a howling wilderness and intolerable dwelling Vanity Fair would be. Every man's hand would be against his neighbor in this case, my dear sir, and the benefits of civilization would be done away with. We should be quarrelling, abusing, avoiding one another. Our houses would become caverns: and we should go in rags because we cared for nobody. Rents would go down. Parties would n't be given any more. All the tradesmen of the town would be bankrupt. Wine, wax-lights, comestibles, rouge, crinoline-petticoats, diamonds, wigs, Louis-Quatorze gimcracks, and old china, park hacks, and splendid high-stepping carriage horses — all the delights of life, I say, — would go to the deuce, if people did but act upon their silly principles, and avoid those whom they dislike and abuse. Whereas, by a little charity and mutual forbearance, things are made to go on pleasantly enough : we may abuse a man as much as we like, and call him the greatest rascal unhung — but do we wish to hang him therefore ? No. We shake hands when we meet. If his cook is good we forgive him, and go and dine with him ; and we expect he will do the same by us. Thus trade flourishes — civilization advances : peace is kept ; new dresses are wanted for new assemblies every week ; and the last year's vintage of Lafitte will remunerate the honest proprietor who reared it.

At the time whereof we are writing, though the Great George was on the throne and ladies wore *gigots* and large combs like tortoise-shell shovels in their hair, instead of the simple sleeves and lovely wreaths which are actually in fashion, the manners of the very polite world were not, I take it, essentially different from those of the present day : and their amusements pretty similar. To us, from the outside, gazing over the policeman's shoulders at the bewildering beauties as they pass into court or ball, they may seem beings of unearthly splendor, and in the enjoyment of an exquisite happiness by us unattainable. It is to console some of these dissatisfied beings, that we are narrating our dear Becky's struggles, and triumphs, and disappointments, of all of which, indeed, as is the case with all persons of merit, she had her share.

At this time the amiable amusement of acting charades had come among us from France : and was considerably in vogue in this country, enabling the many ladies amongst us who had beauty to display their charms, and the fewer number who had cleverness, to exhibit their wit. My Lord Steyne was incited by Becky, who perhaps believed herself endowed with both the above qualifications, to give an entertainment at Gaunt House, which should include some of these little dramas — and we must take leave to introduce the reader to this brilliant *réunion*, and, with a melancholy welcome too, for it will be among the very last of the fashionable entertainments to which it will be our fortune to conduct him.

A portion of that splendid room, the picture gallery of Gaunt House, was arranged as the charade theatre. It had been so used when George III. was king; and a picture of the Marquis of Gaunt is still extant, with his hair in powder and a pink ribbon, in a Roman shape, as it was called, enacting the part of Cato in Mr. Addison's tragedy of that name, performed before their Royal Highnesses the Prince of Wales, the Bishop of Osnaburgh, and Prince William Henry, then children like the actor. One or two of the old properties were drawn out of the garrets, where they had lain ever since, and furbished up anew for the present festivities.

Young Bedwin Sands, then an elegant dandy and Eastern traveller, was manager of the revels. An Eastern traveller was somebody in those days, and the adventurous Bedwin, who had published his quarto, and passed some months under the tents in the desert, was a personage of no small importance. — In his volume there were several pictures of Sands in various Oriental costumes; and he travelled about with a black attendant of most unprepossessing appearance, just like another Brian de Bois Guilbert. Bedwin, his costumes, and black man, were hailed at Gaunt House as very valuable acquisitions.

He led off the first charade. A Turkish officer with an immense plume of feathers (the Janizaries were supposed to be still in existence, and the tarboosh had not as yet displaced the ancient and majestic head-dress of the true believers) was seen couched on a divan, and making believe to puff at a narghile, in which, however, for the sake of the ladies, only a fragrant pastille was allowed to smoke. The Turkish dignitary yawns and expresses signs of weariness and idleness. He claps his hands and Mesrour the Nubian appears, with bare arms, bangles, yataghans, and every Eastern ornament — gaunt, tall, and hideous. He makes a salaam before my lord the Aga.

A thrill of terror and delight runs through the assembly. The ladies whisper to one another. The black slave was given to Bedwin Sands by an Egyptian Pasha in exchange for three dozen of Maraschino. He has sewn up ever so many odalisques in sacks and tilted them into the Nile.

"Bid the slave-merchant enter," says the Turkish voluptuary with a wave of his hand. Mesrour conducts the slave-merchant into my lord's presence; he brings a veiled female with him. He removes the veil. A thrill of applause bursts through the house. It is Mrs. Winkworth (she was a Miss Absolom) with the beautiful eyes and hair. She is in a gorgeous Oriental costume; the black braided locks are twined with innumerable jewels; her dress is covered over with gold piastres. The odious Mahometan expresses himself charmed by her beauty. She falls down on her knees, and entreats him to restore her to the mountains where she was born, and where her Circassian lover is still deploring the absence of his Zuleikah. No entreaties will move the obdurate Hassan. He laughs at the notion of the Circassian bridegroom. Zuleikah covers her face with her hands, and drops down in an attitude of the most beautiful despair. There seems to be no hope for her, when — when the Kislar Aga appears.

The Kislar Aga brings a letter from the Sultan.

Hassan receives and places on his head the dread firman. A ghastly terror seizes him, while on the negro's face (it is Mesrour again in another costume) appears a ghastly joy. "Mercy! mercy!" cries the Pasha: while the Kislar Aga, grinning horribly, pulls out — a *bow-string*.

The curtain draws just as he is going to use that awful weapon. Hassan from within bawls out, "First two syllables" — and Mrs. Rawdon Crawley, who is going to act in the charade, comes forward and compliments Mrs. Winkworth on the admirable taste and beauty of her costume.

The second part of the charade takes place. It is still an Eastern scene. Hassan, in another dress, is in an attitude by Zuleikah, who is perfectly reconciled to him. The Kislar Aga has become a peaceful black slave. It is sunrise on the desert, and the Turks turn their heads eastwards and bow to the sand. As there are no dromedaries at hand, the band facetiously plays "The Camels are coming." An enormous Egyptian head figures in the scene. It is a musical one, — and, to the surprise of the Oriental travellers, sings a comic song, composed by Mr. Wagg. The Eastern voyagers go off dancing, like Papageno and the Moorish King, in the "Magic Flute." "Last two syllables" roars the head.

The last act opens. It is a Grecian tent this time. A tall and stalwart man reposes on a couch there. Above him hang his helmet and shield. There is no need for them now. Ilium is down. Iphigenia is slain. Cassandra is a prisoner in his outer halls. The king of men (it is Colonel Crawley, who, indeed, has no notion about the sack of Ilium or the conquest of Cassandra), the *anax andrôn* is asleep in his chamber at Argos. A lamp casts the broad shadow of the sleep⌐

ing warrior flickering on the wall — the sword and shield of Troy glitter in its light. The band plays the awful music of "Don Juan," before the statue enters.

Ægisthus steals in pale and on tiptoe. What is that ghastly face looking out balefully after him from behind the arras? He raises his dagger to strike the sleeper, who turns in his bed, and opens his broad chest as if for the blow. He cannot strike the noble slumbering chieftain. Clytemnestra glides swiftly into the room like an apparition — her arms are bare and white, — her tawny hair floats down her shoulders, — her face is deadly pale, — and her eyes are lighted up with a smile so ghastly, that people quake as they look at her.

A tremor ran through the room. "Good God!" somebody said, "it's Mrs. Rawdon Crawley."

Scornfully she snatches the dagger out of Ægisthus's hand, and advances to the bed. You see it shining over her head in the glimmer of the lamp, and — and the lamp goes out, with a groan, and all is dark.

The darkness and the scene frightened people. Rebecca performed her part so well, and with such ghastly truth, that the spectators were all dumb, until, with a burst, all the lamps of the hall blazed out again, when everybody began to shout applause. "Brava! brava!" old Steyne's strident voice was heard roaring over all the rest. "By ——, she'd do it too," he said between his teeth. The performers were called by the whole house, which sounded with cries of "Manager! Clytemnestra!" AGAMEMNON could not be got to show in his classical tunic, but stood in the background with Ægisthus and others of the performers of the little play. Mr. Bedwin Sands led on Zuleikah and Clytemnestra. A great personage insisted on being presented to the charming Clytem-

THE TRIUMPH OF CLYTEMNESTRA.

nestra. "Heigh ha? Run him through the body. Marry somebody else, hay?" was the apposite remark made by His Royal Highness.

"Mrs. Rawdon Crawley was quite killing in the part," said Lord Steyne. Becky laughed; gay, and saucy looking, and swept the prettiest little curtsy ever seen.

Servants brought in salvers covered with numerous cool dainties, and the performers disappeared to get ready for the second charade-tableau.

The three syllables of this charade were to be depicted in pantomime, and the performance took place in the following wise:—

First syllable. Colonel Rawdon Crawley, C.B., with a slouched hat and a staff, a great-coat, and a lantern borrowed from the stables, passed across the stage bawling out, as if warning the inhabitants of the hour. In the lower window are seen two bag-men playing apparently at the game of cribbage, over which they yawn much. To them enters one looking like Boots (the Honorable G. Ringwood) which character the young gentleman performed to perfection, and divests them of their lower coverings; and presently Chambermaid (the Right Honorable Lord Southdown) with two candlesticks, and a warm-ing-pan. She ascends to the upper apartment, and warms the bed. She uses the warming-pan as a weapon wherewith she wards off the attention of the bagmen. She exits. They put on their night-caps, and pull down the blinds. Boots comes out and closes the shutters of the ground-floor chamber. You hear him bolting and chaining the door within. All the lights go out. The music plays *Dormez, dormez, chers Amours.* A voice from behind the curtain says, "First syllable."

Second syllable. The lamps are lighted up all of a sudden. The music plays the old air from John of Paris, *Ah quel plaisir d' être en voyage.* It is the same scene. Between the first and second floors of the house represented, you behold a sign on which the Steyne arms are painted. All the bells are ringing all over the house. In the lower apartment you see a man with a long slip of paper presenting it to another, who shakes his fist, threatens and vows that it is monstrous. "Ostler, bring round my gig," cries another at the door. He chucks Chambermaid (the Right Honorable Lord Southdown) under the chin; she seems to deplore his absence, as Calypso did that of that other eminent traveller Ulysses. Boots (the Honorable G. Ringwood) passes with a wooden box, containing silver flagons, and cries "Pots" with such exquisite humor and naturalness, that the whole house rings with applause, and a bouquet is thrown to him. Crack, crack, crack, go the whips. Landlord, chambermaid, waiter rush to the door; but just as some distinguished guest is arriving, the curtains close, and the invisible theatrical manager cries out "Second syllable."

"I think it must be 'Hotel,'" says Captain Grigg of the Life Guards; there is a general laugh at the Captain's cleverness. He is not very far from the mark.

While the third syllable is in preparation, the band begins a nautical medley — "All in the Downs," "Cease Rude Boreas." "Rule Britannia," "In the Bay of Biscay O!" — some maritime event is about to take place. A bell is heard ringing as the curtain draws aside. "Now, gents, for the shore!" a voice exclaims. People take leave of each other. They point anxiously as if towards the clouds, which are represented by a dark curtain, and they nod their heads in fear. Lady Squeams (the Right Honorable Lord Southdown), her lap-dog, her bags, reticules, and husband ·sit down, and cling hold of some ropes. It is evidently a ship.

The Captain (Colonel Crawley, C.B.), with a cocked hat and a telescope, comes in, holding his hat on his head, and looks out; his coat-tails fly about as if in the wind. When he leaves go of his hat to use his telescope, his hat flies off, with immense applause. It is blowing fresh. The music rises and whistles louder and louder; the mariners go across the stage staggering, as if the ship was in severe motion. The Steward (the Honorable G. Ringwood) passes reeling by, holding six basins. He puts one rapidly by Lord Squeams — Lady Squeams, giving a pinch to her dog, which begins to howl piteously, puts her pocket-handkerchief to her face, and rushes away as for the cabin. The music rises up to the wildest pitch of stormy excitement, and the third syllable is concluded.

There was a little ballet, " Le Rossignol," in which Montessu and Noblet used to be famous in those days, and which Mr. Wagg transferred to the English stage as an opera, putting his verse, of which he was a skilful writer, to the pretty airs of the ballet. It was dressed in old French costume, and little Lord Southdown now appeared admirably attired in the disguise of an old woman hobbling about the stage with a faultless crooked stick.

Trills of melody were heard behind the scenes, and gurgling from a sweet pasteboard cottage covered with roses and trellis work. " Philomèle, Philomèle," cries the old woman, and Philomèle comes out.

More applause — it is Mrs. Rawdon Crawley in

powder and patches, the most *ravissante* little
Marquise in the world.

She comes in laughing, humming, and frisks about
the stage with all the innocence of theatrical youth
— she makes a curtsy. Mamma says, "Why, child,
you are always laughing and singing," and away she
goes, with —

THE ROSE UPON MY BALCONY.

The rose upon my balcony the morning air perfuming,
Was leafless all the winter time and pining for the spring;
You ask me why her breath is sweet and why her cheek is
    blooming,
It is because the sun is out and birds begin to sing.

The nightingale, whose melody is through the greenwood
    ringing,
Was silent when the boughs were bare and winds were blow-
    ing keen.
And if, Mamma, you ask of me the reason of his singing,
It is because the sun is out and all the leaves are green.

Thus each performs his part, Mamma, the birds have found
    their voices,
The blowing rose a flush, Mamma, her bonny cheek to dye;
And there's sunshine in my heart, Mamma, which wakens and
    rejoices,
And so I sing and blush, Mamma, and that's the reason why.

During the intervals of the stanzas of this ditty, the
good-natured personage addressed as mamma by the
singer, and whose large whiskers appeared under her
cap, seemed very anxious to exhibit her maternal affection by embracing the innocent creature who performed
the daughter's part. Every caress was received with
loud acclamations of laughter by the sympathizing

audience. At its conclusion (while the music was performing a symphony as if ever so many birds were warbling) the whole house was unanimous for an *encore*: and applause and bouquets without end were showered upon the NIGHTINGALE of the evening. Lord Steyne's voice of applause was loudest of all. Becky, the nightingale, took the flowers which he threw to her, and pressed them to her heart with the air of a consummate comedian. Lord Steyne was frantic with delight. His guests' enthusiasm harmonized with his own. Where was the beautiful black-eyed Houri whose appearance in the first charade had caused such delight? She was twice as handsome as Becky, but the brilliancy of the latter had quite eclipsed her. All voices were for her. Stephens, Caradori, Ronzi de Begnis, people compared her to one or the other, and agreed with good reason, very likely, that had she been an actress none on the stage could have surpassed her. She had reached her culmination: her voice rose trilling and bright over the storm of applause: and soared as high and joyful as her triumph. There was a ball after the dramatic entertainments, and everybody pressed round Becky as the great point of attraction of the evening. The Royal Personage declared with an oath, that she was perfection, and engaged her again and again in conversation. Little Becky's soul swelled with pride and delight at these honors; she saw fortune, fame, fashion before her. Lord Steyne was her slave; followed her everywhere, and scarcely spoke to any one in the room besides; and paid her the most marked compliments and attention. She still appeared in her Marquise costume, and danced a minuet with Monsieur de Truffigny, Monsieur Le Duc de la Jabotière's *attaché*; and the Duke, who had all the traditions of the ancient court, pronounced that

Madame Crawley was worthy to have been a pupil of Vestris, or to have figured at Versailles. Only a feeling of dignity, the gout, and the strongest sense of duty and personal sacrifice, prevented his Excellency from dancing with her himself; and he declared in public, that a lady who could talk and dance like Mrs. Rawdon, was fit to be ambassadress at any court in Europe. He was only consoled when he heard that she was half a Frenchwoman by birth. "None but a compatriot," his Excellency declared, "could have performed that majestic dance in such a way."

Then she figured in a waltz with Monsieur de Klingenspohr, the Prince of Peterwaradin's cousin and *attaché*. The delighted Prince, having less *retenue* than his French diplomatic colleague, insisted upon taking a turn with the charming creature, and twirled round the ball-room with her, scattering the diamonds out of his boot-tassels and hussar jacket until His Highness was fairly out of breath. Papoosh Pasha himself would have liked to dance with her if that amusement had been the custom of his country. The company made a circle round her, and applauded as wildly as if she had been a Noblet or a Taglioni. Everybody was in ecstasy; and Becky too, you may be sure. She passed by Lady Stunnington with a look of scorn. She patronized Lady Gaunt and her astonished and mortified sister-in-law — she *écraséd* all rival charmers. As for poor Mrs. Winkworth, and her long hair and great eyes, which had made such an effect at the commencement of the evening; where was she now? Nowhere in the race. She might tear her long hair and cry her great eyes out; but there was not a person to heed or to deplore the discomfiture.

The greatest triumph of all was at supper time. She was placed at the grand exclusive table with His

Royal Highness the exalted personage before mentioned, and the rest of the great guests. She was
served on gold plate. She might have had pearls
melted into her champagne if she liked — another
Cleopatra; and the potentate of Peterwaradin would
have given half the brilliants off his jacket for a kind
glance from those dazzling eyes. Jabotière wrote
home about her to his government. The ladies at the
other tables, who supped off mere silver, and marked
Lord Steyne's constant attention to her, vowed it was
a monstrous infatuation, a gross insult to ladies of
rank. If sarcasm could have killed, Lady Stunnington would have slain her on the spot.

Rawdon Crawley was scared at these triumphs.
They seemed to separate his wife farther than ever
from him somehow. He thought with a feeling very
like pain how immeasurably she was his superior.

When the hour of departure came, a crowd of
young men followed her to her carriage, for which
the people without bawled, the cry being caught up
by the link-men who were stationed outside the tall
gates of Gaunt House, congratulating each person
who issued from the gate and hoping his lordship
had enjoyed this noble party.

Mrs. Rawdon Crawley's carriage, coming up to the
gate after due shouting, rattled into the illuminated
court-yard, and drove up to the covered way. Rawdon
put his wife into the carriage, which drove off. Mr.
Wenham had proposed to him to walk home, and
offered the Colonel the refreshment of a cigar.

They lighted their cigars by the lamp of one of the
many link-boys outside, and Rawdon walked on with
his friend Wenham. Two persons separated from
the crowd and followed the two gentlemen; and
when they had walked down Gaunt Square a few

score of paces, one of the men came up, and touching Rawdon on the shoulder, said, "Beg your pardon, Colonel, I vish to speak to you most particular." This gentleman's acquaintance gave a loud whistle as the latter spoke, at which signal a cab came clattering up from those stationed at the gate of Gaunt House — and the *aide-de-camp* ran round and placed himself in front of Colonel Crawley.

That gallant officer at once knew what had befallen him. He was in the hands of the bailiffs. He started back, falling against the man who had first touched him.

"We're three on us — it's no use bolting," the man behind said.

"It's you, Moss, is it?" said the Colonel, who appeared to know his interlocutor. "How much is it?"

"Only a small thing," whispered Mr. Moss, of Cursitor Street, Chancery Lane, and assistant officer to the Sheriff of Middlesex — "One hundred and sixty-six, six and eightpence, at the suit of Mr. Nathan."

"Lend me a hundred, Wenham, for God's sake," poor Rawdon said — "I've got seventy at home."

"I've not got ten pounds in the world," said poor Mr. Wenham — "Good-night, my dear fellow."

"Good-night," said Rawdon ruefully. And Wenham walked away — and Rawdon Crawley finished his cigar as the cab drove under Temple Bar.

CHAPTER XXIV.

WHEN Lord Steyne was benevolently disposed, he did nothing by halves, and his kindness towards the Crawley family did the greatest honor to his benevolent discrimination. His lordship extended his good-will to little Rawdon: he pointed out to the boy's parents the necessity of sending him to a public school; that he was of an age now when emulation, the first principles of the Latin language, pugilistic exercises, and the society of his fellow-boys would be of the greatest benefit to the boy. His father objected that he was not rich enough to send the child to a good public school; his mother, that Briggs was a capital mistress for him, and had brought him on (as indeed was the fact) famously in English, the Latin rudiments, and in general learning: but all these objections disappeared before the generous perseverance of the Marquis of Steyne. His lordship was one of the governors of that famous old collegiate institution called the Whitefriars. It had been a Cistercian Convent in old days, when the Smithfield, which is contiguous to it, was a tournament ground. Obstinate heretics used to be brought thither convenient for burning hard by. Henry VIII., the Defender of the Faith, seized upon the monastery and its possessions, and hanged and tortured some of the monks who could not accommodate themselves to the pace of his reform. Finally, a great merchant bought the house and land adjoining, in which, and with the help of other wealthy endowments of land and money, he established a famous foundation hospital for old men and children. An extern school grew round the old almost monastic foundation, which subsists still with its middle-age costume and usages : and all Cistercians pray that it may long flourish.

Of this famous house, some of the greatest noblemen, prelates, and dignitaries in England are governors : and as the boys are very comfortably lodged, fed, and educated, and subsequently inducted to good scholarships at the University and livings in the Church, many little gentlemen are devoted to the ecclesiastical profession from their tenderest years, and there is considerable emulation to procure nominations for the foundation. It was originally intended for the sons of poor and deserving clerics and laics ; but many of the noble governors of the Institution, with an enlarged and rather capricious benevolence, selected all sorts of objects for their bounty. To get an education for nothing, and a future livelihood and profession assured, was so excellent a scheme that some of the richest people did not disdain it ; and not only great men's relations, but great men themselves, sent their sons to profit by the chance — Right Rev. Prelates sent their own kinsmen or the sons of their clergy, while, on the other hand, some great noblemen did not disdain to patronize the children of their confidential servants, — so that a lad entering this establishment had every variety of youthful society wherewith to mingle.

Rawdon Crawley, though the only book which he studied was the Racing Calendar, and though his chief recollections of polite learning were connected with the floggings which he received at Eton in his early youth, had that decent and honest reverence for classical learning which all English gentlemen feel, and was glad to think that his son was to have a provision for life, perhaps, and a certain opportunity of becoming a scholar. And although his boy was his chief solace and companion, and endeared to him by a thousand small ties, about which he did not care to speak to his wife, who had all along shown the utmost indifference to their son, yet Rawdon agreed at once to part with him, and to give up his own greatest comfort and benefit for the sake of the welfare of the little lad. He did not know how fond he was of the child until it became necessary to let him go away. When he was gone, he felt more sad and downcast than he cared to own — far sadder than the boy himself, who was happy enough to enter a new career, and find companions of his own age. Becky burst out laughing once or twice, when the Colonel, in his clumsy, incoherent way, tried to express his sentimental sorrows at the boy's departure. The poor fellow felt that his dearest pleasure and closest friend was taken from him. He looked often and wistfully at the little vacant bed in his dressing-room, where the child used to sleep. He missed him sadly of mornings, and tried in vain to walk in the Park without him. He did not know how solitary he was until little Rawdon was gone. He liked the people who were fond of him ; and would go and sit for long hours with his good-natured sister Lady Jane, and talk to her about the virtues, and good looks, and hundred good qualities of the child.

Young Rawdon's aunt, we have said, was very fond of him, as was her little girl, who wept copiously when the time for her cousin's departure came. The elder Rawdon was thankful for the fondness of mother and daughter. The very best and honestest feelings of the man came out in these artless outpourings of paternal feeling in which he indulged in their presence, and encouraged by their sympathy. He secured not only Lady Jane's kindness, but her sincere regard, by the feelings which he manifested, and which he could not show to his own wife. The two kinswomen met as seldom as possible. Becky laughed bitterly at Jane's feelings and softness; the other's kindly and gentle nature could not but revolt at her sister's callous behavior.

It estranged Rawdon from his wife more than he knew or acknowledged to himself. She did not care for the estrangement. Indeed, she did not miss him or anybody. She looked upon him as her errand-man and humble slave. He might be ever so depressed or sulky, and she did not mark his demeanor, or only treated it with a sneer. She was busy thinking about her position, or her pleasures, or her advancement in society; she ought to have held a great place in it, that is certain.

It was honest Briggs who made up the little kit for the boy which he was to take to school. Molly, the housemaid, blubbered in the passage when he went away — Molly kind and faithful in spite of a long arrear of unpaid wages. Mrs. Becky could not let her husband have the carriage to take the boy to school. Take the horses into the City ! — such a thing was never heard of. Let a cab be brought. She did not offer to kiss him when he went : nor did the child propose to embrace her : but gave a kiss to old Briggs (whom, in general, he was very shy of caressing), and consoled her by pointing out that he was to come home on Saturdays, when she would have the benefit of seeing him. As the cab rolled towards the City, Becky's carriage rattled off to the Park. She was chattering and laughing with a score of young dandies by the Serpentine, as the father and son entered at the old gates of the school — where Rawdon left the child, and came away with a sadder purer feeling in his heart than perhaps that poor battered fellow had ever known since he himself came out of the nursery.

He walked all the way home very dismally, and dined alone with Briggs. He was very kind to her, and grateful for her love and watchfulness over the boy. His conscience smote him that he had borrowed Briggs's money and aided in deceiving her. They talked about little Rawdon a long time, for Becky only came home to dress and go out to dinner — and then he went off uneasily to drink tea with Lady Jane, and tell her of what had happened, and how little Rawdon went off like a trump, and how he was to wear a gown and little knee-breeches, and how young Blackball, Jack Blackball's son, of the old regiment, had taken him in charge and promised to be kind to him.

In the course of a week, young Blackball had constituted little Rawdon his fag, shoe-black, and breakfast toaster; initiated him into the mysteries of the Latin Grammar, and thrashed him three or four times; but not severely. The little chap's good-natured honest face won his way for him. He only got that degree of beating which was, no doubt, good for him; and as for blacking shoes, toasting bread, and fagging in general, were these offices not deemed to be necessary parts of every young English gentleman's education?

Our business does not lie with the second generation and Master Rawdon's life at school, otherwise the present tale might be carried to any indefinite length.

The Colonel went to see his son a short time afterwards, and found the lad sufficiently well and happy,
grinning and laughing in his little black gown and
little breeches.

His father sagaciously tipped Blackball, his master,
a sovereign, and secured that young gentleman's good
will towards his fag. As a *protégé* of the great Lord
Steyne, the nephew of a County member, and son of
a Colonel and C. B., whose name appeared in some of
the most fashionable parties in the "Morning Post,"
perhaps the school authorities were disposed not to
look unkindly on the child. He had plenty of pocket-
money, which he spent in treating his comrades roy-
ally to raspberry tarts, and he was often allowed to
come home on Saturdays to his father, who always
made a jubilee of that day. When free, Rawdon
would take him to the play, or send him thither with
the footman ; and on Sundays he went to church with
Briggs and Lady Jane and his cousins. Rawdon mar-
velled over his stories about school, and fights, and
fagging. Before long, he knew the names of all the
masters and the principal boys as well as little Rawdon himself. He invited little Rawdon's crony from
school, and made both the children sick with pastry,
and oysters, and porter after the play. He tried to
look knowing over the Latin Grammar when little
Rawdon showed him what part of that work he was
"in." "Stick to it, my boy," he said to him with
much gravity, "there's nothing like a good classical
education ! nothing !"

Becky's contempt for her husband grew greater
every day. "Do what you like, — dine where you
please, — go and have ginger-beer and sawdust at
Astley's, or psalm-singing with Lady Jane, — only
don't expect *me* to busy myself with the boy. I have

your interests to attend to, as you can't attend to them yourself. I should like to know where you would have been now, and in what sort of a position in society, if I had not looked after you?" Indeed, nobody wanted poor old Rawdon at the parties whither Becky used to go. She was often asked without him now. She talked about great people as if she had the fee-simple of May Fair; and when the court went into mourning, she always wore black.

Little Rawdon being disposed of, Lord Steyne, who took such a parental interest in the affairs of this amiable poor family, thought that their expenses might be very advantageously curtailed by the departure of Miss Briggs; and that Becky was quite clever enough to take the management of her own house. It has been narrated in a former chapter, how the benevolent nobleman had given his *protégée* money to pay off her little debt to Miss Briggs, who however still remained behind with her friends; whence my lord came to the painful conclusion that Mrs. Crawley had made some other use of the money confided to her than that for which her generous patron had given the loan. However, Lord Steyne was not so rude as to impart his suspicions upon this head to Mrs. Becky, whose feelings might be hurt by any controversy on the money-question, and who might have a thousand painful reasons for disposing otherwise of his lordship's generous loan. But he determined to satisfy himself of the real state of the case: and instituted the necessary inquiries in a most cautious and delicate manner.

In the first place he took an early opportunity of pumping Miss Briggs. That was not a difficult operation. A very little encouragement would set that worthy woman to talk volubly, and pour out all within her. And one day when Mrs. Rawdon had gone out to drive (as Mr. Fiche, his lordship's confidential servant, easily learned at the livery stables where the Crawleys kept their carriage and horses, or rather, where the livery-man kept a carriage and horses for Mr. and Mrs. Crawley) — my lord dropped in upon the Curzon Street house — asked Briggs for a cup of coffee — told her that he had good accounts of the little boy at school — and in five minutes found out from her that Mrs. Rawdon had given her nothing except a black silk gown, for which Miss Briggs was immensely grateful.

He laughed within himself at this artless story. For the truth is, our dear friend Rebecca had given him a most circumstantial narration of Briggs's delight at receiving her money — eleven hundred and twenty-five pounds — and in what securities she had invested it; and what a pang Becky herself felt in being obliged to pay away such a delightful sum of money. "Who knows," the dear woman may have thought within herself, "perhaps he may give me a little more?" My lord, however, made no such proposal to the little schemer — very likely thinking that he had been sufficiently generous already.

He had the curiosity, then, to ask Miss Briggs about the state of her private affairs — and she told his lordship candidly what her position was — how Miss Crawley had left her a legacy — how her relatives had had part of it — how Colonel Crawley had put out another portion, for which she had the best security and interest — and how Mr. and Mrs. Rawdon had kindly busied themselves with Sir Pitt, who was to dispose of the remainder most advantageously for her, when he had time. My lord asked how much the

Colonel had already invested for her, and Miss Briggs at once and truly told him that the sum was six hundred and odd pounds.

But as soon as she had told her story, the voluble Briggs repented of her frankness, and besought my lord not to tell Mr. Crawley of the confessions which she had made. "The Colonel was so kind — Mr. Crawley might be offended and pay back the money, for which she could get no such good interest anywhere else." Lord Steyne, laughing, promised he never would divulge their conversation, and when he and Miss Briggs parted he laughed still more.

"What an accomplished little devil it is!" thought he. "What a splendid actress and manager! She had almost got a second supply out of me the other day, with her coaxing ways. She beats all the women I have ever seen in the course of all my well-spent life. They are babies compared to her. I am a greenhorn myself, and a fool in her hands — an old fool. She is unsurpassable in lies." His lordship's admiration for Becky rose immeasurably at this proof of her cleverness. Getting the money was nothing — but getting double the sum she wanted, and paying nobody — it was a magnificent stroke. And Crawley, my lord thought — Crawley is not such a fool as he looks and seems. He has managed the matter cleverly enough on his side. Nobody would ever have supposed from his face and demeanor that he knew anything about this money business; and yet he put her up to it, and has spent the money, no doubt. In this opinion my lord, we know, was mistaken; but it influenced a good deal his behavior towards Colonel Crawley, whom he began to treat with even less than that semblance of respect which he had formerly shown towards that gentleman. It never entered into the head of Mrs. Crawley's patron that the little lady might be making a purse for herself; and, perhaps, if the truth must be told, he judged of Colonel Crawley by his experience of other husbands, whom he had known in the course of the long and well-spent life which had made him acquainted with a great deal of the weakness of mankind. My lord had bought so many men during his life, that he was surely to be pardoned for supposing that he had found the price of this one.

He taxed Becky upon the point on the very first occasion when he met her alone, and he complimented her, good-humoredly, on her cleverness in getting more than the money which she required. Becky was only a little taken aback. It was not the habit of this dear creature to tell falsehoods, except when necessity compelled, but in these great emergencies it was her practice to lie very freely; and in an instant she was ready with another neat, plausible circumstantial story which she administered to her patron. The previous statement which she had made to him was a falsehood — a wicked falsehood: she owned it; but who had made her tell it? "Ah, my lord," she said, "you don't know all I have to suffer and bear in silence: you see me gay and happy before you — you little know what I have to endure when there is no protector near me. It was my husband, by threats and the most savage treatment, forced me to ask for that sum about which I deceived you. It was he, who, foreseeing that questions might be asked regarding the disposal of the money, forced me to account for it as I did. He took the money. He told me he had paid Miss Briggs; I did not want, I did not dare to doubt him. Pardon the wrong which a desperate man is forced to commit, and pity a miserable, miserable woman." She burst into

tears as she spoke. Persecuted virtue never looked
more bewitchingly wretched.

They had a long conversation, driving round and
round the Regent's Park in Mrs. Crawley's carriage
together, a conversation of which it is not necessary
to repeat the details: but the upshot of it was, that,
when Becky came home, she flew to her dear Briggs
with a smiling face, and announced that she had some
very good news for her. Lord Steyne had acted in
the noblest and most generous manner. He was always
thinking how and when he could do good. Now that
little Rawdon was gone to school, a dear companion
and friend was no longer necessary to her. She was
grieved beyond measure to part with Briggs; but her
means required that she should practise every retrench-
ment, and her sorrow was mitigated by the idea that
her dear Briggs would be far better provided for by
her generous patron than in her humble home. Mrs.
Pilkington, the housekeeper at Gauntly Hall, was
growing exceedingly old, feeble, and rheumatic: she
was not equal to the work of superintending that vast
mansion, and must be on the lookout for a successor.
It was a splendid position. The family did not go to
Gauntly once in two years. At other times the housekeeper was the mistress of the magnificent mansion —
had four covers daily for her table; was visited by the
clergy and the most respectable people of the county —
was the lady of Gauntly, in fact; and the two last
housekeepers before Mrs. Pilkington had married rec-
tors of Gauntly: but Mrs. P. could not, being the
aunt of the present Rector. The place was not to be
hers yet; but she might go down on a visit to Mrs.
Pilkington, and see whether she would like to succeed her.

What words can paint the ecstatic gratitude of

Briggs! All she stipulated for was that little Rawdon should be allowed to come down and see her at the Hall. Becky promised this — anything. She ran up to her husband when he came home, and told him the joyful news. Rawdon was glad, deuced glad; the weight was off his conscience about poor Briggs's money. She was provided for, at any rate, but — but his mind was disquiet. He did not seem to be all right somehow. He told little Southdown what Lord Steyne had done, and the young man eyed Crawley with an air which surprised the latter.

He told Lady Jane of this second proof of Steyne's bounty, and she, too, looked odd and alarmed; so did Sir Pitt. "She is too clever and — and gay to be allowed to go from party to party without a companion," both said. "You must go with her, Rawdon, wherever she goes, and you *must* have somebody with her — one of the girls from Queen's Crawley, perhaps, though they were rather giddy guardians for her."

Somebody Becky should have. But in the meantime it was clear that honest Briggs must not lose her chance of settlement for life; and so she and her bags were packed, and she set off on her journey. And so. two of Rawdon's out-sentinels were in the hands of the enemy.

Sir Pitt went and expostulated with his sister-in-law upon the subject of the dismissal of Briggs, and other matters of delicate family interest. In vain she pointed out to him how necessary was the protection of Lord Steyne for her poor husband; how cruel it would be on their part to deprive Briggs of the position offered to her. Cajolements, coaxings, smiles, tears could not satisfy Sir Pitt, and he had something very like a quarrel with his once admired Becky. He spoke of the honor of the family: the unsullied repu-

tation of the Crawleys : expressed himself in indignant tones about her receiving those young Frenchmen — those wild young men of fashion, my Lord
Steyne himself, whose carriage was always at her
door, who passed hours daily in her company, and
whose constant presence made the world talk about
her. As the head of the house he implored her to be
more prudent. Society was already speaking lightly
of her. Lord Steyne, though a nobleman of the
greatest station and talents, was a man whose attentions would compromise any woman ; he besought, he
implored, he commanded his sister-in-law to be watchful in her intercourse with that nobleman.

Becky promised anything and everything Pitt
wanted ; but Lord Steyne came to her house as often
as ever, and Sir Pitt's anger increased. I wonder
was Lady Jane angry or pleased that her husband at
last found fault with his favorite Rebecca ? Lord
Steyne's visits continuing, his own ceased ; and his
wife was for refusing all further intercourse with
that nobleman, and declining the invitation to the
Charade-night which the Marchioness sent to her ; but
Sir Pitt thought it was necessary to accept it, as his
Royal Highness would be there.

Although he went to the party in question, Sir Pitt
quitted it very early, and his wife, too, was very glad
to come away. Becky hardly so much as spoke to
him or noticed her sister-in-law. Pitt Crawley declared her behavior was monstrously indecorous, repro-
bated in strong terms the habit of play-acting and
fancy dressing, as highly unbecoming a British female ; and after the charades were over, took his
brother Rawdon severely to task for appearing himself, and allowing his wife to join in such improper
exhibitions

Rawdon said she should not join in any more such amusements; but indeed, and perhaps from hints from his elder brother and sister, he had already become a very watchful and exemplary domestic character. He left off his clubs and billiards. He never left home. He took Becky out to drive; he went laboriously with her to all her parties. Whenever my Lord Steyne called, he was sure to find the Colonel. And when Becky proposed to go out without her husband, or received invitations for herself, he peremptorily ordered her to refuse them; and there was that in the gentleman's manner which enforced obedience. Little Becky, to do her justice, was charmed with Rawdon's gallantry. If he was surly, she never was. Whether friends were present or absent, she had always a kind smile for him, and was attentive to his pleasure and comfort. It was the early days of their marriage over again: the same good-humor, *prévenances*, merriment, and artless confidence and regard. "How much pleasanter it is," she would say, "to have you by my side in the carriage than that foolish old Briggs! Let us always go on so, dear Rawdon. How nice it would be, and how happy we should always be, if we had but the money!" He fell asleep after dinner in his chair; he did not see the face opposite to him, haggard, weary, and terrible; it lighted up with fresh candid smiles when he woke. It kissed him gayly. He wondered that he had ever had suspicions. No, he never had suspicions; all those dumb doubts and surly misgivings which had been gathering on his mind were mere idle jealousies. She was fond of him; she always had been. As for her shining in society it was no fault of hers; she was formed to shine there. Was there any woman who could talk, or sing, or do anything like her? If she would but like the boy! Rawdon thought. But the mother and son never could be brought together.

And it was while Rawdon's mind was agitated with these doubts and perplexities that the incident occurred which was mentioned in the last chapter; and the unfortunate Colonel found himself a prisoner away from home.

CHAPTER XXV.

A RESCUE AND A CATASTROPHE.

FRIEND RAWDON drove on then to Mr. Moss's mansion in Cursitor Street, and was duly inducted into that dismal place of hospitality. Morning was breaking over the cheerful housetops of Chancery Lane as the rattling cab woke up the echoes there. A little pink-eyed Jew-boy, with a head as ruddy as the rising morn, let the party into the house, and Rawdon was welcomed to the ground-floor apartments by Mr. Moss, his travelling companion and host, who cheerfully asked him if he would like a glass of something warm after his drive.

The Colonel was not so depressed as some mortals would be, who, quitting a palace and a *placens uxor*, find themselves barred into a spunging-house, for, if the truth must be told, he had been a lodger at Mr. Moss's establishment once or twice before. We have not thought it necessary in the previous course of this narrative to mention these trivial little domestic incidents: but the reader may be assured that they can't unfrequently occur in the life of a man who lives on nothing a-year.

Upon his first visit to Mr. Moss, the Colonel, then a bachelor, had been liberated by the generosity of his aunt; on the second mishap, little Becky, with the greatest spirit and kindness, had borrowed a sum of money from Lord Southdown, and had coaxed her husband's creditor (who was her shawl, velvet-gown, lace pocket-handkerchief, trinket, and gimcrack purveyor, indeed) to take a portion of the sum claimed, and Rawdon's promissory note for the remainder: so on both these occasions the capture and release had been conducted with the utmost gallantry on all sides, and Moss and the Colonel were therefore on the very best of terms.

"You'll find your old bed, Colonel, and everything comfortable," that gentleman said, "as I may honestly say. You may be pretty sure its kep aired, and by the best of company, too. It was slep in the night afore last by the Honorable Capting Famish, of the Fiftieth Dragoons, whose Mar took him out, after a fortnight, jest to punish him, she said. But, Law bless you, I promise you, he punished my champagne, and had a party 'ere every night — reg'lar tip-top swells, down from the clubs and the West End — Captain Ragg, the Honorable Deuceace, who lives in the Temple, and some fellers as knows a good glass of wine, I warrant you. I've got a Doctor of Diwinity up stairs, five gents in the coffee-room, and Mrs. Moss has a tably-dy-hoty at half-past five, and a little cards or music afterwards, when we shall be most happy to see you."

"I'll ring when I want anything," said Rawdon, and went quietly to his bed-room. He was an old soldier, we have said, and not to be disturbed by any little shocks of fate. A weaker man would have sent off a letter to his wife on the instant of his capture. "But what is the use of disturbing her night's rest?" thought Rawdon. "She won't know whether I am in my room or not. It will be time enough to write to her when she has had her sleep out, and I have had mine. It's only a hundred and seventy, and the deuce is in it if we can't raise that." And so, thinking about little

Rawdon (whom he would not have know that he was in such a queer place), the Colonel turned into the bed lately occupied by Captain Famish, and fell asleep. It was ten o'clock when he woke up, and the ruddy-headed youth brought him, with conscious pride, a fine silver dressing-case, wherewith he might perform the operation of shaving. Indeed Mr. Moss's house, though somewhat dirty, was splendid throughout. There were dirty trays, and wine-coolers *en permanence* on the side-board, huge dirty gilt cornices, with dingy yellow satin hangings to the barred windows which looked into Cursitor Street — vast and dirty gilt picture-frames surrounding pieces sporting and sacred, all of which works were by the greatest masters; and fetched the greatest prices, too, in the bill transactions, in the course of which they were sold and bought over and over again. The Colonel's breakfast was served to him in the same dingy and gorgeous plated ware. Miss Moss, a dark-eyed maid in curl-papers, appeared with the teapot, and, smiling, asked the Colonel how he had slep? and she brought him in the "Morning Post," with the names of all the great people who had figured at Lord Steyne's entertainment the night before. It contained a brilliant account of the festivi-ties, and of the beautiful and accomplished Mrs. Raw-don Crawley's admirable personifications.

After a lively chat with this lady (who sat on the edge of the breakfast table in an easy attitude dis-playing the drapery of her stocking and an ex-white satin shoe, which was down at heel), Colonel Crawley called for pens and ink, and paper; and being asked how many sheets, chose one which was brought to him between Miss Moss's own finger and thumb. Many a sheet had that dark-eyed damsel brought in; many a poor fellow had scrawled and blotted hurried lines of entreaty, and paced up and down that awful room until his messenger brought back the reply. Poor men always use messengers instead of the post. Who has not had their letters, with the wafers wet, and the announcement that a person is waiting in the hall?

Now on the score of his application, Rawdon had not many misgivings.

"DEAR BECKY" (Rawdon wrote):

"*I hope you slept well.* Don't be *frightened* if I don't bring you in your *coffy.* Last night as I was coming home smoking, I met with an *accident.* I was *nabbed* by Moss of Cursitor Street — from whose *gilt and splendid parler* I write this — the same that had me this time two years. Miss Moss brought in my tea — she is grown very *fat,* and, as usual, had *her stockens down at heal.*

"It's Nathan's business — a hundred-and-fifty — with costs, hundred-and-seventy. Please send me my desk and some *cloths* — I'm in pumps and a white tye (something like Miss M.'s stockings) — I've seventy in it. And as soon as you get this, Drive to Nathan's — offer him seventy-five down, and ask *him to renew* — say I'll take wine — we may as well have some dinner sherry; but not *pictures,* they're too dear.

"If he won't stand it. Take my ticker and such of your things as you can *spare,* and send them to Balls — we must, of course, have the sum to-night. It won't do to let it stand over, as to-morrow's Sunday; the beds here are not very *clean,* and there may be other things out against me. I'm glad it ain't Rawdon's Saturday for coming home. God bless you.

"Yours in haste,

"R. C.

"P. S. Make haste and come."

This letter, sealed with a wafer, was despatched by one of the messengers who are always hanging about Mr. Moss's establishment; and Rawdon, having seen him depart, went out in the court-yard, and smoked his cigar with a tolerably easy mind — in spite of

the bars overhead; for Mr. Moss's court-yard is railed
in like a cage, lest the gentlemen who are boarding with him should take a fancy to escape from his
hospitality.

Three hours, he calculated, would be the utmost
time required, before Becky should arrive and open
his prison doors: and he passed these pretty cheerfully in smoking, in reading the paper, and in the
coffee-room with an acquaintance, Captain Walker,
who happened to be there, and with whom he cut for
sixpences for some hours, with pretty equal luck on
either side.

But the day passed away and no messenger returned, — no Becky. Mr. Moss's tably-dy-hoty was
served at the appointed hour of half-past five, when
such of the gentlemen lodging in the house as could
afford to pay for the banquet, came and partook of it
in the splendid front parlor before described, and
with which Mr. Crawley's temporary lodging communicated, when Miss M. (Miss Hem as her papa called
her) appeared without the curl-papers of the morning,
and Mrs. Hem did the honors of a prime boiled leg
of mutton and turnips, of which the Colonel ate
with a very faint appetite. Asked whether he would
"stand" a bottle of champagne for the company, he
consented, and the ladies drank to his 'ealth, and Mr.
Moss, in the most polite manner "looked towards
him."

In the midst of this repast, however, the door-bell
was heard, — young Moss of the ruddy hair, rose up
with the keys and answered the summons, and coming
back, told the Colonel that the messenger had returned with a bag, a desk and a letter, which he gave
him. "No ceremony, Colonel, I beg," said Mrs. Moss
with a wave of her hand, and he opened the letter

rather tremulously. It was a beautiful letter, highly scented, on a pink paper, and with a light green seal.

"MON PAUVRE CHER PETIT" (Mrs. Crawley wrote):

"I could not sleep *one wink* for thinking of what had become of *my odious old monstre:* and only got to rest in the morning after sending for Mr. Blench (for I was in a fever), who gave me a composing draught and left orders with Finette that I should be disturbed *on no account.* So that my poor old man's messenger, who had *bien mauvaise mine* Finette says, and *sentoit le Genièvre,* remained in the hall for some hours waiting my bell. You may fancy my state when I read your poor dear old ill-spelt letter.

"Ill as I was, I instantly called for the carriage, and as soon as I was dressed (though I could n't drink a drop of chocolate — I assure you I could n't without my *monstre* to bring it to me), I drove *ventre à terre* to Nathan's. I saw him — I wept — I cried — I fell at his odious knees. Nothing would mollify the horrid man. He would have all the money, he said, or keep my poor *monstre* in prison. I drove home with the intention of paying that *triste visite chez mon oncle* (when every trinket I have should be at your disposal though they would not fetch a hundred pounds, for some, you know, are with *ce cher oncle* already), and found Milor there with the Bulgarian old sheep-faced monster, who had come to compliment me upon last night's performances. Paddington came in, too, drawling and lisping and twiddling his hair; so did Champignac, and his *chef* — everybody with *foison* of compliments and pretty speeches — plaguing poor me, who longed to be rid of them, and was thinking *every moment of the time of mon pauvre prisonnier.*

"When they were gone, I went down on my knees to Milor; told him we were going to pawn everything, and begged and prayed him to give me two hundred pounds. He pish'd and psha'd in a fury — told me not to be such a fool as to pawn — and said he would see whether he could lend me the money. At last he went away, promising that he

would send it me in the morning : when I will bring it to my
poor old monster with a kiss from his affectionate

" BECKY.

"I am writing in bed. Oh, I have such a headache and
such a heartache ! "

When Rawdon read over this letter, he turned so
red and looked so savage, that the company at the
table d'hôte easily perceived that bad news had
reached him. All his suspicions, which he had been
trying to banish, returned upon him. She could not
even go out and sell her trinkets to free him. She
could laugh and talk about compliments paid to her,
whilst he was in prison. Who had put him there?
Wenham had walked with him. Was there — He
could hardly bear to think of what he suspected.
Leaving the room hurriedly, he ran into his own —
opened his desk, wrote two hurried lines, which he
directed to Sir Pitt or Lady Crawley, and bade the
messenger carry them at once to Gaunt Street, bidding him to take a cab, and promising him a guinea
if he was back in an hour.

In the note he besought his dear brother and sister,
for the sake of God ; for the sake of his dear child
and his honor ; to come to him and relieve him from
his difficulty. He was in prison : he wanted a hundred pounds to set him free — he entreated them to
come to him.

He went back to the dining-room after despatch-
ing his messenger, and called for more wine. He
laughed and talked with a strange boisterousness, as
the people thought. Sometimes he laughed madly
at his own fears, and went on drinking for an hour ;
listening all the while for the carriage which was to
bring his fate back.

At the expiration of that time, wheels were heard whirling up to the gate — the young janitor went out with his gate-keys. It was a lady whom he let in at the bailiff's door.

"Colonel Crawley," she said, trembling very much. He, with a knowing look, locked the outer door upon her — then unlocked and opened the inner one, and calling out, "Colonel, you're wanted," led her into the back parlor, which he occupied.

Rawdon came in from the dining-parlor where all those people were carousing, into his back room; a flare of coarse light following him into the apartment where the lady stood, still very nervous.

"It is I, Rawdon," she said, in a timid voice, which she strove to render cheerful. "It is Jane." Rawdon was quite overcome by that kind voice and presence. He ran up to her — caught her in his arms — gasped out some inarticulate words of thanks, and fairly sobbed on her shoulder. She did not know the cause of his emotion.

The bills of Mr. Moss were quickly settled, perhaps to the disappointment of that gentleman, who had counted on having the Colonel as his guest over Sunday at least; and Jane, with beaming smiles and happiness in her eyes, carried away Rawdon from the bailiff's house, and they went homewards in the cab in which she had hastened to his release. "Pitt was gone to a parliamentary dinner," she said, "when Rawdon's note came, and so, dear Rawdon, I — I came myself;" and she put her kind hand in his. Perhaps it was well for Rawdon Crawley that Pitt was away at that dinner. Rawdon thanked his sister a hundred times, and with an ardor of gratitude which touched and almost alarmed that soft-hearted woman. "Oh," said he in his rude, artless way, "you — you don't know how I'm changed since I've known you, and — and little Rawdy. I — I'd like to change somehow. You see I want — I want — to be — ." He did not finish the sentence, but she could interpret it. And that night after he left her, and as she sat by her own little boy's bed, she prayed humbly for that poor way-worn sinner.

Rawdon left her and walked home rapidly. It was nine o'clock at night. He ran across the streets, and the great squares of Vanity Fair, and at length came up breathless opposite his own house. He started back and fell against the railings, trembling as he looked up. The drawing-room windows were blazing with light. She had said that she was in bed and ill. He stood there for some time, the light from the rooms on his pale face.

He took out his door-key and let himself into the house. He could hear laughter in the upper rooms. He was in the ball-dress in which he had been captured the night before. He went silently up the stairs; leaning against the banisters at the stair-head. — Nobody was stirring in the house besides — all the servants had been sent away. Rawdon heard laughter within — laughter and singing. Becky was singing a snatch of the song of the night before; a hoarse voice shouted "Brava! Brava!" — it was Lord Steyne's.

Rawdon opened the door and went in. A little table with a dinner was laid out — and wine and plate. Steyne was hanging over the sofa on which Becky sat. The wretched woman was in a brilliant full toilette, her arms and all her fingers sparkling with bracelets and rings; and the brilliants on her breast which Steyne had given her. He had her hand in his, and was bowing over it to kiss it, when

Becky started up with a faint scream as she caught sight of Rawdon's white face. At the next instant she tried a smile, a horrid smile, as if to welcome her husband: and Steyne rose up, grinding his teeth, pale, and with fury in his looks.

He, too, attempted a laugh — and came forward holding out his hand. "What, come back! How d'ye do, Crawley?" he said, the nerves of his mouth twitching as he tried to grin at the intruder.

There was that in Rawdon's face which caused Becky to fling herself before him. "I am innocent, Rawdon," she said; "before God, I am innocent." She clung hold of his coat, of his hands; her own were all covered with serpents, and rings, and bawbles. "I am innocent. — Say I am innocent," she said to Lord Steyne.

He thought a trap had been laid for him, and was as furious with the wife as with the husband. "You innocent! Damn you," he screamed out. "You innocent! Why every trinket you have on your body is paid for by me. I have given you thousands of pounds which this fellow has spent, and for which he has sold you. Innocent, by ——! You're as innocent as your mother, the ballet-girl, and your husband the bully. Don't think to frighten me as you have done others. Make way, sir, and let me pass;" and Lord Steyne seized up his hat, and, with flame in his eyes, and looking his enemy fiercely in the face, marched upon him, never for a moment doubting that the other would give way.

But Rawdon Crawley springing out, seized him by the neckcloth, until Steyne, almost strangled, writhed, and bent under his arm. "You lie, you dog!" said Rawdon. "You lie, you coward and villain!" And he struck the Peer twice over the face with his open hand, and flung him bleeding to the ground. It was all done before Rebecca could interpose. She stood there trembling before him. She admired her husband, strong, brave, and victorious.

"Come here," he said. — She came up at once.

"Take off those things." — She began, trembling, pulling the jewels from her arms, and the rings from her shaking fingers, and held them all in a heap, quivering and looking up at him. "Throw them down," he said, and she dropped them. He tore the diamond ornament out of her breast, and flung it at Lord Steyne. It cut him on his bald forehead. Steyne wore the scar to his dying day.

"Come up stairs," Rawdon said to his wife. "Don't kill me, Rawdon," she said. He laughed savagely. — "I want to see if that man lies about the money as he has about me. Has he given you any?"

"No," said Rebecca, "that is —"

"Give me your keys," Rawdon answered, and they went out together.

Rebecca gave him all the keys but one: and she was in hopes that he would not have remarked the absence of that. It belonged to the little desk which Amelia had given her in early days, and which she kept in a secret place. But Rawdon flung open boxes and wardrobes, throwing the multifarious trumpery of their contents here and there, and at last he found the desk. The woman was forced to open it. It contained papers, love-letters many years old — all sorts of small trinkets and woman's memoranda. And it contained a pocket-book with bank-notes. Some of these were dated ten years back, too, and one was quite a fresh one — a note for a thousand pounds which Lord Steyne had given her.

"Did he give you this?" Rawdon said.

"Yes;" Rebecca answered.

"I'll send it to him to-day," Rawdon said (for day had dawned again, and many hours had passed in this search), "and I will pay Briggs, who was kind to the boy, and some of the debts. You will let me know where I shall send the rest to you. You might have spared me a hundred pounds, Becky, out of all this — I have always shared with you."

"I am innocent," said Becky. And he left her without another word.

What were her thoughts when he left her? She remained for hours after he was gone, the sunshine pouring into the room, and Rebecca sitting alone on the bed's edge. The drawers were all opened and their contents scattered about, — dresses and feathers, scarfs and trinkets, a heap of tumbled vanities lying in a wreck. Her hair was falling over her shoulders; her gown was torn where Rawdon had wrenched the brilliants out of it. She heard him go down stairs a few minutes after he left her, and the door slamming and closing on him. She knew he would never come back. He was gone forever. Would he kill himself? — she thought — not until after he had met Lord Steyne. She thought of her long past life, and all the dismal incidents of it. Ah, how dreary it seemed, how miserable, lonely and profitless! Should she take laudanum, and end it, too — have done with all hopes, schemes, debts, and triumphs? The French maid found her in this position — sitting in the midst of her miserable ruins with clasped hands and dry eyes. The woman was her accomplice and in Steyne's pay. "*Mon Dieu*, Madame, what has happened?" she asked.

What *had* happened? Was she guilty or not?

She said not; but who could tell what was truth which came from those lips; or if that corrupt heart was in this case pure? All her lies and her schemes, all her selfishness and her wiles, all her wit and genius had come to this bankruptcy. The woman closed the curtains, and with some entreaty and show of kindness, persuaded her mistress to lie down on the bed. Then she went below and gathered up the trinkets which had been lying on the floor since Rebecca dropped them there at her husband's orders, and Lord Steyne went away.

CHAPTER XXVI.

SUNDAY AFTER THE BATTLE.

THE mansion of Sir Pitt Crawley in Great Gaunt Street, was just beginning to dress itself for the day, as Rawdon, in his evening costume, which he had now worn two days, passed by the scared female who was scouring the steps, and entered into his brother's study. Lady Jane in her morning-gown, was up and above stairs in the nursery, superintending the toilettes of her children, and listening to the morning prayers which the little creatures performed at her knee. Every morning she and they performed this duty privately, and before the public ceremonial at which Sir Pitt presided, and at which all the people of the household were expected to assemble. Rawdon sat down in the study before the Baronet's table, set out with the orderly blue books and the letters, the neatly docketed bills and symmetrical pamphlets; the locked account-books, desks, and despatch boxes, the Bible, the "Quarterly Review," and the "Court Guide," which all stood as if on parade awaiting the inspection of their chief.

A book of family sermons, one of which Sir Pitt was in the habit of administering to his family on Sunday mornings, lay ready on the study table, and awaiting his judicious selection. And by the sermon-book was the "Observer" newspaper, damp and neatly folded, and for Sir Pitt's own private use. His gentleman alone took the opportunity of perusing

the newspaper before he laid it by his master's desk.
Before he had brought it into the study that morning,
he had read in the journal a flaming account of "Festivities at Gaunt House," with the names of all the
distinguished personages invited by the Marquis of
Steyne to meet his Royal Highness. Having made
comments upon this entertainment to the housekeeper
and her niece as they were taking early tea and hot
buttered toast in the former lady's apartment, and
wondered how the Rawding Crawleys could git on,
the valet had damped and folded the paper once more,
so that it looked quite fresh and innocent against the
arrival of the master of the house.

Poor Rawdon took up the paper and began to try
and read it until his brother should arrive. But the
print fell blank upon his eyes; and he did not know
in the least what he was reading. The Government
news and appointments (which Sir Pitt as a public
man was bound to peruse, otherwise he would by no
means permit the introduction of Sunday papers into
his household), the theatrical criticisms, the fight for
a hundred pounds a-side between the Barking Butcher
and the Tutbury Pet, the Gaunt House chronicle itself, which contained a most complimentary though
guarded account of the famous charades of which
Mrs. Becky had been the heroine — all these passed
as in a haze before Rawdon, as he sat waiting the
arrival of the chief of the family.

Punctually, as the shrill-toned bell of the black
marble study clock began to chime nine, Sir Pitt
made his appearance, fresh, neat, smugly shaved,
with a waxy clean face, and stiff shirt collar, his
scanty hair combed and oiled, trimming his nails as
he descended the stairs majestically, in a starched
cravat and a gray flannel dressing-gown, — a real old

SIR PITT'S STUDY CHAIR.

English gentleman, in a word, — a model of neatness and every propriety. He started when he saw poor Rawdon in his study in tumbled clothes, with blood-shot eyes, and his hair over his face. He thought his brother was not sober, and had been out all night on some orgy. "Good gracious, Rawdon," he said, with a blank face, "what brings you here at this time of the morning? Why ain't you at home?"

"Home," said Rawdon, with a wild laugh. "Don't be frightened, Pitt. I'm not drunk. Shut the door; I want to speak to you."

Pitt closed the door and came up to the table, where he sat down in the other arm-chair, — that one placed for the reception of the steward, agent, or confidential visitor who came to transact business with the Baronet, — and trimmed his nails more vehemently than ever.

"Pitt, it's all over with me," the Colonel said, after a pause. "I'm done."

"I always said it would come to this," the Baronet cried, peevishly, and beating a tune with his clean-trimmed nails. "I warned you a thousand times. I can't help you any more. Every shilling of my money is tied up. Even the hundred pounds that Jane took you last night were promised to my lawyer to-morrow morning; and the want of it will put me to great inconvenience. I don't mean to say that I won't assist you ultimately. But as for paying your creditors in full, I might as well hope to pay the National Debt. It is madness, sheer madness, to think of such a thing. You must come to a com-promise. It's a painful thing for the family; but everybody does it. There was George Kitely, Lord Ragland's son, went through the Court last week, and was what they call white-washed, I believe.

Lord Ragland would not pay a shilling for him, and —"

"It's not money I want," Rawdon broke in. "I'm not come to you about myself. Never mind what happens to me —"

"What is the matter, then?" said Pitt, somewhat relieved.

"It's the boy," said Rawdon, in a husky voice. "I want you to promise me that you will take charge of him when I'm gone. That dear good wife of yours has always been good to him; and he's fonder of her than he is of his — Damn it. Look here, Pitt — you know that I was to have had Miss Crawley's money. I wasn't brought up like a younger brother: but was always encouraged to be extravagant, and kep idle. But for this I might have been quite a different man. I didn't do my duty with the regiment so bad. You know how I was thrown over about the money, and who got it."

"After the sacrifices I have made, and the manner in which I have stood by you, I think this sort of reproach is useless," Sir Pitt said. "Your marriage was your own doing, not mine."

"That's over now," said Rawdon. "That's over now." And the words were wrenched from him with a groan, which made his brother start.

"Good God! is she dead?" Sir Pitt said, with a voice of genuine alarm and commiseration.

"I wish *I* was," Rawdon replied. "If it wasn't for little Rawdon I'd have cut my throat this morning — and that damned villain's too."

Sir Pitt instantly guessed the truth, and surmised that Lord Steyne was the person whose life Rawdon wished to take. The Colonel told his senior briefly, and in broken accents, the circumstances of the case. "It was a regular plan between that scoundrel and her," he said. "The bailiffs were put upon me: I was taken as I was going out of his house: when I wrote to her for money, she said she was ill in bed, and put me off to another day. And when I got home I found her in diamonds and sitting with that villain alone." He then went on to describe hurriedly the personal conflict with Lord Steyne. To an affair of that nature, of course, he said, there was but one issue; and after his conference with his brother, he was going away to make the necessary arrangements for the meeting which must ensue. "And as it may end fatally with me," Rawdon said with a broken voice, "and as the boy has no mother, I must leave him to you and Jane, Pitt — only it will be a comfort to me if you will promise me to be his friend.

The elder brother was much affected, and shook Rawdon's hand with a cordiality seldom exhibited by him. Rawdon passed his hand over his shaggy eyebrows. "Thank you, brother," said he. "I know I can trust your word."

"I will, upon my honor," the Baronet said. And thus, and almost mutely, this bargain was struck between them.

Then Rawdon took out of his pocket the little pocket-book which he had discovered in Becky's desk: and from which he drew a bundle of the notes which it contained. "Here's six hundred," he said — "you didn't know I was so rich. I want you to give the money to Briggs, who lent it to us — and who was kind to the boy — and I've always felt ashamed of having taken the poor old woman's money. And here's some more — I've only kept back a few pounds — which Becky may as well have, to get on with." As he spoke he took hold of the other notes to give to his brother; but his hands shook, and he was so agitated that the pocket-book fell from him, and out of it the thousand-pound note which had been the last of the unlucky Becky's winnings.

Pitt stooped and picked them up, amazed at so much wealth. "Not that," Rawdon said — "I hope to put a bullet into the man whom that belongs to." He had thought to himself, it would be a fine revenge to wrap a ball in the note, and kill Steyne with it.

After this colloquy the brothers once more shook hands and parted. Lady Jane had heard of the Colonel's arrival and was waiting for her husband in the adjoining dining-room, with female instinct, auguring evil. The door of the dining-room happened to be left open, and the lady of course was issuing from it as the two brothers passed out of the study. She held out her hand to Rawdon, and said she was glad he was come to breakfast; though she could perceive, by his haggard unshorn face, and the dark looks of her husband, that there was very little question of breakfast between them. Rawdon muttered some excuses about an engagement, squeezing hard the timid little hand which his sister-in-law reached out to him. Her imploring eyes could read nothing but calamity in his face; but he went away without another word. Nor did Sir Pitt vouchsafe her any explanation. The children came up to salute him, and he kissed them in his usual frigid manner. The mother took both of them close to herself, and held a hand of each of them as they knelt down to prayers, which Sir Pitt read to them, and to the servants in their Sunday suits or liveries, ranged upon chairs on the other side of the hissing tea-urn. Breakfast was so late that day, in consequence of the delays which had occurred, that the church-bells began to ring whilst they were sitting over their meal : and Lady Jane was too ill, she said, to go to church, though her thoughts had been entirely astray during the period of family devotion.

Rawdon Crawley meanwhile hurried on from Great Gaunt Street, and knocking at the great bronze Medusa's head which stands on the portal of Gaunt House, brought out the purple Silenus in a red and silver waistcoat, who acts as porter of that palace. The man was scared also by the Colonel's dishevelled appearance, and barred the way as if afraid that the other was going to force it. But Colonel Crawley only took out a card and enjoined him particularly to send it in to Lord Steyne, and to mark the address written on it, and say that Colonel Crawley would be all day after one o'clock at the Regent Club in St. James's Street — not at home. The fat red-faced man looked after him with astonishment as he strode away; so did the people in their Sunday clothes who were out so early; the charity boys with shining faces, the green-grocer lolling at his door, and the publican shutting his shutters in the sunshine, against service commenced. The people joked at the cab-stand about his appearance, as he took a carriage there, and told the driver to drive him to Knightsbridge Barracks.

All the bells were jangling and tolling as he reached that place. He might have seen his old acquaintance Amelia on her way from Brompton to Russell Square had he been looking out. Troops of schools were on their march to church, the shiny pavement and outsides of coaches in the suburbs were thronged with people out upon their Sunday pleasure; but the Colonel was much too busy to take any heed of these phenomena, and, arriving at Knightsbridge, speedily made his way up to the room of his old friend and comrade Captain Macmurdo who Crawley found, to his satisfaction, was in barracks.

Captain Macmurdo, a veteran officer and Waterloo man, greatly liked by his regiment, in which want of money alone prevented him from attaining the highest ranks, was enjoying the forenoon calmly in bed. He had been at a fast supper-party, given the night before by Captain the Honorable George Cinqbars, at his house in Brompton Square, to several young men of the regiment, and a number of ladies of the *corps de ballet*, and old Mac, who was at home with people of all ages and ranks, and consorted with generals, dog-fanciers, opera-dancers, bruisers, and every kind of person, in a word, was resting himself after the night's labors, and, not being on duty, was in bed.

His room was hung round with boxing, sporting, and dancing pictures, presented to him by comrades as they retired from the regiment, and married and settled into quiet life. And as he was now nearly fifty years of age, twenty-four of which he had passed in the corps, he had a singular museum. He was one of the best shots in England, and, for a heavy man, one of the best riders; indeed, he and Crawley had been rivals when the latter was in the army. To be brief, Mr. Macmurdo was lying in bed, reading in "Bell's Life" an account of that very fight between the Tutbury Pet and the Barking Butcher, which has been before mentioned — a venerable bristly warrior, with a little close-shaved gray head, with a silk night-cap, a red face and nose, and a great dyed mustache.

When Rawdon told the Captain he wanted a friend,

the latter knew perfectly well on what duty of friendship he was called to act, and indeed had conducted scores of affairs for his acquaintances with the greatest prudence and skill. His Royal Highness the late lamented Commander-in-Chief had had the greatest regard for Macmurdo on this account; and he was the common refuge of gentlemen in trouble.

"What's the row about, Crawley, my boy?" said the old warrior. "No more gambling business, hay, like that when we shot Captain Marker?"

"It's about — about my wife," Crawley answered, casting down his eyes and turning very red.

The other gave a whistle. "I always said she'd throw you over," he began: — indeed there were bets in the regiment and at the clubs regarding the probable fate of Colonel Crawley, so lightly was his wife's character esteemed by his comrades and the world; but seeing the savage look with which Rawdon answered the expression of this opinion, Macmurdo did not think fit to enlarge upon it further.

"Is there no way out of it, old boy?" the Captain continued in a grave tone. "Is it only suspicion, you know, or — or what is it? Any letters? Can't you keep it quiet? Best not make any noise about a thing of that sort if you can help it." "Think of his only finding her out now," the Captain thought to himself, and remembered a hundred particular conversations at the mess-table, in which Mrs. Crawley's reputation had been torn to shreds.

"There's no way but one out of it," Rawdon replied — "and there's only a way out of it for one of us, Mac — do you understand? I was put out of the way: arrested: I found 'em alone together. I told him he was a liar and a coward, and knocked him down and thrashed him."

"Serve him right," Macmurdo said. "Who is it?"

Rawdon answered it was Lord Steyne.

"The deuce! a Marquis! they said he — that is, they said you —"

"What the devil do you mean?" roared out Rawdon; "do you mean that you ever heard a fellow doubt about my wife, and did n't tell me, Mac?"

"The world's very censorious, old boy," the other replied. "What the deuce was the good of my telling you what any tomfools talked about?"

"It was damned unfriendly, Mac," said Rawdon, quite overcome; and, covering his face with his hands, he gave way to an emotion, the sight of which caused the tough old campaigner opposite him to wince with sympathy. "Hold up, old boy," he said; "great man or not, we 'll put a bullet in him, damn him. As for women, they 're all so."

"You don't know how fond I was of that one," Rawdon said, half inarticulately. "Damme, I followed her like a footman. I gave up everything I had to her. I 'm a beggar because I would marry her. By Jove, sir, I 've pawned my own watch in order to get her anything she fancied: and she — she 's been making a purse for herself all the time, and grudged me a hundred pound to get me out of quod." He then fiercely and incoherently, and with an agitation under which his counsellor had never before seen him labor, told Macmurdo the circumstances of the story. His adviser caught at some stray hints in it.

"She may be innocent, after all," he said. "She says so. Steyne has been a hundred times alone with her in the house before."

"It may be so," Rawdon answered sadly; "but this don't look very innocent:" and he showed the Captain the thousand-pound note which he had found in Becky's pocket-book. "This is what he gave her, Mac: and she kep it unknown to me: and with this money in the house, she refused to stand by me when I was locked up." The Captain could not but own that the secreting of the money had a very ugly look.

Whilst they were engaged in their conference, Rawdon despatched Captain Macmurdo's servant to Curzon Street, with an order to the domestic there to give up a bag of clothes of which the Colonel had great need. And during the man's absence, and with great labor and a Johnson's Dictionary, which stood them in much stead, Rawdon and his second composed a letter, which the latter was to send to Lord Steyne. Captain Macmurdo had the honor of waiting upon the Marquis of Steyne, on the part of Colonel Rawdon Crawley, and begged to intimate that he was empowered by the Colonel to make any arrangements for the meeting which, he had no doubt, it was his lordship's intention to demand, and which the circumstances of the morning had rendered inevitable. Captain Macmurdo begged Lord Steyne, in the most polite manner, to appoint a friend, with whom he (Captain M'M.) might communicate, and desired that the meeting might take place with as little delay as possible.

In a postscript the Captain stated that he had in his possession a bank-note for a large amount, which Colonel Crawley had reason to suppose was the property of the Marquis of Steyne. And he was anxious, on the Colonel's behalf, to give up the note to its owner.

By the time this note was composed, the Captain's servant returned from his mission to Colonel Crawley's house in Curzon Street, but without the carpet-bag and portmanteau, for which he had been sent: and with a very puzzled and odd face.

"They won't give 'em up," said the man; there's a regular shinty in the house; and everything at sixes and sevens. The landlord's come in and took possession. The servants was a-drinkin' up in the drawing-room. They said — they said you had gone off with the plate, Colonel," the man added after a pause: — "One of the servants is off already. And Simpson, the man as was very noisy and drunk indeed, says nothing shall go out of house until his wages is paid up."

The account of this little revolution in May Fair astonished and gave a little gayety to an otherwise very *triste* conversation. The two officers laughed at Rawdon's discomfiture.

"I'm glad the little 'un is n't at home," Rawdon said, biting his nails. "You remember him, Mac, don't you, in the Riding School? How he sat the kicker to be sure! did n't he?"

"That he did, old boy," said the good-natured Captain.

Little Rawdon was then sitting, one of fifty gown boys, in the Chapel of Whitefriars School: thinking, not about the sermon, but about going home next Saturday, when his father would certainly tip him, and perhaps would take him to the play.

"He's a regular trump, that boy," the father went on, still musing about his son. "I say, Mac, if anything goes wrong — if I drop — I should like you to — to go and see him, you know: and say that I was very fond of him, and that. And — dash it — old chap, give him these gold sleeve-buttons: it's all I've got." He covered his face with his black hands: over which the tears rolled and made furrows of white. Mr. Macmurdo had also occasion to take off his silk night-cap and rub it across his eyes.

"Go down and order some breakfast," he said to his man in a loud cheerful voice, — "What 'll you have, Crawley? Some devilled kidneys and a herring — let 's say — And, Clay, lay out some dressing things for the Colonel; we were always pretty much of a size, Rawdon, my boy, and neither of us ride so light as we did when we first entered the corps." With which, and leaving the Colonel to dress himself, Macmurdo turned round towards the wall, and resumed the perusal of "Bell's Life," until such time as his friend's toilette was complete, and he was at liberty to commence his own.

This, as he was about to meet a lord, Captain Macmurdo performed with particular care. He waxed his mustachios into a state of brilliant polish, and put on a tight cravat and a trim buff waistcoat: so that all the young officers in the mess-room, whither Crawley had preceded his friend, complimented Mac on his appearance at breakfast, and asked if he was going to be married that Sunday.

VOLUME III.

CONTENTS.

VOL. III.

LOVEL THE WIDOWER.

CONTENTS

Vol. II

YOUTH THE IMPROVER

VANITY FAIR.

A NOVEL WITHOUT A HERO.

———◆———

CHAPTER I.

IN WHICH THE SAME SUBJECT IS PURSUED.

BECKY did not rally from the state of stupor and confusion in which the events of the previous night had plunged her intrepid spirit, until the bells of the Curzon Street Chapels were ringing for afternoon service, and rising from her bed she began to ply her own bell, in order to summon the French maid who had left her some hours before.

Mrs. Rawdon Crawley rang many times in vain; and though, on the last occasion, she rang with such vehemence as to pull down the bell-rope, Mademoiselle Fifine did not make her appearance, — no, not though her mistress, in a great pet, and with the bell-rope in her hand, came out to the landing-place with her hair over her shoulders, and screamed out repeatedly for her attendant.

The truth is, she had quitted the premises for many hours, and upon that permission which is called French leave among us. After picking up the trinkets in the drawing-room, Mademoiselle had ascended to her own apartments, packed and corded her own boxes there, tripped out and called a cab for herself, brought down her trunks with her own hand, and without ever so much as asking the aid of any of the other servants, who would probably have refused it, as they hated her cordially, and without wishing any one of them good-by, had made her exit from Curzon Street.

The game, in her opinion, was over in that little domestic establishment. Fifine went off in a cab, as we have known more exalted persons of her nation to do under similar circumstances : but, more provident or lucky than these, she secured not only her own property, but some of her mistress's (if indeed that lady could be said to have any property at all) — and not only carried off the trinkets before alluded to, and some favorite dresses on which she had long kept her eye, but four richly gilt Louis Quatorze candlesticks, six gilt Albums, Keepsakes, and Books of Beauty, a gold enamelled snuff-box which had once belonged to Madame du Barri, and the sweetest little ink-stand and mother-of-pearl blotting-book, which Becky used when she composed her charming little pink notes, had vanished from the premises in Curzon Street together with Mademoiselle Fifine, and all the silver laid on the table for the little *festin* which Rawdon interrupted. The plated ware Mademoiselle left behind her was too cumbrous probably, for which reason, no doubt, she also left the fire irons, the chimney-glasses, and the rosewood cottage piano.

A lady very like her subsequently kept a milliner's shop in the Rue du Helder at Paris, where she lived with great credit and enjoyed the patronage of my Lord Steyne. This person always spoke of England as of the most treacherous country in the world, and stated to her young pupils that she had been *affreusement volé* by natives of that island. It was no doubt compassion for her misfortunes which induced the Marquis of Steyne to be so very kind to Madame de Saint Amaranthe. May she flourish as she deserves, — she appears no more in our quarter of Vanity Fair.

Hearing a buzz and a stir below, and indignant at the impudence of those servants who would not answer her summons, Mrs. Crawley flung her morning robe round her, and descended majestically to the drawing-room, whence the noise proceeded.

The cook was there with blackened face, seated on the beautiful chintz sofa by the side of Mrs. Raggles, to whom she was administering Maraschino. The page with the sugar-loaf buttons, who carried about Becky's pink notes, and jumped about her little carriage with such alacrity, was now engaged putting his fingers into a cream dish; the footman was talking to Raggles, who had a face full of perplexity and woe — and yet, though the door was open, and Becky had been screaming a half-dozen of times a few feet off, not one of her attendants had obeyed her call. "Have a little drop, do 'ee now, Mrs. Raggles," the cook was saying as Becky entered, the white cashmere dressing-gown flouncing around her.

"Simpson! Trotter!" the mistress of the house cried in great wrath. "How dare you stay here when you heard me call? How dare you sit down in my presence? Where's my maid?" The page withdrew his fingers from his mouth with a momentary terror: but the cook took off a glass of Maraschino, of which Mrs. Raggles had had enough, staring at Becky over the little gilt glass as she drained its contents. The liquor appeared to give the odious rebel courage.

"*Your* sofy, indeed!" Mrs. Cook said. "I'm a settin' on Mrs. Raggles's sofy. Don't you stir, Mrs. Raggles, Mum. I'm a settin' on Mr. and Mrs.

Raggles's sofy, which they bought with honest money, and very dear it cost 'em, too. And I 'm thinkin' if I set here until I 'm paid my wages, I shall set a precious long time, Mrs. Raggles ; and set I will, too — ha ! ha ! " and with this she filled herself another glass of the liquor, and drank it with a more hideously satirical air.

"Trotter ! Simpson ! turn that drunken wretch out," screamed Mrs. Crawley.

"I shawn't," said Trotter the footman; "turn out yourself. Pay our selleries, and turn me out too. *We 'll* go fast enough."

" Are you all here to insult me ? " cried Becky in a fury ; " when Colonel Crawley comes home I 'll — "

At this the servants burst into a horse haw-haw, in which, however, Raggles, who still kept a most melancholy countenance, did not join. " He ain't a coming back," Mr. Trotter resumed. " He sent for his things, and I would n't let 'em go, although Mr. Raggles would : and I don't b'lieve he 's no more a Colonel than I am. He 's hoff : and I suppose you 're a goin' after him. You 're no better than swindlers, both on you. Don't be a bullyin' *me*. I won't stand it. Pay us our selleries, I say. Pay us our selleries." It was evident, from Mr. Trotter's flushed countenance and defective intonation, that he, too, had had recourse to vinous stimulus.

" Mr. Raggles," said Becky, in a passion of vexation, " you will not surely let me be insulted by that drunken man ? " " Hold your noise, Trotter ; do now," said Simpson the page. He was affected by his mistress's deplorable situation, and succeeded in preventing an outrageous denial of the epithet " drunken " on the footman's part.

" O Mam," said Raggles, " I never thought to live to see this year day. I 've known the **Crawley family**

ever since I was born. I lived butler with Miss
Crawley for thirty years; and I little thought one of
that family was a goin' to ruing me — yes, ruing me "
— said the poor fellow with tears in his eyes. "Har
you a goin' to pay me? You've lived in this 'ouse
four year. You've 'ad my substance: my plate and
linning. You ho me a milk and butter bill of two
'undred pound, you must 'ave noo laid heggs for your
homlets, and cream for your spanil dog."

"She did n't care what her own flesh and blood
had," interposed the cook. "Many's the time, he'd
have starved but for me."

"He's a charaty boy now, Cooky," said Mr. Trotter,
with a drunken "ha! ha!" — and honest Raggles
continued, in a lamentable tone, an enumeration of
his griefs. All he said was true. Becky and her
husband had ruined him. He had bills coming due
next week and no means to meet them. He would
be sold up and turned out of his shop and his house,
because he had trusted to the Crawley family. His
tears and lamentations made Becky more peevish
than ever.

"You all seem to be against me," she said, bitterly.
"What do you want? I can't pay you on Sunday.
Come back to-morrow and I'll pay you everything.
I thought Colonel Crawley had settled with you. He
will to-morrow. I declare to you upon my honor that
he left home this morning with fifteen hundred
pounds in his pocket-book. He has left me nothing.
Apply to him. Give me a bonnet and shawl and let
me go out and find him. There was a difference
between us this morning. You all seem to know it.
I promise you upon my word that you shall all be
paid. He has got a good appointment. Let me go
out and find him."

This audacious statement caused Raggles and the other personages present to look at one another with a wild surprise, and with it Rebecca left them. She went up stairs and dressed herself this time without the aid of her French maid. She went into Rawdon's room, and there saw that a trunk and bag were packed ready for removal, with a pencil direction that they should be given when called for; then she went into the Frenchwoman's garret; everything was clean, and all the drawers emptied there. She bethought herself of the trinkets which had been left on the ground, and felt certain that the woman had fled. "Good Heavens! was ever such ill luck as mine?" she said; "to be so near, and to lose all. Is it all too late? No; there was one chance more."

She dressed herself, and went away unmolested this time, but alone. It was four o'clock. She went swiftly down the streets (she had no money to pay for a carriage), and never stopped until she came to Sir Pitt Crawley's door, in Great Gaunt Street. Where was Lady Jane Crawley? She was at church. Becky was not sorry. Sir Pitt was in his study, and had given orders not to be disturbed — she must see him — she slipped by the sentinel in livery at once, and was in Sir Pitt's room before the astonished Baronet had even laid down the paper.

He turned red and started back from her with a look of great alarm and horror.

"Do not look so," she said. "I am not guilty, Pitt, dear Pitt; you were my friend once. Before God, I am not guilty. I seem so. Everything is against me. And oh, at such a moment! just when all my hopes were about to be realized: just when happiness was in store for us."

"Is this true, what I see in the paper then?" Sir Pitt said — a paragraph in which had greatly surprised him.

"It is true. Lord Steyne told me on Friday night, the night of that fatal ball. He has been promised an appointment any time these six months. Mr. Martyr, the Colonial Secretary, told him yesterday that it was made out. That unlucky arrest ensued; that horrible meeting. I was only guilty of too much devotedness to Rawdon's service. I have received Lord Steyne alone a hundred times before. I confess I had money of which Rawdon knew nothing. Don't you know how careless he is of it, and could I dare to confide it to him?" And so she went on with a perfectly connected story, which she poured into the ears of her perplexed kinsman.

It was to the following effect. Becky owned, and with perfect frankness, but deep contrition, that having remarked Lord Steyne's partiality for her (at the mention of which Pitt blushed), and being secure of her own virtue, she had determined to turn the great peer's attachment to the advantage of herself and her family. "I looked for a peerage for you, Pitt," she said (the brother-in-law again turned red). "We have talked about it. Your genius and Lord Steyne's interest made it more than probable, had not this dreadful calamity come to put an end to all our hopes. But, first, I own that it was my object to rescue my dear husband, — him whom I love in spite of all his ill usage and suspicions of me, — to remove him from the poverty and ruin which was impending over us. I saw Lord Steyne's partiality for me," she said, casting down her eyes. "I own that I did everything in my power to make myself pleasing to him, and as far as an honest woman may, to secure his — his esteem.

It was only on Friday morning that the news arrived
of the death of the Governor of Coventry Island, and
my lord instantly secured the appointment for my
dear husband. It was intended as a surprise for him,
— he was to see it in the papers to-day. Even after
that horrid arrest took place (the expenses of which
Lord Steyne generously said he would settle, so that I
was in a manner prevented from coming to my husband's assistance), my lord was laughing with me,
and saying that my dearest Rawdon would be consoled when he read of his appointment in the paper,
in that shocking spun — bailiff's house. And then
— then he came home. His suspicions were excited
— the dreadful scene took place between my lord
and my cruel, cruel Rawdon — and, O my God, what
will happen next? Pitt, dear Pitt! pity me, and
reconcile us!" And as she spoke she flung herself
down on her knees, and bursting into tears, seized
hold of Pitt's hand, which she kissed passionately.

It was in this very attitude that Lady Jane, who,
returning from church, ran to her husband's room
directly she heard Mrs. Rawdon Crawley was closeted
there, found the Baronet and his sister-in-law.

"I am surprised that woman has the audacity to
enter this house," Lady Jane said, trembling in every
limb, and turning quite pale. (Her ladyship had
sent out her maid directly after breakfast, who had
communicated with Raggles and Rawdon Crawley's
household, who had told her all, and a great deal
more than they knew, of that story, and many others
besides.) "How dare Mrs. Crawley to enter the house
of — of an honest family?"

Sir Pitt started back, amazed at his wife's display
of vigor. Becky still kept her kneeling posture, and
clung to Sir Pitt's hand.

"Tell her that she does not know all. Tell her that I am innocent, dear Pitt," she whimpered out.

"Upon my word, my love, I think you do Mrs. Crawley injustice," Sir Pitt said; at which speech Rebecca was vastly relieved. "Indeed I believe her to be — "

"To be what?" cried out Lady Jane, her clear voice thrilling, and her heart beating violently as she spoke. "To be a wicked woman — a heartless mother, a false wife? She never loved her dear little boy, who used to fly here and tell me of her cruelty to him. She never came into a family but she strove to bring misery with her, and to weaken the most sacred affections with her wicked flattery and falsehoods. She has deceived her husband, as she has deceived everybody; her soul is black with vanity, worldliness, and all sorts of crime. I tremble when I touch her. I keep my children out of her sight. I — "

"Lady Jane!" cried Sir Pitt, starting up, "this is really language — "

"I have been a true and faithful wife to you, Sir Pitt," Lady Jane continued, intrepidly; "I have kept my marriage vow as I made it to God, and have been obedient and gentle as a wife should. But righteous obedience has its limits, and I declare that I will not bear that — that woman again under my roof: if she enters it, I and my children will leave it. She is not worthy to sit down with Christian people. You — you must choose, sir, between her and me;" and with this my lady swept out of the room, fluttering with her own audacity, and leaving Rebecca and Sir Pitt not a little astonished at it.

As for Becky, she was not hurt; nay, she was pleased. "It was the diamond-clasp you gave me," she said to Sir Pitt, reaching him out her hand; and

before she left him (for which event you may be sure
my Lady Jane was looking out from her dressing-
room window in the upper story) the Baronet had
promised to go and seek out his brother, and endeavor
to bring about a reconciliation.

Rawdon found some of the young fellows of the
regiment seated in the mess-room at breakfast, and
was induced without much difficulty to partake of
that meal, and of the devilled legs of fowls and soda-
water with which these young gentlemen fortified
themselves. Then they had a conversation befitting
the day and their time of life: about the next pigeon-
match at Battersea, with relative bets upon Ross and
Osbaldiston: about Mademoiselle Ariane of the French
Opera, and who had left her, and how she was consoled by Panther Carr; and about the fight between
the Butcher and the Pet, and the probabilities that it
was a cross. Young Tandyman, a hero of seventeen,
laboriously endeavoring to get up a pair of mustachios,
had seen the fight, and spoke in the most scientific
manner about the battle, and the condition of the
men. It was he who had driven the Butcher on to the
ground in his drag, and passed the whole of the previous night with him. Had there not been foul play
he must have won it. All the old files of the Ring
were in it: and Tandyman would n't pay; no, dammy,
he would n't pay. — It was but a year since the
young Cornet, now so knowing a hand in Cribb's
parlor, had a still lingering liking for toffy, and used
to be birched at Eton.

So they went on talking about dancers, fights, drinking, demireps, until Macmurdo came down and joined
the boys and the conversation. He did not appear to
think that any especial reverence was due to their

boyhood; the old fellow cut in with stories, to the full as choice as any the youngest rake present had to tell; — nor did his own gray hairs, nor their smooth faces detain him. Old Mac was famous for his good stories. He was not exactly a lady's man; that is, men asked him to dine rather at the houses of their mistresses than of their mothers. There can scarcely be a life lower, perhaps, than his; but he was quite contented with it, such as it was, and led it in perfect good-nature, simplicity, and modesty of demeanor.

By the time Mac had finished a copious breakfast, most of the others had concluded their meal. Young Lord Varinas was smoking an immense Meerschaum pipe, while Captain Hugues was employed with a cigar: that violent little devil Tandyman, with his little bull-terrier between his legs, was tossing for shillings with all his might (that fellow was always at some game or other) against Captain Deuceace; and Mac and Rawdon walked off to the Club, neither, of course, having given any hint of the business which was occupying their minds.

Both, on the other hand, had joined pretty gayly in the conversation; for why should they interrupt it? Feasting, drinking, ribaldry, laughter, go on alongside of all sorts of other occupations in Vanity Fair, — the crowds were pouring out of church as Rawdon and his friend passed down St. James's Street and entered into their Club.

The old bucks and *habitués*, who ordinarily stand gaping and grinning out of the great front window of the Club, had not arrived at their posts as yet, — the newspaper-room was almost empty. One man was present whom Rawdon did not know; another to whom he owed a little score for whist, and whom, in consequence, he did not care to meet; a third was reading the "Royalist" (a periodical famous for its scandal and its attachment to Church and King) Sunday paper at the table, and, looking up at Crawley with some interest, said, "Crawley, I congratulate you."

"What do you mean?" said the Colonel.

"It's in the 'Observer' and the 'Royalist' too," said Mr. Smith.

"What?" Rawdon cried, turning very red. He thought that the affair with Lord Steyne was already in the public prints. Smith looked up wondering and smiling at the agitation which the Colonel exhibited as he took up the paper, and, trembling, began to read.

Mr. Smith and Mr. Brown (the gentleman with whom Rawdon had the outstanding whist account) had been talking about the Colonel just before he came in.

"It is come just in the nick of time," said Smith. "I suppose Crawley had not a shilling in the world."

"It's a wind that blows everybody good," Mr. Brown said. "He can't go away without paying me a pony he owes me."

"What's the salary?" asked Smith.

"Two or three thousand," answered the other. "But the climate's so infernal, they don't enjoy it long. Liverseege died after eighteen months of it: and the man before went off in six weeks, I hear."

"Some people say his brother is a very clever man. I always found him a d——bore," Smith ejaculated. "He must have good interest, though. He must have got the Colonel the place."

"*He!*" said Brown, with a sneer — "Pooh. — It was Lord Steyne got it."

"How do you mean?"

"A virtuous woman is a crown to her husband," answered the other, enigmatically, and went to read his papers.

Rawdon, for his part, read in the "Royalist" the following astonishing paragraph : —

"GOVERNORSHIP OF COVENTRY ISLAND. — H.M.S. Yellow-jack, Commander Jaunders, has brought letters and papers from Coventry Island. H. E. Sir Thomas Liverseege had fallen a victim to the prevailing fever at Swamp Town. His loss is deeply felt in the flourishing colony. We hear that the Governorship has been offered to Colonel Rawdon Crawley, C.B., a distinguished Waterloo officer. We need not only men of acknowledged bravery, but men of administrative talents to superintend the affairs of our colonies ; and we have no doubt that the gentleman selected by the Colonial Office to fill the lamented vacancy which has occurred at Coventry Island is admirably calculated for the post which he is about to occupy."

"Coventry Island! where was it? who had appointed him to the government? You must take me out as your secretary, old boy," Captain Macmurdo said laughing; and as Crawley and his friend sat wondering and perplexed over the announcement, the Club waiter brought in to the Colonel a card, on which the name of Mr. Wenham was engraved, who begged to see Colonel Crawley.

The Colonel and his *aide-de-camp* went out to meet the gentleman, rightly conjecturing that he was an emissary of Lord Steyne. "How d' ye do, Crawley? I am glad to see you," said Mr. Wenham, with a bland smile, and grasping Crawley's hand with great cordiality.

"You come, I suppose, from — "

"Exactly," said Mr. Wenham.

"Then this is my friend Captain Macmurdo, of the Life Guards Green."

"Delighted to know Captain Macmurdo, I'm sure,"
Mr. Wenham said, and tendered another smile and
shake of the hand to the second, as he had done to
the principal. Mac put out one finger, armed with a
buckskin glove, and made a very frigid bow to Mr.
Wenham over his tight cravat. He was, perhaps,
discontented at being put in communication with a
pékin, and thought that Lord Steyne should have
sent him a Colonel at the very least.

"As Macmurdo acts for me, and knows what I
mean," Crawley said, "I had better retire and leave
you together."

"Of course," said Macmurdo.

"By no means, my dear Colonel," Mr. Wenham
said; "the interview which I had the honor of requesting was with you personally, though the company of Captain Macmurdo cannot fail to be also
most pleasing. In fact, Captain, I hope that our
conversation will lead to none but the most agreeable results, very different from those which my
friend Colonel Crawley appears to anticipate."

"Humph!" said Captain Macmurdo. — Be hanged
to these civilians, he thought to himself, they are
always for arranging and speechifying. Mr. Wenham took a chair which was not offered to him —
took a paper from his pocket, and resumed —

"You have seen this gratifying announcement in
the papers this morning, Colonel? Government has
secured a most valuable servant, and you, if you accept office, as I presume you will, an excellent appointment. Three thousand a year, delightful climate,
excellent government-house, all your own way in
the Colony, and a certain promotion. I congratulate you with all my heart. I presume you know,
gentlemen, to whom my friend is indebted for this
piece of patronage?"

"Hanged if I know," the Captain said: his principal turned very red.

"To one of the most generous and kindest men in the world, as he is one of the greatest — to my excellent friend, the Marquis of Steyne."

"I'll see him d—— before I take his place," growled out Rawdon.

"You are irritated against my noble friend," Mr. Wenham calmly resumed: "and now, in the name of common sense and justice, tell me why?"

"*Why?*" cried Rawdon in surprise.

"Why? Dammy!" said the Captain, ringing his stick on the ground.

"Dammy, indeed," said Mr. Wenham, with the most agreeable smile; "still, look at the matter as a man of the world — as an honest man, and see if you have not been in the wrong. You come home from a journey, and find — what? — my Lord Steyne supping at your house in Curzon Street with Mrs. Crawley. Is the circumstance strange or novel? Has he not been a hundred times before in the same position? Upon my honor and word as a gentleman," (Mr. Wenham here put his hand on his waistcoat with a parliamentary air,) "I declare I think that your suspicions are monstrous and utterly unfounded, and that they injure an honorable gentleman who has proved his good will towards you by a thousand benefactions — and a most spotless and innocent lady."

"You don't mean to say that — that Crawley's mistaken?" said Mr. Macmurdo.

"I believe that Mrs. Crawley is as innocent as my wife, Mrs. Wenham," Mr. Wenham said, with great energy. "I believe that, misled by an infernal jealousy, my friend here strikes a blow against not only

an infirm and old man of high station, his constant
friend and benefactor, but against his wife, his own
dearest honor, his son's future reputation, and his
own prospects in life.

"I will tell you what happened," Mr. Wenham continued with great solemnity; "I was sent for this
morning by my Lord Steyne, and found him in a
pitiable state, as, I need hardly inform Colonel Crawley, any man of age and infirmity would be after a
personal conflict with a man of your strength. I
say to your face; it was a cruel advantage you took
of that strength, Colonel Crawley. It was not only
the body of my noble and excellent friend which was
wounded — his heart, sir, was bleeding. A man whom
he had loaded with benefits and regarded with affection, had subjected him to the foulest indignity. What
was this very appointment, which appears in the
journals of to-day, but a proof of his kindness to
you? When I saw his lordship this morning I found
him in a state pitiable indeed to see: and as anxious
as you are to revenge the outrage committed upon
him, by blood. You know he has given his proofs,
I presume, Colonel Crawley?"

"He has plenty of pluck," said the Colonel. "Nobody ever said he had n't."

"His first order to me was to write a letter of challenge, and to carry it to Colonel Crawley. One or
other of us," he said, "must not survive the outrage
of last night."

Crawley nodded. "You 're coming to the point,
Wenham," he said.

"I tried my utmost to calm Lord Steyne. Good
God! sir," I said, "how I regret that Mrs. Wenham
and myself had not accepted Mrs. Crawley's invitation to sup with her!"

"She asked you to sup with her?" Captain Macmurdo said.

"After the Opera. Here's the note of invitation — stop — no, this is another paper — I thought I had it, but it's of no consequence, and I pledge you my word to the fact. If we had come — and it was only one of Mrs. Wenham's headaches which prevented us — she suffers under them a good deal, especially in the spring — if we had come, and you had returned home, there would have been no quarrel, no insult, no suspicion — and so it is positively because my poor wife has a headache that you are to bring death down upon two men of honor, and plunge two of the most excellent and ancient families in the kingdom into disgrace and sorrow."

Mr. Macmurdo looked at his principal with the air of a man profoundly puzzled: and Rawdon felt with a kind of rage that his prey was escaping him. He did not believe a word of the story, and yet, how discredit or disprove it?

Mr. Wenham continued with the same fluent oratory, which in his place in parliament he had so often practised — "I sat for an hour or more by Lord Steyne's bedside, beseeching, imploring Lord Steyne to forego his intention of demanding a meeting. I pointed out to him that the circumstances were after all suspicious — they were suspicious. I acknowledge it, — any man in your position might have been taken in — I said that a man furious with jealousy is to all intents and purposes a madman, and should be as such regarded — that a duel between you must lead to the disgrace of all parties concerned — that a man of his lordship's exalted station had no right in these days, when the most atrocious revolutionary principles, and the most dangerous levelling doctrines are preached, among the vulgar, to create a public scandal; and that, however innocent, the common people would insist that he was guilty. In fine, I implored him not to send the challenge."

"I don't believe one word of the whole story," said Rawdon, grinding his teeth. "I believe it a d—— lie, and that you're in it, Mr. Wenham. If the challenge don't come from him, by Jove it shall come from me."

Mr. Wenham turned deadly pale at this savage interruption of the Colonel, and looked towards the door.

But he found a champion in Captain Macmurdo. That gentleman rose up with an oath, and rebuked Rawdon for his language. "You put the affair into my hands, and you shall act as I think fit, by Jove, and not as you do. You have no right to insult Mr. Wenham with this sort of language; and dammy, Mr. Wenham, you deserve an apology. And as for a challenge to Lord Steyne, you may get somebody else to carry it, I won't. If my lord, after being thrashed, chooses to sit still, dammy let him. And as for the affair with — with Mrs. Crawley, my belief is, there's nothing proved at all: that your wife's innocent, as innocent as Mr. Wenham says she is: and at any rate, that you would be a d—— fool not to take the place and hold your tongue."

"Captain Macmurdo, you speak like a man of sense," Mr. Wenham cried out, immensely relieved — "I forget any words that Colonel Crawley has used in the irritation of the moment."

"I thought you would," Rawdon said, with a sneer.

"Shut your mouth, you old stoopid," the Captain said, good-naturedly. "Mr. Wenham ain't a fighting man; and quite right, too."

"This matter, in my belief," the Steyne emissary cried, "ought to be buried in the most profound oblivion. A word concerning it should never pass these doors. I speak in the interest of my friend, as well as of Colonel Crawley, who persists in considering me his enemy."

"I suppose Lord Steyne won't talk about it very much," said Captain Macmurdo; "and I don't see why our side should. The affair ain't a very pretty one, any way you take it; and the less said about it the better. It's you are thrashed, and not us; and if you are satisfied, why, I think, we should be."

Mr. Wenham took his hat, upon this, and Captain Macmurdo following him to the door, shut it upon himself and Lord Steyne's agent, leaving Rawdon chafing within. When the two were on the other side, Macmurdo looked hard at the other ambassador, and with an expression of anything but respect on his round jolly face.

"You don't stick at a trifle, Mr. Wenham," he said.

"You flatter me, Captain Macmurdo," answered the other, with a smile. "Upon my honor and conscience now, Mrs. Crawley did ask us to sup after the Opera."

"Of course; and Mrs. Wenham had one of her headaches. I say, I've got a thousand-pound note here, which I will give you if you will give me a receipt, please; and I will put the note up in an envelope for Lord Steyne. My man sha'n't fight him. But we had rather not take his money."

"It was all a mistake, — all a mistake, my dear sir," the other said, with the utmost innocence of manner; and was bowed down the Club steps by Captain Macmurdo, just as Sir Pitt Crawley ascended them. There was a slight acquaintance between these two gentlemen; and the Captain, going back with the Baronet to the room where the latter's brother was, told Sir Pitt, in confidence, that he had made the affair all right between Lord Steyne and the Colonel.

Sir Pitt was well pleased, of course, at this intelligence; and congratulated his brother warmly upon the peaceful issue of the affair, making appropriate moral remarks upon the evils of duelling, and the unsatisfactory nature of that sort of settlement of disputes.

And after this preface, he tried with all his eloquence to effect a reconciliation between Rawdon and his wife. He recapitulated the statements which Becky had made, pointed out the probabilities of their truth, and asserted his own firm belief in her innocence.

But Rawdon would not hear of it. "She has kept money concealed from me these ten years," he said. "She swore, last night only, she had none from Steyne. She knew it was all up, directly I found it. If she's not guilty, Pitt, she's as bad as guilty; and I'll never see her again, — never." His head sank down on his chest as he spoke the words; and he looked quite broken and sad.

"Poor old boy," Macmurdo said, shaking his head.

Rawdon Crawley resisted for some time the idea of taking the place which had been procured for him by so odious a patron: and was also for removing the boy from the school where Lord Steyne's interest had placed him. He was induced, however, to acquiesce in these benefits by the entreaties of his brother and Macmurdo: but mainly by the latter pointing out to him what a fury Steyne would be in, to think that his enemy's fortune was made through his means.

When the Marquis of Steyne came abroad after his accident, the Colonial Secretary bowed up to him and congratulated himself and the Service upon having made so excellent an appointment. These congratulations were received with a degree of gratitude which may be imagined on the part of Lord Steyne.

The secret of the *rencontre* between him and Colonel Crawley was buried in the profoundest oblivion, as Wenham said; that is by the seconds and the principals. But before that evening was over it was talked of at fifty dinner-tables in Vanity Fair. Little Cackleby himself went to seven evening parties, and told the story with comments and emendations at each place. How Mrs. Washington White revelled in it! The Bishopess of Ealing was shocked beyond expression: the Bishop went and wrote his name down in the visiting-book at Gaunt House that very day. Little Southdown was sorry: so you may be sure was his sister Lady Jane, very sorry. Lady Southdown wrote it off to her other daughter at the Cape of Good Hope. It was town-talk for at least three days, and was only kept out of the newspapers by the exertions of Mr. Wagg, acting upon a hint from Mr. Wenham.

The bailiffs and brokers seized upon poor Raggles in Curzon Street, and the late fair tenant of that poor little mansion was in the meanwhile — where? Who cared? Who asked after a day or two? Was she guilty or not? We all know how charitable the world is, and how the verdict of Vanity Fair goes when there is a doubt. Some people said she had gone to Naples in pursuit of Lord Steyne; whilst others averred that his lordship quitted that city, and fled to Palermo on hearing of Becky's arrival; some said she was living in Bierstadt, and had become a *dame d' honneur* to the Queen of Bulgaria; some that she was at Boulogne; and others, at a boarding-house at Cheltenham.

Rawdon made her a tolerable annuity; and we may be sure that she was a woman who could make a little money go a great way, as the saying is. He would have paid his debts on leaving England, could he have got any Insurance Office to take his life; but the climate of Coventry Island was so bad that he could borrow no money on the strength of his salary. He remitted, however, to his brother punctually, and wrote to his little boy regularly every mail. He kept Macmurdo in cigars; and sent over quantities of shells, cayenne pepper, hot pickles, guava jelly, and colonial produce to Lady Jane. He sent his brother home the "Swamp Town Gazette," in which the new Governor was praised with immense enthusiasm; whereas the "Swamp Town Sentinel," whose wife was not asked to Government House, declared that his Excellency was a tyrant, compared to whom Nero was an enlightened philanthropist. Little Rawdon used to like to get the papers and read about his Excellency.

His mother never made any movement to see the child. He went home to his aunt for Sundays and holidays; he soon knew every bird's nest about Queen's Crawley, and rode out with Sir Huddlestone's hounds, which he admired so on his first well-remembered visit to Hampshire.

CHAPTER II.

GEORGY OSBORNE was now fairly established in his grandfather's mansion in Russell Square : occupant of his father's room in the house, and heir-apparent of all the splendors there. The good looks, gallant bearing, and gentlemanlike appearance of the boy won the grandsire's heart for him. Mr. Osborne was as proud of him as ever he had been of the elder George.

The child had many more luxuries and indulgences than had been awarded to his father. Osborne's commerce had prospered greatly of late years. His wealth and importance in the City had very much increased. He had been glad enough in former days to put the elder George to a good private school ; and a commission in the army for his son had been a source of no small pride to him : for little George and his future prospects the old man looked much higher. He would make a gentleman of the little chap, was Mr. Osborne's constant saying regarding little Georgy. He saw him in his mind's eye, a collegian, a parliament-man, — a Baronet, perhaps. The old man thought he would die contented if he could see his grandson in a fair way to such honors. He would have none but a tip-top college man to educate him, — none of your quacks and pretenders, — no, no. A few years before, he used to be savage, and inveigh against all parsons, scholars, and the like, — declaring that they

were a pack of humbugs, and quacks, that were n't fit
to get their living but by grinding Latin and Greek,
and a set of supercilious dogs, that pretended to look
down upon British merchants and gentlemen, who
could buy up half a hundred of 'em. He would mourn
now, in a very solemn manner, that his own education
had been neglected, and repeatedly point out, in pompous orations to Georgy, the necessity and excellence
of classical acquirements.

When they met at dinner the grandsire used to ask
the lad what he had been reading during the day, and
was greatly interested at the report the boy gave
of his own studies; pretending to understand little
George when he spoke regarding them. He made a
hundred blunders, and showed his ignorance many a
time. It did not increase the respect which the child
had for his senior. A quick brain and a better education elsewhere showed the boy very soon that his
grandsire was a dullard; and he began accordingly to
command him and to look down upon him; for his
previous education, humble and contracted as it had
been, had made a much better gentleman of Georgy
than any plans of his grandfather could make him.
He had been brought up by a kind, weak, and tender
woman, who had no pride about anything, but about
him, and whose heart was so pure and whose bearing
was so meek and humble, that she could not but needs
be a true lady. She busied herself in gentle offices
and quiet duties; if she never said brilliant things,
she never spoke or thought unkind ones: guileless
and artless, loving and pure, indeed how could our
poor little Amelia be other than a real gentlewoman.

Young Georgy lorded over this soft and yielding
nature: and the contrast of its simplicity and delicacy
with the coarse pomposity of the dull old man with

whom he next came in contact, made him lord over the latter too. If he had been a Prince Royal he could not have been better brought up to think well of himself.

Whilst his mother was yearning after him at home, and I do believe every hour of the day, and during most hours of the sad lonely nights, thinking of him, this young gentleman had a number of pleasures and consolations administered to him, which made him for his part bear the separation from Amelia very easily. Little boys who cry when they are going to school — cry because they are going to a very uncomfortable place. It is only a very few who weep from sheer affection. When you think that the eyes of your childhood dried at the sight of a piece of gingerbread, and that a plum-cake was a compensation for the agony of parting with your mamma and sisters; O my friend and brother, you need not be too confident of your own fine feelings.

Well, then, Master George Osborne had every comfort and luxury that a wealthy and lavish old grandfather thought fit to provide. The coachman was instructed to purchase for him the handsomest pony which could be bought for money; and on this George was taught to ride, first at a riding-school, whence, after having performed satisfactorily without stirrups, and over the leaping-bar, he was conducted through the New Road to Regent's Park, and then to Hyde Park, where he rode in state with Martin the coachman behind him. Old Osborne, who took matters more easily in the City now, where he left his affairs to his junior partners, would often ride out with Miss O. in the same fashionable direction. As little Georgy came cantering up with his dandified air, and his heels down, his grandfather would nudge the lad's aunt, and say, "Look, Miss O." And he would laugh, and his face would grow red with pleasure, as he nodded out of the window to the boy, as the groom saluted the carriage, and the footman saluted Master George. Here too his aunt, Mrs. Frederick Bullock, (whose chariot might daily be seen in the Ring, with bullocks *or* emblazoned on the panels and harness, and three pasty-faced little Bullocks, covered with cockades and feathers, staring from the windows,) — Mrs. Frederick Bullock, I say, flung glances of the bitterest hatred at the little upstart as he rode by with his hand on his side and his hat on one ear, as proud as a lord.

Though he was scarcely eleven years of age, Master George wore straps and the most beautiful little boots like a man. He had gilt spurs, and a gold-headed whip, and a fine pin in his handkerchief; and the neatest little kid gloves which Lamb's Conduit Street could furnish. His mother had given him a couple of neck-cloths, and carefully hemmed and made some little shirts for him; but when her Samuel came to see the widow, they were replaced by much finer linen. He had little jewelled buttons in the lawn shirt-fronts. Her humble presents had been put aside — I believe Miss Osborne had given them to the coach-man's boy. Amelia tried to think she was pleased at the change. Indeed, she was happy and charmed to see the boy looking so beautiful.

She had had a little black profile of him done for a shilling; and this was hung up by the side of another portrait over her bed. One day the boy came on his accustomed visit, galloping down the little street at Brompton, and bringing, as usual, all the inhabitants to the windows to admire his splendor, and with great eagerness, and a look of triumph in his face, he pulled a case out of his great-coat — (it was a natty white great-coat, with a cape and a velvet collar) — pulled out a red morocco case, which he gave her.

"I bought it with my own money, Mamma," he said. "I thought you'd like it."

Amelia opened the case, and giving a little cry of delighted affection, seized the boy and embraced him a hundred times. It was a miniature of himself, very prettily done (though not half handsome enough, we may be sure, the widow thought).

His grandfather had wished to have a picture of him by an artist whose works, exhibited in a shop-window, in Southampton Row, had caught the old gentleman's eyes; and George, who had plenty of money, bethought him of asking the painter how much a copy of the little portrait would cost, saying that he would pay for it out of his own money, and that he wanted to give it to his mother. The pleased painter executed it for a small price; and old Osborne himself, when he heard of the incident, growled out his satisfaction, and gave the boy twice as many sovereigns as he paid for the miniature.

But what was the grandfather's pleasure compared to Amelia's ecstasy? That proof of the boy's affection charmed her so, that she thought no child in the world was like hers for goodness. For long weeks after, the thought of his love made her happy. She slept better with the picture under her pillow; and how many many times did she kiss it, and weep and pray over it! A small kindness from those she loved made that timid heart grateful. Since her parting with George she had had no such joy and consolation.

At his new home Master George ruled like a lord; at dinner he invited the ladies to drink wine with the utmost coolness, and took off his champagne in a way which charmed his old grandfather. "Look at him," the old man would say, nudging his neighbor with a delighted purple face, "did you ever see such a chap? Lord, Lord! he'll be ordering a dressing-case next, and razors to shave with; I'm blessed if he won't."

The antics of the lad did not, however, delight Mr. Osborne's friends so much as they pleased the old gentleman. It gave Mr. Justice Coffin no pleasure to hear Georgy cut into the conversation and spoil his stories. Colonel Fogey was not interested in seeing the little boy half tipsy. Mr. Sergeant Toffy's lady felt no particular gratitude when, with a twist of his elbow, he tilted a glass of port-wine over her yellow satin, and laughed at the disaster; nor was she better pleased, although old Osborne was highly delighted, when Georgy "whopped" her third boy (a young gentleman a year older than Georgy, and by chance home for the holidays from Dr. Tickleus's at Ealing School) in Russell Square. George's grandfather gave the boy a couple of sovereigns for that feat, and promised to reward him further for every boy above his own size and age whom he whopped in a similar manner. It is difficult to say what good the old man saw in these combats; he had a vague notion that quarrelling made boys hardy, and that tyranny was a useful accomplishment for them to learn. English youth have been so educated time out of mind, and we have hundreds of thousands of apologists and admirers of injustice, misery, and brutality, as perpetrated among children. Flushed with praise and victory over Master Toffy, George wished naturally to pursue his conquests further, and one day as he was strutting about in prodigiously dandified new clothes, near St. Pancras, and a young baker's boy made sarcastic comments upon his appearance, the youthful patrician pulled off his dandy jacket with great spirit, and giving it in charge to the friend who accompanied him (Master Todd, of Great Coram Street, Russell Square, son of the junior partner of the house of Osborne and Co.) — George tried to whop the little baker. But the chances of war were unfavorable this time, and the little baker whopped Georgy : who came home with a rueful black eye and all his fine shirt frill dabbled with the claret drawn from his own little nose. He told his grandfather that he had been in combat with a giant; and frightened his poor mother at Brompton with long, and by no means authentic, accounts of the battle.

This young Todd, of Coram Street, Russell Square, was Master George's great friend and admirer. They both had a taste for painting theatrical characters; for hard-bake and raspberry tarts; for sliding and skating in the Regent's Park and the Serpentine, when the weather permitted; for going to the play, whither they were often conducted, by Mr. Osborne's orders, by Rowson, Master George's appointed body-servant, with whom they sat in great comfort in the pit.

In the company of this gentleman they visited all the principal theatres of the metropolis — knew the names of all the actors from Drury Lane to Sadler's Wells; and performed, indeed, many of the plays to the Todd family and their youthful friends, with West's famous characters, on their pasteboard theatre. Rowson, the footman, who was of a generous disposition, would not unfrequently, when in cash, treat his young master to oysters after the play, and to a glass of rum-shrub for a night-cap. We may be pretty certain that Mr. Rowson profited in his turn, by his young master's liberality and gratitude for the pleasures to which the footman inducted him.

A famous tailor from the West End of the town, —
Mr. Osborne would have none of your City or Holborn
bunglers, he said, for the boy (though a City tailor
was good enough for *him*), — was summoned to ornament little George's person, and was told to spare no
expense in so doing. So, Mr. Woolsey, of Conduit
Street, gave a loose to his imagination, and sent the
child home fancy trowsers, fancy waistcoats, and
fancy jackets enough to furnish a school of little
dandies. Georgy had little white waistcoats for evening parties and little cut velvet waistcoats for dinners, and a dear little darling shawl dressing-gown,
for all the world like a little man. He dressed for
dinner every day, "like a regular West End Swell,"
as his grandfather remarked; one of the domestics
was affected to his special service, attended him at
his toilette, answered his bell, and brought him his
letters always on a silver tray.

Georgy, after breakfast, would sit in the arm-chair
in the dining-room, and read the "Morning Post,"
just like a grown-up man. "How he *du* damn and
swear," the servants would cry, delighted at his precocity. Those who remembered the Captain his
father, declared Master George was his Pa every
inch of him. He made the house lively by his activity, his imperiousness, his scolding, and his good
nature.

George's education was confided to a neighboring
scholar and private pedagogue who "prepared young
noblemen and gentlemen for the Universities, the
senate, and the learned professions: whose system
did not embrace the degrading corporal severities still
practised at the ancient places of education, and in
whose family the pupils would find the elegances of
refined society and the confidence and affection of a

home." It was in this way that the Rev. Lawrence
Veal of Hart Street, Bloomsbury, and domestic Chaplain to the Earl of Bareacres, strove with Mrs. Veal
his wife to entice pupils.

By thus advertising and pushing sedulously, the
domestic Chaplain and his lady generally succeeded
in having one or two scholars by them: who paid a
high figure: and were thought to be in uncommonly
comfortable quarters. There was a large West Indian,
whom nobody came to see, with a mahogany complexion, a woolly head, and an exceedingly dandified
appearance; there was another hulking boy of three-
and-twenty whose education had been neglected, and
whom Mr. and Mrs. Veal were to introduce into the
polite world: there were two sons of Colonel Bangles
of the East India Company's Service: these four sat
down to dinner at Mrs. Veal's genteel board, when
Georgy was introduced to her establishment.

Georgy was, like some dozen other pupils, only a
day boy; he arrived in the morning under the guardianship of his friend Mr. Rowson, and if it was fine,
would ride away in the afternoon on his pony, followed by the groom. The wealth of his grandfather
was reported in the school to be prodigious. The Rev.
Mr. Veal used to compliment Georgy upon it personally, warning him that he was destined for a high station; that it became him to prepare, by sedulity and
docility in youth, for the lofty duties to which he would
be called in mature age; that obedience in the child
was the best preparation for command in the man;
and that he therefore begged George would not bring
toffy into the school, and ruin the health of the Masters Bangles, who had everything they wanted at the
elegant and abundant table of Mrs. Veal.

With respect to learning, "the Curriculum," as Mr.

Veal loved to call it, was of prodigious extent: and the young gentlemen in Hart Street might learn a something of every known science. The Rev. Mr. Veal had an orrery, an electrifying machine, a turning lathe, a theatre (in the wash-house), a chemical apparatus, and what he called a select library of all the works of the best authors of ancient and modern times and languages. He took the boys to the British Museum, and descanted upon the antiquities and the specimens of natural history there, so that audiences would gather round him as he spoke, and all Bloomsbury highly admired him as a prodigiously well-informed man. And whenever he spoke (which he did almost always), he took care to produce the very finest and longest words of which the vocabulary gave him the use ; rightly judging, that it was as cheap to employ a handsome, large, and sonorous epithet, as to use a little stingy one.

Thus he would say to George in school, "I observed on my return home from taking the indulgence of an evening's scientific conversation with my excellent friend Doctor Bulders — a true archæologian, gentlemen, a true archæologian — that the windows of your venerated grandfather's almost princely mansion in Russell Square were illuminated as if for the purposes of festivity. Am I right in my conjecture, that Mr. Osborne entertained a society of chosen spirits round his sumptuous board last night ? "

Little Georgy, who had considerable humor, and used to mimic Mr. Veal to his face with great spirit and dexterity, would reply, that Mr. V. was quite correct in his surmise.

"Then those friends who had the honor of partaking of Mr. Osborne's hospitality, gentlemen, had no reason, I will lay any wager, to complain of their repast. I myself have been more than once so favored. (By the way, Master Osborne, you came a little late this morning, and have been a defaulter in this respect more than once.) I myself, I say, gentlemen, humble as I am, have been found not unworthy to share Mr. Osborne's elegant hospitality. And though I have feasted with the great and noble of the world — for I presume that I may call my excellent friend and patron, the Right Honorable George Earl of Bareacres, one of the number — yet I assure you that the board of the British merchant was to the full as richly served, and his reception as gratifying and noble. Mr. Bluck, sir, we will resume, if you please, that passage of Eutropius, which was interrupted by the late arrival of Master Osborne."

To this great man George's education was for some time intrusted. Amelia was bewildered by his phrases, but thought him a prodigy of learning. That poor widow made friends of Mrs. Veal, for reasons of her own. She liked to be in the house, and see Georgy coming to school there. She liked to be asked to Mrs. Veal's *conversazioni*, which took place once a month (as you were informed on pink cards, with "Athene" engraved on them), and where the professor welcomed his pupils and their friends to weak tea and scientific conversation. Poor little Amelia never missed one of these entertainments, and thought them delicious so long as she might have Georgy sitting by her. And she would walk from Brompton in any weather, and embrace Mrs. Veal with tearful gratitude for the delightful evening she had passed, when, the company having retired and Georgy gone off with Mr. Rowson, his attendant, poor Mrs. Osborne put on her cloaks and her shawls preparatory to walking home.

As for the learning which Georgy imbibed **under**

this valuable master of a hundred sciences, to judge
from the weekly reports which the lad took home to
his grandfather, his progress was remarkable. The
names of a score or more of desirable branches of
knowledge were printed in a table, and the pupil's
progress in each was marked by the professor. In
Greek Georgy was pronounced *aristos*, in Latin *opti-
mus*, in French *très bien*, and so forth; and everybody
had prizes for everything at the end of the year.
Even Mr. Swartz, the woolly-headed young gentleman, and half-brother to the Honorable Mrs. Mc-
Mull, and Mr. Bluck, the neglected young pupil of
three-and-twenty from the agricultural districts, and
that idle young scapegrace of a Master Todd before
mentioned, received little eighteen-penny books,
with "Athene" engraved on them, and a pompous
Latin inscription from the Professor to his young
friends.

The family of this Master Todd were hangers-on of
the house of Osborne. The old gentleman had advanced Todd from being a clerk to be a junior partner
in his establishment.

Mr. Osborne was the godfather of young Master
Todd (who in subsequent life wrote Mr. Osborne
Todd on his cards, and became a man of decided
fashion), while Miss Osborne had accompanied Miss
Maria Todd to the font, and gave her *protégée* a
prayer-book, a collection of tracts, a volume of very
low-church poetry, or some such memento of her
goodness every year. Miss O. drove the Todds out in
her carriage now and then: when they were ill, her
footman, in large plush smalls and waistcoat, brought
jellies and delicacies from Russell Square to Coram
Street. Coram Street trembled and looked up to
Russell Square indeed; and Mrs. Todd, who had a

pretty hand at cutting out paper trimmings for haunches of mutton, and could make flowers, ducks, etc., out of turnips and carrots in a very creditable manner, would go to "the Square," as it was called, and assist in the preparations incident to a great dinner, without even so much as thinking of sitting down to the banquet. If any guest failed at the eleventh hour, Todd was asked to dine. Mrs. Todd and Maria came across in the evening, slipped in with a muffled knock, and were in the drawing-room by the time Miss Osborne and the ladies under her convoy reached that apartment; and ready to fire off duets and sing until the gentlemen came up. Poor Maria Todd; poor young lady! How she had to work and thrum at these duets and sonatas in the Street, before they appeared in public in the Square!

Thus it seemed to be decreed by fate, that Georgy was to domineer over everybody with whom he came in contact, and that friends, relatives, and domestics were all to bow the knee before the little fellow. It must be owned that he accommodated himself very willingly to this arrangement. Most people do so. And Georgy liked to play the part of master, and perhaps had a natural aptitude for it.

In Russell Square everybody was afraid of Mr. Osborne, and Mr. Osborne was afraid of Georgy. The boy's dashing manners, and off-hand rattle about books and learning, his likeness to his father (dead unreconciled in Brussels yonder), awed the old gentleman, and gave the young boy the mastery. The old man would start at some hereditary feature or tone unconsciously used by the little lad, and fancy that George's father was again before him. He tried by indulgence to the grandson to make up for harshness to the elder George. People were surprised at his

gentleness to the boy. He growled and swore at Miss
Osborne as usual: and would smile when George
came down late for breakfast.

Miss Osborne, George's aunt, was a faded old
spinster, broken down by more than forty years of
dulness and coarse usage. It was easy for a lad of
spirit to master *her*. And whenever George wanted
anything from her, from the jam-pots in her cupboards, to the cracked and dry old colors in her
paint-box (the old paint-box which she had had when
she was a pupil of Mr. Smee, and was still almost
young and blooming), Georgy took possession of the
object of his desire, which obtained, he took no further notice of his aunt.

For his friends and cronies, he had a pompous old
schoolmaster, who flattered him, and a toady, his
senior, whom he could thrash. It was dear Mrs.
Todd's delight to leave him with her youngest daughter, Rosa Jemima, a darling child of eight years old.
The little pair looked so well together, she would say
(but not to the folks in "the Square," we may be
sure), — "Who knows what might happen? Don't
they make a pretty little couple?" the fond mother
thought.

The broken-spirited, old, maternal grandfather was
likewise subject to the little tyrant. He could not
help respecting a lad who had such fine clothes, and
rode with a groom behind him. Georgy, on his side,
was in the constant habit of hearing coarse abuse and
vulgar satire levelled at John Sedley, by his pitiless
old enemy, Mr. Osborne. Osborne used to call the
other the old pauper, the old coal-man, the old bankrupt, and by many other such names of brutal contumely. How was little George to respect a man so
prostrate? A few months after he was with his

paternal grandfather, Mrs. Sedley died. There had been little love between her and the child. He did not care to show much grief. He came down to visit his mother in a fine new suit of mourning, and was very angry that he could not go to a play upon which he had set his heart.

The illness of that old lady had been the occupation and perhaps the safeguard of Amelia. What do men know about women's martyrdoms? We should go mad had we to endure the hundredth part of those daily pains which are meekly borne by many women. Ceaseless slavery meeting with no reward; constant gentleness and kindness met by cruelty as constant; love, labor, patience, watchfulness, without even so much as the acknowledgment of a good word; all this, how many of them have to bear in quiet, and appear abroad with cheerful faces as if they felt nothing. Tender slaves that they are, they must needs be hypocrites and weak.

From her chair Amelia's mother had taken to her bed, which she had never left: and from which Mrs. Osborne herself was never absent except when she ran to see George. The old lady grudged her even those rare visits; she, who had been a kind, smiling, good-natured mother once, in the days of her prosperity, but whom poverty and infirmities had broken down. Her illness or estrangement did not affect Amelia. They rather enabled her to support the other calamity under which she was suffering, and from the thoughts of which she was kept by the ceaseless calls of the invalid. Amelia bore her harshness quite gently; smoothed the uneasy pillow; was always ready with a soft answer to the watchful, querulous voice; soothed the sufferer with words of hope, such as her pious simple heart could best feel and utter, and closed the eyes that had once looked so tenderly upon her.

Then all her time and tenderness were devoted to the consolation and comfort of the bereaved old father, who was stunned by the blow which had befallen him, and stood utterly alone in the world. His wife, his honor, his fortune, everything he loved best had fallen away from him. There was only Amelia to stand by and support with her gentle arms the tottering, heart-broken, old man. We are not going to write the history: it would be too dreary and stupid. I can see Vanity Fair yawning over it *d'avance*.

One day as the young gentlemen were assembled in the study at the Rev. Mr. Veal's, and the domestic Chaplain to the Right Honorable the Earl of Bareacres was spouting away as usual — a smart carriage drove up to the door decorated with the statue of Athene, and two gentlemen stepped out. The young Masters Bangles rushed to the window, with a vague notion that their father might have arrived from Bombay. The great hulking scholar of three-and-twenty, who was crying secretly over a passage of Eutropius, flattened his neglected nose against the panes, and looked at the drag, as the *laquais de place* sprang from the box and let out the persons in the carriage.

"It's a fat one and a thin one," Mr. Bluck said, as a thundering knock came to the door.

Everybody was interested, from the domestic Chaplain himself, who hoped he saw the fathers of some future pupils, down to Master Georgy, glad of any pretext for laying his book down.

The boy in the shabby livery, with the faded copper-buttons, who always thrust himself into the tight coat to open the door, came into the study and said, "Two gentlemen want to see Master Osborne." The Professor had had a trifling altercation in the morning with that young gentleman, owing to a difference about the introduction of crackers in school-time; but his face resumed its habitual expression of bland courtesy, as he said, "Master Osborne, I give you full permission to go and see your carriage friends, — to whom I beg you to convey the respectful compliments of myself and Mrs. Veal."

Georgy went into the reception-room, and saw two strangers, whom he looked at with his head up, in his usual haughty manner. One was fat, with mustachios, and the other was lean and long, in a blue frock-coat, with a brown face, and a grizzled head.

"My God, how like he is!" said the long gentleman, with a start. "Can you guess who we are, George?"

The boy's face flushed up, as it did usually when he was moved, and his eyes brightened. "I don't know the other," he said, "but I should think you must be Major Dobbin."

Indeed it was our old friend. His voice trembled with pleasure as he greeted the boy, and taking both the other's hands in his own, drew the lad to him.

"Your mother has talked to you about me — has she?" he said.

"That she has," Georgy answered, "hundreds and hundreds of times."

CHAPTER III.

It was one of the many causes for personal pride with which old Osborne chose to recreate himself, that Sedley, his ancient rival, enemy, and benefactor, was in his last days so utterly defeated and humiliated, as to be forced to accept pecuniary obligations at the hands of the man who had most injured and insulted him. The successful man of the world cursed the old pauper, and relieved him from time to time. As he furnished George with money for his mother, he gave the boy to understand by hints, delivered in his brutal, coarse way, that George's maternal grandfather was but a wretched old bankrupt and dependant, and that John Sedley might thank the man to whom he already owed ever so much money, for the aid which his generosity now chose to administer. George carried the pompous supplies to his mother and the shattered old widower whom it was now the main business of her life to tend and comfort. The little fellow patronized the feeble and disappointed old man.

It may have shown a want of "proper pride" in Amelia that she chose to accept these money benefits at the hands of her father's enemy. But proper pride and this poor lady had never had much acquaintance together. A disposition naturally simple and demanding protection; a long course of poverty and humility, of daily privations, and hard words, of kind offices and no returns, had been her lot ever since womanhood almost, or since her luckless marriage with George Osborne. You who see your betters, bearing up under this shame every day, meekly suffering under the slights of fortune, gentle and unpitied, poor, and rather despised for their poverty, do you ever step down from your prosperity and wash the feet of these poor wearied beggars? The very thought of them is odious and low. "There must be classes — there must be rich and poor," Dives says, smacking his claret — (it is well if he even sends the broken meat out to Lazarus sitting under the window). Very true; but think how mysterious and often unaccountable it is — that lottery of life which gives to this man the purple and fine linen, and sends to the other rags for garments and dogs for comforters.

So I must own, that without much repining, on the contrary, with something akin to gratitude, Amelia took the crumbs that her father-in-law let drop now and then and with them fed her own parent. Directly she understood it to be her duty, it was this young woman's nature (ladies, she is but thirty still, and we choose to call her a young woman even at that age) — it was, I say, her nature to sacrifice herself and to fling all that she had at the feet of the beloved object. During what long thankless nights had she worked out her fingers for little Georgy whilst at home with her; what buffets, scorns, privations, poverties had she endured for father and mother! And in the midst of all these solitary resignations and unseen sacrifices, she did not respect herself any more than the world respected her; but I believe thought in her heart that she was a poor-spirited, despicable little creature, whose luck in life was only too good for her merits. O you poor women! O you poor secret martyrs and victims, whose life is a torture, who are stretched on

racks in your bed-rooms, and who lay your heads down
on the block daily at the drawing-room table; every
man who watches your pains, or peers into those dark
places where the torture is administered to you, must
pity you — and — and thank God that he has a beard.
I recollect seeing, years ago, at the prisons for idiots
and madmen at Bicêtre, near Paris, a poor wretch bent
down under the bondage of his imprisonment and his
personal infirmity, to whom one of our party gave a
half pennyworth of snuff in a *cornet* or "screw" of
paper. The kindness was too much for the poor epileptic creature. He cried in an anguish of delight and
gratitude: if anybody gave you and me a thousand a
year, or saved our lives, we could not be so affected.
And so, if you properly tyrannize over a woman, you
will find a halfp'orth of kindness act upon her, and
bring tears into her eyes, as though you were an angel
benefiting her.

Some such boons as these were the best which Fortune allotted to poor little Amelia. Her life, begun
not unprosperously, had come down to this — to a
mean prison and a long, ignoble bondage. Little
George visited her captivity sometimes, and consoled
it with feeble gleams of encouragement. Russell
Square was the boundary of her prison: she might
walk thither occasionally, but was always back to
sleep in her cell at night; to perform cheerless duties; to watch by thankless sick-beds; to suffer the
harassment and tyranny of querulous disappointed old
age. How many thousands of people are there, women
for the most part, who are doomed to endure this long
slavery? — who are hospital nurses without wages, —
sisters of Charity, if you like, without the romance and
the sentiment of sacrifice, — who strive, fast, watch,
and suffer, unpitied; and fade away ignobly and

unknown. The hidden and awful wisdom which apportions the destinies of mankind is pleased so to humiliate and cast down the tender, good, and wise; and to set up the selfish, the foolish, or the wicked. Oh, be humble, my brother, in your prosperity! Be gentle with those who are less lucky, if not more deserving. Think, what right have you to be scornful, whose virtue is a deficiency of temptation, whose success may be a chance, whose rank may be an ancestor's accident, whose prosperity is very likely a satire.

They buried Amelia's mother in the church-yard at Brompton; upon just such a rainy, dark day, as Amelia recollected when first she had been there to marry George. Her little boy sat by her side in pompous new sables. She remembered the old pew-woman and clerk. Her thoughts were away in other times as the parson read. But that she held George's hand in her own, perhaps she would have liked to change places with . . . Then, as usual, she felt ashamed of her selfish thoughts, and prayed inwardly to be strengthened to do her duty.

So she determined with all her might and strength to try and make her old father happy. She slaved, toiled, patched, and mended, sang and played backgammon, read out the newspaper, cooked dishes, for old Sedley, walked him out sedulously into Kensington Gardens or the Brompton Lanes, listened to his stories with untiring smiles and affectionate hypocrisy, or sat musing by his side and communing with her own thoughts and reminiscences, as the old man, feeble and querulous, sunned himself on the garden benches and prattled about his wrongs or his sorrows. What sad, unsatisfactory thoughts those of the widow were! The children running up and down the slopes and broad paths in the gardens, reminded her of George who was taken from her: the first George was taken from her: her selfish, guilty love, in both instances, had been rebuked and bitterly chastised. She strove to think it was right that she should be so punished. She was such a miserable wicked sinner. She was quite alone in the world.

I know that the account of this kind of solitary imprisonment is insufferably tedious, unless there is some cheerful or humorous incident to enliven it, — a tender gaoler, for instance, or a waggish commandant of the fortress, or a mouse to come out and play about Latude's beard and whiskers, or a subterranean passage under the castle, dug by Trenck with his nails and a toothpick: the historian has no such enlivening incident to relate in the narrative of Amelia's captivity. Fancy her, if you please, during this period, very sad, but always ready to smile when spoken to; in a very mean, poor, not to say vulgar position of life; singing songs, making puddings, playing cards, mending stockings, for her old father's benefit. So, never mind, whether she be a heroine or no; or you and I, however old, scolding and bankrupt; — may we have in our last days a kind soft shoulder on which to lean, and a gentle hand to soothe our gouty old pillows.

Old Sedley grew very fond of his daughter after his wife's death; and Amelia had her consolation in doing her duty by the old man.

But we are not going to leave these two people long in such a low and ungenteel station of life. Better days, as far as worldly prosperity went, were in store for both. Perhaps the ingenious reader has guessed who was the stout gentleman who called upon Georgy at his school in company with our old friend Major Dobbin. It was another old acquaintance returned to England, and at a time when his presence was likely to be of great comfort to his relatives there.

Major Dobbin having easily succeeded in getting leave from his good-natured commandant to proceed to Madras, and thence probably to Europe, on urgent private affairs, never ceased travelling night and day until he reached his journey's end, and had directed his march with such celerity, that he arrived at Madras in a high fever. His servants who accompanied him, brought him to the house of the friend with whom he had resolved to stay until his departure for Europe in a state of delirium: and it was thought for many, many days that he would never travel farther than the burying-ground of the church of St. George's, where the troops should fire a salvo over his grave, and where many a gallant officer lies far away from his home.

Here, as the poor fellow lay tossing in his fever, the people who watched him might have heard him raving about Amelia. The idea that he should never see her again depressed him in his lucid hours. He thought his last day was come; and he made his solemn preparations for departure: setting his affairs in this world in order, and leaving the little property of which he was possessed to those whom he most desired to benefit. The friend in whose house he was located witnessed his testament. He desired to be buried with a little brown hair-chain which he wore round his neck, and which, if the truth must be known, he had got from Amelia's maid at Brussels, when the young widow's hair was cut off, during the fever which prostrated her after the death of George Osborne on the plateau at Mount St. John.

He recovered, rallied, relapsed again, having undergone such a process of blood-letting and calomel as

showed the strength of his original constitution. He
was almost a skeleton when they put him on board
the Ramchunder East Indiaman, Captain Bragg, from
Calcutta, touching at Madras; and so weak and prostrate, that his friend who had tended him through his
illness, prophesied that the honest Major would never
survive the voyage, and that he would pass some
morning, shrouded in flag and hammock, over the
ship's side, and carrying down to the sea with him the
relic that he wore at his heart. But whether it was
the sea air, or the hope which sprung up in him afresh,
from the day that the ship spread her canvas and
stood out of the roads towards *home*, our friend began
to amend, and he was quite well (though as gaunt as a
greyhound) before they reached the Cape. "Kirk will
be disappointed of his majority this time," he said,
with a smile: "he will expect to find himself gazetted
by the time the regiment reaches home." For it must
be premised that while the Major was lying ill at
Madras, having made such prodigious haste to go
thither, the gallant — th, which had passed many
years abroad, which after its return from the West
Indies had been baulked of its stay at home by the
Waterloo campaign, and had been ordered from Flan-
ders to India, had received orders home; and the
Major might have accompanied his comrades, had he
chosen to wait for their arrival at Madras.

Perhaps he was not inclined to put himself in
his exhausted state again under the guardianship of
Glorvina. "I think Miss O'Dowd would have done
for me," he said, laughingly, to a fellow-passenger,
"if we had had her on board, and when she had sunk
me, she would have fallen upon you, depend upon it,
and carried you in as a prize to Southampton, Jos,
my boy."

For indeed it was no other than our stout friend who was also a passenger on board the Ramchunder. He had passed ten years in Bengal. — Constant dinners, tiffins, pale ale and claret, the prodigious labor of cutchery, and the refreshment of brandy-pawnee which he was forced to take there, had their effect upon Waterloo Sedley. A voyage to Europe was pronounced necessary for him — and having served his full time in India, and had fine appointments which had enabled him to lay by a considerable sum of money, he was free to come home and stay with a good pension, or to return and resume that rank in the service to which his seniority and his vast talents entitled him.

He was rather thinner than when we last saw him, but had gained in majesty and solemnity of demeanor. He had resumed the mustachios to which his services at Waterloo entitled him, and swaggered about on deck in a magnificent velvet cap with a gold band, and a profuse ornamentation of pins and jewelry about his person. He took breakfast in his cabin, and dressed as solemnly to appear on the quarter-deck, as if he were going to turn out for Bond Street, or the Course at Calcutta. He brought a native servant with him, who was his valet and pipe-bearer; and who wore the Sedley crest in silver on his turban. That oriental menial had a wretched life under the tyranny of Jos Sedley. Jos was as vain of his person as a woman, and took as long a time at his toilette as any fading beauty. The youngsters among the passengers, Young Chaffers of the 150th, and poor little Ricketts, coming home after his third fever, used to draw out Sedley at the cuddy-table, and make him tell prodigious stories about himself and his exploits against tigers and Napoleon. He was great when he visited

the Emperor's tomb at Longwood, when to these
gentlemen and the young officers of the ship, Major
Dobbin not being by, he described the whole battle
of Waterloo, and all but announced that Napoleon
never would have gone to St. Helena at all but for
him, Jos Sedley.

After leaving St. Helena he became very generous,
disposing of a great quantity of ship stores, claret,
preserved meats, and great casks packed with soda-
water, brought out for his private delectation.   There
were no ladies on board: the Major gave the *pas* of
precedency to the civilian, so that he was the first dignitary at table; and treated by Captain Bragg, and the
officers of the Ramchunder, with the respect which his
rank warranted. He disappeared rather in a panic
during a two-days' gale, in which he had the portholes
of his cabin battened down; and remained in his cot
reading the "Washerwoman of Finchley Common,"
left on board the Ramchunder by the Right Honorable
the Lady Emily Hornblower, wife of the Rev. Silas
Hornblower, when on their passage out to the Cape,
where the Reverend gentleman was a missionary: but,
for common reading, he had brought a stock of novels
and plays which he lent to the rest of the ship, and
rendered himself agreeable to all by his kindness and
condescension.

Many and many a night as the ship was cutting
through the roaring dark sea, the moon and stars
shining over head, and the bell singing out the watch,
Mr. Sedley and the Major would sit on the quarter-
deck of the vessel talking about home, as the Major
smoked his cheroot, and the civilian puffed at the
hookah which his servant prepared for him.

In these conversations it was wonderful with what
perseverance and ingenuity Major Dobbin would

manage to bring the talk round to the subject of
Amelia and her little boy. Jos, a little testy about
his father's misfortunes and unceremonious applica-
tions to him, was soothed down by the Major, who
pointed out the elder's ill fortunes and old age. He
would not perhaps like to live with the old couple:
whose ways and hours might not agree with those of
a younger man, accustomed to different society (Jos
bowed at this compliment) : but, the Major pointed
out, how advantageous it would be for Jos Sedley to
have a house of his own in London, and not a mere
bachelor's establishment as before : how his sister
Amelia would be the very person to preside over it ;
how elegant, how gentle she was, and of what refined
good manners. He recounted stories of the success
which Mrs. George Osborne had had in former days
at Brussels, and in London, where she was much
admired by people of very great fashion : and he
then hinted how becoming it would be for Jos to send
Georgy to a good school and make a man of him ; for
his mother and her parents would be sure to spoil
him. In a word, this artful Major made the civilian
promise to take charge of Amelia and her unprotected
child. He did not know as yet what events had
happened in the little Sedley family : and how death
had removed the mother, and riches had carried off
George from Amelia. But the fact is, that every day
and always, this love-smitten and middle-aged gentleman was thinking about Mrs. Osborne, and his whole
heart was bent upon doing her good. He coaxed,
wheedled, cajoled, and complimented Jos Sedley with
a perseverance and cordiality of which he was not
aware himself, very likely ; but some men who have
unmarried sisters or daughters even, may remember
how uncommonly agreeable gentlemen are to the

male relations when they are courting the females; and perhaps this rogue of a Dobbin was urged by a similar hypocrisy.

The truth is, when Major Dobbin came on board the Ramchunder, very sick, and for the three days she lay in the Madras Roads, he did not begin to rally, nor did even the appearance and recognition of his old acquaintance, Mr. Sedley, on board much cheer him, until after a conversation which they had one day, as the Major was laid languidly on the deck. He said then he thought he was doomed; he had left a little something to his godson in his will; and he trusted Mrs. Osborne would remember him kindly, and be happy in the marriage she was about to make. "Married? not the least," Jos answered: "he had heard from her: she made no mention of the marriage, and by the way, it was curious, she wrote to say that Major Dobbin was going to be married, and hoped that *he* would be happy." What were the dates of Sedley's letters from Europe? The civilian fetched them. They were two months later than the Major's; and the ship's surgeon congratulated himself upon the treatment adopted by him towards his new patient, who had been consigned to ship-board by the Madras practitioner with very small hopes indeed; for, from that day, the very day that he changed the draught, Major Dobbin began to mend. And thus it was that deserving officer, Captain Kirk, was disappointed of his majority.

After they passed St. Helena, Major Dobbin's gayety and strength was such as to astonish all his fellow-passengers. He larked with the midshipmen, played single-stick with the mates, ran up the shrouds like a boy, sang a comic song one night to the amusement of the whole party assembled over their grog after supper, and rendered himself so gay, lively, and amiable, that even Captain Bragg, who thought there was nothing in his passenger, and considered he was a poor-spirited feller at first, was constrained to own that the Major was a reserved but well-informed and meritorious officer. "He ain't got distangy manners, dammy," Bragg observed to his first mate; "he would n't do at Government House, Roper, where his Lordship and Lady William was as kind to me, and shook hands with me before the whole company, and asking me at dinner to take beer with him, before the Commander-in-Chief himself; he ain't got manners, but there's something about him — " And thus Captain Bragg showed that he possessed discrimination as a man, as well as ability as a commander.

But a calm taking place when the Ramchunder was within ten days' sail of England, Dobbin became so impatient and ill-humored as to surprise those comrades who had before admired his vivacity and good temper. He did not recover until the breeze sprang up again, and was in a highly excited state when the pilot came on board. Good God, how his heart beat as the two friendly spires of Southampton came in sight.

CHAPTER IV.

OUR Major had rendered himself so popular on
board the Ramchunder, that when he and Mr. Sedley descended into the welcome shore-boat which was
to take them from the ship, the whole crew, men and
officers, the great Captain Bragg himself leading off,
gave three cheers for Major Dobbin, who blushed
very much, and ducked his head in token of thanks.
Jos, who very likely thought the cheers were for himself, took off his gold-laced cap and waved it majestically to his friends, and they were pulled to shore
and landed with great dignity at the pier, whence
they proceeded to the Royal George Hotel.

Although the sight of that magnificent round of
beef, and the silver tankard suggestive of real British
home-brewed ale and porter, which perennially greet
the eyes of the traveller returning from foreign parts,
who enters the coffee-room of the George, are so in-
vigorating and delightful, that a man entering such
a comfortable snug homely English inn, might well
like to stop some days there, yet Dobbin began to talk
about a post-chaise instantly, and was no sooner at
Southampton than he wished to be on the road to
London. Jos, however, would not hear of moving
that evening. Why was he to pass a night in a
post-chaise instead of a great large undulating downy
feather-bed which was there ready to replace the horrid
little narrow crib in which the portly Bengal gentleman had been confined during the voyage ? He could

MR. JOS'S HOOKAHBADAR.

not think of moving till his baggage was cleared, or
of travelling until he could do so with his chillum.
So the Major was forced to wait over that night, and
despatched a letter to his family announcing his arrival; entreating from Jos a promise to write to his
own friends. Jos promised, but did n't keep his promise. The Captain, the surgeon, and one or two passengers came and dined with our two gentlemen at
the inn; Jos exerting himself in a sumptuous way in
ordering the dinner: and promising to go to town the
next day with the Major. The landlord said it did
his eyes good to see Mr. Sedley take off his first pint
of porter. If I had time and dared to enter into di-
gressions, I would write a chapter about that first pint
of porter drunk upon English ground. Ah, how good
it is! It is worth while to leave home for a year, just
to enjoy that one draught.

Major Dobbin made his appearance the next morning very neatly shaved and dressed, according to his
wont. Indeed, it was so early in the morning, that
nobody was up in the house except that wonderful
Boots of an inn who never seems to want sleep: and
the Major could hear the snores of the various inmates of the house roaring through the corridors as
he creaked about in those dim passages. Then the
sleepless Boots went shirking round from door to
door, gathering up at each the Bluchers, Welling-
tons, Oxonians, which stood outside. Then Jos's
native servant arose and began to get ready his master's ponderous dressing apparatus, and prepare his
hookah: then the maid-servants got up, and meeting the dark man in the passages, shrieked, and mistook him for the devil. He and Dobbin stumbled
over their pails in the passages as they were scouring the decks of the Royal George. When the first

unshorn waiter appeared and unbarred the door of
the inn, the Major thought that the time for departure was arrived, and ordered a post-chaise to be
fetched instantly, that they might set off.

He then directed his steps to Mr. Sedley's room,
and opened the curtains of the great large family
bed wherein Mr. Jos was snoring. "Come, up!
Sedley," the Major said, "it's time to be off; the
chaise will be at the door in half an hour."

Jos growled from under the counterpane to know
what the time was; but when he at last extorted from
the blushing Major (who never told fibs, however they
might be to his advantage) what was the real hour of
the morning, he broke out into a volley of bad language, which we will not repeat here, but by which
he gave Dobbin to understand that he would jeopardy
his soul if he got up at that moment, that the Major
might go and be hanged, that he would not travel
with Dobbin, and that it was most unkind and un-
gentlemanlike to disturb a man out of his sleep in
that way; on which the discomfited Major was
obliged to retreat, leaving Jos to resume his interrupted slumbers.

The chaise came up presently, and the Major would
wait no longer.

If he had been an English nobleman travelling on
a pleasure tour, or a newspaper courier bearing de-
spatches (government messages are generally carried
much more quietly), he could not have travelled more
quickly. The post-boys wondered at the fees he flung
amongst them. How happy and green the country
looked as the chaise whirled rapidly from mile-stone
to mile-stone, through neat country towns where landlords came out to welcome him with smiles and bows;
by pretty road-side inns, where the signs hung on the

elms, and horses and wagoners were drinking under the checkered shadow of the trees; by old halls and parks; rustic hamlets clustered round ancient gray churches — and through the charming friendly English landscape. Is there any in the world like it? To a traveller returning home it looks so kind — it seems to shake hands with you as you pass through it. Well, Major Dobbin passed through all this from Southampton to London, and without noting much beyond the mile-stones along the road. You see he was so eager to see his parents at Camberwell.

He grudged the time lost between Piccadilly and his old haunt at the Slaughters', whither he drove faithfully. Long years had passed since he saw it last, since he and George, as young men, had enjoyed many a feast, and held many a revel there. He had now passed into the stage of old-fellowhood. His hair was grizzled, and many a passion and feeling of his youth had grown gray in that interval. There, however, stood the old waiter at the door, in the same greasy black suit, with the same double chin and flaccid face, with the same huge bunch of seals at his fob, rattling his money in his pockets as before, and receiving the Major as if he had gone away only a week ago. "Put the Major's things in twenty-three, that's his room," John said, exhibiting not the least surprise. "Roast fowl for your dinner, I suppose. You ain't got married? They said you was married — the Scotch surgeon of yours was here. No, it was Captain Humby of the Thirty-third, as was quartered with the — th in Injee. Like any warm water? What do you come in a chay for — ain't the coach good enough?" And with this, the faithful waiter, who knew and remembered every officer who used the house, and with whom ten years were but as yesterday, led the way up to Dobbin's old room, where stood the great moreen bed, and the shabby carpet, a thought more dingy, and all the old black furniture covered with faded chintz, just as the Major recollected them in his youth.

He remembered George pacing up and down the room, and biting his nails, and swearing that the Governor must come round, and that if he did n't, he did n't care a straw, on the day before he was married. He could fancy him walking in, banging the door of Dobbin's room, and his own hard by —

" You ain't got young," John said, calmly surveying his friend of former days.

Dobbin laughed. " Ten years and a fever don't make a man young, John," he said. " It is you that are always young : — No, you are always old."

" What became of Captain Osborne's widow ? " John said. " Fine young fellow that. Lord, how he used to spend his money. He never came back after that day he was married from here. He owes me three pound at this minute. Look here, I have it in my book. 'April 10, 1815, Captain Osborne : 3*l*.' I wonder whether his father would pay me," and so saying, John of the Slaughters' pulled out the very morocco pocket-book in which he had noted his loan to the Captain, upon a greasy faded page still extant, with many other scrawled memoranda regarding the bygone frequenters of the house.

Having inducted his customer into the room, John retired with perfect calmness ; and Major Dobbin, not without a blush and a grin at his own absurdity, chose out of his kit the very smartest and most becoming civil costume he possessed, and laughed at his own tanned face and gray hair, as he surveyed them in the dreary little toilette-glass on the dressing-table.

" I 'm glad old John did n't forget me," he thought.

"She'll know me, too, I hope." And he sallied out of the inn, bending his steps once more in the direction of Brompton.

Every minute incident of his last meeting with Amelia was present to the constant man's mind as he walked towards her house. The arch and the Achilles statue were up since he had last been in Piccadilly; a hundred changes had occurred which his eye and mind vaguely noted. He began to tremble as he walked up the lane from Brompton, that well-remembered lane leading to the street where she lived. Was she going to be married or not? If he were to meet her with the little boy — Good God, what should he do? He saw a woman coming to him with a child of five years old — was that she? He began to shake at the mere possibility. When he came up to the row of houses, at last, where she lived, and to the gate, he caught hold of it and paused. He might have heard the thumping of his own heart. "May God Almighty bless her, whatever has happened," he thought to himself. "Psha! she may be gone from here," he said, and went in through the gate.

The window of the parlor which she used to occupy was open, and there were no inmates in the room. The Major thought he recognized the piano, though, with the picture over it, as it used to be in former days, and his perturbations were renewed. Mr. Clapp's brass plate was still on the door, at the knocker of which Dobbin performed a summons.

A buxom-looking lass of sixteen, with bright eyes and purple cheeks, came to answer the knock, and looked hard at the Major as he leaned back against the little porch.

He was as pale as a ghost, and could hardly falter out the words — "Does Mrs. Osborne live here?"

She looked him hard in the face for a moment —
and then turning white too — said, "Lord bless me —
it's Major Dobbin." She held out both her hands
shaking — "Don't you remember me?" she said. "I
used to call you Major Sugarplums." On which, and
I believe it was for the first time that he ever so conducted himself in his life, the Major took the girl in
his arms and kissed her. She began to laugh and cry
hysterically, and calling out "Ma, Pa!" with all her
voice, brought up those worthy people, who had already
been surveying the Major from the casement of the
ornamental kitchen, and were astonished to find their
daughter in the little passage in the embrace of a
great tall man in a blue frock-coat and white duck
trousers.

"I'm an old friend," he said — not without blushing though. "Don't you remember me, Mrs. Clapp,
and those good cakes you used to make for tea? —
Don't you recollect me, Clapp? I'm George's godfather, and just come back from India." A great
shaking of hands ensued — Mrs. Clapp was greatly
affected and delighted; she called upon Heaven to interpose a vast many times in that passage.

The landlord and landlady of the house led the
worthy Major into the Sedleys' room (whereof he remembered every single article of furniture, from the
old brass ornamented piano, once a natty little instrument, Stothard maker, to the screens and the alabaster
miniature tombstone, in the midst of which ticked Mr.
Sedley's gold watch), and there as he sat down in the
lodger's vacant arm-chair, the father, the mother, and
the daughter, with a thousand ejaculatory breaks in
the narrative, informed Major Dobbin of what we
know already, but of particulars in Amelia's history
of which he was not aware — namely of Mrs. Sedley's

death, of George's reconcilement with his grandfather
Osborne, of the way in which the widow took on at
leaving him, and of other particulars of her life.
Twice or thrice he was going to ask about the marriage question, but his heart failed him. He did not
care to lay it bare to these people. Finally, he was
informed that Mrs. O. was gone to walk with her pa
in Kensington Gardens, whither she always went with
the old gentleman (who was very weak and peevish
now, and led her a sad life, though she behaved to him
like an angel, to be sure), of a fine afternoon after
dinner.

"I 'm very much pressed for time," the Major said,
"and have business to-night of importance. I should
like to see Mrs. Osborne tho'. Suppose Miss Polly
would come with me and show me the way."

Miss Polly was charmed and astonished at this proposal. She knew the way. She would show Major
Dobbin. She had often been with Mr. Sedley when
Mrs. O. was gone — was gone Russell Square way:
and knew the bench where he liked to sit. She
bounced away to her apartment, and appeared presently in her best bonnet and her mamma's yellow
shawl and large pebble brooch, of which she assumed
the loan in order to make herself a worthy companion
for the Major.

That officer, then, in his blue frock-coat and buckskin gloves, gave the young lady his arm, and they
walked away very gayly. He was glad to have a
friend at hand for the scene which he dreaded somehow. He asked a thousand more questions from his
companion about Amelia: his kind heart grieved to
think that she should have had to part with her son.
How did she bear it? Did she see him often? Was
Mr. Sedley pretty comfortable now in a worldly point

of view? Polly answered all these questions of Major
Sugarplums to the very best of her power.

And in the midst of their walk an incident occurred
which, though very simple in its nature, was productive of the greatest delight to Major Dobbin. A pale
young man with feeble whiskers and a stiff white neckcloth came walking down the lane, *en sandwich :* —
having a lady, that is, on each arm. One was a tall
and commanding middle-aged female, with features
and a complexion similar to those of the clergyman
of the Church of England by whose side she marched,
and the other a stunted little woman with a dark face,
ornamented by a fine new bonnet and white ribbons,
and in a smart pelisse with a rich gold watch in the
midst of her person. The gentleman, pinioned as he
was by these two ladies, carried further a parasol,
shawl, and basket, so that his arms were entirely engaged, and of course he was unable to touch his hat
in acknowledgment of the curtsy with which Miss
Mary Clapp greeted him.

He merely bowed his head in reply to her salutation, which the two ladies returned with a patronizing
air, and at the same time looking severely at the individual in the blue coat and bamboo cane, who accompanied Miss Polly.

"Who's that?" asked the Major, amused by the
group, and after he had made way for the three
to pass up the lane. Mary looked at him rather
roguishly.

"That is our curate, the Reverend Mr. Binny (a
twitch from Major Dobbin), and his sister Miss B.
Lord bless us, how she did use to worret us at Sunday-
school; and the other lady, the little one with a cast
in her eye, and the handsome watch, is Mrs. Binny —
Miss Grits that was; her pa was a grocer, and kept

the Little Original Gold Tea Pot in Kensington Gravel Pits. They were married last month, and are just come back from Margate. She's five thousand pound to her fortune; but her and Miss B., who made the match, have quarrelled already."

If the Major had twitched before, he started now, and slapped the bamboo on the grouud with an emphasis which made Miss Clapp cry "Law," and laugh too. He stood for a moment silent with open mouth looking after the retreating young couple, while Miss Mary told their history; but he did not hear beyond the announcement of the reverend gentleman's marriage; his head was swimming with felicity. After this rencontre he began to walk double quick toward the place of his destination; and yet they were too soon (for he was in a great tremor at the idea of a meeting for which he had been longing any time these ten years) — through the Brompton lanes, and entering at the little old portal in Kensington Garden wall.

"There they are," said Miss Polly, and she felt him again start back on her arm. She was a confidante at once of the whole business. She knew the story as well as if she had read it in one of her favorite novel-books — "Fatherless Fanny," or the "Scottish Chiefs."

"Suppose you were to run on and tell her," the Major said. Polly ran forward, her yellow shawl streaming in the breeze.

Old Sedley was seated on a bench, his handkerchief placed over his knees, prattling away according to his wont, with some old story about old times, to which Amelia had listened, and awarded a patient smile many a time before. She could of late think of her own affairs, and smile or make other marks of recognition of her father's stories, scarcely hearing

a word of the old man's tales. As Mary came bouncing along, and Amelia caught sight of her, she started
up from her bench. Her first thought was, that something had happened to Georgy; but the sight of the
messenger's eager and happy face dissipated that fear
in the timorous mother's bosom.

"News! News!" cried the emissary of Major
Dobbin. "He's come! He's come!"

"Who is come?" said Emmy, still thinking of
her son.

"Look there," answered Miss Clapp, turning round
and pointing; in which direction Amelia looking, saw
Dobbin's lean figure and long shadow stalking across
the grass. Amelia started in her turn, blushed up,
and, of course, began to cry. At all this simple little
creature's fêtes, the *grandes eaux* were accustomed
to play.

He looked at her — oh, how fondly — as she came
running toward him, her hands before her, ready to
give them to him. She wasn't changed. She was
a little pale; a little stouter in figure. Her eyes were
the same, the kind trustful eyes. There were scarce
three lines of silver in her soft brown hair. She gave
him both her hands as she looked up flushing and
smiling through her tears into his honest homely
face. He took the two little hands between his two,
and held them there. He was speechless for a moment. Why did he not take her in his arms, and
swear that he would never leave her? She must have
yielded: she could not but have obeyed him.

"I — I've another arrival to announce," he said,
after a pause.

"Mrs. Dobbin?" Amelia said, making a movement
back — Why didn't he speak?

"No," he said, letting her hands go: "Who has told

you those lies ? — I mean, your brother Jos came in the same ship with me, and is come home to make you all happy."

"Papa, papa!" Emmy cried out, "here are news! My brother is in England. He is come to take care of you. — Here is Major Dobbin."

Mr. Sedley started up, shaking a great deal, and gathering up his thoughts. Then he stepped forward and made an old-fashioned bow to the Major, whom he called Mr. Dobbin, and hoped his worthy father, Sir William, was quite well. He proposed to call upon Sir William, who had done him the honor of a visit a short time ago. Sir William had not called upon the old gentleman for eight years — it was that visit he was thinking of returning.

"He is very much shaken," Emmy whispered, as Dobbin went up and cordially shook hands with the old man.

Although he had such particular business in London that evening, the Major consented to forego it upon Mr. Sedley's invitation to him to come home and partake of tea. Amelia put her arm under that of her young friend with the yellow shawl, and headed the party on their return homewards, so that Mr. Sedley fell to Dobbin's share. The old man walked very slowly, and told a number of ancient histories about himself and his poor Bessy, his former prosperity, and his bankruptcy. His thoughts, as is usual with failing old men, were quite in former times. The present, with the exception of the one catastrophe which he felt, he knew little about. The Major was glad to let him talk on. His eyes were fixed upon the figure in front of him — the dear little figure always present to his imagination and in his prayers, and visiting his dreams wakeful or slumbering.

Amelia was very happy, smiling, and active all that evening; performing her duties as hostess of the little entertainment with the utmost grace and propriety, as Dobbin thought. His eyes followed her about as they sat in the twilight. How many a time had he longed for that moment, and thought of her far away under hot winds and in weary marches, gentle and happy, kindly ministering to the wants of old age, and decorating poverty with sweet submission — as he saw her now. I do not say that his taste was the highest, or that it is the duty of great intellects to be content with a bread-and-butter paradise, such as sufficed our simple old friend; but his desires were of this sort whether for good or bad; and, with Amelia to help him, he was as ready to drink as many cups of tea as Dr. Johnson.

Amelia seeing this propensity, laughingly encouraged it; and looked exceedingly roguish as she administered to him cup after cup. It is true she did not know that the Major had had no dinner, and that the cloth was laid for him at the Slaughters', and a plate laid thereon to mark that the table was retained, in that very box in which the Major and George had sat many a time carousing, when she was a child just come home from Miss Pinkerton's school.

The first thing Mrs. Osborne showed the Major was Georgy's miniature, for which she ran up stairs on her arrival at home. It was not half handsome enough of course for the boy, but wasn't it noble of him to think of bringing it to his mother? Whilst her papa was awake she did not talk much about Georgy. To hear about Mr. Osborne and Russell Square was not agreeable to the old man, who very likely was unconscious that he had been living for some months past mainly on the bounty of his richer rival; and lost his temper if allusion was made to the other.

Dobbin told him all, and a little more perhaps than all, that had happened on board the "Ramchunder;" and exaggerated Jos's benevolent dispositions towards his father, and resolution to make him comfortable in his old days. The truth is, that during the voyage the Major had impressed this duty most strongly upon his fellow passenger and extorted promises from him that he would take charge of his sister and her child. He soothed Jos's irritation with regard to the bills which the old gentleman had drawn upon him, gave a laughing account of his own sufferings on the same score, and of the famous consignment of wine with which the old man had favored him: and brought Mr. Jos, who was by no means an ill-natured person when well pleased and moderately flattered, to a very good state of feeling regarding his relatives in Europe.

And in fine I am ashamed to say that the Major stretched the truth so far as to tell old Mr. Sedley that it was mainly a desire to see his parent which brought Jos once more to Europe.

At his accustomed hour Mr. Sedley began to doze in his chair, and then it was Amelia's opportunity to commence her conversation, which she did with great eagerness; — it related exclusively to Georgy. She did not talk at all about her own sufferings at breaking from him, for indeed this worthy woman, though she was half-killed by the separation from the child, yet thought it was very wicked in her to repine at losing him; but everything concerning him, his virtues, talents, and prospects, she poured out. She described his angelic beauty; narrated a hundred instances of his generosity and greatness of mind

whilst living with her: how a Royal Duchess had
stopped and admired him in Kensington Gardens;
how splendidly he was cared for now, and how he had
a groom and a pony; what quickness and cleverness
he had, and what a prodigiously well-read and delightful person the Rev. Lawrence Veal was, George's
master. "He knows *everything,*" Amelia said. "He
has the most delightful parties. You who are so
learned yourself, and have read so much, and are so
clever and accomplished — don't shake your head and
say no — *he* always used to say you were — you will
be charmed with Mr. Veal's parties. The last Tues-
day in every month. He says there is no place in the
bar or the senate that Georgy may not aspire to.
Look here," and she went to the piano-drawer and
drew out a theme of Georgy's composition. This
great effort of genius, which is still in the possession
of George's mother, is as follows: —

On Selfishness. — Of all the vices which degrade the human character, Selfishness is the most odious and contemptible.
An undue love of Self leads to the most monstrous crimes ;
and occasions the greatest misfortunes both in *States and
Families.* As a selfish man will impoverish his family and
often bring them to ruin: so a selfish king brings ruin on his
people and often plunges them into war.

Example: The selfishness of Achilles, as remarked by the
poet Homer, occasioned a thousand woes to the Greeks —
μυρί Αχαιοῖς ἄλγε' ἔθηκε — (Hom. Il. A. 2). The selfishness
of the late Napoleon Bonaparte occasioned innumerable wars
in Europe, and caused him to perish, himself, in a miserable
island — that of Saint Helena in the Atlantic Ocean.

We see by these examples that we are not to consult our
own interest and ambition, but that we are to consider the interests of others as well as our own.

                                    George S. Osborne.

Athene House, 24 April, 1827.

"Think of him writing such a hand, and quoting Greek too, at his age," the delighted mother said. "O William," she added, holding out her hand to the Major — "what a treasure Heaven has given me in that boy ! He is the comfort of my life — and he is the image of — of him that 's gone !"

"Ought I to be angry with her for being faithful to him ?" William thought. "Ought I to be jealous of my friend in the grave, or hurt that such a heart as Amelia's can love only once and forever ? Oh, George, George, how little you knew the prize you had, though." This sentiment passed rapidly through William's mind, as he was holding Amelia's hand, whilst the handkerchief was veiling her eyes.

"Dear friend," she said, pressing the hand which held hers, "how good, how kind you always have been to me ! See ! Papa is stirring. You will go and see Georgy to-morrow, won't you ?"

"Not to-morrow," said poor old Dobbin. "I have business." He did not like to own that he had not as yet been to his parents' and his dear sister Ann — a remissness for which I am sure every well-regulated person will blame the Major. And presently he took his leave, leaving his address behind him for Jos, against the latter's arrival. And so the first day was over, and he had seen her.

When he got back to the Slaughters' the roast fowl was of course cold, in which condition he ate it for supper. And knowing what early hours his family kept, and that it would be needless to disturb their slumbers at so late an hour, it is on record, that Major Dobbin treated himself to half-price at the Haymarket Theatre that evening, where let us hope he enjoyed himself.

CHAPTER V.

THE OLD PIANO.

THE Major's visit left old John Sedley in a great state of agitation and excitement. His daughter could not induce him to settle down to his customary occupations or amusements that night. He passed the evening fumbling amongst his boxes and desks, untying his papers with trembling hands, and sorting and arranging them against Jos's arrival. He had them in the greatest order — his tapes and his files, his receipts, and his letters with lawyers and correspondents; the documents relative to the Wine Project (which failed from a most unaccountable accident, after commencing with the most splendid prospects), the Coal Project (which only a want of capital prevented from becoming the most successful scheme ever put before the public), the Patent Saw-mills and Sawdust Consolidation Project, etc., etc. — All night, until a very late hour, he passed in the preparation of these documents, trembling about from one room to another, with a quivering candle and shaky hands. — Here's the wine papers, here's the sawdust, here's the coals; here's my letters to Calcutta and Madras, and replies from Major Dobbin, C. B., and Mr. Joseph Sedley to the same. "He shall find no irregularity about *me*, Emmy," the old gentleman said.

Emmy smiled. "I don't think Jos will care about seeing those papers, Papa," she said.

"You don't know anything about business, my dear," answered the sire, shaking his head with an important air. And it must be confessed, that on this point Emmy was very ignorant; and that is a pity, some people are so knowing. All these twopenny documents arranged on a side table, old Sedley covered them carefully over with a clean bandanna handkerchief (one out of Major Dobbin's lot), and enjoined the maid and landlady of the house, in the most solemn way, not to disturb those papers, which were arranged for the arrival of Mr. Joseph Sedley the next morning; "Mr. Joseph Sedley of the Honorable East India Company's Bengal Civil Service."

Amelia found him up very early the next morning, more eager, more hectic, and more shaky than ever. "I did n't sleep much, Emmy my dear," he said. "I was thinking of my poor Bessy. I wish she was alive, to ride in Jos's carriage once again. She kept her own, and became it very well." And his eyes filled with tears, which trickled down his furrowed old face. Amelia wiped them away, and smilingly kissed him, and tied the old man's neckcloth in a smart bow, and put his brooch into his best shirt-frill, in which, in his Sunday suit of mourning, he sat from six o'clock in the morning awaiting the arrival of his son.

There are some splendid tailors' shops in the High Street of Southampton, in the fine plate-glass windows of which hang gorgeous waistcoats of all sorts, of silk and velvet, and gold and crimson, and pictures of the last new fashions in which those wonderful gentlemen with quizzing glasses, and holding on to little boys with the exceeding large eyes and curly hair, ogle ladies in riding-habits prancing by the Statue of Achilles at Apsley House. Jos, although provided with some of the most splendid vests that Calcutta could furnish, thought he could not go to town until he was supplied with one or two of these garments, and selected a crimson satin, embroidered with gold butterflies, and a black and red velvet tartan with white stripes and a rolling collar, with which, and a rich blue satin stock and a gold pin, consisting of a five-barred gate with a horseman in pink enamel jumping over it, he thought he might make his entry into London with some dignity. For Jos's former shyness and blundering blushing timidity had given way to a more candid and courageous self-assertion of his worth. "I don't care about owning it," Waterloo Sedley would say to his friends, "I am a dressy man:" and though rather uneasy if the ladies looked at him at the Government House balls, and though he blushed and turned away alarmed under their glances, it was chiefly from a dread lest they should make love to him, that he avoided them, being averse to marriage altogether. But there was no such swell in Calcutta as Waterloo Sedley, I have heard say: and he had the handsomest turnout, gave the best bachelor dinners, and had the finest plate in the whole place.

To make these waistcoats for a man of his size and dignity took at least a day, part of which he employed in hiring a servant to wait upon him and his native; and in instructing the agent who cleared his baggage, his boxes, his books, which he never read; his chests of mangoes, chutney, and currie-powders; his shawls for presents to people whom he didn't know as yet; and the rest of his *Persicos apparatus*.

At length, he drove leisurely to London on the third day, and in the new waistcoat: the native, with chattering teeth, shuddering in a shawl on the box by the side of the new European servant; Jos puffing his pipe at intervals within, and looking so majestic, that the little boys cried Hooray, and many people thought he must be a Governor-General. *He*, I promise, did not decline the obsequious invitation of the landlords to alight and refresh himself in the neat country towns. Having partaken of a copious breakfast, with fish, and rice, and hard eggs, at Southampton, he had so far rallied at Winchester as to think a glass of sherry necessary. At Alton he stepped out of the carriage, at his servant's request, and imbibed some of the ale for which the place is famous. At Farnham he stopped to view the Bishop's Castle, and to partake of a light dinner of stewed eels, veal cutlets, and French beans, with a bottle of claret. He was cold over Bagshot Heath, where the native chattered more and more, and Jos Sahib took some brandy-and-water; in fact, when he drove into town, he was as full of wine, beer, meat, pickles, cherry-brandy, and tobacco, as the steward's cabin of a steam-packet. It was evening when his carriage thundered up to the little door in Brompton, whither the affectionate fellow drove first, and before hieing to the apartments secured for him by Mr. Dobbin at the Slaughters'.

All the faces in the street were in the windows; the little maid-servant flew to the wicket-gate, the Mesdames Clapp looked out from the casement of the ornamented kitchen; Emmy, in a great flutter, was in the passage among the hats and coats, and old Sedley in the parlor inside, shaking all over. Jos descended from the post-chaise and down the creaking swaying steps in awful state, supported by the new valet from Southampton and the shuddering native, whose brown face was now livid with cold, and of the color of a turkey's gizzard. He created an immense sensation in the passage presently, where Mrs. and Miss Clapp, coming perhaps to listen at the parlor door, found Loll Jewab shaking upon the hall-bench under the coats, moaning in a strange piteous way, and showing his yellow eyeballs and white teeth.

For, you see, we have adroitly shut the door upon the meeting between Jos and the old father, and the poor little gentle sister inside. The old man was very much affected : so, of course, was his daughter : nor was Jos without feeling. In that long absence of ten years, the most selfish will think about home and early ties. Distance sanctifies both. Long brooding over those lost pleasures exaggerates their charm and sweetness. Jos was unaffectedly glad to see and shake the hand of his father, between whom and himself there had been a coolness — glad to see his little sister, whom he remembered so pretty and smiling, and pained at the alteration which time, grief, and misfortune had made in the shattered old man. Emmy had come out to the door in her black clothes and whispered to him of her mother's death, and not to speak of it to their father. There was no need of this caution, for the elder Sedley himself began immediately to speak of the event, and prattled about it, and wept over it plenteously. It shocked the Indian not a little, and made him think of himself less than the poor fellow was accustomed to do.

The result of the interview must have been very satisfactory, for when Jos had reascended his post-chaise, and had driven away to his hotel, Emmy embraced her father tenderly, appealing to him with an air of triumph, and asking the old man whether she did not always say that her brother had a good heart ?

Indeed, Joseph Sedley, affected by the humble position in which he found his relations, and in the

expansiveness and overflowing of heart occasioned
by the first meeting, declared that they should
never suffer want or discomfort any more, that he
was at home for some time at any rate, during
which his house and everything he had should be
theirs: and that Amelia would look very pretty at
the head of his table — until she would accept one
of her own.

She shook her head sadly, and had, as usual, recourse to the water-works   She knew what he meant.
She and her young confidante, Miss Mary, had talked
over the matter most fully, the very night of the
Major's visit: beyond which time the impetuous
Polly could not refrain from talking of the discovery
which she had made, and describing the start and
tremor of joy by which Major Dobbin betrayed him
self when Mr. Binny passed with his bride, and the
Major learned that he had no longer a rival to fear.
"Did n't you see how he shook all over when you
asked if he was married, and he said, 'Who told you
those lies?'   O Ma'am," Polly said, "he never kept
his eyes off you; and I 'm sure he 's grown gray
a-thinking of you."

But Amelia, looking up at her bed, over which hung
the portraits of her husband and son, told her young
protégée, never, never, to speak on that subject again;
that Major Dobbin had been her husband's dearest
friend, and her own and George's most kind and
affectionate guardian; that she loved him as a
brother — but that a woman who had been married
to such an angel as that, and she pointed to the wall,
could never think of any other union.   Poor Polly
sighed: she thought what she should do if young Mr.
Tomkins, at the surgery, who always looked at her so
at church, and who, by those mere aggressive glances

had put her timorous little heart into such a flutter that she was ready to surrender at once, — what she should do if he were to die? She knew he was consumptive, his cheeks were so red, and he was so uncommon thin in the waist.

Not that Emmy, being made aware of the honest Major's passion, rebuffed him in any way, or felt displeased with him. Such an attachment from so true and loyal a gentleman could make no woman angry. Desdemona was not angry with Cassio, though there is very little doubt she saw the Lieutenant's partiality for her (and I for my part believe that many more things took place in that sad affair than the worthy Moorish officer ever knew of); why, Miranda was even very kind to Caliban, and we may be pretty sure for the same reason. Not that she would encourage him in the least, — the poor uncouth monster — of course not. No more would Emmy by any means encourage her admirer, the Major. She would give him that friendly regard, which so much excellence and fidelity merited; she would treat him with perfect cordiality and frankness until he made his proposals; and *then* it would be time enough for her to speak, and to put an end to hopes which never could be realized.

She slept, therefore, very soundly that evening, after the conversation with Miss Polly, and was more than ordinarily happy, in spite of Jos's delaying. "I am glad he is not going to marry that Miss O'Dowd," she thought. "Colonel O'Dowd never could have a sister fit for such an accomplished man as Major William." Who was there amongst her little circle, who would make him a good wife? Not Miss Binny, she was too old and ill-tempered; Miss Osborne? — too old too. Little Polly was too young. Mrs. Osborne could not find anybody to suit the Major before she went to sleep.

However, when the postman made his appearance, the little party were put out of suspense by the receipt of a letter from Jos to his sister, who announced, that he felt a little fatigued after his voyage, and should not be able to move on that day, but that he would leave Southampton early the next morning, and be with his father and mother at evening. Amelia, as she read out the letter to her father, paused over the latter word; her brother, it was clear, did not know what had happened in the family. Nor could he; for the fact is that though the Major rightly suspected that his travelling companion never would be got into motion in so short a space as twenty-four hours, and would find some excuse for delaying, yet Dobbin had not written to Jos to inform him of the calamity which had befallen the Sedley family; being occupied in talking with Amelia until long after post-hour.

The same morning brought Major Dobbin a letter to the Slaughters' Coffee-house from his friend at Southampton; begging dear Dob to excuse Jos for being in a rage when awakened the day before (he had a confounded headache, and was just in his first sleep), and entreating Dob to engage comfortable rooms at the Slaughters' for Mr. Sedley and his servants. The Major had become necessary to Jos during the voyage. He was attached to him, and hung upon him. The other passengers were away to London. Young Ricketts and little Chaffers went away on the coach that day — Ricketts on the box, and taking the reins from Botley; the Doctor was off to his family at Portsea; Bragg gone to town to his co-partners: and the first mate busy in the unloading of the "Ramchunder." Mr. Jos was

very lonely at Southampton, and got the landlord of
the George to take a glass of wine with him that day;
at the very hour at which Major Dobbin was seated
at the table of his father, Sir William, where his sister found out (for it was impossible for the Major
to tell fibs) that he had been to see Mrs. George
Osborne.

Jos was so comfortably situated in St. Martin's
Lane, he could enjoy his hookah there with such perfect ease, and could swagger down to the theatres,
when minded, so agreeably, that, perhaps, he would
have remained altogether at the Slaughters' had not
his friend, the Major, been at his elbow. That gentleman would not let the Bengalee rest until he had executed his promise of having a home for Amelia and his
father. Jos was a soft fellow in anybody's hands;
Dobbin most active in anybody's concerns but his
own; the civilian was, therefore, an easy victim to
the guileless arts of this good-natured diplomatist, and
was ready to do, to purchase, hire, or relinquish whatever his friend thought fit. Loll Jewab, of whom the
boys about St. Martin's Lane used to make cruel fun
whenever he showed his dusky countenance in the
street, was sent back to Calcutta in the "Lady Kickle-
bury" East Indiaman, in which Sir William Dobbin
had a share; having previously taught Jos's European
the art of preparing curries, pilaus, and pipes. It was
a matter of great delight and occupation to Jos to superintend the building of a smart chariot, which he
and the Major ordered in the neighboring Long Acre:
and a pair of handsome horses were jobbed, with which
Jos drove about in state in the Park, or to call upon
his Indian friends. Amelia was not seldom by his
side on these excursions, when also Major Dobbin

would be seen in the back seat of the carriage. At other times old Sedley and his daughter took advantage of it: and Miss Clapp, who frequently accompanied her friend, had great pleasure in being recognized as she sat in the carriage, dressed in the famous yellow shawl, by the young gentleman at the surgery, whose face might commonly be seen over the window-blinds as she passed.

Shortly after Jos's first appearance at Brompton, a dismal scene, indeed, took place at that humble cottage, at which the Sedleys had passed the last ten years of their life. Jos's carriage (the temporary one, not the chariot under construction) arrived one day and carried off old Sedley and his daughter — to return no more. The tears that were shed by the landlady and the landlady's daughter at that event were as genuine tears of sorrow as any that have been outpoured in the course of this history. In their long acquaintanceship and intimacy they could not recall a harsh word that had been uttered by Amelia. She had been all sweetness and kindness, always thankful, always gentle, even when Mrs. Clapp lost her own temper, and pressed for the rent. When the kind creature was going away for good and all, the landlady reproached herself bitterly for ever having used a rough expression to her — how she wept, as they stuck up with wafers on the window, a paper notifying that the little rooms so long occupied were to let! They never would have such lodgers again, that was quite clear. After-life proved the truth of this melancholy prophecy: and Mrs. Clapp revenged herself for the deterioration of mankind by levying the most savage contributions upon the tea-caddies and legs of mutton of her *locataires*. Most of them scolded and grumbled; some of them did not pay: none of them stayed. The landlady might well regret those old, old friends, who had left her.

As for Miss Mary, her sorrow at Amelia's departure was such as I shall not attempt to depict. From childhood upwards she had been with her daily, and had attached herself so passionately to that dear good lady, that when the grand barouche came to carry her off into splendor, she fainted in the arms of her friend, who was indeed scarcely less affected than the good-natured girl. Amelia loved her like a daughter. During eleven years the girl had been her constant friend and associate. The separation was a very painful one indeed to her. But it was of course arranged that Mary was to come and stay often at the grand new house whither Mrs. Osborne was going; and where Mary was sure she would never be so happy as she had been in their humble cot, as Miss Clapp called it, in the language of the novels which she loved.

Let us hope she was wrong in her judgment. Poor Emmy's days of happiness had been very few in that humble cot. A gloomy Fate had oppressed her there. She never liked to come back to the house after she had left it, or to face the landlady who had tyrannized over her when ill-humored and unpaid, or when pleased had treated her with a coarse familiarity scarcely less odious. Her servility and fulsome compliments when Emmy was in prosperity were not more to that lady's liking. She cast about notes of admiration all over the new house, extolling every article of furniture or ornament; she fingered Mrs. Osborne's dresses, and calculated their price. Nothing could be too good for that sweet lady, she vowed and protested. But in the vulgar sycophant who now paid court to her, Emmy always remembered the coarse tyrant who had made her miserable many a time, to whom she had been forced to put up petitions for time, when the rent was overdue; who cried out at her extravagance if she bought delicacies for her ailing mother or father; who had seen her humble and trampled upon her.

Nobody ever heard of these griefs, which had been part of our poor little woman's lot in life. She kept them secret from her father, whose improvidence was the cause of much of her misery. She had to bear all the blame of his misdoings, and indeed was so utterly gentle and humble as to be made by nature for a victim.

I hope she is not to suffer much more of that hard usage. And, as in all griefs there is said to be some consolation, I may mention that poor Mary, when left at her friend's departure in a hysterical condition, was placed under the medical treatment of the young fellow from the surgery, under whose care she rallied after a short period. Emmy, when she went away from Brompton, endowed Mary with every article of furniture that the house contained: only taking away her pictures (the two pictures over the bed) and her piano — that little old piano which had now passed into a plaintive jingling old age, but which she loved for reasons of her own. She was a child when first she played on it: and her parents gave it her. It had been given to her again since, as the reader may remember, when her father's house was gone to ruin, and the instrument was recovered out of the wreck.

Major Dobbin was exceedingly pleased when, as he was superintending the arrangements of Jos's new house, which the Major insisted should be very handsome and comfortable, the cart arrived from

Brompton, bringing the trunks and band-boxes of the emigrants from that village, and with them the old piano. Amelia would have it up in her sitting-room, a neat little apartment on the second floor, adjoining her father's chamber: and where the old gentleman sat commonly of evenings.

When the men appeared, then, bearing this old music-box, and Amelia gave orders that it should be placed in the chamber aforesaid, Dobbin was quite elated. "I'm glad you've kept it," he said in a very sentimental manner. "I was afraid you didn't care about it."

"I value it more than anything I have in the world," said Amelia.

"*Do* you, Amelia?" cried the Major. The fact was, as he had bought it himself, though he never said anything about it, it never entered into his head to suppose that Emmy should think anybody else was the purchaser, and as a matter of course he fancied that she knew the gift came from him. "Do you, Amelia?" he said; and the question, the great question of all, was trembling on his lips, when Emmy replied —

"Can I do otherwise? — did not *he* give it me?"

"I did not know," said poor old Dob, and his countenance fell.

Emmy did not note the circumstance at the time, nor take immediate heed of the very dismal expression which honest Dobbin's countenance assumed; but she thought of it afterwards. And then it struck her, with inexpressible pain and mortification too, that it was William who was the giver of the piano; and not George, as she had fancied. It was not George's gift; the only one which she had received from her lover, as she thought — the thing she had cherished beyond all others — her dearest relic and prize. She had spoken to it about George; played his favorite airs upon it: sat for long evening hours, touching, to the best of her simple art, melancholy harmonies on the keys, and weeping over them in silence. It was not George's relic. It was valueless now. The next time that old Sedley asked her to play, she said it was shockingly out of tune, that she had a headache, that she could n't play.

Then, according to her custom, she rebuked herself for her pettishness and ingratitude, and determined to make a reparation to honest William for the slight she had not expressed to him, but had felt for his piano. A few days afterwards, as they were seated in the drawing-room, where Jos had fallen asleep with great comfort after dinner, Amelia said with rather a faltering voice to Major Dobbin, —

"I have to beg your pardon for something."

"About what?" said he.

"About — about that little square piano. I never thanked you for it when you gave it me; many, many years ago, before I was married. I thought somebody else had given it. Thank you, William." She held out her hand; but the poor little woman's heart was bleeding; and as for her eyes, of course they were at their work.

But William could hold no more. "Amelia, Amelia," he said, "I did buy it for you. I loved you then as I do now. I must tell you. I think I loved you from the first minute that I saw you, when George brought me to your house, to show me the Amelia whom he was engaged to. You were but a girl, in white, with large ringlets; you came down singing — do you remember? — and we went to Vauxhall. Since then I have thought of but one woman in the

world, and that was you. I think there is no hour in
the day has passed for twelve years that I have n't
thought of you. I came to tell you this before I
went to India, but you did not care, and I had n't the
heart to speak. You did not care whether I stayed
or went."

"I was very ungrateful," Amelia said.

"No; only indifferent," Dobbin continued desperately. "I have nothing to make a woman to be otherwise. I know what you are feeling now. You are
hurt in your heart at the discovery about the piano;
and that it came from me and not from George. I
forgot, or I should never have spoken of it so. It is
for me to ask your pardon for being a fool for a
moment, and thinking that years of constancy and
devotion might have pleaded with you."

"It is you who are cruel now," Amelia said with
some spirit. "George is my husband, here and in
heaven. How could I love any other but him? I am
his now as when you first saw me, dear William. It
was he who told me how good and generous you were,
and who taught me to love you as a brother. Have
you not been everything to me and my boy? Our
dearest, truest, kindest friend and protector? Had
you come a few months sooner perhaps you might
have spared me that — that dreadful parting. Oh, it
nearly killed me, William — but you did n't come,
though I wished and prayed for you to come, and
they took him too away from me. Is n't he a noble
boy, William? Be his friend still and mine" — and
here her voice broke, and she hid her face on his
shoulder.

The Major folded his arms round her, holding her
to him as if she was a child, and kissed her head. "I
will not change, dear Amelia," he said. "I ask for

no more than your love. I think I would not have it
otherwise. Only let me stay near you, and see you
often."

"Yes, often," Amelia said. And so William was at
liberty to look and long: as the poor boy at school
who has no money may sigh after the contents of the
tart-woman's tray.

CHAPTER VI.

RETURNS TO THE GENTEEL WORLD.

GOOD fortune now begins to smile upon Amelia. We are glad to get her out of that low sphere in which she has been creeping hitherto, and introduce her into a polite circle; not so grand and refined as that in which our other female friend, Mrs. Becky, has appeared, but still having no small pretensions to gentility and fashion. Jos's friends were all from the three presidencies, and his new house was in the comfortable Anglo-Indian district of which Moira Place is the centre. Minto Square, Great Clive Street, Warren Street, Hastings Street, Ochterlony Place, Plassy Square, Assaye Terrace ("Gardens" was a felicitous word not applied to stucco houses with asphalte terraces in front, so early as 1827) — who does not know these respectable abodes of the retired Indian aristocracy, and the quarter which Mr. Wenham calls the Black Hole, in a word? Jos's position in life was not grand enough to entitle him to a house in Moira Place, where none can live but retired Members of Council, and partners of Indian firms (who break after having settled a hundred thousand pounds on their wives, and retire into comparative penury to a country place and four thousand a-year): he engaged a comfortable house of a second or third-rate order in Gillespie Street, purchasing the carpets, costly mirrors, and handsome and appropriate planned furniture by Seddons, from the assignees of Mr.

Scape, lately admitted partner into the great Calcutta
House of Fogle, Fake, and Cracksman, in which poor
Scape had embarked seventy thousand pounds, the
earnings of a long and honorable life, taking Fake's
place, who retired to a princely Park in Sussex
(the Fogles have been long out of the firm, and Sir
Horace Fogle is about to be raised to the peerage as
Baron Bandanna) — admitted, I say, partner into the
great agency house of Fogle and Fake two years before it failed for a million, and plunged half the
Indian public into misery and ruin.

Scape, ruined, honest, and broken-hearted at sixty-
five years of age, went out to Calcutta to wind up
the affairs of the house. Walter Scape was withdrawn from Eton, and put into a merchant's house.
Florence Scape, Fanny Scape, and their mother faded
away to Boulogne, and will be heard of no more.
To be brief, Jos stepped in and bought their carpets
and sideboards, and admired himself in the mirrors
which had reflected their kind handsome faces. The
Scape tradesmen, all honorably paid, left their cards,
and were eager to supply the new household. The
large men in white waistcoats, who waited at Scape's
dinners, green-grocers, bank-porters, and milk-men in
their private capacity, left their addresses, and ingra-
tiated themselves with the butler. Mr. Chummy, the
chimney-purifier, who had swept the last three families, tried to coax the butler and the boy under
him, whose duty it was to go out covered with buttons and with stripes down his trousers, for the
protection of Mrs. Amelia whenever she chose to
walk abroad.

It was a modest establishment. The butler was
Jos's valet also, and never was more drunk than a
butler in a small family should be who has a proper

regard for his master's wine. Emmy was supplied
with a maid, grown on Sir William Dobbin's subur-
ban estate; a good girl, whose kindness and humility
disarmed Mrs. Osborne, who was at first terrified at
the idea of having a servant to wait upon herself,
who did not in the least know how to use one, and
who always spoke to domestics with the most rever-
ential politeness. But this maid was very useful in
the family, in dexterously tending old Mr. Sedley,
who kept almost entirely to his own quarter of the
house, and never mixed in any of the gay doings
which took place there.

Numbers of people came to see Mrs. Osborne.
Lady Dobbin and daughters were delighted at her
change of fortune, and waited upon her. Miss
Osborne from Russell Square came in her grand
chariot with the flaming hammercloth emblazoned
with the Leeds arms. Jos was reported to be immensely rich. Old Osborne had no objection that
Georgy should inherit his uncle's property as well
as his own. "Damn it, we will make a man of the
feller," he said; "and I'll see him in Parliament
before I die. *You* may go and see his mother, Miss
O., though I'll never set eyes on her:" and Miss
Osborne came. Emmy, you may be sure, was very
glad to see her, and so be brought nearer to George.
That young fellow was allowed to come much more
frequently than before to visit his mother. He
dined once or twice a week in Gillespie Street, and
bullied the servants and his relations there, just as
he did in Russell Square.

He was always respectful to Major Dobbin, however, and more modest in his demeanor when that
gentleman was present. He was a clever lad, and
afraid of the Major. George could not help admir-

ing his friend's simplicity, his good-humor, his various learning quietly imparted, his general love of truth and justice. He had met no such man as yet in the course of his experience, and he had an instinctive liking for a gentleman. He hung fondly by his god-father's side; and it was his delight to walk in the Parks and hear Dobbin talk. William told George about his father, about India and Waterloo, about everything but himself. When George was more than usully pert and conceited, the Major made jokes at him, which Mrs. Osborne thought very cruel. One day, taking him to the play, and the boy declining to go into the pit because it was vulgar, the Major took him to the boxes, left him there, and went down himself to the pit. He had not been seated there very long, before he felt an arm thrust under his, and a dandy little hand in a kid-glove squeezing his arm. George had seen the absurdity of his ways, and come down from the upper region. A tender laugh of benevolence lighted up old Dobbin's face and eyes as he looked at the repentant little prodigal. He loved the boy, as he did everything that belonged to Amelia. How charmed she was when she heard of this instance of George's goodness! Her eyes looked more kindly on Dobbin than they ever had done. She blushed, he thought, after looking at him so.

Georgy never tired of his praises of the Major to his mother. "I like him, Mamma, because he knows such lots of things; and he ain't like old Veal, who is always bragging and using such long words, don't you know? The chaps call him 'Longtail' at school. I gave him the name; ain't it capital? But Dob reads Latin like English, and French and that; and when we go out together he tells me stories about

my Papa, and never about himself; though I heard
Colonel Buckler, at Grandpapa's, say that he was
one of the bravest officers in the army, and had distinguished himself ever so much.   Grandpapa was
quite surprised, and said, ' *That* feller! why, I didn't
think he could say Bo to a goose' — but *I* know he
could, couldn't he, Mamma?"

Emmy laughed : she thought it was very likely the
Major could do thus much.

If there was a sincere liking between George and
the Major, it must be confessed that between the boy
and his uncle no great love existed.   George had got
a way of blowing out his cheeks, and putting his
hands in his waistcoat pockets, and saying, "God
bless my soul, you don't say so," so exactly after the
fashion of old Jos, that it was impossible to refrain
from laughter.   The servants would explode at dinner if the lad, asking for something, which wasn't at
table, put on that countenance and used that favorite
phrase.   Even Dobbin would shoot out a sudden peal
at the boy's mimicry.   If George did not mimic his
uncle to his face, it was only by Dobbin's rebukes and
Amelia's terrified entreaties that the little scapegrace
was induced to resist.   And the worthy civilian being
haunted by a dim consciousness that the lad thought
him an ass, and was inclined to turn him into ridicule, used to be extremely timorous and, of course,
doubly pompous and dignified in the presence of Master Georgy.   When it was announced that the young
gentleman was expected in Gillespie Street to dine
with his mother, Mr. Jos commonly found that he
had an engagement at the club.   Perhaps nobody
was much grieved at his absence.   On those days Mr.
Sedley would commonly be induced to come out from
his place of refuge in the upper stories; and there

would be a small family party, whereof Major Dobbin
pretty generally formed one. He was the *ami de la
maison ;* old Sedley's friend, Emmy's friend, Georgy's
friend, Jos's counsel and adviser. "He might almost
as well be at Madras for anything *we* see of him,"
Miss Ann Dobbin remarked, at Camberwell. Ah!
Miss Ann, did it not strike you that it was not *you*
whom the Major wanted to marry?

Joseph Sedley then led a life of dignified otiosity
such as became a person of his eminence. His very
first point, of course, was to become a member of the
Oriental Club: where he spent his mornings in the
company of his brother Indians, where he dined, or
whence he brought home men to dine.

Amelia had to receive and entertain these gentle-
men and their ladies. From these she heard how
soon Smith would be in Council; how many lacs
Jones had brought home with him, how Thomson's
House in London had refused the bills drawn by
Thomson, Kibobjee, and Co., the Bombay House, and
how it was thought the Calcutta House must go too:
how very imprudent, to say the least of it, Mrs.
Brown's conduct (wife of Brown of the Ahmednuggur
Irregulars) had been with young Swankey of the
Body Guard, sitting up with him on deck until all
hours, and losing themselves as they were riding out
at the Cape; how Mrs. Hardyman had had out her
thirteen sisters, daughters of a country curate, the
Rev. Felix Rabbits, and married eleven of them,
seven high up in the service; how Hornby was wild
because his wife would stay in Europe, and Trotter
was appointed Collector at Ummerapoora. This and
similar talk took place, at the grand dinners all
round. They had the same conversation; the same
silver dishes; the same saddles of mutton, boiled tur-

keys, and *entrées*. Politics set in a short time after dessert, when the ladies retired up stairs and talked about their complaints and their children.

Mutato nomine, it is all the same. Don't the barristers' wives talk about Circuit? — Don't the soldiers' ladies gossip about the Regiment? — don't the clergymen's ladies discourse about Sunday-schools, and who takes whose duty? — don't the very greatest ladies of all talk about that small clique of persons to whom they belong, and why should our Indian friends not have their own conversation? — only I admit it is slow for the laymen whose fate it sometimes is to sit by and listen.

Before long Emmy had a visiting-book, and was driving about regularly in a carriage, calling upon Lady Bludyer (wife of Major-General Sir Roger Bludyer, K.C.B., Bengal Army); Lady Huff, wife of Sir G. Huff, Bombay ditto; Mrs. Pice, the Lady of Pice the Director, etc. We are not long in using ourselves to changes in life. That carriage came round to Gillespie Street every day: that buttony boy sprang up and down from the box with Emmy's and Jos's visiting-cards; at stated hours Emmy and the carriage went for Jos to the club, and took him an airing; or, putting old Sedley into the vehicle, she drove the old man round the Regent's Park. The lady's-maid and the chariot, the visiting-book and the buttony page, became soon as familiar to Amelia as the humble routine of Brompton. She accommodated herself to one as to the other. If Fate had ordained that she should be a duchess, she would even have done that duty too. She was voted, in Jos's female society, rather a pleasing young person — not much in her, but pleasing, and that sort of thing.

The men, as usual, liked her artless kindness and

simple refined demeanor.   The gallant young Indian
dandies at home on furlough — immense dandies
these — chained and mustached — driving in tearing
cabs, the pillars of the theatres, living at West End
hotels, — nevertheless admired Mrs. Osborne, liked
to bow to her carriage in the Park, and to be admitted to have the honor of paying her a morning
visit.   Swankey of the Body Guard himself, that dangerous youth, and the greatest buck of all the Indian
army now on leave, was one day discovered by Major
Dobbin *tête-à-tête* with Amelia, and describing the
sport of pig-sticking to her with great humor and eloquence: and he spoke afterwards of a d—d King's
officer that's always hanging about the house — a
long, thin, queer-looking oldish fellow — a dry fellow
though, that took the shine out of a man in the
talking line.

Had the Major possessed a little more personal
vanity he would have been jealous of so dangerous a
young buck as that fascinating Bengal Captain.   But
Dobbin was of too simple and generous a nature to
have any doubts about Amelia.   He was glad that the
young men should pay her respect; and that others
should admire her.   Ever since her womanhood almost, had she not been persecuted and undervalued.
It pleased him to see how kindness brought out her
good qualities, and how her spirits gently rose with
her prosperity.   Any person who appreciated her paid
a compliment to the Major's good judgment — that is,
if a man may be said to have good judgment who is
under the influence of Love's delusion.

After Jos went to court, which we may be sure he
did as a loyal subject of his Sovereign (showing himself in his full court suit at the club, whither Dobbin

came to fetch him in a very shabby old uniform), he who had always been a stanch Loyalist and admirer of George IV., became such a tremendous Tory and pillar of the State, that he was for having Amelia to go to a Drawing-room too. He somehow had worked himself up to believe that he was implicated in the maintenance of the public welfare, and that the Sovereign would not be happy unless Jos Sedley and his family appeared to rally round him at St. James's.

Emmy laughed. "Shall I wear the family diamonds, Jos?" she said.

"I wish you would let me buy you some," thought the Major. "I should like to see any that were too good for you."

CHAPTER VII.

IN WHICH TWO LIGHTS ARE PUT OUT.

THERE came a day when the round of decorous pleasures and solemn gayeties in which Mr. Jos Sedley's family indulged, was interrupted by an event which happens in most houses. As you ascend the staircase of your house from the drawing towards the bed-room floors, you may have remarked a little arch in the wall right before you, which at once gives light to the stair which leads from the second story to the third (where the nursery and servants' chambers commonly are) and serves for another purpose of utility of which the undertaker's men can give you a notion. They rest the coffins upon that arch, or pass them through it so as not to disturb in any unseemly manner the cold tenant slumbering within the black arch.

That second-floor arch in a London house, looking up and down the well of the staircase, and commanding the main thoroughfare by which the inhabitants are passing; by which cook lurks down before daylight to scour her pots and pans in the kitchen; by which young master stealthily ascends, having left his boots in the hall, and let himself in after dawn from a jolly night at the club; down which Miss comes rustling in fresh ribbons and spreading muslins, brilliant and beautiful, and prepared for conquest and the ball; or Master Tommy slides, preferring the banisters for a mode of conveyance, and disdaining danger and the

stair ; down which the mother is fondly carried smiling
in her strong husband's arms, as he steps steadily step
by step, and followed by the monthly nurse, on the
day when the medical man has pronounced that the
charming patient may go down stairs ; up which John
lurks to bed, yawning with a sputtering tallow candle,
and to gather up before sunrise the boots which are
awaiting him in the passages ; — that stair, up or down
which babies are carried, old people are helped, guests
are marshalled to the ball, the parson walks to the
christening, the doctor to the sick-room, and the undertaker's men to the upper floor — what a memento
of Life, Death, and Vanity it is — that arch and
stair — if you choose to consider it, and sit on the
landing, looking up and down the well ! The doctor
will come up to us too for the last time there, my
friend in motley. The nurse will look in at the curtains, and you take no notice — and then she will fling
open the windows for a little, and let in the air. Then
they will pull down all the front blinds of the house
and live in the back rooms — then they will send for
the lawyer and other men in black, etc. — Your comedy and mine will have been played then, and we shall
be removed, oh how far, from the trumpets, and the
shouting, and the posture-making. If we are gentlefolks they will put hatchments over our late domicile,
with gilt cherubim, and mottoes stating that there is
" Quiet in Heaven." Your son will new furnish the
house, or perhaps let it, and go into a more modern
quarter ; your name will be among the " Members
Deceased," in the lists of your clubs next year. However much you may be mourned, your widow will like
to have her weeds neatly made — the cook will send
or come up to ask about dinner — the survivor will
soon bear to look at your picture over the mantel-

piece, which will presently be deposed from the place of honor, to make way for the portrait of the son who reigns.

Which of the dead are most tenderly and passionately deplored? Those who love the survivors the least, I believe. The death of a child occasions a passion of grief and frantic tears, such as your end, brother reader, will never inspire. The death of an infant which scarce knew you, which a week's absence from you would have caused to forget you, will strike you down more than the loss of your closest friend, or your first-born son — a man grown like yourself, with children of his own. We may be harsh and stern with Judah and Simeon — our love and pity gush out for Benjamin, the little one. And if you are old, as some reader of this may be or shall be — old and rich, or old and poor — you may one day be thinking for yourself — "These people are very good round about me; but they won't grieve too much when I am gone. I am very rich, and they want my inheritance — or very poor, and they are tired of supporting me."

The period of mourning for Mrs. Sedley's death was only just concluded, and Jos scarcely had had time to cast off his black and appear in the splendid waistcoats which he loved, when it became evident to those about Mr. Sedley, that another event was at hand, and that the old man was about to go seek for his wife in the dark land whither she had preceded him. "The state of my father's health," Jos Sedley solemnly remarked at the club, "prevents me from giving any *large* parties this season: but if you will come in quietly at half-past six, Chutney, my boy, and take a homely dinner with one or two of the old set — I shall be always glad to see you." So Jos and his acquaintances dined and drank their claret among themselves in silence; whilst the sands of life were running out in the old man's glass up stairs. The velvet-footed butler brought them their wine; and they composed themselves to a rubber after dinner: at which Major Dobbin would sometimes come and take a hand: and Mrs. Osborne would occasionally descend, when her patient above was settled for the night, and had commenced one of those lightly troubled slumbers which visit the pillow of old age.

The old man clung to his daughter during this sickness. He would take his broths and medicines from scarcely any other hand. To tend him became almost the sole business of her life. Her bed was placed close by the door which opened into his chamber, and she was alive at the slightest noise or disturbance from the couch of the querulous invalid. Though, to do him justice, he lay awake many an hour, silent and without stirring, unwilling to awaken his kind and vigilant nurse.

He loved his daughter with more fondness now, perhaps, than ever he had done since the days of her childhood. In the discharge of gentle offices and kind filial duties, this simple creature shone most especially. "She walks into the room as silently as a sunbeam," Mr. Dobbin thought, as he saw her passing in and out from her father's room; a cheerful sweetness lighting up her face as she moved to and fro, graceful and noiseless. When women are brooding over their children, or busied in a sick-room, who has not seen in their faces those sweet angelic beams of love and pity?

A secret feud of some years' standing was thus healed: and with a tacit reconciliation. In these last hours, and touched by her love and goodness, the old man forgot all his grief against her, and wrongs which he and his wife had many a long night debated: how she had given up everything for her boy: how she was careless of her parents in their old age and misfortune, and only thought of the child: how absurdly and foolishly, impiously indeed, she took on, when George was removed from her. Old Sedley forgot these charges as he was making up his last account, and did justice to the gentle and uncomplaining little martyr. One night when she stole into his room, she found him awake, when the broken old man made his confession. "Oh, Emmy, I've been thinking we were very unkind and unjust to you," he said, and put out his cold and feeble hand to her. She knelt down and prayed by his bedside, as he did too, having still hold of her hand. When our turn comes, friend, may we have such company in our prayers.

Perhaps as he was lying awake then, his life may have passed before him — his early hopeful struggles, his manly successes and prosperity, his downfall in his declining years, and his present helpless condition — no chance of revenge against Fortune, which had had the better of him — neither name nor money to bequeath — a spent-out, bootless life of defeat and disappointment, and the end here! Which, I wonder, brother reader, is the better lot, to die prosperous and famous, or poor and disappointed? To have, and to be forced to yield; or to sink out of life, having played and lost the game? That must be a strange feeling, when a day of our life comes and we say, "*To-morrow*, success or failure won't matter much: and the sun will rise, and all the myriads of mankind go to their work or their pleasure as usual, but I shall be out of the turmoil."

So there came one morning and sunrise, when all

the world got up and set about its various works and
pleasures, with the exception of old John Sedley, who
was not to fight with fortune, or to hope or scheme
any more : but to go and take up a quiet and utterly
unknown residence in a churchyard at Brompton by
the side of his old wife.

Major Dobbin, Jos, and Georgy followed his remains
to the grave, in a black cloth coach. Jos came on
purpose from the Star and Garter at Richmond,
whither he retreated after the deplorable event. He
did not care to remain in the house, with the — under
the circumstances, you understand. But Emmy
stayed and did her duty as usual. She was bowed
down by no especial grief, and rather solemn than
sorrowful. She prayed that her own end might be as
calm and painless, and thought with trust and rever-
erence of the words which she had heard from her
father during his illness, indicative of his faith, his
resignation, and his future hope.

Yes, I think that will be the better ending of the
two, after all. Suppose you are particularly rich and
well-to-do, and say on that last day, "I am very rich ; I
am tolerably well known ; I have lived all my life in
the best society, and thank Heaven, come of a most
respectable family. I have served my King and
country with honor. I was in Parliament for several
years, where, I may say, my speeches were listened to,
and pretty well received. I don't owe any man a
shilling : on the contrary, I lent my old college friend,
Jack Lazarus, fifty pounds, for which my executors
will not press him. I leave my daughters with ten
thousand pounds apiece — very good portions for girls :
I bequeath my plate and furniture, my house in Baker
Street, with a handsome jointure, to my widow for
her life; and my landed property, besides money in

the funds, and my cellar of well-selected wine in Baker Street, to my son. I leave twenty pound a-year to my valet; and I defy any man after I am gone to find anything against my character." Or suppose, on the other hand, your swan sings quite a different sort of dirge, and you say, "I am a poor blighted, disappointed old fellow, and have made an utter failure through life. I was not endowed either with brains or with good fortune: and confess that I have committed a hundred mistakes and blunders. I own to having forgotten my duty many a time. I can't pay what I owe. On my last bed I lie utterly helpless and humble: and I pray forgiveness for my weakness, and throw myself with a contrite heart, at the feet of the Divine Mercy." Which of these two speeches, think you, would be the best oration for your own funeral? Old Sedley made the last; and in that humble frame of mind, and holding by the hand of his daughter, life and disappointment and vanity sank away from under him.

"You see," said old Osborne to George, "what comes of merit and industry, and judicious speculations, and that. Look at me and my banker's account. Look at your poor grandfather, Sedley, and his failure. And yet he was a better man than I was, this day twenty years — a better man, I should say, by ten thousand pound."

Beyond these people and Mr. Clapp's family, who came over from Brompton to pay a visit of condolence, not a single soul alive ever cared a penny piece about old John Sedley, or remembered the existence of such a person.

When old Osborne first heard from his friend Colonel Buckler (as little Georgy has already informed us) how distinguished an officer Major Dobbin was, he exhibited a great deal of scornful incredulity, and expressed his surprise how ever such a feller as that should possess either brains or reputation. But he heard of the Major's fame from various members of his society. Sir William Dobbin had a great opinion of his son, and narrated many stories illustrative of the Major's learning, valor, and estimation in the world's opinion. Finally, his name appeared in the lists of one or two great parties of the nobility; and this circumstance had a prodigious effect upon the old aristocrat of Russell Square.

The Major's position as guardian to Georgy, whose possession had been ceded to his grandfather, rendered some meetings between the two gentlemen inevitable; and it was in one of these that old Osborne, a keen man of business, looking into the Major's accounts with his ward and the boy's mother, got a hint which staggered him very much, and at once pained and pleased him, that it was out of William Dobbin's own pocket that a part of the fund had been supplied upon which the poor widow and the child had subsisted.

When pressed upon the point, Dobbin, who could not tell lies, blushed and stammered a good deal, and finally confessed. "The marriage," he said (at which his interlocutor's face grew dark), "was very much my doing. I thought my poor friend had gone so far, that retreat from his engagement would have been dishonor to him, and death to Mrs. Osborne; and I could do no less, when she was left without resources, than give what money I could spare to maintain her."

"Major D.," Mr. Osborne said, looking hard at him, and turning very red too — "you did me a great injury; but give me leave to tell you, sir, you are an honest feller. There's my hand, sir, though I little thought that my flesh and blood was living on you—" and the pair shook hands, with great confusion on Major Dobbin's part, thus found out in his act of charitable hypocrisy.

He strove to soften the old man, and reconcile him towards his son's memory. "He was such a noble fellow," he said, "that all of us loved him, and would have done anything for him. I, as a young man in those days, was flattered beyond measure by his preference for me; and was more pleased to be seen in his company than in that of the Commander-in-Chief. I never saw his equal for pluck and daring, and all the qualities of a soldier;" and Dobbin told the old father as many stories as he could remember regarding the gallantry and achievements of his son. "And Georgy is so like him," the Major added.

"He's so like him that he makes me tremble sometimes," the grandfather said.

On one or two evenings the Major came to dine with Mr. Osborne (it was during the time of the sickness of Mr. Sedley), and as the two sat together in the evening after dinner all their talk was about the departed hero. The father boasted about him according to his wont, glorifying himself in recounting his son's feats and gallantry, but his mood was at any rate better and more charitable than that in which he had been disposed until now to regard the poor fellow; and the Christian heart of the kind Major was pleased at these symptoms of returning peace and good will. On the second evening old Osborne called Dobbin, William, just as he used to do at the time when Dobbin and George were boys together: and the honest gentleman was pleased by that mark of reconciliation.

On the next day at breakfast when Miss Osborne, with the asperity of her age and character, ventured to make some remark reflecting slightingly upon the Major's appearance or behavior — the master of the house interrupted her. "You'd have been glad enough to git him for yourself, Miss O. But them grapes are sour. Ha! ha! Major William is a fine feller."

"That he is, Grandpapa," said Georgy, approvingly: and going up close to the old gentleman he took a hold of his large gray whiskers, and laughed in his face good-humoredly and kissed him. And he told the story at night to his mother: who fully agreed with the boy. "Indeed he is," she said. "Your dear father always said so. He is one of the best and most upright of men." Dobbin happened to drop in very soon after this conversation, which made Amelia blush perhaps: and the young scapegrace increased the confusion by telling Dobbin the other part of the story. "I say, Dob," he said, "there's such an uncommon nice girl wants to marry you. She's plenty of tin: she wears a front: and she scolds the servants from morning till night." "Who is it?" asked Dobbin.

"It's aunt O.," the boy answered. "Grandpapa said so. And I say, Dob, how prime it would be to have you for my uncle." Old Sedley's quavering voice from the next room at this moment weakly called for Amelia and the laughing ended.

That old Osborne's mind was changing, was pretty clear. He asked George about his uncle sometimes, and laughed at the boy's imitation of the way in which Jos said, "God bless my soul," and gobbled his soup. Then he said, "It's not respectful, sir, of you younkers to be imitating of your relations. Miss O., when you go out a-driving to-day, leave my card upon Mr.

Sedley, do you hear? There's no quarrel betwigst me and him anyhow."

The card was returned, and Jos and the Major were asked to dinner, — to a dinner the most splendid and stupid that perhaps ever Mr. Osborne gave; every inch of the family plate was exhibited, and the best company was asked. Mr. Sedley took down Miss O. to dinner, and she was very gracious to him; whereas she hardly spoke to the Major, who sat apart from her, and by the side of Mr. Osborne, very timid. Jos said, with great solemnity, it was the best turtle soup he had ever tasted in his life; and asked Mr. Osborne where he got his Madeira?

"It is some of Sedley's wine," whispered the butler to his master. "I've had it a long time, and paid a good figure for it too," Mr. Osborne said aloud to his guest; and then whispered to his right-hand neighbor how he had got it "at the old chap's sale."

More than once he asked the Major about — about Mrs. George Osborne — a theme on which the Major could be very eloquent when he chose. He told Mr. Osborne of her sufferings — of her passionate attachment to her husband, whose memory she worshipped still — of the tender and dutiful manner in which she had supported her parents, and given up her boy, when it seemed to her her duty to do so. "You don't know what she endured, sir," said honest Dobbin with a tremor in his voice; "and I hope and trust you will be reconciled to her. If she took your son away from you, she gave hers to you; and however much you loved your George, depend on it, she loved hers ten times more."

"By God, you are a good feller, sir," was all Mr. Osborne said. It had never struck him that the widow would feel any pain at parting from the boy, or that his having a fine fortune could grieve her. A reconciliation was announced as speedy and inevitable; and Amelia's heart already began to beat at the notion of the awful meeting with George's father.

It was never, however, destined to take place. Old Sedley's lingering illness and death supervened, after which a meeting was for some time impossible. That catastrophe and other events may have worked upon Mr. Osborne. He was much shaken of late, and aged, and his mind was working inwardly. He had sent for his lawyers, and probably changed something in his will. The medical man who looked in, pronounced him shaky, agitated, and talked of a little blood and the sea-side; but he took neither of these remedies.

One day when he should have come down to breakfast, his servant missing him, went into his dressing-room and found him lying at the foot of the dressing-table in a fit. Miss Osborne was apprised; the doctors were sent for, Georgy stopped away from school; the bleeders and cuppers came. Osborne partially regained cognizance; but never could speak again, though he tried dreadfully once or twice, and in four days he died. The doctors went down, and the undertaker's men went up the stairs; and all the shutters were shut towards the garden in Russell Square. Bullock rushed from the city in a hurry. "How much money had he left to that boy? — not half, surely? Surely share and share alike between the three?" It was an agitating moment.

What was it that poor old man tried once or twice in vain to say? I hope it was that he wanted to see Amelia, and be reconciled before he left the world to the dear and faithful wife of his son: it was most likely that; for his will showed that the hatred which he had so long cherished had gone out of his heart.

They found in the pocket of his dressing-gown the letter with the great red seal, which George had written him from Waterloo. He had looked at the other papers too, relative to his son, for the key of the box in which he kept them was also in his pocket, and it was found the seals and envelopes had been broken — very likely on the night before the seizure — when the butler had taken him tea into his study, and found him reading in the great red family Bible.

When the will was opened, it was found that half the property was left to George, and the remainder between the two sisters. Mr. Bullock to continue, for their joint benefit, the affairs of the commercial house, or to go out, as he thought fit. An annuity of five hundred pounds, chargeable on George's property, was left to his mother, "the widow of my beloved son, George Osborne," who was to resume the guardianship of the boy.

"Major William Dobbin, my beloved son's friend," was appointed executor; "and as out of his kindness and bounty, and with his own private funds, he maintained my grandson and my son's widow, when they were otherwise without means of support" (the testator went on to say), "I hereby thank him heartily for his love and regard for them: and beseech him to accept such a sum as may be sufficient to purchase his commission as a Lieutenant-Colonel, or to be disposed of in any way he may think fit."

When Amelia heard that her father-in-law was reconciled to her, her heart melted, and she was grateful for the fortune left to her. But when she heard how Georgy was restored to her, and knew how and by whom, and how it was William's bounty that supported her in poverty, how it was William who gave her her husband and her son — oh, then she sank on her knees, and prayed for blessings on that constant and kind heart. She bowed down and humbled herself, and kissed the feet, as it were, of that beautiful and generous affection.

And gratitude was all that she had to pay back for such admirable devotion and benefits — only gratitude! If she thought of any other return, the image of George stood up out of the grave, and said, "You are mine, and mine only, now and forever."

William knew her feelings: had he not passed his whole life in divining them?

When the nature of Mr. Osborne's will became known to the world, it was edifying to remark how Mrs. George Osborne rose in the estimation of the people forming her circle of acquaintance. The servants of Jos's establishment, who used to question her humble orders, and say they would "ask Master," whether or not they could obey, never thought now of that sort of appeal. The cook forgot to sneer at her shabby old gowns (which, indeed, were quite eclipsed by that lady's finery when she was dressed to go to church of a Sunday evening), the others no longer grumbled at the sound of her bell, or delayed to answer that summons. The coachman, who grumbled that his 'osses should be brought out, and his carriage made into an hospital for that old feller and Mrs. O., drove her with the utmost alacrity now, and trembling lest he should be superseded by Mr. Osborne's coachman, asked "what them there Russell Square coachmen knew about town, and whether *they* was fit to sit on a box before a lady?" Jos's friends, male and female, suddenly became interested about Emmy, and cards of condolence multiplied on her hall table. Jos himself, who had looked on her as a good-natured harmless pauper, to whom it was his duty to give victuals and shelter, paid her and the rich little boy, his nephew, the greatest respect — was anxious that she should have change and amusement after her troubles and trials, "poor dear girl" — and began to appear at the breakfast-table, and most particularly to ask how she would like to dispose of the day.

In her capacity of guardian to Georgy, she, with the consent of the Major, her fellow-trustee, begged Miss Osborne to live in the Russell Square house as long as ever she chose to dwell there; but that lady, with thanks, declared that she never could think of remaining alone in that melancholy mansion, and departed in deep mourning to Cheltenham, with a couple of her old domestics. The rest were liberally paid and dismissed; the faithful old butler, whom Mrs. Osborne proposed to retain, resigning and preferring to invest his savings in a public-house, where, let us hope, he was not unprosperous. Miss Osborne not choosing to live in Russell Square, Mrs. Osborne also, after consultation, declined to occupy the gloomy old mansion there. The house was dismantled; the rich furniture and effects, the awful chandeliers and dreary blank mirrors packed away and hidden, the rich rosewood drawing-room suite was muffled in straw, the carpets were rolled up and corded, the small select library of well-bound books was stowed into two wine-chests, and the whole paraphernalia rolled away in several enormous vans to the Pantechnicon, where they were to lie until Georgy's majority. And the great heavy dark plate-chests went off to Messrs. Stumpy and Rowdy, to lie in the cellars of those eminent bankers until the same period should arrive.

One day Emmy with George in her hand and clad in deep sables went to visit the deserted mansion which she had not entered since she was a girl. The

place in front was littered with straw where the vans
had been laden and rolled off. They went into the
great blank rooms, the walls of which bore the marks
where the pictures and mirrors had hung.   Then they
went up the great blank stone staircases into the upper
rooms, into that where grandpapa died, as George said
in a whisper, and then higher still into George's own
room. The boy was still clinging by her side, but she
thought of another besides him.   She knew that it had
been his father's room as well as his own.

She went up to one of the open windows (one of
those at which she used to gaze with a sick heart when
the child was first taken from her), and thence as she
looked out she could see, over the trees of Russell
Square, the old house in which she herself was born,
and where she had passed so many happy days of sacred
youth.   They all came back to her, the pleasant holidays, the kind faces, the careless, joyful past times :
and the long pains and trials that had since cast her
down.   She thought of these and of the man who had
been her constant protector, her good genius, her sole
benefactor, her tender and generous friend.

"Look here, mother," said Georgy, "here 's a G. O.
scratched on the glass with a diamond; I never saw it
before, *I* never did it."

"It was your father's room long before you were
born, George," she said, and she blushed as she kissed
the boy.

She was very silent as they drove back to Richmond
where they had taken a temporary house : where the
smiling lawyers used to come bustling over to see her
(and we may be sure noted the visit in the bill) : and
where of course there was a room for Major Dobbin
too, who rode over frequently, having much business
to transact on behalf of his little ward.

Georgy at this time was removed from Mr. Veal's on an unlimited holiday, and that gentleman was engaged to prepare an inscription for a fine marble slab, to be placed up in the Foundling under the monument of Captain George Osborne.

The female Bullock, aunt of Georgy, although despoiled by that little monster of one half of the sum which she expected from her father, nevertheless showed her charitableness of spirit by being reconciled to the mother and the boy. Roehampton is not far from Richmond, and one day the chariot, with the golden bullocks emblazoned on the panels, and the flaccid children within, drove to Amelia's house at Richmond; and the Bullock family made an irruption into the garden, where Amelia was reading a book, Jos was in an arbor placidly dipping strawberries into wine, and the Major in one of his Indian jackets was giving a back to Georgy, who chose to jump over him. He went over his head, and bounded into the little advance of Bullocks, with immense black bows in their hats, and huge black sashes, accompanying their mourning mamma.

"He is just of the age for Rosa," the fond parent thought, and glanced towards that dear child, an unwholesome little Miss of seven years of age.

"Rosa, go and kiss your dear cousin," Mrs. Frederick said. "Don't you know me, George? — I am your aunt."

"*I* know you well enough," George said; "but I don't like kissing, please;" and he retreated from the obedient caresses of his cousin.

"Take me to your dear mamma, you droll child," Mrs. Frederick said; and those ladies accordingly met, after an absence of more than fifteen years.

During Emmy's cares and poverty the other had
never once thought about coming to see her; but now
that she was decently prosperous in the world, her
sister-in-law came to her as a matter of course.

So did numbers more. Our old friend, Miss Swartz,
and her husband came thundering over from Hampton
Court, with flaming yellow liveries, and was as im-
petuously fond of Amelia as ever. Miss Swartz
would have liked her always if she could have seen
her. One must do her that justice. But, *que voulez
vous?* — in this vast town one has not the time to go
and seek one's friends; if they drop out of the rank
they disappear, and we march on without them.
Who is ever missed in Vanity Fair.

But so, in a word, and before the period of grief
for Mr. Osborne's death had subsided, Emmy found
herself in the centre of a very genteel circle indeed;
the members of which could not conceive that anybody belonging to it was not very lucky. There was
scarce one of the ladies that had n't a relation a peer,
though the husband might be a drysalter in the City.
Some of the ladies were very blue and well informed;
reading Mrs. Somerville, and frequenting the Royal
Institution; others were severe and Evangelical, and
held by Exeter Hall. Emmy, it must be owned,
found herself entirely at a loss in the midst of their
clavers, and suffered wofully on the one or two occasions on which she was compelled to accept Mrs.
Frederick Bullock's hospitalities. That lady persisted
in patronizing her, and determined most graciously
to form her. She found Amelia's milliners for her,
and regulated her household and her manners. She
drove over constantly from Roehampton, and entertained her friend with faint fashionable fiddlefaddle
and feeble court slipslop. Jos liked to hear it, but

the Major used to go off growling at the appearance
of this woman, with her twopenny gentility. He
went to sleep under Frederick Bullock's bald head,
after dinner, at one of the banker's best parties,
(Fred was still anxious that the balance of the Osborne property should be transferred from Stumpy
and Rowdy's to them), and whilst Amelia, who did
not know Latin, or who wrote the last crack article
in the Edinburgh, and did not in the least deplore,
or otherwise, Mr. Peel's late extraordinary tergiver-
sation on the fatal Catholic Relief Bill, sat dumb
amongst the ladies in the grand drawing-room, looking out upon velvet lawns, trim gravel walks, and
glistening hot-houses.

"She seems good-natured but insipid," said Mrs.
Rowdy; "that Major seems to be particularly *épris.*"

"She wants *ton* sadly," said Mrs. Hollyock. "My
dear creature, you never will be able to form her."

"She is dreadfully ignorant or indifferent," said
Mrs. Glowry, with a voice as if from the grave, and
a sad shake of the head and turban. — "I asked her
if she thought that it was in 1836, according to Mr.
Jowls, or in 1839, according to Mr. Wapshot, that the
Pope was to fall: and she said — 'Poor Pope! I
hope not. — What has he done?'"

"She is my brother's widow, my dear friends,"
Mrs. Frederick replied, "and as such I think we're
all bound to give her every attention and instruction
on entering into the world. You may fancy there
can be no *mercenary* motives in those whose *disappointments* are well known."

"That poor dear Mrs. Bullock," said Rowdy to
Hollyock, as they drove away together — "she is
always scheming and managing. She wants Mrs.
Osborne's account to be taken from our house to hers

— and the way in which she coaxes that boy, and makes him sit by that blear-eyed little Rosa, is perfectly ridiculous."

"I wish Glowry was choked with her 'Man of Sin' and her 'Battle of Armageddon,'" cried the other; and the carriage rolled away over Putney Bridge.

But this sort of society was too cruelly genteel for Emmy: and all jumped for joy when a foreign tour was proposed.

CHAPTER . VIII.

AM RHEIN.

THE above every-day events had occurred, and a few weeks had passed, when, on one fine morning, Parliament being over, the summer advanced, and all the good company in London about to quit that city for their annual tour in search of pleasure or health, the 'Batavier' steamboat left the Tower-stairs laden with a goodly company of English fugitives. The quarter-deck awnings were up, and the benches and gangways crowded with scores of rosy children, bustling nurse-maids, ladies in the prettiest pink bonnets and summer dresses, gentlemen in travelling caps and linen jackets, whose mustachios had just begun to sprout for the ensuing tour; and stout trim old veterans with starched neckcloths and neat-brushed hats, such as have invaded Europe any time since the conclusion of the war, and carry the national Goddem into every city of the Continent. The congregation of hat-boxes, and Bramah desks, and dressing-cases was prodigious. There were jaunty young Cambridge-men travelling with their tutor, and going for a reading excursion to Nonnenwerth or Königswinter: there were Irish gentlemen, with the most dashing whiskers and jewelry, talking about horses incessantly, and prodigiously polite to the young ladies on board, whom, on the contrary, the Cambridge lads and their pale-faced tutor avoided with maiden coyness: there were old Pall Mall loungers bound for Ems and Wiesbaden, and a course of waters to clear off the dinners of the season,

and a little *roulette* and *trente-et-quarante* to keep the
excitement going; there was old Methuselah, who had
married his young wife, with Captain Papillon of the
Guards holding her parasol and guide-books: there
was young May who was carrying off his bride on a
pleasure tour (Mrs. Winter that was, and who had
been at school with May's grandmother); there was
Sir John and my lady with a dozen children, and
corresponding nursemaids; and the great grandee
Bareacres family that sat by themselves near the
wheel, stared at everybody, and spoke to no one.
Their carriages, emblazoned with coronets, and heaped
with shining imperials, were on the fore-deck; locked
in with a dozen more such vehicles: it was difficult to
pass in and out amongst them: and the poor inmates
of the fore-cabin had scarcely any space for locomo-
tion. These consisted of a few magnificently attired
gentlemen from Houndsditch, who brought their own
provisions, and could have bought half the gay people
in the grand saloon; a few honest fellows with mustachios and portfolios, who set to sketching before
they had been half an hour on board; one or two
French *femmes de chambre* who began to be dreadfully
ill by the time the boat had passed Greenwich; a
groom or two who lounged in the neighborhood of the
horse-boxes under their charge, or leaned over the
side by the paddle-wheels, and talked about who was
good for the Leger, and what they stood to win or
lose for the Goodwood cup.

All the couriers, when they had done plunging
about the ship, and had settled their various masters
in the cabins or on the deck, congregated together
and began to chatter and smoke; the Hebrew gentlemen joining them and looking at the carriages. There
was Sir John's great carriage that would hold thirteen

people; my Lord Methuselah's carriage, my Lord Bareacres's chariot, britzska, and *fourgon*, that anybody might pay for who liked. It was a wonder how my lord got the ready money to pay for the expenses of the journey. The Hebrew gentlemen knew how he got it. They knew what money his lordship had in his pocket at that instant, and what interest he paid for it, and who gave it him. Finally there was a very neat, handsome travelling carriage, about which the gentlemen speculated.

"*A qui cette voiture là?*" said one gentleman-courier with a large morocco money-bag and ear-rings, to another with ear-rings and a large morocco money-bag.

"*C'est à Kirsch je bense — je l'ai vu toute à l'heure — qui brenoit des sangviches dans la voiture,*" said the courier in a fine German French.

Kirsch emerging presently from the neighborhood of the hold, where he had been bellowing instructions intermingled with polyglot oaths to the ship's men engaged in secreting the passengers' luggage, came to give an account of himself to his brother interpreters. He informed them that the carriage belonged to a Nabob from Calcutta and Jamaica, enormously rich, and with whom he was engaged to travel; and at this moment a young gentleman who had been warned off the bridge between the paddle-boxes, and who had dropped thence on to the roof of Lord Methuselah's carriage, from which he made his way over other carriages and imperials until he had clambered on to his own, descended thence and through the window into the body of the carriage to the applause of the couriers looking on.

"*Nous allons avoir une belle traversée,* Monsieur George," said the courier with a grin, as he lifted his gold-laced cap.

"D—— your French," said the young gentleman, "where's the biscuits, ay?" Whereupon, Kirsch answered him in the English language or in such an imitation of it as he could command, — for though he was familiar with all languages, Mr. Kirsch was not acquainted with a single one, and spoke all with indifferent volubility and incorrectness.

The imperious young gentleman who gobbled the biscuits (and indeed it was time to refresh himself, for he had breakfasted at Richmond full three hours before), was our young friend George Osborne. Uncle Jos and his mamma were on the quarter-deck with a gentleman of whom they used to see a good deal, and the four were about to make a summer tour.

Jos was seated at that moment on deck under the awning, and pretty nearly opposite to the Earl of Bareacres and his family, whose proceedings absorbed the Bengalee almost entirely. Both the noble couple looked rather younger than in the eventful year '15, when Jos remembered to have seen them at Brussels (indeed he always gave out in India that he was intimately acquainted with them). Lady Bareacres's hair which was then dark was now a beautiful golden auburn, whereas Lord Bareacres's whiskers, formerly red, were at present of a rich black with purple and green reflections in the light. But changed as they were, the movements of the noble pair occupied Jos's mind entirely. The presence of a lord fascinated him, and he could look at nothing else.

"Those people seem to interest you a good deal," said Dobbin, laughing and watching him. Amelia too laughed. She was in a straw bonnet with black ribbons, and otherwise dressed in mourning: but the little bustle and holiday of the journey pleased and excited her, and she looked particularly happy.

A fine Summer Evening.

"What a heavenly day!" Emmy said, and added, with great originality, "I hope we shall have a calm passage."

Jos waved his hand, scornfully glancing at the same time under his eyelids at the great folks opposite. "If you had made the voyages we have," he said, "you wouldn't much care about the weather." But nevertheless, traveller as he was, he passed the night direfully sick in his carriage, where his courier tended him with brandy-and-water and every luxury.

In due time this happy party landed at the quays of Rotterdam, whence they were transported by another steamer to the city of Cologne. Here the carriage and the family took to the shore, and Jos was not a little gratified to see his arrival announced in the Cologne newspapers as "Herr Graf Lord von Sedley nebst Begleitung aus London." He had his court dress with him: he had insisted that Dobbin should bring his regimental paraphernalia: he announced that it was his intention to be presented at some foreign courts, and pay his respects to the sovereigns of the countries which he honored with a visit.

Wherever the party stopped, and an opportunity was offered, Mr. Jos left his own card and the Major's upon "Our Minister." It was with great difficulty that he could be restrained from putting on his cocked hat and tights to wait upon the English consul at the Free City of Judenstadt, when that hospitable functionary asked our travellers to dinner. He kept a journal of his voyage, and noted elaborately the defects or excellences of the various inns at which he put up, and of the wines and dishes of which he partook.

As for Emmy, she was very happy and pleased. Dobbin used to carry about for her her stool and

sketch-book, and admired the drawings of the good-
natured little artist, as they never had been admired
before. She sat upon steamers' decks and drew crags
and castles, or she mounted upon donkeys and ascended to ancient robber-towers, attended by her two
aides-de-camp, Georgy and Dobbin. She laughed, and
the Major did too, at his droll figure on donkey-back,
with his long legs touching the ground. He was the
interpreter for the party, having a good military
knowledge of the German language ; and he and the
delighted George fought the campaigns of the Rhine
and the Palatinate. In the course of a few weeks, and
by assiduously conversing with Herr Kirsch on the
box of the carriage, Georgy made prodigious advance
in the knowledge of High Dutch, and could talk to
hotel waiters and postilions in a way that charmed
his mother, and amused his guardian.

Mr. Jos did not much engage in the afternoon
excursions of his fellow-travellers. He slept a good
deal after dinner, or basked in the arbors of the
pleasant inn-gardens. Pleasant Rhine gardens ! Fair
scenes of peace and sunshine — noble purple mountains, whose crests are reflected in the magnificent
stream — who has ever seen you, that has not a grateful memory of those scenes of friendly repose and
beauty ? To lay down the pen, and even to think of
that beautiful Rhineland makes one happy. At this
time of summer evening, the cows are trooping down
from the hills, lowing and with their bells tinkling,
to the old town, with its old moats, and gates, and
spires, and chestnut-trees, with long blue shadows
stretching over the grass ; the sky and the river below
flame in crimson and gold ; and the moon is already
out, looking pale towards the sunset. The sun sinks
behind the great castle-crested mountains, the night

falls suddenly, the river grows darker and darker, lights quiver in it from the windows in the old ramparts, and twinkle peacefully in the villages under the hills on the opposite shore.

So Jos used to go to sleep a good deal with his bandanna over his face and be very comfortable, and read all the English news, and every word of Galignani's admirable newspaper (may the blessings of all Englishmen who have ever been abroad rest on the founders and proprietors of that piratical print!) and whether he woke or slept his friends did not very much miss him. Yes, they were very happy. They went to the Opera often of evenings — to those snug, unassuming, dear old operas in the German towns, where the *noblesse* sits and cries, and knits stockings on the one side, over against the *bourgeoisie* on the other; and His Transparency the Duke and his Transparent family, all very fat and good-natured, come and occupy the great box in the middle; and the pit is full of the most elegant slim-waisted officers with straw-colored mustachios, and twopence a-day on full pay. Here it was that Emmy found her delight, and was introduced for the first time to the wonders of Mozart and Cimarosa. The Major's musical taste has been before alluded to, and his performances on the flute commended. But perhaps the chief pleasure he had in these operas was in watching Emmy's rapture while listening to them. A new world of love and beauty broke upon her when she was introduced to those divine compositions: this lady had the keenest and finest sensibility, and how could she be indifferent when she heard Mozart? The tender parts of "Don Juan" awakened in her raptures so exquisite that she would ask herself when she went to say her prayers of a night, whether it was not wicked to feel so much delight as that with which "Vedrai Carino" and "Batti Batti" filled her gentle little bosom? But the Major, whom she consulted upon this head, as her theological adviser (and who himself had a pious and reverent soul), said that for his part, every beauty of art or nature made him thankful as well as happy; and that the pleasure to be had in listening to fine music, as in looking at the stars in the sky, or at a beautiful landscape or picture, was a benefit for which we might thank Heaven as sincerely as for any other worldly blessing. And in reply to some faint objections of Mrs. Amelia's (taken from certain theological works like the "Washerwoman of Finchley Common" and others of that school, with which Mrs. Osborne had been furnished during her life at Brompton) he told her an Eastern fable of the Owl who thought that the sunshine was unbearable for the eyes, and that the Nightingale was a most overrated bird. "It is one's nature to sing and the other's to hoot," he said laughing, "and with such a sweet voice as you have yourself, you must belong to the Bulbul faction."

I like to dwell upon this period of her life, and to think that she was cheerful and happy. You see she has not had too much of that sort of existence as yet, and has not fallen in the way of means to educate her tastes or her intelligence. She has been domineered over hitherto by vulgar intellects. It is the lot of many a woman. And as every one of the dear sex is the rival of the rest of her kind, timidity passes for folly in their charitable judgments; and gentleness for dulness; and silence — which is but timid denial of the unwelcome assertion of ruling folks, and tacit protestantism — above all, finds no mercy at the hands of the female Inquisition. Thus, my dear and civilized reader, if you and I were to find ourselves this evening in a society of green-grocers, let us say, it is probable that our conversation would not be brilliant; if, on the other hand, a green-grocer should find himself at your refined and polite tea-table, where everybody was saying witty things, and everybody of fashion and repute tearing her friends to pieces in the most delightful manner, it is possible that the stranger would not be very talkative, and by no means interesting or interested.

And it must be remembered, that this poor lady had never met a gentleman in her life until this present moment. Perhaps these are rarer personages than some of us think for. Which of us can point out many such in his circle — men whose aims are generous, whose truth is constant, and not only constant in its kind but elevated in its degree; whose want of meanness makes them simple : who can look the world honestly in the face with an equal manly sympathy for the great and the small ? We all know a hundred whose coats are very well made, and a score who have excellent manners, and one or two happy beings who are what they call, in the inner circles, and have shot into the very centre and bull's-eye of the fashion; but of gentlemen how many ? Let us take a little scrap of paper and each make out his list.

My friend the Major I write, without any doubt, in mine. He had very long legs, a yellow face, and a slight lisp, which at first was rather ridiculous. But his thoughts were just, his brains were fairly good, his life was honest and pure, and his heart warm and humble. He certainly had very large hands and feet, which the two George Osbornes used to caricature and laugh at; and their jeers and laughter perhaps led poor little Emmy astray as to his worth. But have we not all been misled about our heroes, and changed our opinions a hundred times? Emmy, in this happy time, found that hers underwent a very great change in respect of the merits of the Major.

Perhaps it was the happiest time of both their lives indeed, if they did but know it — and who does? Which of us can point out and say that was the culmination — that was the summit of human joy? But at all events, this couple were very decently contented, and enjoyed as pleasant a summer tour as any pair that left England that year. Georgy was always present at the play, but it was the Major who put Emmy's shawl on after the entertainment; and in the walks and excursions the young lad would be on a-head, and up a tower-stair or a tree, whilst the soberer couple were below, the Major smoking his cigar with great placidity and constancy, whilst Emmy sketched the site or the ruin. It was on this very tour that I, the present writer of a history of which every word is true, had the pleasure to see them first, and to make their acquaintance.

It was at the little comfortable Ducal town of Pumpernickel (that very place where Sir Pitt Crawley had been so distinguished as an *attaché*; but that was in early early days, and before the news of the battle of Austerlitz sent all the English diplomatists in Germany to the right about) that I first saw Colonel Dobbin and his party. They had arrived with the carriage and courier at the Erbprinz Hotel, the best of the town, and the whole party dined at the *table d'hôte*. Everybody remarked the majesty of Jos, and the knowing way in which he sipped, or rather sucked, the Johannisberger, which he ordered for dinner. The little boy, too, we observed, had a famous appetite, and consumed *schinken*, and *braten*, and *kart offeln,* and cranberry jam, and salad, and pudding, and roast fowls, and sweetmeats, with a gallantry that did honor to his nation. After about fifteen dishes, he concluded the repast with dessert, some of which he even carried out of doors; for some young gentlemen at table, amused with his coolness and gallant free and easy manner, induced him to pocket a handful of macaroons, which he discussed on his way to the theatre, whither everybody went in the cheery social little German place. The lady in black, the boy's mamma, laughed and blushed, and looked exceedingly pleased and shy as the dinner went on, and at the various feats and instances of *espièglerie* on the part of her son. The Colonel — for so he became very soon afterwards — I remember joked the boy with a great deal of grave fun, pointing out dishes which he *had n't* tried, and entreating him not to balk his appetite, but to have a second supply of this or that.

It was what they call a *gast-rolle* night at the Royal Grand Ducal Pumpernickelisch Hof, — or Court Theatre; and Madame Schroeder Devrient, then in the bloom of her beauty and genius, performed the part of the heroine in the wonderful opera of "Fidelio." From our places in the stalls we could see our four friends of the *table d'hôte,* in the loge which Schwendler of the Erbprinz kept for his best guests; and I could not help remarking the effect which the magnificent actress and music produced upon Mrs. Osborne, for so we heard the stout gentleman in the mustachios call her. During the astonishing Chorus of the Prisoners, over which the delightful voice of the actress rose and soared in the most ravishing harmony, the English lady's face wore such an expression of wonder and delight that it struck even little Fipps, the *blasé attaché,* who drawled out, as he fixed his glass upon her, "Gayd, it really does one good to see a woman caypable of that stayt of excaytement." And in the Prison Scene where Fidelio, rushing to her husband, cries, *Nichts nichts mein Florestan,* she fairly lost herself and covered her face with her handkerchief. Every woman in the house was snivelling at the time : but I suppose it was because it was predestined that I was to write this particular lady's memoirs that I remarked her.

The next day they gave another piece of Beethoven, "Die Schlacht bei Vittoria." "Malbrook" is introduced at the beginning of the performance, as indicative of the brisk advance of the French Army. Then come drums, trumpets, thunders of artillery, and groans of the dying, and at last in a grand triumphant swell, "God Save the King" is performed.

There may have been a score of Englishmen in the house, but at the burst of that beloved and well-known music, every one of them, — we young fellows in the stalls, Sir John and Lady Bullminster (who had taken a house at Pumpernickel for the education of their nine children), the fat gentleman with the mustachios, the long Major in white duck trousers, and the lady with the little boy upon whom he was so sweet : even Kirsch, the courier in the gallery, stood bolt upright in their places, and proclaimed themselves to be members of the dear old British nation. As for Tapeworm, the *Chargé d'Affaires,* he rose up in his box and bowed and simpered, as if he would represent the whole empire. Tapeworm was nephew and heir of old Marshal Tiptoff, who has been introduced in this story as General Tiptoff, just before Waterloo, who was Colonel of the — th regiment in which Major Dobbin served, and who died in this year full of honors, and of an aspic of plovers' eggs ; when the regiment was graciously given by his Majesty to Colonel Sir Michael O'Dowd, K. C. B., who had commanded it in many glorious fields.

Tapeworm must have met with Colonel Dobbin at the house of the Colonel's Colonel, the Marshal, for he recognized him on this night at the theatre; and with the utmost condescension, his Majesty's minister came over from his own box, and publicly shook hands with his new-found friend.

"Look at that infernal sly-boots of a Tapeworm," Fipps whispered, examining his chief from the stalls. "Wherever there's a pretty woman he always twists himself in." And I wonder what were diplomatists made for but for that?

"Have I the honor of addressing myself to Mrs. Dobbin?" asked the Secretary, with a most insinuating grin.

Georgy burst out laughing, and said, "By Jove, that *is* a good un." — Emmy and the Major blushed: we saw them from the stalls.

"This lady is Mrs. George Osborne," said the Major, "and this is her brother, Mr. Sedley, a distinguished officer of the Bengal Civil Service: permit me to introduce him to your lordship."

My lord nearly sent Jos off his legs, with the most fascinating smile. "Are you going to stop in Pumpernickel?" he said. "It is a dull place: but we want some nice people, and we would try and make it *so* agreeable to you. Mr. — Ahum — Mrs. — Oho. I shall do myself the honor of calling upon you to-morrow at your inn." And he went away with a Parthian grin and glance, which he thought must finish Mrs. Osborne completely.

The performance over, the young fellows lounged about the lobbies, and we saw the society take its de-

parture.   The Duchess Dowager went off in her jingling old coach, attended by two faithful and withered
old maids-of-honor, and a little snuffy spindle-shanked
gentleman-in-waiting, in a brown jasey and a green
coat covered with orders — of which the star and the
grand yellow cordon of the order of Saint Michael of
Pumpernickel were most conspicuous.   The drums
rolled, the guards saluted, and the old carriage drove
away.

Then came his Transparency, the Duke and Transparent family, with his great officers of state and
household.   He bowed serenely to everybody.   And
amid the saluting of the guards, and the flaring of the
torches of the running footmen, clad in scarlet, the
Transparent carriages drove away to the old Ducal
Schloss, with its towers and pinnacles standing on the
Schlossberg.   Everybody in Pumpernickel knew everybody.   No sooner was a foreigner seen there, than the
Minister of Foreign Affairs, or some other great or
small officer of state, went round to the Erbprinz, and
found out the name of the new arrivals.

We watched them, too, out of the theatre.   Tapeworm had just walked off, enveloped in his cloak, with
which his gigantic *chasseur* was always in attendance,
and looking as much as possible like Don Juan.   The
Prime Minister's lady had just squeezed herself into
her sedan, and her daughter, the charming Ida, had
put on her calash and clogs : when the English party
came out, the boy yawning drearily, the Major taking
great pains in keeping the shawl over Mrs. Osborne's
head, and Mr. Sedley, looking grand, with a crush
opera-hat on one side of his head, and his hand in the
stomach of a voluminous white waistcoat.   We took
off our hats to our acquaintances of the *table d'hôte*,
and the lady, in return, presented us with a little

smile and a curtsy, for which everybody might be thankful.

The carriage from the inn, under the superintendence of the bustling Mr. Kirsch, was in waiting to convey the party; but the fat man said he would walk, and smoke his cigar on his way homeward; so the other three, with nods and smiles to us, went without Mr. Sedley; Kirsch, with the cigar-case, following in his master's wake.

We all walked together, and talked to the stout gentleman about the *agrémens* of the place. It was very agreeable for the English. There were shooting-parties and *battues;* there was a plenty of balls and entertainments at the hospitable court; the society was generally good; the theatre excellent, and the living cheap.

"And our Minister seems a most delightful and affable person," our new friend said. "With such a representative, and — and a good medical man, I can fancy the place to be most eligible. Good night, gentlemen." And Jos creaked up the stairs to bedward, followed by Kirsch with a flambeau. We rather hoped that nice-looking woman would be induced to stay some time in the town.

CHAPTER IX.

Such polite behavior as that of Lord Tapeworm did not fail to have the most favorable effect upon Mr. Sedley's mind, and the very next morning, at breakfast, he pronounced his opinion that Pumpernickel was the pleasantest little place of any which he had visited on their tour. Jos's motives and artifices were not very difficult of comprehension: and Dobbin laughed in his sleeve, like a hypocrite as he was, when he found by the knowing air of the civilian and the off-hand manner in which the latter talked about Tapeworm Castle, and the other members of the family, that Jos had been up already in the morning, consulting his travelling Peerage. Yes, he had seen the Right Honorable the Earl of Bagwig, his lordship's father; he was sure he had, he had met him at — at the levee — didn't Dob remember? and when the Diplomatist called on the party, faithful to his promise, Jos received him with such a salute and honors as were seldom accorded to the little Envoy. He winked at Kirsch on his Excellency's arrival, and that emissary instructed beforehand, went out and superintended an entertainment of cold meats, jellies, and other delicacies, brought in upon trays, and of which Mr. Jos absolutely insisted that his noble guest should partake.

Tapeworm, so long as he could have an opportunity of admiring the bright eyes of Mrs. Osborne (whose freshness of complexion bore daylight remarkably well) was not ill pleased to accept any invitation to stay in Mr. Sedley's lodgings; he put one or two dexterous questions to him about India and the dancing-girls there; asked Amelia about that beautiful boy who had been with her, and complimented the astonished little woman upon the prodigious sensation which she had made in the house; and tried to fascinate Dobbin by talking of the late war, and the exploits of the Pumpernickel contingent under the command of the Hereditary Prince, now Duke of Pumpernickel.

Lord Tapeworm inherited no little portion of the family gallantry, and it was his happy belief, that almost every woman upon whom he himself cast friendly eyes, was in love with him. He left Emmy under the persuasion that she was slain by his wit and attractions, and went home to his lodgings to write a pretty little note to her. She was not fascinated; only puzzled by his grinning, his simpering, his scented cambric handkerchief, and his high-heeled lacquered boots. She did not understand one half the compliments which he paid; she had never, in her small experience of mankind, met a professional ladies' man as yet, and looked upon my lord as something curious rather than pleasant; and if she did not admire, certainly wondered at him. Jos, on the contrary, was delighted. "How very affable his lordship is," he said; "How very kind of his lordship to say he would send his medical man! Kirsch, you will carry our cards to the Count de Schlüsselback directly: the Major and I will have the greatest pleasure in paying our respects at court as soon as possible. Put out my uniform, Kirsch, — both our uniforms. It is a mark of politeness which

every English gentleman ought to show to the countries which he visits, to pay his respects to the sovereigns of those countries as to the representatives
of his own."

When Tapeworm's doctor came, Doctor von Glauber, Body Physician to H. S. H. the Duke, he speedily convinced Jos that the Pumpernickel mineral
springs and the doctor's particular treatment would
infallibly restore the Bengalee to youth and slim-
ness. "Dere came here last year," he said, "Sheneral Bulkeley, an English Sheneral, tvice so pic as
you, sir. I sent him back qvite tin after tree months,
and he danced vid Baroness Glauber at the end of
two."

Jos's mind was made up, the springs, the doctor,
the court, and the *Chargé d' Affaires* convinced him,
and he proposed to spend the autumn in these
delightful quarters. — And punctual to his word, on
the next day the *Chargé d' Affaires* presented Jos and
the Major to Victor Aurelius XVII., being conducted
to their audience with that sovereign by the Count
de Schlüsselback, Marshal of the Court.

They were straightway invited to dinner at court,
and their intention of staying in the town being
announced, the politest ladies of the whole town
instantly called upon Mrs. Osborne; and as not one
of these, however poor they might be, was under the
rank of a Baroness, Jos's delight was beyond expression. He wrote off to Chutney at the club to say that
the Service was highly appreciated in Germany, that
he was going to show his friend, the Count de Schlüsselback, how to stick a pig in the Indian fashion, and
that his august friends, the Duke and Duchess, were
everything that was kind and civil.

Emmy, too, was presented to the august family,

Jos performs a Polonaise.

then the waters of Monblaisir begin to play (it is lucky that there is company to behold them, for one would be afraid to see them alone) — then there come mountebanks and riding troops (the way in which his Transparency was fascinated by one of the horse-riders, is well known, and it is believed that *La Petite Vivandière,* as she was called, was a spy in the French interest), and the delighted people are permitted to march through room after room of the Grand Ducal palace, and admire the slippery floor, the rich hangings, and the spittoons at the doors of all the innumerable chambers. There is one Pavilion at Monblaisir which Aurelius Victor XV. had arranged — a great Prince but too fond of pleasure — and which I am told is a perfect wonder of licentious elegance. It is painted with the story of Bacchus and Ariadne, and the table works in and out of the room by means of a windlass so that the company was served without any intervention of domestics. But the place was shut up by Barbara, Aurelius XV.'s widow, a severe and devout Princess of the House of Bolkum and Regent of the Duchy during her son's glorious minority, and after the death of her husband, cut off in the pride of his pleasures.

The theatre of Pumpernickel is known and famous in that quarter of Germany. It languished a little when the present Duke in his youth insisted upon having his own operas played there, and it is said one day, in a fury, from his place in the orchestra, when he attended a rehearsal, broke a bassoon on the head of the Chapel Master, who was conducting, and led too slow; and during which time the Duchess Sophia wrote domestic comedies which must have been very dreary to witness. But the Prince executes his music in private now, and the Duchess only gives away her plays to the foreigners of distinction who visit her kind little court.

It is conducted with no small comfort and splendor. When there are balls, though there may be four hundred people at supper, there is a servant in scarlet and lace to attend upon every four, and every one is served on silver. There are festivals and entertainments going continually on; and the Duke has his chamberlains and equerries, and the Duchess her mistress of the wardrobe and ladies-of-honor just like any other and more potent potentates.

The Constitution is or was a moderate despotism, tempered by a Chamber that might or might not be elected. I never certainly could hear of its sitting in my time at Pumpernickel. The Prime Minister had lodgings in a second floor; and the Foreign Secretary occupied the comfortable lodgings over Zwieback's Conditorey. The army consisted of a magnificent band that also did duty on the stage, where it was quite pleasant to see the worthy fellows marching in Turkish dresses with rouge on and wooden scimitars, or as Roman warriors with ophicleides and trombones, — to see them again, I say, at night, after one had listened to them all the morning in the Aurelius Platz, where they performed opposite the Café where we breakfasted. Besides the band, there was a rich and numerous staff of officers, and, I believe, a few men. Besides the regular sentries, three or four men, habited as hussars, used to do duty at the Palace, but I never saw them on horseback, and *au fait*, what was the use of cavalry in a time of profound peace? — and whither the deuce should the hussars ride?

Everybody — everybody that was noble of course, for as for the *bourgeois* we could not quite be ex-

pected to take notice of *them* — visited his neighbor.
H. E. Madame de Burst received once a week, H. E.
Madame de Schnurrbart had her night — the theatre
was open twice a week, the court graciously received
once, so that a man's life might in fact be a perfect
round of pleasure in the unpretending Pumpernickel
way.

That there were feuds in the place, no one can
deny. Politics ran very high at Pumpernickel, and
parties were very bitter. There was the Strumpff
faction and the Lederlung party, the one supported
by our Envoy and the other by the French *Chargé
d'Affaires*, M. de Macabau. Indeed it sufficed for
our Minister to stand up for Madame Strumpff, who
was clearly the greater singer of the two, and had
three more notes in her voice than Madame Lederlung her rival — it sufficed, I say, for our Minister to
advance *any* opinion to have it instantly contradicted
by the French diplomatist.

Everybody in the town was ranged in one or other
of these factions. The Lederlung was a prettyish little creature certainly, and her voice (what there was
of it) was very sweet, and there is no doubt that the
Strumpff was not in her first youth and beauty, and
certainly too stout; when she came on in the last
scene of the "Sonnambula" for instance, in her night-
chemise with a lamp in her hand, and had to go out
of the window, and pass over the plank of the mill,
it was all she could do to squeeze out of the window,
and the plank used to bend and creak again under her
weight — but how she poured out the finale of the
opera! and with what a burst of feeling she rushed
into Elvino's arms — almost fit to smother him!
Whereas the little Lederlung — but a truce to this
gossip — the fact is, that these two women were the

two flags of the French and the English party at Pumpernickel, and the society was divided in its allegiance to those two great nations.

We had on our side the Home Minister, the Master of the Horse, the Duke's Private Secretary, and the Prince's Tutor: whereas of the French party were the Foreign Minister, the Commander-in-Chief's lady, who had served under Napoleon, and the *Hof-Marschall* and his wife, who was glad enough to get the fashions from Paris, and always had them and her caps by M. de Macabau's courier. The Secretary of his Chancery was little Grignac, a young fellow, as malicious as Satan, and who made caricatures of Tapeworm in all the albums of the place.

Their headquarters and *table d'hôte* were established at the Pariser Hof, the other inn of the town; and though, of course, these gentlemen were obliged to be civil in public, yet they cut at each other with epigrams that were as sharp as razors, as I have seen a couple of wrestlers in Devonshire, lashing at each other's shins, and never showing their agony upon a muscle of their faces. Neither Tapeworm nor Macabau ever sent home a despatch to his government, without a most savage series of attacks upon his rival. For instance, on our side we would write, "The interests of Great Britain in this place, and throughout the whole of Germany, are perilled by the continuance in office of the present French envoy; this man is of a character so infamous that he will stick at no falsehood, or hesitate at no crime, to attain his ends. He poisons the mind of the court against the English minister, represents the conduct of Great Britain in the most odious and atrocious light, and is unhappily backed by a minister whose ignorance and necessities are as notorious as his influence is fatal." On their side they would say, "M. de Tapeworm continues his system of stupid insular arrogance and vulgar falsehood against the greatest nation in the world. Yesterday he was heard to speak lightly of Her Royal Highness Madame the Duchess of Berri : on a former occasion he insulted the heroic Duke of Angoulême, and dared to insinuate that H.R. H. the Duke of Orleans was conspiring against the august throne of the lilies. His gold is prodigated in every direction which his stupid menaces fail to frighten. By one and the other, he has won over creatures of the court here, — and, in fine, Pumpernickel will not be quiet, Germany tranquil, France respected, or Europe content, until this poisonous viper be crushed under heel : " and so on. When one side or the other had written any particularly spicy despatch, news of it was sure to slip out.

Before the winter was far advanced it is actually on record that Emmy took a night and received company with great propriety and modesty. She had a French master who complimented her upon the purity of her accent and her facility of learning; the fact is she had learned long ago, and grounded herself subsequently in the grammar so as to be able to teach it to George ; and Madame Strumpff came to give her lessons in singing, which she performed so well and with such a true voice that the Major's windows, who had lodgings opposite under the Prime Minister, were always open to hear the lesson. Some of the German ladies, who are very sentimental and simple in their tastes, fell in love with her and began to call her *du* at once. These are trivial details, but they relate to happy times. The Major made himself George's tutor, and read Cæsar and mathematics with him, and they had a German master, and rode out of

evenings by the side of Emmy's carriage — she was
always too timid, and made a dreadful outcry at the
slightest disturbance on horseback. So she drove
about with one of her dear German friends, and Jos
asleep on the back-seat of the barouche.

He was becoming very sweet upon the Gräfinn
Fanny de Butterbrod, a very gentle tender-hearted
and unassuming young creature, a Canoness and
Countess in her own right, but with scarcely ten
pounds per year to her fortune, and Fanny for her
part declared that to be Amelia's sister was the greatest delight that Heaven could bestow on her, and Jos
might have put a Countess's shield and coronet by
the side of his own arms on his carriage and forks;
when — when events occurred, and those grand fêtes
given upon the marriage of the Hereditary Prince of
Pumpernickel with the lovely Princess Amelia of
Humbourg-Schlippenschloppen took place.

At this festival the magnificence displayed was
such as had not been known in the little German
place since the days of the prodigal Victor XIV. All
the neighboring Princes, Princesses, and Grandees
were invited to the feast. Beds rose to half-a-crown
per night in Pumpernickel, and the army was exhausted in providing guards of honor for the Highnesses, Serenities, and Excellencies, who arrived from
all quarters. The Princess was married by proxy,
at her father's residence, by the Count de Schlüsselback. Snuff-boxes were given away in profusion (as
we learned from the court-jeweller, who sold and
afterwards bought them again), and bushels of the
Order of Saint Michael of Pumpernickel were sent to
the nobles of the court, while hampers of the cordons
and decorations of the Wheel of Saint Catherine of
Schlippenschloppen were brought to ours. The

French envoy got both. "He is covered with ribbons like a prize cart-horse," Tapeworm said, who was not allowed by the rules of his service to take any decorations: "Let him have the cordons; but with whom is the victory?" The fact is, it was a triumph of British diplomacy: the French party having proposed and tried their utmost to carry a marriage with a Princess of the house of Potztausend-Donnerwetter, whom, as a matter of course, we opposed.

Everybody was asked to the fêtes of the marriage. Garlands and triumphal arches were hung across the road to welcome the young bride. The great Saint Michael's Fountain ran with uncommonly sour wine, while that in the Artillery Place frothed with beer. The great waters played; and poles were put up in the park and gardens for the happy peasantry, which they might climb at their leisure, carrying off watches, silver forks, prize sausages hung with pink ribbon, etc., at the top. Georgy got one, wrenching it off, having swarmed up the pole to the delight of the spectators, and sliding down with the rapidity of a fall of water. But it was for the glory's sake merely. The boy gave the sausage to a peasant, who had very nearly seized it, and stood at the foot of the mast, blubbering, because he was unsuccessful.

At the French *Chancellerie* they had six more lampions in their illumination than ours had; but our transparency, which represented the young Couple advancing, and Discord flying away, with the most ludicrous likeness to the French ambassador, beat the French picture hollow; and I have no doubt got Tapeworm the advancement and the Cross of the Bath, which he subsequently attained.

Crowds of foreigners arrived for the fêtes: and of English of course. Besides the court balls, public

balls were given at the Town Hall and the *Redoute*,
and in the former place there was a room for *trente-et-
quarante* and *roulette* established, for the week of the
festivities only, and by one of the great German companies from Ems, or Aix-la-Chapelle. The officers
or inhabitants of the town were not allowed to play
at these games, but strangers, peasants, ladies were
admitted, and any one who chose to lose or win
money.

The little scapegrace Georgy Osborne amongst
others, whose pockets were always full of dollars, and
whose relations were away at the grand festival of
the court, came to the Stadthaus ball in company of
his uncle's courier, Mr. Kirsch, and having only
peeped into a play-room at Baden Baden when he
hung on Dobbin's arm, and where, of course, he was
not permitted to gamble, came eagerly to this part of
the entertainment, and hankered round the tables
where the croupiers and the punters were at work.
Women were playing; they were masked, some of
them; this license was allowed in these wild times
of carnival.

A woman with light hair, in a low dress, by no
means so fresh as it had been, and with a black mask
on, through the eyelets of which her eyes twinkled
strangely, was seated at one of the roulette-tables
with a card and a pin, and a couple of florins before
her. As the croupier called out the color and number, she pricked on the card with great care and
regularity, and only ventured her money on the colors
after the red or black had come up a certain number
of times. It was strange to look at her.

But in spite of her care and assiduity she guessed
wrong, and the last two florins followed each other
under the croupier's rake, as he cried out with his

inexorable voice, the winning color and number. She
gave a sigh, a shrug with her shoulders, which were
already too much out of her gown, and dashing the
pin through the card on to the table, sat thrumming
it for a while. Then she looked round her, and saw
Georgy's honest face staring at the scene. The little
scamp! what business had he to be there?

When she saw the boy, at whose face she looked
hard through her shining eyes and mask, she said,
" *Monsieur n'est pas joueur?* "

" *Non, Madame,*" said the boy: but she must have
known, from his accent, of what country he was, for
she answered him with a slight foreign tone. "You
have nevare played — will you do me a littl' favor?"

"What is it?" said Georgy, blushing again. Mr.
Kirsch was at work for his part at the *rouge et noir,*
and did not see his young master.

"Play this for me, if you please, put it on any
number, any number." And she took from her bosom
a purse, and out of it a gold piece, the only coin
there, and she put it into George's hand. The boy
laughed, and did as he was bid.

The number came up, sure enough. There is a
power that arranges that, they say, for beginners.

"Thank you," said she, pulling the money towards
her; "thank you. What is your name?"

"My name 's Osborne," said Georgy, and was fingering in his own pockets for dollars, and just about
to make a trial, when the Major, in his uniform, and
Jos, *en Marquis,* from the court ball, made their appearance. Other people finding the entertainment
stupid, and preferring the fun at the Stadthaus, had
quitted the Palace ball earlier; but it is probable the
Major and Jos had gone home and found the boy's
absence, for the former instantly went up to him, and

taking him by the shoulder, pulled him briskly back
from the place of temptation. Then, looking round
the room, he saw Kirsch employed as we have said,
and going up to him, asked how he dared to bring
Mr. George to such a place.

"*Laissez-moi tranquille*," said Mr. Kirsch, very much
excited by play and wine. "*Il faut s'amuser, parbleu.
Je ne suis pas au service de Monsieur.*"

Seeing his condition the Major did not choose to
argue with the man; but contented himself with
drawing away George, and asking Jos if he would
come away. He was standing close by the lady in the
mask, who was playing with pretty good luck now;
and looking on much interested at the game.

"Had n't you better come, Jos," the Major said,
"with George and me?"

"I'll stop and go home with that rascal, Kirsch,"
Jos said; and for the same reason of modesty, which
he thought ought to be preserved before the boy,
Dobbin did not care to remonstrate with Jos, but left
him and walked home with Georgy.

"Did you play?" asked the Major when they were
out, and on their way home.

The boy said "No."

"Give me your word of honor as a gentleman, that
you never will."

"Why?" said the boy: "It seems very good fun."
And, in a very eloquent and impressive manner, the
Major showed him why he should n't, and would have
enforced his precepts by the example of Georgy's
own father, had he liked to say anything that
should reflect on the other's memory. When he
had housed him he went to bed, and saw his light,
in the little room outside of Amelia's, presently
disappear. Amelia's followed half an hour after-

wards. I don't know what made the Major note it so accurately.

Jos, however, remained behind over the play-table; he was no gambler, but not averse to the little excitement of the sport now and then; and he had some Napoleons chinking in the embroidered pockets of his court waistcoat. He put down one over the fair shoulder of the little gambler before him, and they won. She made a little movement to make room for him by her side, and just took the skirt of her gown from a vacant chair there.

"Come and give me good luck," she said, still in a foreign accent, quite different from that frank and perfectly English "Thank you," with which she had saluted George's *coup* in her favor. The portly gentleman, looking round to see that nobody of rank observed him, sat down; he muttered — "Ah, really, well now, God bless my soul. I'm very fortunate; I'm sure to give you good fortune," and other words of compliment and confusion.

"Do you play much?" the foreign mask said.

"I put a Nap or two down," said Jos, with a superb air, flinging down a gold piece.

"Yes; ay nap after dinner," said the mask, archly. But Jos looking frightened, she continued in her pretty French accent, "You do not play to win. No more do I. I play to forget, but I cannot. I cannot forget old times, Monsieur. Your little nephew is the image of his father; and you — you are not changed — but yes, you are. Everybody changes, everybody forgets; nobody has any heart."

"Good God, who is it?" asked Jos in a flutter.

"Can't you guess, Joseph Sedley?" said the little woman, in a sad voice, and undoing her mask, she looked at him. "You have forgotten me."

"Good heavens! Mrs. Crawley!" gasped out Jos.

"Rebecca," said the other, putting her hand on his; but she followed the game still, all the time she was looking at him.

"I am stopping at the Elephant," she continued. "Ask for Madame de Raudon. I saw my dear Amelia to-day; how pretty she looked, and how happy! So do you! Everybody but me, who am wretched, Joseph Sedley." And she put her money over from the red to the black, as if by a chance movement of her hand, and while she was wiping her eyes with a pocket-handkerchief fringed with torn lace.

The red came up again, and she lost the whole of that stake. "Come away," she said. "Come with me a little — we are old friends, are we not, dear Mr. Sedley?"

And Mr. Kirsch having lost all his money by this time, followed his master out into the moonlight, where the illuminations were winking out, and the transparency over our mission was scarcely visible.

CHAPTER X.

A VAGABOND CHAPTER.

WE must pass over a part of Mrs. Rebecca Crawley's biography with that lightness and delicacy which the world demands — the moral world, that has, perhaps, no particular objection to vice, but an insuperable repugnance to hearing vice called by its proper name. There are things we do and know perfectly well in Vanity Fair, though we never speak of them: as the Ahrimanians worship the devil, but don't mention him: and a polite public will no more bear to read an authentic description of vice than a truly-refined English or American female will permit the word breeches to be pronounced in her chaste hearing. And yet, Madam, both are walking the world before our faces every day, without much shocking us. If you were to blush every time they went by, what complexions you would have! It is only when their naughty names are called out that your modesty has any occasion to show alarm or sense of outrage, and it has been the wish of the present writer, all through this story, deferentially to submit to the fashion at present prevailing, and only to hint at the existence of wickedness in a light, easy, and agreeable manner, so that nobody's fine feelings may be offended. I defy any one to say that our Becky, who has certainly some vices, has not been presented to the public in a perfectly genteel and inoffensive manner. In describing this siren, singing and smiling, coaxing and cajoling, the author, with modest pride, asks his readers all round, has he once forgotten the laws of politeness, and showed the monster's hideous tail above water? No! Those who like may peep down under waves that are pretty transparent, and see it writhing and twirling, diabolically hideous and slimy, flapping amongst bones, or curling round corpses; but above the water-line, I ask, has not everything been proper, agreeable, and decorous, and has any the most squeamish immoralist in Vanity Fair a right to cry fie? When, however, the siren disappears and dives below, down among the dead men, the water of course grows turbid over her, and it is labor lost to look into it ever so curiously. They look pretty enough when they sit upon a rock, twanging their harps and combing their hair, and sing, and beckon to you to come and hold the looking-glass; but when they sink into their native element, depend on it those mermaids are about no good, and we had best not examine the fiendish marine cannibals, revelling and feasting on their wretched pickled victims. And so, when Becky is out of the way, be sure that she is not particularly well employed, and that the less that is said about her doings is in fact the better.

If we were to give a full account of her proceedings during a couple of years that followed after the Curzon Street catastrophe, there might be some reason for people to say this book was improper. The actions of very vain, heartless, pleasure-seeking people are very often improper (as are many of yours, my friend with the grave face and spotless reputation; — but that is merely by the way); and what are those of a woman without faith — or love — or character? And I am inclined to think that there was a period in Mrs. Becky's life, when she was seized, not by remorse, but by a kind of despair, and absolutely neglected her person, and did not even care for her reputation.

This *abattement* and degradation did not take place all at once : it was brought about by degrees, after her calamity, and after many struggles to keep up — as a man who goes overboard hangs on to a spar whilst any hope is left, and then flings it away and goes down, when he finds that struggling is in vain.

She lingered about London whilst her husband was making preparations for his departure to his seat of government : and it is believed made more than one attempt to see her brother-in-law, Sir Pitt Crawley, and to work upon his feelings, which she had almost enlisted in her favor. As Sir Pitt and Mr. Wenham were walking down to the House of Commons, the latter spied Mrs. Rawdon in a black veil, and lurking near the palace of the legislature. She sneaked away when her eyes met those of Wenham, and indeed never succeeded in her designs upon the Baronet.

Probably Lady Jane interposed. I have heard that she quite astonished her husband by the spirit which she exhibited in this quarrel, and her determination to disown Mrs. Becky. Of her own movement, she invited Rawdon to come and stop in Gaunt Street until his departure for Coventry Island, knowing that with him for a guard Mrs. Becky would not try to force her door : and she looked curiously at the superscriptions of all the letters which arrived for Sir Pitt, lest he and his sister-in-law should be corresponding. Not but that Rebecca could have written had she a mind : but she did not try to see or to write to Pitt at his own house, and after one or two attempts consented to his demand that the correspondence regarding her conjugal differences should be carried on by lawyers only.

The fact was, that Pitt's mind had been poisoned against her. A short time after Lord Steyne's accident Wenham had been with the Baronet; and given him such a biography of Mrs. Becky as had astonished the member for Queen's Crawley. He knew everything regarding her: who her father was; in what year her mother danced at the Opera; what had been her previous history, and what her conduct during her married life:—as I have no doubt that the greater part of the story was false and dictated by interested malevolence, it shall not be repeated here. But Becky was left with a sad sad reputation in the esteem of a country gentleman and relative who had been once rather partial to her.

The revenues of the Governor of Coventry Island are not large. A part of them were set aside by his Excellency for the payment of certain outstanding debts and liabilities, the charges incident on his high situation required considerable expense; finally, it was found that he could not spare to his wife more than three hundred pounds a year, which he proposed to pay to her on an undertaking that she would never trouble him. Otherwise: scandal, separation, Doctors' Commons would ensue. But it was Mr. Wenham's business, Lord Steyne's business, Rawdon's, everybody's — to get her out of the country, and hush up a most disagreeable affair.

She was probably so much occupied in arranging these affairs of business with her husband's lawyers, that she forgot to take any step whatever about her son, the little Rawdon, and did not even once propose to go and see him. That young gentleman was consigned to the entire guardianship of his aunt and uncle, the former of whom had always possessed a great share of the child's affection. His mamma wrote

him a neat letter from Boulogne when she quitted
England, in which she requested him to mind his
book, and said she was going to take a continental
tour, during which she would have the pleasure of
writing to him again. But she never did for a year
afterwards, and not, indeed, until Sir Pitt's only boy,
always sickly, died of hooping-cough and measles; —
then Rawdon's mamma wrote the most affectionate
composition to her darling son, who was made heir
of Queen's Crawley by this accident, and drawn more
closely than ever to the kind lady, whose tender
heart had already adopted him. Rawdon Crawley,
then grown a tall, fine lad, blushed when he got the
letter. "Oh, Aunt Jane, you are my mother!" he
said; "and not — and not that one." But he wrote
back a kind and respectful letter to Mrs. Rebecca,
then living at a boarding-house at Florence. — But we
are advancing matters.

Our darling Becky's first flight was not very far.
She perched upon the French coast at Boulogne, that
refuge of so much exiled English innocence; and
there lived in rather a genteel, widowed manner, with
a *femme de chambre* and a couple of rooms, at an hotel.
She dined at the *table d'hôte*, where people thought
her very pleasant, and where she entertained her
neighbors by stories of her brother, Sir Pitt, and
her great London acquaintance; talking that easy,
fashionable slipslop, which has so much effect upon
certain folks of small breeding. She passed with
many of them for a person of importance; she gave
little tea-parties in her private room, and shared in
the innocent amusements of the place, — in sea-bath-
ing, and in jaunts in open carriages, in strolls on
the sands, and in visits to the play. Mrs. Burjoice, the printer's lady, who was boarding with her

family at the hotel for the summer, and to whom her
Burjoice came of a Saturday and Sunday, voted her
charming, until that little rogue of a Burjoice began
to pay her too much attention. But there was nothing
in the story, only that Becky was always affable, easy,
and good-natured — and with men especially.

Numbers of people were going abroad as usual at
the end of the season, and Becky had plenty of
opportunities of finding out by the behavior of her
acquaintances of the great London world the opinion
of "society" as regarded her conduct. One day it
was Lady Partlet and her daughters whom Becky
confronted as she was walking modestly on Boulogne
pier, the cliffs of Albion shining in the distance across
the deep blue sea. Lady Partlet marshalled all her
daughters round her with a sweep of her parasol, and
retreated from the pier darting savage glances at poor
little Becky who stood alone there.

On another day the packet came in. It had been
blowing fresh, and it always suited Becky's humor to
see the droll woe-begone faces of the people as they
emerged from the boat. Lady Slingstone happened to
be on board this day. Her ladyship had been exceedingly ill in her carriage, and was greatly exhausted
and scarcely fit to walk up the plank from the ship
to the pier. But all her energies rallied the instant
she saw Becky smiling roguishly under a pink bon
net: and giving her a glance of scorn, such as would
have shrivelled up most women, she walked into
the Custom House quite unsupported. Becky only
laughed: but I don't think she liked it. She felt she
was alone, quite alone: and the far-off shining cliffs
of England were impassable to her.

The behavior of the men had undergone too I don't
know what change. Grinstone showed his teeth and

laughed in her face with a familiarity that was not pleasant. Little Bob Suckling, who was cap in hand to her three months before, and would walk a mile in the rain to see for her carriage in the line at Gaunt House, was talking to Fitzoof of the Guards (Lord Heehaw's son) one day upon the jetty, as Becky took her walk there. Little Bobby nodded to her over his shoulder without moving his hat, and continued his conversation with the heir of Heehaw. Tom Raikes tried to walk into her sitting-room at the inn with a cigar in his mouth; but she closed the door upon him and would have locked it only that his fingers were inside. She began to feel that she was very lonely indeed. "If *he'd* been here," she said, "those cowards would never have dared to insult me." She thought about "him" with great sadness, and perhaps longing — about his honest, stupid, constant kindness and fidelity: his never-ceasing obedience; his good humor; his bravery and courage. Very likely she cried, for she was particularly lively, and had put on a little extra rouge when she came down to dinner.

She rouged regularly now: and — and her maid got Cognac for her besides that which was charged in the hotel bill.

Perhaps the insults of the men were not, however, so intolerable to her as the sympathy of certain women. Mrs. Crackenbury and Mrs. Washington White passed through Boulogne on their way to Switzerland. (The party were protected by Colonel Horner, young Beaumoris, and of course old Crackenbury, and Mrs. White's little girl.) *They* did not avoid her. They giggled, cackled, tattled, condoled, consoled, and patronized her until they drove her almost wild with rage. To be patronized by *them!* she thought, as they went away simpering after kissing her. And she heard Beaumoris's laugh ringing on the stair, and knew quite well how to interpret his hilarity.

It was after this visit that Becky, who had paid her weekly bills, Becky who had made herself agreeable to everybody in the house, who smiled at the landlady, called the waiters "Monsieur," and paid the chambermaids in politeness and apologies, what far more than compensated for a little niggardliness in point of money (of which Becky never was free), that Becky, we say, received a notice to quit from the landlord, who had been told by some one that she was quite an unfit person to have at his hotel, where English ladies would not sit down with her. And she was forced to fly into lodgings, of which the dulness and solitude were most wearisome to her.

Still she held up, in spite of these rebuffs, and tried to make a character for herself, and conquer scandal. She went to church very regularly, and sang louder than anybody there. She took up the cause of the widows of the shipwrecked fishermen, and gave work and drawings for the Quashyboo Mission; she subscribed to the Assembly and *would n't* waltz. In a word, she did everything that was respectable, and that is why we dwell upon this part of her career with more fondness than upon subsequent parts of her history, which are not so pleasant. She saw people avoiding her, and still laboriously smiled upon them; you never could suppose from her countenance what pangs of humiliation she might be enduring inwardly.

Her history was after all a mystery. Parties were divided about her. Some people, who took the trouble to busy themselves in the matter, said that she was the criminal; whilst others vowed that she was as innocent as a lamb, and that her odious husband was in fault. She won over a good many by bursting into tears about her boy, and exhibiting the most frantic grief when his name was mentioned, or she saw anybody like him. She gained good Mrs. Alderney's heart in that way, who was rather the Queen of British Boulogne, and gave the most dinners and balls of all the residents there, by weeping when Master Alderney came from Dr. Swishtail's academy to pass his holidays with his mother. "He and her Rawdon were of the same age, and *so* like," Becky said, in a voice choking with agony; whereas there was five years' difference between the boys' ages, and no more likeness between them than between my respected reader and his humble servant. Wenham, when he was going abroad, on his way to Kissengen to join Lord Steyne, enlightened Mrs. Alderney on this point, and told her how he was much more able to describe little Rawdon than his mamma, who notoriously hated him, and never saw him; how he was thirteen years old, while little Alderney was but nine; fair, while the other darling was dark, — in a word, caused the lady in question to repent of her good-humor.

Whenever Becky made a little circle for herself with incredible toils and labor, somebody came and swept it down rudely, and she had all her work to begin over again. It was very hard; very hard; lonely and disheartening.

There was Mrs. Newbright, who took her up for some time, attracted by the sweetness of her singing at church, and by her proper views upon serious subjects, concerning which in former days, at Queen's Crawley, Mrs. Becky had had a good deal of instruction. — Well, she not only took tracts, but she read them. She worked flannel petticoats for the Quashyboos — cotton night-caps for the Cocoanut Indians — painted hand-screens for the conversion of the Pope and the Jews — sat under Mr. Rowls on Wednesdays, Mr. Huggleton on Thursdays, attended two Sunday services at church, besides Mr. Bawler, the Darbyite, in the evening, and all in vain. Mrs. Newbright had occasion to correspond with the Countess of Southdown about the Warmingpan Fund for the Feejee Islanders (for the management of which admirable charity both these ladies formed part of a female committee), and having mentioned her "sweet friend," Mrs. Rawdon Crawley, the Dowager Countess wrote back such a letter regarding Becky, with such particulars, hints, facts, falsehoods, and general comminations, that intimacy between Mrs. Newbright and Mrs. Crawley ceased forthwith : and all the serious world of Tours, where this misfortune took place, immediately parted company with the reprobate. Those who know the English Colonies abroad know that we carry with us our pride, pills, prejudices, Harveysauces, cayenne-peppers, and other Lares, making a little Britain wherever we settle down.

From one colony to another Becky fled uneasily. From Boulogne to Dieppe, from Dieppe to Caen, from Caen to Tours — trying with all her might to be respectable, and alas ! always found out some day or other, and pecked out of the cage by the real daws.

Mrs. Hook Eagles took her up at one of these places : —a woman without a blemish in her character, and a house in Portman Square. She was staying at the hotel at Dieppe, whither Becky fled, and they made each other's acquaintance first at sea, where they were swimming together, and subsequently at the *table d' hôte* of the hotel. Mrs. Eagles had heard, — who indeed had not ? — some of the scandal of the Steyne affair ; but after a conversation with Becky, she pronounced that Mrs. Crawley was an angel, her husband a ruffian, Lord Steyne an unprincipled wretch, as everybody knew, and the whole case against Mrs. Crawley, an infamous and wicked conspiracy of that rascal Wenham. "If you were a man of any spirit, Mr. Eagles, you would box the wretch's ears the next time you see him at the Club," she said to her husband. But Eagles was only a quiet old gentleman, husband to Mrs. Eagles, with a taste for geology, and not tall enough to reach anybody's ears.

The Eagles then patronized Mrs. Rawdon, took her to live with her at her own house at Paris, quarrelled with the ambassador's wife because she would not receive her *protégée;* and did all that lay in woman's power to keep Becky straight in the paths of virtue and good repute.

Becky was very respectable and orderly at first, but the life of humdrum virtue grew utterly tedious to her before long. It was the same routine every day, the same dulness and comfort, the same drive over the same stupid Bois de Boulogne, the same company of an evening, the same Blair's Sermon of a Sunday night — the same opera always being acted over and over again : Becky was dying of weariness, when, luckily for her, young Mr. Eagles came from Cambridge, and his mother, seeing the impression which her little friend made upon him, straightway gave Becky warning.

Then she tried keeping house with a female friend ; then the double *ménage* began to quarrel and get into debt. Then she determined upon a boarding-house existence, and lived for some time at that famous mansion kept by Madame de Saint Amour, in the Rue Royale, at Paris, where she began exercising her graces and fascinations upon the shabby dandies and fly-blown beauties who frequented her landlady's *salons.* Becky loved society, and, indeed, could no more exist without it than an opium-eater without his dram, and she was happy enough at the period of her boarding-house life. "The women here are as amusing as those in May Fair," she told an old London friend who met her — "only, their dresses are not quite so fresh. The men wear cleaned gloves, and are sad rogues, certainly, but they are not worse than Jack This and Tom That. The mistress of the house is a little vulgar, but I don't think she is so vulgar as Lady —— " and here she named the name of a great leader of fashion that I would die rather than reveal. In fact, when you saw Madame de Saint Amour's rooms lighted up of a night, men with *plaques* and *cordons* at the *écarté* tables, and the women at a little distance, you might fancy yourself for a while in good society, and that Madame was a real Countess. Many people did so fancy : and Becky was for a while one of the most dashing ladies of the Countess's *salons*.

But it is probable that her old creditors of 1815 found her out and caused her to leave Paris, for the poor little woman was forced to fly from the city rather suddenly ; and went thence to Brussels.

How well she remembered the place ! She grinned as she looked up at the little *entresol* which she had occupied, and thought of the Bareacres family, bawling for horses and flight, as their carriage stood in the *porte-cochère* of the hotel. She went to Waterloo and to Lacken, where George Osborne's monument much struck her. She made a little sketch of it. "That poor Cupid !" she said ; "how dreadfully he was in love with me, and what a fool he was ! I wonder whether little Emmy is alive. It was a good little creature : and that fat brother of hers. I have his funny fat picture still among my papers. They were kind simple people."

At Brussels Becky arrived, recommended by Madame de Saint Amour to her friend, Madame la Comtesse de Borodino, widow of Napoleon's General, the famous Count de Borodino, who was left with no resource by the deceased hero but that of a *table d' hôte* and an *écarté* table. Second-rate dandies and *roués*, widow-ladies who always have a law-suit, and very simple English folks, who fancy they see "continental society" at these houses, put down their money, or ate their meals, at Madame de Borodino's tables. The gallant young fellows treated the company round to champagne at the *table d' hôte*, rode out with the women, or hired horses on country excursions, clubbed money to take boxes at the play or the Opera, betted over the fair shoulders of the ladies at the *écarté* tables, and wrote home to their parents, in Devonshire, about their felicitous introduction to foreign society.

Here, as at Paris, Becky was a boarding-house queen : and ruled in select *pensions*. She never refused the champagne, or the bouquets, or the drives into the country, or the private boxes; but what she preferred was the *écarté* at night, — and she played audaciously. First she played only for a little, then for five-franc pieces, then for Napoleons, then for notes : then she would not be able to pay her month's *pension :* then she borrowed from the young gentlemen : then she got into cash again, and bullied Madame de Borodino, whom she had coaxed and wheedled before : then she was playing for ten sous at a time, and in a dire state of poverty : then her quarter's allowance would come in, and she would pay off Madame de Borodino's score : and would once more take the cards against Monsieur de Rossignol, or the Chevalier de Raff.

When Becky left Brussels, the sad truth is, that she

owed three months' *pension* to Madame de Borodino,
of which fact, and of the gambling, and of the drinking, and of the going down on her knees to the Rev.
Mr. Muff, Ministre Anglican, and borrowing money
of him, and of her coaxing and flirting with Milor
Noodle, son of Sir Noodle, pupil of the Rev. Mr.
Muff, whom she used to take into her private room,
and of whom she won large sums at *écarté* — of which
fact, I say, and of a hundred of her other knaveries,
the Countess de Borodino informs every English person who stops at her establishment, and announces
that Madame Rawdon was no better than a *vipère*.

So our little wanderer went about setting up her
tent in various cities of Europe, as restless as Ulysses
or Bampfylde Moore Carew. Her taste for disre-
pectability grew more and more remarkable. She
became a perfect Bohemian ere long, herding with
people whom it would make your hair stand on end
to meet.

There is no town of any mark in Europe but it has
its little colony of English raffs — men whose names
Mr. Hemp the officer reads out periodically at the
Sheriffs' Court — young gentlemen of very good family
often, only that the latter disowns them; frequenters
of billiard-rooms and *estaminets*, patrons of foreign
races and gaming-tables. They people the debtors'
prisons — they drink and swagger — they fight and
brawl — they run away without paying — they have
duels with French and German officers — they cheat
Mr. Spooney at *écarté* — they get the money, and
drive off to Baden in magnificent britzkas — they try
their infallible martingale, and lurk about the tables
with empty pockets, shabby bullies, penniless bucks,
until they can swindle a Jew banker with a sham bill
of exchange, or find another Mr. Spooney to rob.

The alternations of splendor and misery which these people undergo are very queer to view. Their life must be one of great excitement. Becky — must it be owned ? — took to this life, and took to it not unkindly. She went about from town to town among these Bohemians. The lucky Mrs. Rawdon was known at every play-table in Germany. She and Madame de Cruchecassée kept house at Florence together. It is said she was ordered out of Munich; and my friend Mr. Frederick Pigeon avers that it was at her house at Lausanne that he was hocussed at supper and lost eight hundred pounds to Major Loder and the Hon. Mr. Deuceace. We are bound, you see, to give some account of Becky's biography ; but of this part, the less, perhaps, that is said the better.

They say, that when Mrs. Crawley was particularly down on her luck, she gave concerts and lessons in music here and there. There was a Madame de Raudon, who certainly had a *matinée musicale* at Wildbad, accompanied by Herr Spoff, premier pianist to the Hospodar of Wallachia, and my little friend Mr. Eaves, who knew everybody, and had travelled everywhere, always used to declare that he was at Strasburg in the year 1830, when a certain Madame Rebecque made her appearance in the opera of the " Dame Blanche," giving occasion to a furious row in the theatre there. She was hissed off the stage by the audience, partly from her own incompetency, but chiefly from the ill-advised sympathy of some persons in the *parquet,* (where the officers of the garrison had their admissions) ; and Eaves was certain that the unfortunate *débutante* in question was no other than Mrs. Rawdon Crawley.

She was, in fact, no better than a vagabond upon this earth. When she got her money she gambled ;

when she had gambled it she was put to shifts to live; who knows how or by what means she succeeded? It is said that she was once seen at St. Petersburg, but was summarily dismissed from that capital by the police, so that there cannot be any possibility of truth in the report that she was a Russian spy at Töplitz and Vienna afterwards. I have even been informed, that at Paris she discovered a relation of her own, no less a person than her maternal grandmother, who was not by any means a Montmorency, but a hideous old box-opener at a theatre on the Boulevards. The meeting between them, of which other persons, as it is hinted elsewhere, seem to have been acquainted, must have been a very affecting interview. The present historian can give no certain details regarding the event.

It happened at Rome once, that Mrs. de Raudon's half-year's salary had just been paid into the principal bankers there, and, as everybody who had a balance of above five hundred scudi was invited to the balls which this prince of merchants gave during the winter, Becky had the honor of a card, and appeared at one of the Prince and Princess Polonia's splendid evening entertainments. The Princess was of the family of Pompili, lineally descended from the second king of Rome, and Egeria of the house of Olympus, while the Prince's grandfather, Alessandro Polonia, sold wash-balls, essences, tobacco, and pocket-handkerchiefs, ran errands for gentlemen, and lent money in a small way. All the great company in Rome thronged to his saloons — Princes, Dukes, Ambassadors, artists, fiddlers, monsignori, young bears with their leaders — every rank and condition of man. His halls blazed with light and magnificence: were resplendent with gilt frames (containing pictures),

and dubious antiques: and the enormous gilt crown
and arms of the princely owner, a gold mushroom on
a crimson field (the color of the pocket-handkerchiefs
which he sold), and the silver fountain of the Pompili
family shone all over the roof, doors, and panels of
the house, and over the grand velvet baldaquins prepared to receive Popes and Emperors.

So Becky, who had arrived in the diligence from
Florence, and was lodged at an inn in a very modest
way, got a card for Prince Polonia's entertainment,
and her maid dressed her with unusual care, and she
went to this fine ball leaning on the arm of Major
Loder, with whom she happened to be travelling at
the time — (the same man who shot Prince Ravoli
at Naples the next year, and was caned by Sir John
Buckskin for carrying four kings in his hat beside
those which he used in playing at *écarté*) — and this
pair went into the rooms together, and Becky saw a
number of old faces which she remembered in happier
days, when she was not innocent, but not found out.
Major Loder knew a great number of foreigners,
keen-looking whiskered men with dirty striped ribbons in their button-holes, and a very small display
of linen; but his own countrymen, it might be remarked, eschewed the Major. Becky, too, knew
some ladies here and there — French widows, dubious Italian countesses, whose husbands had treated
them ill — faugh — what shall we say, we who have
moved among some of the finest company of Vanity
Fair, of this refuse and sediment of rascals? If we
play, let it be with clean cards, and not with this
dirty pack. But every man who has formed one of
the innumerable army of travellers has seen these
marauding irregulars hanging on, like Nym and Pis-
tol, to the main force; wearing the king's colors, and

boasting of his commission, but pillaging for themselves, and occasionally gibbeted by the roadside.

Well, she was hanging on the arm of Major Loder, and they went through the rooms together, and drank a great quantity of champagne at the buffet, where the people, and especially the Major's irregular corps, struggled furiously for refreshments, of which when the pair had had enough, they pushed on until they reached the Duchess's own pink velvet saloon, at the end of the suite of apartments (where the statue of the Venus is, and the great Venice looking-glasses, framed in silver), and where the princely family were entertaining their most distinguished guests at a round table at supper. It was just such a little select banquet as that of which Becky recollected that she had partaken at Lord Steyne's — and there he sat at Polonia's table, and she saw him.

The scar cut by the diamond on his white, bald, shining forehead, made a burning red mark; his red whiskers were dyed of a purple hue, which made his pale face look still paler. He wore his collar and orders, his blue ribbon and garter. He was a greater prince than any there, though there was a reigning duke and a royal highness, with their princesses, and near his lordship was seated the beautiful Countess of Belladonna, *née* de Glandier, whose husband (the Count Paolo della Belladonna) so well known for his brilliant entomological collections, had been long absent on a mission to the Emperor of Morocco.

When Becky beheld that familiar and illustrious face, how vulgar all of a sudden did Major Loder appear to her, and how that odious Captain Rook did smell of tobacco! In one instant she reassumed her fine-ladyship, and tried to look and feel as if she was

in May Fair once more. "That woman looks stupid
and ill-humored," she thought; "I am sure she can't
amuse him. No, he must be bored by her — he never
was by me." A hundred such touching hopes, fears,
and memories palpitated in her little heart, as she
looked with her brightest eyes (the rouge which she
wore up to her eyelids made them twinkle) towards
the great nobleman. Of a Star and Garter night
Lord Steyne used also to put on his grandest manner, and to look and speak like a great prince, as he
was. Becky admired him smiling sumptuously, easy,
lofty, and stately. Ah, *bon dieu*, what a pleasant
companion he was, what a brilliant wit, what a rich
fund of talk, what a grand manner! — and she had
exchanged this for Major Loder, reeking of cigars
and brandy-and-water, and Captain Rook with his
horse-jockey jokes and prize-ring slang, and their
like. "I wonder whether he will know me," she
thought. Lord Steyne was talking and laughing
with a great and illustrious lady at his side, when
he looked up and saw Becky.

She was all over in a flutter as their eyes met, and
she put on the very best smile she could muster, and
dropped him a little, timid, imploring curtsy. He
stared aghast at her for a minute, as Macbeth might
on beholding Banquo's sudden appearance at his
ball-supper; and remained looking at her with open
mouth, when that horrid Major Loder pulled her
away.

"Come away into the supper-room, Mrs. R.," was
that gentleman's remark: "seeing these nobs grub-
bing away has made me peckish too. Let's go and
try the old governor's champagne." Becky thought
the Major had had a great deal too much already.

The day after she went to walk on the Pincian

Hill — the Hyde Park of the Roman idlers — possibly in hopes to have another sight of Lord Steyne. But she met another acquaintance there: it was Mr. Fiche, his lordship's confidential man, who came up nodding to her rather familiarly, and putting a finger to his hat. "I knew that Madame was here," he said; "I followed her from her hotel. I have some advice to give Madame."

"From the Marquis of Steyne?" Becky asked, resuming as much of her dignity as she could muster, and not a little agitated by hope and expectation.

"No," said the valet; "it is from me. Rome is very unwholesome."

"Not at this season, Monsieur Fiche, — not till after Easter."

"I tell Madame it is unwholesome now. There is always malaria for some people. That cursed marsh wind kills many at all seasons. Look, Madame Crawley, you were always *bon enfant*, and I have an interest in you, *parole d'honneur*. Be warned. Go away from Rome, I tell you — or you will be ill and die."

Becky laughed, though in rage and fury. "What! assassinate poor little me?" she said. "How romantic. Does my lord carry bravos for couriers, and stilettos in the *fourgons*? Bah! I will stay, if but to plague him. I have those who will defend me whilst I am here."

It was Monsieur Fiche's turn to laugh now. "Defend you," he said, "and who? The Major, the Captain, any one of those gambling men whom Madame sees, would take her life for a hundred Louis. We know things about Major Loder (he is no more a Major than I am my Lord the Marquis) which would send him to the galleys or worse. We know everything, and have friends everywhere. We know whom you saw at Paris, and what relations you found there. Yes, Madame may stare but we do. How was it that no minister on the Continent would receive Madame? She has offended somebody: who never forgives — whose rage redoubled when he saw you. He was like a madman last night when he came home. Madame de Belladonna made him a scene about you, and fired off in one of her furies."

"Oh, it was Madame de Belladonna, was it?" Becky said, relieved a little, for the information she had just got had scared her.

"No — she does not matter — she is always jealous. I tell you it was Monseigneur. You did wrong to show yourself to him. And if you stay here you will repent it. Mark my words. Go. Here is my lord's carriage" — and seizing Becky's arm, he rushed down an alley of the garden as Lord Steyne's barouche, blazing with heraldic devices, came whirling along the avenue, borne by the almost priceless horses, and bearing Madame de Belladonna lolling on the cushions, dark, sulky, and blooming, a King Charles in her lap, a white parasol swaying over her head, and old Steyne stretched at her side with a livid face and ghastly eyes. Hate, or anger, or desire, caused them to brighten now and then still; but ordinarily, they gave no light, and seemed tired of looking out on a world of which almost all the pleasure and all the best beauty had palled upon the worn-out wicked old man.

"Monseigneur has never recovered the shock of that night, never," Monsieur Fiche whispered to Mrs. Crawley as the carriage flashed by, and she peeped out at it from behind the shrubs that hid her. "That was a consolation at any rate," Becky thought.

Whether my lord really had murderous intentions

towards Mrs. Becky as Monsieur Fiche said —
(since Monseigneur's death he has returned to his
native country, where he lives much respected and
has purchased from his Prince the title of Baron
Ficci), — and the factotum objected to have to do with
assassination; or whether he simply had a commission
to frighten Mrs. Crawley out of a city where his lordship proposed to pass the winter, and the sight of
her would be eminently disagreeable to the great
nobleman, is a point which has never been ascertained: but the threat had its effect upon the little
woman, and she sought no more to intrude herself
upon the presence of her old patron.

Everybody knows the melancholy end of that noble-
man, which befell at Naples two months after the
French Revolution of 1830: when the Most Honor-
able George Gustavus, Marquis of Steyne, Earl of
Gaunt and of Gaunt Castle, in the Peerage of Ireland,
Viscount Hellborough, Baron Pitchley and Grillsby,
a Knight of the Most Noble Order of the Garter, of
the Golden Fleece of Spain, of the Russian Order of
Saint Nicholas of the First Class, of the Turkish
Order of the Crescent, First Lord of the Powder
Closet and Groom of the Back Stairs, Colonel of the
Gaunt or Regent's Own Regiment of Militia, a Trustee
of the British Museum, an elder Brother of the Trinity
House, a Governor of the White Friars and D.C.L., —
died after a series of fits, brought on, as the papers
said, by the shock occasioned to his lordship's
sensibilities by the downfall of the ancient French
monarchy.

An eloquent catalogue appeared in a weekly print,
describing his virtues, his magnificence, his talents, and
his good actions. His sensibility, his attachment to
the illustrious House of Bourbon, with which he

claimed an alliance, were such that he could not survive the misfortunes of his august kinsmen. His body was buried at Naples, and his heart — that heart which always beat with every generous and noble emotion — was brought back to Castle Gaunt in a silver urn. "In him," Mr. Wagg said, "the poor and the Fine Arts have lost a beneficent patron, society one of its most brilliant ornaments, and England one of her loftiest patriots and statesmen," etc., etc.

His will was a good deal disputed, and an attempt was made to force from Madame de Belladonna the celebrated jewel called the "Jew's-eye" diamond, which his lordship always wore on his forefinger, and which it was said that she removed from it after his lamented demise. But his confidential friend and attendant, Monsieur Fiche, proved that the ring had been presented to the said Madame de Belladonna two days before the Marquis's death; as were the bank-notes, jewels, Neapolitan and French bonds, etc., found in his lordship's secretaire, and claimed by his heirs from that injured woman.

CHAPTER XI.

FULL OF BUSINESS AND PLEASURE.

THE day after the meeting at the play-table, Jos had himself arrayed with unusual care and splendor, and without thinking it necessary to say a word to any member of his family regarding the occurrences of the previous night, or asking for their company in his walk, he sallied forth at an early hour, and was presently seen making inquiries at the door of the Elephant Hotel. In consequence of the fêtes the house was full of company, the tables in the street were already surrounded by persons smoking and drinking the national small-beer, the public rooms were in a cloud of smoke, and Mr. Jos having, in his pompous way, and with his clumsy German, made inquiries for the person of whom he was in search, was directed to the very top of the house, above the first-floor rooms where some travelling peddlers had lived, and were exhibiting their jewelry and brocades; above the second-floor apartments occupied by the *état major* of the gambling firm; above the third-floor rooms, tenanted by the band of renowned Bohemian vaulters and tumblers; and so on to the little cabins of the roof, where, among students, bagmen, small tradesmen, and country-folks, come in for the festival, Becky had found a little nest; — as dirty a little refuge as ever beauty lay hid in.

Becky liked the life. She was at home with every-body in the place, peddlers, punters, tumblers, students,

and all. She was of a wild, roving nature, inherited
from father and mother, who were both Bohemians,
by taste and circumstance; if a lord was not by, she
would talk to his courier with the greatest pleasure;
the din, the stir, the drink, the smoke, the tattle of
the Hebrew peddlers, the solemn, braggart ways of the
poor tumblers, the *sournois* talk of the gambling-table
officials, the songs and swagger of the students, and
the general buzz and hum of the place had pleased
and tickled the little woman, even when her luck was
down, and she had not wherewithal to pay her bill.
How pleasant was all the bustle to her now that her
purse was full of the money which little Georgy had
won for her the night before.

As Jos came creaking and puffing up the final
stairs, and was speechless when he got to the landing, and began to wipe his face and then to look for
No. 92, the room where he was directed to seek for
the person he wanted, the door of the opposite chamber, No. 90, was opened, and a student, in jack-boots
and a dirty *schlafrock*, was lying on the bed smoking
a long pipe; whilst another student in long yellow
hair and a braided coat, exceeding smart and dirty too,
was actually on his knees at No. 92, bawling through
the keyhole supplications to the person within.

"Go away," said a well-known voice, which made
Jos thrill, "I expect somebody; I expect my grandpapa. He mustn't see you there."

"Angel *Engländerinn!*" bellowed the kneeling
student with the whity-brown ringlets and the large
finger-ring, "do take compassion upon us. Make an
appointment. Dine with me and Fritz at the inn in
the park. We will have roast pheasants and porter,
plum-pudding and French wine. We shall die if
you don't."

" That we will," said the young nobleman on the bed; and this colloquy Jos overheard, though he did not comprehend it, for the reason that he had never studied the language in which it was carried on.

" *Newmero kattervang dooze, si vous plait,*" Jos said in his grandest manner, when he was able to speak.

" *Quater fang tooce!*" said the student, starting up, and he bounced into his own room, where he locked the door, and where Jos heard him laughing with his comrade on the bed.

The gentleman from Bengal was standing disconcerted by this incident, when the door of the 92 opened of itself, and Becky's little head peeped out full of archness and mischief. She lighted on Jos. " It's you," she said, coming out. " How I have been waiting for you! Stop! not yet — in one minute you shall come in." In that instant she put a rouge-pot, a brandy-bottle, and a plate of broken meat into the bed, gave one smooth to her hair, and finally let in her visitor.

She had, by way of morning robe, a pink domino, a trifle faded and soiled, and marked here and there with pomatum; but her arms shone out from the loose sleeves of the dress very white and fair, and it was tied round her little waist, so as not ill to set off the trim little figure of the wearer. She led Jos by the hand into her garret. " Come in," she said. " Come, and talk to me. Sit yonder on the chair;" and she gave the civilian's hand a little squeeze, and laughingly placed him upon it. As for herself, she placed herself on the bed — not on the bottle and plate, you may be sure — on which Jos might have reposed had he chosen that seat: and so there she sat and talked with her old admirer.

"How little years have changed you," she said, with a look of tender interest. "I should have known you anywhere. What a comfort it is amongst strangers to see once more the frank honest face of an old friend!"

The frank honest face, to tell the truth, at this moment bore any expression but one of openness and honesty: it was, on the contrary, much perturbed and puzzled in look. Jos was surveying the queer little apartment in which he found his old flame. One of her gowns hung over the bed, another depending from a hook of the door: her bonnet obscured half the looking-glass, on which, too, lay the prettiest little pair of bronze boots; a French novel was on the table by the bedside, with a candle, not of wax. Becky thought of popping that into the bed too, but she only put in the little paper night-cap with which she had put the candle out on going to sleep.

"I should have known you anywhere," she continued; "a woman never forgets some things. And you were the first man I ever — I ever saw."

"Was I, really?" said Jos. "God bless my soul, you — you don't say so."

"When I came with your sister from Chiswick, I was scarcely more than a child," Becky said. "How is that dear love? Oh, her husband was a sad wicked man, and of course it was of me that the poor dear was jealous. As if I cared about him, heigho! when there was somebody — but no — don't let us talk of old times;" and she passed her handkerchief with the tattered lace across her eyelids.

"Is not this a strange place," she continued, "for a woman, who has lived in a very different world too, to be found in? I have had so many griefs and wrongs, Joseph Sedley, I have been made to suffer so cruelly, that I am almost made mad sometimes. I can't stay still in any place, but wander about always restless and unhappy. All my friends have been false to me — all. There is no such thing as an honest man in the world. I was the truest wife that ever lived, though I married my husband out of pique, because somebody else — but never mind that. I was true, and he trampled upon me, and deserted me. I was the fondest mother. I had but one child, one darling, one hope, one joy, which I held to my heart with a mother's affection, which was my life, my prayer, my — my blessing; and they — they tore it from me — tore it from me;" and she put her hand to her heart with a passionate gesture of despair, burying her face for a moment on the bed.

The brandy-bottle inside clinked up against the plate which held the cold sausage. Both were moved, no doubt, by the exhibition of so much grief. Max and Fritz were at the door listening with wonder to Mrs. Becky's sobs and cries. Jos, too, was a good deal frightened and affected at seeing his old flame in this condition. And she began, forthwith, to tell her story, — a tale so neat, simple, and artless, that it was quite evident from hearing her, that if ever there was a white-robed angel escaped from heaven to be subject to the infernal machinations and villany of fiends here below, that spotless being — that miserable unsullied martyr was present on the bed before Jos — on the bed, sitting on the brandy-bottle.

They had a very long, amicable, and confidential talk there; in the course of which, Jos Sedley was somehow made aware (but in a manner that did not in the least scare or offend him) that Becky's heart had first learned to beat at his enchanting presence: that George Osborne had certainly paid an unjustifiable court to *her*, which might account for Amelia's jealousy, and their little rupture; but that Becky never gave the least encouragement to the unfortunate officer, and that she had never ceased to think about Jos from the very first day she had seen him, though, of course, her duties as a married woman were paramount — duties which she had always preserved, and would, to her dying day, or until the proverbially bad climate in which Colonel Crawley was living, should release her from a yoke which his cruelty had rendered odious to her.

Jos went away, convinced that she was the most virtuous, as she was one of the most fascinating of women, and revolving in his mind all sorts of benevolent schemes for her welfare. Her persecutions ought to be ended; she ought to return to the society of which she was an ornament. He would see what ought to be done. She must quit that place, and take a quiet lodging. Amelia must come and see her, and befriend her. He would go and settle about it, and consult with the Major. She wept tears of heartfelt gratitude as she parted from him, and pressed his hand as the gallant stout gentleman stooped down to kiss hers.

So Becky bowed Jos out of her little garret with as much grace as if it was a palace of which she did the honors; and that heavy gentleman having disappeared down the stairs, Hans and Fritz came out of their hole, pipe in mouth, and she amused herself by mimicking Jos to them as she munched her cold bread and sausage and took draughts of her favorite brandy-and-water.

Jos walked over to Dobbin's lodgings with great solemnity, and there imparted to him the affecting history with which he had just been made acquainted, without, however, mentioning the play-business of the night before. And the two gentlemen were laying their heads together, and consulting as to the best means of being useful to Mrs. Becky, while she was finishing her interrupted *déjeuner à la fourchette.*

How was it she had come to that little town? How was it that she had no friends and was wandering about alone? Little boys at school are taught in their earliest Latin book, that the path of Avernus is very easy of descent. Let us skip over the interval in the history of her downward progress. She was not worse now than she had been in the days of her prosperity : — only a little down on her luck.

As for Mrs. Amelia, she was a woman of such a soft and foolish disposition, that when she heard of anybody unhappy, her heart straightway melted towards the sufferer; and as she had never thought or done anything mortally guilty herself, she had not that abhorrence for wickedness which distinguishes moralists much more knowing. If she spoiled everybody who came near her with kindness and compliments, — if she begged pardon of all her servants for troubling them to answer the bell, — if she apologized to a shop-boy who showed her a piece of silk, or made a curtsy to a street-sweeper, with a complimentary remark upon the elegant state of his crossing — and she was almost capable of every one of these follies — the notion that an old acquaintance was miserable was sure to soften her heart; nor would she hear of anybody's being deservedly unhappy. A world under such legislation as hers would not be a very orderly place of abode; but there are not many women, at least not of the rulers, who are of her sort. This lady, I believe, would have abolished all gaols, punishments, handcuffs, whippings, poverty, sickness, hunger, in the world; and was such a mean-spirited creature, that — we are obliged to confess it — she could even forget a mortal injury.

When the Major heard from Jos of the sentimental adventure which had just befallen the latter, he was not, it must be owned, nearly as much interested as the gentleman from Bengal. On the contrary, his excitement was quite the reverse from a pleasurable one; he made use of a brief but improper expression regarding a poor woman in distress, saying, in fact, — "the little minx, has she come to light again?" He never had had the slightest liking for her; but had heartily mistrusted her from the very first moment when her green eyes had looked at, and turned away from, his own.

"That little devil brings mischief wherever she goes," the Major said, disrespectfully. "Who knows what sort of life she has been leading? and what business has she here abroad and alone? Don't tell me about persecutors and enemies; an honest woman always has friends, and never is separated from her family. Why has she left her husband? He may have been disreputable and wicked, as you say. He always was. I remember the confounded blackleg, and the way in which he used to cheat and hoodwink poor George. Was n't there a scandal about their separation? I think I heard something," cried out Major Dobbin, who did not care much about gossip; and whom Jos tried in vain to convince that Mrs. Becky was in all respects a most injured and virtuous female.

"Well, well; let 's ask Mrs. George," said that arch-diplomatist of a Major. "Only let us go and consult *her*. I suppose you will allow that *she* is a good judge at any rate, and knows what is right in such matters."

"Hm! Emmy is very well," said Jos, who did not happen to be in love with his sister.

"Very well? by Gad, sir, she's the finest lady I ever met in my life," bounced out the Major. "I say at once, let us go and ask her if this woman ought to be visited or not — I will be content with her verdict." Now this odious, artful rogue of a Major was thinking in his own mind that he was sure of his case. Emmy, he remembered, was at one time cruelly and deservedly jealous of Rebecca, never mentioned her name but with a shrinking and terror — a jealous woman never forgives, thought Dobbin; and so the pair went across the street to Mrs. George's house, where she was contentedly warbling at a music-lesson with Madame Strumpff.

When that lady took her leave, Jos opened the business with his usual pomp of words. "Amelia, my dear," said he, "I have just had the most extraordinary — yes — God bless my soul! the most extraordinary adventure — an old friend — yes, a most interesting old friend of yours, and I may say in old times, has just arrived here, and I should like you to see her."

"Her!" said Amelia, "who is it? Major Dobbin, if you please not to break my scissors." The Major was twirling them round by the little chain from which they sometimes hung to their lady's waist, and was thereby endangering his own eye.

"It is a woman whom I dislike very much," said the Major, doggedly; "and whom you have no cause to love."

"It is Rebecca, I'm sure it is Rebecca," Amelia said blushing, and being very much agitated.

"You are right; you always are," Dobbin answered. Brussels, Waterloo, old, old times, griefs, pangs, remembrances, rushed back into Amelia's gentle heart, and caused a cruel agitation there.

"Don't let me see her," Emmy continued. "I could n't see her."

"I told you so," Dobbin said to Jos.

"She is very unhappy, and — and that sort of thing," Jos urged. "She is very poor and unprotected: and has been ill — exceedingly ill — and that scoundrel of a husband has deserted her."

"Ah!" said Amelia.

"She has n't a friend in the world," Jos went on, not undexterously; "and she said she thought she might trust in you. She 's so miserable, Emmy. She has been almost mad with grief. Her story quite affected me : — 'pon my word and honor, it did — never was such a cruel persecution borne so angelically, I may say. Her family has been most cruel to her."

"Poor creature!" Amelia said.

"And if she can get no friend, she says she thinks she 'll die," Jos proceeded, in a low tremulous voice. — "God bless my soul! do you know that she tried to kill herself? She carries laudanum with her — I saw the bottle in her room — such a miserable little room — at a third-rate house, the Elephant, up in the roof at the top of all. I went there."

This did not seem to affect Emmy. She even smiled a little. Perhaps she figured Jos to herself panting up the stair.

"She 's beside herself with grief," he resumed. "The agonies that woman has endured are quite frightful to hear of. She had a little boy, of the same age as Georgy."

"Yes, yes, I think I remember," Emmy remarked. "Well?"

"The most beautiful child ever seen," Jos said, who was very fat, and easily moved, and had been touched by the story Becky told; "a perfect angel, who adored his mother. The ruffians tore him shrieking out of her arms, and have never allowed him to see her."

"Dear Joseph," Emmy cried out, starting up at once, "let us go and see her this minute." And she ran into her adjoining bedchamber, tied on her bonnet in a flutter, came out with her shawl on her arm, and ordered Dobbin to follow.

He went and put her shawl — it was a white cashmere, consigned to her by the Major himself from India — over her shoulders. He saw there was nothing for it but to obey; and she put her hand into his arm, and they went away.

"It is number 92, up four pair of stairs," Jos said perhaps not very willing to ascend the steps again; but he placed himself in the window of his drawing-room, which commands the place on which the Elephant stands, and saw the pair marching through the market.

It was as well that Becky saw them too from her garret; for she and the two students were chattering and laughing there; they had been joking about the appearance of Becky's grandpapa — whose arrival and departure they had witnessed — but she had time to dismiss them, and have her little room clear before the landlord of the Elephant, who knew that Mrs. Osborne was a great favorite at the Serene Court, and respected her accordingly, led the way up the stairs to the roof-story, encouraging Miladi and the Herr Major as they achieved the ascent.

"Gracious lady, gracious lady!" said the landlord, knocking at Becky's door; he had called her Madame the day before, and was by no means courteous to her.

"Who is it?" Becky said, putting out her head, and she gave a little scream. There stood Emmy in a tremble, and Dobbin, the tall Major, with his cane.

He stood still watching, and very much interested at the scene; but Emmy sprang forward with open arms towards Rebecca, and forgave her at that moment, and embraced her and kissed her with all her heart. Ah, poor wretch, when was your lip pressed before by such pure kisses?

CHAPTER XII.

AMANTIUM IRÆ.

FRANKNESS and kindness like Amelia's were likely to touch even such a hardened little reprobate as Becky. She returned Emmy's caresses and kind speeches with something very like gratitude, and an emotion which, if it was not lasting, for a moment was almost genuine. That was a lucky stroke of hers about the child "torn from her arms shrieking." It was by that harrowing misfortune that Becky had won her friend back, and it was one of the very first points, we may be certain, upon which our poor simple little Emmy began to talk to her new-found acquaintance.

"And so they took your darling child from you," our simpleton cried out. "Oh, Rebecca, my poor dear suffering friend, I know what it is to lose a boy, and to feel for those who have lost one. But please Heaven yours will be restored to you, as a merciful merciful Providence has brought me back mine."

"The child, my child? Oh, yes, my agonies were frightful," Becky owned, not perhaps without a twinge of conscience. It jarred upon her, to be obliged to commence instantly to tell lies in reply to so much confidence and simplicity. But that is the misfortune of beginning with this kind of forgery. When one fib becomes due as it were, you must forge another to take up the old acceptance; and so the stock of your lies in circulation inevitably multiplies, and the danger of detection increases every day.

"My agonies," Becky continued, "were terrible (I hope she won't sit down on the bottle) when they took him away from me; I thought I should die; but I fortunately had a brain fever, during which my doctor gave me up, and — and I recovered, and — and here I am, poor and friendless."

"How old is he?" Emmy asked.

"Eleven," said Becky.

"Eleven!" cried the other. "Why, he was born the same year with Georgy, who is —"

"I know, I know," Becky cried out, who had in fact quite forgotten all about little Rawdon's age. "Grief has made me forget so many things, dearest Amelia. I am very much changed; half wild sometimes. He was eleven when they took him away from me. Bless his sweet face; I have never seen it again."

"Was he fair or dark?" went on that absurd little Emmy. "Show me his hair."

Becky almost laughed at her simplicity. "Not to-day, love, — some other time, when my trunks arrive from Leipzig, whence I came to this place, — and a little drawing of him, which I made in happy days."

"Poor Becky, poor Becky!" said Emmy. "How thankful, how thankful I ought to be!" (though I doubt whether that practice of piety inculcated upon us by our womankind in early youth, namely, to be thankful because we are better off than somebody else, be a very rational religious exercise); and then she began to think as usual, how her son was the handsomest, the best, and the cleverest boy in the whole world.

"You will see my Georgy," was the best thing Emmy could think of to console Becky. If anything could make her comfortable that would.

And so the two women continued talking for an hour or more, during which Becky had the opportunity of giving her new friend a full and complete version of her private history. She showed how her marriage with Rawdon Crawley had always been viewed by the family with feelings of the utmost hostility; how her sister-in-law (an artful woman) had poisoned her husband's mind against her; how he had formed odious connections, which had estranged his affections from her; how she had borne everything — poverty, neglect, coldness from the being whom she most loved — and all for the sake of her child; how, finally, and by the most flagrant outrage, she had been driven into demanding a separation from her husband, when the wretch did not scruple to ask that she should sacrifice her own fair fame so that he might procure advancement through the means of a very great and powerful but unprincipled man — the Marquis of Steyne, indeed. The atrocious monster!

This part of her eventful history Becky gave with the utmost feminine delicacy, and the most indignant virtue. Forced to fly her husband's roof by this insult, the coward had pursued his revenge by taking her child from her. And thus Becky said she was a wanderer, poor, unprotected, friendless, and wretched.

Emmy received this story, which was told at some length, as those persons who are acquainted with her character may imagine that she would. She quivered with indignation at the account of the conduct of the miserable Rawdon and the unprincipled Steyne. Her

eyes made notes of admiration for every one of the
sentences in which Becky described the persecutions
of her aristocratic relatives, and the falling away of
her husband. (Becky did not abuse him. She spoke
rather in sorrow than in anger. She had loved him
only too fondly : and was he not the father of her
boy ?) And as for the separation-scene from the
child, while Becky was reciting it, Emmy retired
altogether behind her pocket-handkerchief, so that
the consummate little tragedian must have been
charmed to see the effect which her performance
produced on her audience.

Whilst the ladies were carrying on their conversation, Amelia's constant escort, the Major (who, of
course, did not wish to interrupt their conference, and
found himself rather tired of creaking about the narrow stair passage of which the roof brushed the nap
from his hat), descended to the ground-floor of the
house and into the great room common to all the frequenters of the Elephant, out of which the stair led.
This apartment is always in a fume of smoke, and
liberally sprinkled with beer. On a dirty table stand
scores of corresponding brass-candlesticks with tallow
candles for the lodgers, whose keys hang up in rows
over the candles. Emmy had passed blushing through
the room anon, where all sorts of people were col-
lected ; Tyrolese glove-sellers and Danubian linen-
merchants, with their packs ; students recruiting
themselves with *butterbrods* and meat ; idlers, playing
cards or dominos on the sloppy, beery tables ; tumblers refreshing during the cessation of their performances ; — in a word, all the *fumum* and *strepitus*
of a German inn in fair time. The waiter brought
the Major a mug of beer, as a matter of course ; and
he took out a cigar, and amused himself with that

pernicious vegetable and a newspaper until his charge
should come down to claim him.

Max and Fritz came presently down stairs, their
caps on one side, their spurs jingling, their pipes
splendid with coats-of-arms and full-blown tassels,
and they hung up the key of No. 90 on the board,
and called for the ration of *butterbrod* and beer. The
pair sat down by the Major, and fell into a conversation of which he could not help hearing somewhat.
It was mainly about "Fuchs" and "Philister," and
duels and drinking-bouts at the neighboring University of Schoppenhausen, from which renowned seat of
learning they had just come in the *Eilwagen*, with
Becky, as it appeared, by their side, and in order to
be present at the bridal fêtes at Pumpernickel.

"The little *Engländerinn* seems to be *en bays de
gonnoisance*," said Max, who knew the French language, to Fritz, his comrade. "After the fat grandfather went away, there came a pretty little compatriot. I heard them chattering and whimpering
together in the little woman's chamber."

"We must take the tickets for her concert," Fritz
said. "Hast thou any money, Max ?"

"Bah," said the other, "the concert is a concert *in
nubibus*. Hans said that she advertised one at Leipzig :
and the Burschen took many tickets. But she went
off without singing. She said in the coach yesterday
that her pianist had fallen ill at Dresden. She cannot
sing, it is my belief : her voice is as cracked as thine,
O thou beer-soaking Renowner !"

"It is cracked ; *I* hear her trying out of her window
a *schrecklich* English ballad, called 'De Rose upon
de Balgony.'"

"*Saufen* and *singen* go not together," observed
Fritz with the red nose, who evidently preferred the

former amusement.   " No, thou shalt take none of her
tickets. She won money at the *trente* and *quarante*
last night.   I saw her: she made a little English boy
play for her.   We will spend thy money there or at
the theatre, or we will treat her to French wine or
cognac in the Aurelius Garden, but the tickets we
will not buy.   What sayest thou ?   Yet, another mug
of beer ? " and one and another successively having
buried their blond whiskers in the mawkish draught,
curled them and swaggered off into the fair.

The Major, who had seen the key of No. 90 put up
on its hook, and had heard the conversation of the two
young university bloods, was not at a loss to understand that their talk related to Becky.   " The little
devil is at her old tricks," he thought, and he smiled
as he recalled old days, when he had witnessed the
desperate flirtation with Jos, and the ludicrous end of
that adventure.   He and George had often laughed
over it subsequently, and until a few weeks after
George's marriage, when he also was caught in the
little Circe's toils, and had an understanding with her
which his comrade certainly suspected, but preferred
to ignore.   William was too much hurt or ashamed to
ask to fathom that disgraceful mystery, although
once, and evidently with remorse on his mind, George
had alluded to it.   It was on the morning of Waterloo, as the young men stood together in front of their
line, surveying the black masses of Frenchmen who
crowned the opposite heights, and as the rain was
coming down, " I have been mixing in a foolish in-
trigue with a woman," George said.   " I am glad we
were marched away.   If I drop, I hope Emmy will
never know of that business.   I wish to God it had
never been begun ! "   And William was pleased to
think, and had more than once soothed poor George's

widow with the narrative, that Osborne, after quitting his wife, and after the action of Quatre Bras, on the first day, spoke gravely and affectionately to his comrade of his father and his wife. On these facts, too, William had insisted very strongly in his conversations with the elder Osborne : and had thus been the means of reconciling the old gentleman to his son's memory, just at the close of the elder man's life.

"And so this devil is still going on with her intrigues," thought William. "I wish she were a hundred miles from here. She brings mischief wherever she goes." And he was pursuing these forebodings and this uncomfortable train of thought, with his head between his hands, and the "Pumpernickel Gazette" of last week unread under his nose, when somebody tapped his shoulder with a parasol, and he looked up and saw Mrs. Amelia.

This woman had a way of tyrannizing over Major Dobbin (for the weakest of all people will domineer over somebody), and she ordered him about, and patted him, and made him fetch and carry just as if he was a great Newfoundland dog. He liked, so to speak, to jump into the water if she said "High, Dobbin!" and to trot behind her with her reticule in his mouth. This history has been written to very little purpose if the reader has not perceived that the Major was a spooney.

"Why did you not wait for me, sir, to escort me down stairs ?" she said, giving a little toss of her head, and a most sarcastic curtsy.

"I could n't stand up in the passage," he answered, with a comical deprecatory look ; and, delighted to give her his arm, and to take her out of the horrid smoky place, he would have walked off without even so much as remembering the waiter, had not the young fellow run after him and stopped him on the threshold of the Elephant, to make him pay for the beer which he had not consumed. Emmy laughed: she called him a naughty man, who wanted to run away in debt: and, in fact, made some jokes suitable to the occasion and the small-beer. She was in high spirits and good humor, and tripped across the market-place very briskly. She wanted to see Jos that instant. The Major laughed at the impetuous affection Mrs. Amelia exhibited; for, in truth, it was not very often that she wanted her brother "that instant."

They found the civilian in his saloon on the first floor; he had been pacing the room, and biting his nails, and looking over the market-place towards the Elephant a hundred times at least during the past hour, whilst Emmy was closeted with her friend in the garret, and the Major was beating the tattoo on the sloppy tables of the public room below, and he was, on his side too, very anxious to see Mrs. Osborne.

"Well?" said he.

"The poor dear creature, how she has suffered!" Emmy said.

"God bless my soul, yes," Jos said, wagging his head, so that his cheeks quivered like jellies.

"She may have Payne's room, who can go up stairs," Emmy continued. Payne was a staid English maid and personal attendant upon Mrs. Osborne, to whom the courier, as in duty bound, paid court, and whom Georgy used to "lark" dreadfully with accounts of German robbers and ghosts. She passed her time chiefly in grumbling, in ordering about her mistress, and in stating her intention to return the next morning to her native village of Clapham. "She may have Payne's room," Emmy said.

"Why, you don't mean to say you are going to

have that woman into the *house?*" bounced out the Major, jumping up.

"Of course we are," said Amelia in the most inno-cent way in the world. "Don't be angry, and break the furniture, Major Dobbin. Of course we are going to have her here."

"Of course, my dear," Jos said.

"The poor creature, after all her sufferings," Emmy continued: "her horrid banker broken and run away: her husband — wicked wretch — having deserted her and taken her child away from her (here she doubled her two little fists and held them in a most menacing attitude before her, so that the Major was charmed to see such a dauntless virago), the poor dear thing! quite alone, and absolutely forced to give lessons in singing to get her bread — and not have her here!"

"Take lessons, my dear Mrs. George," cried the Major, "but don't have her in the house. I implore you, don't."

"Pooh," said Jos.

"You who are always good and kind: always used to be at any rate: I'm astonished at you, Major Wil-liam," Amelia cried. "Why, what is the moment to help her but when she is so miserable? Now is the time to be of service to her. The oldest friend I ever had, and not —"

"She was not always your friend, Amelia," the Major said, for he was quite angry. This allusion was too much for Emmy, who, looking the Major almost fiercely in the face, said, "For shame, Major Dobbin!" and after having fired this shot, she walked out of the room with a most majestic air, and shut her own door briskly on herself and her outraged dignity.

"To allude to *that!*" she said, when the door was

closed. " Oh, it was cruel of him to remind me of it,"
and she looked up at George's picture, which hung
there as usual, with the portrait of the boy underneath. " It was cruel of him. If I had forgiven it,
ought he to have spoken ? No. And it is from his
own lips that I know how wicked and groundless my
jealousy was ; and that you were pure — Oh, yes, you
were pure, my saint in heaven ! "

She paced the room trembling and indignant. She
went and leaned on the chest of drawers over which
the picture hung, and gazed and gazed at it. Its eyes
seemed to look down on her with a reproach that
deepened as she looked. The early dear, dear memories of that brief prime of love rushed back upon her.
The wound which years had scarcely cicatrized bled
afresh, and oh, how bitterly ! She could not bear the
reproaches of the husband there before her. It
could n't be. Never, never.

Poor Dobbin ; poor old William ! That unlucky
word had undone the work of many a year — the long
laborious edifice of a life of love and constancy —
raised too upon what secret and hidden foundations,
wherein lay buried passions, uncounted struggles, unknown sacrifices — a little word was spoken, and down
fell the fair palace of hope — one word, and away
flew the bird which he had been trying all his life
to lure !

William, though he saw by Amelia's looks that a
great crisis had come, nevertheless continued to implore Sedley, in the most energetic terms, to beware of
Rebecca : and he eagerly, almost frantically, adjured
Jos not to receive her. He besought Mr. Sedley to
inquire at least regarding her : told him how he had
heard that she was in the company of gamblers and
people of ill repute ; pointed out what evil she had

done in former days : how she and Crawley had misled poor George into ruin : how she was now parted
from her husband, by her own confession, and, perhaps, for good reason.   What a dangerous companion
she would be for his sister, who knew nothing of the
affairs of the world!   William implored Jos, with all
the eloquence which he could bring to bear, and a
great deal more energy than this quiet gentleman was
ordinarily in the habit of showing, to keep Rebecca
out of his household.

Had he been less violent, or more dexterous, he
might have succeeded in his supplications to Jos; but
the civilian was not a little jealous of the airs of superiority which the Major constantly exhibited towards
him, as he fancied (indeed, he had imparted his opinions to Mr. Kirsch, the courier, whose bills Major
Dobbin checked on this journey, and who sided with
his master), and he began a blustering speech about
his competency to defend his own honor, his desire
not to have his affairs meddled with, his intention, in
fine, to rebel against the Major, when the colloquy —
rather a long and stormy one — was put an end to in
the simplest way possible, namely, by the arrival of
Mrs. Becky, with a porter from the Elephant Hotel,
in charge of her very meagre baggage.

She greeted her host with affectionate respect, and
made a shrinking, but amicable, salutation to Major
Dobbin, who, as her instinct assured her at once, was
her enemy, and had been speaking against her; and
the bustle and clatter consequent upon her arrival
brought Amelia out of her room.   Emmy went up
and embraced her guest with the greatest warmth,
and took no notice of the Major, except to fling him
an angry look — the most unjust and scornful glance
that had perhaps ever appeared in that poor little

woman's face since she was born. But she had private reasons of her own, and was bent upon being
angry with him. And Dobbin, indignant at the injustice, not at the defeat, went off, making her a bow
quite as haughty as the killing curtsy with which the
little woman chose to bid him farewell.

He being gone, Emmy was particularly lively and
affectionate to Rebecca, and bustled about the apartments and installed her guest in her room with an
eagerness and activity seldom exhibited by our placid
little friend. But when an act of injustice is to be
done, especially by weak people, it is best that it
should be done quickly; and Emmy thought she was
displaying a great deal of firmness and proper feeling
and veneration for the late Captain Osborne in her
present behavior.

Georgy came in from the fêtes for dinner-time, and
found four covers laid as usual; but one of the places
was occupied by a lady, instead of by Major Dobbin.
"Hullo! where's Dob?" the young gentleman asked,
with his usual simplicity of language. "Major Dobbin is dining out, I suppose," his mother said; and,
drawing the boy to her, kissed him a great deal, and
put his hair off his forehead, and introduced him to
Mrs. Crawley. "This is my boy, Rebecca," Mrs.
Osborne said — as much as to say — can the world
produce anything like that? Becky looked at him
with rapture, and pressed his hand fondly. "Dear
boy!" she said — "he is just like my —" Emotion
choked her further utterance; but Amelia understood, as well as if she had spoken, that Becky was
thinking of her own blessed child. However, the
company of her friend consoled Mrs. Crawley, and
she ate a very good dinner.

During the repast, she had occasion to speak sev-

eral times, when Georgy eyed her and listened to her.
At the dessert Emmy was gone out to superintend
further domestic arrangements : Jos was in his great
chair dozing over "Galignani : " Georgy and the new
arrival sat close to each other : he had continued to
look at her knowingly more than once, and at last, he
laid down the nut-crackers.

"I say," said Georgy.

"What do you say ? " Becky said, laughing.

"You are the lady I saw in the mask at the *rouge
et noir.*"

"Hush ! you little sly creature," Becky said, taking up his hand and kissing it. "Your uncle was
there too, and Mamma must n't know."

"Oh no — not by no means," answered the little
fellow.

"You see we are quite good friends already, Becky
said to Emmy, who now re-entered ; and it must be
owned that Mrs. Osborne had introduced a most
judicious and amiable companion into her house.

William, in a state of great indignation, though
still unaware of all the treason that was in store for
him, walked about the town wildly until he fell upon
the Secretary of Legation, Tapeworm, who invited
him to dinner. As they were discussing that meal,
he took occasion to ask the Secretary whether he
knew anything about a certain Mrs. Rawdon Crawley,
who had, he believed, made some noise in London ;
and then Tapeworm, who of course knew all the
London gossip, and was besides a relative of Lady
Gaunt, poured out into the astonished Major's ears
such a history about Becky and her husband as astonished the querist, and supplied all the points of this
narrative, for it was at that very table years ago that

the present writer had the pleasure of hearing the
tale. Tufto, Steyne, the Crawleys, and their history
— everything connected with Becky and her previous
life passed under the record of the bitter diplomatist.
He knew everything and a great deal besides, about
all the world ; — in a word, he made the most astound-
ing revelations to the simple-hearted Major. When
Dobbin said that Mrs. Osborne and Mr. Sedley had
taken her into their house, Tapeworm burst into a
peal of laughter which shocked the Major, and asked
if they had not better send into the prison, and take
in one or two of the gentlemen in shaved heads and
yellow jackets, who swept the streets of Pumpernickel, chained in pairs, to board and lodge, and act
as tutor to that little scapegrace Georgy.

This information astonished and horrified the Major
not a little. It had been agreed in the morning (before meeting with Rebecca) that Amelia should go to
the court ball that night. There would be the place
where he should tell her. The Major went home
and dressed himself in his uniform, and repaired to
court in hopes to see Mrs. Osborne. She never came.
When he returned to his lodgings all the lights in the
Sedley tenement were put out. He could not see her
till the morning. I don't know what sort of a night's
rest he had with this frightful secret in bed with
him.

At the earliest convenient hour in the morning he
sent his servant across the way with a note, saying,
that he wished very particularly to speak with her.
A message came back to say, that Mrs. Osborne was
exceedingly unwell, and was keeping her room.

She too, had been awake all that night. She had
been thinking of a thing which had agitated her mind
a hundred times before. A hundred times on the

point of yielding, she had shrunk back from a sacrifice which she felt was too much for her. She
could n't, in spite of his love and constancy, and her
own acknowledged regard, respect, and gratitude.
What are benefits, what is constancy, or merit? One
curl of a girl's ringlet, one hair of a whisker, will turn
the scale against them all in a minute. They did not
weigh with Emmy more than with other women. She
had tried them; wanted to make them pass; could
not; and the pitiless little woman had found a pretext, and determined to be free.

When at length, in the afternoon, the Major gained
admission to Amelia, instead of the cordial and affectionate greeting, to which he had been accustomed
now for many a long day, he received the salutation
of a curtsy, and of a little gloved hand, retracted the
moment after it was accorded to him.

Rebecca, too, was in the room, and advanced to
meet him with a smile and an extended hand. Dobbin drew back rather confusedly. "I — I beg your
pardon, Ma'am," he said; "but I am bound to tell
you that it is not as your friend that I am come
here now."

"Pooh! damn; don't let us have this sort of
thing!" Jos cried out, alarmed, and anxious to get
rid of a scene.

"I wonder what Major Dobbin has to say against
Rebecca?" Amelia said in a low, clear voice with a
slight quiver in it, and a very determined look about
the eyes.

"I will *not* have this sort of thing in my house,"
Jos again interposed. "I say I will not have it: and
Dobbin, I beg, sir, you 'll stop it." And he looked
round trembling and turning very red, and gave a
great puff, and made for his door.

"Dear friend!" Rebecca said with angelic sweetness, "do hear what Major Dobbin has to say against me."

"I will *not* hear it, I say," squeaked out Jos at the top of his voice, and, gathering up his dressing-gown, he was gone.

"We are only two women," Amelia said. "You can speak now, sir."

"This manner towards me is one which scarcely becomes you, Amelia," the Major answered haughtily; "nor I believe am I guilty of habitual harshness to women. It is not a pleasure to me to do the duty which I am come to do."

"Pray proceed with it quickly, if you please, Major Dobbin," said Amelia, who was more and more in a pet. The expression of Dobbin's face, as she spoke in this imperious manner, was not pleasant.

"I came to say — and as you stay, Mrs. Crawley, I must say it in your presence — that I think you — you ought not to form a member of the family of my friends. A lady who is separated from her husband, who travels not under her own name, who frequents public gaming-tables — "

"It was to the ball I went," cried out Becky.

" — is not a fit companion for Mrs. Osborne and her son," Dobbin went on: "and I may add that there are people here who know you, and who profess to know that regarding your conduct, about which I don't even wish to speak before — before Mrs. Osborne."

"Yours is a very modest and convenient sort of calumny, Major Dobbin," Rebecca said. "You leave me under the weight of an accusation which, after all, is unsaid. What is it? Is it unfaithfulness to my husband? I scorn it, and defy anybody to prove it — I defy you, I say. My honor is as untouched as that of the bitterest enemy who ever maligned me. Is it of being poor, forsaken, wretched, that you accuse me? Yes, I am guilty of those faults, and punished for them every day. Let me go, Emmy. It is only to suppose that I have not met you, and I am no worse to-day than I was yesterday. It is only to suppose that the night is over and the poor wanderer is on her way. Don't you remember the song we used to sing in old, dear old days? I have been wandering ever since then — a poor castaway, scorned for being miserable, and insulted because I am alone. Let me go: my stay here interferes with the plans of this gentleman."

"Indeed it does, Madam," said the Major. "If I have any authority in this house — "

"Authority, none!" broke out Amelia. "Rebecca, you stay with me. *I* won't desert you, because you have been persecuted, or insult you, because — because Major Dobbin chooses to do so. Come away, dear." And the two women made towards their door.

William opened it. As they were going out, however, he took Amelia's hand, and said — "Will you stay a moment and speak to me?"

"He wishes to speak to you away from me," said Becky, looking like a martyr. Amelia griped her hand in reply.

"Upon my honor it is not about you that I am going to speak," Dobbin said. "Come back, Amelia," and she came. Dobbin bowed to Mrs. Crawley, as he shut the door upon her. Amelia looked at him, leaning against the glass: her face and her lips were quite white.

"I was confused when I spoke just now," the Major said, after a pause; "and I misused the word authority."

"You did," said Amelia, with her teeth chattering.

"At least I have claims to be heard," Dobbin continued.

"It is generous to remind me of our obligations to you," the woman answerd.

"The claims I mean, are those left me by George's father," William said.

"Yes, and you insulted his memory. You did yesterday. You know you did. And I will never forgive you. Never!" said Amelia. She shot out each little sentence in a tremor of anger and emotion.

"You don't mean that, Amelia?" William said, sadly. "You don't mean that these words, uttered in a hurried moment, are to weigh against a whole life's devotion? I think that George's memory has not been injured by the way in which I have dealt with it, and if we are come to bandying reproaches, I at least merit none from his widow and the mother of his son. Reflect, afterwards when — when you are at leisure, and your conscience will withdraw this accusation. It does even now." Amelia held down her head.

"It is not that speech of yesterday," he continued, "which moves you. That is but the pretext, Amelia, or I have loved you and watched you for fifteen years in vain. Have I not learned in that time to read all your feelings, and look into your thoughts? I know what your heart is capable of: it can cling faithfully to a recollection, and cherish a fancy; but it can't feel such an attachment as mine deserves to mate with, and such as I would have won from a woman more generous than you. No, you are not worthy of the love which I have devoted to you. I knew all along that the prize I had set my life on was not worth the winning; that I was a fool, with fond fan-

cies, too, bartering away my all of truth and ardor
against your little feeble remnant of love. I will bargain no more : I withdraw. I find no fault with you.
You are very good-natured, and have done your best ;
but you could n't — you could n't reach up to the height
of the attachment which I bore you, and which a
loftier soul than yours might have been proud to
share. Good-by, Amelia ! I have watched your
struggle. Let it end. We are both weary of it."

Amelia stood scared and silent as William thus
suddenly broke the chain by which she held him,
and declared his independence and superiority. He
had placed himself at her feet so long that the poor
little woman had been accustomed to trample upon
him. She did n't wish to marry him, but she wished
to keep him. She wished to give him nothing, but
that he should give her all. It is a bargain not
unfrequently levied in love.

William's sally had quite broken and cast her down.
Her assault was long since over and beaten back.

" Am I to understand then, — that you are going —
away, — William ? " she said.

He gave a sad laugh. " I went once before," he
said, " and came back after twelve years. We were
young then, Amelia. Good-by. I have spent enough
of my life at this play."

Whilst they had been talking, the door into Mrs.
Osborne's room had opened ever so little ; indeed,
Becky had kept a hold of the handle, and had turned
it on the instant when Dobbin quitted it ; and she
heard every word of the conversation that had passed
between these two. " What a noble heart that man
has," she thought, " and how shamefully that woman
plays with it." She admired Dobbin ; she bore him
no rancor for the part he had taken against her. It

was an open move in the game, and played fairly. "Ah!" she thought, "if I could have had such a husband as that — a man with a heart and brains too! I would not have minded his large feet;" and running into her room, she absolutely bethought herself of something, and wrote him a note, beseeching him to stop for a few days — not to think of going — and that she could serve him with A.

The parting was over. Once more poor William walked to the door and was gone; and the little widow, the author of all this work, had her will, and had won her victory, and was left to enjoy it as she best might. Let the ladies envy her triumph.

At the romantic hour of dinner, Mr. Georgy made his appearance, and again remarked the absence of "Old Dob." The meal was eaten in silence by the party. Jos's appetite not being diminished, but Emmy taking nothing at all.

After the meal, Georgy was lolling in the cushions of the old window, a large window, with three sides of glass abutting from the gable, and commanding on one side the market-place, where the Elephant is, his mother being busy hard by, when he remarked symptoms of movement at the Major's house on the other side of the street.

"Hullo!" said he, "there's Dob's trap — they are bringing it out of the court-yard." The "trap" in question was a carriage which the Major had bought for six pounds sterling, and about which they used to rally him a good deal.

Emmy gave a little start but said nothing.

"Hullo!" Georgy continued, "there's Francis coming out with the portmanteaus, and Kunz, the one-eyed postilion, coming down the market with three *schimmels*. Look at his boots and yellow jacket, —

ain't he a rum one ?   Why — they 're putting the
horses to Dob's carriage.   Is he going anywhere ? "

"Yes," said Emmy, "he is going on a journey."

"Going a journey ; and when is he coming back ? "

"He is — not coming back," answered Emmy.

"Not coming back !" cried out Georgy, jumping up.
"Stay here, sir," roared out Jos.   "Stay, Georgy,"
said his mother, with a very sad face.   The boy
stopped ; kicked about the room ; jumped up and
down from the window-seat with his knees, and
showed every symptom of uneasiness and curiosity.

The horses were put to.   The baggage was strapped
on.   Francis came out with his master's sword, cane,
and umbrella tied up together, and laid them in the
well, and his desk and old tin cocked-hat case, which
he placed under the seat.   Francis brought out the
stained old blue cloak lined with red camlet, which
had wrapped the owner up any time these fifteen
years, and had *manchen Sturm erlebt*, as a favorite
song of those days said.   It had been new for the
campaign of Waterloo, and had covered George and
William after the night of Quatre Bras.

Old Burcke, the landlord of the lodgings, came out,
then Francis, with more packages — final packages —
then Major William, — Burcke wanted to kiss him.
The Major was adored by all people with whom he
had to do.   It was with difficulty he could escape
from this demonstration of attachment.

"By Jove, I *will* go ! " screamed out George.   "Give
him this," said Becky, quite interested, and put a
paper into the boy's hand.   He had rushed down the
stairs and flung across the street in a minute — the
yellow postilion was cracking his whip gently.

William had got into the carriage, released from
the embraces of his landlord.   George bounded in

afterwards and flung his arms round the Major's neck
(as they saw from the window), and began asking him
multiplied questions. Then he felt in his waistcoat-
pocket and gave him a note. William seized at it
rather eagerly, he opened it trembling, but instantly
his countenance changed, and he tore the paper in two,
and dropped it out of the carriage. He kissed Georgy
on the head, and the boy got out, doubling his fists into
his eyes, and with the aid of Francis. He lingered
with his hand on the panel. Fort Schwager! The
yellow postilion cracked his whip prodigiously, up
sprang Francis to the box, away went the *schimmels*,
and Dobbin with his head on his breast. He never
looked up as they passed under Amelia's window:
and Georgy, left alone in the street, burst out crying
in the face of all the crowd.

Emmy's maid heard him howling again during the
night, and brought him some preserved apricots to
console him. She mingled her lamentations with his.
All the poor, all the humble, all honest folks, all good
men who knew him, loved that kind-hearted and
simple gentleman.

As for Emmy, had she not done her duty? She
had her picture of George for a consolation.

CHAPTER XIII.

WHICH CONTAINS BIRTHS, MARRIAGES, AND DEATHS.

WHATEVER Becky's private plan might be by which Dobbin's true love was to be crowned with success, the little woman thought that the secret might keep, and indeed, being by no means so much interested about anybody's welfare as about her own, she had a great number of things pertaining to herself to consider, and which concerned her a great deal more than Major Dobbin's happiness in this life.

She found herself suddenly and unexpectedly in snug comfortable quarters: surrounded by friends, kindness, and good-natured simple people, such as she had not met with for many a long day; and, wanderer as she was by force and inclination, there were moments when rest was pleasant to her. As the most hardened Arab that ever careered across the Desert over the hump of a dromedary, likes to repose sometimes under the date-trees by the water; or to come into the cities, walk in the bazaars, refresh himself in the baths, and say his prayers in the mosques, before he goes out again marauding; Jos's tents and *pilau* were pleasant to this little Ishmaelite. She picketed her steed, hung up her weapons, and warmed herself comfortably by his fire. The halt in that roving, restless life, was inexpressibly soothing and pleasant to her.

So, pleased herself, she tried with all her might to please everybody; and we know that she was eminent and successful as a practitioner in the art of giving pleasure. As for Jos, even in that little interview in the garret at the Elephant Inn, she had found means to win back a great deal of his good-will. In the course of a week, the civilian was her sworn slave and frantic admirer. He did n't go to sleep after dinner, as his custom was, in the much less lively society of Amelia. He drove out with Becky in his open carriage. He asked little parties and invented festivities to do her honor.

Tapeworm, the *Chargé d'Affaires*, who had abused her so cruelly, came to dine with Jos, and then came every day to pay his respects to Becky. Poor Emmy, who was never very talkative, and more glum and silent than ever after Dobbin's departure, was quite forgotten when this superior genius made her appearance. The French minister was as much charmed with her as his English rival. The German ladies, never particularly squeamish as regards morals, especially in English people, were delighted with the cleverness and wit of Mrs. Osborne's charming friend; and though she did not ask to go to court, yet the most august and Transparent Personages there heard of her fascinations, and were quite curious to know her. When it became known that she was noble, of an ancient English family, that her husband was a Colonel of the Guard, Excellenz and Governor of an island, only separated from his lady by one of those trifling differences which are of little account in a country where "Werther" is still read, and the "Wahlverwandschaften" of Goethe is considered an edifying moral book, nobody thought of refusing to receive her in the very highest society of the little

Duchy; and the ladies were even more ready to call her *du*, and to swear eternal friendship for her, than they had been to bestow the same inestimable benefits upon Amelia. Love and Liberty are interpreted by those simple Germans in a way which honest folks in Yorkshire and Somersetshire little understand; and a lady might, in some philosophic and civilized towns, be divorced ever so many times from her respective husbands, and keep her character in society. Jos's house never was so pleasant since he had a house of his own, as Rebecca caused it to be. She sang, she played, she laughed, she talked in two or three languages; she brought everybody to the house: and she made Jos believe that it was his own great social talents and wit which gathered the society of the place round about him.

As for Emmy, who found herself not in the least mistress of her own house, except when the bills were to be paid, Becky soon discovered the way to soothe and please her. She talked to her perpetually about Major Dobbin sent about his business, and made no scruple of declaring her admiration for that excellent, high-minded gentleman, and of telling Emmy that she had behaved most cruelly regarding him. Emmy defended her conduct, and showed that it was dictated only by the purest religious principles; that a woman once, etc., and to such an angel as him whom she had had the good fortune to marry, was married forever; but she had no objection to hear the Major praised as much as ever Becky chose to praise him; and indeed brought the conversation round to the Dobbin subject a score of times every day.

Means were easily found to win the favor of Georgy and the servants. Amelia's maid, it has been said, was heart and soul in favor of the generous Major.

Having at first disliked Becky for being the means of dismissing him from the presence of her mistress, she was reconciled to Mrs. Crawley subsequently, because the latter became William's most ardent admirer and champion.   And in those nightly conclaves in which the two ladies indulged after their parties, and while Miss Payne was " brushing their 'airs," as she called the yellow locks of the one, and the soft brown tresses of the other, this girl always put in her word for that dear good gentleman Major Dobbin. Her advocacy did not make Amelia angry any more than Rebecca's admiration of him.   She made George write to him constantly, and persisted in sending Mamma's kind love in a postscript.   And as she looked at her husband's portrait of nights, it no longer reproached her — perhaps she reproached it, now William was gone.

Emmy was not very happy after her heroic sacrifice. She was very *distraite*, nervous, silent, and ill to please. The family had never known her so peevish.   She grew pale and ill.   She used to try and sing certain songs (" Einsam bin ich nicht alleine," was one of them ; that tender love-song of Weber's, which, in old-fashioned days, young ladies, and when you were scarcely born, showed that those who lived before you knew too how to love and to sing) ; — certain songs, I say, to which the Major was partial ; and as she warbled them in the twilight in the drawing-room, she would break off in the midst of the song, and walk into her neighboring apartment, and there, no doubt, take refuge in the miniature of her husband.

Some books still subsisted, after Dobbin's departure, with his name written in them ; a German Dictionary, for instance, with " William Dobbin, — th Reg.," in the fly-leaf ; a guide-book with his initials, and one or two

other volumes which belonged to the Major. Emmy
cleared these away, and put them on the drawers,
where she placed her work-box, her desk, her Bible,
and Prayer-book, under the pictures of the two Georges.
And the Major, on going away, having left his gloves
behind him, it is a fact that Georgy, rummaging his
mother's desk some time afterwards, found the gloves
neatly folded up, and put away in what they call the
secret drawers of the desk.

Not caring for society, and moping there a great
deal, Emmy's chief pleasure in the summer evenings
was to take long walks with Georgy (during which
Rebecca was left to the society of Mr. Joseph), and
then the mother and son used to talk about the Major
in a way which even made the boy smile. She told
him that she thought Major William was the best man
in all the world; the gentlest and the kindest, the
bravest and the humblest. Over and over again, she
told him how they owed everything which they possessed in the world to that kind friend's benevolent
care of them; how he had befriended them all through
their poverty and misfortunes; watched over them
when nobody cared for them; how all his comrades
admired him though he never spoke of his own gallant actions; how Georgy's father trusted him beyond
all other men, and had been constantly befriended by
the good William.   "Why, when your papa was a
little boy," she said, "he often told me that it was
William who defended him against a tyrant at the
school where they were; and their friendship never
ceased from that day until the last, when your dear
father fell."

"Did Dobbin kill the man who killed Papa?"
Georgy said.   "I'm sure he did, or he would if he
could have caught him; would n't he, Mother?   When

I'm in the army, won't I hate the French? — that's all."

In such colloquies the mother and the child passed a great deal of their time together. The artless woman had made a confidant of the boy. He was as much William's friend as everybody else who knew him well.

By the way, Mrs. Becky, not to be behind-hand in sentiment, had got a miniature too hanging up in her room, to the surprise and amusement of most people, and the delight of the original, who was no other than our friend Jos. On her first coming to favor the Sedleys with a visit, the little woman, who had arrived with a remarkably small shabby kit, was perhaps ashamed of the meanness of her trunks and band-boxes, and often spoke with great respect about her baggage left behind at Leipzig, which she must have from that city. When a traveller talks to you perpetually about the splendor of his luggage, which he does not happen to have with him; my son, beware of that traveller! He is, ten to one, an impostor.

Neither Jos nor Emmy knew this important maxim. It seemed to them of no consequence whether Becky had a quantity of very fine clothes in invisible trunks; but as her present supply was exceedingly shabby, Emmy supplied her out of her own stores, or took her to the best milliner in the town, and there fitted her out. It was no more torn collars now, I promise you, and faded silks trailing off at the shoulder. Becky changed her habits with her situation in life — the rouge-pot was suspended — another excitement to which she had accustomed herself was also put aside, or at least only indulged in in privacy; as when she was prevailed on by Jos of a summer evening, Emmy and the boy being absent on their walks, to take a lit-

tle spirit-and-water. But if she did not indulge — the
courier did : that rascal Kirsch could not be kept from
the bottle, nor could he tell how much he took when
he applied to it. He was sometimes surprised himself at the way in which Mr. Sedley's cognac diminished. Well, well; this is a painful subject. Becky
did not very likely indulge so much as she used before
she entered a decorous family.

At last the much-bragged-about boxes arrived from
Leipzig, — three of them not by any means large or
splendid ; — nor did Becky appear to take out any
sort of dresses or ornaments from the boxes when
they did arrive. But out of one, which contained a
mass of her papers (it was that very box which Rawdon Crawley had ransacked in his furious hunt for
Becky's concealed money), she took a picture with
great glee, which she pinned up in her room, and to
which she introduced Jos. It was the portrait of a
gentleman in pencil, his face having the advantage of
being painted up in pink. He was riding on an elephant away from some cocoanut-trees, and a pagoda :
it was an Eastern scene.

"God bless my soul, it is my portrait," Jos cried
out. It was he indeed, blooming in youth and beauty,
in a nankeen jacket of the cut of 1804. It was the
old picture that used to hang up in Russell Square.

"I bought it," said Becky, in a voice trembling with
emotion; "I went to see if I could be of any use to
my kind friends. I have never parted with that picture — I never will."

"Won't you?" Jos cried, with a look of unutterable rapture and satisfaction. "Did you really now
value it for my sake?"

"You know I did, well enough," said Becky; "but
why speak, — why think, — why look back ! It is
too late now!"

That evening's conversation was delicious for Jos. Emmy only came in to go to bed very tired and unwell. Jos and his fair guest had a charming *tête-à-tête*, and his sister could hear, as she lay awake in her adjoining chamber, Rebecca singing over to Jos the old songs of 1815. He did not sleep, for a wonder, that night, any more than Amelia.

It was June, and, by consequence, high season in London; Jos, who read the incomparable "Galignani" (the exile's best friend) through every day, used to favor the ladies with extracts from his paper during their breakfast. Every week in this paper there is a full account of military movements, in which Jos, as a man who had seen service, was especially interested. On one occasion he read out — " Arrival of the — th regiment. Gravesend, June 20. The 'Ramchunder,' East Indiaman, came into the river this morning, having on board fourteen officers, and one hundred and thirty-two rank and file of this gallant corps. They have been absent from England fourteen years, having been embarked the year after Waterloo, in which glorious conflict they took an active part, and having subsequently distinguished themselves in the Burmese war. The veteran colonel, Sir Michael O'Dowd, K.C.B., with his lady and sister, landed here yesterday, with Captains Posky, Stubble, Macraw, Malony; Lieutenants Smith, Jones, Thompson, F. Thomson; Ensigns Hicks and Grady; the band on the pier playing the national anthem, and the crowd loudly cheering the gallant veterans as they went into Wayte's hotel, where a sumptuous banquet was provided for the defenders of Old England. During the repast, which we need not say was served up in Wayte's best style, the cheering continued so enthusiastically, that Lady O'Dowd and the Colonel came forward to the balcony, and drank the healths of their fellow-countrymen in a bumper of Wayte's best claret."

On a second occasion Jos read a brief announcement — Major Dobbin had joined the — th regiment at Chatham; and subsequently he promulgated accounts of the presentations at the Drawing-room, of Colonel Sir Michael O'Dowd, K.C.B., Lady O'Dowd (by Mrs. Molloy Malony of Ballymalony), and Miss Glorvina O'Dowd (by Lady O'Dowd). Almost directly after this, Dobbin's name appeared among the Lieutenant-Colonels: for old Marshall Tiptoff had died during the passage of the — th from Madras, and the Sovereign was pleased to advance Colonel Sir Michael O'Dowd to the rank of Major-General on his return to England, with an intimation that he should be Colonel of the distinguished regiment which he had so long commanded.

Amelia had been made aware of some of these movements. The correspondence between George and his guardian had not ceased by any means: William had even written once or twice to her since his departure, but in a manner so unconstrainedly cold, that the poor woman felt now in her turn that she had lost her power over him, and that, as he had said, he was free. He had left her, and she was wretched. The memory of his almost countless services, and lofty and affectionate regard, now presented itself to her, and rebuked her day and night. She brooded over those recollections according to her wont; saw the purity and beauty of the affection with which she had trifled, and reproached herself for having flung away such a treasure.

It was gone indeed. William had spent it all out. He loved her no more, he thought, as he had loved her. He never could again. That sort of regard, which he had proffered to her for so many faithful years, can't be flung down and shattered, and mended so as to show no scars. The little heedless tyrant had so destroyed it. No, William thought again and again, "It was myself I deluded, and persisted in cajoling; had she been worthy of the love I gave her, she would have returned it long ago. It was a fond mistake. Is n't the whole course of life made up of such? and suppose I had won her, should I not have been disenchanted the day after my victory? Why pine, or be ashamed of my defeat?" The more he thought of this long passage of his life, the more clearly he saw his deception. "I 'll go into harness again," he said, "and do my duty in that state of life in which it has pleased Heaven to place me. I will see that the buttons of the recruits are properly bright, and that the sergeants make no mistakes in their accounts. I will dine at mess, and listen to the Scotch surgeon telling his stories. When I am old and broken, I will go on half-pay, and my old sisters shall scold me. I have 'geliebt and gelebet' as the girl in 'Wallenstein' says. I am done. — Pay the bills, and get me a cigar: find out what there is at the play to-night, Francis; to-morrow we cross by the 'Batavier.'" He made the above speech, whereof Francis only heard the last two lines, pacing up and down the Boompjes at Rotterdam. The "Batavier" was lying in the basin. He could see the place on the quarter-deck, where he and Emmy had sat on the happy voyage out. What had that little Mrs. Crawley to say to him? Psha! to-morrow we will put to sea, and return to England, home, and duty!

After June all the little court society of Pumpernickel used to separate, according to the German plan, and make for a hundred watering-places, where they drank at the wells; rode upon donkeys; gambled at the *redoutes*, if they had money and a mind; rushed with hundreds of their kind, to gormandize at the *tables d'hôte;* and idled away the summer. The English diplomatists went off to Toeplitz and Kissengen, their French rivals shut up their *Chancellerie* and whisked away to their darling Boulevard de Gand. The Transparent reigning family took too to the waters, or retired to their hunting-lodges. Everybody went away having any pretensions to politeness, and, of course, with them, Doctor von Glauber, the court doctor, and his Baroness. The seasons for the baths were the most productive periods of the doctor's practice — he united business with pleasure, and his chief place of resort was Ostend, which is much frequented by Germans, and where the doctor treated himself and his spouse to what he called a "dib" in the sea.

His interesting patient, Jos, was a regular milch cow to the doctor, and he easily persuaded the civilian, both for his own health's sake and that of his charming sister, which was really very much shattered, to pass the summer at that hideous seaport town. Emmy did not care where she went much. Georgy jumped at the idea of a move. As for Becky, she came as a matter of course in the fourth place inside of the fine barouche Mr. Jos had bought: the two domestics being on the box in front. She might have some misgivings about the friends whom she should meet at Ostend, and who might be likely to tell ugly stories — but bah! she was strong enough to hold her own. She had cast such an anchor in Jos now as would require a strong storm to shake. That incident of the picture had finished him. Becky took down her elephant, and put it into the little box which she had had from Amelia ever so many years ago. Emmy also came off with her Lares, — her two pictures, — and the party, finally, were lodged in an exceedingly dear and uncomfortable house at Ostend.

There Amelia began to take baths, and get what good she could from them, and though scores of people of Becky's acquaintance passed her and cut her, yet Mrs. Osborne, who walked about with her, and who knew nobody, was not aware of the treatment experienced by the friend whom she had chosen so judiciously as a companion; indeed, Becky never thought fit to tell her what was passing under her innocent eyes.

Some of Mrs. Rawdon Crawley's acquaintances, however, acknowledged her readily enough, — perhaps more readily than she would have desired. Among those were Major Loder (unattached), and Captain Rook (late of the Rifles), who might be seen any day on the Dyke, smoking and staring at the women, and who speedily got an introduction to the hospitable board and select circle of Mr. Joseph Sedley. In fact, they would take no denial; they burst into the house whether Becky was at home or not, walked into Mrs. Osborne's drawing-room, which they perfumed with their coats and mustachios, called Jos "old buck," and invaded his dinner-table, and laughed and drank for long hours there.

"What can they mean?" asked Georgy, who did not like these gentlemen. "I heard the Major say to Mrs. Crawley yesterday, 'No, no, Becky, you sha'n't keep the old buck to yourself. We must have the bones in, or dammy, I'll split.' What could the Major mean, Mamma?"

"Major! don't call *him* Major!" Emmy said. "I 'm sure I can't tell what he meant." His presence and that of his friend inspired the little lady with intolerable terror and aversion. They paid her tipsy compliments; they leered at her over the dinner-table. And the Captain made her advances that filled her with sickening dismay, nor would she ever see him unless she had George by her side.

Rebecca, to do her justice, never would let either of these men remain alone with Amelia; the Major was disengaged too, and swore he would be the winner of her. A couple of ruffians were fighting for this innocent creature, gambling for her at her own table; and though she was not aware of the rascals' designs upon her, yet she felt a horror and uneasiness in their presence, and longed to fly.

She besought, she entreated Jos to go. Not he. He was slow of movement, tied to his doctor, and perhaps to some other leading-strings. At least Becky was not anxious to go to England.

At last she took a great resolution — made the great plunge. She wrote off a letter to a friend whom she had on the other side of the water; a letter about which she did not speak a word to anybody, which she carried herself to the post under her shawl, nor was any remark made about it; only that she looked very much flushed and agitated when Georgy met her; and she kissed him and hung over him a great deal that night. She did not come out of her room after her return from her walk. Becky thought it was Major Loder and the Captain who frightened her.

"She mustn't stop here," Becky reasoned with herself. "She must go away, the silly little fool. She is still whimpering after that gaby of a husband — dead (and served right!) these fifteen years. She sha'n't marry either of these men. It's too bad of

Loder. No; she shall marry the bamboo cane, I'll settle it this very night."

So Becky took a cup of tea to Amelia in her private apartment, and found that lady in the company of her miniatures, and in a most melancholy and nervous condition. She laid down the cup of tea.

"Thank you," said Amelia.

"Listen to me, Amelia," said Becky, marching up and down the room before the other, and surveying her with a sort of contemptuous kindness. "I want to talk to you. You must go away from here and from the impertinences of these men. I won't have you harassed by them: and they will insult you if you stay. I tell you they are rascals; men fit to send to the hulks. Never mind how I know them. I know everybody. Jos can't protect you, he is too weak, and wants a protector himself. You are no more fit to live in the world than a baby in arms. You must marry, or you and your precious boy will go to ruin. You must have a husband, you fool; and one of the best gentlemen I ever saw has offered you a hundred times, and you have rejected him, you silly, heartless, ungrateful little creature!"

"I tried — I tried my best, indeed I did, Rebecca," said Amelia, deprecatingly, "but I couldn't forget — " and she finished the sentence by looking up at the portrait.

"Couldn't forget *him!*" cried out Becky, "that selfish humbug, that low-bred cockney-dandy, that padded booby, who had neither wit, nor manners, nor heart, and was no more to be compared to your friend with the bamboo cane than you are to Queen Elizabeth. Why, the man was weary of you, and would have jilted you, but that Dobbin forced him to keep his word. He owned it to me. He never cared for you. He used to sneer about you to me, time after time; and made love to me the week after he married you."

"It's false! It's false! Rebecca," cried out Amelia, starting up.

"Look there, you fool," Becky said, still with provoking good-humor, and taking a little paper out of her belt, she opened it and flung it into Emmy's lap. "You know his handwriting. He wrote that to me — wanted me to run away with him — gave it me under your nose, the day before he was shot — and served him right!" Becky repeated.

Emmy did not hear her; she was looking at the letter. It was that which George had put into the bouquet and given to Becky on the night of the Duchess of Richmond's ball. It was as she said: the foolish young man had asked her to fly.

Emmy's head sank down, and for almost the last time in which she shall be called upon to weep in this history, she commenced that work. Her head fell to her bosom, and her hands went up to her eyes; and there for a while, she gave way to her emotions, as Becky stood on and regarded her. Who shall analyze those tears, and say whether they were sweet or bitter? Was she most grieved, because the idol of her life was tumbled down and shivered at her feet, or indignant that her love had been so despised, or glad because the barrier was removed which modesty had placed between her and a new, a real affection? "There is nothing to forbid me now," she thought. "I may love him with all my heart now. Oh, I will, I will, if he will but let me, and forgive me." I believe it was this feeling rushed over all the others which agitated that gentle little bosom.

Indeed, she did not cry so much as Becky expected

The Letter before Waterloo.

— the other soothed and kissed her — a rare mark of sympathy with Mrs. Becky. She treated Emmy like a child, and patted her head. "And now let us get pen and ink, and write to him to come this minute," she said.

"I — I wrote to him this morning," Emmy said, blushing exceedingly. Becky screamed with laughter — "*Un biglietto*," she sang out with Rosina, "*eccolo quà!*" — the whole house echoed with her shrill singing.

Two mornings after this little scene, although the day was rainy and gusty, and Amelia had had an exceedingly wakeful night, listening to the wind roaring, and pitying all travellers by land and by water, yet she got up early, and insisted upon taking a walk on the Dyke with Georgy; and there she paced as the rain beat into her face, and she looked out westward across the dark sea-line, and over the swollen billows which came tumbling and frothing to the shore. Neither spoke much, except now and then, when the boy said a few words to his timid companion, indicative of sympathy and protection.

"I hope he won't cross in such weather," Emmy said.

"I bet ten to one he does," the boy answered. "Look, Mother, there's the smoke of the steamer." It was that signal, sure enough.

But though the steamer was under weigh, he might not be on board; he might not have got the letter; he might not choose to come. — A hundred fears poured one over the other into the little heart, as fast as the waves on to the Dyke.

The boat followed the smoke into sight. Georgy had a dandy telescope, and got the vessel under view in the most skilful manner. And he made appropriate nautical comments upon the manner of the approach of the steamer as she came nearer and nearer, dipping and rising in the water. The signal of an English steamer in sight went fluttering up to the mast on the pier. I dare say Mrs. Amelia's heart was in a similar flutter.

Emmy tried to look through the telescope over George's shoulder, but she could make nothing of it. She only saw a black eclipse bobbing up and down before her eyes.

George took the glass again and raked the vessel. "How she does pitch!" he said. "There goes a wave slap over her bows. There's only two people on deck besides the steersman. "There's a man lying down, and a — chap in a — cloak with a — Hooray! — It's Dob by Jingo!" He clapped to the telescope and flung his arms round his mother. As for that lady: let us say what she did in the words of a favorite poet — Δακρυοεν γελασασα. She was sure it was William. It could be no other. What she had said about hoping that he would not come was all hypocrisy. Of course he would come: what could he do else but come? She knew he would come.

The ship came swiftly nearer and nearer. As they went in to meet her at the landing-place at the quay, Emmy's knees trembled so that she scarcely could run. She would have liked to kneel down and say her prayers of thanks there. Oh, she thought, she would be all her life saying them!

It was such a bad day that as the vessel came alongside of the quay there were no idlers abroad; scarcely even a commissioner on the lookout for the few passengers in the steamer. That young scapegrace George had fled too: and as the gentleman in the old cloak lined with red stuff stepped on to the shore, there was scarcely any one present to see what took place, which was briefly this :

A lady in a dripping white bonnet and shawl, with her two little hands out before her, went up to him, and in the next minute she had altogether disappeared under the folds of the old cloak, and was kissing one of his hands with all her might; whilst the other, I suppose, was engaged in holding her to his heart (which her head just about reached) and in preventing her from tumbling down. She was murmuring something about — forgive — dear William — dear, dear, dearest friend — kiss, kiss, kiss, and so forth — and in fact went on under the cloak in an absurd manner.

When Emmy emerged from it, she still kept tight hold of one of William's hands, and looked up in his face. It was full of sadness and tender love and pity. She understood its reproach and hung down her head.

"It was time you sent for me, dear Amelia," he said.

"You will never go again, William."

"No, never," he answered: and pressed the dear little soul once more to his heart.

As they issued out of the Custom-house precincts, Georgy broke out on them, with his telescope up to his eye, and a loud laugh of welcome; he danced round the couple, and performed many facetious antics as he led them up to the house. Jos was n't up yet; Becky not visible (though she looked at them through the blinds). Georgy ran off to see about breakfast. Emmy, whose shawl and bonnet were off in the passage in the hands of Miss Payne, now went to undo the clasp of William's cloak, and — we will, if you please, go with George, and look after

breakfast for the Colonel. The vessel is in port. He
has got the prize he has been trying for all his life.
The bird has come in at last. There it is with its
head on his shoulder, billing and cooing close up to
his heart, with soft outstretched fluttering wings.
This is what he has asked for every day and hour
for eighteen years. This is what he pined after.
Here it is — the summit, the end — the last page of
the third volume. Good-by, Colonel — God bless
you, honest William! — Farewell, dear Amelia —
Grow green again, tender little parasite, round the
rugged old oak to which you cling!

Perhaps it was compunction towards the kind and
simple creature, who had been the first in life to defend her, perhaps it was a dislike to all such sentimental scenes, — but Rebecca, satisfied with her part
of the transaction, never presented herself before
Colonel Dobbin and the lady whom he married.
"Particular business," she said, took her to Bruges,
whither she went; and only Georgy and his uncle
were present at the marriage ceremony. When it
was over, and Georgy had rejoined his parents, Mrs.
Becky returned (just for a few days) to comfort the
solitary bachelor, Joseph Sedley. He preferred a
continental life, he said, and declined to join in
housekeeping with his sister and her husband.

Emmy was very glad in her heart to think that she
had written to her husband before she read or knew
of that letter of George's. "I knew it all along,"
William said; "but could I use that weapon against
the poor fellow's memory? It was that which made
me suffer so when you — "

"Never speak of that day again," Emmy cried out,

so contrite and humble, that William turned off the conversation, by his account of Glorvina and dear old Peggy O'Dowd, with whom he was sitting when the letter of recall reached him. "If you had n't sent for me," he added with a laugh, "who knows what Glorvina's name might be now?"

At present it is Glorvina Posky (now Mrs. Major Posky), she took him on the death of his first wife, having resolved never to marry out of the regiment. Lady O'Dowd is also so attached to it that, she says, if anything were to happen to Mick, bedad she'd come back and marry some of 'em. But the Major-General is quite well, and lives in great splendor at O'Dowdstown, with a pack of beagles, and (with the exception of perhaps their neighbor, Hoggarty of Castle Hoggarty) he is the first man of his county. Her ladyship still dances jigs, and insisted on standing up with the Master of the Horse at the Lord Lieutenant's last ball. Both she and Glorvina declared that Dobbin had used the latter *sheamfully,* but Posky falling in, Glorvina was consoled, and a beautiful turban from Paris appeased the wrath of Lady O'Dowd.

When Colonel Dobbin quitted the service, which he did immediately after his marriage, he rented a pretty little country place in Hampshire, not far from Queen's Crawley, where, after the passing of the Reform Bill, Sir Pitt and his family constantly resided now. All idea of a Peerage was out of the question, the Baronet's two seats in Parliament being lost. He was both out of pocket and out of spirits by that catastrophe, failed in his health, and prophesied the speedy ruin of the Empire.

Lady Jane and Mrs. Dobbin became great friends — there was a perpetual crossing of pony-chaises between the Hall and the Evergreens, the Colonel's place (rented of his friend Major Ponto, who was abroad with his family). Her ladyship was godmother to Mrs. Dobbin's child, which bore her name, and was christened by the Rev. James Crawley, who succeeded his father in the living; and a pretty close friendship subsisted between the two lads, George and Rawdon, who hunted and shot together in the vacations, were both entered of the same College at Cambridge, and quarrelled with each other about Lady Jane's daughter, with whom they were both, of course, in love. A match between George and that young lady was long a favorite scheme of both the matrons, though I have heard that Miss Crawley herself inclined towards her cousin.

Mrs. Rawdon Crawley's name was never mentioned by either family. There were reasons why all should be silent regarding her. For wherever Mr. Joseph Sedley went, she travelled likewise; and that infatuated man seemed to be entirely her slave. The Colonel's lawyers informed him that his brother-in-law had effected a heavy insurance upon his life, whence it was probable that he had been raising money to discharge debts. He procured prolonged leave of absence from the East India House, and indeed his infirmities were daily increasing.

On hearing the news about the insurance, Amelia, in a good deal of alarm, entreated her husband to go to Brussels, where Jos then was, and inquire into the state of his affairs. The Colonel quitted home with reluctance (for he was deeply immersed in his "History of the Punjaub," which still occupies him, and much alarmed about his little daughter, whom he idolizes, and who was just recovering from the chicken-pox), and went to Brussels and found Jos living at one of

BECKY'S SECOND APPEARANCE IN THE CHARACTER OF
CLYTEMNESTRA.

the enormous hotels in that city. Mrs. Crawley, who had her carriage, gave entertainments, and lived in a very genteel manner, occupied another suite of apartments in the same hotel.

The Colonel, of course, did not desire to see that lady, or even think proper to notify his arrival at Brussels, except privately to Jos by a message through his valet. Jos begged the Colonel to come and see him that night, when Mrs. Crawley would be at a *soirée*, and when they could meet *alone*. He found his brother-in-law in a condition of pitiable infirmity; and dreadfully afraid of Rebecca, though eager in his praises of her. She tended him through a series of unheard-of illnesses, with a fidelity most admirable. She had been a daughter to him. "But — but — oh, for God's sake, do come and live near me, and — and — see me sometimes," whimpered out the unfortunate man.

The Colonel's brow darkened at this. "We can't, Jos," he said. "Considering the circumstances, Amelia can't visit you."

"I swear to you — I swear to you on the Bible," gasped out Joseph, wanting to kiss the book, "that she is as innocent as a child, as spotless as your own wife."

"It may be so," said the Colonel, gloomily; "but Emmy can't come to you. Be a man, Jos : break off this disreputable connection. Come home to your family. We hear your affairs are involved."

"Involved!" cried Jos. "Who has told such calumnies? All my money is placed out most advantageously. Mrs. Crawley — that is — I mean, — it is laid out to the best interest."

"You are not in debt, then? Why did you insure your life?"

"I thought — a little present to her — in case anything happened; and you know my health is so delicate — common gratitude you know — and I intend to
leave all my money to you — and I can spare it out
of my income, indeed I can," cried out William's
weak brother-in-law.

The Colonel besought Jos to fly at once — to go
back to India, whither Mrs. Crawley could not follow
him; to do anything to break off a connection which
might have the most fatal consequences to him.

Jos clasped his hands, and cried, — "He would go
back to India. He would do anything: only he must
have time: they must n't say anything to Mrs. Crawley: — she'd — she'd kill me if she knew it. You
don't know what a terrible woman she is," the poor
wretch said.

"Then, why not come away with me?" said Dobbin in reply; but Jos had not the courage. "He
would see Dobbin again in the morning; he must on
no account say that he had been there. He must go
now. Becky might come in." And Dobbin quitted
him full of forebodings.

He never saw Jos more. Three months afterwards
Joseph Sedley died at Aix-la-Chapelle. It was found
that all his property had been muddled away in speculations, and was represented by valueless shares in
different bubble companies. All his available assets
were the two thousand pounds for which his life was
insured, and which were left equally between his beloved "sister Amelia, wife of, etc., and his friend and
invaluable attendant during sickness, Rebecca, wife
of Lieutenant-Colonel Rawdon Crawley, C.B.," who
was appointed administratrix.

The solicitor of the Insurance Company swore it
was the blackest case that ever had come before him;

talked of sending a commission to Aix to examine into the death, and the Company refused payment of
the policy. But Mrs., or Lady Crawley, as she styled
herself, came to town at once (attended with her soli-
citors, Messrs. Burke, Thurtell, and Hayes, of Tha-
vies Inn), and dared the Company to refuse the
payment. They invited examination, they declared
that she was the object of an infamous conspiracy,
which had been pursuing her all through life, and
triumphed finally. The money was paid, and her
character established, but Colonel Dobbin sent back
his share of the legacy to the Insurance Office, and
rigidly declined to hold any communication with
Rebecca.

She never was Lady Crawley, though she continued
so to call herself. His Excellency Colonel Rawdon
Crawley died of yellow fever at Coventry Island,
most deeply beloved and deplored, and six weeks
before the demise of his brother, Sir Pitt. The estate consequently devolved upon the present Sir
Rawdon Crawley, Bart.

He, too, has declined to see his mother, to whom he
makes a liberal allowance; and who, besides, appears
to be very wealthy. The Baronet lives entirely at
Queen's Crawley, with Lady Jane and her daughter;
whilst Rebecca, Lady Crawley, chiefly hangs about
Bath and Cheltenham, where a very strong party of
excellent people consider her to be a most injured
woman. She has her enemies. Who has not? Her
life is her answer to them. She busies herself in
works of piety. She goes to church, and never
without a footman. Her name is in all the Charity
Lists. The Destitute Orange-girl, the Neglected
Washerwoman, the Distressed Muffin-man, find in
her a fast and generous friend. She is always hav-

ing stalls at Fancy Fairs for the benefit of these hapless beings. Emmy, her children, and the Colonel, coming to London some time back, found themselves suddenly before her at one of these fairs. She cast down her eyes demurely and smiled as they started away from her; Emmy skurrying off on the arm of George (now grown a dashing young gentleman), and the Colonel seizing up his little Janey of whom he is fonder than of anything in the world — fonder even than of his "History of the Punjaub."

"Fonder than he is of me," Emmy thinks, with a sigh. But he never said a word to Amelia that was not kind and gentle; or thought of a want of hers that he did not try to gratify.

Ah! *Vanitas Vanitatum!* which of us is happy in this world? Which of us has his desire? or having it, is satisfied? — come, children, let us shut up the box and the puppets, for our play is played out.

THE END.

LOVEL THE WIDOWER.

LOVEL THE WIDOWER.

CHAPTER I.

THE BACHELOR OF BEAK STREET.

WHO shall be the hero of this tale? Not I who write it. I am but the Chorus of the Play. I make remarks on the conduct of the characters: I narrate their simple story. There is love and marriage in it: there is grief and disappointment: the scene is in the parlor, and the region beneath the parlor. No: it may be the parlor and kitchen, in this instance, are on the same level. There is no high life, unless, to be sure, you call a baronet's widow a lady in high life; and some ladies may be, while some certainly are not. I don't think there's a villain in the whole performance. There is an abominable selfish old woman, certainly; an old highway robber; an old sponger on other people's kindness; an old haunter of Bath and Cheltenham boarding-houses (about which how can I know anything, never having been in a boarding-house at Bath or Cheltenham in my life?); an old swindler of tradesmen, tyrant of servants, bully of the poor — who, to be sure, might do duty for a villain, but she considers herself as virtuous a woman as ever was born. The heroine is not faultless (ah! that will be a great relief to some folks, for many writers' good women are, you know, so *very* insipid). The

principal personages you may very likely think to be
no better than a muff.   But is many a respectable man
of our acquaintance much better? and do muffs know
that they are what they are, or, knowing it, are they
unhappy?   Do girls decline to marry one if he is
rich?   Do we refuse to dine with one?   I listened to
one at Church last Sunday, with all the women crying and sobbing; and, oh, dear me! how finely he
preached!   Don't we give him great credit for wisdom
and eloquence in the House of Commons?   Don't we
give him important commands in the army?   Can
you, or can you not, point out one who has been made
a peer?   Does n't your wife call one in the moment
any of the children are ill?   Don't we read his dear
poems, or even novels?   Yes; perhaps even this one
is read and written by — Well?   *Quid rides?*   Do
you mean that I am painting a portrait which hangs
before me every morning in the looking-glass when I
am shaving?   *Après?*   Do you suppose that I suppose that I have not infirmities like my neighbors?
Am I weak?   It is notorious to all my friends there
is a certain dish I can't resist: no, not if I have
already eaten twice too much at dinner.   So, dear sir,
or madam, have *you* your weakness — *your* irresistible
dish of temptation (or if you don't know it, your
friends do).   No, dear friend, the chances are that
you and I are not people of the highest intellect, of
the largest fortune, of the most ancient family, of the
most consummate virtue, of the most faultless beauty
in face and figure.   We are no heroes nor angels;
neither are we fiends from abodes unmentionable,
black assassins, treacherous Iagos, familiar with stab-
bing and poison — murder our amusement, daggers
our playthings, arsenic our daily bread, lies our conversation, and forgery our common handwriting.   No,

we are not monsters of crime, or angels walking the
earth — at least I know *one* of us who is n't, as can be
shown any day at home if the knife won't cut or the
mutton comes up raw. But we are not altogether
brutal and unkind, and a few folks like us. Our
poetry is not as good as Alfred Tennyson's but we
can turn a couplet for Miss Fanny's album : our jokes
are not always first-rate, but Mary and her mother
smile very kindly when papa tells his story or makes
his pun. We have many weaknesses, but we are not
ruffians of crime. No more was my friend Lovel.
On the contrary, he was as harmless and kindly a fellow as ever lived when I first knew him. At present,
with his changed position, he is, perhaps, rather *fine*
(and certainly, I am not asked to his *best* dinner-
parties as I used to be, where you hardly see a com-
moner — but stay ! I am advancing matters). At
the time when this story begins, I say, Lovel had his
faults — which of us has not ? He had buried his
wife, having notoriously been henpecked by her.
How many men and brethren are like him ! He had
a good fortune — I wish I had as much — though I
dare say many people are ten times as rich. He was
a good-looking fellow enough ; though that depends,
ladies, upon whether you like a fair man or a dark
one. He had a country house, but it was only at Putney. In fact, he was in business in the city, and being a hospitable man, and having three or four spare
bed-rooms, some of his friends were always welcome
at Shrublands, especially after Mrs. Lovel's death,
who liked me pretty well at the period of her early
marriage with my friend, but got to dislike me at last
and to show me the cold shoulder. That is a joint I
never could like (though I have known fellows who
persist in dining off it year after year, who cling hold

of it, and refuse to be separated from it). I say,
when Lovel's wife began to show me that she was
tired of my company, I made myself scarce : used to
pretend to be engaged when Fred faintly asked me to
Shrublands ; to accept his meek apologies, proposals
to dine *en garçon* at Greenwich, the club, and so forth ;
and never visit upon him my wrath at his wife's indifference — for, after all, he had been my friend at
many a pinch : he never stinted at "Harts's" or
"Lovegrove's," and always made a point of having
the wine I liked, never mind what the price was. As
for his wife, there was, assuredly, no love lost between
us — I thought her a lean, scraggy, lackadaisical,
egotistical, consequential, insipid creature : and as for
his mother-in-law, who stayed at Fred's as long and as
often as her daughter would endure her, has any one
who ever knew that notorious old Lady Baker at Bath,
at Cheltenham, at Brighton, — wherever trumps and
frumps were found together ; wherever scandal was
cackled ; wherever fly-blown reputations were assembled, and dowagers with damaged titles trod over
each other for the *pas ;* — who, I say, ever had a good
word for that old woman ? What party was not
bored where she appeared ? What tradesman was
not done with whom she dealt ? I wish with all my
heart I was about to narrate a story with a good
mother-in-law for a character ; but then you know, my
dear madam, all good women in novels are insipid.
This woman certainly was not. She was not only not
insipid, but exceedingly bad-tasted. She had a foul,
loud tongue, a stupid head, a bad temper, an immense pride and arrogance, an extravagant son, and
very little money. Can I say much more of a woman
than this ? Aha ! my good Lady Baker ! I was a
mauvais sujet, was I ? — I was leading Fred into

smoking, drinking, and low bachelor habits, was I?
I, his old friend, who have borrowed money from him
any time these twenty years, was not fit company for
you and your precious daughter? Indeed! *I* paid
the money I borrowed from him like a man; but did
you ever pay him, I should like to know? When
Mrs. Lovel was in the first column of "The Times,"
then Fred and I used to go off to Greenwich and
Blackwall, as I said; then his kind old heart was
allowed to feel for his friend; *then* we could have the
other bottle of claret without the appearance of Bedford and the coffee, which in Mrs. L.'s time used to be
sent in to us before we could ring for a second bottle,
although she and Lady Baker had had three glasses
each out of the first. Three full glasses each, I give
you my word! No, Madam, it was your turn to bully
me once — now it is mine and I use it. No, you old
catamaran, though you pretend you never read novels,
some of your confounded good-natured friends will let
you know of *this* one. Here you are, do you hear?
Here you shall be shown up. And so I intend to
show up *other* women and *other* men who have offended me. Is one to be subject to slights and scorn,
and not have revenge? Kindnesses are easily forgotten; but injuries! — what worthy man does not
keep *those* in mind?

Before entering upon the present narrative, may I
take leave to inform a candid public that, though it
is all true, there is not a word of truth in it; that
though Lovel is alive and prosperous, and you very
likely have met him, yet I defy you to point him out;
that his wife (for he is Lovel the Widower no more)
is not the lady you imagine her to be, when you say
(as you will persist in doing), "Oh, that character is
intended for Mrs. Thingamy, or was notoriously drawn

from Lady So-and-So. No. You are utterly mistaken.
Why, even the advertising-puffers have almost given
up that stale stratagem of announcing " REVELATIONS
FROM HIGH LIFE.— The *beau monde* will be startled
at recognizing the portraits of some of its brilliant
leaders in Miss Wiggins's forthcoming *roman de
société*." Or, " We suspect a certain ducal house will
be puzzled to guess how the pitiless author of ' May
Fair Mysteries' has become acquainted with (and
exposed with a fearless hand) *certain family secrets*
which were thought only to be known to a few of the
very highest members of the aristocracy." No, I say ;
these silly baits to catch an unsuspecting public shall
not be our arts. If you choose to occupy yourself
with trying to ascertain if a certain cap fits one
amongst ever so many thousand heads, you *may*
possibly pop it on the right one : but the cap-maker
will perish before he tells you ; unless, of course, he
has some private pique to avenge, or malice to wreak,
upon some individual who can't by any possibility
hit again ; — *then*, indeed, he will come boldly forward
and seize upon his victim — (a bishop, say, or a
woman without coarse, quarrelsome male relatives,
will be best) — and clap on him, or her, such a cap,
with such ears, that all the world shall laugh at the
poor wretch, shuddering, and blushing beet-root red,
and whimpering deserved tears of rage and vexation
at being made the common butt of society. Besides,
I dine at Lovel's still ; his company and cuisine are
amongst the best in London. If they suspected I was
taking them off, he and his wife would leave off inviting me. Would any man of a generous disposition
lose such a valued friend for a joke, or be so foolish
as to show him up in a story ? All persons with a
decent knowledge of the world will at once banish

the thought, as not merely base, but absurd. I am
invited to his house one day next week ; *vous concevez*
I can't mention the very day, for then he would find
me out — and of course there would be no more cards
for his old friend. He would not like appearing, as
it must be owned he does in this memoir, as a man
of not very strong mind. He believes himself to be
a most determined, resolute person. He is quick in
speech, wears a fierce beard, speaks with asperity
to his servants (who liken him to a — to that before-
named sable or ermine contrivance, in which ladies
insert their hands in winter), and takes his wife to
task so smartly, that I believe she believes he believes
he is the master of the house. "Elizabeth, my love,
he must mean A, or B, or D," I fancy I hear Lovel
say ; and she says, "Yes ; oh ! it is certainly D, —
his very image ! " " D to a T," says Lovel (who is a
neat wit). *She* may know that I mean to depict her
husband in the above unpretending lines : but she
will never let me know of her knowledge except by
a little extra courtesy ; except (may I make this
pleasing exception ?) by a few more invitations ;
except by a look of those unfathomable eyes (gracious
goodness ! to think she wore spectacles ever so long,
and put a lid over them as it were !), into which,
when you gaze sometimes, you may gaze so deep, and
deep, and deep, that I defy you to plumb half-way
down into their mystery.

When I was a young man, I had lodgings in Beak
Street, Regent Street (I no more have lived in Beak
Street than in Belgrave Square : but I choose to say
so, and no gentleman will be so rude as to contradict
another) — I had lodgings, I say, in Beak Street,
Regent Street. Mrs. Prior was the landlady's name.
She had seen better days — landladies frequently

have. Her husband — he could not be called the landlord, for Mrs. P. was manager of the place — had
been, in happier times, captain or lieutenant in the
militia; then of Diss, in Norfolk, of no profession;
then of Norwich Castle, a prisoner for debt; then of
Southampton Buildings, London, law-writer; then
of the Bom-Retiro Caçadores, in the service of H. M.
the Queen of Portugal, lieutenant and paymaster;
then of Melina Place, St. George's Fields, etc. — I
forbear to give the particulars of an existence which
a legal biographer has traced step by step, and which
has more than once been the subject of judicial inves-
tigation by certain commissioners in Lincoln's Inn
Fields. Well, Prior, at this time, swimming out of
a hundred shipwrecks, had clambered on to a lighter,
as it were, and was clerk to a coal-merchant, by the
river-side. "You conceive, sir," he would say, "my
employment is only temporary — the fortune of war,
the fortune of war!" He smattered words in not a
few foreign languages. His person was profusely
scented with tobacco. Bearded individuals, padding
the muddy hoof in the neighboring Regent Street,
would call sometimes of an evening, and ask for "the
Captain." He was known at many neighboring bill-
iard-tables, and, I imagine, not respected. You will
not see enough of Captain Prior to be very weary of
him and his coarse swagger, to be disgusted by his repeated requests for small money-loans, or to deplore
his loss, which you will please to suppose has happened before the curtain of our present drama draws
up. I think two people in the world were sorry for
him: his wife, who still loved the memory of the
handsome young man who had wooed and won her;
his daughter Elizabeth, whom for the last few months
of his life, and up to his fatal illness, he every even-

ing conducted to what he called her "academy."
You are right. Elizabeth is the principal character
in this story. When I knew her, a thin, freckled
girl of fifteen, with a lean frock, and hair of a reddish
hue, she used to borrow my books, and play on the
First Floor's piano, when he was from home —
Slumley his name was. He was editor of the "Swell,"
a newspaper then published : author of a great number of popular songs, a friend of several music-sell-
ing houses ; and it was by Mr. Slumley's interest
that Elizabeth was received as a pupil at what the
family called "the academy."

Captain Prior then used to conduct his girl to
the Academy, but she often had to conduct him home
again. Having to wait about the premises for two,
or three, or five hours sometimes, whilst Elizabeth
was doing her lessons, he would naturally desire to
shelter himself from the cold at some neighboring
house of entertainment. Every Friday, a prize of a
golden medal, nay, I believe sometimes of twenty-
five silver medals, was awarded to Miss Bellenden
and other young ladies for their good conduct and
assiduity at this academy. Miss Bellenden gave her
gold medal to her mother, only keeping five shillings
for herself, with which the poor child bought gloves,
shoes, and her humble articles of millinery.

Once or twice the Captain succeeded in intercepting
that piece of gold, and I dare say treated some of his
whiskered friends, the clinking trampers of the Quad-
rant pavement. He was a free-handed fellow when
he had anybody's money in his pocket. It was owing
to differences regarding the settlement of accounts
that he quarrelled with the coal-merchant, his very
last employer. Bessy, after yielding once or twice
to his importunity, and trying to believe his solemn

promises of repayment, had strength of mind to refuse her father the pound which he would have
taken. Her five shillings — her poor little slender
pocket-money, the representative of her charities and
kindnesses to the little brothers and sisters, of her
little toilette ornaments, nay, necessities; of those
well-mended gloves, of those oft-darned stockings, of
those poor boots, which had to walk many a weary
mile after midnight; of those little knickknacks, in
the shape of brooch or bracelet, with which the poor
child adorned her homely robe or sleeve — her poor
five shillings, out of which Mary sometimes found a
pair of shoes, or Tommy a flannel jacket, and little
Bill a coach and horse — this wretched sum, this
mite, which Bessy administered among so many poor
— I very much fear her father sometimes confiscated.
I charged the child with the fact, and she could not
deny me. I vowed a tremendous vow, that if ever I
heard of her giving Prior money again, I would quit
the lodgings, and never give those children lollipop,
nor pegtop, nor sixpence; nor the pungent marmalade, nor the biting gingerbread-nut, nor the theatre-
characters, nor the paint-box to illuminate the same;
nor the discarded clothes, which became smaller
clothes upon the persons of little Tommy and little
Bill, for whom Mrs. Prior, and Bessy, and the little
maid, cut, clipped, altered, ironed, darned, mangled,
with the greatest ingenuity. I say, considering what
had passed between me and the Priors — considering
those money transactions, and those clothes, and my
kindness to the children — it was rather hard that
my jam-pots were poached, and my brandy-bottles
leaked. And then to frighten her brother with the
story of the inexorable creditor — oh, Mrs. Prior! —
oh, fie, Mrs. P.!

So Bessy went to her school in a shabby shawl, a
faded bonnet, and a poor little lean dress flounced
with the mud and dust of all weathers, whereas there
were some other young ladies, fellow-pupils of her,
who laid out their gold medals to much greater advantage.   Miss Delamere, with her eighteen shillings
a week (calling them *"silver medals"* was only my
wit, you see), had twenty new bonnets, silk and satin
dresses for all seasons, feathers in abundance, swans-
down muffs and tippets, lovely pocket-handkerchiefs
and trinkets, and many and many a half-crown mould
of jelly, bottle of sherry, blanket, or what not, for a
poor fellow-pupil in distress; and as for Miss Montanville, who had exactly the same sal — well, who
had a scholarship of exactly the same value, viz.
about fifty pounds yearly — she kept an elegant little
cottage in the Regent's Park, a brougham with a
horse all over brass harness, and a groom with a
prodigious gold lace hat-band, who was treated with
frightful contumely at the neighboring cabstand; an
aunt or a mother, I don't know which (I hope it was
only an aunt), always comfortably dressed, and who
looked after Montanville : and she herself had bracelets, brooches, and velvet pelisses of the very richest
description.   But then Miss Montanville was a good
economist.   *She* was never known to help a poor
friend in distress, or give a fainting brother and sister
a crust or a glass of wine.   She allowed ten shillings
a week to her father, whose name was Boskinson,
said to be a clerk to a chapel in Paddington; but she
would never see him — no, not when he was in hospital where he was so ill; and though she certainly
lent Miss Wilder thirteen pounds, she had Wilder
arrested upon her promissory note for twenty-four,
and sold up every stick of Wilder's furniture, so that

the whole academy cried shame! Well, an accident
occurred to Miss Montanville, for which those may be
sorry who choose. On the evening of the 26th of De-
cember, Eighteen hundred and something, when the
conductors of the academy were giving their grand
annual Christmas Pant — I should say examination of
the academy pupils before their numerous friends,
Montanville, who happened to be present, not in her
brougham this time, but in an aerial chariot of splendor drawn by doves, fell off a rainbow, and through
the roof of the Revolving Shrine of the Amaranthine
Queen, thereby very nearly damaging Bellenden, who
was occupying the shrine, attired in a light-blue span-
gled dress, waving a wand, and uttering some idiotic
verses composed for her by the Professor of Literature
attached to the academy. As for Montanville, let her
go shrieking down that trap-door, break her leg, be
taken home, and never more be character of ours. She
never could speak. Her voice was as hoarse as a fish-
woman's. Can that immense stout old box-keeper at
the —— theatre, who limps up to ladies on the first
tier, and offers that horrible footstool, which everybody stumbles over, and makes a clumsy curtsy, and
looks so knowing and hard, as if she recognized an
acquaintance in the splendid lady who enters the box
— can that old female be the once brilliant Emily
Montanville? I am told there are *no* lady box-
keepers in the English theatres. This, I submit, is a
proof of my consummate care and artifice in rescuing
from a prurient curiosity the individual personages
from whom the characters of the present story are
taken. Montanville is *not* a box-opener. She *may*,
under another name, keep a trinket-shop in the Bur-
lington Arcade, for what you know: but this secret
no torture shall induce me to divulge. Life has its

rises and its downfalls, and you have had yours, you
hobbling old creature. Montanville indeed! Go thy
ways! Here is a shilling for thee. (Thank you, sir.)
Take away that confounded footstool, and never let
us see thee more!

Now the fairy Amarantha was like a certain dear
young lady of whom we have read in early youth.
Up to twelve o'clock, attired in sparkling raiment, she
leads the dance with the prince (Gradini known as
Grady in his days of banishment at the T. R. Dublin).
At supper, she takes her place by the prince's royal
father (who is alive now, and still reigns occasionally,
so that we will not mention his revered name). She
makes believe to drink from the gilded pasteboard,
and to eat of the mighty pudding. She smiles as the
good old irascible monarch knocks the prime minister
and the cooks about: she blazes in splendor: she
beams with a thousand jewels, in comparison with
which the Koh-i-noor is a wretched lustreless little
pebble: she disappears in a chariot, such as a Lord
Mayor never rode in: — and at midnight, who is that
young woman tripping homeward through the wet
streets in a battered bonnet, a cotton shawl, and a
lean frock fringed with the dreary winter flounces?

Our Cinderella is up early in the morning: she does
no little portion of the house-work: she dresses her
sisters and brothers: she prepares papa's breakfast.
On days when she has not to go to morning lessons at
her academy, she helps with the dinner. Heaven help
us! She has often brought mine when I have dined
at home, and owns to having made that famous
mutton-broth when I had a cold. Foreigners come to
the house — professional gentlemen — to see Slumley
on the first floor; exiled captains of Spain and
Portugal, companions of the warrior her father. It is

surprising how she has learned their accents, and has
picked up French, and Italian, too.   And she played
the piano in Mr. Slumley's room sometimes, as I have
said; but refrained from that presently, and from
visiting him altogether.   I suspect he was not a man
of principle.   His paper used to make direful attacks
upon individual reputations; and you would find
theatre and opera people most curiously praised and
assaulted in the "Swell."   I recollect meeting him,
several years after, in the lobby of the opera, in a
very noisy frame of mind, when he heard a certain
lady's carriage called, and cried out with exceeding
strong language, which need not be accurately reported. "Look at that woman! Confound her! I
made her, sir! Got her an engagement when the
family was starving, sir! Did you see her, sir? She
would n't even look at me!"   Nor indeed was Mr. S.
at that moment a very agreeable object to behold.

Then I remembered that there had been some
quarrel with this man, when we lodged in Beak
Street together.   If difficulty there was, it was solved
ambulando.   He quitted the lodgings, leaving an excellent and costly piano as security for a heavy bill
which he owed to Mrs. Prior, and the instrument was
presently fetched away by the music-sellers, its
owners.   But regarding Mr. S——'s valuable biography, let us speak very gently.   You see it is "an
insult to literature" to say that there are disreputable
and dishonest persons who write in newspapers.

Nothing, dear friend, escapes your penetration: if a
joke is made in your company, you are down upon it
instanter, and your smile rewards the wag who amuses
you : so you knew at once, whilst I was talking of
Elizabeth and her academy, that a theatre was meant,
where the poor child danced for a guinea or five-and-

twenty shillings per week. Nay, she must have had
not a little skill and merit to advance to the quarter
of a hundred: for she was not pretty at this time, only
a rough, tawny-haired filly of a girl, with great eyes.
Dolphin, the manager, did not think much of her, and
she passed before him in his regiment of Sea-nymphs,
or Bayadères, or Fairies, or Mazurka maidens (with
their fluttering lances and little scarlet slyboots!)
scarcely more noticed than private Jones standing
under arms in his company when his Royal Highness
the Field-Marshal gallops by. There were no dramatic
triumphs for Miss Bellenden: no bouquets were flung
at her feet: no cunning Mephistopheles — the emissary
of some philandering Faustus outside — corrupted her
duenna, or brought her caskets of diamonds. Had
there been any such admirer for Bellenden, Dolphin
would not only not have been shocked, but he would
very likely have raised her salary. As it was, though
himself, I fear, a person of loose morals, he respected
better things. "That Bellenden's a good hhonest
gurl," he said to the present writer: "works hard:
gives her money to her family: father a shy old cove.
Very good family I hear they are!" and he passes on
to some other of the innumerable subjects which
engage a manager.

"Now, why should a poor lodging-house keeper make
such a mighty secret of having a daughter earning an
honest guinea by dancing at a theatre? Why persist
in calling the theatre an academy? Why did Mrs.
Prior speak of it as such, to me who knew what the
truth was, and to whom Elizabeth herself made no mystery of her calling?

There are actions and events in its life over which
decent Poverty often chooses to cast a veil that is not
unbecoming wear. We can all, if we are minded, peer

through this poor flimsy screen: often there is no
shame behind it: — only empty platters, poor scraps,
and other threadbare evidence of want and cold.   And
who is called on to show his rags to the public, and
cry out his hunger in the street?   At this time (her
character has developed itself not so amiably since),
Mrs. Prior was outwardly respectable; and yet, as I
have said, my groceries were consumed with remarkable rapidity; my wine and brandy bottles were all
leaky, until they were excluded from air under a patent lock · — my Morel's raspberry jam, of which I was
passionately fond, if exposed on the table for a few
hours, was always eaten by the cat, or that wonderful
little wretch of a maid-of-all-work, so active, yet so
patient, so kind, so dirty, so obliging.   Was it *the maid*
who took those groceries?   I have seen the " Gazza
Ladra," and know that poor little maids are sometimes
wrongfully accused; and besides, in my particular case,
I own I don't care who the culprit was.   At the year's
end, a single man is not much poorer for this house-
tax which he pays.   One Sunday evening, being confined with a cold, and partaking of that mutton-broth
which Elizabeth made so well, and which she brought
me, I entreated her to bring from the cupboard, of
which I gave her the key, a certain brandy-bottle.
She saw my face when I looked at her: there was
no mistaking its agony.   There was scarce any brandy
left: it had all leaked away: and it was Sunday, and
no good brandy was to be bought that evening.

Elizabeth, I say, saw my grief.   She put down the
bottle, and she cried: she tried to prevent herself from
doing so at first, but she fairly burst into tears.

" My dear — dear child," says I, seizing her hand,
" you don't suppose I fancy you — "

" No — no! " she says, drawing the large hand over

her eyes. "No — no! but I saw it when you and Mr. Warrington last 'ad some. Oh! do have a patting lock!"

"A patent lock, my dear!" I remarked. "How odd that you, who have learned to pronounce Italian and French words so well, should make such strange slips in English! Your mother speaks well enough."

"She was born a lady. She was not sent to be a milliner's girl, as I was, and then among those noisy girls at that — oh! that *place!*" cries Bessy, in a sort of desperation, clinching her hand.

Here the bells of St. Beak's began to ring quite cheerily for evening service. I heard "Elizabeth!" cried out from the lower regions by Mrs. Prior's cracked voice. And the maiden went her way to church, which she and her mother never missed of a Sunday; and I dare say I slept just as well without the brandy-and-water.

Slumley being gone, Mrs. Prior came to me rather wistfully one day, and wanted to know whether I would object to Madame Bentivoglio, the opera-singer, having the first floor? This was too much, indeed! How was my work to go on with that woman practising all day and roaring underneath me? But, after sending away so good a customer, I could not refuse to lend the Priors a little more money; and Prior insisted upon treating me to a new stamp, and making out a new and handsome bill for an amount nearly twice as great as the last; which he had no doubt under heaven, and which he pledged his honor as an officer and a gentleman, that he would meet. Let me see: That was how many years ago? — Thirteen, fourteen, twenty? Never mind. My fair Elizabeth, I think if you saw your poor old father's signature now, you would pay it. I came upon it lately in an old box I

have n't opened these fifteen years, along with some
letters written — never mind by whom — and an old
glove that I used to set an absurd value by; and that
emerald-green tabinet waistcoat which kind old Mrs.
Macmanus gave me, and which I wore at the L—d
L—t—nt's ball, Ph-n-x Park, Dublin, once, when I
danced with *her* there! Lord! — Lord! It would no
more meet round my waist now than round Daniel
Lambert's. How we outgrow things!

But as I never presented this united bill of £43 odd
(the first portion of £23, etc. was advanced by me in
order to pay an execution out of the house) — as I never
expected to have it paid any more than I did to be
Lord Mayor of London, — I say it was a little hard
that Mrs. Prior should write off to her brother (she
writes a capital letter), blessing Providence that had
given him a noble income, promising him the benefit
of her prayers, in order that he should long live to
enjoy his large salary, and informing him that an obdurate creditor, who shall be nameless (meaning me),
who had Captain Prior *in his power* (as if, being in
possession of that dingy scrawl, I should have known
what to do with it), who held Mr. Prior's acceptance
for £43 14s. 4d. due on the 3rd July (my bill), would
infallibly bring their family to RUIN, unless a part of
the money was paid up. When I went up to my old
college, and called on Sargent, at Boniface Lodge, he
treated me as civilly as if I had been an undergraduate; scarcely spoke to me in hall, where, of course, I
dined at the Fellows' table; and only asked me to one
of Mrs. Sargent's confounded tea-parties during the
whole time of my stay. Now, it was by this man's
entreaty that I went to lodge at Prior's; he talked
to me after dinner one day, he hummed, he ha'd, he
blushed, he prated in his pompous way, about an un-

fortunate sister in London — fatal early marriage —
husband, Captain Prior, Knight of the Swan with Two
Necks of Portugal, most distinguished officer, but imprudent speculator — advantageous lodgings in the centre of London, quiet, though near the clubs — if I was
ill (I am a confirmed invalid), Mrs. Prior, his sister,
would nurse me like a mother.   So, in a word, I went
to Prior's: I took the rooms: I was attracted by some
children: Amelia Jane (that little dirty maid before
mentioned) dragging a go-cart, containing a little dirty
pair; another marching by them, carrying a fourth
wellnigh as big as himself.   These little folks, having
threaded the mighty flood of Regent Street, debouched
into the quiet creek of Beak Street, just as I happened
to follow them.   And the door at which the small
caravan halted, — the very door I was in search of, —
was opened by Elizabeth, then only just emerging
from childhood, with tawny hair falling into her solemn
eyes.

The aspect of these little people, which would have
deterred many, happened to attract me. I am a lonely
man. I may have been ill-treated by some one once,
but that is neither here nor there. If I had had
children of my own, I think I should have been good
to them. I thought Prior a dreadful vulgar wretch,
and his wife a scheming, greedy little woman. But
the children amused me: and I took the rooms, liking
to hear overhead in the morning the patter of their
little feet. The person I mean has several; husband,
judge in the West Indies. *Allons!* now you know
how I came to live at Mrs. Prior's.

Though I am now a steady, a *confirmed* old bachelor
(I shall call myself Mr. Batchelor, if you please, in
this story; and there is some one far — far away who
knows why I will NEVER take another title), I was a

gay young fellow enough once. I was not above the
pleasures of youth : In fact, I learned quadrilles on
purpose to dance with her that long vacation when I
went to read with my young friend, Lord Viscount
Poldoody at Dub — psha ! Be still, thou foolish
heart ! Perhaps I misspent my time as an undergraduate. Perhaps I read too many novels, occupied
myself too much with "elegant literature" (that used
to be our phrase), and spoke too often at the Union,
where I had a considerable reputation. But those
fine words got me no college prizes : I missed my
fellowship : was rather in disgrace with my relations
afterwards, but had a small independence of my own,
which I eked out by taking a few pupils for little-goes
and the common degree. At length, a relation dying,
and leaving me a further small income, I left the university, and came to reside in London.

Now, in my third year at college, there came to St.
Boniface a young gentlemen, who was one of the few
gentleman-pensioners of our society. His popularity
speedily was great. A kindly and simple youth, he
would have been liked, I dare say, even though he
had been no richer than the rest of us; but this is
certain, that flattery, worldliness, mammon-worship,
are vices as well known to young as to old boys ; and
a rich lad at school or college has his followers, tuft-
hunters, led-captains, little courts, just as much as any
elderly millionnaire of Pall Mall, who gazes round his
club to see whom he shall take home to dinner ! while
humble trencher-men wait anxiously, thinking — Ah !
will he take me this time ? or will he ask that abominable sneak and toady Henchman again ? Well —
well ! this is an old story about parasites and flatterers. My dear good sir, I am not for a moment
going to say that *you* ever were one; and I dare say

it was very base and mean of us to like a man chiefly
on account of his money. "I know" — Fred Lovel
used to say — "I know fellows come to my rooms because I have a large allowance, and plenty of my poor
old governor's wine, and give good dinners: I am not
deceived; but, at least, it is pleasanter to come to me
and have good dinners, and good wine, than to go to
Jack Highson's dreary tea and turnout, or to Ned
Roper's abominable Oxbridge port." And so I admit
at once that Lovel's parties *were* more agreeable than
most men's in the college. Perhaps the goodness of
the fare, by pleasing the guests, made them more
pleasant. A dinner in hall, and a pewter plate is all
very well, and I can say grace before it with all my
heart; but a dinner with fish from London, game, and
two or three nice little *entrées*, is better — and there
was no better cook in the university than ours at
St. Boniface, and ah me! there were appetites then,
and digestions which rendered the good dinner doubly
good.

Between me and young Lovel a friendship sprang
up, which, I trust, even the publication of this story
will not diminish. There is a period, immediately
after the taking of his bachelor's degree, when many
a university-man finds himself embarrassed. The
tradesmen rather rudely press for a settlement of
their accounts. Those prints we ordered *calidi ju-
ventâ ;* those shirt-studs and pins which the jewellers
would persist in thrusting into our artless bosoms;
those fine coats we would insist on having for our
books, as well as ourselves; all these have to be paid
for by the graduate. And my father, who was then
alive, refusing to meet these demands, under the — I
own — just plea, that my allowance had been ample,
and that my half-sisters ought not to be mulcted of

their slender portions in consequence of my extravagance, I should have been subject to very serious inconvenience — nay, possibly, to personal incarceration — had not Lovel, at the risk of rustication, rushed up to London to his mother (who then had *especial reasons* for being very gracious with her son), obtained a supply of money from her, and brought it to me at Mr. Shackell's horrible hotel, where I was lodged. He had tears in his kind eyes; he grasped my hand a hundred and hundred times as he flung the notes into my lap; and the recording tutor (Sargent was only tutor then), who was going to bring him up before the master for breach of discipline, dashed away a drop from his own lid, when, with a moving eloquence, I told what had happened, and blotted out the transaction with some particular old 1811 port, of which we freely partook in his private rooms that evening. By laborious instalments, I had the happiness to pay Lovel back. I took pupils as I said; I engaged in literary pursuits: I became connected with a literary periodical, and, I am ashamed to say, I imposed myself upon the public as a good classical scholar. I was not thought the less learned, when, my relative dying, I found myself in possession of a small independency; and my "Translations from the Greek," my "Poems by Beta," and my articles in the paper of which I was part proprietor for several years, have had their little success in their day.

Indeed at Oxbridge, if I did not obtain university honors, at least I showed literary tastes. I got the prize essay one year at Boniface, and plead guilty to having written essays, poems, and a tragedy. My college friends had a joke at my expense (a very small joke serves to amuse those port-wine-bibbing fogies, and keeps them laughing for ever so long a time) — they are welcome, I say, to make merry at my charges — in respect of a certain bargain which I made on coming to London, and in which, had I been Moses Primrose purchasing green spectacles, I could scarcely have been more taken in. *My* Jenkinson was an old college acquaintance, whom I was idiot enough to imagine a respectable man: the fellow had a very smooth tongue, and sleek, sanctified exterior. He was rather a popular preacher, and used to cry a good deal in the pulpit. He, and a queer wine-merchant and bill-discounter, Sherrick by name, had somehow got possession of that neat little literary paper, the "Museum," which, perhaps, you remember; and this eligible literary property my friend Honeyman, with his wheedling tongue, induced me to purchase. I bear no malice: the fellow is in India now, where I trust he pays his butcher and baker. He was in dreadful straits for money when he sold me the "Museum." He began crying when I told him some short time afterwards that he was a swindler, and from behind his pocket-handkerchief sobbed a prayer that I should one day think better of him; whereas my remarks to the same effect produced an exactly contrary impression upon his accomplice, Sherrick, who burst out laughing in my face, and said, "The more fool you." Mr. Sherrick was right. He was a fool, without mistake, who had any money-dealing with him; and poor Honeyman was right, too; I don't think so badly of him as I did. A fellow so hardly pinched for money could not resist the temptation of extracting it from such a greenhorn. I dare say I gave myself airs as editor of that confounded "Museum," and proposed to educate the public taste, to diffuse morality and sound literature throughout the nation, and to pocket a liberal salary

in return for my services. I dare say I printed my own
sonnets, my own tragedy, my own verses (to a Being
who shall be nameless, but whose conduct has caused
a faithful heart to bleed not a little). I dare say I
wrote satirical articles, in which I piqued myself upon the fineness of my wit, and criticisms, got up for
the nonce out of encyclopædias and biographical dic-
tionaries; so that I would be actually astounded at
my own knowledge. I dare say I made a gaby of
myself to the world: pray, my good friend, hast thou
never done likewise? If thou hast never been a fool,
be sure thou wilt never be a wise man.

I think it was my brilliant *confrère* on the first
floor (he had pecuniary transactions with Sherrick,
and visited two or three of her Majesty's metropoli-
tan prisons at that gentleman's suit) who first showed
me how grievously I had been cheated in the newspaper matter. Slumley wrote for a paper printed at
our office. The same boy often brought proofs to both
of us — a little bit of a puny bright-eyed chap, who
looked scarce twelve years old, when he was sixteen;
who in wit was a man, when in stature he was a
child, — like many other children of the poor.

This little Dick Bedford used to sit many hours
asleep on my landing-place or Slumley's whilst we
were preparing our invaluable compositions within
our respective apartments. S—— was a good-natured
reprobate, and gave the child of his meat and his
drink. I used to like to help the little man from my
breakfast, and see him enjoy the meal. As he sat,
with his bag on his knees, his head sunk in sleep, his
little high-lows scarce reaching the floor, Dick made a
touching little picture. The whole house was fond of
him. The tipsy Captain nodded him a welcome as he
swaggered down stairs, stock, and coat, and waistcoat

in hand, to his worship's toilette in the back kitchen. The children and Dick were good friends; and Elizabeth patronized him, and talked with him now and again, in her grave way. You know Clancy the composer? — know him better, perhaps, under his name of Friederich Donner? Donner used to write music to Slumley's words, or *vice versâ;* and would come now and again to Beak Street, where he and his poet would try their joint work at the piano. At the sound of that music, little Dick's eyes used to kindle. "Oh, it's prime!" said the young enthusiast. And I will say, that good-natured miscreant of a Slumley not only gave the child pence, but tickets for the play, concerts, and so forth. Dick had a neat little suit of clothes at home; his mother made him a very nice little waistcoat out of my undergraduate's gown, and he and she, a decent woman, when in their best raiment, looked respectable enough for any theatre-pit in England.

Amongst other places of public amusement which he attended, Mr. Dick frequented the academy where Miss Bellenden danced, and whence poor Elizabeth Prior issued forth after midnight in her shabby frock. And once, the Captain, Elizabeth's father and protector, being unable to walk very accurately, and noisy and incoherent in his speech, so that the attention, of Messieurs of the police was directed towards him, Dick came up, placed Elizabeth and her father in a cab, paid the fare with his own money, and brought the whole party home in triumph, himself sitting on the box of the vehicle. I chanced to be coming home myself (from one of Mrs. Wateringham's elegant tea *soirées*, in Dorset Square), and reached my door just at the arrival of Dick and his caravan. "Here, cabby!" says Dick, handing out the fare, and looking with his brightest eyes. It is pleasanter to look at that beaming little face, than at the Captain yonder, reeling into his house, supported by his daughter. Dick cried, Elizabeth told me, when, a week afterwards, she wanted to pay him back his shilling; and she said he was a strange child, that he was.

I revert to my friend Lovel. I was coaching Lovel for his degree (which, between ourselves, I think he never would have attained), when he suddenly announced to me, from Weymouth, where he was passing the vacation, his intention to quit the university, and to travel abroad. "Events have happened, dear friend," he wrote, "which will make my mother's home miserable to me (I little knew when I went to town about your business, what caused her *wonderful complaisance* to me). She would have broken my heart, Charles " (my Christian name is Charles), " but its wounds have found *a consoler!* "

Now, in this little chapter, there are some little mysteries propounded, upon which, were I not above any such artifice, I might easily leave the reader to ponder for a month.

1. Why did Mrs. Prior, at the lodgings, persist in calling the theatre at which her daughter danced the academy?

2. What were the special reasons why Mrs. Lovel should be very gracious with her son, and give him £150 as soon as he asked for the money?

3. Why was Fred Lovel's heart nearly broken? And 4. Who was his consoler?

I answer these at once, and without the slightest attempt at delay or circumlocution. 1. Mrs. Prior, who had repeatedly received money from her brother, John Erasmus Sargent, D.D., Master of St. Boniface College, knew perfectly well that if the Master (whom she already pestered out of his life) heard that she had sent a niece of his on the stage, he would never give her another shilling.

2. The reason why Emma, widow of the late Adolphus Loeffel, of Whitechapel Road, sugar-baker, was so particularly gracious to her son, Adolphus Frederick Lovel, Esq., of St. Boniface College, Oxbridge, and principal partner in the house of Loeffel aforesaid, an infant, was that she, Emma, was about to contract a second marriage with the Rev. Samuel Bonnington.

3. Fred Lovel's heart was so very much broken by this intelligence, that he gave himself airs of Hamlet, dressed in black, wore his long fair hair over his eyes, and exhibited a hundred signs of grief and desperation : until —

4. Louisa (widow of the late Sir Popham Baker, of Bakerstown, co. Kilkenny, Baronet) induced Mr. Lovel to take a trip on the Rhine with her and Cecilia, fourth and only unmarried daughter of the aforesaid Sir Popham Baker, deceased.

My opinion of Cecilia I have candidly given in a previous page. I adhere to that opinion. I shall not repeat it. The subject is disagreeable to me, as the woman herself was in life. What Fred found in her to admire I cannot tell : lucky for us all that tastes, men, women, vary. You will never see her alive in this history. That is her picture, painted by the late Mr. Gandish. She stands fingering that harp with which she has often driven me half mad with her "Tara's Halls" and her "Poor Marianne." She used to bully Fred so, and be so rude to his guests, that in order to pacify her, he would meanly say, "Do, my love, let us have a little music!" and thrumpty —

thrumpty, off would go her gloves, and "Tara's Halls" would begin. "The harp that *once*," indeed! the accursed catgut scarce knew any other music, and "once" was a hundred times at least in *my* hearing. Then came the period when I was treated to the cold joint which I have mentioned; and, not liking it, I gave up going to Shrublands.

So, too, did my Lady Baker, but not of *her own free will*, mind you. *She* did not quit the premises because her reception was too cold, but because the house was made a great deal too hot for her. I remember Fred coming to me in high spirits, and describing to me, with no little humor, a great battle between Cecilia and Lady Baker, and her ladyship's defeat and flight. She fled, however, only as far as Putney village, where she formed again, as it were, and fortified herself in a lodging. Next day she made a desperate and feeble attack, presenting herself at Shrubland's lodge-gate, and threatening that she and sorrow would sit down before it; and that all the world should know how a daughter treated her mother. But the gate was locked, and Barnet, the gardener, appeared behind it, saying, "Since you *are* come, my lady, perhaps you will pay my missis the four-and-twenty shillings you borrowed of her." And he grinned at her through the bars, until she fled before him, cowering. Lovel paid the little forgotten account; the best four-and-twenty shillings he had ever laid out, he said.

Eight years passed away; during the last four of which I scarce saw my old friend, except at clubs and taverns, where we met privily, and renewed, not old warmth and hilarity, but old kindness. One winter he took his family abroad; Cecilia's health was delicate, Lovel told me, and the doctor had advised that

I AM REFERRED TO CECILIA.

she should spend a winter in the south. He did not
stay with them: he had pressing affairs at home; he
had embarked in many businesses besides the paternal sugar-bakery; was concerned in companies, a
director of a joint-stock bank, a man in whose fire
were many irons. A faithful governess was with the
children; a faithful man and maid were in attendance on the invalid; and Lovel, adoring his wife, as
he certainly did, yet supported her absence with great
equanimity.

In the spring I was not a little scared to read
amongst the deaths in the newspaper: — " At Naples,
of scarlet fever, on the 25th ult., Cecilia, wife of
Frederick Lovel, Esq., and daughter of the late Sir
Popham Baker, Bart." I knew what my friend's
grief would be. He had hurried abroad at the news
of her illness; he did not reach Naples in time to
receive the last words of his poor Cecilia.

Some months after the catastrophe, I had a note
from Shrublands. Lovel wrote quite in the old affectionate tone. He begged his dear old friend to go
to him, and console him in his solitude. Would I
come to dinner that evening?

Of course I went off to him straightway. I found
him in deep sables in the drawing-room with his
children, and I confess I was not astonished to see
my Lady Baker once more in that room.

" You seem surprised to see me here, Mr. Batchelor ? " says her ladyship, with that grace and good-
breeding which she generally exhibited; for if she
accepted benefits, she took care to insult those from
whom she received them.

" Indeed, no," said I, looking at Lovel, who piteously
hung down his head. He had his little Cissy at his
knee: he was sitting under the portrait of the defunct

musician, whose harp, now muffled in leather, stood dimly in the corner of the room.

"I am here not at my own wish, but from a feeling of duty towards that — departed — angel!" says Lady Baker, pointing to the picture.

"I am sure when Mamma was here, you were always quarrelling," says little Popham, with a scowl.

"This is the way those innocent children have been taught to regard me," cries grandmamma.

"Silence, Pop," says Papa, and don't be a rude boy."

"Isn't Pop a rude boy?" echoes Cissy.

"Silence, Pop," continues Papa, "or you must go up to Miss Prior."

CHAPTER II.

Of course we all know who she was, the Miss Prior of Shrublands, whom papa and grandmamma called to the unruly children. Years had passed since I had shaken the Beak Street dust off my feet. The brass plate of " Prior " was removed from the once familiar door, and screwed, for what I can tell, on to the late reprobate owner's coffin. A little eruption of mushroom-formed brass knobs I saw on the door-post when I passed by it last week, and " Café des Ambassadeurs " was thereon inscribed, with three fly-blown blue tea-cups, a couple of coffee-pots of the well-known Britannia metal, and two freckled copies of the *Indépendance Belge* hanging over the window-blind. Were those their Excellencies the Ambassadors at the door, smoking cheroots ? Pool and billiards were written on their countenances, their hats, their elbows. They may have been ambassadors down on their luck, as the phrase is. They were in disgrace, no doubt, at the court of her imperial majesty, Queen Fortune. Men as shabby have retrieved their disgraces ere now, washed their cloudy faces, strapped their dingy waistcoats with cordons, and stepped into fine carriages from quarters not a whit more reputable than the " Café des Ambassadeurs." If I lived in the Leicester Square neighborhood, and kept a café, I would always treat foreigners with respect. They may be billiard-markers now, or doing a little shady police business ; but why should

they not afterwards be generals and great officers of
state ?   Suppose that gentleman is at present a bar-
ber, with his tongs and stick of fixature for the mus-
taches, how do you know he has not his epaulettes and
his *bâton de maréchal* in the same pouch ?   I see engraven on the second-floor bell, on my rooms, " Plugwell."   Who can Plugwell be, whose feet now warm at
the fire where I sat many a long evening ?   And this
gentleman with the fur collar, the straggling beard, the
frank and engaging leer, the somewhat husky voice,
who is calling out on the doorstep, " Step in, and 'ave
it done.   Your correct likeness, only one shilling " —
is he an ambassador too ?   Ah, no : he is only the
chargé d' affaires of a photographer who lives up stairs :
no doubt where the little ones used to be.   Bless me !
Photography was an infant, and in the nursery, too,
when *we* lived in Beak Street.

Shall I own that, for old time's sake, I went up
stairs, and " 'ad it done " — that correct likeness, price
one shilling.   Would Some One (I have said, I think,
that the party in question is well married in a distant
island) like to have the thing, I wonder, and be reminded of a man whom she knew in life's prime, with
brown curly locks, as she looked on the effigy of this
elderly gentleman, with a forehead as bare as a
billiard-ball ?

As I went up and down that darkling stair, the
ghosts of the Prior children peeped out from the banisters ; the little faces smiled in the twilight : it may
be wounds (of the heart) throbbed and bled again, —
oh, how freshly and keenly !   How infernally I have
suffered behind that door in that room — I mean that
one where Plugwell now lives.   Confound Plugwell !
I wonder what that woman thinks of me as she sees
me shaking my fist at the door ?   Do you think me

mad, Madam? I don't care if you do. Do you think
when I spoke anon of the ghosts of Prior's children, I
mean that any of them are dead? None are, that I
know of. A great hulking Bluecoat boy, with fluffy
whiskers, spoke to me not long since, in an awful bass
voice, and announced his name as "Gus Prior." And
"How's Elizabeth?" he added, nodding his bullet
head. Elizabeth, indeed, you great vulgar boy! Elizabeth, — and, by the way, how long we have been
keeping her waiting!

You see, as I beheld her, a heap of memories struck
upon me, and I could not help chattering; when of
course — and you are perfectly right, only you might
just as well have left the observation alone: for I
knew quite well what you were going to say — when
I had much better have held my tongue. Elizabeth
means a history to me. She came to me at a critical
period of my life. Bleeding and wounded from the
conduct of that other individual (by her present name
of Mrs. O'D — her present *O'D*-ous name — I say, I
will never — never call her) — desperately wounded
and miserable on my return from a neighboring capital, I went back to my lodgings in Beak Street, and
there there grew up a strange intimacy between me
and my landlady's young daughter. I told her my
story — indeed, I believe I told anybody who would
listen. She seemed to compassionate me. She would
come wistfully into my rooms, bringing me my gruel and
things (I could scarcely bear to eat for a while after
— after that affair to which I may have alluded before) — she used to come to me, and she used to pity
me, and I used to tell her all, and to tell her over and
over again. Days and days have I passed tearing my
heart out in that second-floor room which answers to
the name of Plugwell now. Afternoon after afternoon

have I spent there, and poured out my story of love
and wrong to Elizabeth, showed her that waistcoat I
told you of — that glove (her hand was n't so very
small either) — her letters, those two or three vacuous,
meaningless letters, with "My dear sir — Mamma
hopes you will come to tea ; " or, "If dear Mr. Batchelor *should* be riding in the Phœnix Park near the
Long Milestone, about two, my sister and I will be in
the car, and, " etc.; or, "Oh, you kind man ! the tickets " (she called it *tickuts* — by heaven ! she did)
" were too welcome, and the *bouquays* too lovely " (this
word, I saw, had been operated on with a penknife.
I found no faults, not even in her spelling — then) ;
or, never mind what more.   But more of this *puling*,
of this *humbug*, of this *bad spelling*, of this infernal
jilting, swindling, heartless hypocrisy (all her mother's
doing, I own ; for until he *got his place*, my rival was
not so well received as I was) — more of this RUBBISH,
I say, I showed Elizabeth, and she pitied me !

She used to come to me day after day, and I used
to talk to her. She used not to say much. Perhaps
she did not listen ; but I did not care for that.   On —
and on — and on I would go with my prate about
my passion, my wrongs, and despair ; and untiring
as my complaints were, still more constant was my
little hearer's compassion.   Mamma's shrill voice
would come to put an end to our conversation, and
she would rise up with an " Oh, bother ! " and go
away : but the next day the good girl was sure to
come to me again, when we would have another repe-
tition of our tragedy.

I dare say you are beginning to suppose (what,
after all, is a very common case, and certainly *no con-
jurer* is wanted to make the guess) that out of all this
crying and sentimentality, which a soft-hearted old

fool of a man poured out to a young girl — out of all
this whimpering and pity, something which is said to
be akin to pity might arise. But in this, my good
madam, you are utterly wrong. Some people have
the small-pox twice; *I do not.* In my case, if a heart
is broke, it's broke: if a flower is withered, it's
withered. If I choose to put my grief in a ridiculous
light, why not? why do you suppose I am going to
make a tragedy of such an old used-up, battered,
stale, vulgar, trivial every-day subject as a jilt who
plays with a man's passion, and laughs at him, and
leaves him? Tragedy indeed! Oh, yes! poison —
black-edged note-paper — Waterloo Bridge — one more
unfortunate, and so forth! No: if she goes, let her
go! — *si celeres quatit pennas,* I puff the what-d'ye-call-
it away! But I'll have no *tragedy,* mind you.

Well, it must be confessed that a man desperately
in love (as I fear I must own I then was, and a good
deal cut up by Glorvina's conduct) is a most selfish
being: whilst women are so soft and unselfish that
they can forget or disguise their own sorrows for a
while, whilst they minister to a friend in affliction. I
did not see, though I talked with her daily, on my
return from that accursed Dublin, that my little Elizabeth was pale and *distraite,* and sad, and silent. She
would sit quite dumb whilst I chattered, her hands
between her knees, or draw one of them over her
eyes. She would say, "Oh, yes! Poor fellow — poor
fellow!" now and again, as giving a melancholy
confirmation of my dismal stories; but mostly she remained quiet, her head drooping towards the ground,
a hand to her chin, her feet to the fender.

I was one day harping on the usual string. I
was telling Elizabeth how, after presents had been
accepted, after letters had passed between us (if her

scrawl could be called letters, if my impassioned song could be so construed), after everything but the actual word had passed our lips — I was telling Elizabeth how, on one accursed day, Glorvina's mother greeted me on my arrival in M-rr-n Square, by saying, "Dear, dear Mr. Batchelor, we look on you quite as one of the family! Congratulate me — congratulate my child! Dear Tom has got his appointment as Recorder of Tobago; and it is to be a match between him and his cousin Glory."

"His cousin *What!*" I shriek with a maniac laugh.

"My poor Glorvina! Sure the children have been fond of each other ever since they could speak. I knew your kind heart would be the first to rejoice in their happiness."

And so, say I — ending the story — I, who thought myself loved, was left without a pang of pity: I, who could mention a hundred reasons why I thought Glorvina well disposed to me, was told she regarded me as an *uncle!* Were her letters such as nieces write? Who ever heard of an uncle walking round Merrion Square for hours of a rainy night, and looking up to a bed-room window, because his *niece*, forsooth, was behind it? I had set my whole heart on the cast, and this was the return I got for it. For months she cajoles me — her eyes follow me, her cursed smiles welcome and fascinate me, and at a moment, at the beck of another — she laughs at me and leaves me!

At this, my little pale Elizabeth, still hanging down, cries, "Oh, the villain! the villain!" and sobs so that you might have thought her little heart would break.

"Nay," said I, "my dear, Mr. O'Dowd is no villain. His uncle, Sir Hector, was as gallant an old officer as any in the service. His aunt was a Malloy, of Mol-

loystown, and they are of excellent family, though, I
believe, of embarrassed circumstances; and young
Tom —"

"*Tom?*" cries Elizabeth, with a pale, bewildered
look. "*His name was n't Tom,* dear Mr. Batchelor;
his name was Woo-woo-illiam!" and the tears begin
again.

Ah, my child! my child! my poor young creature!
and you, too, have felt the infernal stroke. You, too,
have passed the tossing nights of pain — have heard
the dreary hours toll — have looked at the cheerless
sunrise with your blank sleepless eyes — have woke
out of dreams, mayhap, in which the beloved one was
smiling on you, whispering love-words — oh! how
sweet and fondly remembered! What! — your heart
has been robbed, too, and your treasury is rifled and
empty! — poor girl! And I looked in that sad face,
and saw no grief there! You could do your little
sweet endeavor to soothe my wounded heart, and I
never saw yours was bleeding! Did you suffer more
than I did, my poor little maid? I hope not. Are
you so young, and is all the flower of life blighted for
you? the cup without savor, the sun blotted, or almost
invisible over your head? The truth came on me all
at once: I felt ashamed that my own selfish grief
should have made me blind to hers.

"What!" said I, "my poor child? Was it — ?"
and I pointed with my finger *downwards.*

She nodded her poor head.

I knew it was the lodger who had taken the first
floor shortly after Slumley's departure. He was an
officer in the Bombay Army. He had had the lodgings for three months. He had sailed for India
shortly before I returned home from Dublin.

Elizabeth is waiting all this time — shall she come

in ? No, not yet. I have still a little more to say
about the Priors.

You understand that she was no longer Miss Prior
of Beak Street, and that mansion, even at the time of
which I write, had been long handed over to other
tenants. The Captain dead, his widow with many
tears pressed me to remain with her, and I did, never
having been able to resist that kind of appeal. Her
statements regarding her affairs were not strictly correct. — Are not women sometimes incorrect about
money matters ? — A landlord (not unjustly indignant) quickly handed over the mansion in Beak Street
to other tenants. The Queen's taxes swooped down
on poor Mrs. Prior's scanty furniture — on hers ? — on
mine likewise : on my neatly bound college books,
emblazoned with the effigy of Bonifacius, our patron,
and of Bishop Budgeon, our founder ; on my elegant
Raphael Morghen prints, purchased in undergraduate
days — (ye Powers ! what *did* make us boys go tick
for fifteen-guinea proofs of Raphael, Dying Stags,
Duke of Wellington Banquets, and the like ?) ; my
harmonium, at which SOME ONE has warbled songs of
my composition — (I mean the words, artfully describing my passion, my hopes, or my despair) ; on my
rich set of Bohemian glass, bought on the Zeil, Frank-
fort O. M. ; on my picture of my father, the late Captain Batchelor (Hoppner), R. N., in white ducks, and
a telescope, pointing, of course, to a tempest, in the
midst of which was a naval engagement ; on my poor
mother's miniature, by old Adam Buck, in pencil and
pink, with no waist to speak of at all ; my tea and
cream pots (bullion), with a hundred such fond knickknacks as decorate the chamber of a lonely man. I
found all these household treasures in possession of
the myrmidons of the law, and had to pay the Priors'

taxes with this hand, before I could be redintegrated in my own property. Mrs. Prior could only pay me back with a widow's tears and blessings (Prior having quitted a world where he had long ceased to be of use or ornament). The tears and blessings, I say, she offered me freely, and they were all very well. But why go on tampering with the tea-box, Madam? Why put your finger — your finger? — your whole paw — in the jam-pot? And it is a horrible fact that the wine and spirit bottles were just as leaky after Prior's decease as they had been during his disreputable lifetime. One afternoon, having a sudden occasion to return to my lodgings, I found my wretched landlady in the very act of marauding sherry. She gave an hysterical laugh, and then burst into tears. She declared that since her poor Prior's death she hardly knew what she said or did. She may have been incoherent; she was; but she certainly spoke truth on *this* occasion.

I am speaking lightly — flippantly, if you please — about this old Mrs. Prior, with her hard, eager smile, her wizened face, her frowning look, her cruel voice; and yet, goodness knows, I could, if I liked, be serious as a sermonizer. Why, this woman had once red cheeks, and was well-looking enough, and told few lies, and stole no sherry, and felt the tender passions of the heart, and I dare say kissed the weak old beneficed clergyman her father very fondly and remorsefully that night when she took leave of him to skip round to the back garden-gate and run away with Mr. Prior. Maternal instinct she had, for she nursed her young as best she could from her lean breast, and went about hungrily, robbing and pilfering for them. On Sundays she furbished up that threadbare black silk gown and bonnet, ironed the

collar, and clung desperately to church. She had a
feeble pencil-drawing of the vicarage in Dorsetshire,
and *silhouettes* of her father and mother, which were
hung up in the lodgings wherever she went. She
migrated much : wherever she went she fastened on
the gown of the clergyman of the parish ; spoke of
her dear father the vicar, of her wealthy and gifted
brother the Master of Boniface, with a reticence
which implied that Dr. Sargent might do more for his
poor sister and her family, if he would. She plumed
herself (oh! those poor moulting old plumes !) upon
belonging to the clergy ; had read a good deal of good
sound old-fashioned theology in early life, and wrote
a noble hand, in which she had been used to copy
her father's sermons. She used to put cases of conscience, to present her humble duty to the Rev. Mr.
Green, and ask explanation of such and such a passage of his admirable sermon, and bring the subject
round so as to be reminded of certain quotations of
Hooker, Beveridge, Jeremy Taylor. I think she had
an old commonplace book with a score of these
extracts, and she worked them in very amusingly and
dexterously into her conversation. Green would be
interested : perhaps pretty young Mrs. Green would
call, secretly rather shocked at the coldness of old Dr.
Brown, the rector, about Mrs. Prior. Between Green
and Mrs. Prior money transactions would ensue : Mrs.
Green's visits would cease : Mrs. Prior was an expen-
sive woman to know. I remember Pye of Maudlin,
just before he "went over," was perpetually in
Mrs. Prior's back parlor with little books, pictures,
medals, etc., etc., — you know. They called poor
Jack a Jesuit at Oxbridge ; but one year at Rome I
met him (with a half-crown shaved out of his head,
and a hat as big as Don Basilio's) ; and he said, " My

dear Batchelor, do you know that person at your
lodgings? I think she was an artful creature! She
borrowed fourteen pounds of me, and I forget how
much of — seven, I think — of Barfoot, of Corpus,
just — just before we were received. And I believe
she absolutely got another loan from Pummel, to be
able to get out of the hands of us Jesuits. Are you
going to hear the Cardinal? Do — do go and hear
him — everybody does: it's the most fashionable thing
in Rome." And from this I opine that there are sly-
boots in other communions besides that of Rome.

Now Mamma Prior had not been unaware of the
love-passages between her daughter and the fugitive
Bombay captain. Like Elizabeth, she called Captain
Walkingham "villain" readily enough; but, if I
know woman's nature in the least (and I don't), the
old schemer had thrown her daughter only too frequently in the officer's way, had done no small portion of the flirting herself, had allowed poor Bessy to
receive presents from Captain Walkingham, and had
been the manager and directress of much of the mischief which ensued. You see, in this humble class of
life, unprincipled mothers *will* coax and wheedle and
cajole gentlemen whom they suppose to be eligible,
in order to procure an establishment for their darling
children! What the Prioress did was done from the
best motives of course. "Never — never did the monster see Bessy without me, or one or two of her brothers and sisters, and Jack and dear Ellen are as sharp
children as any in England!" protested the indignant
Mrs. Prior to me; "and if one of my boys had been
grown up, Walkingham never would have dared to
act as he did — the unprincipled wretch! My poor
husband would have punished the villain as he
deserved; but what could he do in his shattered

state of health? Oh! you men, — you men, Mr.
Batchelor! how *unprincipled* you are!"

"Why, my good Mrs. Prior," said I, "you let
Elizabeth come to my room often enough."

"To have the conversation of her uncle's friend, of
an educated man, of a man so much older than herself! Of course, dear sir! Would not a mother
wish every advantage for her child? and whom
could I trust, if not you, who have ever been such a
friend to me and mine?" asks Mrs. Prior, wiping her
dry eyes with the corner of her handkerchief, as she
stands by my fire, my monthly bills in hand, — written in her neat old-fashioned writing, and calculated
with that prodigal liberality which she always exer-
cised in compiling the little accounts between us.
"Why, bless me!" says my cousin, little Mrs. Skinner,
coming to see me once when I was unwell, and examining one of the just-mentioned documents, —
"bless me! Charles, you consume more tea than all
my family, though we are seven in the parlor, and as
much sugar and butter, — well, it's no wonder you are
bilious!"

"But then, my dear, I like my tea so *very* strong,"
said I; "and you take yours uncommonly mild. I
have remarked it at your parties."

"It's a shame that a man should be robbed so,"
cried Mrs. S.

"How kind it is of you to cry thieves, Flora!" I
reply.

"It's my duty, Charles!" exclaims my cousin.
"And I should like to know who that great, tall,
gawky, red-haired girl in the passage is!"

Ah me! the name of the only woman who ever had
possession of this heart was not Elizabeth; though I
own I did think at one time that my little schemer

of a landlady would not have objected if I had proposed to make Miss Prior Mrs. Batchelor. And it is not only the poor and needy who have this mania, but the rich, too. In the very highest circles, as I am informed by the best authorities, this match-making goes on. Ah woman — woman! — ah wedded wife! — ah fond mother of fair daughters! how strange thy passion is to add to thy titles that of mother-in-law! I am told, when you have got the title, it is often but a bitterness and a disappointment. Very likely the son-in-law is rude to you, the coarse, ungrateful brute! and very possibly the daughter rebels, the thankless serpent! And yet you will go on scheming: and having met only with disappointment from Louisa and her husband, you will try and get one for Jemima, and Maria, and down even to little Toddles coming out of the nursery in her red shoes! When you see her with little Tommy, your neighbor's child, fighting over the same Noah's ark, or clambering on the same rocking-horse, I make no doubt, in your fond silly head, you are thinking, "Will those little people meet some twenty years hence?" And you give Tommy a very large piece of cake, and have a fine present for him on the Christmas tree — you know you do, though he is but a rude, noisy child, and has already beaten Toddles, and taken her doll away from her, and made her cry. I remember, when I myself was suffering from the conduct of a young woman in — in a capital which is distinguished by a viceregal court — and from *her* heartlessness, as well as that of her relative, who I once thought would be *my* mother-in-law — shrieking out to a friend who happened to be spouting some lines from Tennyson's "Ulysses:" — "By George! Warrington, I have no doubt that when the young sirens set their green caps at the old Greek captain and his crew, waving and beckoning him with their white arms and glancing smiles, and wheedling him with their sweetest pipes — I make no doubt, sir, that *the mother sirens* were behind the rocks (with their dyed fronts and cheeks painted, so as to resist water), and calling out — 'Now, Halcyone, my child, that air from the "Pirata!"' Now, Glaukopis, dear, look well at that old gentleman at the helm! Bathykolpos, love, there's a young sailor on the maintop, who will tumble right down into your lap if you beckon him!' And so on — and so on." And I laughed a wild shriek of despair. For I, too, have been on the dangerous island, and come away thence, mad, furious, wanting a strait-waistcoat.

And so, when a white-armed siren, named Glorvina, was bedevilling *me* with her all too tempting ogling and singing, I did not see at the time, but *now* I know, that her artful mother was egging that artful child on.

How, when the Captain died, bailiffs and executions took possession of his premises, I have told in a previous page, nor do I care to enlarge much upon the odious theme. I think the bailiffs were on the premises before Prior's exit; but he did not know of their presence. If I had to buy them out, 'twas no great matter: only I say it *was* hard of Mrs. Prior to represent me in the character of Shylock to the Master of Boniface. Well — well! I suppose there are other gentlemen besides Mr. Charles Batchelor who have been misrepresented in this life. Sargent and I made up matters afterwards, and Miss Bessy was the cause of our coming together again. "Upon my word, my dear Batchelor," says he one Christmas, when I went up to the old college, "I did not know how

much my — ahem! — my family was obliged to you!
My — ahem! — niece, Miss Prior, has informed me
of various acts of — ahem! — generosity which you
showed to my poor sister, and her still more wretched
husband.   You got my second — ahem! — nephew —
pardon me if I forget his Christian name — into the
what-d'-you-call-'em — Bluecoat School; you have
been, on various occasions, of considerable pecuniary
service to my sister's family.   A man need not take
high university honors to have a good — ahem! —
heart; and, upon my word, Batchelor, I and my —
ahem! — wife are sincerely obliged to you."

"I tell you what, Master," said I, "there *is* a point
upon which you ought really to be obliged to me, and
in which I have been the means of putting money into
your pocket, too."

"I confess I fail to comprehend you," says the
Master, with his grandest air.

"I have got you and Mrs. Sargent a very good governess for your children, at the very smallest remu-
neration," say I.

"Do you know the charges that unhappy sister of
mine and her family have put me to already?" says
the Master, turning as red as his hood.

"They have formed the frequent subject of your
conversation," I replied.   "You have had Bessy as a
governess —"

"A nursery governess — she has learned Latin and
a great deal more since she has been in my house!"
cries the Master.

"A nursery governess at the wages of a housemaid," I continued, as bold as Corinthian brass.

"Does my niece, does my — ahem! — children's
governess, complain of my treatment in my college?"
cries the Master.

"My dear Master," I asked, "you don't suppose I would have listened to her complaints, or, at any rate, have repeated them, until now?"

"And why now, Batchelor, I should like to know?" says the Master, pacing up and down his study in a fume, under the portraits of Holy Bonifacius, Bishop Budgeon, and all the defunct bigwigs of the college. "And why now, Batchelor, I should like to know?" says he.

"Because — though after staying with you for three years, and having improved herself greatly, as every woman must in your society, my dear Master, Miss Prior is worth at least fifty guineas a year more than you give her — I would not have had her speak until she had found a better place."

"You mean to say she proposes to go away?"

"A wealthy friend of mine, who was a member of our college by the way, wants a nursery governess, and I have recommended Miss Prior to him, at seventy guineas a year."

"And pray who's the member of my college who will give my niece seventy guineas?" asks the Master, fiercely.

"You remember Lovel, the gentleman-pensioner?"

"The sugar-baking man — the man who took you out of ja— ?"

"One good turn deserves another," says I, hastily. "I have done as much for some of your family, Sargent!"

The red Master, who had been rustling up and down his study in his gown and bands, stopped in his walk as if I had struck him. He looked at me. He turned redder than ever. He drew his hand over his eyes. "Batchelor," says he, "I ask your pardon. It was I who forgot myself — may Heaven forgive me!

— forgot how good you have been to my family, to my — ahem! — *humble* family, and — and how devoutly thankful I ought to be for the protection which they have found in you." His voice quite fell as he spoke: and of course any little wrath which I might have felt was disarmed before his contrition. We parted the best friends. He not only shook hands with me at the study-door, but he actually followed me to the hall-door, and shook hands at his lodge-porch, *sub Jove*, in the quadrangle. Huckles, the tutor (Highlow Huckles we used to call him in our time), and Botts (Trumperian professor), who happened to be passing through the court at the time, stood aghast as they witnessed the phenomenon.

"I say, Batchelor," asks Huckles, "have you been made a marquis by any chance?"

"Why a marquis, Huckles?" I ask.

"Sargent never comes to his lodge-door with any man under a marquis," said Huckles, in a low whisper.

"Or a pretty woman," says that Botts (he *will* have his joke). "Batchelor, my elderly Tiresias, are you turned into a lovely young lady *par hasard?*"

"Get along, you absurd Trumperian professor!" say I. But the circumstance was the talk not only in Compotation Room that evening over our wine, but of the whole college. And further, events happened which made each man look at his neighbor with wonder. For that whole term Sargent did not ask our nobleman Lord Sackville (Lord Wigmore's son) to the lodge. (Lord W.'s father, you know, Duff, was baker to the college.) For that whole term he was rude but twice to Perks, the junior tutor, and then only in a very mild way: and what is more, he gave his niece a present of a gown, of his blessing, of a

kiss, and a high character, when she went away; —
and promised to put one of her young brothers to
school — which promise, I need not say, he faithfully
kept: for he has good principles, Sargent has.   He is
rude: he is ill-bred: he is *bumptious* beyond almost
any man I ever knew; he is spoiled not a little by
prosperity; — but he is magnanimous: he can own
that he has been in the wrong; and oh me! what a
quantity of Greek he knows!

Although my late friend the Captain never seemed
to do aught but spend the family money, his disreputable presence somehow acted for good in the household.   "My dear husband kept our family together,"
Mrs. Prior said, shaking her lean head under her
meagre widow's cap.   "Heaven knows how I shall
provide for these lambs now he is gone."   Indeed, it
was not until after the death of that tipsy shepherd
that the wolves of the law came down upon the lambs
— myself included, who have passed the age of lamb-
hood and mint sauce a long time.   They came down
upon our fold in Beak Street, I say, and ravaged it.
What was I to do?   Could I leave that widow and
children in their distress?   I was not ignorant of
misfortune, and knew how to succor the miserable.
Nay, I think, the little excitement attendant upon the
seizure of my goods, etc., the insolvent vulgarity of
the low persons in possession — with one of whom I
was very near coming to a personal encounter — and
other incidents which occurred in the bereft household, served to rouse me, and dissipate some of the
languor and misery under which I was suffering in
consequence of Miss Mulligan's conduct to me.   I
know I took the late Captain to his final abode.   My
good friends the printers of the "Museum" took one of
his boys into their counting-house.   A blue coat and a

pair of yellow stockings were procured for Augustus ;
and seeing the Master's children walking about in
Boniface gardens with a glum-looking old wretch of a
nurse, I bethought me of proposing to him to take his
niece Miss Prior — and, Heaven be good to me ! never
said one word to her uncle about Miss Bellenden and
the Academy.   I dare say I drew a number of long
bows about her.   I managed about the bad grammar
pretty well, by lamenting that Elizabeth's poor mother
had been forced to allow the girl to keep company
with ill-educated people : and added, that she could
not fail to mend her English in the house of one of
the most distinguished scholars in Europe, and one of
the best-bred women.   I did say so, upon my word,
looking that half-bred, stuck-up Mrs. Sargent gravely
in the face ; and I humbly trust, if that bouncer has been
registered against me, the Recording Angel will be
pleased to consider that the motive was good, though
the statement was unjustifiable.   But I don't think it
was the compliment : I think it was the temptation of
getting a governess for next to nothing that operated
upon Madam Sargent.   And so Bessy went to her
aunt, partook of the bread of dependence, and drank
of the cup of humiliation, and ate the pie of humility,
and brought up her odious little cousins to the best of
her small power, and bowed the head of hypocrisy
before the don her uncle, and the pompous little upstart her aunt.   *She* the best-bred woman in England,
indeed !   She, the little vain skinflint !

   Bessy's mother was not a little loath to part with the
fifty pounds a year which the child brought home
from the Academy ; but her departure thence was inevitable.   Some quarrel had taken place there, about
which the girl did not care to talk.   Some rudeness
had been offered to Miss Bellenden, to which Miss

Prior was determined not to submit: or was it that
she wanted to go away from the scenes of her own
misery, and to try and forget that Indian captain?
Come, fellow-sufferer! Come, child of misfortune,
come hither! Here is an old bachelor who will weep
with thee tear for tear!

I protest here is Miss Prior coming into the room
at last. A pale face, a tawny head of hair combed
back, under a black cap: a pair of blue spectacles, as
I live! a tight mourning dress, buttoned up to her
white throat; a head hung meekly down: such is
Miss Prior. She takes my hand when I offer it. She
drops me a demure little curtsy, and answers my many
questions with humble monosyllabic replies. She
appeals constantly to Lady Baker for instruction, or
for confirmation of her statements. What! have six
years of slavery so changed the frank daring young
girl whom I remember in Beak Street? She is taller
and stouter than she was. She is awkward and high-
shouldered, but surely she has a very fine figure.

"Will Miss Cissy and Master Popham have their
teas here or in the schoolroom?" asks Bedford, the
butler, of his master. Miss Prior looks appealingly
to Lady Baker.

"In the sch —" Lady Baker is beginning.

"Here — here!" bawl out the children. "Much
better fun down here: and you'll send us out some
fruit and things from dinner, Papa!" cries Cissy.

"It's time to dress for dinner," says her ladyship.

"Has the first bell rung?" asks Lovel.

"Yes, the first bell has rung, and grandmamma
must go, for it always takes her a precious long time
to dress for dinner!" cries Pop. And, indeed, on
looking at Lady Baker, the connoisseur might perceive
that her ladyship was a highly composite person,

whose charms required very much care and arrangement. There are some cracked old houses where the painters and plumbers and puttyers are always at work.

"Have the goodness to ring the bell!" she says, in a majestic manner, to Miss Prior, though I think Lady Baker herself was nearest.

I sprang towards the bell myself, and my hand meets Elizabeth's there, who was obeying her ladyship's summons, and who retreats, making me the demurest curtsy. At the summons, enter Bedford the butler (he was an old friend of mine too) and young Buttons, the page under that butler.

Lady Baker points to a heap of articles on a table, and says to Bedford: "If you please, Bedford, tell my man to give those things to Pincott, my maid, to be taken to my room."

"Shall not I take them up, dear Lady Baker?" says Miss Prior.

But Bedford, looking at his subordinate, says: "Thomas! tell Bulkeley, her ladyship's man, to take her ladyship's things, and give them to her ladyship's maid." There was a tone of sarcasm, even of parody, in Monsieur Bedford's voice; but his manner was profoundly grave and respectful. Drawing up her person, and making a motion, I don't know whether of politeness or defiance, exit Lady Baker, followed by page, bearing bandboxes, shawls, paper parcels, parasols — I know not what. Dear Popham stands on his head as grandmamma leaves the room. "Don't be vulgar!" cries little Cissy (the dear child is always acting as a little Mentor to her brother). "I shall, if I like," says Pop; and he makes faces at her.

"You know your room, Batch?" asks the master of the house.

"Mr. Batchelor's old room — always has the blue room," says Bedford, looking very kindly at me.

"Give us," cries Lovel, "a bottle of that Sau—"

"—terne Mr. Batchelor used to like. Château Yquen. All right!" says Mr. Bedford. "How will you have the turbot done you brought down? — Dutch sauce? — Make lobster into salad? Mr. Bonnington likes lobster-salad," says Bedford. Pop is winding up the butler's back at this time. It is evident Mr. Bedford is a privileged person in the family. As he had entered it on my nomination, several years ago, and had been ever since the faithful valet, butler, and major-domo of Lovel, Bedford and I were always good friends when we met.

"By the way, Bedford, why was n't the barouche sent for me to the bridge?" cries Lovel. "I had to walk all the way home, with a bat and stumps for Pop, with the basket of fish, and that bandbox with my lady's—"

"He — he!" grins Bedford.

"'He — he!' Confound you, why do you stand grinning there? Why did n't I have the carriage, I say?" bawls the master of the house.

"*You* know, sir," says Bedford. "*She* had the carriage." And he indicated the door through which Lady Baker had just retreated.

"Then why did n't I have the phaeton?" asks Bedford's master.

"Your ma and Mr. Bonnington had the phaeton."

"And why should n't they, pray? Mr. Bonnington is lame: I'm at my business all day. I should like to know why they *should n't* have the phaeton?" says Lovel, appealing to me. As we had been sitting talking together previous to Miss Prior's appearance, Lady Baker had said to Lovel, "Your mother and

Mr. Bonnington are coming to dinner *of course*, Frederick?" and Lovel had said, "Of course they are," with a peevish bluster, whereof I now began to understand the meaning. The fact was, these two women were fighting for the possession of this child; but who was the Solomon to say which should have him? Not I. *Nenni.* I put my oar in no man's boat. Give me an easy life, my dear friends, and row me gently over.

"You had better go and dress," says Bedford sternly, looking at his master; "the first bell has rung this quarter of an hour. Will you have some '34?"

Lovel started up; he looked at the clock. "You are all ready, Batch, I see. I hope you are going to stay some time, ain't you?" And he disappeared to array himself in his sables and starch. I was thus alone with Miss Prior and her young charges, who resumed straightway their infantine gambols and quarrels.

"My dear Bessy!" I cry, holding out both hands, "I am heartily glad to—"

"Ne m'appelez que de mon nom paternel devant tout ce monde s'il vous plait, mon cher ami, mon bon protecteur!" she says hastily, in very good French, folding her hands and making a curtsy.

"Oui, oui, oui! Parlez-vous Français? J'aime, tu aimes, il aime!" cries out dear Master Popham. "What are you talking about? Here's the phaeton!" and the young innocent dashes through the open window on to the lawn, whither he is followed by his sister, and where we see the carriage containing Mr. and Mrs. Bonnington rolling over the smooth walk.

Bessy advances towards me, and gives me readily enough now the hand she had refused anon.

"I never thought you would have refused it, Bessy," said I.

"Refuse it to the best friend I ever had!" she says, pressing my hand. "Ah, dear Mr. Batchelor, what an ungrateful wretch I should be, if I did!"

"Let me see your eyes. Why do you wear spectacles? You never wore them in Beak Street," I say. You see I was very fond of the child. She had wound herself around me in a thousand fond ways. Owing to a certain Person's conduct my heart may be a ruin — a Persepolis, sir — a perfect Tadmor. But what then? May not a traveller rest under its shattered columns? May not an Arab maid repose there till the morning dawns and the caravan passes on? Yes, my heart is a Palmyra, and once a Queen inhabited me (O Zenobia! Zenobia! to think thou shouldst have been led away captive by an O'D—!). Now I am alone, alone in the solitary wilderness. Nevertheless, if a stranger comes to me I have a spring for his weary feet, I will give him the shelter of my shade. Rest thy cheek awhile, young maiden, on my marble — then go thy ways and leave me.

This I thought, or something to this effect, as in reply to my remark, "Let me see your eyes," Bessy took off her spectacles, and I took them up and looked at her. Why did n't I say to her, "My dear brave Elizabeth! as I look in your face, I see you have had an awful deal of suffering. Your eyes are inscrutably sad. We who are initiated, know the members of our Community of Sorrow. We have both been wrecked in different ships, and been cast on this shore. Let us go hand-in-hand, and find a cave and a shelter somewhere together"? I say, why did n't I say this to her? She would have come, I feel sure she would.

BESSY'S SPECTACLES.

We would have been semi-attached as it were. We would have locked up that room in either heart where the skeleton was, and said nothing about it, and pulled down the party-wall and taken our mild tea in the garden. I live in Pump Court now. It would have been better than this dingy loneliness and a snuffy laundress who bullies me. But for Bessy? Well — well, perhaps better for her too.

I remember these thoughts rushing through my mind whilst I held the spectacles. What a number of other things too? I remember two canaries making a tremendous concert in their cage. I remember the voices of the two children quarrelling on the lawn, the sound of the carriage-wheels grinding over the gravel; and then of a little old familiar cracked voice in my ear, with a "La, Mr. Batchelor! are *you* here?" And a sly face looks up at me from under an old bonnet.

"It is mamma," says Bessy.

"And I'm come to tea with Elizabeth and the dear children; and while you are at dinner, dear Mr. Batchelor, thankful — thankful for all mercies! And, dear me! here is Mrs. Bonnington, I do declare! Dear madam, how well you look — not twenty, I declare! And dear Mr. Bonnington! Oh, sir! let me — let me, I *must* press your hand. What a sermon last Sunday! All Putney was in tears!"

And the little woman, flinging out her lean arms, seizes portly Mr. Bonnington's fat hand: as he and kind Mrs. Bonnington enter at the open casement. The little woman seems inclined to do the honors of the house. "And won't you go up stairs, and put on your cap? Dear me, what a lovely ribbon! How blue does become Mrs. Bonnington! I always say so to Elizabeth," she cries, peeping into a little packet which Mrs. Bonnington bears in her hand. After exchanging friendly words and greetings with me, that lady retires to put the lovely cap on, followed by her little jackal of an aide-de-camp. The portly clergyman surveys his pleased person in the spacious mirror. "Your things are in your old room — like to go in, and brush up a bit?" whispers Bedford to me. I am obliged to go, you see, though, for my part, I had thought, until Bedford spoke, that the ride on the top of the Putney omnibus had left me without any need of brushing; having aired my clothes, and given my young cheek a fresh and agreeable bloom.

My old room, as Bedford calls it, was that snug apartment communicating by double doors with the drawing-room, and whence you can walk on to the lawn out of the windows.

"Here's your books, here's your writing-paper," says Bedford, leading the way into the chamber. "Does sore eyes good to see *you* down here again, sir. You may smoke now. Clarence Baker smokes when he comes. Go and get some of that wine you like for dinner." And the good fellow's eyes beam kindness upon me as he nods his head, and departs to superintend the duties of his table. Of course you understand that this Bedford was my young printer's boy of former days. What a queer fellow! I had not only been kind to him, but he was grateful.

CHAPTER III.

IN WHICH I PLAY THE SPY.

THE room to which Bedford conducted me I hold
to be the very pleasantest chamber in all the mansion
of Shrublands. To lie on that comfortable, cool
bachelor's bed there, and see the birds hopping about
on the lawn; to peep out of the French window at
early morning, inhale the sweet air, mark the dewy
bloom on the grass, listen to the little warblers performing their chorus, step forth in your dressing-gown
and slippers, pick a strawberry from the bed, or an
apricot in its season; blow one, two, three, just half
a dozen puffs of a cigarette; hear the venerable
towers of Putney toll the hour of six (three hours
from breakfast, by consequence), and pop back into
bed again with a favorite novel, or review, to set you
off (you see I am not malicious, or I could easily
insert here the name of some twaddler against whom
I have a grudgekin): to pop back into bed again, I
say, with a book which sets you off into that dear,
invaluable second sleep, by which health, spirits, appetite are so prodigiously improved : — all these I
hold to be most cheerful and harmless pleasures, and
have partaken of them often at Shrublands with a
grateful heart. That heart may have had its griefs,
but is yet susceptible of enjoyment and consolation.
That bosom may have been lacerated, but is not
therefore and henceforward a stranger to comfort.

After a certain affair in Dublin — nay, very soon
after, three months after — I recollect remarking to
myself: "Well, thank my stars, I still have a relish
for '34 claret." Once at Shrublands I heard steps
pacing overhead at night, and the feeble but continued wail of an infant. I wakened from my sleep,
was sulky, but turned and slept again. Biddlecombe
the barrister I knew was the occupant of the upper
chamber. He came down the next morning looking
wretchedly yellow about the cheeks, and livid round
the eyes. His teething infant had kept him on the
march all night, and Mrs. Biddlecombe, I am told,
scolds him frightfully besides. He munched a shred
of toast, and was off by the omnibus to chambers.
I chipped a second egg; I may have tried one or two
other nice little things on the table (Strasbourg pâté
I know I never can resist, and am convinced it is
perfectly wholesome). I could see my own sweet
face in the mirror opposite, and my gills were as
rosy as any broiled salmon. "Well — well!" I
thought, as the barrister disappeared on the roof of
the coach, "he has *domus* and *placens uxor* — but is
she *placens*? *Placetne* to walk about all night with a
roaring baby? Is it pleasing to go to bed after a
long hard day's work, and have your wife nagnagging
you because she has not been invited to the Lady
Chancelloress's *soirée*, or what not? Suppose the
Glorvina whom you loved so had been yours? Her
eyebrows looked as if they could scowl, her eyes as
if they could flash with anger. Remember what a
slap she gave the little knife-boy for upsetting the
butter-boat over her tabinet. Suppose *parvulus aulâ*,
a little Batchelor your son, who had the toothache all
night in your bedroom?" These thoughts passed
rapidly through my mind as I helped myself to the

comfortable meal before me. "I say, what a lot of
muffins you're eating!" cried innocent Master Lovel.
Now the married, the wealthy, the prosperous Biddlecombe only took his wretched scrap of dry toast.
"Aha!" you say, "this man is consoling himself
after his misfortune." O churl! and do you grudge
me consolation? "Thank you, dear Miss Prior.
Another cup, and plenty of cream, if you please."
Of course, Lady Baker was not at table when I said,
"Dear Miss Prior," at breakfast. Before her ladyship I was as mum as a mouse. Elizabeth found
occasion to whisper to me during the day, in her
demure way: "This is a very rare occasion. Lady
B—— never allows me to breakfast alone with Mr.
Lovel, but has taken her extra nap, I suppose, because
you and Mr. and Mrs. Biddlecombe were here.

Now it may be that one of the double doors of the
room which I inhabited was occasionally open, and
that Mr. Batchelor's eyes and ears are uncommonly
quick, and note a number of things which less obser-
vant persons would never regard or discover; but out
of this room, which I occupied for some few days,
now and subsequently, I looked forth as from a little
ambush upon the proceedings of the house, and got a
queer little insight into the history and characters of
the personages round about me. The two grandmothers of Lovel's children were domineering over
that easy gentleman, as women — not grandmothers
merely, but sisters, wives, aunts, daughters, when the
chance is given them — will domineer. Ah! Glorvina, what a gray mare you might have become had
you chosen Mr. Batchelor for your consort! (But
this I only remark with a parenthetic sigh.) The
two children had taken each the side of a grandmamma, and whilst Master Pop was declared by his

maternal grandmother to be a Baker all over, and
taught to despise sugar-baking and trade, little Cecilia
was Mrs. Bonnington's favorite, repeated Watts's
hymns with fervent precocity; declared that she
would marry none but a clergyman; preached infantine sermons to her brother and maid about worldliness; and somewhat wearied me, if the truth must
be told, by the intense self-respect with which she
regarded her own virtues. The old ladies had that
love for each other, which one may imagine that their
relative positions would engender. Over the bleeding
and helpless bodies of Lovel and his worthy and kind
step-father, Mr. Bonnington, they skirmished, and
fired shots at each other. Lady B—— would give
hints about second marriages, and second families,
and so forth, which of course made Mrs. Bonnington
wince. Mrs. B—— had the better of Lady Baker, in
consequence of the latter's notorious pecuniary irregu-
larities. *She* had never had recourse to her son's
purse, she could thank heaven. She was not afraid
of meeting any tradesman in Putney or London : she
had never been ordered out of the house in the late
Cecilia's lifetime : *she* could go to Boulogne and enjoy
the *fresh air* there. This was the terrific whip she
had over Baker. Lady B——, I regret to say, in
consequence of the failure of remittances, had been
locked up in prison, just at a time when she was in a
state of violent quarrel with her late daughter, and
good Mr. Bonnington had helped her out of durance.
How did I know this ? Bedford, Lovel's factotum,
told me : and how the old ladies were fighting like
two cats.

There was one point on which the two ladies
agreed. A very wealthy widower, young still, good-
looking, and good-tempered, we know can sometimes

find a dear woman to console his loneliness, and protect his motherless children. From the neighboring Heath, from Wimbledon, Roehampton, Barnes, Mortlake, Richmond, Esher, Walton, Windsor, nay, Reading, Bath, Exeter, and Penzance itself, or from any other quarter of Britain, over which your fancy may please to travel, families would have come ready with dear young girls to take charge of that man's future happiness; but it is a fact that these two dragons kept all women off from their ward. An unmarried woman, with decent good looks, was scarce ever allowed to enter Shrublands gate. If such an one appeared, Lovel's two mothers sallied out, and crunched her hapless bones. Once or twice he dared to dine with his neighbors, but the ladies led him such a life that the poor creature gave up the practice, and faintly announced his preference for home. "My dear Batch," says he, "what do I care for the dinners of the people round about? Has any one of them got a better cook or better wine than mine? When I come home from business, it is an intolerable nuisance to have to dress and go out seven or eight miles to cold *entrées*, and loaded claret, and sweet port. I can't stand it, sir. I *won't* stand it" (and he stamps his foot in a resolute manner). "Give me an easy life, a wine-merchant I can trust, and my own friends, by my own fireside. Shall we have some more? We can manage another bottle between us three, Mr. Bonnington?"

"Well," says Mr. Bonnington, winking at the ruby goblet, "I am sure I have no objection, Frederick, to another bo —"

"Coffee is served, sir," cries Bedford, entering.

"Well — well, perhaps we have had enough," says worthy Bonnington.

"We *have* had enough; we all drink too much,"
says Lovel, briskly. "Come in to coffee."

We go to the drawing-room. Fred and I, and the
two ladies, sit down to a rubber, whilst Miss Prior
plays a piece of Beethoven to a slight warbling accompaniment from Mr. Bonnington's handsome nose,
who has fallen asleep over the newspaper. During
our play, Bessy glides out of the room — a gray
shadow. Bonnington wakens up when the tray is
brought in. Lady Baker likes that good old custom:
it was always the fashion at the Castle, and she takes
a good glass of negus too; and so do we all; and the
conversation is pretty merry, and Fred Lovel hopes
I shall sleep better to-night, and is very facetious
about poor Biddlecombe, and the way in which that
eminent Q. C. is henpecked by his wife.

From my bachelor's room, then, on the ground-
floor; or from my solitary walks in the garden,
whence I could oversee many things in the house;
or from Bedford's communications to me, which were
very friendly, curious, and unreserved; or from my
own observation, which I promise you can see as far
into the millstones of life as most folks', I grew to
find the mysteries of Shrublands no longer mysterious to me; and, like another *Diable Boiteux*, had
the roofs of a pretty number of the Shrublands rooms
taken off for me.

For instance, on that very first day of my stay,
whilst the family were attiring themselves for dinner,
I chanced to find two secret cupboards of the house
unlocked, and the contents unveiled to me. Pinhorn,
the children's maid, a giddy little flirting thing in a
pink ribbon, brought some articles of the toilette
into my worship's apartment, and as she retired did
not shut the door behind her. I might have thought

that pert little head had never been made to ache by any care ; but ah! black care sits behind the horseman as Horace remarks, and not only behind the horseman, but behind the footman; and not only on the footman, but on the buxom shoulders of the lady's-maid. So with Pinhorn. You surely have remarked respecting domestic servants that they address you in a tone utterly affected and unnatural — adopting, when they are amongst each other, voices and gestures entirely different to those which their employers see and hear. Now, this little Pinhorn, in her occassional intercourse with your humble servant, had a brisk, quick, fluttering toss of the head, and a frisky manner, no doubt capable of charming some persons. As for me, ancillary allurements have, I own, had but small temptations. If Venus brought me a bedroom candle and a jug of hot water, I should give her sixpence, and no more. Having, you see, given my all to one wom — Psha! never mind *that* old story. — Well, I dare say this little creature may have been a flirt, but I took no more notice of her than if she had been a coal-scuttle.

Now, suppose she *was* a flirt. Suppose, under a mask of levity, she hid a profound sorrow. Do you suppose she was the first woman who ever has done so ? Do you suppose because she has fifteen pounds a year, her tea, sugar, and beer, and told fibs to her masters and mistresses, she had not a heart. She went out of the room absolutely coaxing and leering at me as she departed, with a great counterpane over her arm ; but in the next apartment I heard her voice quite changed, and another changed voice too — though not so much altered — interrogating her. My friend Dick Bedford's voice, in addressing those whom Fortune had pleased to make his superiors, was gruff

and brief. He seemed to be anxious to deliver himself of his speech to you as quickly as possible ; and
his tone always seemed to hint, " There — there is my
message, and I have delivered it ; but you know perfectly well that I am as good as you."   And so he
was, and so I always admitted : so even the trembling,
believing, flustering, suspicious Lady Baker herself
admitted, when she came into communication with
this man.   I have thought of this little Dick as of
Swift at Sheen hard by, with Sir William Temple :
or Spartacus when he was as yet the servant of the
fortunate Roman gentleman who owned him.   Now if
Dick was intelligent, obedient, useful, only not rebellious, with his superiors, I should fancy that
amongst his equals he was by no means pleasant
company, and that most of them hated him for his
arrogance, his honesty, and his scorn of them all.

But women do not always hate a man for scorning
and despising them.   Women do not revolt at the
rudeness and arrogance of us their natural superiors.
Women, if properly trained, come down to heel at the
master's bidding, and lick the hand that has been
often raised to hit them.   I do not say the brave little
Dick Bedford ever raised an actual hand to this poor
serving-girl, but his tongue whipped her, his behavior
trampled on her, and she cried, and came to him
whenever he lifted a finger.   Psha ! Don't tell *me*.
If you want a quiet, contented, orderly home, and
things comfortable about you, that is the way you
must manage your women.

Well, Bedford happens to be in the next room.   It
is the morning-room at Shrublands.   You enter the
dining-room from it, and they are in the habit of laying out the dessert there, before taking it in for dinner.
Bedford is laying out his dessert as Pinhorn enters

from my chamber, and he begins upon her with a sarcastic sort of grunt, and a "Ho! suppose you've been making up to B., have you?"

"Oh, Mr. Bedford, *you* know very well who it is I cares for!" she says, with a sigh.

"Bother!" Mr. B. remarks.

"Well, Richard, then!" (here she weeps.)

"Leave go my 'and!—leave go my a-hand, I say!" (What *could* she have been doing to cause this exclamation?)

"Oh, Richard, it's not your *'and* I want—it's your ah-ah-art, Richard!"

"Mary Pinhorn," exclaims the other, "what's the use of going on with this game? You know we couldn't be a-happy together—you know your ideers ain't no good, Mary. It ain't your fault. *I* don't blame you for it, my dear. Some people are born clever, some are born tall: I ain't tall."

"Oh, you're tall enough for me, Richard!"

Here Richard again found occasion to cry out: "*Don't*, I say! Suppose Baker was to come in and find you squeezing of my hand in this way? I say, some people are born with big brains, Miss Pinhorn, and some with big figures. Look at that ass, Bulkeley, Lady B.'s man! He is as big as a Lifeguardsman, and he has no more education, nor no more ideas, than the beef he feeds on."

"La! Richard, whatever do you mean?"

"Pooh! How should *you* know what I mean? Lay them books straight. Put the volumes together, stupid! and the papers, and get the table ready for nursery tea, and don't go on there mopping your eyes, and making a fool of yourself, Mary Pinhorn!"

"Oh, your heart is a stone—a stone—a stone!" cries Mary, in a burst of tears. "And I wish it was

hung round my neck, and I was at the bottom of the
well, and — there's the hupstairs bell!" with which
signal I suppose Mary disappeared, for I only heard a
sort of grunt from Mr. Bedford; then the clatter of a
dish or two, the wheeling of chairs and furniture, and
then came a brief silence, which lasted until the entry
of Dick's subordinate, Buttons, who laid the table for
the children's and Miss Prior's tea.

So here was an old story told over again. Here
was love unrequited, and a little passionate heart
wounded and unhappy. My poor little Mary! As I
am a sinner, I will give thee a crown when I go away,
and not a couple of shillings, as my wont has been.
Five shillings will not console thee much, but they
will console thee a little. Thou will not imagine that I
bribe thee with any privy thought of evil? Away! *Ich
habe genossen das irdische Glück — ich habe — geliebt!*

At this juncture I suppose Mrs. Prior must have
entered the apartment, for though I could not hear
her noiseless step, her little cracked voice came pretty
clearly to me with a "Good afternoon, Mr. Bedford!
Oh, dear me! what a many — many years we have
been acquainted. To think of the pretty little printer's
boy who used to come to Mr. Batchelor, and see you
grown such a fine man!"

Bedford. — "How? I'm only five foot four."

Mrs. P. — "But such a fine figure, Bedford! You
are — now indeed you are! Well, you are strong and
I am weak. You are well, and I am weary and faint."

Bedford. — "The tea's a-coming directly, Mrs.
Prior."

Mrs. P. — "Could you give me a glass of water
first — and perhaps a little sherry in it, please. Oh,
thank you. How good it is! How it revives a poor
old wretch! — and your cough, Bedford? How is your

cough? I have brought you some lozenges for it —
some of Sir Henry Halford's own prescribing for my
dear husband, and — "

Bedford (abruptly). — "I must go — never mind
the cough now, Mrs. P."

Mrs. Prior. — "What's here? almonds and raisins,
macaroons, preserved apricots, biscuits for dessert —
and — la bless the man! how you sta — artled me!"

Bedford. — "Don't! Mrs. Prior: I beg and implore
of you, keep your 'ands out of the dessert. I can't
stand it. I *must* tell the governor if this game goes
on."

Mrs. P. — "Ah! Mr. Bedford, it is for my poor —
poor child at home: the doctor recommended her
apricots. Ay, indeed, dear Bedford; he did, for her
poor chest!"

Bedford. — "And I'm blest if you have n't been at
the sherry-bottle again! Oh, Mrs. P., you drive me
wild — you do. I can't see Lovel put upon in this
way. You know it's only last week I whopped the
boy for stealing the sherry, and 't was you done it."

Mrs. Prior (passionately). — "For a sick child,
Bedford. What won't a mother do for her sick
child?"

Bedford. — "Your children's always sick. You're
always taking things for 'em. I tell you, by the laws,
I won't and must n't stand it, Mrs. P."

Mrs. Prior (with much spirit). — "Go and tell your
master, Bedford! Go and tell tales of me, sir. Go
and have me dismissed out of this house. Go and
have my daughter dismissed out of this house, and her
poor mother brought to disgrace."

Bedford. — "Mrs. Prior — Mrs. Prior! you *have*
been a-taking the sherry. A glass I don't mind: but
you've been a-bringing that bottle again."

Mrs. P. (whimpering). — "It's for Charlotte, Bedford! my poor delicate angel of a Shatty! she's ordered it, indeed she is!"

Bedford. — "Confound your Shatty! I can't stand it, I must n't and won't, Mrs. P.!"

Here a noise and clatter of other persons arriving interrupted the conversation between Lovel's major-domo and the mother of the children's governess, and I presently heard Master Pop's voice saying, "You 're going to tea with us, Mrs. Prior?"

Mrs. P. — "Your kind dear grandmammas have asked me, dear Master Popham."

Pop. — "But you'd like to go to dinner best, would n't you? I dare say you have doosid bad dinners at your house. Have n't you, Mrs. Prior?"

Cissy. — "Don't say doosid. It's a naughty word, Popham!"

Pop. — "I *will* say doosid. Doo-oo-oosid! There! And I'll say worse words too, if I please, and you hold *your* tongue. What's there for tea? jam for tea? strawberries for tea? muffins for tea? That's it: strawberries and muffins for tea. And we'll go in to dessert besides: that's prime. I say, Miss Prior?"

Miss Prior. — "What do you say, Popham?"

Pop. — "Should n't you like to go in to dessert? — there's lots of good things there, — and have wine. Only when grandmamma tells her story about — about my grandfather and King George the what-d'ye-call-'im: King George the Fourth — "

Cis. — "Ascended the throne, 1820; died at Windsor, 1830."

Pop. — "Bother Windsor! Well, when she tells that story, I can tell you *that* ain't very good fun."

Cis. — "And it's rude of you to speak in that way of your grandmamma, Pop!"

"WHERE THE SUGAR GOES."

Pop. — "And you'll hold *your* tongue, Miss! And I shall speak as I like. And I'm a man, and I don't want any of your stuff and nonsense. I say, Mary, give us the marmalade!"

Cis. — "You have had plenty to eat, and boys ought not to have so much."

Pop. — "Boys may have what they like. Boys can eat twice as much as women. There, I don't want any more. Anybody may have the rest."

Mrs. Prior. — "What nice marmalade! I know some children, my dears, who —"

Miss P. (imploringly). — "Mamma, I beseech you —"

Mrs. P. — "I know three dear children who very — very seldom have nice marmalade and delicious cake."

Pop. — "I know whom you mean: you mean Augustus, and Frederick, and Fanny — your children? Well, they shall have marmalade and cake."

Cis. — "Oh, yes, I will give them all mine."

Pop. (who speaks, I think, as if his mouth was full). — "I won't give 'em mine; but they can have another pot, you know. You have always got a basket with you; you know you have, Mrs. Prior. You had it the day you took the cold fowl."

Mrs. P. — "For the poor blind black man! Oh, how thankful he was to his dear young benefactors! He is a man and a brother, and to help him was most kind of you, dear Master Popham!"

Pop. — "That black beggar my brother? He ain't my brother."

Mrs. P. — "No, dears, you have both the most lovely complexions in the world."

Pop. — "Bother complexions! I say Mary, another pot of marmalade."

Mary. — "I don't know, Master Pop — "

Pop. — "I *will* have it, I say. If you don't, I 'll smash everything, I will."

Cis. — "Oh, you naughty, rude boy!"

Pop. — "Hold your tongue, stupid! I will have it, I say."

Mrs. P. — "Do humor him, Mary, please. And I 'm sure my dear children at home will be better for it."

Pop. — "There 's your basket. Now put this cake in, and this bit of butter, and this sugar on the top of the butter. Hurray! hurray! Oh, what jolly fun! Here 's some cake — no, I think I 'll keep that; and, Mrs. Prior, tell Gus, and Fanny, and Fred, I sent it to 'em, and they shall never want for anything as long as Frederick Popham Baker Lovel, Esquire, can give it them. Did Gus like my gray great-coat that I did n't want?"

Miss P. — "You did not give him your new great-coat?"

Pop. — "It was beastly ugly, and I did give it him; and I 'll give him this if I choose. And don't you speak to me; I 'm going to school, and I ain't going to have no governesses soon."

Mrs. Prior. — "Ah, dear child! what a nice coat it is; and how well my poor boy looks in it!"

Miss Prior. — "Mother, mother! I implore you — mother — !"

Mr. Lovel enters. — "So the children at high tea! How d'ye do, Mrs. Prior? I think we shall be able to manage that little matter for your second boy, Mrs. Prior."

Mrs. Prior. — Heaven bless you, — bless you, my dear, kind benefactor! Don't prevent me, Elizabeth: I *must* kiss his hand. There!"

And here the second bell rings, and I enter the
morning-room, and can see Mrs. Prior's great basket
popped cunningly under the table-cloth.   Her basket?
— her *porte-manteau*, her *porte-bouteille*, her *porte
gâteau*, her *porte-pantalon*, her *porte-butin* in general.
Thus I could see that every day Mrs. Prior visited
Shrublands she gleaned greedily of the harvest.   Well,
Boaz was rich, and this ruthless Ruth was hungry
and poor.

At the welcome summons of the second bell, Mr.
and Mrs. Bonnington also made their appearance; the
latter in the new cap which Mrs. Prior had admired,
and which she saluted with a nod of smiling recognition: "Dear madam, it *is* lovely — I told you it was,"
whispers Mrs. P., and the wearer of the blue ribbons
turned her bonny, good-natured face towards the looking-glass, and I hope saw no reason to doubt Mrs.
Prior's sincerity.   As for Bonnington, I could perceive that he had been taking a little nap before dinner, — a practice by which the appetite is improved,
I think, and the intellect prepared for the bland pran-
dial conversation.

"Have the children been quite good?" asks papa,
of the governess.

"There are worse children, sir," says Miss Prior,
meekly.

"Make haste and have your dinner; we are coming
in to dessert!" cries Pop.

"You would not have us go to dine without your
grandmother?" papa asks.   Dine without Lady
Baker, indeed!   I should have liked to see him go
to dinner without Lady Baker.

Pending her ladyship's arrival, papa and Mr. Bonnington walk to the open window, and gaze on the
lawn and the towers of Putney rising over the wall.

"Ah, my good Mrs. Prior," cries Mrs Bonnington, "those grandchildren of mine are sadly spoiled."

"Not by *you*, dear madam," says Mrs. Prior, with a look of commiseration. "Your dear children at home are, I am sure, perfect models of goodness. Is Master Edward well, ma'am? and Master Robert, and Master Richard, and dear funny little Master William? Ah, what blessings those children are to you! If a certain wilful little nephew of theirs took after them!"

"The little naughty wretch!" cried Mrs. Bonnington; "do you know, Prior, my grandson Frederick — (I don't know why they call him Popham in this house, or why he should be ashamed of his father's name) — do you know that Popham spilt the ink over my dear husband's bands, which he keeps in his great dictionary, and fought with my Richard, who is three years older than Popham, and actually beat his own uncle!"

"Gracious goodness!" I cried; "you don't mean to say ma'am, that Pop has been laying violent hands upon his venerable relative?" I feel ever so gentle a pull at my coat. Was it Miss Prior who warned me not to indulge in the sarcastic method with good Mrs. Bonnington?

"I don't know why you call my poor child a venerable relative," Mrs. B. remarks. "I know that Popham was very rude to him; and then Robert came to his brother, and that graceless little Popham took a stick, and my husband came out, and do you know Popham Lovel actually kicked Mr. Bonnington on the shins, and butted him like a little naughty ram; and if you think such conduct is a subject for ridicule — I *don't*, Mr. Batchelor."

"My dear — dear lady!" I cried, seizing her hand;

for she was going to cry, and in woman's eye the un-
answerable tear always raises a deuce of a commotion
in my mind. "I would not for the world say a word
that should willingly vex you; and as for Popham, I
give you my honor, I think nothing would do that
child so much good as a good whipping."

"He is spoiled, Madam; we know by *whom*," says
Mrs. Prior. "Dear Lady Baker! how that red does
become your ladyship." In fact, Lady B. sailed in
at this juncture, arrayed in ribbons of scarlet; with
many brooches, bangles, and other gimcracks orna-
menting her plenteous person. And now her ladyship
having arrived, Bedford announced that dinner was
served, and Lovel gave his mother-in-law an arm,
whilst I offered mine to Mrs. Bonnington to lead her
to the adjoining dining-room. And the pacable kind
soul speedily made peace with me. And we ate and
drank of Lovel's best. And Lady Baker told us her
celebrated anecdote of George the Fourth's compliment to her late dear husband, Sir Popham, when his
Majesty visited Ireland. Mrs. Prior and her basket
were gone when we repaired to the drawing-room:
having been hunting all day, the hungry mother had
returned with her prey to her wide-mouthed birdikins.
Elizabeth looked very pale and handsome, reading at
her lamp. And whist and the little tray finished the
second day at Shrublands.

I paced the moonlit walk alone when the family
had gone to rest; and smoked my cigar under the
tranquil stars. I had been some thirty hours in the
house, and what a queer little drama was unfolding
itself before me! What struggles and passions were
going on here — what *certamina* and *motus animo-
rum!* Here was Lovel, this willing horse; and what
a crowd of relations, what a heap of luggage had the

honest fellow to carry! How that little Mrs. Prior
was working, and scheming, and tacking, and flatter-
ing, and fawning, and plundering, to be sure! And
that serene Elizabeth, with what consummate skill,
art, and prudence, had she to act, to keep her place
with two such rivals reigning over her. And Elizabeth not only kept her place, but she actually was
liked by those two women! Why, Elizabeth Prior,
my wonder and respect for thee increase with every
hour during which I contemplate thy character! How
is it that you live with those lionesses, and are not
torn to pieces? What sops of flattery do you cast to
them to appease them? Perhaps I do not think my
Elizabeth brings up her two children very well, and,
indeed, have seldom become acquainted with young
people more odious. But is the fault hers, or is it
Fortune's spite? How, with these two grandmothers
spoiling the children alternately, can the governess do
better than she does? How has she managed to lull
their natural jealousy? I will work out that intricate
problem, that I will, ere many days are over. And
there are other mysteries which I perceive. There is
poor Mary breaking her heart for the butler. That
butler, why does he connive at the rogueries of Mrs.
Prior? Ha! herein lies a mystery too; and I vow I
will penetrate it ere long. So saying, I fling away the
butt-end of the fragrant companion of my solitude,
and enter into my room by the open French window
just as Bedford walks in at the door. I had heard
the voice of that worthy domestic warbling a grave
melody from his pantry window as I paced the lawn.
When the family goes to rest, Bedford passes a couple
of hours in study in his pantry, perusing the newspapers and the new works, and forming his opinion
on books and politics. Indeed I have reason to be-

lieve that the letters in the "Putney Herald" and "Mortlake Monitor," signed "A Voice from the Basement," were Mr. Bedford's composition.

"Come to see all safe for the night, sir, and the windows closed before you turn in," Mr. Dick remarks. "Best not leave 'em open, even if you are asleep inside — catch cold — many bad people about. Remember Bromley murder! — Enter at French windows — you cry out — cut your throat — and there's a fine paragraph for papers next morning!"

"What a good voice you have, Bedford," I say; "I heard you warbling just now — a famous bass, on my word!"

"Always fond of music — sing when I'm cleaning my plate — learned in Old Beak Street. *She* used to teach me," and he points towards the upper floors.

"What a little chap you were then! — when you came for my proofs for the 'Museum,'" I remark.

"I ain't a very big one now, sir; but it ain't the big ones that do the best work," remarks the butler.

"I remember Miss Prior saying that you were as old as she was."

"Hm! and I scarce came up to her — eh — elbow." (Bedford had constantly to do battle with the aspirates. He conquered them, but you could see there was a struggle.)

"And it was Miss Prior taught you to sing?" I say, looking him full in the face.

He dropped his eyes — he could not bear my scrutiny. I knew the whole story now.

"When Mrs. Lovel died at Naples, Miss Prior brought home the children, and you acted as courier to the whole party?"

"Yes, sir," says Bedford. "We had the carriage, and of course poor Mrs. L. was sent home by sea, and

I brought home the young ones, and — and the rest of the family. I could say *Avanti! avanti!* to the Italian postilions, and ask for *des chevaux* when we crossed the Halps — the Alps, — I beg your pardon, sir."

"And you used to see the party to their rooms at the inns, and call them up in the morning, and you had a blunderbuss in the rumble to shoot the robbers ? "

" Yes," says Bedford.

" And it was a pleasant time ? "

" Yes," says Bedford, groaning, and hanging down his miserable head. "Oh, yes, it was a pleasant time."

He turned away; he stamped his foot; he gave a sort of imprecation; he pretended to look at some books, and dust them with a napkin which he carried. I saw the matter at once. "Poor Dick!" says I.

" It 's the old — old story," says Dick. " It 's you and the Hirish girl over again, sir. I 'm only a servant, I know; but I 'm a — Confound it!" And here he stuck his fists into his eyes.

"And this is the reason you allow old Mrs. Prior to steal the sherry and the sugar ? " I ask.

" How do you know that? — you remember how she prigged in Beak Street ? " asks Bedford, fiercely.

" I overheard you and her just before dinner," I said.

" You had better go and tell Lovel — have me turned out of the house. That 's the best thing that can be done," cries Bedford again, fiercely, stamping his feet.

" It is always my custom to do as much mischief as I possibly can, Dick Bedford," I say, with fine irony.

He seizes my hand. "No, you're a trump — everybody knows that; beg pardon, sir; but you see I'm so — so — dash! — miserable, that I hardly know whether I'm walking on my head or my heels."

"You haven't succeeded in touching her heart, then, my poor Dick?" I said.

Dick shook his head. "She has no heart," he said. If she ever had any, that fellar in India took it away with him. She don't care for anybody alive. She likes me as well as any one. I think she appreciates me, you see, sir; she can't 'elp it — I'm blest if she can. She knows I am a better man than most of the chaps that come down here, — I am, if I wasn't a servant. If I were only an apothecary — like that grinning jackass who comes here from Barnes in his gig, and wants to marry her — she'd have me. She keeps him on, and encourages him — she can do that cleverly enough. And the old dragon fancies she is fond of him. Psha! Why am I making a fool of myself? — I am only a servant. Mary's good enough for me; *she'll* have me fast enough. I beg your pardon, sir; I am making a fool of myself; I ain't the first, sir. Good-night, sir; hope you'll sleep well." And Dick departs to his pantry and his private cares, and I think, "Here is another victim who is writhing under the merciless arrows of the universal torturer."

"He is a very singular person," Miss Prior remarked to me, as, next day, I happened to be walking on Putney Heath by her side, while her young charges trotted on and quarrelled in the distance. "I wonder where the world will stop next, dear Mr. Batchelor, and how far the march of intellect will proceed! Any one so free, and easy, and cool, as this Mr. Bedford I never saw. When we were abroad with poor Mrs.

Lovel, he picked up French and Italian in quite a surprising way. He takes books down from the library
now: the most abstruse works — works that *I* could n't
pretend to read, I 'm sure. Mr. Bonnington says he
has taught himself history, and Horace in Latin, and
algebra, and I don't know what besides. He talked
to the servants and tradespeople at Naples much
better than *I* could, I assure you." And Elizabeth
tosses up her head heavenwards, as if she would ask
of yonder skies how such a man could possibly be as
good as herself.

She stepped along the Heath — slim, stately, healthy,
tall, — her firm, neat foot treading swiftly over the
grass. She wore her blue spectacles, but I think she
could have looked at the sun without the glasses and
without wincing. That sun was playing with her
tawny, wavy ringlets, and scattering gold-dust over
them.

"It is wonderful," said I, admiring her, "how
these people give themselves airs, and try to imitate
their betters!"

"Most extraordinary!" says Bessy. She had not
one particle of humor in all her composition. I think
Dick Bedford was right; and she had no heart. Well,
she had famous lungs, health, appetite, and with these
one may get through life not uncomfortably.

"You and Saint Cecilia got on pretty well, Bessy?"
I ask.

"Saint who?"

"The late Mrs. L."

"Oh, Mrs. Lovel: — yes. What an odd person you
are! I did not understand whom you meant," says
Elizabeth the downright.

"Not a good temper, I should think? She and
Fred fought?"

"*He* never fought."

"I think a little bird has told me that she was not adverse to the admiration of our sex?"

"I don't speak ill of my friends, Mr. Batchelor," replies Elizabeth the prudent.

"You must have difficult work with the two old ladies at Shrublands?"

Bessy shrugs her shoulders. "A little management is necessary in all families," she says. "The ladies are naturally a little jealous one of the other; but they are both of them not unkind to me in the main; and I have to bear no more than other women in my situation. It was not all pleasure at St. Boniface, Mr. Batchelor, with my uncle and aunt. I suppose all governesses have their difficulties; and I must get over mine as best I can, and be thankful for the liberal salary which your kindness procured for me, and which enables me to help my poor mother and my brothers and sisters."

"I suppose you give all your money to her?"

"Nearly all. They must have it; poor mamma has so many mouths to feed."

"And *notre petit cœur*, Bessy?" I ask, looking in her fresh face. "Have we replaced the Indian officer?"

Another shrug of the shoulders. "I suppose we all get over those follies, Mr. Batchelor. I remember somebody else was in a sad way too," — and she looks askance at the victim of Glorvina. "*My* folly is dead and buried long ago. I have to work so hard for Mamma, and my brothers and sisters, that I have no time for such nonsense."

Here a gentleman in a natty gig, with a high-trotting horse, came spanking towards us over the common, and with my profound knowledge of human nature, I saw at once that the servant by the driver's side was a little doctor's boy, and the gentleman himself was a neat and trim general practitioner.

He stared at me grimly, as he made a bow to Miss Bessy. I saw jealousy and suspicion in his aspect.

"Thank you, dear Mr. Drencher," says Bessy, "for your kindness to Mamma and our children. You are going to call at Shrublands? Lady Baker was indisposed this morning. She says when she can't have Dr. Piper, there's nobody like you." And this artful one smiles blandly on Mr. Drencher.

"I have got the workhouse, and a case at Roehampton, and I shall be at Shrublands *about two*, Miss Prior," says that young doctor, whom Bedford had called a grinning jackass. He laid an eager emphasis on the *two*. Go to! I know what two and two mean as well as most people, Mr. Drencher! Glances of rage he shot at me from out his gig. The serpents of that miserable Æsculapius unwound themselves from his rod, and were gnawing at his swollen heart!

"He has a good practice, Mr. Drencher?" I ask, sly rogue as I am.

"He is very good to Mamma and our children. His practice with *them* does not profit him much," says Bessy.

"And I suppose our walk will be over before two o'clock?" remarks that slyboots who is walking with Miss Prior.

"I hope so. Why, it is our dinner-time; and this walk on the Heath does make one so hungry!" cries the governess.

"Bessy Prior," I said, "it is my belief that you no more want spectacles than a cat in the twilight." To

which she replied, that I was such a strange, odd man,
she really could not understand me.

We were back at Shrublands at two. Of course we
must not keep the children's dinner waiting: and of
course Mr. Drencher drove up at five minutes past
two, with his gig-horse all in a lather. I, who knew
the secrets of the house, was amused to see the furious
glances which Bedford darted from the sideboard, or
as he served the doctor with cutlets. Drencher, for
his part, scowled at me. I, for my part, was easy,
witty, pleasant, and I trust profoundly wicked and
malicious. I bragged about my aristocratic friends to
Lady Baker. I trumped her old-world stories about
George the Fourth at Dublin with the latest dandified
intelligence I had learned at the club. That the
young doctor should be dazzled and disgusted was, I
own, my wish; and I enjoyed his rage as I saw him
choking with jealousy over his victuals.

But why was Lady Baker sulky with me? How
came it, my fashionable stories had no effect upon
that polite matron? Yesterday at dinner she had
been gracious enough: and turning her back upon
those poor simple Bonningtons, who knew nothing of
the *beau monde* at all, had condescended to address
herself specially to me several times with an " I need
not tell *you*, Mr. Batchelor, that the Duchess of Dorsetshire's maiden name was De Bobus;" or, " You
know very well that the etiquette at the Lord Lieutenant's balls, at Dublin Castle, is for the wives of
baronets to " — etc. etc.

Now whence, I say, did it arise that Lady Baker,
who had been kind and familiar with me on Sunday,
should on Monday turn me a shoulder as cold as that
lamb which I offered to carve for the family, and
which remained from yesterday's quarter? I had

thought of staying but two days at Shrublands. I
generally am bored at country-houses. I was going
away on the Monday morning, but Lovel, when he
and I and the children and Miss Prior breakfasted
together before he went to business, pressed me to
stay so heartily and sincerely that I agreed, gladly
enough, to remain. I could finish a scene or two of
my tragedy at my leisure ; besides, there were one or
two little comedies going on in the house which inspired me with no little curiosity.

Lady Baker growled at me, then, during lunch-time.
She addressed herself in whispers and hints to Mr.
Drencher. She had in her own man Bulkeley, and
bullied him. She desired to know whether she was
to have the barouche or not : and when informed
that it was at her ladyship's service, said it was a
great deal too cold for the open carriage, and that
she would have the brougham. When she was told
that Mr. and Mrs. Bonnington had impounded the
brougham, she said she had no idea of people taking
other people's carriages : and when Mr. Bedford remarked that her ladyship had her choice that morning,
and had chosen the barouche, she said, "I did n't speak
to you, sir ; and I will thank you not to address me until you are spoken to !" She made the place so hot
that I began to wish I had quitted it.

"And pray, Miss Prior, where is Captain Baker to
sleep," she asked, "now that the ground-floor room is
engaged ? "

Miss Prior meekly said, " Captain Baker would have
the pink room."

" The room on my landing-place, without double
doors ? Impossible ! Clarence is always smoking.
Clarence will fill the whole house with his smoke.
He shall *not* sleep in the pink room. I expected the

ground-floor room for him, which — a — this gentleman persists in not vacating." And the dear creature looked me full in the face.

"This gentleman smokes, too, and is so comfortable where he is that he proposes to remain there," I say, with a bland smile.

"Haspic of plovers' eggs, sir," says Bedford, handing a dish over my back. And he actually gave me a little dig, and growled, "Go it — give it her!"

"There is a capital inn on the Heath," I continue, peeling one of my opal favorites. "If Captain Baker must smoke, he may have a room there."

"Sir! my son does not live at inns," cries Lady Baker.

"Oh, Grandma! don't he though? And was n't there a row at the 'Star and Garter;' and did n't Pa pay Uncle Clarence's bill there, though?"

"Silence, Popham! Little boys should be seen and not heard," says Cissy. "Should n't little boys be seen and not heard, Miss Prior?"

"They should n't insult their grandmothers. O my Cecilia — my Cecilia!" cries Lady Baker, lifting her hand.

"You sha'n't hit me! I say, you sha'n't hit me!" roars Pop, starting back, and beginning to square at his enraged ancestress. The scene was growing painful. And there was that rascal of a Bedford choking with suppressed laughter at the sideboard. Bulkeley, her ladyship's man, stood calm as fate; but young Buttons burst out in a guffaw; on which, I assure you, Lady Baker looked as savage as Lady Macbeth.

"Am I to be insulted by my daughter's servants?" cries Lady Baker. "I will leave the house this instant."

"At what hour will your ladyship have the barouche?" says Bedford, with perfect gravity.

If Mr. Drencher had whipped out a lancet and bled
Lady B—— on the spot, he would have done her
good.   I shall draw the curtain over this sad —
this humiliating scene.   Drop, little curtain, on this
absurd little act.

CHAPTER IV.

The being for whom my friend Dick Bedford seemed to have a special contempt and aversion, was Mr. Bulkeley, the tall footman in attendance upon Lovel's dear mother-in-law. One of the causes of Bedford's wrath, the worthy fellow explained to me. In the servants' hall, Bulkeley was in the habit of speaking in disrespectful and satirical terms of his mistress, enlarging upon her many foibles, and describing her pecuniary difficulties to the many *habitués* of that second social circle at Shrublands. The hold which Mr. Bulkeley had over his lady lay in a long unsettled account of wages, which her ladyship was quite disinclined to discharge. And, in spite of this insolvency, the footman must have found his profit in the place, for he continued to hold it from year to year, and to fatten on his earnings, such as they were. My lady's dignity did not allow her to travel without this huge personage in her train ; and a great comfort it must have been to her, to reflect that in all the country-houses which she visited (and she would go wherever she could force an invitation), her attendant freely explained himself regarding her peculiarities, and made his brother servants aware of his mistress's embarrassed condition. And yet the woman, whom I suppose no soul alive respected (unless, haply, she herself had a hankering delusion that she was a respectable woman), thought that her position in life forbade her to move abroad without a maid, and this hulking encumbrance in plush ; and never was seen anywhere, in watering-place, country-house, hotel, unless she was so attended.

Between Bedford and Bulkeley, then, there was feud and mutual hatred. Bedford chaffed the big man by constant sneers and sarcasms, which penetrated the other's dull hide, and caused him frequently to assert that he would punch Dick's ugly head off. The housekeeper had frequently to interpose, and fling her matronly arms between these men of war ; and perhaps Bedford was forced to be still at times, for Bulkeley was nine inches taller than himself, and was perpetually bragging of his skill and feats as a bruiser. This sultan may also have wished to fling his pocket-handkerchief to Miss Mary Pinhorn, who, though she loved Bedford's wit and cleverness, might also be not insensible to the magnificent chest, calves, whiskers, of Mr. Bulkeley. On this delicate subject, however, I can't speak. The men hated each other. You have, no doubt, remarked, in your experience of life, that when men *do* hate each other, about a woman, or some other cause, the real reason is never assigned. You say, " The conduct of such and such a man to his grandmother — his behavior in selling that horse to Benson — his manner of brushing his hair down the middle " — or what you will, " makes him so offensive to me that I can't endure him." His verses, therefore, are mediocre ; his speeches in Parliament are utter failures ; his practice at the bar is dwindling every year ; his powers (always small) are utterly leaving him, and he is repeating his confounded jokes until they quite nauseate. Why, only about myself, and within these three days, I read a nice little article — written in sorrow, you know, not in anger — by our eminent *confrère* Wiggins, deploring

the decay of, etc., etc. And Wiggins's little article
which was not found suitable for a certain magazine ?
— *Allons donc !* The drunkard says the pickled salmon
gave him the headache ; the man who hates us gives *a*
reason, but not *the* reason. Bedford was angry with
Bulkeley for abusing his mistress at the servants'
table ? Yes. But for what else besides ? I don't
care — nor possibly does your worship, the exalted
reader, for these low vulgar kitchen quarrels.

Out of that ground-floor room, then, I would not
move in spite of the utmost efforts of my Lady Baker's
broad shoulder to push me out ; and with many grins
that evening, Bedford complimented me on my gallantry in routing the enemy at luncheon. I think he
may possibly have told his master, for Lovel looked
very much alarmed and uneasy when we greeted each
other on his return from the city, but became more
composed when Lady Baker appeared at the second
dinner-bell, without a trace on her fine countenance of
that storm which had caused all her waves to heave
with such commotion at noon. How finely some people, by the way, can hang up quarrels — or pop them
into a drawer — as they do their work, when dinner is
announced, and take them out again at a convenient
season ! Baker was mild, gentle, a thought sad and
sentimental — tenderly interested about her dear son
and daughter, in Ireland, whom she *must* go and see —
quite easy in hand, in a word, and to the immense relief
of all of us. She kissed Lovel on retiring, and prayed
blessings on her Frederick. She pointed to the picture : nothing could be more melancholy or more
gracious.

" *She* go ! " says Mr. Bedford to me at night —
" not she. She knows when she 's well off ; was
obliged to turn out of Bakerstown before she came

here : that brute Bulkeley told me so. She's always
quarrelling with her son and his wife. Angels don't
grow everywhere as they do at Putney, Mr. B.! You
gave it her well to-day at lunch, you did though!"
During my stay at Shrublands, Mr. Bedford payed
me a regular evening visit in my room, set the *carte
du pays* before me, and in his curt way acquainted
me with the characters of the inmates of the house,
and the incidents occurring therein.

Captain Clarence Baker did not come to Shrublands
on the day when his anxious mother wished to clear
out my nest (and expel the amiable bird in it) for her
son's benefit. I believe an important fight, which
was to come off in the Essex Marshes, and which was
postponed in consequence of the interposition of the
county magistrates, was the occasion, or at any rate
the pretext, of the Captain's delay. "He likes seeing fights better than going to 'em, the Captain does,"
my major-domo remarked. "His regiment was ordered to India, and he sold out: climate don't agree
with his precious health. The Captain ain't been
here ever so long, not since poor Mrs. L.'s time, before Miss P. came here: Captain Clarence and his
sister had a tremendous quarrel together. He was
up to all sorts of pranks, the Captain was. Not a
good lot, by any means, I should say, Mr. Batchelor." And here Bedford begins to laugh. "Did you
ever read, sir, a farce called 'Raising the Wind?'
There's plenty of Jeremy Diddlers now, Captain
Jeremy Diddlers and Lady Jeremy Diddlers too.
Have you such a thing as half a crown about you?
If you have, don't invest it in some folks' pockets —
that's all. Beg your pardon, sir, if I am bothering
you with talking."

As long as I was at Shrublands, and ready to par-

take of breakfast with my kind host and his children
and their governess, Lady Baker had her own breakfast taken to her room. But when there were no
visitors in the house, she would come groaning out of
her bed-room to be present at the morning meal ; and
not uncommonly would give the little company anecdotes of the departed saint, under whose invocation,
as it were, we were assembled, and whose simpering
effigy looked down upon us, over her harp, and from
the wall. The eyes of the portrait followed you
about, as portraits' eyes so painted will ; and those
glances, as it seemed to me, still domineered over
Lovel, and made him quail as they had done in life.
Yonder, in the corner, was Cecilia's harp, with its
leathern cover. I likened the skin to that drum
which the dying Zisca ordered should be made out of
his hide, to be beaten before the hosts of his people
and inspire terror. *Vous concevez*, I did not say to
Lovel at breakfast, as I sat before the ghostly musical
instrument, "My dear fellow, that skin of Cordovan
leather belonging to your defunct Cecilia's harp is
like the hide which," etc. ; but I confess, at first, I
used to have a sort of *crawly* sensation, as of a sickly
genteel ghost flitting about the place, in an exceedingly peevish humor, trying to scold and command,
and finding her defunct voice could n't be heard —
trying to re-illumine her extinguished leers and faded
smiles and ogles, and finding no one admired or took
note. In the gray of the gloaming, in the twilight
corner where stands the shrouded companion of song
— what is that white figure flickering round the
silent harp ? Once, as we were assembled in the
room at afternoon tea, a bird, entering at the open
window, perched on the instrument. Popham dashed
at it. Lovel was deep in conversation upon the wine-

duties with a Member of Parliament he had brought
down to dinner. Lady Baker, who was, if I may use
the expression, "jawing," as usual, and telling one of
her tremendous stories about the Lord Lieutenant to
Mr. Bonnington, took no note of the incident. Elizabeth did not seem to remark it : what was a bird on a
harp to her, but a sparrow perched on a bit of leather-
casing! All the ghosts in Putney church-yard might
rattle all their bones, and would not frighten that
stout spirit!

I was amused at a precaution which Bedford took,
and somewhat alarmed at the distrust towards Lady
Baker which he exhibited, when, one day on my return
from town — whither I had made an excursion of four
or five hours — I found my bed-room door locked,
and Dick arrived with the key. "He's wrote to say
he's coming this evening, and if he had come when
you was away, Lady B. was capable of turning your
things out, and putting his in, and taking her oath
she believed you was going to leave. The long-bows
Lady B. do pull are perfectly awful, Mr. B.! So it
was long-bow to long-bow, Mr. Batchelor; and I said
you had took the key in your pocket, not wishing to
have your papers disturbed. She tried the lawn window, but I had bolted that, and the Captain will have
the pink room, after all, and must smoke up the
chimney. I should have liked to see him, or you,
or any one do it in poor Mrs. L.'s time — I just
should!"

During my visit to London, I had chanced to meet
my friend Captain Fitzb—dle, who belongs to a dozen
clubs, and knows something of every man in London.
"Know anything of Clarence Baker?" "Of course,
I do," says Fitz; "and if you want any *renseignement*,
my dear fellow, I have the honor to inform you that

a blacker little sheep does not trot the London *pavé*.
Wherever that ingenious officer's name is spoken —
at Tattersall's, at his clubs, in his late regiments, in
men's society, in ladies' society, in that expanding and
most agreeable circle which you may call no society at
all — a chorus of maledictions rises up at the mention
of Baker. Know anything of Clarence Baker! My
dear fellow, enough to make your hair turn white,
unless (as I sometimes fondly imagine) nature has
already performed that process, when of course I
can't pretend to act upon mere hair-dye." (The
whiskers of the individual who addressed me, innocent, stared me in the face as he spoke, and were
dyed of the most unblushing purple.) "Clarence
Baker, sir, is a young man who would have been invaluable in Sparta as a warning against drunkenness
and an exemplar of it. He has helped the regimental surgeon to some most interesting experiments in
delirium tremens. He is known, and not in the least
trusted, in every billiard-room in Brighton, Canter-
bury, York, Sheffield — on every pavement which has
rung with the clink of dragoon boot-heels. By a wise
system of revoking at whist he has lost games which
have caused not only his partners, but his opponents
and the whole club, to admire him and to distrust
him: long before and since he was of age, he has
written his eminent name to bills which have been
dishonored, and has nobly pleaded his minority as a
reason for declining to pay. From the garrison towns
where he has been quartered, he has carried away not
only the hearts of the milliners, but their gloves,
haberdashery, and perfumery. He has had contro-
versies with Cornet Green, regarding horse transactions; disputed turf accounts with Lieutenant Brown;
and betting and backgammon differences with Captain

Black. From all I have heard he is the worthy son
of his admirable mother. And I bet you even on the
four events, if you stay three days in a country-house
with him — which appears to be your present happy
idea — that he will quarrel with you, insult you, and
apologize; that he will intoxicate himself more than
once; that he will offer to play cards with you, and
not pay on losing (if he wins, I perhaps need not
state what his conduct will be); and that he will try
to borrow money from you, and most likely from your
servant, before he goes away." So saying, the sen-
tentious Fitz strutted up the steps of one of his many
club-haunts in Pall Mall, and left me forewarned, and
I trust forearmed, against Captain Clarence and all
his works.

The adversary, when at length I came in sight of
him, did not seem very formidable. I beheld a weakly
little man with Chinese eyes, and pretty little feet and
hands, whose pallid countenance told of Finishes and
Casinos. His little chest and fingers were decorated
with many jewels. A perfume of tobacco hung round
him. His little mustache was twisted with an elaborate gummy curl. I perceived that the little hand
which twirled the mustache shook wofully: and
from the little chest there came a cough surprisingly
loud and dismal.

He was lying on a sofa as I entered, and the children of the house were playing round him. "If you
are our uncle, why did n't you come to see us oftener?"
asks Popham.

"How should I know that you were such uncommonly nice children?" asks the Captain.

"We're not nice to you," says Popham. "Why
do you cough so? Mamma used to cough. And
why does your hand shake so?"

"My hand shakes because I am ill: and I cough because I'm ill. Your mother died of it, and I dare say I shall too."

"I hope you'll be good, and repent before you die, Uncle, and I will lend you some nice books," says Cecilia.

"Oh, bother books!" cries Pop.

"And I hope *you'll* be good, Popham," and "You hold *your* tongue, Miss," and "I shall," and "I sha'n't," and "You're another," and "I'll tell Miss Prior," — "Go and tell, tell-tale," — "Boo" — "Boo" — "Boo" — "Boo" — and I don't know what more exclamations came tumultuously and rapidly from these dear children, as their uncle lay before them, a handkerchief to his mouth, his little feet high raised on the sofa cushions.

Captain Baker turned a little eye towards me, as I entered the room, but did not change his easy and elegant posture. When I came near to the sofa where he reposed, he was good enough to call out:

"Glass of sherry!"

"It's Mr. Batchelor; it is n't Bedford, Uncle," says Cissy.

"Mr. Batchelor ain't got any sherry in his pocket: — have you, Mr. Batchelor? You ain't like old Mrs. Prior, always pocketing things, are you?" cries Pop, and falls a-laughing at the ludicrous idea of my being mistaken for Bedford.

"Beg your pardon. How should I know, you know?" drawls the invalid on the sofa. "Everybody's the same now, you see."

"Sir!" says I, and "sir" was all I could say. The fact is, I could have replied with something remarkably neat and cutting, which would have transfixed the languid little jackanapes who dared to mistake me for a footman : but, you see, I only thought of my repartee some eight hours afterwards when I was lying in bed, and I am sorry to own that a great number of my best *bonmots* have been made in that way. So, as I had not the pungent remark ready when wanted, I can't say I said it to Captain Baker, but I dare say I turned very red, and said, "Sir !" and — and in fact that was all.

"You were goin' to say somethin' ?" asked the Captain, affably.

"You know my friend Mr. Fitzboodle, I believe ?" said I; the fact is, I really did not know what to say.

"Some mistake — think not."

"He is a member of the Flag Club," I remarked, looking my young fellow hard in the face.

"I ain't. There's a set of cads in that club that will say anything."

"You may not know him, sir, but he seemed to know you very well. Are we to have any tea, children ?" I say, flinging myself down on an easy-chair, taking up a magazine, and adopting an easy attitude, though I dare say my face was as red as a turkey-cock's, and I was boiling over with rage.

As we had a very good breakfast and a profuse luncheon at Shrublands, of course we could not support nature till dinner-time without a five-o'clock tea ; and this was the meal for which I pretended to ask. Bedford, with his silver kettle, and his buttony satellite, presently brought in this refection, and of course the children bawled out to him —

"Bedford — Bedford ! Uncle mistook Mr. Batchelor for you."

"I could not be mistaken for a more honest man, Pop," said I. And the bearer of the tea-urn gave me a look of gratitude and kindness which, I own, went far to restore my ruffled equanimity.

"Since you are the butler, will you get me a glass of sherry and a biscuit?" says the Captain. And Bedford, retiring, returned presently with the wine.

The young gentleman's hand shook so, that, in order to drink his wine, he had to surprise it, as it were, and seize it with his mouth, when a shake brought the glass near his lips. He drained the wine, and held out his hand for another glass. The hand was steadier now.

"You the man who was here before?" asks the Captain.

"Six years ago, when you were here, sir," says the butler.

"What! I ain't changed, I suppose?"

"Yes, you are, sir."

"Then, how the dooce do you remember me?"

"You forgot to pay me some money you borrowed of me, one pound five, sir," says Bedford, whose eyes slyly turned in my direction.

And here, according to her wont at this meal, the dark-robed Miss Prior entered the room. She was coming forward with her ordinarily erect attitude and firm step, but paused in her walk an instant, and when she came to us, I thought, looked remarkably pale. She made a slight curtsy, and it must be confessed that Captain Baker rose up from his sofa for a moment when she appeared. She then sat down, with her back towards him, turning towards herself the table and its tea apparatus.

At this board my Lady Baker found us assembled when she returned from her afternoon drive. She flew to her darling reprobate of a son. She took his hand, she smoothed back his hair from his damp forehead. "My darling child," cries this fond mother, "what a pulse you have got!"

"I suppose, because I 've been drinking," says the prodigal.

"Why did n't you come out driving with me? The afternoon was lovely!"

"To pay visits at Richmond? Not as I knows on, Ma'am," says the invalid. "Conversation with elderly ladies about poodles, Bible societies, that kind of thing? It must be a doosid lovely afternoon that would make me like that sort of game." And here comes a fit of coughing, over which mamma ejaculates her sympathy.

"Kick — kick — killin' myself!" gasps out the Captain; "know I am. No man *can* lead my life, and stand it. Dyin' by inches! Dyin' by whole yards, by Jo — ho — hove, I am!" Indeed, he was as bad in health as in morals, this graceless Captain.

"That man of Lovel's seems a d—— insolent beggar," he presently and ingenuously remarks.

"Oh, Uncle, you must n't say those words!" cries niece Cissy.

"He 's a man, and may say what he likes, and so will I, when I 'm a man. Yes, and I 'll say it now, too, if I like," cries Master Popham.

"Not to give me pain, Popham? Will you?" asks the governess.

On which the boy says — "Well, who wants to hurt you, Miss Prior?"

And our colloquy ends by the arrival of the man of the house from the city.

What I have admired in some dear women is their capacity for quarrelling and for reconciliation. As I saw Lady Baker hanging round her son's neck, and fondling his scanty ringlets, I remembered the awful stories with which in former days she used to entertain us regarding this reprobate. Her heart was pincushioned with his filial crimes. Under her chestnut front her ladyship's real head of hair was gray, in consequence of his iniquities. His precocious appetite had devoured the greater part of her jointure. He had treated her many dangerous illnesses with indifference : had been the worst son, the worst brother, the most ill-conducted schoolboy, the most immoral young man — the terror of households, the Lovelace of garrison towns, the perverter of young officers ; in fact, Lady Baker did not know how she supported existence at all under the agony occasioned by his crimes, and it was only from the possession of a more than ordinarily strong sense of religion that she was enabled to bear her burden.

The Captain himself explained these alternating maternal caresses and quarrels in his easy way.

"Saw how the old lady kissed and fondled me ?" says he to his brother-in-law. "Quite refreshin', ain't it ? Hang me, I thought she was goin' to send me a bit of sweetbread off her own plate. Came up to my room last night, wanted to tuck me up in bed, and abused my brother to me for an hour. You see, when I'm in favor, she always abuses Baker; when *he's* in favor she abuses me to him. And my sister-in-law, did n't she give it my sister-in-law ! Oh! I'll trouble you ! And poor Cecilia — why, hang me, Mr. Batchelor, she used to go on — this bottle's corked, I'm hanged if it is n't — to go on about Cecilia, and call her — Hullo !"

Here he was interrupted by our host, who said sternly —

"Will you please to forget those quarrels, or not mention them here ? Will you have more wine, Batchelor ?"

And Lovel rises, and haughtily stalks out of the

room. To do Lovel justice, he had a great contempt and dislike for his young brother-in-law, which, with his best magnanimity, he could not at all times conceal.

So our host stalks towards the drawing-room, leaving Captain Clarence sipping wine.

"Don't go, too," says the Captain. "He's a confounded rum fellow, my brother-in-law is. He's a confounded ill-conditioned fellow, too. They always are, you know, these tradesmen fellows, these half-bred uns. I used to tell my sister so; but she *would* have him, because he had such lots of money, you know. And she threw over a fellar she was very fond of; and I told her she'd regret it. I told Lady B. she'd regret it. It was all Lady B.'s doing. She made Cissy throw the fellar over. He was a bad match, certainly, Tom Mountain was; and not a clever fellow, you know, or that sort of thing; but, at any rate, he was a gentleman, and better than a confounded sugar-baking beggar out Ratcliff Highway."

"You seem to find that claret very good," I remark, speaking, I may say, Socratically, to my young friend, who had been swallowing bumper after bumper.

"Claret good! Yes, doosid good!"

"Well, you see our confounded sugar-baker gives you his best."

"And why shouldn't he, hang him? Why, the fellow chokes with money. What does it matter to him how much he spends? You're a poor man, I dare say. You don't look as if you were overflush of money. Well, if *you* stood a good dinner, it would be all right — I mean it would show — you understand me, you know. But a sugar-baker with ten thousand a year, what does it matter to him, bottle of claret more — less?"

"Let us go in to the ladies," I say.

"Go in to Mother! *I* don't want to go in to my mother," cries out the artless youth. "And I don't want to go in to the sugar-baker, hang him! and I don't want to go in to the children; and I'd rather have a glass of brandy-and-water with you, old boy. Here you! What's your name? Bedford! I owe you five-and-twenty shillings, do I, old Bedford? Give us a glass of Schnaps, and I'll pay you! Look here, Batchelor. I hate that sugar-baker. Two years ago, I drew a bill on him, and he wouldn't pay it — perhaps he would have paid it, but my sister wouldn't let him. And, I say, shall we go and have a cigar in your room? My mother's been abusing you to me like fun this morning. She abuses everybody. She used to abuse Cissy. Cissy used to abuse her — used to fight like two cats — "

And if I narrate this conversation, dear Spartan youth! if I show thee this Helot maundering in his cups, it is that from his odious example thou mayst learn to be moderate in the use of thine own. Has the enemy who has entered thy mouth ever stolen away thy brains? Has wine ever caused thee to blab secrets; to utter egotisms and follies? Beware of it. Has it ever been thy friend at the end of the hard day's work, the cheery companion of thy companions, the promoter of harmony, kindness, harmless social pleasure? Be thankful for it. Three years since, when the comet was blazing in the autumnal sky, I stood on the château-steps of a great claret proprietor. "Boirai-je de ton vin, O comète?" I said, addressing the luminary with the flaming tail. "Shall those generous bunches which you ripen yield their juices for me *morituro?*" It was a solemn thought. Ah! my dear brethren! who knows the Order of the Fates?

When shall we pass the Gloomy Gates? Which of us goes, which of us waits to drink those famous Fifty-eights? A sermon, upon my word! And pray why not a little homily on an autumn eve over a purple cluster? — If that rickety boy had only drunk claret, I warrant you his tongue would not have blabbed, his hand would not have shaken, his wretched little brain and body would not have reeled with fever.

"'Gad," said he next day to me, "cut again last night. Have an idea that I abused Lovel. When I have a little wine on board, always speak my mind, don't you know? Last time I was here in my poor sister's time, said somethin' to her, don't quite know what it was, somethin' confoundedly true and unpleasant I dare say. I think it was about a fellow she used to go on with before she married the sugar-baker. And I got orders to quit, by Jove, sir — neck and crop, sir, and no mistake! And we gave it one another over the stairs. Oh, my! we did pitch in! — And that was the last time I ever saw Cecilia — give you my word. A doosid unforgiving woman my poor sister was, and between you and me, Batchelor, as great a flirt as ever threw a fellar over. You should have heard her and my Lady B. go on, that's all! — Well, Mamma, are you going out for a drive in the coachy-poachy? Not as I knows on, thank you, as I before had the honor to observe. Mr. Batchelor and me are going to play a little game at billiards." We did, and I won; and, from that day to this, have never been paid my little winnings.

On the day after the doughty captain's arrival, Miss Prior, in whose face I had remarked a great expression of gloom and care, neither made her appearance at breakfast nor at the children's dinner. "Miss Prior was a little unwell," Lady Baker said, with an air of most perfect satisfaction. "Mr. Drencher will come to see her this afternoon, and prescribe for her, I dare say," adds her ladyship, nodding and winking a roguish eye at me. I was at a loss to understand what was the point of humor which amused Lady B., until she herself explained it.

"My good sir," she said, "I think Miss Prior is not at all *averse* to being ill." And the nods recommenced.

"As how?" I ask.

"To being ill, or at least to calling in the medical man."

"Attachment between governess and Sawbones, I make bold for to presume?" says the Captain.

"Precisely, Clarence — a very fitting match. I saw the affair, even before Miss Prior owned it — that is to say, she has not denied it. She says she can't afford to marry, that she has children enough at home in her brothers and sisters. She is a well-principled young woman, and does credit, Mr. Batchelor, to your recommendation, and the education she has received from her uncle, the master of St. Boniface."

"Cissy to school; Pop to Eton; and Miss What-d'-you-call to grind the pestle in Sawbones's back-shop: I see!" says Captain Clarence. "He seems a low, vulgar blackguard, that Sawbones."

"Of course, my love, what can you expect from that sort of person?" asks mamma, whose own father was a small attorney in a small Irish town.

"I wish I had his confounded good health," cries Clarence, coughing.

"My poor darling!" says mamma.

I said nothing. And so Elizabeth was engaged to that great, broad-shouldered, red-whiskered young surgeon with the huge appetite and the dubious *h's!* Well, why not? What was it to me? Why

should n't she marry him ? Was he not an honest
man, and a fitting match for her ? Yes. Very good.
Only if I *do* love a bird or flower to glad me with its
dark blue eye, it is the first to fade away. If I *have*
a partiality for a young gazelle it is the first to —
psha ! What have I to do with this namby-pamby ?
Can the heart that has truly loved ever forget, and
does n't it as truly love on to the — stuff ! I am past
the age of such follies. I might have made a woman
happy; I think I should. But the fugacious years
have lapsed, my Posthumus ! My waist is now a
good bit wider than my chest, and it is decreed that I
shall be alone !

My tone, then, when next I saw Elizabeth, was sorrowful — not angry. Drencher, the young doctor,
came punctually enough, you may be sure, to look
after his patient. Little Pinhorn, the children's
maid, led the young practitioner smiling towards the
schoolroom regions. His creaking highlows sprang
swiftly up the stairs. I happened to be in the hall
and surveyed him with a grim pleasure. "Now he is
in the schoolroom," I thought. "Now he is taking
her hand — it is very white — and feeling her pulse.
And so on, and so on. Surely, surely Pinhorn remains in the room ? " I am sitting on a hall-table as
I muse plaintively on these things, and gaze up the
stairs by which the Hakeem (great carroty-whiskered
cad !) has passed into the sacred precincts of the
harem. As I gaze up the stair, another door opens
into the hall; a scowling face peeps through that
door, and looks up the stair, too. 'T is Bedford, who
has slid out of his pantry, and watches the doctor.
And thou, too, my poor Bedford ! Oh ! the whole
world throbs with vain heart-pangs, and tosses and
heaves with longing, unfulfilled desires ! All night,

and all over the world, bitter tears are dropping as
regular as the dew, and cruel memories are haunting
the pillow. Close my hot eyes, kind Sleep! Do not
visit it, dear delusive images out of the Past! Often
your figure shimmers through my dreams, Glorvina.
Not as you are now, the stout mother of many children — you always had an alarming likeness to your
own mother, Glorvina — but as you were — slim,
black-haired, blue-eyed — when your carnation lips
warbled the "Vale of Avoca" or the "Angel's Whisper." "What!" I say then, looking up the stair,
"am I absolutely growing jealous of yon apothecary?
— O fool!" And at this juncture, out peers Bedford's face from the pantry, and I see he is jealous
too. I tie my shoe as I sit on the table; I don't
affect to notice Bedford in the least (who, in fact,
pops his own head back again as soon as he sees
mine). I take my wide-awake from the peg, set it on
one side my head, and strut whistling out of the
hall-door. I stretch over Putney Heath, and my
spirit resumes its tranquillity.

I sometimes keep a little journal of my proceedings, and on referring to its pages, the scene rises
before me pretty clearly to which the brief notes
allude. On this day I find noted: "*Friday, July
14. — B. came down to-day. Seems to require a great
deal of attendance from Dr. — Row between dowagers
after dinner.*" "B.," I need not remark, is Bessy.
"Dr.," of course, you know. "Row between dowagers" means a battle royal between Mrs. Bonnington
and Lady Baker, such as not unfrequently raged
under the kindly Lovel's roof.

Lady Baker's gigantic menial Bulkeley condescended to wait at the family dinner at Shrublands,
when perforce he had to put himself under Mr. Bed-

ford's orders. Bedford would gladly have dispensed with the London footman, over whose calves, he said, he and his boy were always tumbling; but Lady Baker's dignity would not allow her to part from her own man; and her good-natured son-in-law allowed her, and indeed almost all other persons, to have their own way. I have reason to fear Mr. Bulkeley's morals were loose. Mrs. Bonnington had a special horror of him; his behavior in the village public-houses, where his powder and plush were forever visible — his freedom of conduct and conversation before the good lady's nurse and parlor-maids — provoked her anger and suspicion. More than once she whispered to me her loathing of this flour-besprinkled monster; and, as much as such a gentle creature could, she showed her dislike to him by her behavior. The flunky's solemn equanimity was not to be disturbed by any such feeble indications of displeasure. From his powdered height, he looked down upon Mrs. Bonnington, and her esteem or her dislike was beneath him.

Now on this Friday night the 14th, Captain Clarence had gone to pass the day in town, and our Bessy made her appearance again, the doctor's prescriptions having, I suppose, agreed with her. Mr. Bulkeley, who was handing coffee to the ladies, chose to offer none to Miss Prior, and I was amused when I saw Bedford's heel scrunch down on the flunky's right foot, as he pointed towards the governess. The oaths which Bulkeley had to devour in silence must have been frightful. To do the gallant fellow justice, I think he would have died rather than speak before company in a drawing-room. He limped up and offered the refreshment to the young lady, who bowed and declined it.

"Frederick," Mrs. Bonnington begins, when the coffee-ceremony is over, "now the servants are gone, I must scold you about the waste at your table, my dear. What was the need of opening that great bottle of champagne? Lady Baker only takes two glasses. Mr. Batchelor does n't touch it." (No, thank you, my dear Mrs. Bonnington: too old a stager.) "Why not have a little bottle instead of that great, large, immense one? Bedford is a tee-totaler. I suppose it is *that London footman who likes it.*"

"My dear mother, I have n't really ascertained his tastes," says Lovel.

"Then why not tell Bedford to open a pint, dear?" pursues mamma.

"Oh, Bedford — Bedford, we must not mention *him,* Mrs. Bonnington!" cries Lady Baker. "Bedford is faultless. Bedford has the keys of everything. Bedford is not to be controlled in anything. Bedford is to be at liberty to be rude to my servant."

"Bedford was admirably kind in his attendance on your daughter, Lady Baker," says Lovel, his brow darkening: "and as for your man, I should think he was big enough to protect himself from any rudeness of poor Dick!" The good fellow had been angry for one moment, at the next he was all for peace and conciliation.

Lady Baker puts on her superfine air. With that air she had often awe-stricken good, simple Mrs. Bonnington; and she loved to use it whenever city folks or humble people were present. You see she thought herself your superior and mine, as *de par le monde* there are many artless Lady Bakers who do. "My dear Frederick!" says Lady B. then, putting on her best Mayfair manner, "excuse me for saying, but you don't know the — the class of servant to which Bulkeley belongs. I had him as a great favor from Lord Toddleby's. That — that class of servant is not generally accustomed to go out single."

"Unless they are two behind a carriage-perch they pine away, I suppose," remarks Mr. Lovel, "as one love-bird does without his mate."

"No doubt — no doubt," says Lady B., who does not in the least understand him; "I only say you are not accustomed here — in this kind of establishment, you understand — to that class of — "

But here Mrs. Bonnington could contain her wrath no more. "Lady Baker!" cries that injured mother, "is my son's establishment not good enough for any powdered wretch in England? Is the house of a British merchant — "

"My dear creature — my dear creature!" interposes her ladyship, "it *is* the house of a British merchant, and a most comfortable house too."

"Yes, *as you find it*," remarks mamma.

"Yes, as I find it, when I come to take care of that *departed angel's children*, Mrs. Bonnington!" — (Lady B. here indicates the Cecilian effigy) — "of that dear seraph's orphans, Mrs. Bonnington! *You* cannot. You have other duties — other children — a husband, whom you have left at home in delicate health, and who — "

"Lady Baker!" exclaims Mrs. Bonnington, "no one shall say I don't take care of my dear husband!"

"My dear Lady Baker! — my dear — dear mother!" cries Lovel, *éploré*, and whimpers aside to me, "They spar in this way every night, when we're alone. It's too bad, ain't it, Batch?"

"I say you *do* take care of Mr. Bonnington," Baker blandly resumes (she has hit Mrs. Bonnington on the raw place, and smilingly proceeds to thong again) : " I say you *do* take care of your husband, my dear creature, and that is why you can't attend to Frederick! And as he is of a very easy temper, — except sometimes with his poor Cecilia's mother, — he allows all his tradesmen to cheat him; all his servants to cheat him; Bedford to be rude to everybody ; and if to me, why not to my servant Bulkeley, with whom Lord Toddleby's groom of the chambers gave me the very highest character ? "

Mrs. Bonnington in a great flurry broke in by saying she was surprised to hear that noblemen *had* grooms in their chambers : and she thought they were much better in the stables : and when they dined with Captain Huff, you know, Frederick, *his* man always brought such a dreadful smell of the stable in with him, that — here she paused. Baker's eye was on her ; and that dowager was grinning a cruel triumph.

" He ! — he ! You mistake, my good Mrs. Bonnington ! " says her ladyship. " Your poor mother mistakes, my dear Frederick. You have lived in a quiet and most respectable sphere, but not, you understand, not — "

" Not what, pray, Lady Baker ? We have lived in this neighborhood twenty years : in my late husband's time, when *we saw a great deal of company*, and this dear Frederick was a boy at Westminster School. And we have *paid* for everything we have had for twenty years ; and we have not owed a penny to any *tradesman*. And we may not have had *powdered footmen*, six feet high, impertinent beasts, who were rude to all the maids in the place. Don't — I *will* speak, Frederick ! But servants who loved us, and who were *paid their wages*, and who — o — ho — ho — ho ! "

Wipe your eyes, dear friends! out with all your pocket-handkerchiefs. I protest I cannot bear to see a woman in distress. Of course Fred Lovel runs to console his dear old mother, and vows Lady Baker meant no harm.

"Meant harm! My dear Frederick, what harm can I mean? I only said your poor mother did not seem to know what a groom of the chambers was! How should she?"

"Come — come," says Frederick, "enough of this! Miss Prior, will you be so kind as to give us a little music?"

Miss Prior was playing Beethoven at the piano, very solemnly and finely, when our Black Sheep returned to this quiet fold, and, I am sorry to say, in a very riotous condition. The brilliancy of his eye, the purple flush on his nose, the unsteady gait, and uncertain tone of voice, told tales of Captain Clarence, who stumbled over more than one chair before he found a seat near me.

"Quite right, old boy," says he, winking at me. "Cut again — dooshid good fellosh. Better than being along with you shtoopid-old-fogish." And he began to warble wild "Fol-de-rol-lolls" in an insane accompaniment to the music.

"By heavens, this is too bad!" growls Lovel. "Lady Baker, let your big man carry your son to bed. Thank you, Miss Prior!"

At a final yell, which the unlucky young scapegrace gave, Elizabeth stopped, and rose from the piano, looking very pale. She made her curtsy, and was departing, when the wretched young captain sprang up, looked at her, and sank back on the sofa with another wild laugh. Bessy fled away scared, and white as a sheet.

"TAKE THE BRUTE TO BED!" roars the master of

the house, in great wrath.   And scapegrace was conducted to his apartment, whither he went laughing
wildly, and calling out, "Come on, old sh-sh-shugar-
baker!"

The morning after this fine exhibition, Captain Clarence Baker's mamma announced to us that her poor
dear suffering boy was too ill to come to breakfast,
and I believe he prescribed for himself devilled drum-
stick and soda-water, of which he partook in his bed-
room.   Lovel, seldom angry, was violently wroth with
his brother-in-law; and, almost always polite, was at
breakfast scarcely civil to Lady Baker.   I am bound
to say that female abused her position.   She appealed
to Cecilia's picture a great deal too much during the
course of breakfast.   She hinted, she sighed, she wag-
gled her head at me, and spoke about "that angel" in
the most tragic manner.   Angel is all very well: but
your angel brought in *à tout propos ;* your departed
blessing called out of her grave ever so many times a
day ; when grandmamma wants to carry a point of her
own ; when the children are naughty, or noisy ; when
papa betrays a flickering inclination to dine at his club,
or to bring home a bachelor friend or two to Shrublands ; — I say your angel always dragged in by the
wings into the conversation loses her effect.   No man's
heart put on wider crape than Lovel's at Cecilia's loss.
Considering the circumstances, his grief was most creditable to him ; but at breakfast, at lunch, about Bulkeley the footman, about the barouche or the phaeton, or
any trumpery domestic perplexity, to have a *Deus in-
tersit* was too much.   And I observed, with some inward satisfaction, that when Baker uttered her pompous
funereal phrases, rolled her eyes up to the ceiling, and
appealed to that quarter, the children ate their jam
and quarrelled and kicked their little shins under the

table, Lovel read his paper and looked at his watch to
see if it was omnibus time; and Bessy made the tea,
quite undisturbed by the old lady's tragical prattle.

When Baker described her son's fearful cough and
dreadfully feverish state, I said, "Surely, Lady Baker,
Mr. Drencher had better be sent for;" and I suppose
I uttered the disgusting dissyllable Drencher with a
fine sarcastic accent; for once, just once, Bessy's gray
eyes rose through the spectacles and met mine with a
glance of unutterable sadness, then calmly settled down
on to the slop-basin again, or the urn, in which her
pale features, of course, were odiously distorted.

"You will not bring anybody home to dinner, Frederick, in my poor boy's state?" asks Lady B.

"He may stay in his bed-room I suppose," replied
Lovel.

"He is Cecilia's brother, Frederick!" cries the
lady.

"Conf —" Lovel was beginning. What was he
about to say?

"If you are going to confound your angel in heaven,
I have nothing to say, sir!" cries the mother of
Clarence.

"*Parbleu, Madame!*" cried Lovel in French; "if
he were not my wife's brother, do you think I would
let him stay here?"

"*Parly Français? Oui, oui, oui!*" cries Pop. "I
know what Pa means!"

"And so do *I* know. And I shall lend Uncle Clarence some books which Mr. Bonnington gave me,
and —"

"Hold your tongue all!" shouts Lovel, with a
stamp of his foot.

"You will, perhaps, have the great kindness to
allow me the use of your carriage — or, at least, to

wait here until my poor suffering boy can be moved,
Mr. Lovel?" says Lady B., with the airs of a martyr.

Lovel rang the bell. "The carriage for Lady Baker
—at her ladyship's hour, Bedford: and the cart for
her luggage. Her ladyship and Captain Baker are
going away."

"I have lost one child, Mr. Lovel, whom some
people seem to forget. I am not going to murder
another! I will not leave this house, sir, *unless you
drive me from it by force,* until the medical man has
seen my boy!" And here she and sorrow sat down
again. She was always giving warning. She was
always fitting the halter and traversing the cart, was
Lady B., but she forever declined to drop the handkerchief and have the business over. I saw by a
little shrug in Bessy's shoulders, what the governess's
views were of the matter; and, in a word, Lady B. no
more went away on this day, than she had done on
forty previous days when she announced her intention
of going. She would accept benefits, you see, but then
she insulted her benefactors, and so squared accounts.

That great healthy, florid, scarlet-whiskered medical
wretch came at about twelve, saw Mr. Baker and
prescribed for him: and *of course* he must have a few
words with Miss Prior, and inquire into the state of
her health. Just as on the previous occasion, I happened to be in the hall when Drencher went up stairs;
Bedford happened to be looking out of his pantry-
door: I burst into a yell of laughter when I saw
Dick's livid face—the sight somehow suited my
savage soul.

No sooner was Medicus gone than Bessy, grave and
pale, in bonnet and spectacles, came sliding down
stairs. I do not mean down the banister, which was
Pop's favorite method of descent; but slim, tall,

noiseless, in a nunlike calm, she swept down the steps.
Of course, I followed her. And there was Master
Bedford's nose peeping through the pantry-door at us,
as we went out with the children. Pray, what business of *his* was it to be always watching anybody who
walked with Miss Prior ?

"So, Bessy," I said, "what report does Mr. — hem !
— Mr. Drencher — give of the interesting invalid ? "

"Oh, the most horrid ! He says that Captain
Baker has several times had a dreadful disease brought
on by drinking, and that he is mad when he has it.
He has delusions, sees demons, when he is in this
state — wants to be watched."

"Drencher tells you everything ? "

She says meekly : "He attends us when we are ill."

I remark, with fine irony : "He attends the whole
family : he is always coming to Shrublands ! "

"He comes very often," Miss Prior says gravely.

"And do you mean to say, Bessy," I cry, madly
cutting off two or three heads of yellow broom with
my stick — "do you mean to say a fellow like that,
who drops his *h's* about the room, is a welcome
visitor ? "

"I should be very ungrateful if he were not welcome, Mr. Batchelor," says Miss Prior. "And call
me by my surname, please — and he has taken care
of all my family — and — "

"And, of course, of course, of course, Miss Prior ! "
say I, brutally ; "and this is the way the world wags ;
and this is the way we are ill, and are cured ; and we
are grateful to the doctor that cures us ! "

She nods her grave head. "You used to be kinder
to me once, Mr. Batchelor, in old days — in your — in
my time of trouble ! Yes, my dear, that is a beautiful
bit of broom ! Oh, what a fine butterfly ! " (Cecilia

scours the plain after the butterfly.)   " You used to
be kinder to me once — when we were both unhappy."

"I was unhappy," I say, "but I survived. I was
ill, but I am now pretty well, thank you. I was jilted
by a false, heartless woman. Do you suppose there
are no other heartless women in the world ? " And I
am confident, if Bessy's breast had not been steel, the
daggers which darted out from my eyes would have
bored frightful stabs in it.

But she shook her head, and looked at me so sadly
that my eye-daggers tumbled down to the ground at
once ; for you see, though I am a jealous Turk, I am
a very easily appeased jealous Turk ; and if I had
been Bluebeard, and my wife, just as I was going to
decapitate her, had lifted up her head from the block
and cried a little, I should have dropped my scimitar,
and said, " Come, come, Fatima, never mind for the
present about that key and closet business, and I 'll
chop your head off some other morning." I say
Bessy disarmed me. Pooh ! I say, women will make
a fool of me to the end. Ah ! ye gracious Fates !
Cut my thread of life ere it grow too long. Suppose
I were to live till seventy, and some little wretch of
a woman were to set her cap at me ? She would
catch me — I know she would. All the males of our
family have been spooney and soft, to a degree perfectly ludicrous and despicable to contemplate —
Well, Bessy Prior, putting a hand out, looked at me,
and said —

" You are the oldest and best friend I have ever
had, Mr. Batchelor — the only friend."

" Am I, Elizabeth ? " I gasp, with a beating heart.

" Cissy is running back with a butterfly." (Our
hands unlock.) " Don't you see the difficulties of my
position ? Don't you know that ladies are often jeal-

ous of governesses; and that unless — unless they imagined I was — I was favorable to Mr. Drencher, who is very good and kind — the ladies of Shrublands might not like my remaining alone in the house with — with — you understand?" A moment the eyes look over the spectacles: at the next, the meek bonnet bows down towards the ground.

I wonder did she hear the bump — bumping of my heart! O heart! — O wounded heart! did I ever think thou wouldst bump — bump again? "Egl — Egl — izabeth," I say, choking with emotion, "do, do, do you — te — tell me — you don't — don't — don't — lo — love that apothecary?"

She shrugs her shoulder — her charming shoulder.

"And if," I hotly continue, "if a gentleman — if a man of mature age certainly, but who has a kind heart and four hundred a year of his own — were to say to you, 'Elizabeth! will you bid the flowers of a blighted life to bloom again? — Elizabeth! will you soothe a wounded heart?' — "

"Oh, Mr. Batchelor!" she sighed, and then added quickly, "Please, don't take my hand. Here's Pop."

And that dear child (bless him!) came up at the moment, saying, "Oh, Miss Prior, look here! I've got such a jolly big toadstool!" And next came Cissy, with a confounded butterfly. O Richard the Third! Haven't you been maligned because you smothered two little nuisances in a Tower? What is to prove to me that you did not serve the little brutes right, and that you weren't a most humane man? Darling Cissy coming up, then, in her dear, charming way, says, "You sha'n't take Mr. Batchelor's hand, you shall take *my* hand!" And she tosses up her little head, and walks with the instructress of her youth.

Bessy's Reflections.

"Ces enfans ne comprennent guère le Français," says Miss Prior, speaking very rapidly.

"Après lonche?" I whisper. The fact is, I was so agitated I hardly knew what the French for lunch was. And then our conversation dropped: and the beating of my own heart was all the sound I heard.

Lunch came. I couldn't eat a bit: I should have choked. Bessy ate plenty, and drank a glass of beer. It was her dinner, to be sure. Young *Blacksheep* did not appear. We did not miss him. When Lady Baker began to tell her story of George IV. at Slane Castle, I went into my own room. I took a book. Books? Psha! I went into the garden. I took out a cigar. But no, I would not smoke it. Perhaps she — many people don't like smoking.

I went into the garden. "Come into the garden, Maud." I sat by a large lilac-bush. I waited. Perhaps she would come? The morning-room windows were wide open on the lawn. Will she never come? Ah! what is that tall form advancing? gliding — gliding into the chamber like a beauteous ghost? "Who most does like an angel show, you may be sure 't is she." She comes up to the glass. She lays her spectacles down on the mantel-piece. She puts a slim white hand over her auburn hair and looks into the mirror. Elizabeth, Elizabeth! I come!

As I came up, I saw a horrid little grinning, debauched face surge over the back of a great arm-chair and look towards Elizabeth. It was Captain Blacksheep, of course. He laid his elbows over the chair. He looked keenly and with a diabolical smile at the unconscious girl; and just as I reached the window, he cried out, "*Bessy Bellenden, by Jove!*"

Elizabeth turned round, gave a little cry, and — but what happened I shall tell in the ensuing chapter."

CHAPTER V.

IF, when I heard Baker call out Bessy Bellenden, and adjure Jove, he had run forward and seized Elizabeth by the waist, or offered her other personal indignity, I too should have run forward on my side and engaged him. Though I am a stout elderly man, short in stature and in wind, I know I am a match for *that* rickety little captain on his high-heeled boots. A match for him? I believe Miss Bessy would have been a match for both of us. Her white arm was as hard and polished as ivory. Had she held it straight pointed against the rush of the dragoon, he would have fallen backwards before his intended prey: I have no doubt he would. It was the hen, in this case, was stronger than the libertine fox, and *au besoin* would have pecked the little marauding vermin's eyes out. Had, I say, Partlet been weak, and Reynard strong, I *would* have come forward: I certainly would. Had he been a wolf now, instead of a fox, I am certain I should have run in upon him, grappled with him, torn his heart and tongue out of his black throat, and trampled the lawless brute to death.

Well, I did n't do any such thing. I was just *going* to run in, — and I did n't. I was just going to rush to Bessy's side to clasp her (I have no doubt) to my heart: to beard the whiskered champion who was before her, and perhaps say, "Cheer thee — cheer thee, my persecuted maiden, my beauteous love — my

Rebecca! Come on, Sir Brian de Bois Guilbert, thou
dastard Templar! It is I, Sir Wilfrid of Ivanhoe."
(By the way, though the fellow was not a *Templar*, he
was a *Lincoln's-Inn man*, having passed twice through
the Insolvent Court there with infinite discredit.) But
I made no heroic speeches. There was no need for
Rebecca to jump out of window and risk her lovely
neck. How could she, in fact, the French window being flush with the ground-floor? And I give you my
honor, just as I was crying my war-cry, couching my
lance, and rushing *à la recousse* upon Sir Baker, a
sudden thought made me drop my (figurative) point:
a sudden idea made me rein in my galloping (meta-
phorical) steed and spare Baker for that time.

Suppose I had gone in? But for that sudden precaution, there might have been a Mrs. Batchelor. I
might have been a bullied father of ten children.
(Elizabeth has a fine high temper of her own.) What
is four hundred and twenty a year, with a wife and
perhaps half a dozen children? Should I have been
a whit the happier? Would Elizabeth? Ah! no.
And yet I feel a certain sort of shame, even now,
when I think that I did n't go in. Not that I was in
a fright, as some people choose to hint. I swear I
was not. But the reason why I did not charge was
this —

Nay, I *did* charge part of the way, and then, I own,
stopped. It was an error in judgment. It was n't a
want of courage. Lord George Sackville was a brave
man, and as cool as a cucumber under fire. Well, *he*
did n't charge at the battle of Minden, and Prince
Ferdinand made the deuce and all of a disturbance,
as we know. Byng was a brave man, — and I ask,
was n't it a confounded shame executing him? So
with respect to myself. Here is my statement. I

make it openly. I don't care. I am accused of seeing
a woman insulted, and not going to her rescue. I am
not guilty, I say. That is, there were reasons which
caused me not to attack. Even putting aside the superior strength of Elizabeth herself to the enemy, —
I vow there were cogent and honorable reasons why
I did not charge home.

You see I happened to be behind a blue lilac-bush
(and was turning a rhyme — heaven help us! — in
which *death* was only to part me and Elizabeth) when
I saw Baker's face surge over the chair-back. I rush
forward as he cries " by Jove." Had Miss Prior cried
out on her part, the strength of twenty Heenans, I
know, would have nerved this arm; but all she did
was to turn pale, and say, " Oh, mercy! Captain
Baker! Do pity me!"

" What! you remember me, Bessy Bellenden, do
you?" asks the Captain, advancing.

" Oh, not that name! please, not that name!" cries
Bessy.

" I thought I knew you yesterday," says Baker.
" Only, gad, you see, I had so much claret on board, I
did not much know what was what. And oh! Bessy,
I have got such a splitter of a headache."

" Oh! please — please, my name is Miss Prior.
Pray! pray, sir, don't — "

" You've got handsomer — doosid deal handsomer.
Know you now well, your spectacles off. You come
in here, — teach my nephew and niece, humbug my
sister, make love to the sh— Oh! you uncommon sly
little toad!"

" Captain Baker! I beg — I implore you," says
Bessy, or something of the sort: for the white hands
assumed an attitude of supplication.

" Pooh! don't gammon *me!*" says the rickety Cap-

tain (or words to that effect), and seizes those two
firm white hands in his moist, trembling palms.

Now do you understand why I paused ? When the
dandy came grinning forward, with looks and gestures
of familiar recognition : when the pale Elizabeth implored him to spare her : — a keen arrow of jealousy
shot whizzing through my heart, and caused me wellnigh to fall backwards as I ran forwards. I bumped
up against a bronze group in the garden. The group
represented a lion stung by a serpent. *I* was a lion
stung by a serpent too. Even Baker could have
knocked me down. Fiends and anguish ! he had
known her before. The Academy, the life she had
led, the wretched old tipsy ineffective guardian of a
father — all these antecedents in poor Bessy's history
passed through my mind. And I had offered my heart
and troth to this woman!' Now, my dear sir, I appeal
to you. What would *you* have done ? Would *you*
have liked to have such a sudden suspicion thrown
over the being of your affection ? "Oh ! spare me —
spare me !" I heard her say, in clear — too clear —
pathetic tones. And then there came rather a shrill
"Ah !" and then the lion was up in my breast again ;
and I give you my honor, just as I was going to step
forward — to step ? — to *rush* forward from behind
the urn where I had stood for a moment with thumping heart, Bessy's "Ah !" or little cry was followed by
a *whack*, which I heard as clear as anything I ever
heard in my life ; — and I saw the little Captain spin
back, topple over a chair heels up, and in this posture heard him begin to scream and curse in shrill
tones.

Not for long, for as the Captain and the chair
tumble down, a door springs open ; — a man rushes
in, who pounces like a panther upon the prostrate

Captain, pitches into his nose and eyes, and chokes his bad language by sending a fist down his naughty throat.

"Oh! thank you, Bedford!—please leave him, Bedford! that's enough. There, don't hurt him any more!" says Bessy, laughing — laughing, upon my word.

"Ah! will you?" says Bedford. "Lie still, you little beggar, or I'll knock your head off. Look here, Miss Prior! — Elizabeth — dear — dear Elizabeth! I love you with all my heart, and soul, and strength — I do."

"O Bedford! Bedford!" warbles Elizabeth.

"I do! I can't help it. I must say it! Ever since Rome, I do. Lie still, you drunken little beast! It's no use. But I adore you, O Elizabeth! Elizabeth!" And there was Dick, who was always following Miss P. about, and poking his head into keyholes to spy her, actually making love to her over the prostrate body of the Captain.

Now, what was I to do? Wasn't I in a most confoundedly awkward situation? A lady had been attacked — a lady? — the lady, and I hadn't rescued her. Her insolent enemy was overthrown, and I hadn't done it. A champion, three inches shorter than myself, had come in and dealt the blow. I was in such a rage of mortification, that I should have liked to thrash the Captain and Bedford too. The first I know I could have matched: the second was a tough little hero. And it was he who rescued the damsel, whilst I stood by! In a strait so odious, sudden, and humiliating, what should I, what could I, what did I do?

Behind the lion and snake there is a brick wall and marble balustrade, built for no particular reason, but

BEDFORD TO THE RESCUE.

flanking three steps and a grassy terrace, which then rises up on a level to the house-windows. Beyond the balustrade is a shrubbery of more lilacs and so forth, by which you can walk round into another path, which also leads up to the house. So as I had not charged — ah! woe is me! — as the battle was over, I — I just went round that shrubbery into the other path, and so entered the house, arriving like Fortinbras in "Hamlet," when everybody is dead and sprawling, you know, and the whole business is done.

And was there to be no end to my shame, or to Bedford's laurels? In that brief interval, whilst I was walking round the bypath (just to give myself a pretext for entering coolly into the premises), this fortunate fellow had absolutely engaged another and larger champion. This was no other than Bulkeley, my Lady B.'s first-class attendant. When the Captain fell, amidst his screams and curses, he called for Bulkeley: and that individual made his appearance, with a little Scotch cap perched on his powdered head.

"Hullo! what's the row year?" says Goliath, entering.

"Kill that blackguard! Hang him, kill him!" screams Captain Blacksheep, rising with bleeding nose.

"I say, what's the row year?" asks the grenadier.

"Off with your cap, sir, before a lady!" calls out Bedford.

"Hoff with my cap! you be blo — "

But he said no more, for little Bedford jumped some two feet from the ground, and knocked the cap off, so that a cloud of ambrosial powder filled the room with violet odors. The immense frame of the giant shook at this insult: "I will be the death on you, you little beggar!" he grunted out; and was advancing to destroy Dick, just as I entered in the cloud which his head had raised.

"I'll knock the brains as well as the powder out of your ugly head!" says Bedford, springing at the poker. At which juncture I entered.

"What — what is this disturbance?" I say, advancing with an air of mingled surprise and resolution.

"You git out of the way till I knock his 'ead off!" roars Bulkeley.

"Take up your cap, sir, and leave the room," I say, still with the same elegant firmness.

"Put down that there poker, you coward!" bellows the monster on board wages.

"Miss Prior!" I say (like a dignified hypocrite, as I own I was), "I hope no one has offered you a rudeness?" And I glare round, first at the knight of the bleeding nose, and then at his squire.

Miss Prior's face, as she replied to me, wore a look of awful scorn.

"Thank you, sir," she said, turning her head over her shoulder, and looking at me with her gray eyes. "Thank you, Richard Bedford! God bless you! I shall ever be thankful to you, wherever I am." And the stately figure swept out of the room.

She had seen me behind that confounded statue, then, and I had not come to her! O torments and racks! O scorpions, fiends, and pitchforks! The face of Bedford, too (flashing with knightly gratitude anon as she spoke kind words to him and passed on), wore a look of scorn as he turned towards me, and then stood, his nostrils distended, and breathing somewhat hard, glaring at his enemies, and still grasping his mace of battle.

When Elizabeth was gone, there was a pause of a moment, and then Blacksheep, taking his bleeding cambric from his nose, shrieks out, "Kill him, I say! A fellow that dares to hit one in my condition, and when I'm down! Bulkeley, you great hulking jackass! kill him, I say!"

"Jest let him put that there poker down, that's hall," growls Bulkeley.

"You're afraid, you great cowardly beast! You shall go; Mr. What-d'-ye-call-'im — Mr. Bedford — you shall have the sack, sir, as sure as your name is what it is! I'll tell my brother-in-law everything; and as for that woman —"

"If you say a word against her, I'll cane you wherever I see you, Captain Baker!" I cry out.

"Who spoke to *you?*" says the Captain, falling back and scowling at me.

"Who hever told you to put *your* foot in?" says the squire.

I was in such a rage, and so eager to find an object on which I might wreak my fury, that I confess I plunged at this Bulkeley. I gave him two most violent blows on the waistcoat, which caused him to double up with such frightful contortions, that Bedford burst out laughing; and even the Captain with the damaged eye and nose began to laugh too. Then, taking a lesson from Dick, as there was a fine shining dagger on the table, used for the cutting open of reviews and magazines, I seized and brandished this weapon, and I dare say would have sheathed it in the giant's bloated corpus, had he made any movement towards me. But he only called out, "hI'll be the death on you, you cowards! hI'll be the death of both on you!" and snatching up his cap from the carpet, walked out of the room.

"Glad you did that, though," says Baker, nodding his head. "Think I'd best pack up."

And now the Devil of Rage which had been swelling within me gave place to a worse devil — the Devil of Jealousy — and I turned on the Captain, who was also just about to slink away : —

"Stop!" I cried out — I screamed out, I may say.

"Who spoke to you, I should like to know? and who the dooce dares to speak to me in that sort of way?" says Clarence Baker, with a plentiful garnish of expletives, which need not be here inserted. But he stopped, nevertheless, and turned slouching round.

"You spoke just now of Miss Prior?" I said. "Have you anything against her?"

"What's that to you?" he asked.

"I am her oldest friend. I introduced her into this family. *Dare* you say a word against her?"

"Well, who the dooce has!"

"You knew her before?"

"Yes, I did, then."

"When she went by the name of Bellenden?"

"Of course I did. And what's that to you?" he screams out.

"I this day asked her to be my wife, sir! *That's* what it is to me!" I replied with severe dignity.

Mr. Clarence began to whistle. "Oh! if that's it — of course not!" he says.

The jealous demon writhed within me and rent me.

"You mean that there *is* something, then?" I asked, glaring at the young reprobate.

"No, I don't," says he, looking very much frightened. "No, there is nothin'. Upon my sacred honor, there is n't, that I know." (I was looking uncommonly fierce at this time, and, I must own, would rather have quarrelled with somebody than not.)

"No, there is nothin' that I know. Ever so many years ago, you see, I used to go with Tom Papillion, Turkington, and two or three fellows, to that theatre. Dolphin had it. And we used to go behind the scenes — and — and I own I had a row with her. And I was in the wrong. There now, I own I was. And she left the theatre. And she behaved quite right. And I was very sorry. And I believe she is as good a woman as ever stepped now. And the father was a disreputable old man, but most honorable — I know he was. And there was a fellow in the Bombay service — a fellow by the name of Walker or Walkingham — yes, Walkingham; and I used to meet him at the 'Cave of Harmony,' you know; and he told me that she was as right as right could be. And he was doosidly cut up about leaving her. And he would have married her, I dessay, only for his father the General, who would n't stand it. And he was ready to hang himself when he went away. He used to drink awfully, and then he used to swear about her; and we used to chaff him, you know. Low, vulgarish sort of man he was; and a very passionate fellow. And if you 're goin' to marry her, you know — of course, I ask your pardon, and that; and upon the honor of a gentleman I know nothin' against her. And I wish you joy and all that sort of thing. I do now, really now!" And so saying, the mean, mischievous little monkey sneaked away, and clambered up to his own perch in his own bed-room.

Worthy Mrs. Bonnington, with a couple of her young ones, made her appearance at this juncture. She had a key, which gave her a free pass through the garden door, and brought her children for an afternoon's play and fighting with their little nephew and niece. Decidedly, Bessy did not bring up her

young folks well. Was it that their grandmothers
spoiled them, and undid the governess's work? Were
those young people odious (as they often were) by
nature, or rendered so by the neglect of their guardians? If Bessy had loved her charges more, would
they not have been better? Had she a kind, loving,
maternal heart? Ha! This thought — this jealous
doubt — smote my bosom: and were she mine, and
the mother of many possible little Batchelors, would
she be kind to *them?* Would they be wilful, and
selfish, and abominable little wretches, in a word,
like these children? Nay — nay! Say that Elizabeth has but a cold heart; we cannot be all perfection. But, *per contra,* you must admit that, cold as
she is, she does her duty. How good she has been to
her own brothers and sisters: how cheerfully she has
given away her savings to them: how admirably she
has behaved to her mother, hiding the iniquities of
that disreputable old schemer, and covering her im-
proprieties with decent filial screens and pretexts.
Her mother? *Ah! grands dieux!* You want to
marry, Charles Batchelor, and you will have that
greedy pauper for a mother-in-law; that fluffy Bluecoat boy, those hobnailed taw-players, top-spinners,
toffee-eaters, those underbred girls, for your brothers
and sisters-in-law! They will be quartered upon you.
You are so absurdly weak and good-natured — you
know you are — that you will never be able to resist.
Those boys will grow up: they will go out as clerks
or shop-boys: get into debt, and expect you to pay
their bills: want to be articled to attorneys and so
forth, and call upon you for the premium. Their
mother will never be out of your house. She will
ferret about in your drawers and wardrobes, filch
your haberdashery, and cast greedy eyes on the very

shirts and coats on your back, and calculate when she
can get them for her boys. Those vulgar young mis-
creants will never fail to come and dine with you on
a Sunday. They will bring their young linendraper
or articled friends. They will draw bills on you, or
give their own to money-lenders, and unless you take
up those bills they will consider you a callous, avari-
cious brute, and the heartless author of their ruin.
The girls will come and practise on your wife's piano.
They won't come to you on Sundays only; they will
always be staying in the house. They will always be
preventing a *tête-à-tête* between your wife and you.
As they grow old, they will want her to take them
out to tea-parties, and to give such entertainments,
where they will introduce their odious young men.
They will expect you to commit meannesses, in order
to get theatre tickets for them from the newspaper
editors of your acquaintance. You will have to sit
in the back seat: to pay the cab to and from the
play: to see glances and bows of recognition passing
between them and dubious bucks in the lobbies: and
to lend the girls your wife's gloves, scarfs, ornaments,
smelling-bottles, and handkerchiefs, which of course
they will never return. If Elizabeth is ailing from
any circumstance, they will get a footing in your
house, and she will be jealous of them. The ladies
of your own family will quarrel with them of course;
and very likely your mother-in-law will tell them a
piece of her mind. And you bring this dreary cer-
tainty upon you, because, forsooth, you fall in love
with a fine figure, a pair of gray eyes, and a head of
auburn (not to say red) hair! O Charles Batchelor!
in what a galley hast thou seated thyself, and what
a family is crowded in thy boat!

All these thoughts are passing in my mind, as good

Mrs. Bonnington is prattling to me — I protest I don't
know about what. I think I caught some faint sentences about the Patagonian mission, the National
schools, and Mr. Bonnington's lumbago; but I can't
say for certain. I was busy with my own thoughts.
I had asked the awful question — I was not answered.
Bessy had even gone away in a huff about my want
of gallantry, but I was easy on that score. As for
Mr. Drencher, she had told me her sentiments regarding him; "and though I am considerably older,
yet," thought I, "I need not be afraid of *that* rival.
But when she says *yes?* Oh, dear! oh, dear! *Yes*
means Elizabeth — certainly, a brave young woman
— but it means Mrs. Prior, and Gus, and Amelia Jane,
and the whole of that dismal family." No wonder,
with these dark thoughts crowding my mind, Mrs.
Bonnington found me absent; and, as a comment
upon some absurd reply of mine, said, "La! Mr.
Batchelor, you must be crossed in love?" Crossed
in love! It might be as well for some folks if they
were crossed in love. At my age, and having loved
madly, as I did, that party in Dublin, a man does n't
take the second fit by any means so strongly. Well!
well! the die was cast, and I was there to bide the
hazard. What can be the matter? I look pale and
unwell, and had better see Mr. D.? Thank you, my
dear Mrs. Bonnington. I had a violent — a violent
toothache last night — yes, toothache; and was kept
awake, thank you. And there's nothing like having
it out? and Mr. D. draws them beautifully, and has
taken out six of your children's? It's better now; I
dare say it will be better still, soon. I retire to my
chamber : I take a book — can't read one word of it.
I resume my tragedy. Tragedy? Bosh!

I suppose Mr. Drencher thought his yesterday's

patient would be better for a little more advice and
medicine, for he must pay a second visit to Shrublands on this day, just after the row with the Captain had taken place, and walked up to the upper
regions, as his custom was. Very likely he found
Mr. Clarence bathing his nose there, and prescribed
for the injured organ. Certainly he knocked at the
door of Miss Prior's schoolroom (the fellow was
always finding a pretext for entering *that* apartment),
and Master Bedford comes to me, with a woe-begone,
livid countenance, and a "Ha! ha! young Sawbones
is up with her!"

"So, my poor Dick," I say, "I heard your confession as I was myself running in to rescue Miss P.
from that villain."

"My blood was hup," groans Dick, — "up, I beg
your pardon. When I saw that young rascal lay a
hand on her I could not help flying at him. I would
have hit him if he had been my own father. And I
could not help saying what was on my mind. It
would come out; I knew it would some day. I might
as well wish for the moon as hope to get her. She
thinks herself superior to me, and perhaps she is
mistaken. But it's no use; she don't care for me;
she don't care for anybody. Now the words are out,
in course I must n't stay here."

"You may get another place easily enough with
your character, Bedford!"

But he shook his head. "I'm not disposed to black
nobody else's boots no more. I have another place.
I have saved a bit of money. My poor old mother is
gone, whom you used to be so kind to, Mr. B. I'm
alone now. Confound that Sawbones, will he *never*
come away? I'll tell you about my plans some day,
sir, and I know you'll be so good as to help me."

And away goes Dick, looking the picture of woe and despair.

Presently, from the upper rooms, Sawbones descends. I happened to be standing in the hall, you see, talking to Dick. Mr. Drencher scowls at me fiercely, and I suppose I return him haughty glance for glance. He hated me: I him: I liked him to hate me.

"How is your patient, Mr. — a — Drencher?" I ask.

"Trifling contusion of the nose — brown paper and vinegar," says the doctor.

"Great powers! did the villain strike her on the nose?" I cry in terror.

"*Her* — whom?" says he.

"Oh — ah — yes — indeed; it's nothing," I say, smiling. The fact is I had forgotten about Baker in my natural anxiety for Elizabeth.

"I don't know what you mean by laughing, sir?" says the red-haired practitioner. "But if you mean chaff, Mr. Batchelor, let me tell you I don't want chaff, and I won't have chaff!" and herewith, exit Sawbones, looking black doses at me.

Jealous of me, think I, as I sink down in a chair in the morning-room, where the combat had just taken place. And so thou, too, art fever-caught my poor physician! What a fascination this girl has! Here's the butler: here's the medical man: here am I: here is the Captain has been smitten — smitten on the nose. Has the gardener been smitten too, and is the page gnawing his buttons off for jealousy, and is Mons. Bulkeley equally in love with her? I take up a review, and think over this, as I glance through its pages.

As I am lounging and reading, Mons. Bulkeley himself makes his appearance, bearing in cloaks and

packages belonging to his lady. "Have the goodness to take that cap off," I say, coolly.

" *You* 'ave the goodness to remember that if hever
I see you hout o' this 'ouse I 'll punch your hugly
'ead off," says the monstrous menial. But I poise
my paper-cutter, and he retires growling.

From despondency I pass to hope; and the prospect
of marriage, which before appeared so dark to me,
assumes a gayer hue. I have four hundred a year,
and that house in Devonshire Street, Bloomsbury
Square, of which the upper part will be quite big
enough for us. If we have children, there is Queen
Square for them to walk and play in. Several genteel families I know, who still live in the neighborhood, will come and see my wife, and we shall have a
comfortable, cosy little society, suited to our small
means. The tradesmen in Lamb's Conduit Street are
excellent, and the music at the Foundling always
charming. I shall give up one of my clubs. The
other is within an easy walk.

No: my wife's relations will *not* plague me. Bessy
is a most sensible, determined woman, and as cool a
hand as I know. She will only see Mrs. Prior at
proper (and, I trust, distant) intervals. Her brothers
and sisters will learn to know their places, and not
obtrude upon me or the company which I keep. My
friends, who are educated people and gentlemen, will
not object to visit me because I live over a shop (my
ground-floor and spacious back premises in Devonshire Street are let to a German toy-warehouse). I
shall add a hundred or two at least to my income by
my literary labor; and Bessy, who has practised
frugality all her life, and been a good daughter and a
good sister, I know will prove a good wife, and, please
heaven! a good mother. Why, four hundred a year,

plus two hundred, is a nice little income. And my old college friend, Wigmore, who is just on the Bench? He will, he must get me a place — say three hundred a year. With nine hundred a year we can do quite well.

Love is full of elations and despondencies. The future, over which such a black cloud of doubt lowered a few minutes since, blushed a sweet rose-color now. I saw myself happy, beloved, with a competence, and imagined myself reposing in the delightful garden of Red Lion Square on some summer evening, and half a dozen little Batchelors frisking over the flower-bespangled grass there.

After our little colloquy, Mrs. Bonnington, not finding much pleasure in my sulky society, had gone to Miss Prior's room with her young folks, and as the door of the morning-room opened now and again, I could hear the dear young ones scuttling about the passages, where they were playing at horses, and fighting, and so forth. After a while good Mrs. B. came down from the schoolroom. "Whatever has happened, Mr. Batchelor?" she said to me, in her passage through the morning-room. "Miss Prior is very pale and absent. *You* are very pale and absent. Have you been courting her, you naughty man, and trying to supplant Mr. Drencher? There now, you turn as red as my ribbon! Ah! Bessy is a good girl, and *so* fond of my dear children. 'Ah, dear Mrs. Bonnington,' she says to me — but of course you won't tell Lady B.: it would make Lady B. perfectly furious. 'Ah!' says Miss P. to me, 'I wish, ma'am, that my little charges were like their dear little uncles and aunts — so exquisitely brought up!' Pop again wished to beat his uncle. I wish — I wish Frederick would send that child to school! Miss P. owns that he is too much for her. Come, children, it is time to go to dinner." And, with more of this prattle, the good lady summons her young ones, who descend from the schoolroom with their nephew and niece.

Following nephew and niece, comes demure Miss Prior, to whom I fling a knowing glance, which says, plain as eyes can speak — Do, Elizabeth, come and talk for a little to your faithful Batchelor! She gives a sidelong look of intelligence, leaves a parasol and a pair of gloves on a table, accompanies Mrs. Bonnington and the young ones into the garden, sees the clergyman's wife and children disappear through the garden gate, and her own youthful charges engaged in the strawberry-beds; and, of course, returns to the morning-room for her parasol and gloves, which she had forgotten. There is a calmness about that woman — an easy, dauntless dexterity, which frightens me — *ma parole d'honneur.* In that white breast is there a white marble stone in place of the ordinary cordial apparatus? Under the white velvet glove of that cool hand are there bones of cold steel?

"So, Drencher has again been here, Elizabeth?" I say.

She shrugs her shoulders. "To see that wretched Captain Baker. The horrid little man will die! He was not actually sober just now when he — when I — when you saw him. How I wish you had come sooner — to prevent that horrible, tipsy, disreputable quarrel. It makes me very, very thoughtful, Mr. Batchelor. He will speak to his mother — to Mr. Lovel. I shall have to go away. I know I must."

"And don't you know where you can find a home, Elizabeth? Have the words I spoke this morning been so soon forgotten?"

"Oh! Mr. Batchelor! you spoke in a heat. You

could not think seriously of a poor girl like me, so
friendless and poor, with so many family ties. Pop
is looking this way, please. To a man bred like you,
what can I be?"

"You may make the rest of my life happy, Elizabeth!" I cry. "We are friends of such old—old
date, that you know what my disposition is."

"Oh! indeed," says she, "it is certain that there
never was a sweeter disposition or a more gentle
creature." (Somehow I thought she said the words
"gentle creature" with rather a sarcastic tone of
voice.) "But consider your habits, dear sir. I remember how in Beak Street you used to be always
giving, and, in spite of your income, always poor.
You love ease and elegance; and having, I dare say,
not too much for yourself now, would you encumber
yourself with — with me and the expenses of a household? I shall always regard you, esteem you, love
you as the best friend I ever had, and — *voici venir la
mère du vaurien.*"

Enter Lady Baker. "Do I interrupt a *tête-à-tête*,
pray?" she asks.

"My benefactor has known me since I was a child,
and befriended me since then," says Elizabeth, with
simple kindness beaming in her look. "We were just
speaking—I was just—ah!—telling him that my
uncle has invited me most kindly to St. Boniface,
whenever I can be spared; and if you and the family
go to the Isle of Wight this autumn, perhaps you will
intercede with Mr. Lovel, and let me have a little
holiday. Mary will take every charge of the children,
and I do so long to see my dear aunt and cousins!
And I was begging Mr. Batchelor to use his interest
with you, and to entreat you to use *your* interest to
get me leave. That was what our talk was about."

The deuce it was! I could n't say No, of course; but I protest I had no idea until that moment that our conversation had been about aunt and uncle at St. Boniface. Again came the horrible suspicion, the dreadful doubt — the chill as of a cold serpent crawling down my back — which had made me pause, and gasp, and turn pale, anon when Bessy and Captain Clarence were holding colloquy together. What *has* happened in this woman's life? *Do* I know all about her, or anything; or only just as much as she chooses? O Batch — Batch! I suspect you are no better than an old gaby!

"And Mr. Drencher has just been here and seen your son," Bessy continues, softly; "and he begs and entreats your ladyship to order Captain Baker to be more prudent. Mr. D. says Captain Baker is shortening his life, indeed he is, by his carelessness."

There is Mr. Lovel coming from the city, and the children are running to their papa! And Miss Prior makes her patroness a meek curtsy, and demurely slides away from the room. With a sick heart I say to myself, "She has been — yes — humbugging is the word — humbugging Lady B. Elizabeth! Elizabeth! can it be possible thou art humbugging *me* too?"

Before Lovel enters, Bedford rapidly flits through the room. He looks as pale as a ghost. His face is awfully gloomy.

"Here's the governor come," Dick whispers to me. "It must all come hout now — out, I beg your pardon. So she's caught *you*, has she? I thought she would." And he grins a ghastly grin.

"What do you mean?" I ask, and I dare say turn rather red.

"I know all about it. I'll speak to you to-night,

sir. Confound her! confound her!" and he doubles his knuckles into his eyes, and rushes out of the room over Buttons entering with the afternoon tea.

"What on earth's the matter, and why are you knocking the things about?" Lovel asks at dinner of his butler, who, indeed, acted as one distraught. A savage gloom was depicted on Bedford's usually melancholy countenance, and the blunders in his service were many. With his brother-in-law Lovel did not exchange many words. Clarence was not yet forgiven for his escapade two days previous. And when Lady Baker cried, "Mercy, child! what have you done to yourself?" and the Captain replied, "Knocked my face against a dark door — made my nose bleed," Lovel did not look up or express a word of sympathy. "If the fellow knocked his worthless head off, I should not be sorry," the widower murmured to me. Indeed, the tone of the Captain's voice, his *ton*, and his manners in general, were specially odious to Mr. Lovel, who could put up with the tyranny of women, but revolted against the vulgarity and assumption of certain men.

As yet nothing had been said about the morning's quarrel. Here we were all sitting with a sword hanging over our heads, smiling and chatting, and talking cookery, politics, the weather, and what not. Bessy was perfectly cool and dignified at tea. Danger or doubt did not seem to affect *her*. If she had been ordered for execution at the end of the evening she would have made the tea, played her Beethoven, answered questions in her usual voice, and glided about from one to another with her usual dignified calm, until the hour of decapitation came, when she would have made her curtsy, and gone out, and had the amputation performed quite quietly and neatly. I

admired her, I was frightened before her. The cold
snake crept more than ever down my back as I meditated on her. I made such awful blunders at whist
that even good Mrs. Bonnington lost her temper with
her fourteen shillings. Miss Prior would have played
her hand out, and never made a fault, you may be
sure. She retired at her accustomed hour. Mrs.
Bonnington had her glass of negus, and withdrew too.
Lovel keeping his eyes sternly on the Captain, that
officer could only get a little sherry and seltzer, and
went to bed sober. Lady Baker folded Lovel in her
arms, a process to which my poor friend very humbly
submitted. Everybody went to bed, and no tales were
told of the morning's doings. There was a respite,
and no execution could take place till to-morrow at
any rate. Put on thy nightcap, Damocles, and slumber
for to-night at least. Thy slumbers will not be cut
short by the awful Chopper of Fate.

Perhaps you may ask what need had *I* to be alarmed?
Nothing could happen to me. I was not going to lose
a governess's place. Well, if I must tell the truth, I
had not acted with entire candor in the matter of
Bessy's appointment. In recommending her to Lovel
and the late Mrs L., I had answered for her probity,
and so forth, with all my might. I had described the
respectability of her family, her father's campaigns,
her grandfather's (old Dr. Sargent's) celebrated sermons; and had enlarged with the utmost eloquence
upon the learning and high character of her uncle, the
Master of Boniface, and the deserved regard he bore
his niece. But that part of Bessy's biography which
related to the Academy I own I had not touched upon.
A quoi bon? Would every gentleman or lady like to
have everything told about him or her? I had kept
the Academy dark then; and so had brave Dick Bed

ford the butler; and should that miscreant Captain reveal the secret, I knew there would be an awful commotion in the building. I should have to incur Lovel's not unjust reproaches for *suppressio veri,* and the anger of those two *viragines,* the grandmothers of Lovel's children. I was more afraid of the women than of him, though conscience whispered me that I had not acted quite rightly by my friend.

When, then, the bed-candles were lighted, and every one said good-night, "Oh! Captain Baker," say I, gayly, and putting on a confoundedly hypocritical grin, "if you will come into my room, I will give you that book."

"What book?" says Baker.

"The book we were talking of this morning."

"Hang me, if I know what you mean," says he. And luckily for me, Lovel, giving a shrug of disgust, and a good-night to me, stalked out of the room, bed-candle in hand. No doubt he thought his wretch of a brother-in-law did not well remember after dinner what he had done or said in the morning.

As I now had the Blacksheep to myself, I said calmly, "You are quite right. There was no talk about a book at all, Captain Baker. But I wished to see you alone, and impress upon you my earnest wish that everything which occurred this morning — mind, *everything* — should be considered as strictly private, and should be confided to *no person whatever* — you understand? — to no person."

"Confound me," Baker breaks out, "if I understand what you mean by your books and your 'strictly private.' I shall speak what I choose — hang me!"

"In that case, sir," I said, "will you have the goodness to send a friend of yours to my friend Captain Fitzboodle? I must consider the matter as personal

between ourselves. You insulted — and, as I find now,
for the second time — a lady whose relations to me
you know. You have given neither to her, nor to me,
the apology to which we are both entitled. You refuse even to promise to be silent regarding a painful
scene which was occasioned by your own brutal and
cowardly behavior; and you must abide by the consequences, sir! you must abide by the consequences!"
And I glared at him over my flat candlestick.

"Curse me! — and hang me! — and, etc., etc., etc.,"
he says, "if I know what all this is about. What the
dooce do you talk to *me* about books, and about silence,
and apologies, and sending Captain Fitzboodle to me?
I don't want to see Captain Fitzboodle — great fat
brute! *I* know him perfectly well."

"Hush!" say I, "here's Bedford." In fact, Dick
appeared at this juncture, to close the house and put
the lamps out.

But Captain Clarence only spoke or screamed louder.
"What do I care about who hears me? That fellow
insulted me already to-day, and I'd have pitched his
life out of him, only I was down, and I'm so confounded weak and nervous, and just out of my fever
— and — and hang it all! what are you driving at,
Mr. What's-your-name?" And the wretched little
creature cries almost as he speaks.

"Once for all, will you agree that the affair about
which we spoke shall go no further?" I say, as stern
as Draco.

"I sha'n't say anythin' about it. I wish you'd
leave me alone, you fellows, and not come botherin'.
I wish I could get a glass of brandy-and-water up in
my bedroom, I tell you I can't sleep without it,"
whimpers the wretch.

"Sorry I laid hands on you, sir," says Bedford,

sadly. "It was n't worth the while. Go to bed, and I 'll get you something warm."

"Will you, though? I could n't sleep without it. Do now — do now! and I won't say anythin' — I won't now — on the honor of a gentleman, I won't. Good-night, Mr. What-d'-ye-call." And Bedford leads the helot to his chamber.

"I 've got him in bed; and I 've given him a dose; and I put some laudanum in it. He ain't been out. He has not had much to-day," says Bedford, coming back to my room, with his face ominously pale.

"You have given him laudanum?" I ask.

"*Sawbones* gave him some yesterday, — told me to give him a little — forty drops," growls Bedford.

Then the gloomy major-domo puts a hand into each waistcoat pocket, and looks at me. "You want to fight for her, do you, sir? Calling out, and that sort of game? Phoo!" — and he laughs scornfully.

"The little miscreant is too despicable, I own," say I, "and it 's absurd for a peaceable fellow like me to talk about powder and shot at this time of day. But what could I do?"

"I say it 's SHE ain't worth it," says Bedford, lifting up both clenched fists out of the waistcoat pockets.

"What do you mean, Dick?" I ask.

"She 's humbugging you, — she 's humbugging me, — she 's humbugging everybody," roars Dick. "Look here, sir!" and out of one of the clenched fists he flings a paper down on the table.

"What is it?" I ask. It 's her handwriting. I see the neat trim lines on the paper.

"It 's not to you; nor yet to me," says Bedford.

"Then how dare you read it, sir?" I ask, all of a tremble.

"It's to him. It's to Sawbones," hisses out Bedford. "Sawbones dropt it as he was getting into his gig: and I read it. *I* ain't going to make no bones about whether it's wrote to me or not. She tells him how you asked her to marry you. (Ha!) That's how I came to know it. And do you know what she calls you, and what *he* calls you, — that castor-hoil beast? And do you know what she says of you? That you hadn't pluck to stand by her to-day. There, — it's all down under her hand and seal. You may read it, or not, if you like. And if poppy or mandragora will medicine you to sleep afterwards, I just recommend you to take it. *I* shall go and get a drop out of the Captain's bottle — I shall.

And he leaves me, and the fatal paper on the table.

Now, suppose you had been in my case — would you, or would you not, have read the paper? Suppose there is some news — bad news — about the woman you love, will you, or will you not, hear it? Was Othello a rogue because he let Iago speak to him? There was the paper. It lay there glimmering under the light, with all the house quiet.

CHAPTER VI.

CECILIA'S SUCCESSOR.

MONSIEUR ET HONORÉ LECTEUR! I see, as perfectly as if you were sitting opposite to me, the scorn depicted on your noble countenance when you read my confession that I, Charles Batchelor, Esquire, did burglariously enter the premises of Edward Drencher, Esquire, M.R.C.S.I. (phew! the odious pestle-grinder, I never could bear him!) and break open, and read a certain letter, his property. I may have been wrong, but I am candid. I tell my misdeeds; some fellows hold their tongues. Besides, my good man, consider the temptation, and the horrid insight into the paper which Bedford's report had already given me. Would *you* ike to be told that the girl of your heart was playing fast and loose with it, had none of her own, or had given hers to another? I don't want to make a Mrs. Robin Gray of any woman, and merely because "her mither presses her sair" to marry against her will. "If Miss Prior," thought I, "prefers this lint-scraper to me, ought I to balk her? He is younger, and stronger, certainly, than myself. Some people may consider him handsome. (By the way, what a remarkable thing it is about many women, that, in affairs of the heart, they don't seem to care or understand whether a man is a gentleman or not.) It may be it is my superior fortune and social station which may induce Elizabeth to waver in her choice between me and my bleeding, bolusing, tooth-drawing rival.

If so, and I am only taken from mercenary considerations, what a pretty chance of subsequent happiness do either of us stand! Take the vaccinator, girl, if thou preferrest him! I know what it is to be crossed in love already. It's hard, but I can bear it! I ought to know, I must know, I *will* know what is in that paper!" So saying, as I pace round and round the table where the letter lies flickering white under the midnight taper, I stretch out my hand — I seize the paper — I — well, I own it — there — yes — I took it, and I read it.

Or rather, I may say, I read that part of IT which the bleeder and blisterer had flung down. It was but a fragment of a letter — a fragment — oh! how bitter to swallow! A lump of Epsom salt could not have been more disgusting. It appeared (from Bedford's statement) that Æsculapius, on getting into his gig, had allowed this scrap of paper to whisk out of his pocket — the rest he read, no doubt, under the eyes of the writer. Very likely during the perusal, he had taken and squeezed the false hand which wrote the lines. Very likely the first part of the *precious document* contained compliments to him — from the horrible context I judge so — compliments to that vendor of leeches and bandages, into whose heart I dare say I wished ten thousand lancets might be stuck, as I perused the FALSE ONE's wheedling address to him! So ran the document. How well every word of it was engraven on my anguished heart! If page *three*, which I suppose was about the bit of the letter which I got, was as it was — what must pages *one* and *two* have been? The dreadful document began, then, thus : —

"— dear hair in the locket, which I shall *ever* wear for the sake of *him who gave it*" — (dear hair! in

deed — disgusting carrots! She should have been
ashamed to call it "dear hair") — "for the sake of
him who gave it, and whose *bad temper* I shall pardon,
because I think in spite of his faults he is a *little fond*
of his poor Lizzie! Ah! Edward! how *could* you go
on so the last time about poor Mr. B.! Can you imagine that I can ever have more than a filial regard
for the kind old gentleman?" (*Il était question de
moi, ma parole d'honneur. I* was the kind old gentleman!) "I have known him since my childhood.
He was intimate in our family in earlier and happier
days; made our house his home; and, I must say,
was most kind to all of us children. If he has vanities, you naughty boy, is he the only one of his sex
who is vain? Can you fancy that such an old creature (an *old muff,* as you call him, you wicked, satirical man!) could ever make an impression on my
heart? No, sir!" (Aha! So I was an old muff, was
I?) "Though I don't wish to make *you* vain too, or
that other people should laugh at you, as you do at
poor dear Mr. B., I think, sir, you need but look *in
your glass* to see that you need not be afraid of such a
rival as *that.* You fancy he is attentive to me? If
you looked only a little angrily at him, he would fly
back to London. To-day, when your *horrid little
patient* did presume to offer to take my hand, when I
boxed his little wicked ears and sent him *spinning* to
the end of the room — poor Mr. Batch was so *frightened* that he did not *dare* to come into the room, and
I saw him peeping behind a statue on the lawn, and
he would not come in until the *servants arrived.*
Poor man! We cannot all of us have courage like *a
certain Edward,* who I know is as *bold as a lion.*
Now, sir, you must not be quarrelling with that
wretched little captain for being rude. I have shown

him that I can very well *take care of myself.* I knew
the *odious thing* the first moment I set eyes on him,
though he had forgotten me. Years ago I met him,
and I remember he was equally *rude and tips —*"

Here the letter was torn. Beyond *"tips"* it did
not go. But that was enough, was n't it? To this
woman I had offered a gentle and manly, I may say a
kind and tender heart — I had offered four hundred a
year in funded property, besides my house in Devonshire Street, Bloomsbury — and she preferred *Edward*,
forsooth, at the sign of the Gallipot: and may ten
thousand pestles smash my brains!

You may fancy what a night I had after reading
that scrap. I promise you I did not sleep much. I
heard the hours toll as I kept vigil. I lay amidst
shattered capitals, broken shafts of the tumbled palace
which I had built in imagination — oh! how bright
and stately! I sat amongst the ruins of my own happiness, surrounded by the murdered corpses of innocent visioned domestic joys. Tick — tock! Moment
after moment I heard on the clock the clinking foot-
steps of wakeful grief. I fell into a doze towards
morning, and dreamed that I was dancing with Glorvina, when I woke with a start, finding Bedford
arrived with my shaving-water, and opening the shutters. When he saw my haggard face he wagged his
head.

"You *have* read it, I see, sir," says he.

"Yes, Dick," groaned I, out of bed, "I have swal-
lowed it." And I laughed I may say a fiendish laugh.
"And now I have taken it, not poppy nor mandragora,
nor all the drowsy syrups in his shop (hang him) will
be able to medicine me to sleep for some time to
come!"

"She has no heart, sir. I don't think she cares for

t' other chap much," groans the gloomy butler. "She can't, after having known *us*" — and my companion in grief, laying down my hot-water jug, retreats.

I did not cut any part of myself with my razor. I shaved quite calmly. I went to the family at breakfast. My impression is I was sarcastic and witty. I I smiled most kindly at Miss Prior when she came in. Nobody could have seen from my outward behavior that anything was wrong within. I was an apple. Could you inspect the worm at my core? No, no. Somebody, I think old Baker, complimented me on my good looks. I was a smiling lake. Could you see on my placid surface, amongst my sheeny water lilies, that a corpse was lying under my cool depths? "A bit of devilled chicken?" "No, thank you. By the way, Lovel, I think I must go to town to-day." "You'll come back to dinner, of course?" "Well — no." "Oh, stuff! You promised me to-day and to-morrow. Robinson, Brown, and Jones are coming to-morrow, and you must be here to meet them." Thus we prattle on. I answer, I smile, I say, "Yes, if you please, another cup," or "Be so good as to hand the muffin," or what not. But I am dead. I feel as if I am under ground, and buried. Life, and tea, and clatter, and muffins are going on, of course; and daisies spring, and the sun shines on the grass whilst I am under it. Ah, dear me! it's very cruel: it's very, very lonely: it's very odd! I don't belong to the world any more. I have done with it. I am shelved away. But my spirit returns and flitters through the world, which it has no longer anything to do with: and my ghost, as it were, comes and smiles at my own tombstone. Here lies Charles Batchelor, the Unloved One. Oh! alone, alone, alone! Why, Fate! didst thou ordain that I should be companion-

less ? Tell me where the Wandering Jew is, that I
may go and sit with him. Is there any place at a
light-house vacant ? Who knows where is the Island
of Juan Fernandez ? Engage me a ship and take me
there at once. Mr. R. Crusoe, I think ? My dear
Robinson, have the kindness to hand me over your
goatskin cap, breeches, and umbrella. Go home, and
leave *me* here. Would you know who is the solitari-
est man on earth ? That man am I. Was that cutlet
which I ate at breakfast anon, was that lamb which
frisked on the mead last week (beyond yon wall where
the unconscious cucumber lay basking which was to
form his sauce) — I say, was that lamb made so tender, that I might eat him ? And my heart, then ?
Poor heart ! wert thou so softly constituted only that
women might stab thee ? So I am a Muff, am I ?
And she will always wear a lock of his "dear hair,"
will she ? Ha ! ha ! The men on the omnibus looked
askance as they saw me laugh. They thought it was
from Hanwell, not Putney, I was escaping. Escape ?
Who can escape ? I went into London. I went to
the clubs. Jawkins, of course, was there ; and my impression is that he talked as usual. I took another
omnibus, and went back to Putney. "I will go back
and revisit my grave," I thought. It is said that
ghosts loiter about their former haunts a good deal
when they are first dead ; flit wistfully among their
old friends and companions, and, I dare say, expect to
hear a plenty of conversation and friendly tearful
remark about themselves. But suppose they return,
and find nobody talking of them at all ? Or, suppose,
Hamlet (*Père*, and Royal Dane) comes back and finds
Claudius and Gertrude very comfortable over a piece
of cold meat, or what not ! Is the late gentleman's
present position as a ghost a very pleasant one ?

Crow, Cocks! Quick, Sundawn! Open, Trap-door!
Allons: it's best to pop under ground again. So I
am a Muff, am I? What a curious thing that walk
up the hill to the house was! What a different place
Shrublands was yesterday to what it is to-day! Has
the sun lost its light, and the flowers their bloom, and
the joke its sparkle, and the dish its savor? Why,
bless my soul! what is Lizzy herself — only an ordinary woman — freckled certainly — incorrigibly dull,
and without a scintillation of humor: and you mean
to say, Charles Batchelor, that your heart once beat
about *that* woman? Under the intercepted letter of
that cold assassin, my heart had fallen down dead, ir-
retrievably dead. I remember, *àpropos* of the occasion
of my first death, that perpetrated by Glorvina — on
my second visit to Dublin — with what a strange sensation I walked under some trees in the Phœnix Park
beneath which it had been my custom to meet my
False One Number I. There were the trees — there
were the birds singing — there was the bench on
which we used to sit — the same, but how different!
The trees had a different foliage, exquisite amaranthine: the birds sang a song paradisiacal; the bench
was a bank of roses and fresh flowers, which young
Love twined in fragrant chaplets around the statue of
Glorvina. Roses and fresh flowers? Rheumatisms
and flannel waistcoats, you silly old man! Foliage
and Song? O namby-pamby driveller! A statue? —
a doll, thou twaddling old dullard! — a doll with car-
mine cheeks, and a heart stuffed with bran — I say,
on the night preceding that ride to and from Putney,
I had undergone death — in that omnibus I had been
carried over to t'other side of the Stygian shore. I
returned but as a passionless ghost, remembering my
life-days, but not feeling any more. Love was dead,

Elizabeth! Why, the doctor came, and partook freely
of lunch, and I was not angry. Yesterday I called
him names, and hated him, and was jealous of him.
To-day I felt no rivalship; and no envy at his success; and no desire to supplant him. No — I swear
— not the slightest wish to make Elizabeth mine if
she would. I might have cared for her yesterday —
yesterday I had a heart. Psha! my good sir or
madam. You sit by me at dinner. Perhaps you are
handsome, and use your eyes. Ogle away. Don't
balk yourself, pray. But if you fancy I care a three-
penny-piece about you — or for your eyes — or for
your bonny brown hair — or for your sentimental
remarks, sidelong warbled — or for your praise to
(not of) my face — or for your satire behind my back
— ah me! — how mistaken you are! *Peine perdue,
ma chère dame!* The digestive organs are still in
good working order — but the heart? *Caret.*

I was perfectly civil to Mr. Drencher, and, indeed,
wonder to think how in my irritation I had allowed
myself to apply (mentally) any sort of disagreeable
phrases to a most excellent and deserving and good-
looking young man, who is beloved by the poor, and
has won the just confidence of an extensive circle of
patients. I made no sort of remark to Miss Prior,
except about the weather and the flowers in the garden. I was bland, easy, rather pleasant, not too high-
spirited, you understand. — No: I vow you could not
have seen a nerve wince, or the slightest alteration in
my demeanor. I helped the two old dowagers; I listened to their twaddle; I gayly wiped up with my
napkin three quarters of a glass of sherry which Popham flung over my trousers. I would defy you to
know that I had gone through the ticklish operation
of an excision of the heart a few hours previously.

Heart — pooh! I saw Miss Prior's lip quiver. Without a word between us, she knew perfectly well that
all was over as regarded her late humble servant.
She winced once or twice. While Drencher was busy
with his plate, the gray eyes cast towards me inter-
jectional looks of puzzled entreaty. *She*, I say,
winced: and I give you my word I did not care a fig
whether she was sorry, or pleased, or happy, or going
to be hung. And I can't give a better proof of my
utter indifference about the matter, than the fact that
I wrote two or three copies of verses descriptive of
my despair. They appeared, you may perhaps remember, in one of the annuals of those days, and were
generally attributed to one of the most sentimental of
our young poets. I remember the reviews said they
were "replete with emotion," "full of passionate and
earnest feeling," and so forth. Feeling, indeed! —
ha! ha! "Passionate outbursts of a grief-stricken
heart!" — Passionate scrapings of a fiddlestick, my
good friend. "Lonely" of course rhymes with
"only," and "gushes" with "blushes," and "despair"
with "hair," and so on. Despair is perfectly com-
patible with a good dinner, I promise you. Hair is
false: hearts are false. Grapes may be sour, but
claret is good, my masters. Do you suppose I am going to cry my eyes out, because Chloe's are turned
upon Strephon? If you find any whimpering in
mine, may they never wink at a bees-wing again.

When the doctor rose presently, saying, he would
go and see the gardener's child, who was ill, and casting longing looks at Miss Prior, I assure you I did
not feel a tittle of jealousy, though Miss Bessy actually followed Mr. Drencher into the lawn, under the
pretext of calling back Miss Cissy, who had run
thither without her bonnet.

"Now, Lady Baker, which was right? you or
I?" asks bonny Mrs. Bonnington, wagging her head
towards the lawn where this couple of innocents were
disporting.

"You thought there was an affair between Miss
Prior and the medical gentleman," I say, smiling.
"It was no secret, Mrs. Bonnington."

"Yes, but there were others who were a little smitten in that quarter, too," says Lady Baker; and she
in turn wags *her* old head towards me.

"You mean me?" I answer, as innocent as a new-
born babe. "I am a burnt child, Lady Baker; I have
been at the fire, and am already thoroughly done,
thank you. One of your charming sex jilted me some
years ago; and once is quite enough, I am much
obliged to you."

This I said, not because it was true; in fact, it was
the reverse of true; but if I choose to lie about my
own affairs, pray, why not? And though a strictly
truth-telling man generally, when I do lie, I promise
you I do it boldly and well.

"If, as I gather from Mrs. Bonnington, Mr. Drencher and Miss Prior like each other, I wish my old
friend joy. I wish Mr. Drencher joy with all my
heart. The match seems to me excellent. He is a
deserving, a clever, and a handsome young fellow;
and I am sure, ladies, you can bear witness to *her*
goodness, after all you have known of her."

"My dear Batchelor," says Mrs. Bonnington, still
smiling and winking, "I don't believe one single
word you say — not one single word!" And she
looks infinitely pleased as she speaks.

"Oh!" cries Lady Baker, "my good Mrs. Bonnington, you are always match-making — don't contradict
me. You know you thought —"

"Oh, please don't," cries Mrs. B.

"I will. She thought, Mr. Batchelor, she actually thought that our son, that my Cecilia's husband, was smitten by the governess. I should like to have seen him dare!" and her flashing eyes turn towards the late Mrs. Lovel's portrait, with its faded simper leering over the harp. "The idea that any woman could succeed that angel, indeed!"

"Indeed, I don't envy her," I said.

"You don't mean, Batchelor, that my Frederick would not make any woman happy?" cries the Bonnington. "He is only seven-and-thirty, very young for his age, and the most affectionate of creatures. I am surprised, and it's most cruel, and most unkind of you, to say that you don't envy any woman that marries my boy!"

"My dear good Mrs. Bonnington, you quite misapprehend me," I remark.

"Why, when his late wife was alive," goes on Mrs. B——, sobbing, "you know with what admirable sweetness and gentleness he bore her — her — bad temper — excuse me, Lady Baker!"

"Oh, pray, abuse my departed angel!" cries the Baker; "say that your son should marry and forget her — say that those darlings should be made to forget their mother. She was a woman of birth, and a woman of breeding, and a woman of family, and the Bakers came in with the Conqueror, Mrs. Bonnington — "

"I think I heard of one in the court of Pharaoh," I interposed.

"And to say that a Baker is not worthy of a Lovel is *pretty* news indeed! Do you hear *that*, Clarence?"

"Hear what, Ma'am?" says Clarence, who enters at this juncture. "You're speakin' loud enough — though blesht if I hear two sh-shyllables."

"You wretched boy, you have been smoking!"

"Shmoking — have n't I?" says Clarence with a laugh; "and I 've been at the 'Five Bells,' and I 've been having a game of billiards with an old friend of mine," and he lurches towards a decanter.

"Ah! don't drink any more, my child!" cries the mother.

"I 'm as sober as a judge, I tell you. You leave so precious little in the bottle at dinner, that I must get it when I can, must n't I, Batchelor, old boy? We had a row yesterday, had n't we? No, it was sugar-baker. I 'm not angry — you 're not angry. Bear no malish. Here 's your health, old boy!"

The unhappy gentleman drank his bumper of sherry, and, tossing his hair off his head, said — "Where 's the governess — where 's Bessy Bellenden? Who 's that kickin' me under the table, I say?"

"Where is who?" asks his mother.

"Bessy Bellenden — the governess — that 's her real name. Known her these ten years. Used to dansh at Prinsh's Theatre. Remember her in the *corps-de-ballet*. Ushed to go behind the shenes. Dooshid pretty girl!" maunders out the tipsy youth; and as the unconscious subject of his mischievous talk enters the room, again he cries out, "Come and sit by me, Bessy Bellenden, I say!"

The matrons rose with looks of horror in their faces. "A ballet-dancer!" cries Mrs. Bonnington. "A ballet-dancer!" echoes Lady Baker. "Young woman, is this true?"

"'The Bulbul and the Roshe' — hay?" laughs the Captain. "Don't you remember you and Fosbery in blue and shpangles? Always all right, though, Bell-enden was. Fosbery wash n't: but Bellenden was. Give you every credit for that, Bellenden. Boxsh my

earsh. Bear no malish — no — no — malish! Get some
more sherry, you — whatsh your name — Bedford,
butler — and I 'll pay you the money I owe you."
And he laughs his wild laugh, utterly unconscious
of the effect he is producing. Bedford stands staring at him as pale as death. Poor Miss Prior is as
white as marble. Wrath, terror, and wonder are in
the countenances of the dowagers. It is an awful
scene!

"Mr. Batchelor knows that it was to help my
family I did it," says the poor governess.

"Yes, by George! and nobody can say a word
against her," bursts in Dick Bedford, with a sob;
"and she is as honest as any woman here."

"Pray, who told you to put your oar in?" cries the
tipsy Captain.

"And you knew that this person was on the stage,
and you introduced her into my son's family. Oh,
Mr. Batchelor, Mr. Batchelor, I did n't think it of
you! Don't speak to me, Miss!" cries the flurried
Bonnington.

"You brought this woman to the children of my
adored Cecilia?" calls out the other dowager. "Serpent, leave the room! Pack your trunks, viper! and
quit the house this instant. Don't touch her, Cissy.
Come to me, my blessing. Go away, you horrid
wretch!"

"She ain't a horrid wretch; and when I was ill she
was very good to us," breaks in Pop, with a roar of
tears: "and you sha'n't go, Miss Prior — my dear,
pretty Miss Prior. You sha'n't go!" and the child
rushes up to the governess, and covers her neck with
tears and kisses.

"Leave her, Popham, my darling blessing! — leave
that woman!" cries Lady Baker.

"I won't, you old beast! — and she sha-a-an't go. And I wish you was dead — and, my dear, you sha'n't go, and Pa sha'n't let you!" — shouts the boy.

"Oh, Popham, if Miss Prior has been naughty, Miss Prior must go!" says Cecilia, tossing up her head.

"Spoken like my daughter's child!" cries Lady Baker: and little Cissy, having flung her little stone, looks as if she had performed a very virtuous action.

"God bless you, Master Pop, — you are a trump, you are!" says Mr. Bedford.

"Yes, that I am, Bedford; and she sha'n't go, shall she?" cries the boy.

But Bessy stooped down sadly, and kissed him. "Yes, I must, dear," she said.

"Don't touch him! Come away, sir! Come away from her this moment!" shrieked the two mothers.

"I nursed him through the scarlet fever, when his own mother would not come near him," says Elizabeth, gently.

"I'm blest if she did n't," sobs Bedford — "and — bub — bub — bless you, Master Pop!"

"That child is wicked enough, and headstrong enough, and rude enough already!" exclaims Lady Baker. "I desire, young woman, you will not pollute him further!"

"That's a hard word to say to an honest woman, Ma'am," says Bedford.

"Pray, Miss, are you engaged to the butler, too?" hisses out the dowager.

"There's very little the matter with Barnet's child — only teeth. — What on earth has happened? My dear Lizzy — my dear Miss Prior — what is it?" cries the doctor, who enters from the garden at this juncture.

"Nothing has happened, only this young woman has

appeared in a new *character*," says Lady Baker. "My
son has just informed us that Miss Prior danced upon
the stage, Mr. Drencher; and if you think such a person is a fit companion for your mother and sisters,
who attend a place of Christian worship, I believe —
I wish you joy."

"Is this — is this — true?" asks the doctor, with
a look of bewilderment.

"Yes, it is true," sighs the girl.

"And you never told me, Elizabeth?" groans the
doctor.

"She's as honest as any woman here," calls out
Bedford. "She gave all the money to her family."

"It wasn't fair not to tell me. It wasn't fair,"
sobs the Doctor. And he gives her a ghastly parting
look, and turns his back.

"I say, you — Hi! What-d'-you-call-'im? Sawbones!" shrieks out Captain Clarence. "Come back,
I say. She's all right, I say. Upon my honor, now,
she's all right."

"Miss P—— shouldn't have kept this from me.
My mother and sisters are Dissenters, and very strict.
I couldn't ask a party into my family who has been
— who has been — I wish you good morning," says the
doctor, and stalks away.

"And now, will you please to get your things ready,
and go, too?" continues Lady Baker. "My dear Mrs.
Bonnington, you think —"

"Certainly, certainly, she must go!" cries Mrs.
Bonnington.

"Don't go till Lovel comes home, Miss. *These* ain't
your mistresses. Lady Baker don't pay your salary.
If you go, I go, too. There!" calls out Bedford, and
mumbles something in her ear about "the end of the
world."

"You go, too; and a good riddance, you insolent brute!" exclaims the dowager.

"Oh, Captain Clarence! you have made a pretty morning's work," I say.

"I don't know what the dooce all the sherry — all the shindy's about," says the Captain, playing with the empty decanter. "Gal's a very good gal — pretty gal. If she choosesh dansh shport her family, why the doosh should n't she dansh shport a family?"

"That is exactly what I recommend this person to do," says Lady Baker, tossing up her head. "And now I will thank you to leave the room. Do you hear?"

As poor Elizabeth obeyed the order, Bedford darted after her; and I know ere she had gone five steps he had offered her his savings and everything he had. She might have had mine yesterday. But she had deceived me. She had played fast and loose with me. She had misled me about this doctor. I could trust her no more. My love of yesterday was dead, I say. The vase was broken, which never could be mended. She knew all was over between us. She did not once look at me as she left the room.

The two dowagers — one of them, I think, a little alarmed at her victory — left the house, and for once went away in the same barouche. The young maniac who had been the cause of the mischief staggered away, I know not whither.

About four o'clock, poor little Pinhorn, the children's maid, came to me, wellnigh choking with tears, as she handed me a letter. "She's goin' away — and she saved both them children's lives, she did. And she've wrote to you, sir. And Bedford's a-goin'. And I'll give warnin', I will, too!" And the weeping handmaiden retires, leaving me, perhaps somewhat frightened, with the letter in my hand.

"Dear sir," she said — "I may write you a line of thanks and farewell. I shall go to my mother. I shall soon find another place. Poor Bedford, who has a generous heart, told me that he had given you a letter of mine to Mr. D——. I saw this morning that you knew everything. I can only say now that for all your long kindnesses and friendship to my family I am always your sincere and grateful — E. P."

Yes: that was all. I think she *was* grateful. But she had not been candid with me, nor with the poor surgeon. I had no anger: far from it: a great deal of regard and good will, nay admiration, for the intrepid girl who had played a long, hard part very cheerfully and bravely. But my foolish little flicker of love had blazed up and gone out in a day; I knew that she never could care for me. In that dismal, wakeful night, after reading the letter, I had thought her character and story over, and seen to what a life of artifice and dissimulation necessity had compelled her. I did not blame her. In such circumstances, with such a family, how could she be frank and open? Poor thing! poor thing! Do we know anybody? Ah! dear me, we are most of us very lonely in the world. You who have any who love you, cling to them, and thank God. I went into the hall towards evening: her poor trunks and packages were there, and the little nurserymaid weeping over them. The sight unmanned me; and I believe I cried myself. Poor Elizabeth! And with these small chests you recommence your life's lonely voyage! I gave the girl a couple of sovereigns. She sobbed a God bless me! and burst out crying more desperately than ever. Thou hast a kind heart, little Pinhorn!

"'Miss Prior — to be called for.' Whose trunks are these?" says Lovel, coming from the city. The dowagers drove up at the same moment.

"Did n't you see us from the omnibus, Frederick?" cries her ladyship, coaxingly. "We followed behind you all the way!"

"We were in the barouche, my dear," remarks Mrs. Bonnington, rather nervously.

"Whose trunks are these? — what 's the matter? — and what 's the girl crying for?" asks Lovel.

"Miss Prior is a-going away," sobs Pinhorn.

"Miss Prior going? Is this your doing, my Lady Baker? — or yours, Mother?" the master of the house says, sternly.

"She is going, my love, because she cannot stay in this family," says mamma.

"That woman is no fit companion for my angel's children, Frederick!" cries Lady B.

"That person has deceived us all, my love!" says mamma.

"Deceived? — how? Deceived whom?" continues Mr. Lovel, more and more hotly.

"Clarence, love! come down, dear! Tell Mr. Lovel everything. Come down and tell him this moment," cries Lady Baker to her son, who at this moment appears on the corridor which was round the hall.

"What 's the row now, pray?" And Captain Clarence descends, breaking his shins over poor Elizabeth's trunks, and calling down on them his usual maledictions.

"Tell Mr. Lovel where you saw that — that person, Clarence? Now, sir, listen to my Cecilia's brother!"

"Saw her — saw her in blue and spangles, in the 'Rose and the Bulbul,' at the Prince's Theatre — and a doosid nice-looking girl she was too!" says the Captain.

" There, sir ! "

" There, Frederick ! " cry the matrons in a breath.

" And what then ? " asks Lovel.

" Mercy ! you ask, What then, Frederick ?   Do you know what a theatre is ?   Tell Frederick what a theatre is, Mr. Batchelor, and that my grandchildren must not be educated by — "

" My grandchildren — my Cecilia's children," shrieks the other, " must not be pol-lut-d by — "

" Silence ! " I say.   " Have you a word against her — have you, pray, Baker ? "

" No.   'Gad ! I never said a word against her," says the Captain.   " No, hang me, you know — but — "

" But suppose I knew the fact the whole time ? " asks Lovel, with rather a blush on his cheek.   " Suppose I knew that she danced to give her family bread ? Suppose I knew that she toiled and labored to support her parents, and brothers and sisters ?   Suppose I know that out of her pittance she has continued to support them ?   Suppose I know that she watched my own children through fever and danger ?   For these reasons I must turn her out of doors, must I ?   No, by heaven ! — No ! — Elizabeth ! — Miss Prior ! — Come down ! — Come here, I beg you ! "

The governess, arrayed as for departure, at this moment appeared on the corridor running round the hall. As Lovel continued to speak very loud and resolute, she came down looking deadly pale.

Still much excited, the widower went up to her and took her hand.   " Dear Miss Prior ! " he said — " dear Elizabeth ! you have been the best friend of me and mine.   You tended my wife in illness, you took care of my children in fever and danger.   You have been an admirable sister, daughter in your own family — and for this, and for these benefits conferred upon us,

LOVEL'S MOTHERS.

my relatives — my mother-in-law — would drive you out of my doors! It shall not be! — by heavens, it shall not be!"

You should have seen little Bedford sitting on the governess's box, shaking his fist, and crying "Hurrah!" as his master spoke. By this time the loud voices and the altercation in the hall had brought a half-dozen of servants from their quarters into the hall. "Go away, all of you!" shouts Lovel; and the domestic *posse* retires, Bedford being the last to retreat, and nodding approval at his master as he backs out of the room.

"You are very good, and kind, and generous, sir," says the pale Elizabeth, putting a handkerchief to her eyes. "But without the confidence of these ladies, I must not stay, Mr. Lovel. God bless you for your goodness to me. I must, if you please, return to my mother."

The worthy gentleman looked fiercely round at the two elder women, and again, seizing the governess's hand, said — "Elizabeth! dear Elizabeth! I implore you not to go! If you love the children — "

"Oh, sir!" (A cambric veil covers Miss Prior's emotion, and the expression of her face, on this ejaculation.)

"If you love the children," gasps out the widower, "stay with them. If you have a regard for — for their father" — (Timanthes, where is thy pocket-handkerchief?) — "remain in this house, with such a title as none can question. Be the mistress of it."

"His mistress — and before me! screams Lady Baker. "Mrs. Bonnington, this depravity is monstrous!'"

"Be my wife, dear Elizabeth!" the widower continues. "Continue to watch over the children, who shall be motherless no more."

"Frederick! Frederick! have n't they got *us?*" shrieks one of the old ladies.

"Oh, my poor dear Lady Baker!" says Mrs. Bonnington.

"Oh, my poor dear Mrs. Bonnington!" says Lady Baker.

"Frederick, listen to your mother," implores Mrs. Bonnington.

"To your mothers," sobs Lady Baker.

And they both go down on their knees, and I heard a boo-hoo of a guffaw behind the green-baized servants' door, where I have no doubt Mons. Bedford was posted.

"Ah, Batchelor! dear Batchelor, speak to him!" cries good Mrs. Bonny. "We are praying this child, Batchelor — this child whom you used to know at college, and when he was a good, gentle, obedient boy. You have influence with my poor Frederick. Exert it for his heart-broken mother's sake; and you shall have my bubble-uble-essings, you shall."

"My dear good lady," I exclaim — not liking to see the kind soul in grief.

"Send for Doctor Straightwaist! Order him to pause in his madness," cries Baker; "or it is I, Cecilia's mother, the mother of that murdered angel, that shall go mad."

"Angel? *Allons!*" I say. "Since his widowhood, you have never given the poor fellow any peace. You have been forever quarrelling with him. You took possession of his house; bullied his servants; spoiled his children — you did, Lady Baker."

"Sir," cries her ladyship, "you are a low, presuming, vulgar man! Clarence, beat this rude man!"

"Nay," I say, "there must be no more quarrelling to-day. And I am sure Captain Baker will not molest me. Miss Prior, I am delighted that my old friend should have found a woman of good sense, good conduct, good temper — a woman who has had many trials, and borne them with very great patience — to take charge of him, and make him happy. I congratulate you both. Miss Prior has borne poverty so well that I am certain she will bear good fortune, for it *is* good fortune to become the wife of such a loyal, honest, kindly gentleman as Frederick Lovel."

After such a speech as that, I think I may say *liberavi animam.* Not one word of complaint, you see, not a hint about "Edward," not a single sarcasm, though I might have launched some terrific shots out of my quiver, and have made Lovel and his bride-elect writhe before me. But what is the need of spoiling sport? Shall I growl out of my sulky manger, because my comrade gets the meat? Eat it, happy dog! and be thankful. Would not that bone have choked me if I had tried it? Besides, I am accustomed to disappointment. Other fellows get the prizes which I try for. I am used to run second in the dreary race of love. Second? Psha! Third, Fourth. *Que sçais-je?* There was the Bombay captain in Bess's early days. There was Edward. Here is Frederick. Go to, Charles Batchelor; repine not at fortune: but be content to be Batchelor still. My sister has children. I will be an uncle, a parent to them. Is n't Edward of the scarlet whiskers distanced? Has not poor Dick Bedford lost the race — poor Dick, who never had a chance, and is the best of us all? Besides, what fun it is to see Lady Baker deposed: think of Mrs. Prior coming in and reigning over her! The purple-faced old fury of a Baker, never will she bully, and rage, and trample more. She must pack up her traps and be off. I know she must. I *can* congratulate Lovel sincerely, and that's the fact.

And here at this very moment, and as if to add to the comicality of the scene, who should appear but mother-in-law No. 2, Mrs. Prior, with her Bluecoat boy, and two or three of her children, who had been invited, or had invited themselves, to drink tea with Lovel's young ones, as their custom was whenever they could procure an invitation. Master Prior had a fine "copy" under his arm, which he came to show to his patron Lovel. His mamma, entirely ignorant of what had happened, came fawning in with her old poke-bonnet, her old pocket, that vast depository of all sorts of stores, her old umbrella, and her usual dreary smirk. She made her obeisance to the matrons, — she led up her Bluecoat boy to Mr. Lovel, in whose office she hoped to find a clerk's place for her lad, on whose very coat and waistcoat she had designs whilst they were yet on his back : and she straightway began business with the dowagers —

"My lady, I hope your ladyship is quite well ? " (A curtsy.) "Dear, kind Mrs. Bonnington ! I came to pay my duty to you, Mum. This is Louisa, my lady, the great girl for whom your ladyship so kindly promised the gown. And this is my little girl, Mrs. Bonnington, Mum, please ; and this is my big Blue. Go and speak to dear, kind Mr. Lovel, Gus, our dear good friend and protector, — the son and son-in-law of these dear ladies. Look, sir, he has brought his copy to show you ; and it's creditable to a boy of his age, is n't it, Mr. Batchelor ? You can say, who know so well what writing is, and my kind services to you, sir — and — Elizabeth, Lizzy, my dear ! where 's your spectacles, you — you — "

Here she stopped, and looking alarmed at the

group, at the boxes, at the blushing Lovel, at the pale countenance of the governess, "Gracious goodness!" she said, "what has happened? Tell me, Lizzy, what is it?"

"Is this collusion, pray?" says ruffled Mrs. Bonnington.

"Collusion, dear Mrs. Bonnington?"

"Or insolence?" bawls out my Lady Baker.

"Insolence, your ladyship? What — what is it? What are these boxes — Lizzy's boxes? Ah!" the mother broke out with a scream, "you've not sent the poor girl away? Oh! my poor child — my poor children!"

"The Prince's Theatre has come out, Mrs. Prior," here said I.

The mother clasps her meagre hands. "It wasn't the darling's fault. It was to help her poor father in poverty. It was I who forced her to it. Oh, ladies! ladies! — don't take the bread out of the mouth of these poor orphans!" — and genuine tears rained down her yellow cheeks.

"Enough of this," says Mr. Lovel, haughtily. "Mrs. Prior, your daughter is not going away. Elizabeth has promised to stay with me, and never to leave me — as governess no longer, but as —" and here he takes Miss Prior's hand.

"His wife! Is this — is this true, Lizzy?" gasped the mother.

"Yes, Mamma," meekly said Miss Elizabeth Prior.

At this the old woman flung down her umbrella, and uttering a fine scream, folds Elizabeth in her arms, and then runs up to Lovel: "My son! my son!" says she (Lovel's face was not bad, I promise you, at this salutation and salute). "Come here, children! — come, Augustus, Fanny, Louisa, kiss your dear brother, children! And where are yours, Lizzy? Where are Pop and Cissy? Go and look for your little nephew and niece, dears: Pop and Cissy in the schoolroom, or in the garden, dears. They will be your nephew and niece now. Go and fetch them, I say."

As the young Priors filed off, Mrs. Prior turned to the two other matrons, and spoke to them with much dignity: "Most hot weather, your ladyship, I'm sure! Mr. Bonnington must find it very hot for preaching, Mrs. Bonnington! Lor'! there's that little wretch beating my Johnny on the stairs. Have done, Pop, sir! How ever shall we make those children agree, Elizabeth?"

Quick, come to me, some skilful delineator of the British dowager, and draw me the countenances of Lady Baker and Mrs. Bonnington!

"I call this a jolly game, don't you, Batchelor, old boy?" remarks the Captain to me. "Lady Baker, my dear, I guess your ladyship's nose is out of joint."

"O Cecilia — Cecilia! don't you shudder in your grave?" cries Lady B. "Call my people, Clarence — call Bulkeley — call my maid! Let me go, I say, from this house of horror!" and the old lady dashed into the drawing-room, where she uttered I know not what incoherent shrieks and appeals before that calm, glazed, simpering portrait of the departed Cecilia.

Now this is a truth, for which I call Lovel, his lady, Mrs. Bonnington, and Captain Clarence Baker, as witnesses. Well, then, whilst Lady B. was adjuring the portrait, it is a fact that a string of Cecilia's harp — which has always been standing in the corner of the room under its shroud of Cordovan leather — a string, I say, of Cecilia's harp cracked, and went off with

a loud *bong*, which struck terror into all beholders.
Lady Baker's agitation at the incident was awful; I do
not like to describe it — not having any wish to say
anything tragic in this narrative — though that I *can*
write tragedy, plays of mine (of which envious man-
agers never could be got to see the merit) I think will
prove, when they appear in my posthumous works.

Baker has always averred that at the moment when
the harp-string broke, her heart broke too. But as
she lived for many years, and may be alive now for
what I know; and as she borrowed money repeatedly
from Lovel — he must be acquitted of the charge
which she constantly brings against him of hastening
her own death, and murdering his first wife Cecilia.
"The harp that once through Tara's halls" used to
make such a piteous feeble thrumming, has been carted
off I know not whither; and Cecilia's portrait, though it
has been removed from the post of honor (where, you
conceive, under present circumstances it would hardly
be *àpropos*), occupies a very reputable position in the
pink room up stairs, which that poor young Clarence
inhabited during my visit to Shrublands.

All the house has been altered. There's a fine
organ in the hall, on which Elizabeth performs sacred
music very finely. As for *my* old room, I will trouble
you to smoke *there* under the present government. It
is a library now, with many fine and authentic pictures of the Lovel family hanging up in it, the English branch of the house with the wolf crest, and
Gare à la louve for the motto, and a grand posthumous portrait of a Portuguese officer (Gandish),
Elizabeth's late father.

As for dear old Mrs. Bonnington, she, you may be
sure, would be easily reconciled to any live mortal
who was kind to her, and any plan which should make

her son happy; and Elizabeth has quite won her over. Mrs. Prior, on the deposition of the other dowagers, no doubt expected to reign at Shrublands, but in this object I am not very sorry to say was disappointed. Indeed, I was not a little amused, upon the very first day of her intended reign — that eventful one of which we have been describing the incidents — to see how calmly and gracefully Bessy pulled the throne from under her, on which the old lady was clambering.

Mrs. P. knew the house very well, and everything which it contained; and when Lady Baker drove off with her son and her suite of domestics, Prior dashed through the vacant apartments gleaning what had been left in the flurry of departure — a scarlet feather out of the dowager's room, a shirt-stud and a bottle of hair-oil, the Captain's property. "And now they are gone, and as you can't be alone with him, my dear, I must be with you," says she, coming down to her daughter.

"Of course, Mamma, I must be with you," says obedient Elizabeth.

"And there is the pink room, and the blue room, and the yellow room for the boys — and the chintz boudoir for me — I can put them all away, oh, so comfortably!"

"I can come and share Louisa's room, Mamma," says Bessy. "It will not be proper for me to stay here at all — until afterwards, you know. Or I can go to my uncle at St. Boniface. Don't you think that will be best, eh, Frederick?"

"Whatever you wish, my dear Lizzy!" says Lovel.

"And I dare say there will be some little alterations made in the house. You talked, you know, of painting, Mr. Lovel; and the children can go to their grandmamma Bonnington. And on our return when the alterations are made we shall always be delighted to see *you*, Mr. Batchelor,— our kindest old friend. Shall we not, Frederick ?"

"Always, always," said Frederick.

"Come, children, come to your teas," calls out Mrs. P., in a resolute voice.

"Dear Pop, I'm not going away — that is, only for a few days, dear," says Bessy, kissing the boy; "and you will love me, won't you ?"

"All right," says the boy. But Cissy said, when the same appeal was made to her: "I shall love my dear mamma!" and makes her new mother-in-law a very polite curtsy.

"I think you had better put off those men you expect to dinner to-morrow, Fred," I say to Lovel.

"I think I had, Batch," says the gentleman.

"Or you can dine with them at the club, you know ?" remarks Elizabeth.

"Yes, Bessy."

"And when the children have had their tea I will go with Mamma. My boxes are ready, you know," says arch Bessy.

"And you will stay and dine with Mr. Lovel, won't you, Mr. Batchelor ?" asks the lady.

It was the dreariest dinner I ever had in my life. No undertaker could be more gloomy than Bedford, as he served us. We tried to talk politics and literature. We drank too much, purposely. Nothing would do. "Hang me if I can stand this, Lovel," I said, as we sat mum over our third bottle. "I will go back and sleep at my chambers. I was not a little soft upon her myself, that's the truth. Here's her health, and happiness to both of you, with all my heart." And we drained a great bumper apiece, and I left him. He was very happy I should go.

Bedford stood at the gate, as the little pony-carriage came for me in the dusk. "God bless you, sir," says he. "I can't stand it; I shall go too." And he rubbed his hands over his eyes.

He married Mary Pinhorn, and they have emigrated to Melbourne; whence he sent me, three years ago, an affectionate letter, and a smart gold pin from the diggings.

A month afterwards, a cab might have been seen driving from the Temple to Hanover Square: and a month and a day after that drive, an advertisement might have been read in the "Post" and "Times:" "Married, on Thursday, 10th, at St. George's, Hanover Square, by the Reverend the Master of St. Boniface College, Oxbridge, uncle of the bride, Frederick Lovel, Esquire, of Shrublands, Roehampton, to Elizabeth, eldest daughter of the late Captain Montagu Prior, K. S. F."

We may hear of LOVEL MARRIED some other day, but here is an end of LOVEL THE WIDOWER. *Valete et plaudite*, you good people, who have witnessed the little comedy. Down with the curtain; cover up the boxes; pop out the gas-lights. Ho! cab. Take us home, and let us have some tea, and go to bed. Good-night, my little players. We have been merry together, and we part with softs hearts and somewhat rueful countenances, don't we?

THE END.